THE MARY BROWN BOOKS

BOX SET ONE

BERNICE BLOOM

WHAT'S UP, MARY BROWN?

MEETING MARY

For the love of all that is holy – what was I doing?

It was pouring down with rain on a miserable Thursday evening as I stood alone in the semi-darkness, sheltering under a tree outside a run-down community centre in one of the less salubrious parts of Surrey. Icy cold raindrops rolled across the leaves on the branches above me before dripping onto the top of my neck and crawling slowly down my back.

And all because I was fat.

Sorry, I should explain. I was waiting to go in for my first night at Fat Club. Not that they called it Fat Club, of course; Fat Club was my special name. The course for overweight people was concealed behind a title that made it sound like a jolly feature in a women's magazine: *Six Weeks to a New You!!*

A battered sign hung off the railing beside me urging people to register for the 'hugely successful' six-week course. *'You won't regret it!'* the sign promised.

Oh, God.

I didn't want to go in, of course. Who would?

If your choice was to spend the evening in the pub having a few glasses of wine with your mates or sit around with fat people, crying about how enormous you all are, which one would you choose? That's right – you'd be on your third glass of Sauvignon by now, wouldn't you?

But here I was. I had managed to drag my large bottom off the sagging sofa and made it to the venue on time. And I'd done this despite a large pizza and a bottle of wine beckoning me, siren-like, from the fridge in my warm and cosy flat.

What made me come, in the end, was the realisation that I **needed** to lose weight and couldn't do it alone. I tend to joke around a lot and do a lot of very silly things, but my weight was out of control. I know we all eat too much, but I have some days when I don't stop eating. It's like I'm after an award from the Guinness Book of Records.

And the award for the greatest number of salty snacks eaten in one sitting goes to...Mary Brown, a lady who ate forty times as many treats as her nearest competitor. Well done, Mary. Do you want to waddle up to the stage and collect your award? It's made from potato."

Now all I had to do was force myself to go inside. I walked towards the door, stumbling on exposed roots and slipping on soggy leaves in the semi-darkness. The broken street light directly outside the centre made the experience particularly dismal. I felt around for the cold, wet handle. Finally, I found it, and the door creaked as I turned it. It was like I was in some low-budget 1950s horror film.

Inside, things were considerably brighter. In fact, the fluorescent lighting strips were so overpowering you could have performed major heart surgery in there. I narrowed my eyes, squinting as I adjusted to the brightness, like a small woodland creature coming up from its burrow into daylight.

"Hello, welcome, welcome, welcome," said a woman with a broad, smiling face and ears that stuck out through a plethora of unruly curls. She introduced herself as Liz, explaining that she was the course tutor. She reached out a surprisingly large hand and pulled me into her, hugging me warmly. "Sorry if my outfit's a bit bright; I love colourful clothes."

She wasn't joking. If I were being unkind, I'd say she was dressed like a four-year-old who'd been told she could choose what she wanted to wear to a party. She was wearing a very tight pink dress. And I mean tight (you could practically see the outline of her major internal organs). She styled the dress with red tights and a red cardigan and had lashings of vibrant green eyeshadow thickly painted onto her eyelids. She wore pink lipstick, but most of that appeared to be on her teeth and chin rather than her lips, so she looked like she'd been eating raspberries straight from the bush without using her hands. She even had glitter on her temples. She was a pair of butterfly wings away from winning the prize for the best-dressed little girl at the party.

The childlike nature of her makeup was in contrast to her stature. She was a tall and sturdy woman, carrying quite a few extra pounds. "I'm glad you've decided to join us," she said. "I hope this class will help you change your life for the better. I've lost 13 stone since I first came to the group."

"Wow, well done," I said. The generous side of me thought – that is really impressive. The less generous side thought – blimey, how fat were you before? I decided not to share the more ungenerous thought. In fact, I chose not to share any of my ungenerous thoughts about her makeup or clothing. I was being a real bitch. Sorry if you think me offensive. I'm not generally like this, but I was stressed – I wanted to be at home with pizza and wine, not discussing my food issues with random strangers.

"Take a seat," said Liz, leading me to a circle of chairs and making the compulsory British observations about the weather. We agreed it was miserable and much colder than it usually was for the time of year (I don't know how people remember that sort of thing. Do they keep notes or something? I can't remember the weather last week, let alone last year. I guess she was right, though, so I nodded and smiled, raising my eyebrows in agreement with her). Only two other people were in the room – an older man and a woman who barely looked up. They were tucked into a corner, wearing matching navy blue anoraks and trying to sink into the background. I tried to smile at them, but they didn't smile back. Liz saw me trying to make a connection with them and gave me an enormous grin, revealing just how much lipstick she had smeared across her teeth. I'd rather have been anywhere else on Earth.

"My name's Mary," I said, eventually, when the weight of the silence became too much for me to bear. I walked over and shook hands with the two older people. They didn't offer their names, so I returned to my seat, slightly cross that they didn't have the decency to pretend to be interested in me but also happy that I'd done my bit for group relations. I've never liked to see people looking sad, and those two looked nigh on suicidal. I discovered later that their names were Phil and Philippa.

The Phils were encouraged to come and join me. They sat down without speaking, leaving empty chairs between us, and as other people filtered in, they took the free chairs. A woman called Janice sat to the left of me. She clutched her handbag and whimpered, "I want to go home," which endeared me to her.

"Me too, sister," I said.

What she also had in her favour, as far as our future friendship was concerned, was that she was much larger than me. This gave me a strange sense of confidence and happiness. I know that was selfish and very uncharitable, but I really didn't want to be the fattest person at Fat Club. I mean – no one wants to be the fattest person at Fat Club.

"What on earth is that woman wearing?" she said after Liz had been over to give her a welcome hug. "I didn't realise it was fancy dress."

Opposite me was a very beautiful woman sitting next to the Phils. She was tall and quite big but not as fat as the rest of us: size 14, at a guess. Unnervingly elegant in cream, three-quarter length trousers and a white shirt, she also had a treasure trove of gold accessories to bring the outfit to life. She looked exactly like Kelly Brook. She had no place at a Fat Club, and I longed for bouncers to appear clutching scales and a tape measure and throw her out for not reaching the required obesity level.

Liz wandered over to her, and for one insane moment I thought she was going to do precisely that – chuck the poor woman out because her stomach was too small, and her thighs didn't rub together. But, instead, she told her she was very welcome, hugged her, and invited her to sit down. I watched the alarm spread across the woman's face as she released herself from the compulsory hug she'd just endured and took in Liz's outfit. "My name's Veronica," she said. "I don't know whether I should be here. I used to be a model."

"Everyone's welcome, regardless of who they are or who they used to be. We're simply here to support one another. Why don't you stay and see how you feel," said Liz.

"OK," said Veronica. Liz moved away and the glamour-puss smiled at me, revealing perfect teeth. I smiled back, making sure I didn't show mine.

The club was quite a long way from my home. I couldn't risk going to a club near my house incase someone saw me. It's bad enough being fat without advertising it to all your friends and family. I'd never have lived it down if my boss at the garden centre had seen me walking into a local club. Keith's always been a bit of a clown and would have found it very amusing to mock my efforts to lose weight.

"While we're waiting for the others to get here, does anyone have any questions?" said Liz. "I know you must be wondering about the course and how it works."

"Yes, I'd like to know that." I raised my hand a little, like a child in school. "How does it work? What do we do? How are we all going to lose tonnes of weight? And how quickly will we lose it?" I could hear the urgency and desperation in my own voice. It didn't sound pretty.

"We will go into that in great detail later." Liz gave a warm smile. "But – briefly – this course is about dealing with your issues psychologically, not physically. When you're ready to diet and exercise, you will."

"OK." I tried to stay positive, but this sounded like New Age bullshit. "I'm ready to lose the weight now. I'm sick of being fat. I'd like to get thinner as quickly as possible."

"Amen, sister," said Janice, and I treated her to the biggest smile I could muster.

"OK. I get it, I really do. You desperately want to lose weight, but let's look at the facts," she said calmly, perhaps sensing that I wasn't entirely sold on all this. "You know what you must do to lose weight, don't you? You know that you will lose weight by increasing exercise and reducing your calorie intake. Right?"

"Right," I said.

"But you're not doing it."

"No, I think we can all agree on that." I rubbed my fat stomach and let the ripples provide the evidence.

"Why not?" she asked.

"Um. I don't know." I felt myself go scarlet and wished I'd never asked a bloody question in the first place. I wished I was at home with a bottle of wine.

"Look, I don't want to embarrass you; I'm just trying to explain that losing weight is quite a complicated psychological shift if you want to keep it off, so that takes a bit of time."

She looked at me, and I was sure she could sense my disappointment and frustration.

"There must be a reason you're not cutting back on your calories and losing weight, mustn't there? Or you'd do it. Something's stopping you, and it's not something physical – no one's standing in your way at the gym, not allowing you onto the treadmill or forcing you to eat cake. It's something psychological, and that's what we must sort out.

"This course is to try and understand all the mental processes we go through as overeaters. It will involve working out why you overeat in the first place. This is a gentle, kind environment, and within it, we'll explore your emotions and learn to understand them."

What she said made perfect sense, of course, but I still didn't get it…not really. How would I be filled with positive energy and never eat anything but celery ever again merely by chatting about how fat I was?

"Will you just trust me?" said Liz. "Stay with this, and I can help you."

"OK," I said, though I had reservations about trusting her. I didn't trust anyone, not really. My ability to trust had deserted me along with my innocence all those years ago.

I looked up to see a man walk in; he was one of those very jolly fat guy types – all smiles and laughter and cracking jokes. He didn't seem to fit into this rather dull group. He sat down to the right of me, and I sighed inwardly. I thought I might get an empty seat next to myself, which I'd have liked. I hoped he wouldn't try to jolly me up…no sing-alongs, hand-holding, or anything nasty.

"Am I in the right place?" His voice was barely a whisper. "I am looking for Overeaters Anonymous. How will I know when I find it? You're too thin to be in the group I'm seeking."

It was a valiant attempt at humour in the face of embarrassment, and I did appreciate the compliment, so I smiled at him as he sat down. He removed his glasses that had steamed up when he entered the warm building and wiped them on his checked shirt. He had odd facial hair – not just a simple beard, but a sort of complicated moustache/beard combo that had been shaved into place, like topiary.

There were six of us in the room when Liz decided to start the session. She was expecting 10, but we were already 10 minutes late starting, and she didn't want to keep us waiting.

"I bet they've only got the hall booked for 90 minutes," whispered the man. "Then the 'Under-Eaters Anonymous' group arrive, and they can't risk us all being in the same room at the same time."

I smiled at him. He was ever so slightly bonkers which cheered me up.

I heard Janice giggling to herself at the man's joke. "That's right; the under-eaters are terrified we might eat them."

Liz began by discussing the importance of working together as a group and how we must contact one another during the week. She said she'd give out a list of numbers, and we should text the person on our left during the week just to encourage them.

The very smiley, happy, red-faced man with steamed-up glasses and an odd facial hair arrangement smiled at me. "I'm Ted. I'll text you to check you're OK. Just call me if you need to talk or anything," he said in a kind voice.

BERNICE BLOOM

"Thank you," I replied, and I instantly regretted judging him on the beard thing.

"I'll text you," I said to Janice.

"OK, but will I have to put my bag of chips down to reply?" she said.

I assured her that there was no need for that. "Let's not take this too seriously, Janice. She gave me a lovely big smile.

I guess Janice was in her mid-40s. I'd only just turned 30; she looked about 12 or so years older than me. She was quite plain looking, with short brown hair and very little makeup, but she had such mischief in her eyes that I could imagine men being attracted to her. At a guess, I would say she was a size 22, to my size 18ish, but she wore it well.

"Ted, why don't you lead us off by telling the group something about yourself and why you're here today," said Liz.

"Oh, OK," he said with an embarrassed shrug. He had turned the colour of red wine.

We were all watching him and thinking, 'Thank God I don't have to go first.'

Liz sensed his concern, or perhaps she was just worried about the strange colour he'd turned. Either way, she stepped in.

"Look, you don't have to if you don't want to, but I want everyone in the group to understand one another and be aware of each other's problems. I think it will help you to support one another more effectively if you understand each other's issues."

"Sure," he said in a voice which suggested he'd never been less sure of anything in his life. He stood up.

"OK, here we go then. I never used to have problems. I used to be a very good sportsman," he said, and I immediately looked up. I'd been a good sportswoman many years ago, but I certainly wasn't going to tell them anything about that. I'd never told anyone about the awful things that had happened to me when I was younger.

Ted continued to explain that his life had involved playing county rugby, trials with a range of top English clubs, and being considered a future international.

"It was my life," he said. "All I could think of was that first England cap. I'd dream about it and build it up into a colourful scenario in my mind. It was like playing for England was the only thing worth doing. Nothing else mattered."

But a call-up to the national squad never happened. A freak injury ended his career just when he was on the verge of greatness. Ted told us about the moment a scrum collapsed on him, and he lay on the floor, unable to move.

"Do you all know what a scrum is?" he asked. "Without being too technical, the biggest players on the pitch pile in together to get the ball. The opposition sides push against one another, ramming their shoulders against their opposite number. It's OK if it's done correctly, but I was pushing at an awkward angle, twisted, and was dumped down on the ground neck first. We all winced in support.

"I was only 22," he said. "I fell into a great depression afterwards about being unable to play anymore. I knew I should be grateful to be alive. Certainly, when they took me off the pitch, the doctors were very concerned about whether I'd ever walk again or lead a normal life. My mum said no one knew whether I'd live or die. I was grateful to the doctors for everything they did. I'm thankful to them today – 10 years since the accident – and will be forever more. But I was also desperately sad and felt like my world had collapsed. I couldn't cope without playing the sport that had defined me and was creating a future for me. All I'd ever wanted to be was an international rugby player. I felt as if my past, present, and future had all been snatched away.

"I became useless. Everything felt futile when I couldn't play sport anymore. I tried to eat my way out of sadness, but that didn't work. We all know that doesn't work. I ate more and felt sadder and ate more and felt sadder still; now I'm morbidly obese, and I look at the pictures of me playing rugby, and that feels like another person. I can't play rugby again, but I'd like to be more like the person in the pictures."

Ted stopped, and I reached up to touch his arm, to express sympathy and solidarity. I knew nothing about rugby, but I knew about the pressures of sport and overeating. I understood precisely how food could wrap you in its alluring but dangerous arms and refuse to let you go.

There was a big round of applause when Ted finished… the clapping that said: 'We're with you, we totally understand.' I looked over at him and smiled; he blushed a little, then gave me the biggest smile ever.

Next came Janice. She stood up. "I have a similar story," she said before correcting herself quickly. "Well, not similar – I wasn't a brilliant rugby player or anything like that. What I mean is that I was OK until something major happened. Things were good; life was ticking along, and then my mum died."

Janice took a deep breath. She was finding it hard. "Sorry," she kept saying as she stuttered and breathed heavily, attempting to tell her story. "It was years ago that it happened, just after my 40th birthday, so I don't know why it still affects me so badly today; you'd think I'd be used to it by now, but you never really get used to it. I'm not sure the pain of missing her has got any easier; I've just got used to the pain of being there. This is bringing it all back to the surface. It's difficult."

"Of course it's difficult, and you're doing really well," said Liz. "You're in the best, most supportive company here today." As Liz said that, I realised the pressure on us to look after one another.

"Mum died, and I lost all control," she continued. "I mean – all control – I just ate and ate and ate, and then I ate some more." Janice dissolved into tears.

"You've done really well," said Liz, stroking Janice's shaking back. "Could you go next, please, Mary?"

"Me?"

"Yes, please, Mary, if you don't mind? I think Janice needs to sit down now."

"Right. Um. I don't know what to say," I said, standing up and looking down at the scuffed wooden floor that reminded me so much of school. "I'm embarrassed and ashamed to be this size, and I wish this weren't me here in a church hall talking about how fat I am. I wish I were out with my friends having a lovely time or flirting with the guy who lives in the flat underneath mine because he's bloody gorgeous. You should see him – honestly, he's lovely. Way too lovely for me. Christ, you should see the beautiful women he brings back with him.

But, anyway. Um. Where was I?"

"Just talk us through your issues with food," Liz said gently.

"I guess I'm fat because I eat whenever I feel low or vulnerable."

"OK," said Liz. "So you're using food to comfort yourself? You're convincing yourself that food is the answer to stirred emotions, even when those emotions aren't hunger?"

"Yes. That's right. Deep down, I know I'm not hungry when someone gets cross with me, laughs at me, or makes me feel horrible, but eating sure makes the real feelings go away."

"Does it, though?" asked Liz. "Or is eating just a temporary relief, and then you do the same thing the next time you feel low?"

"Every time I feel low, I eat."

"So it's not really solving any problems, then?"

"No," I said. "None at all."

"OK, Mary. You're doing really well. Is there anything else you'd like to share? Perhaps about your past and when the overeating started?"

"I did sport when I was younger, like Ted. I was a gymnast. You wouldn't believe that now, would you? Gymnastics was a hard sport. I don't want to blame the way I am now on it, but it's tough to spend your whole adolescence running around in a leotard and having to perform and then be marked out of 10. I guess it leaves you feeling like you're always being judged.

"Also, some things happened when I was younger. I mean – one thing in particular happened. I guess it's always haunted me a bit. I haven't always been fat. I started putting on weight when I was about 20, years after stopping gymnastics, but probably because of what happened, but maybe not. I don't know, really.

"Before that, things were different... I was always the successful one... I know it's hard to believe it now, but I was always the prettiest girl, the fittest girl, and the best at school. I was the pretty blonde gymnast who all the boys fancied. I put on a bit of weight, and I was the curvaceous blonde ex-gymnast who'd retired rather suddenly; then, in my early 20s, I became the fat blonde, now I'm just a morbidly obese lump on legs, and I'd be amazed if anyone even noticed my hair colour."

"Don't be daft," said Ted, sounding genuinely moved. "You're beautiful. Everyone can see that." There were general murmurings of approval for Ted's kind words, and I smiled at him before carrying on. "I guess I put enormous pressure on myself to be perfect, and every time things go wrong, I turn to food. That's what we all do, isn't it? As you age, more things go wrong, so you eat more. Then being fat becomes a problem in its own right, so you eat even more because you feel awful about being fat and you need comforting, and the problem exacerbates. You feel like a complete idiot because your reaction to a problem is feeding the problem and making it worse every day.

"Now I'm standing in front of you, and I seem to have eaten myself into a life I don't want to be in anymore, and I don't really know how to get out of it. I feel very ashamed a lot of the time. I'm so ugly and fat I hate to go out, but it's depressing to stay in when all your friends are out. So you eat. You eat because somewhere inside, it feels like the answer to everything…and the problems just grow. Sorry, I'm repeating myself…but that's what happens."

"Well done, Mary," said Liz. "You mentioned that something had happened that you thought might be the cause of your overeating. Something when you were a gymnast, was it? Would you like to share that?"

"No, no," I said. "The only thing is that I eat too much. That's the only 'thing'. That's all I wanted to say."

"OK," said Liz. "Don't worry. Another time, perhaps."

I sat down, and Ted leaned over and lightly touched my hands resting in my lap; it was a warm gesture and surprisingly touching after the stress of talking to everyone. "You're going to do this," he said. "And – please believe me – you are not ugly; you're very pretty."

I smiled at him and squeezed his hand a little. No one had said anything like that to me for about a decade.

They were the sort of words that I'd always fantasised about Dave, my gorgeous neighbour, saying to me, but all Dave wanted to do was fondle my tits. Sorry, I know that's crude, but it's the truth. More of that later.

After me came Phil, the older man opposite. Phil was huge – he must have been six foot six inches and about 25 stone (I'm guessing here – I find it very difficult to guess what men weigh – all I know is that he was super-enormous). He had receding white hair, and he scratched his bald patch nervously. I think he was the one I felt most sorry for. His shyness was crippling, and he really didn't want to talk. He still had his anorak on, zipped up to his neck, when he stood up and mumbled about how difficult he was finding everything, then how he didn't like to talk in front of strangers.

"Just tell us about something you like. Anything at all?" tried Liz.

"I like Star Wars," he said before returning to his chair.

I felt myself shift a little in my seat. My heart beat a little faster.

"You OK?" asked Ted.

"Sure," I replied.

"You've gone pale," he said.

"It's nothing. It's just that I absolutely hate the theme from Star Wars. HATE it."

"Right," he replied uncomprehendingly. "I'll remember never to play it at Fat Club."

"Philippa, would you like to go next?" asked Liz, smiling warmly at the woman I assumed was Phil's wife.

"I won't, thanks," she said, blushing to the roots of her tightly permed, grey hair. It seemed a shame. None of us wanted to share our innermost fears and complexities with a group of overweight strangers, and I confess I held back on a lot of my story. Still, the point of all this was to allow us to bond with one another, support one another and identify with one another, so it was important to say something, if not everything. With every story I heard, I was feeling less of a 'freak'. Not totally unfreaky – I wouldn't go that far – but definitely less freaky. That had to be something, surely?

Next came Veronica. She stood up to reveal a body that was so far from fat that it was ridiculous. It was the body we all wanted. Not tiny, by any means, but these things are relative – she certainly wasn't fat like the rest of us.

"I know I'm not huge," she said, clearing her throat as she looked around the room. Her long, wavy dark hair tumbled over her shoulders. "I appreciate there are a lot of people here who are much larger." I'm sure she looked at me as she said that. "But I'm a lot fatter than I've ever been in my life before, and I feel totally out of control around food. It doesn't matter what size you are if you feel uncomfortable and hate your body.

"I was a model for seven years. You consume nothing but Diet Coke some days and an apple if you're lucky. I spent the best part of a decade feeling starving all the time and eating cotton wool to curb the worst of the hunger pangs. I gave up modelling at 22 when the work started drying up, and realised that I didn't know how to eat. I don't understand how to control myself because I never had to when I wasn't eating. The weight piled on. I've put on six stone since I gave up. Six stone. Can you imagine that?"

I can't have been alone in thinking that she must have been painfully thin before.

"We can help you. We can help you all." Liz looked around at her six chicks with maternal pride. "Now then, everybody up." She clapped her hands loudly, making Phil jump out of his seat. Either he was particularly sensitive, or he was half-asleep. I couldn't rule out either option, to be honest.

"Into pairs, please, and I want you to talk about why you decided to come here today."

I turned to Ted and asked him whether he'd like to be my partner.

He looked remarkably pleased, smiling and glowing red.

"Why did you come here?" he asked.

"Because I realised I couldn't cross my legs properly," I replied, watching his eyebrows raise and a look of confusion spread across his face.

It sounded very silly, but it was the truth. When I realised I couldn't cross my legs, I knew I wasn't just a few pounds over fighting weight, but I was seriously, undeniably and horribly fat. It wasn't a pleasant realisation.

There had been plenty of other unpleasant developments over the years as I'd piled on the pounds. Moments when I was driven to consuming nothing but shakes for a week or proteins for a fortnight, or eating a lemon every morning – wincing and gagging as the bitterness swamped my mouth. Lots of times when I'd not been able to look in the mirror in the changing room because the sight of myself struggling into a pair of size 20 trousers when all the evidence was that a 22 would be ambitious was too much to bear. Every fat girl has cried in a changing room.

But the leg-crossing thing was different. The fact that I couldn't sit in a comfortable position made me feel like I was deformed in some way – or, to put it differently: I had deformed myself in some way. I'd shoved so much food into my mouth that I was unable to function normally – I couldn't sit down properly. Who would do that to herself? I was young, fit, healthy and moderately attractive. I had all the advantages that life could throw at me. Still, I'd put so much food into my mouth that I'd turned myself into a creature unable to walk any distance without panting like an elderly, chain-smoking marathon runner, and now I couldn't sit down properly either. What was I supposed to do – lie down all day? No – I know what you're thinking – what I was supposed to do was get out there and lose some weight.

And I tried. My God, I tried. I tried to exercise more, but my thighs rubbed together when I walked, leaving me so bloody sore and tender that only the application of a bag of frozen peas would calm the redness. No one tells you these things when they're serving you cakes, do they?

Why don't they tell you that a simple walk anywhere will give you such chaffing that it will feel as if someone had taken to your inner thighs with a cheese grater? And that's the trouble with getting fat. The very act of being fat presents, in itself, a whole host of side effects which make losing the fat wildly difficult.

Let's look at the evidence:

1. Walk more.

Not possible: your ankles get sore, and your thighs rub together, causing the sort of rash that would only normally be achieved by rubbing them frantically with sandpaper.

1. Join a gym.

Oh yeah, right. Join a gym and wobble around for two minutes on the treadmill before collapsing in an indecorous heap and lying there crying as all the perfect-bodied people step over me? You need to be fit to join a gym – everyone knows that.

1. Go swimming.

Are you insane? Really – are you? In the interests of public decency, it's impossible for me to wear a swimming costume in public. Christ, no one deserves to have that sight thrust upon them. It's probably illegal for me to be seen in a swimming costume.

Before too long, the only exercise available to me would be rolling.

Eating less would have been one way of solving the problem, of course, but that didn't work. I don't say that flippantly – everyone who has an eating disorder knows that they can't eat less, like they can't breathe less or shiver less when cold. You have no control over it. Or you think you have no control over it, which is exactly the same thing.

I went to talk to my GP on the off-chance that he would have a miracle cure tucked up his sleeve.

"I need to lose weight," I told him.

It turned out he agreed wholeheartedly. He even measured me and weighed me and, yes, confirmed that, indeed, I did need to lose weight. Quite a lot of weight, as it happens. But he had no exciting pills to give me that would help. "Eat less; exercise more," he said. Thanks, doc, revolutionary advice.

"You OK?" asked Ted.

"Yes," I said. "Just thinking – it's all really weird this, isn't it? I mean – thinking about why we are here? Trying to articulate it beyond saying *because I want to lose weight*."

"My dear, it's because we are so dreadfully, dreadfully fat," he replied in a funny voice that made me laugh quite a lot.

"Well, yes, there certainly is that," I replied.

"It would be wrong of you to deny it." He rubbed his stomach, so it all shook like a giant jelly. "We're fat, and we can't hide it, so we need to change it."

He was right that you can't hide it. The horrible thing about eating too much is that everybody knows you have a problem. You can't deny that you're a food addict. You could be a drug addict without people necessarily knowing, certainly until you did yourself real damage, no one would know. The same with alcoholics. It doesn't show until you're really badly affected by it. That's not the same with overeaters, we get fatter and fatter and fatter, and everyone knows that we are eating too much, and everyone is wondering why we don't just cut down.

There's so much judgement of fat people because we're completely out of control around something that everybody else can manage. From the littlest babies to the oldest pensioners, we all eat. But there are some of us who can't control how and when we eat. It seems ridiculous. Of all the problems in the world, all the big things going on, we idiots in the room couldn't stop putting food into our mouths even though it was killing us.

At least now we had each other. It was us against the world – we were valiant, fat, fighting soldiers. And we would stick together and help each other.

I left the meeting feeling pretty bloody wonderful. Really good. I thought the six-week course might get me on track; I could lose a stone in that time and start moving more. I vowed to get off the bus a stop early, drink more water, and make the small changes that would create a real difference. Christ, I was on top of this. I could sort it out.

But the journey home was quite long, and the more I sat there, the more my mind dwelled on things. It was desperate: why did I have to eat nothing but lettuce for the next two years? Why had I got this fat in the first place? I'd never lose it; who was I kidding, thinking that I could? I'd tried so many times, and it hadn't worked; what was so different this time? I watched the world go past from the lower deck of the R49 and felt increasingly sorry for myself. Why did I have this problem and others didn't? Happy, smiley, slim men and women got on and off the bus. It seemed so unfair. They were the sort of people who could open a packet of biscuits and just have one. Why could they do that, and I couldn't? I would never lose weight; why was I even kidding myself?

I stepped off the bus, close to my house, and passed the fish and chip shop on the corner. The waft of vinegar flew out on the night air, its rapacious claws grabbing me around the throat. This is what happens; what always happens. Food has talons…even the smell of food has talons that tear, scratch, seize, and pull at me so I can't escape. The thought of the warmth and comfort of food is so much more powerful than the thought of being thin. Vanity's tentacles are much less sharp than those attached to the comforts of eating.

"Hi, can I get two large portions of chips, please? For me, my husband, and the kids."

"Sure."

Except there was no husband, no children at home waiting for their chips – just a small, empty flat for me to trundle into and gorge myself until I felt like crying. God, I'm lonely. I wish someone loved me.

"Actually, could you add curry sauce?"

This is the thing with being an overeater. I didn't go into the chip shop because I fancied a couple of chips. If that were the case, I'd have eaten a couple of chips and gone on my merry way, and all would have been fine. No – it was different from that – it was like something switched in my brain around food, and I had to keep eating and filling myself until I was so full that I really hurt. It was like I was mentally unwell around food. Like I hated myself through food, but I didn't know why. I was hoping I'd find out on the course, but that night all I was finding out was that things hadn't changed – I needed to feel full up to cover the pain inside…the pain that I could tell no one about. The pain that was caused by the thing that happened so long ago and still hurt so much.

The shop next door sold bottles of wine that went so nicely with chips, and then it was off up the street, tearing the chip paper off and feeling the warmth of the steam rise to bite my hand. I took the chips and fed them into my mouth even though they were piping hot and burnt my tongue as I strode towards my flat. They were also slimy and hot to the touch, so I moved them between my cupped hands to cool them down, then shoved them into my mouth. I was covered in grease and had a mouth full of piping-hot chips and oil all over my face.

That was when Dave from the flat below pulled up and walked to the gate next to me. He was with a beautiful girlfriend who didn't look like she'd ever had a chip in her life. She was wearing a stunning white mini-dress. I never wear white, and I never wear minis. I looked down at my dowdy, old-lady clothes, wondering where to dump the chips before she saw them.

"OK?" asked Dave.

"Sure," I said, spitting bits of fried potato out as I spoke.

"This is Felicity."

I looked over at the vision of feminine beauty and smiled. I couldn't offer her my hand because it was full of chips, so I looked wistfully as she put out her tiny little hand, then withdrew it when she realised I wouldn't be shaking it. Meanwhile, Dave wiped bits of chips off the side of his face.

Eventually, he looked from the bag of chips to the handful of chips to my mouth, and smiled.

"Enjoy your supper. See you soon."

His girlfriend wiggled into his flat, and I waddled into mine.

Fuck it. Fuck all of it.

WEEK TWO AT FAT CLUB

I used to be elegant, you know. Properly nice, with cheekbones and ankles and things. I used to wear my hair up. That's a tell-tale sign of a woman with confidence – when she'll happily pull her fringe back into a clip or twist the back of her hair up into a chignon. Do you know what these women are saying? These women are crying, 'I can pull my hair back and let you see more of my face because I'm not deeply ashamed of what my face looks like.'

Me? I pull it all forward over my face, hoping to hide my puffy cheeks and jowly jawline as much as possible. If I could wear it pulled forward over my face covering it entirely, I would. But then I wouldn't be able to see, and I'd bump into people. Nobody wants a fat woman with hair all over her face bumping into them. So I don't pull it forward, but I don't tie it back, either. Do you see how complicated this all is? It's hard being fat. Don't get fat. It's a pain.

It was quite difficult to persuade myself to go back to Fat Club for the second week.

I had left there the week before feeling so inspired, but after my chip disaster, I'd woken up feeling terrible. This is the trouble with reaching out for help – if you make the effort and it doesn't work, you feel worse than ever. I felt crushed like I'd tried and failed, like nothing could help me. Before I made the effort to ask for help, I could relax in the knowledge that there might be a solution out there. Now it felt as if I'd proven to myself that there was no solution: no help, no hope and no point in trying to convince myself otherwise.

After that dreadful night, the rest of the week did get better, but I certainly didn't feel any different as a result of the course. Going into my job in Fosters DIY & Garden Centre, I was as aware as ever of people around me eating food: food in shops and food on posters.

Food made me feel nice. Why couldn't I have food?

Then I'd go through the process of reminding myself why: because my face was slowly drowning in a pool of fat; all my clothes had gone up six sizes and even my shoes. Shoes! What was that all about? Feet don't get fat. Except mine did. I didn't know whether they were fatter, or whether the pressure exerted on them by the weight of my heavy torso flattened them out. Either way – not good. Not to be recommended.

I'd remind myself that I couldn't bend over since I got fat…not really. That's a horrible thing. The feeling you get when you reach down to tie up your shoes is horrific. Your stomach is in the way and pushes back on your internal organs. You can't breathe. You feel light-headed as if you're about to faint or be sick. As if, to be honest, you're going to die. I'd come up from a basic shoe tie or sock on-put with my face the colour of sun-dried tomato, whining and puffing as if I'd just run a marathon dressed as a polar bear.

The day before the second session, Ted sent me a text saying how much he was looking forward to seeing me at Fat Club. "Well this week it's been an absolute bloody disaster for me," he said. "If you want to see what a very fat man looks like when he eats marshmallows all week and gets even fatter, I suggest you come on Tuesday night. Looking forward to seeing you X."

I laughed out loud when I read it and replied to say I was looking forward to seeing him too. I decided to send a text to Janice.

"Looking forward to seeing you on Tuesday night," I wrote. "I'll be the really fat one who hasn't managed to stop eating chips all week."

Janice replied: "Your chips are nothing compared to my chocolate cake. See you Tuesday."

They call it gallows humour, don't they? That grim and ironic humour you find in a desperate or hopeless situation. I suggest we call this Marshmallows Humour: witticisms born out of the desperation of trying to lose weight. Still, at least by replying to everyone, I was now committed to going back to Fat Club.

When I walked in, I saw Ted straight away. He gave me a cheery smile and a wave and came over to me.

"Thank you for your text," I said. "It really made me laugh."

"You have to laugh about these things, don't you?" he said. "Hard to know what else to do."

"Have you been OK this week?" I asked.

"Kind of terrible," he said. "I just don't seem to be able to sort myself out. I rang Liz in the end because I kept bingeing. Liz said it was only natural, after we'd bared our souls in class we would probably want comforting and our choice of comforting would be food. Today she's going to talk about other ways to comfort ourselves."

"That makes sense. I couldn't stop eating either," I said. "Especially straight after the class, which didn't make me feel great. In fact, it made me feel as if this whole thing was such a hopeless battle. I wasn't going to come back until I got your text."

Ted blushed. "Wow. Then I'm so glad I sent it."

All six of us were there for the second session. Liz looked at us proudly, as if we were all four-year-olds who had just completed our 50m swimming badges. She was wearing a dress with more flowers on it than there are in the whole of Kew Gardens. Her shoes were red.

"You have all come back," she said. "That's a very good start. Mary, how have you got on this week?"

I really wish she hadn't started with me. I didn't want to kick the whole thing off with such negativity.

"I've been fine," I lied. I looked at Ted out of the corner of my eye and I could see him smiling at me.

"Talk us through how you've been fine?" said Liz.

"Well, nothing terrible has happened… No major disasters," I said. "I'm still alive and all that."

"How have you got on with your eating?"

"Oh, that? No, that's been terrible," I said and heard a laugh go around the room.

"Don't worry. Tell me why it's been terrible."

"I just feel like such a failure all the time," I said. "I find myself eating without really knowing I'm doing it, and without meaning to, and I feel such an idiot that I am unable to control myself. After coming here last week I thought things would be different, then on the bus home I started to get so depressed about what an uphill task it was, and how much weight I had to lose, that I lost all my motivation in one second."

"And how did this manifest itself?"

"I bought everything in the chip shop and started eating it all before I'd even walked through the front door, then felt guilty about it, and disgusted with myself. I don't know – I felt horrible all week. The only way I could stop myself from feeling horrible was to eat. It wasn't great, really."

"Thank you for being so honest," said Liz. "What happened to you last week is very typical and I promise you we can sort it out, so don't worry. You were scuppered by the voices in your head telling you that it was too complicated to try to lose weight. The voices said that you could never do it and it was pointless trying. Am I right?"

"Yes," I said. I hate it when people talk about voices in your head as if you're some psycho maniac who is about to kill everybody, but she was right about the feeling I had…that this was all pointless and I was wasting my time.

"One key thing we are going to work on today is controlling the negative voices in your head. You can't let them decide your actions out of fear. You have to make choices out of confidence and positivity have to own them, understand them, be bigger than them and louder than them, and then you CAN be in control of them. That's something we'll work on later. We'll also look at why you are all eating when you need comforting, rather than doing something more constructive.

Why food? We'll discuss that. For now, though, thank you, Mary, please don't worry and think it's all hopeless and helpless. It isn't. Not by a long way. You've only just started – just trust that you'll get there. We are all here to help you and we will."

I felt a tear run down my face as she spoke. It was astonishing how emotional all this was becoming. It was lovely to have someone who cared. Really cared. Cared so much they were trying to help. I know it was her job but she still seemed to care rather than criticise, and that was nice.

It also helped that not many in the group had had a particularly wonderful week (I know that sounds really selfish, but I've got to be honest – if they'd all arrived having lost half a stone each, the voices in my head would have been telling me to murder them).

I left the session feeling confident, understanding why I was reaching for food and determined not to be undone by the voices. I just needed to get myself home without going via the chip shop.

"Fancy a drink?" said Ted.

"Oh I'd like that too," said Janice, overhearing Ted's question to me.

Once Janice said she'd like to go, I was in. I wouldn't have fancied going for a drink on my own with Ted. I mean, he was very nice and everything, but a bit too jolly and happy ALL THE TIME.

We retired to the Shipmate's Arms, just down the road from the centre, all of us waddling in a line. I wondered whether people were looking at us, and thinking that we must have come from Fat Club. I wondered whether it was a fun thing to do locally – to look for the Fat Club people trooping into the pub.

Ted went to the bar, and I sat down next to Janice.

"It's depressing, isn't it?" she said. "I hate being fat. I wish I had a gambling problem or an overspending problem, then at least it wouldn't be blatantly obvious to everyone in the world."

"Unless you gambled away all your money and ended up living in a cardboard box somewhere. Then it would be obvious," I said, but I knew what she meant. On a daily basis, I felt stupid for being so overweight.

"I'm just fed up with being a fat fuck," said Janice. "Fed up with the insults and the way it dominates my life. Fed up with looking dreadful, feeling dreadful and people treating me like I'm dreadful. I'm fed up with all of it. Nothing is nice when you're as fat as I am…nothing at all."

"Here we go," said Ted, returning to the table and putting my drink in front of me before I had the chance to reply to Janice. Ted had a pint, I had a spritzer and Janice had gone for sparkling water. As soon as I saw Janice's drink, I realised that I should have done the same.

"You've done well…having water. Good self-control." I hoped to cheer her up a little, as I swirled my drink around and listened to the ice clinking against the inside of the glass.

"I need to do something," said Janice. "Maybe I should try and get a gastric band?"

"No," said Ted. "Why would you maim yourself like that? Why would you have major bloody surgery when you're on a course that will help you lose it naturally, without some bloody surgeon sticking a knife in you?"

"Ted's right," I said. "I like Liz. I think she's going to be really good for us all."

"I didn't expect to like her much," said Ted. "Especially given the weird outfits she wears, but she's very good at identifying what the problem is and getting to the nub of it, and not letting you wallow in it. I think that's good."

"I don't think I'll ever be able to do it," said Janice. "I really don't. As I said last week, I started eating heavily when my mum died, and I can't sort out the eating without talking about my feelings around Mum's death, which I find difficult. I can't see that changing anytime soon. At least you managed to bring some humour into it, Mary, I just seem to be in floods of tears the whole time."

"Yes, but then she tells me that I'm using humour to hide my anxiety and feelings."

"I think we all do that a bit," said Ted. "I noticed that last week you didn't want to dwell on what you thought had caused your eating problems, and used jokes and quips to avoid talking about it."

"That's what I do," I said, raising my glass.

"If you want to talk about it at any stage. You only have to call."

"OK," I said, but I knew there was no way I could talk about it. "I think it's great that we're all here for one another."

"Amen to that." Ted raised his pint and clinked my wine glass.

"I loved your story about the guy in the flat below seeing you shovelling chips into your mouth, while you were covered in grease," said Janice, with a smile. "That made me laugh a lot. Such bad timing that he came along. What did you say his name was?" "David," said Ted.

Janice and I both looked at him, impressed that he was able to remember Dave's name.

"Yes, Dave," I said. "What a good memory you have, Ted."

Ted nodded. "So what's the story with this Dave then?"

"Nothing," I said. "I've had a few dalliances with him but always end up feeling horrible afterwards. He makes me leave before it's light so that no one sees me coming out of his flat…you know…things like that. All very horrible. I always think that if I was slim it would be different. He wouldn't be ashamed."

"He sounds like an absolute dick," said Ted. "Sorry if that's blunt, but – Christ – no one in the world should be ashamed of being seen with you. You're…well…you're lovely, Mary. He's just using you. Tell him to piss off…you deserve more than that. If he upsets you again I'll go and sit on him, that'll teach him."

"Thank you." I tried to think through the scenario of Ted turning up and sitting on Dave. "But I know he really likes me. I just need to lose weight and everything will be OK."

"I'm with Ted." Janice had returned from the bar with our second drink of the evening. This is the problem with being in a round. You can't go out for one drink, you have to have the number of drinks as there are people around the table.

"You are both really kind, but I know he really likes me. I just need to lose weight." I was aware I was repeating myself and that they both thought I was nuts.

"Nobody needs to lose weight for someone to love them," said Ted. "Lose weight for yourself, for your children or for your future, but not because some dick with an over-inflated view of himself is embarrassed to be seen with you. Tell him to jog on, honestly."

"OK, OK," I said. "Let's leave it with the relationship advice. Janice, are you going to go and get extra help with looking back and understanding how you felt when your mum died, like Liz suggested? Or was that all a bit too much?"

Janice looked down at the table. "I don't know. The truth is that I don't want to think about it or talk about it, and the idea of digging through it and trying to understand it fills me with absolute horror. What do you think?"

"It's a difficult call. You don't want to make yourself feel worse, but I think talking it through with an expert would help in the long-term."

"Did you see a psychologist when you were younger, Mary?" she asked.

"No, I didn't," I replied, as lightly as I could.

It was my turn to go to the bar, so I used the opportunity to escape from the unwelcome conversation. Despite the awkwardness of the last interaction, I was quite enjoying the evening. I could see the boxes of crisps sitting behind the bar staff, but didn't even feel moved to buy some.

Progress, surely?

THE THIRD SESSION AT FAT CLUB

Well, there was good news and bad news to report before returning to Fat Club: I lost six pounds. I know! Huge achievement. I'd been really focused and thinking about the importance of eating healthily and exercising wherever I could. It was amazing.

The bad news… I slept with Dave. I know I shouldn't have, I know I should have persuaded him to make some sort of commitment to me before throwing myself under his duvet, but it doesn't work like that, does it? I thought if I spent a lot of time with him, and showed him it was enormous fun having me around, and how amazing I was in bed, he'd like me regardless of my weight.

So I trouped off to spend the evening with him, and we had an amazing time. He said he really liked me, then at 5 am his alarm went off, and he suggested I might like to leave because he was going to have to get into work early. He stood over me as I scrambled into my clothes, trying to arrange my hair and look as dignified as a woman possibly can while climbing into yesterday's knickers.

He didn't even give me a kiss on the cheek. "I guess you'll know how to get home," he said as I scrambled out of the door, fussing and falling over the complicated locking system before spilling out onto the pavement with my shoes on the wrong feet.

I ambled up the steps to my front door, opened it and burst into tears. I cried quite a lot that day, and it was my day off work, so I had a lot of time on my hands in which to cry, which wasn't helpful. What also wasn't helpful was the fact that I saw Dave leave for work at 8 am. He threw me out at five, having set his alarm clock to go off at that hour, but he didn't leave till eight. It doesn't take a genius to work out what was happening there.

But the good news was, I didn't fall into a fried breakfast, or eat my body weight in crisp sandwiches. I didn't feel the need to fall into food when my mad emotions fell about me. For the first time. It might not sound like much of an achievement, but – honestly – it was one of the greatest achievements of my life.

I had quite a lot of communication with Ted and Janice throughout the week, we phoned each other regularly which was nice and, to be fair, knowing I had got those two on the end of the phone helped a lot with the fight not to eat rubbish all the time. I phoned Ted one night when I'd walked past the chip shop and really wanted to go in. "You need to tell me not to turn round and go back there," I said.

"Don't turn round and go back there," he said, in a very stern voice. "Give me your address and I'll come round now with an apple instead."

We both laughed at the ridiculousness of it all. Why did I have to ring someone and ask them to tell me not to go to the chip shop?

The lovely thing was that I didn't feel as if the battier part of me was being judged by Janice and Ted. My great friends at work and my oldest friends – Sue and Charlie – were brilliant, but they were super slim and couldn't understand what I was going through. They didn't get it at all.

With Ted and Janice, I felt like I was with people who were exactly the same as me. I think that's why this whole group therapy thing works. You stop feeling like a freak who is out of control and needs to keep eating, and you start to feel like a member of a community that understands you have a simple problem that can be easily sorted.

The only issue on which I continued to disagree with Ted and Janice was Dave. Every time his name came up in conversation, Janice would sigh and Ted would bristle.

"Why would anyone treat another human being like that?" he'd ask. Then he'd add, "Actually, scrub that, why would any human being allow herself to be treated like that? That's what you need to ask yourself, young lady."

I knew he was right, but it didn't stop me hanging out of the window, watching Dave go to work, and trying to appear as alluring as possible on the steps of my flat as he returned, in the hope that he would invite me in again.

I arrived at the third session of Fat Club before Janice and Ted. Phil was sitting there on his own because his wife and ever-present companion had gone to the loo.

"Hello," I said as warmly as I could, but he just nodded and looked as if he wanted nothing on earth as much as he wanted me to leave him alone. When Philippa came back in, I retired graciously.

"Hello, trouble, where's Janice today?" said Ted, striding into the room and sitting next to me.

"No sign of her yet," I said.

"Janice said she was definitely coming," chipped in Liz, who was looking vibrant in a dress the colour of bananas. "I talked to her during the week and she was in good spirits."

"Oh good." Janice seemed very depressed last week when we were sitting in the pub. I was glad she was coming. "How are you doing? Good week?" I asked Ted.

"Pretty good," said Ted. "You probably noticed that I'm eight pounds lighter and looking very fly." He was relishing the small weight loss, as we all relished every development, however small, on the road to thinness. "I think I might leave the club now – my body is perfect," he added.

"Indeed," I said. "You don't want to lose any more, you might become anorexic, then you'll have to go to an entirely different support group."

"Yes, good point." He kissed me on the cheek. It was a lovely friendly gesture, but he went scarlet as soon as he'd done it. "Gosh, I'm so sorry," he said. "I didn't mean to do that."

Janice never turned up for the meeting which left me slightly anxious. I kept glancing at my phone to see if she had sent a text but there was nothing from her. As time wore on, the silence from her started to worry me.

In the end, I sent her a note: "Oy, where are you? I can't do this fat girl stuff on my own, you know."

No reply.

The news from within the group was good – people were starting to feel more 'empowered' (sorry, such a horrible word) and were making decisions not to resort to eating all the time.

The meeting finished on a positive note with lots of clapping and smiles and a huge grin of delight from Liz. In fact, the only thing missing from the whole evening was Janice.

"I can't get over how odd it is that she hasn't shown up," I told Liz, as Ted stood by my side, nodding to suggest that he agreed with me.

"I'll text Janice and tell her to meet us for a drink in our regular spot," he said.

"I wasn't thinking of going for a drink tonight, actually," I said.

"I've got quite a lot that I need to do." I saw Ted's face fall.

It was a complete lie. I had nothing I needed to do. The reason I wanted to go home was to see whether I could bump into Dave. I was aware he came back from work at around this time on a Tuesday (I wasn't a stalker…just observant). I hadn't seen him since our drunken fumble and my early exit from his flat, and having lost a bit of weight, and feeling ever so slightly more confident, I thought it would be good to bump into him.

"Just one then." Ted took my arm and led me towards the Shipmate's Arms. I was too weak to refuse, so we sat in the corner of the pub exactly where we'd sat the last time. We left a couple more messages for Janice, and Ted managed to calm me down a bit, reminding me that she was older, and probably had other commitments. It wasn't as easy for her to nip out to Fat Club. He was sure she was OK. He seemed convinced we would have heard from her if there was any problem.

The nice thing about being with Ted was that we were so similar… like brother and sister sometimes – with exactly the same stupid sense of humour. There was something warm and reassuring about him.

Always lovely and greatly entertaining.

When we left, Ted opened the door for me in a very gentlemanly fashion. He managed to tread that thin line between always treating me like an equal, which I loved, while managing to do all the charming, gentlemanly stuff that made me feel special.

His behaviour was a reminder of how long it had been since any man had treated me properly. Men don't open doors for fat girls. Sorry, it might sound like a horrible thing to say, but when I was sweet and pretty and slim, men opened doors. Since I became fat, they take one look at me bulldozing my way down the street and think 'well that one can clearly open the door herself – blimey she might take the whole thing off its hinges.'

I'm joking – sort of – but it's also true that men are more gentlemanly the more delicate and feminine you are, and 16 stone of fat is not considered remotely feminine to most men. The day you can't squeeze into your size 20 jeans is the day you learn to open doors for yourself.

THE VISIT

I was lounging in the bath when the call came through. It was Saturday morning and in traditional fashion, I'd watched all the morning cookery programmes while salivating and fantasising about pies and cakes and. I was now examining the rolls of fat banded around my waist and wishing I could lift them off to reveal a slimmer me underneath.

Wouldn't that be great? You eat as much as you want, then peel the fat off and throw it away when your tummy gets too big.

Ted's number popped up and I answered as cheerily as I could, trying not to splash and reveal that I was in the bath (something a little inappropriate about a man knowing you're wearing nothing but water and bubbles when he talks to you).

"Hello, fellow fatty; how you doing?"

"Not good," he said, and I sat up sharply.

"What's wrong? You sound dreadful." It was very unlike Ted to sound so downcast. He probably had just as many miserable days as the rest of us, but he wore any sadness lightly and presented himself to the world as upbeat and cheery.

"It's Janice."

"Oh no, what happened?"

BERNICE BLOOM

"I'm outside your apartment. I'd rather talk to you about it."

"Sure. How did you find out where I live?"

"Liz told me. Look, I'm sorry to disturb you, I wouldn't be here if it wasn't important."

"No, that's fine. Just give me a minute."

Rather than tell him I was in the bath and that I would be ready in 10 minutes, I jumped out of the bath water at top speed and frantically dried myself while climbing into the plain pyjama bottoms lying on the floor. They could pass for casual trousers – it was fine. I'd been outside in worse. I teamed them with an over-large, long-sleeved t-shirt with a horrible, unflattering picture of Mickey Mouse on the front. It didn't make for an elegant look. If I'd known what information I was about to receive from Ted, I might have rethought the decision to wear a novelty t-shirt.

Ted couldn't hide his surprise when I answered the door. He was used to seeing an extraordinarily large woman once a week when she was wrapped in a voluminous black coat. I suspect that seeing me braless and wet and wearing a t-shirt with a Disney character on it was altogether too much. There was way too much of me on show.

"Oh, have I disturbed you?" he asked, bending to look past me into the hallway as if I might have men gathered there, just waiting for my attention.

"No, not at all. Just out of the bath, no problem. Come in."

As he walked through the flat to the sitting room, I shouted, "I hope you don't mind the mess." Most people say things like: "I hope you don't mind dogs." I'm forced to warn people about the utterly chaotic state in which I live. As I walked along, I grabbed the clothes scattered around the place and shoved them into a corner, wiping the table down with the sleeve of my t-shirt to make it look better.

I could see Ted looking at me with a gentle smile on his lips; either this was because he recognised my behaviour in himself, or he had never seen anything so ludicrous in his life. I was erring towards the latter.

I made coffee while Ted sat in silence – there were no chirpy asides about the horrendous state of the apartment nor any mention of the biscuit barrel on the table.

"I put eight sugars in yours, I hope that's OK," I said when I returned with the drinks, but Ted wasn't listening.

"It's bad news," he said.

"No, I didn't really put eight sugars in – only joking."

"No, not the sugars, nutcase, the news I'm about to tell you."

I sat next to Ted on the sofa. Together we completely filled a sofa which boldly claimed to be able to seat four.

"I called Janice on her mobile," said Ted. "And a guy answered."

"Ooooo...lucky Janice," I said.

"The guy was a nurse. Janice is in hospital."

"Oh no, is she OK?"

"Yes, she's fine now. She took an overdose."

Ted stopped for a while to allow this to sink in. "Mary, she tried to kill herself."

"Shit."

"She'd just had enough of it all...the catcalls, the 'oy fatty' every time she left the house. The fight to be dignified when squeezing into bus seats and the fact that no one wanted to sit next to her on the train."

I could feel the tears stinging in the backs of my eyes. We'd all been there, and I knew how upset Janice was. Those of us struggling to control our weight have all been given the sort of abuse that would see the perpetrator locked up if they said it to someone black, with a disability or mentally impaired. I carry all my weight on my tummy, and I've heard shouts of 'Can someone call a midwife' too many times to mention. When I travel in cars and on planes, I can never get the seat belt around me. It's always mortifyingly embarrassing. But I've never wanted to kill myself.

"I can't believe she was feeling that low," I said, as Ted stared down at the brown and cream carpet on the floor under the coffee table. "She was miserable at Fat Club last week, but – Christ – not that miserable."

BERNICE BLOOM

"We all seem OK on the outside," said Ted. "Don't we? I mean – that's what we do. We all seem *not that miserable*."

"Yes," I said because I didn't know what else to say. No words seemed adequate to express my surprise, upset and bubbling fury inside me. How could Janice have sunk that low?

"Shall we go and visit her?" he asked.

"Yes, definitely. Let's go," I said, standing up and following him without speaking. Our coffee lay undrunk on the table as we filed through the front door.

GOING to the hospital to visit someone who tried to kill themselves because they couldn't stand being fat anymore is not a pleasant thing for anyone to do. I'd suggest it's infinitely harder and more emotionally crucifying when you yourself are obese. We asked which ward she was on, and I'm sure the nurse looked down at my stomach and the way my t-shirt rounded it.

Janice was sitting up in bed when we found her. She looked sheepish when we walked into the room and turned the colour of ham when we approached her.

"Gosh, you didn't have to come," she said, looking at me and then at Ted. "You must have a million things to do. You didn't have to come out here and see me."

I wanted to reach out and hug her, to hold her close and tell her never, ever to hurt herself again. But I didn't. I'm too British for all that. I just reassured her, told her there was nowhere I'd rather be, and sat on the small wooden chair near the bed, handing her a bunch of flowers we had picked up on the way.

"How are you feeling?"

Her eyes filled with tears. "I feel much better; thank you for coming."

"Janice, I'm so sorry, I don't know what to say. You should have rung one of us or talked to us. Perhaps we could have helped?"

"No one could've helped. I was too low to reach out to anyone," she replied.

"But, I wish you'd said something...anything. We could have tried to help."

"Mary, you're lovely, and I cherish your friendship, but there are some things that no one can help with."

"Just as long as you know we're here and care about you," said Ted. He leaned over and kissed Janice on the head so tenderly that I felt my heart shift a little inside me. What good people these were. Really good people.

Since Ted had driven me to the hospital, he drove me back home after the visit. The mood had lifted considerably since confirmation that Janice was OK; she was out of danger and would be fine. She had even talked about coming to the next Fat Club session.

"It's shocking that she got so low, isn't it?" said Ted.

"I think that's the hardest thing for me," I replied. "To think that she could have died. Can you imagine?"

"I know. Promise me that if you ever feel low, you'll call," said Ted. "You know...if you ever fed up. Please just call me."

"I promise I will," I replied as Ted pulled up outside my flat. "And you too. You call me if you feel fed up."

Ted smiled and touched my arm. "Of course."

"Do you want to come in for coffee?" I asked as I pretended to undo the seatbelt. I hadn't even tried to fasten it...ladies with very fat tummies and seat belts are an unhappy combination. But I felt so embarrassed that I always pretended to take it off.

"That would be nice," he replied. "Or we could nip out for something to eat? Let me buy you a late lunch or early dinner. I haven't eaten...most unlike me."

"Neither have I," I lied, hoping he didn't remember the cookie jar on the coffee table and the plates discarded on the side in the kitchen.

"Then, this evening, if you fancy it, we could go to a party at a pub not far from here. It's just a leaving do for a friend who's moving away, but it'll be fun. Come with me. I'll drive and make sure you get home safely afterwards. Anyway, see how you feel after lunch."

"Sure." I wasn't sure about the drinks party, but I fancied lunch. "Let me go in and get changed quickly. I won't be long."

BERNICE BLOOM

"You look absolutely fine like that," he said as I struggled to open the door.

"No, I have to get changed," I said. I'm not the most fashionable girl, but even I would think it inappropriate to go out for lunch with a man dressed in pyjama bottoms and a hideous T-shirt. Even fat girls have standards, you know.

"No problem," said Ted.

I clambered out of the car and walked towards my flat, with Ted following closely behind. As I approached the little gate, I saw Dave coming out of his flat. He looked like he was off to the gym. He was stubbly, unkempt and looked absolutely gorgeous. Dave glanced at me, at Ted, and back again.

"Hello, what have we got here then?" he said.

"This is Ted," I muttered while Dave's handsome face looked at mine. "Ted's just a friend, you know. Just someone I met, not a boyfriend or anything. Just someone I know."

"Oh, I see." Dave gave a smile. "Well then, Ted, you won't mind if I ask Mary whether she fancies coming round for pizza later. Perhaps to watch a film or something?"

"Sure, I'd love to." I didn't stop for even half a second to consider my words.

"Actually, we've got plans," said Ted. He was right, of course, we did have plans, but in that moment, rather shamefully, I just wanted him to go away.

"We'll do that another time," I said, my voice ringing with irritation. I couldn't look Ted in the eye. His shoulders were slouched over, and his face was full of confusion. "You might as well head off now. I'll see you on Tuesday at the club, OK?"

"What club's that?" asked Dave.

"Nothing, really. Just a club," I responded.

"It's a weight loss club," said Ted.

"Ha ha, perfect," said Dave. "That's hysterical. The two tubbies from Fat Club."

Ted looked from me to Dave, and back again, then he walked back out of the gate, across the road and got into his car. My insides felt crushed as I watched him drive away.

Dave also watched Ted leave, smiling victoriously at the departing car. "That's funny: Weight loss Club!" he said. "See you around 4 pm, OK?"

"Looking forward to it," I said seductively, letting myself into my flat. I knew I had treated Ted abysmally, but I had such a thing about Dave, and I desperately wanted to spend the evening with him. I'd lost 10lb. Ten pounds! Dave needed to see my new body. Also, I convinced myself I needed cheering up after the day I'd just endured. A lazy evening on Dave's sofa, with the prospect of a bit of physical action later, was everything I needed. I did feel terrible about Ted though…really bad.

MY HOT DATE WITH DAVE

By the time 4 pm arrived, I was dressed up in the best lingerie you can get in a size 40GG and feeling good. It was a peculiar time to meet for pizza – it wasn't lunch and it wasn't dinner. Still, it was an invitation from Dave, so I wasn't going to question it or analyse it too closely.

I wandered down to his flat in my best black trousers, which were now very loose around my waist. Yes! I could have put smaller ones on, but I decided to go for the bigger pair which were both smarter and gave me the lovely warm feeling of being loose, thus reminding me of the weight I'd lost. I knocked on Dave's door; there was no reply. The lights were off inside, and the flat gave the impression of being entirely empty. I waited for about 20 minutes (I know what you're thinking – who would wait outside someone's door for 20 minutes? Christ, woman, get a grip) and then went back upstairs, got a pen and paper and made a note which I pushed underneath his door. I was just retreating when Dave arrived back from the gym. He looked at me blankly.

"You told me to come down for pizza and video?" I said.

"Oh, OK then, yes – sure, you can come in." He didn't sound overly excited about the prospect.

His flat was in a state of chaos, much like mine, but for some reason – perhaps because I'm female – I admonished him lightly and offered to help clear it up.

"Sure," he said with a smile, removing his t-shirt to display his spectacularly gorgeous torso.

"I'm going to have a quick shower; tidy if you want."

I'd meant that we could tidy up together in a kind of flirting foreplay sort of fashion. I wasn't offering to become his cleaner.

Still, I wanted to get into his good books, so while he showered, I started rounding up all the old packaging, cans and other assorted rubbish that had been thrown around the place. I shoved them into a bin bag. Dave was in his bedroom by now, presumably getting dressed.

"The Hoover is in the cupboard under the stairs," he said.

I knew it was ridiculous to get the Hoover out and clean his flat, but I was also madly happy to be there and thought he would be so grateful it would make everything good between us. I pulled out the Hoover and ran it around the flat, polishing the surfaces as I went, making it look lovely. Dave walked out with his jeans on…no shirt.

Yes.

"You're an angel." He kissed me on the tip of my nose. "One other thing – you aren't any good at ironing, are you?"

"Um, I guess. Why?"

"I have no shirts to wear."

I put up the ironing board and plugged in the iron, and I know what you're thinking – you're thinking; this woman is a bloody moron. Well, yes, perhaps you're right. Dave stood there shirtless (a happy moment in the whole unedifying, desperate mess), and I ironed the shirt he handed to me, taking care to make sure it was perfect. Because somehow, somewhere, in the deep recesses of my soul, I thought he might glance at himself and see how good he looked and feel great, and associate me with that feeling. It was a long shot, but my 'relationship' with Dishy Dave was built on long shots.

I handed him the still-warm shirt and put away the ironing accoutrements.

"The flat looks great," he said. "Emma's coming round later; she'll be very impressed."

"Emma?"

I felt a dagger tear into my heart. Not that I thought he didn't have girlfriends, I knew damn well he had girlfriends – bloody dozens of them – but I thought tonight would just be about me, I also thought that seeing how I was getting slimmer and looking better, this would prompt him to dump all those other idiots, and the two of us would be together, forever.

"Do you mind if we don't get pizza?" he said. "I'm straight from the gym; I might just have a power shake or something."

"No, that's fine by me." It was fine – I didn't want to eat pizza. I'd said yes to pizza because I wanted us to spend the evening together. I fiddled with my hands in my lap and tried to think of something to say…something that would please him.

"I've lost some weight," I said, flinching as I heard the words and the way they rang with desperation.

"Well done," he said. "Where have you lost it from?"

"I mean – I've just lost weight generally, I've been going to this club, and I'm determined to lose loads of weight," I said.

"Of course…Weightloss Club." Dave collapsed with laughter. "Oh my God, that's hysterical," he was wide-eyed with excitement as he got into his stride. "You and that fat bloke from earlier. Just the funniest thing ever. Do they round up all the fatties and put them in one room to talk about food?"

I'd never seen him look so animated or laugh so much, so I joked along with him for a while, trying to smile and giggle. Then I thought about Janice and stopped abruptly. The woman had tried to kill herself because of the nastiness and lack of respect that had become the soundtrack to her life. This wasn't very funny at all.

Then thoughts of Ted came into my mind; lovely, sweet, kind and funny Ted. The look on his face when he'd turned and walked away.

"God, that must be hysterical," said Dave, falling into the recently plumped-up cushions on his sofa and laughing out loud. "Just a whole load of fat people talking about why they can't stop eating. Honestly, that must be so funny. Can you tape it for me?"

"Look, if you've got plans, I'll head off," I said.

"Why?" said Dave. "She is not coming for another hour… We can do that thing I like when you get your enormous titties out, and I cum on them."

"I've got stuff on." I moved towards the door and opened it while he stayed on the sofa.

"Well, thanks for tidying up," he said as I left, pulling the door behind me.

What the hell on earth was wrong with me? Why had I given up a lovely night with a genuinely decent, nice man to go there and be humiliated by that moron? I let myself into my flat and called Ted's number, it rang out and then went to answer phone. He didn't want to talk to me; who could blame him?

Next, I went onto Facebook, and I don't know why but I started looking for him on there. I found Ted's profile fairly easily and smiled as I read his updates. He was really funny. Self-deprecating. Witty. Popular.

There were pictures of him as a sportsman, and he looked bloody gorgeous…much better than Downstairs Dave has ever looked. Then pictures of him having his facial hair shaved into its current state. He'd done it for charity. Three of them had let children at a cancer hospital design their facial hair arrangements to raise money for charity. I'd been mocking that daft facial hair, but it was all for charity. He was such a nice guy.

There were loads of comments on his profile. Many of them from women.

In fact…he had a lot of female friends on Facebook. Loads of them. All the comments after his jokes were from women…all telling him how wonderful he was and what fun he was. They all hoped to bump into him soon.

Bloody hell.

Shit.

He was kind and popular and had female attention coming out of his ears.

There was a reference to a drinks party in a pub. I wondered whether that was the one he'd asked me to go to with him. Bugger – it looked like it would be good fun. His friends had posted funny messages about how much they were looking forward to it and daft pictures of the group together. Ted was at the centre of all the pictures, being silly and having a laugh.

Bollocks. What an idiot I was.

I went into the kitchen and looked around for something to eat. I reached for the chocolate biscuits and stopped myself. Instead, I took two cream crackers and nibbled on them while I returned to the sofa, all while flicking through Google on my phone. I was caught in a stalkerish trance as I tried to discover everything about him. There were pictures of Ted as an aspiring rugby player and articles about how talented he was.

Why hadn't I looked him up before? Presumably, because I wasn't interested in him before. Now I was, though. Quite suddenly, I realised I liked him and was overwhelmed by fascination. I had Google Fever. Nothing could stop me.

It didn't help that Saturday night TV was rubbish. I sat in front of a couple of game shows without really watching them – I was too intent on checking out pictures of Ted on my phone. Then the National Lottery results came on, and I spent a lot of time imagining what I'd do if I won the millions. Perhaps I'd buy the whole house and throw Downstairs-Dave out from his flat below. I fantasised for quite a long time about him lying on the pavement, begging me to throw him crumbs.

I'd phone Ted every so often, but my calls all went unanswered. I'd cocked everything up.

Then, it occurred to me. It was a flash of inspiration: Why didn't I go to the party?

If I turned up and spoke to him, I might be able to persuade him that I was not a horrible person, just an idiot. Directions to get there were fairly simple; two buses and I would be partying with Ted and his friends. Sod it, I was wearing my wonderful (if large) lacy lingerie, and my trousers were loose; what did I have to lose? I picked up my handbag, grabbed my lipstick and covered my lips in scarlet gunk. Now what could possibly go wrong?

As I stepped out of my door, I was greeted by someone who looked like they'd stepped off the pages of a magazine. She was tall, thin and teetering into Dave's flat.

"Hi, are you Emma?" I asked. "Are you heading into Dave's place?"

"Yes," she said, with one of those high-pitched Marilyn Monroe-style voices the men seem to find so appealing.

"I'd give it a few minutes," I said. "His husband has only just left. He asked me to tell you."

Barbie Doll looked at me with eyes as wide as they were blue.

"He still wants to see you, but you should know he's married to a man."

I headed off with a cheery wave, leaving the woman standing on the steps, wondering what to do.

Ha. I felt strong, I felt powerful, and I felt magnificent. Now all I had to do was get myself to Wimbledon. I was quite excited. No, I was very excited; this was a lovely thing – there was a man there who genuinely liked me for me. He had never asked me to iron a shirt or clean his flat. He didn't seem to want anything from me other than my company.

As I thought about the fun times we'd had sitting at Fat Club, laughing our heads off, I started to feel increasingly excited. He was a nice man. Why hadn't I seen that before? What was I doing messing around with Dodgy Dave when I should've been with Super Ted? I changed buses and began getting even more excited. I'd be there in 15 minutes. I checked my makeup in a hand mirror, preening my eyebrows and playing with my hair while adding yet more lipstick, oblivious to the stares of interest from those gathered on seats around me. Nothing mattered but looking as good as I possibly could for Ted.

I stepped off the bus. There was the pub right in front of me. Ted would be in there, and I would be joining him. I had butterflies. When was the last time I'd had butterflies? I couldn't remember the last time

I'd felt so excited. My hands were sticky, so I wiped them against my coat, walked towards the door and forced myself to go inside.

I was so nervous.

I walked in and couldn't see Ted or anyone I recognised from the pictures on Facebook. I approached the bar and ordered a large glass of white wine. I'd just sit and drink it calmly, looking around until I saw someone who looked familiar, and then I'd stroll over and see whether I could see Ted. I hadn't yet decided whether to pretend I was here having a drink and had bumped into him, or confess I'd seen this on Facebook and wanted to come and meet him. I thought I might judge his reaction to my presence before revealing why I was there.

It was odd, but there was no large gathering of people in the pub. It was packed; all the tables and chairs were taken up, but no sign of a big group. I decided to call him again, but there was no answer.

"Excuse me," I said to the barman. "Are there any private parties here today?"

"Yes," he said, pointing to the far door. "Just go through there, up the stairs, push the door on your left, and that's the function room; there's a party going on there."

Ahhhhhh! That made sense. Finally, I would get to see Ted.

"Thank you so much," I said, feeling those butterflies all over again. I stood up, downed the rest of my drink, and headed off. I went up the stairs and into the door on the left to find a party in full swing. Brilliant. This was it. All the people seemed about the right age. Still, walking into a party was quite odd when you were alone, especially when you hadn't been invited and didn't know the person whose party it was.

I tried to look confident as I sat at the bar and ordered a drink. I searched my purse for money, but the barman stopped me. "It's a free bar," he said. That made me feel all the more awkward and embarrassed. I didn't want to steal drinks from these people; I just wanted to see Ted. Luckily, everyone was having such a good time at the free bar that they didn't seem to notice an intruder in their midst.

I sat and drank, playing on my phone, pretending to text someone, laughing to myself and looking as if I was having a jolly good time at the strange party with these people I didn't know. I was fairly sure Ted wasn't in the room, but perhaps he was, and I couldn't see him. Perhaps he was in the loo?

I had another drink, my awkwardness and embarrassment growing even further because, this time, I was ordering a drink when I knew it would be free. It was all too ridiculous, but to insist to the barman that I wanted to pay because I didn't know the person whose party it was, or indeed any of the guests, would be more ridiculous still.

I walked around the room's circumference as groups of drunk friends jostled and took pictures of the partygoers enjoying the night. One guy tried to grab me into a group shot, but I managed to wriggle away. Everyone was drunk and having a great time; pictures were taken, and jokes were told. It was a lovely party, but Ted wasn't at it. I called his mobile again; no answer.

I had walked around the room three times, stared at everyone until they felt uncomfortable, and avoided about 20 photographs. It was useless…time to go home.

THE FOURTH SESSION AT FAT CLUB

I was sad not to have bumped into Ted at the party, but at least I knew that I would see him at the next Fat Club meeting. He had not responded to any of my calls or texts so this felt like the only way to talk to him.

I just wanted everything to be OK between us again.

I wanted him back in my life.

Janice wasn't going this week so there was no chance of us having our Three Musketeers gathering in the pub afterwards. Perhaps just Ted and I could go? That would be nice. In tribute to that thought, I had dispensed with my usual big black, cover-everything coat, and wore a cherry red cardigan instead. I then put the black coat on top, of course, because I'm not an idiot.

I'd spoken to Janice many times over the week and had met her for a coffee at a small cafe near Hampton Court Palace. It had been lovely to see her walk in looking well and back to her own self. She said she had started seeing a psychiatrist, which was helping her a lot.

When we met, I swore her to secrecy and told her that I liked Ted. I hadn't realised how much I liked him at first, but now I did. I also told her about the night from hell when I'd traipsed all the way over to Wimbledon to see him.

THE MARY BROWN BOOKS

Janice laughed at that bit. She loved the idea of me at the party, not knowing anyone but pretending I did. "My God, woman, you've cheered me up," she said.

"This is the sad bit," I said. "What part of this is cheering you up?" In truth, though, it was so bloody farcical that it was funny.

"You sitting there, drinking free drinks," she said. "If I'd been well, I would have come with you, and we'd have had a right laugh. I think Ted's lovely, and he clearly likes you."

"Do you think?"

"Of course. You can tell a mile off."

"But what about the way I behaved? The way I dismissed him as if he were a piece of tissue stuck on the heel of my shoe. I was so eager to get rid of him that I didn't think about his feelings at all. I behaved so badly. I hate myself."

"Come on now, stop that. You'll be able to apologise to Ted when you see him, and the two of you will soon be bosom buddies again."

"Gosh, I hope so. Roll on Tuesday."

TED WAS ALREADY at Fat Club when I walked in, but people were sitting on either side so I couldn't get right next to him. Instead, I waved and smiled at him from my seat, and he just looked down at his notes. I'd tried to call him so many times and sent dozens of friendly texts, apologising. I left a message saying I couldn't wait to see him on Tuesday night. He didn't reply to anything until this morning when he sent a simple one saying: "See you tonight." Not exactly a ringing endorsement of our friendship, but at least he was communicating with me.

The other thing I should tell you is that I lost more weight, bringing my total weight to 14 lbs. Fourteen pounds! Can you believe that? That's a stone, that is...a bloody stone!

"Come on, Mary," said Liz, running her hands through the new green streaks in her hair and pulling her pink cardigan around her. "Your turn to talk. Tell us how your week went."

BERNICE BLOOM

Ted had spoken before me and updated everyone on Janice, so I added that she sent her love and was feeling much better now.

Everyone clapped, and their murmurs of support filled the room.

"How has your week been apart from that?" asked Liz. "Tell us about your eating."

"OK. I'm managing not to shovel down lots of food, I've lost some weight and feel much better. I'm genuinely feeling like I might be able to do it this time. You know, shift a load of weight and get myself healthier and fitter."

"That's wonderful news," said Liz. "And how is it all making you feel?"

"Good," I said, preparing to sit down.

"Sometimes when people have been using food as a crutch for a long time, they feel the absence when it's taken away, and they need something else... Have you been drinking more? Walking more? Gambling, buying clothes or doing anything else in an obsessive way?" she asked. "Try to share everything so we can all help one another."

"No, I'm OK," I said.

"Good. That's great to hear. You haven't shared with the group quite as much as the others have about your reasons for overeating in the first place. Right at the beginning of the course, you hinted that something had happened to you when you were younger. If you decide to talk about that, we're all here for you."

"I'm OK, thanks," I said.

"Right, well, let's end it there for this week," said Liz.

I turned around to talk to Ted, but he'd jumped up and headed out of the room. No goodbye. Not a word.

"Mary, if you want to talk but don't necessarily want to share your feelings with the group, you can always call me," she said. "Don't ever feel like you're alone, will you?"

"No," I said, still watching the door that had slammed shut after Ted's hasty departure. "I won't. Thank you."

SESSION FIVE OF FAT CLUB

"Hello, anyone there?" I was standing by the bins, shouting up at the window. "Hello."

Silence. Not a whisper.

How odd. Luckily, I was in plenty of time for Fat Club. It didn't start for another half hour, so there was no panic, but it would be useful to get some sort of response. I wandered onto the street and looked up and down it, then sat on the wall and checked through my messages.

"Hi, it's me," I typed in. "I'm outside your flat – am shouting up at your window like some sort of loony but you can't hear me. Please come down soon before someone calls the police and they arrest me."

I put a smiley face after the message, to indicate that I was only joking about the police coming, but I was very serious about wanting her to come out soon.

This is the problem when someone you know has tried to harm herself…you're forever worried that she might do it again. Every time Janice hadn't replied to a text or not taken my call, I'd been thrown into a blind panic about where she was and what she was doing, like now. Janice's house was in darkness in front of me, bar one lit window. I'd spent 15 minutes shouting up at that solitary light, and there had been no response.

I rang the doorbell again while simultaneously calling her. She knew I was coming to meet her so we could travel to Fat Club together. We'd spoken only this morning. Shit, what should I do if she didn't answer? Who should I call?

"Janice, it's me again. Look – no problem if you don't want to come tonight – no pressure. I just need to know you're OK. Please send me a text to tell me that everything is alright x."

Nothing.

It was 10 minutes till Fat Club was due to start and 20 minutes after the time I had arranged to be at Janice's house. This was now odd. Bollocks. I couldn't sit there all evening and miss Fat Club – what would be the point of that? But I had to check that Janice was OK. I couldn't go anywhere until I'd heard from her.

Every part of me wanted to ring Ted. I knew he'd be able to help and know what to do. But I also knew that the last thing he wanted was to get a call from me.

I banged on the door again, shouting at the window, "Hi, Janice, it's me – Mary – I've come to walk to Fat Club with you. Are you there?"

Nothing.

Perhaps if I texted Ted? That wouldn't be so awful, would it?

"Hi, I'm outside Janice's house. I arranged to meet her here 20 minutes ago, but there's no sign of her. Not sure what to do…" I wrote.

He called straight away.

"Ted, I'm really worried," I said. "There's no sign of her, I've shouted and texted, but no one's come to the door."

"OK, don't worry. I'm just pulling up outside the community centre; I'll come over there now. What's the address?"

I gave him the address, and it took about a minute for his car to come screeching down the road. He jumped out, running towards me – a superhero in loose-fitting jogging bottoms.

"I can't get any answer from her," I said.

Ted banged on the door in a very manly fashion, and eventually,

THE MARY BROWN BOOKS

we heard a shout from a lady at the window above. "Will you just go away," she said in an old-sounding voice. I stepped back so I could see.

She was, indeed, very elderly and looked quite scared.

"Is Janice there?" I said.

"No. There's no one called Janice here," she replied. "Stop screeching at my door, will you."

"Are you sure we're at the right place?" asked Ted.

"Yes." I opened my phone and looked at the text Janice sent with her address.

"Yes, this is it," I said triumphantly. "It says 10a Bath Avenue."

"No, this is Bath Road," said Ted. "We're in the wrong place, you numpty."

We moved quickly down the steps, jumped into Ted's car, and whizzed around to Bath Road. There – sure enough – standing outside 10a was Janice, her coat wrapped around her against the cold, looking slightly miffed.

"Sorry, sorry," I said as we stopped beside her. "I went to the wrong address. I'm an idiot. But why haven't you got your phone turned on?"

"Oh shit." Janice looked at her phone and saw the messages I'd left and the calls I tried to make. "I left it on mute from when I was in the hospital earlier. Sorry."

"Hospital?" Ted and I cried, in unison, glancing at each other.

"Just a check-up, nothing to worry about."

All three of us bombed down to the community centre, running through the doors 15 minutes after the class had started.

"I'm so sorry we're late," I said as Liz's face lit up at the sight of us. "It's completely my fault."

"She doesn't know her avenues from her roads," said Ted.

I looked at him and smiled. Ted smiled back. YES!

It was a moving session in which Janice tried to explain to a group of overweight people why she'd tried to take her own life…without saying it was because she was overweight. She talked about her misery and anger and how she felt judged, rejected and horrible. Everyone listened intently. She was preaching to the converted, but every one of us was wondering how she got so low. We'd all had moments of frustration, anger and despair. What had happened to Janice to make her think that death was an alternative to dieting?

Afterwards, we headed for the pub. Janice was emotionally drained after speaking out about her attempted suicide so she stayed quiet for most of the time. Ted seemed relaxed and happy as he downed his pint and flicked through some messages on his phone. It wasn't quite the same as it had been in the past – with Ted and me laughing and joking constantly – but it was a step in the right direction. At least we could get along together.

"Does it help to talk about it like that?" I asked Janice. "You know – share the details of it? I find it really, really hard to go into all my emotions and feelings. I'm happy to tell people about my food intake and weight, but as soon as the questions start about what makes me eat, or anything about the past, I clam up straight away."

"We've noticed." Janice touched my leg affectionately. "I agree with you – it's horrible to talk about it, and you feel very vulnerable and a bit silly at the time, but it does make you feel better afterwards."

"Good," I said. "I'm so glad you're feeling better."

I looked up, and Ted was staring at me with narrowed eyes. "The weirdest thing," he said.

"What?" Janice and I chorused.

"It doesn't matter."

"What doesn't matter?"

"Nothing," he said. "Nothing, it's not important."

"I'm intrigued now," said Janice. "You have to tell us what's on your mind."

"Well, I was just scrolling through Facebook, and some friends have put up pictures from a drinks party they had a couple of weeks ago. I didn't go to it, but there's a woman who seems to be kind of sneaking around in the background but seems to be in every picture. My friends have all circled her and written, 'Anyone know who this is?' And the odd thing is it looks exactly like you, Mary."

THE FINAL SESSION

In total, over the six weeks that the Fat Club sessions had been running, I'd lost 19 lbs. I was comfortably down a dress size, I felt better than ever and I'd met a man I really liked: that was the good news.

The less good news was that I still had about 60lbs to lose, and the man I liked was aware that I may have gate-crashed a party of all his friends that I wasn't invited to and crept around in the background like some sort of lunatic.

I denied everything when Ted mentioned it last week, of course, despite the fact that Janice was sitting there and she knew it to be true.

"But it looks just like you," he'd said, while I tried to change the conversation by asking them both whether they liked my boots. It was only when I realised that the boots I was trying to distract them with were the same ones I was wearing in the picture that I took my foot off the table and downed my wine. "More drinks, anyone?"

Eventually, Ted let it go, though I could see him looking from my handbag to my coat and thinking 'The woman in the picture has exactly the same stuff as you…' He had every right to be confused but

I couldn't offer any sort of explanation that would reassure him about my sanity. So I'd just stayed silent.

That was last week, now we were back in our run-down community centre for the last session of what had been an amazing course. Everyone was there except for Liz. This was the first time that she hadn't been there before us, grinning warmly, while dressed in some peculiar outfit, and waiting to greet us all like toddlers on our first day at nursery.

"I'm sorry," she said, bowling in dressed in a canary yellow coat, clutching piles of literature and folders, looking windswept and unkempt. "I have so many bits of paper to give you and I just went and left them all at home. I had to turn back, and the traffic was terrible. All OK now, though. Right, how's everyone feeling?"

There were mutters of general happiness from people as Liz took off her coat to reveal a bright purple jumper, black trousers and pea-green shoes. It was a fairly moderate outfit for her, but the shoe choice was remarkable, to say the least.

"Let's go round the room one final time, and then I want to tell you about the next stage in the overeaters programme," said Liz. "Janice, let's start with you if that's OK. I know we spoke a little bit during the week, but I'm sure everyone in the room is keen to find out how you're feeling."

"I'm fine, honestly – no one needs to worry," said Janice. "You've all been so incredibly kind and supportive... I can't tell you what a difference it's made. I – um – sorry, this is all very emotional for me to talk about, but I hit a real low point a few weeks ago... I don't know what happened to tip me over the edge, but I had this blinding moment when I just didn't want to be here. Now I look back and I can't quite understand what happened in my head. I don't recognise the person who was so low that she couldn't face the future.

"I promised Liz that if anything like that ever happens again, I will talk to someone. Talk to you guys, to be honest, because what I've learned from all your kind messages and sympathetic calls is that I've met some friends for life on this course. I'm so grateful to you all."

Janice spoke about the psychological help she had been getting and how much she was benefitting from talking through her feelings, worries and concerns. "I know it sounds odd, this whole therapy thing… I mean – how can just talking about an issue make it better? In some ways, you might think it would make things worse. Talking about things might make them bigger in your mind. But it's not like that. I genuinely feel as if the problems and the pressure they exert on me are lifted by talking them through. It's as if you're getting them out of your mind when you share them. And you know what it's like when you have negative thoughts left festering in your mind – they grow and distort and become like little monsters in there. The help you've all given me, coupled with the psychological help I've been getting have made me happier and more content than I've felt for years. Thanks so much, everyone."

There was an enormous round of applause when she finished. I stood up and started clapping above my head, but people looked at me as if I was nuts, so I sat back down again.

Veronica spoke next. I still wasn't sure about her, which was probably a bit mean of me because I didn't know her. I mean, she was probably lovely, but there was something unattractive about the way she seemed to want to talk about her modelling career all the time. I was a really good gymnast when I was younger…I mean – really good. I competed all over the world, but I wouldn't mention that every time I opened my mouth. Somehow it felt wrong, too self-indulgent to be appropriate. You don't stand up and tell everyone how great you were. This was Fat Club, for God's sake, we were all morbidly obese, did we need to hear about her life as a size six model?

"One of the things I find really hard is letting go of the fact that I used to be a model," she said, and I must admit I thought straight away 'Here we go again, Veronica, do tell us all about your modelling career. We're all desperate to hear everything about it.' But she surprised me. "I'm not saying that being a model is important… Gosh, it's not like you're trying to find a cure for cancer or help dying kids, but it's one of those professions that, because it affects you away from work, it starts to seep into your life. If you work in a shop, once that shop's closed, you don't have to work in the shop – it's as simple and straightforward as that. If you want to go out and have a huge take-away and get drunk, it's not going to have any impact on your job at all. But if you're a model, you must live like a model. Even if the catwalk shows are weeks away and you're not earning a penny from the profession, you can't go out for dinner and stuff yourself. You can't do anything that's going to make your skin look bad, make you fat or make you in any way unattractive.

"I'd go on holiday and still be eating cotton wool instead of food and drinking loads of water, and panicking about whether the sun would damage my skin or the salt water affect my hair. If you're a model, you're a model every minute of every day, not just when the shop's open.

"Can you imagine what sort of pressure this creates? No one can live like that, which is why so many models go off the rails and take tonnes of drugs or mainline whisky to cope with the hunger and the pain. The truth is that you can't live a life when you're always on show and constantly being judged, without having something to lean on. Hardly ever eating and being permanently exhausted is a rubbish way to live.

"I coped with it all by binge eating, and because of this, I developed bulimia. Not very good bulimia because I put on a load of weight, as you can see from the state of me, but bulimia nonetheless. I'd binge and binge, usually late at night when everyone else was asleep, then make myself sick and cry myself to sleep. Then I'd shower, eat half an apple and head back to the studio to do more modelling. It was rubbish, and it affected me deeply and now I don't have any idea how to eat properly. I never learned that. Food for me was always a comfort, a warm blanket to wrap around myself when the world felt nasty and cruel.

"I know I can be a bit stand-offish at times, and I don't find it that easy to socialise and meet new people, but it's been lovely to be here and to meet everyone and to realise not only that I'm not alone, but that it's all going to be OK because that's how it feels, you know. It feels like it's all going to be OK. I know that with hard work I can get rid of the demons and I've got some brilliant new friends, so thank you, everyone."

I applauded Veronica wildly when she finished; then it was my turn. I wasn't sure what to say. I felt so drained after the last two talks. It had been so moving to listen to them, but I knew that I wasn't able to share my past with people in the same way. I decided, instead, to share my present and my future.

"These sessions have changed my life," I said. "I came here wanting to lose weight, and I have lost quite a lot, to be fair. I've gone down a dress size and feel about a million times better. But I have also gained more than I have lost. I've gained confidence, and I have realised that I'm not alone. Other people are struggling too, and they – that's you guys – are very inspiring. There are two people who I've become particularly friendly with – Janice and Ted – and I'd like to thank them for their friendship.

"I'd also like to make a bit of a confession – we all make mistakes as we go through life, and I've made a few recently. One massive one. A guy I like – let's call him, um, Tarzan – asked me out, and I said yes, then another guy, a rather vain and idiotic guy – let's call him 'the wanker' – suggested I meet up with him on the same night.

"For reasons I can't possibly explain, I changed my plans and went out with the wanker instead, and I dumped Tarzan. Can you imagine anything more ridiculous? Dumping Tarzan and going out with a wanker?

"Anyway, so I went out with the wanker, and realised he was just using me, and I was bonkers and really liked the first guy – Tarzan. So I rushed out of the wanker's house, and I tried calling Tarzan loads and loads, but he didn't return my calls. I even went out that evening to the party he was supposed to be at, but he wasn't there, and all his friends were looking at me and trying to work out what on earth I was doing there."

I looked at Ted and saw him smile as he realised it had been me in those photos – skulking around at the back of the drinks party.

"Anyway, I don't know why I'm telling you all this," I continued. "I

BERNICE BLOOM

just want you to know that a kind, lovely, genuinely nice guy is better than an arsehole in a nice suit."

I sat down to confused looks and half-claps. No one knew who Tarzan was. Liz was nodding, but I could see she had no idea why I'd shared my bizarre dating story with the group. Ted was looking down at the floor. I might never see him again, but at least he knew the truth – that I liked him and deeply regretted behaving the way I had.

Liz handed out lots of information for us to keep, including the details about the next stage – a 12-week course starting in two months.

I would definitely go, I thought, as I gathered my things together and gave Janice a big hug. It turned out Janice was also going, so that was good – at least I'd know someone. I said goodbye to everyone and went to the coat stand to collect my coat. Ted was standing there.

"You OK, Jane?" he said.

"Jane? No, I'm Mary."

"Oh, for God's sake, woman. Me – Tarzan; you – Jane."

There was a gasp of understanding from all the others in the group. Now they knew why I'd told the story. "Oh, yes, I'm fine." I felt my cheeks scorch and turn an unflattering shade of scarlet.

"If that nickname sticks, I'll never forgive you," said Ted, giving me a little hug that told me everything would be OK. "Look, I have to go away for a few days for work. Do you fancy catching up when I get back? We could go out to dinner or for a drink or something?"

"I'd love that," I said.

"Good." He winked at me and made my insides somersault with joy.

Ted left, and I looked around the room. Veronica was smiling at me.

"He's lovely; you two make a fab couple," she said.

"I know. I'm so excited. We're going to go for a drink when he's back. Is that – like – a date, do you think?"

"God, yes," said Veronica. "You have got yourself a date, young lady. What are you going to wear?"

"I don't know. I might buy something new. I haven't been shopping for ages. I might buy a new dress. What do you think?"

"I think you should definitely do that," said Veronica. "Why don't I come with you? It would be a great chance to get to know one another better, and I know a bit about fashion after all those years of modelling. What do you think?"

"I'd love that."

"Just text me, OK. Let me know when you're free, and we'll meet up and get you the most knockout dress imaginable. We'll make it a fun day with wine as well as shopping."

"But of course," I said. "It's not a shopping trip if it doesn't involve wine."

I hadn't felt so happy for years. But, little did I know, as I smiled and waved goodbye to my new friends, that I was about to get myself into the most extraordinary amount of trouble with them.

WILL ANYONE EVER MAKE A DRESS THAT FITS ME?

There is nothing on earth quite like the terror felt by a large woman in a public changing room trapped inside a small dress.

And, ladies and gentlemen, I speak as someone who knows, because that large woman is me. I don't know quite how it happened; one minute I was inching my way into a lacy, black skater dress; the next I was completely stuck; unable to extricate myself from it.

I knew the dress would be tight on me before I started putting it on, but I was convinced that if I just wriggled around it would fit. I had no idea it would be this tight, with the material stretching as if it might tear entirely at any moment.

Oh, God. The whole thing was bursting at the seams.

"Everything is OK?" came a voice from outside the cubicle. It was the skinny, dark-haired assistant who I'd swept passed earlier.

I froze in terror.

"All fine," I said. But that was a lie… I wasn't fine. I was well and truly stuck. But I couldn't tell her that.

"You manage to get on?" she asked in a soft Spanish accent.

I put my foot against the door.

"Yes, all fine. I've got the dress on."

And, to be fair, that was the truth – I had got the damn thing on. I had managed to squeeze it over my vast bosom and had forced my big arms into the lace sleeves. What was proving much more difficult was getting it off.

I looked at myself in the mirror; I looked like an overstuffed black pudding.

I tried pulling at the sleeves but they wouldn't budge at all. They were made of lace so I was terrified to yank too hard in case the whole thing fell apart in front of me. I tried lifting the dress over my head but the bodice part of the skater dress was staying tight on my body and the zip was stuck fast.

I waited until I heard the assistant leave and called out to my friend Veronica, hovering outside the door waiting to see me emerge, looking delicious and gorgeous in a little black dress.

"Veronica, get in here quickly, I'm stuck."

"What do you mean 'you're stuck'?" Veronica walked in.

"Oh blimey, you're stuck." She smirked, then saw my beetroot red face and flustered disposition and thought better than to laugh at my predicament.

"This stupid dress is too small and won't come off," I said. "It's a complete nightmare."

"They have an odd sizing policy here," said Veronica supportively. "Even really skinny girls find the clothes small. It's not your fault."

In truth, I suspected they had a perfectly reasonable sizing policy.

It was my eating policy that was all wrong.

She suggested that the only way to remove the dress was from the bottom up, so she lifted the skirt of the dress to try and get it over my chest.

"It won't go," I warned her. She pulled so hard that I feared she might take half my internal organs with her. But still, the dress wouldn't budge. Veronica continued to pull, baring her teeth. She yanked at the material with all her might and I pushed back with all mine.

"Try taking the dress from the arms," I suggested. "But be careful with the lace."

Veronica moved her hands to the sleeves and tried pulling from there. This had to work, surely. I pulled back as before, and with hindsight what happened next was probably inevitable; an almighty ripping sound. The pressure around my body disappeared and I felt free. The dress was off – that was the good news. The worse news was that the arm of the dress had almost detached itself from the bodice. Upon closer inspection, I saw that the bodice was also ripped, and the zip was hanging off.

"Oh good God, no," said Veronica as we both stared helplessly at the damaged dress.

"What should I do?"

Veronica didn't answer me, so we both stared at the dress for some considerable time as if we might mend it with the power of concentration.

"Get dressed," said Veronica, leaving the changing room with the badly ripped dress.

Once she was gone, I clambered into my Capri trousers and powder pink A-line top, relieved to be in clothes that fitted. There were welts on my skin where the tight bodice of the dress had dug in around my waist.

I checked myself in the mirror, running my hands through my blonde hair.

This was all so annoying. I'd lost a stone and a half and I'd gone down a dress size on the course, hence my reckless decision to try and buy a dress in Zara. But it was still no good. Still too fat. I walked out of the changing room to see Veronica standing there.

"Where's the dress?" I asked. I knew I'd have to pay for it, I just wanted to get it over with.

"I gave it to the assistant and explained that it didn't fit," she replied. "Let's go."

"I have to pay," I said, but Veronica wasn't having any of it.

"Follow me."

"But I feel terrible," I said. "I ripped the dress. I should've told them."

"The dress was too small."

"No, let's be honest: I was too big."

"Don't worry; this sort of thing happens all the time. They won't mind one bit. Let's go and meet the girls."

Veronica took my arm in a pally fashion and led me to the coffee shop down the road. She chatted happily while we strode along, pointing out beautiful clothes in the shop windows as we went, while I spent all the time envisaging a life behind bars. I kept thinking that the woman from Zara was behind us. Every time I saw a woman in black, I thought she was following me and would arrest me, and I'd be locked away. And what about Ted? I'd spent a lifetime trying to find a decent boyfriend, I couldn't lose him now.

"I need to go back and buy that dress," I declared.

Veronica looked over at me. "What dress?"

"The one I tried on and ripped. I need to buy it."

"What? No, you don't. Why would you buy a ripped dress that never fitted you?"

"Because I don't want to spend the rest of my life behind bars."

"You're not going to end up behind bars. What are you talking about? I used to work in a shop; that sort of thing always happened."

"Did it?"

"All the time. Stop worrying."

"I just don't want the sales assistant to get into trouble."

"She won't."

In the coffee shop, we saw Liz and Janice. It was like a meeting of survivors from the weight loss course. They were tucked away in the corner, chatting and laughing so much that they didn't see us arrive. We ordered coffee and joined them, sliding onto the long, leather bench as Liz licked the foam from her coffee off the back of her spoon.

"You're here," she said, finally looking up from her frothy coffee and noticing. She stood up and wrapped me in a warm embrace. "It's so lovely to see you."

"You look great." Janice reached over to hug me too.

Veronica put our coffees on the table and was enveloped in the same affection.

BERNICE BLOOM

"I'm dying to hear how you've got on since we last saw you," said Liz.

"Not too bad," I said. "Things have been going OK."

"And...?" she said. "Come on, don't be shy - what's happening between you and Ted?"

"You don't want to know about that, do you?"

"Yes!" they chorused. "Of course we do."

"No, I'm sure you don't..."

"Tell us before I stand up and strangle you," said Liz.

"OK, OK. It all worked out...we're together and happy." Janice burst into applause, accompanied by Liz.

"Give us the details. You went on a date...and what happened?"

"We went out for dinner soon after he returned from his trip. Do you remember? He was just leaving to go away for a few days as the course ended. Well, he came back, we went out for dinner and it all kind of happened after that - we met for drinks and the cinema and picnics in the park...all very romantic. We've been having a lovely time. He's so nice."

They all ahhh-ed and coo-ed as I told the story of our romance as if I'd just produced tiny newborn kittens.

"That's so sweet," said Janice, hugging herself.

"I'm so pleased, Mary," said Liz. "You two were so obviously meant to be together, I'm happy it's all worked out for you. Where is he now?"

"Amsterdam," I said. "He's in bloody Amsterdam. It's the first time we've spent more than a day apart, and I miss him."

"What's he gone there for?" asked Liz.

"His company is trying to win a big contract in Amsterdam, Ted's gone over there to meet the managing director. He's so clever; if he pulls this deal off, it'll bring in millions to the company, and he'll get a bonus and pay rise. It's amazing."

"God, that is amazing. Well done him. When's he back?"

"He's back at Heathrow tomorrow night." I gave a slight squeal of excitement at this stage, causing Veronica to turn and look at me sharply.

"I'm excited," I said, trying to explain the mouse-like squeak. "I haven't drunk a drop of alcohol since he left, I have been good with my diet and trying to walk as much as possible. I want to look gorgeous when he returns from his trip tomorrow... like Audrey Hepburn."

"Audrey Hepburn?" queried Veronica.

"OK, maybe more Marilyn Monroe or Diana Dors."

Veronica looked at me sideways. She could be horrible sometimes.

"OK, Diana Dors' big fat older sister."

"Don't be ridiculous," said Janice. "You're a beautiful, sexy, gorgeous woman. You look exactly like Marilyn Monroe. Ted must be delighted to have you by his side."

"Thank you," I said. "I can't say I feel a great deal like Marilyn Monroe at the moment. I just tried to buy a new dress in Zara, and I ripped the thing. It was an XL, and it was still way too small."

Liz stirred sweetener into her coffee as I spoke. Not sugar. None of us would dare touch sugar in public. It would be worse than snorting cocaine publicly or defecating on the table.

"The sizing system in Zara is completely wrong. No one can fit into their clothes."

"I think many people can, or they'd go out of business. Just not me! I had to recruit Veronica to help me escape the damn thing."

"Ahhh," said Janice. "Done that!"

"Have you?" I asked. "I felt awful. I wanted to go back and confess and offer to buy the dress. I felt like a criminal just leaving it there, but Veronica told me about when she worked in a clothes shop and everyone did things like that."

"When did you work in a shop?" asked Janice.

"I've never worked in a shop. But madam here needed a bit of reassurance, so I pretended I did."

"You never worked in a shop?" Oh God, this wasn't good. I should have listened to my instincts and just bought the goddamned dress. "I'm going back."

I know what you're thinking - just let it go - but I couldn't. I know

I bend the rules and lie sometimes, but this felt like stealing. I didn't want to steal something.

So I jumped up. "I'll be back in about five minutes," I said. "Wait here for me."

"Don't be so silly," said Veronica, but it was too late. I was already on my way back there to tell an undersized, gorgeous Spanish girl who didn't appear to speak very much English that the fat woman she'd been concerned about had been unable to get into the black dress with the lace sleeves and had ripped it and therefore now wished to buy it.

I didn't realise that as I left the coffee shop, the girls followed me. One larger-than-average lady marching down the street in the direction of Zara, with three others chasing along behind. I guess there was a funny side to it. The security guy on the door certainly looked twice. He probably thought I'd multiplied.

"Hi," I said to the assistant standing by the changing rooms. It was the same woman who had enquired about my well-being earlier. She smiled in recognition but looked a little worried. She knew that nothing in this shop would fit me.

"Could I take this dress please?" I indicated my dress on the rail.

She reached over and took it off, seeing that it was ripped.

"Is no good," she said. "Is rip here. No good."

"Yes, it's good. I want to take it with the rip," I said, trying to take it from her hands.

"No, no. Is rip," she said slowly, thinking that her accent was the problem. She showed me the way the sleeve hung off. "Is no good."

"Yes, it's fine. I want it."

"You want no good, ripped dress?"

"Yes, I want no good, ripped dress," I confirmed. I could see she thought I was completely mad. I could also see that she had seen my friends collecting behind me.

The commotion had come to the attention of the shop manager, who wandered along, dressed head-to-toe in black, of course, with olive skin, of course. Big brown eyes? Of course. Another example of perfect Spanish beauty.

"Is problem?" said the manager.

"No problem," I said, pointing to the dress. "I want that dress."

The lady who had been serving me explained to the manager that the dress was ripped, so she wouldn't give it to me.

"Ahhh," said the manageress, understanding. She turned to me. "Is ripped." She spoke in the clearest voice she could muster. "No good. Ripped."

"I know," I replied. "I'd like to buy the ripped dress."

"No possible," said the manageress. "This is rubbish now. I take it."

"I would like to buy the ripped dress," I tried, aware that any sane shopper visiting Zara that sunny afternoon would have thought I was losing my mind. "Me want ripped and broken dress. I broke the dress. I need to buy it."

"No," said the assistant, looking at me ever so kindly. "We can order this dress, all new, not broken."

"Come on." Veronica pulled me away. "Let's go. This Zara experiment has failed."

One by one, we trooped out of the shop, watched every inch of the way by two charming and very confused Spanish ladies clutching a ripped, black skater dress.

ARTISTIC ENDEAVOURS

We stood on the street looking at one another, none of us quite sure what to say. "Where shall we go?" asked Veronica.

Liz and Janice looked too shell-shocked by what they had just witnessed to be able to think of anywhere sensible to suggest.

Next to us was a small crowd waiting to go into a white building with a large black door. The mixture of people in the queue was intriguing. Incredibly well-dressed men and women, and then what looked like a hen party of girls about my age – in their late twenties – giggling with excitement as they watched, waiting for the black door to open.

"It's going to open in less than a minute!" declared one of them.

We all stood, suddenly transfixed by the door and what it might reveal.

"Here we go," shouted another of the hen party women. "It's opening."

A man emerged wearing a jacket, black tie and white gloves. He bowed graciously and signalled for the three people at the front to go in.

"Isn't that Ashley Saunders?" I asked.

"Who?" said Veronica.

"The guy who does the travel on BBC Breakfast. You know him... always smiling and dressed in ludicrously bright-coloured jackets. He's right at the front, wearing a blazer."

Veronica stared vacantly at the back of the man who delivered the news about the London traffic in the morning while Janice and Liz watched his glamorous older companion, clothed in fur.

"I want to look like that when I'm older," said Liz.

"I wouldn't mind looking like that now," I offered. "At least she'd be able to get into the goddamned clothes in Zara."

"Are you ever going to shut up about that?" asked Veronica.

The group of younger girls was ushered in, and we watched them giggle as they rushed through the door, thrilled to be granted entry into the inner sanctum.

"Come on, you come too, bring your friends," said the doorman. He was signalling to us, clearly thinking we were with the party that had just gone in.

"Come on," I said to the others. "Let's give it a try. What's the worst thing that can happen?"

Veronica gave me a stern look, but I couldn't be stopped.

"Follow me," I urged, strutting through the door.

Inside was a beautiful room with artwork all over the walls. Waiters wandered around, handing out glasses of champagne while others offered small, beautifully crafted canapés. They looked like pastry macramé. A string quartet played in the corner. It was the loveliest room I'd ever been in. A sudden wave of longing hit me, and I wished, like anything, that Ted was standing next to me.

I wished he were right by my side, smiling down at me, gently putting his arm around me, and hugging me close to him.

The four of us took a glass of champagne each, clinked our glasses together, and wandered to the side of the room to look at the paintings adorning the walls. Some of them were beautiful – spectacular blasts of colour and fantastic images. Others looked like they'd been done by a blind man using only his feet.

BERNICE BLOOM

"It's so beautiful in here," said Liz. "And all the free champagne we want. How did we get invited?"

"Because we're fabulous." I winked at Liz. She smiled and regarded me with new respect as we marvelled at the beautiful works of art and the immaculately dressed people wandering around and drinking the complimentary champagne.

"Thank you very much," I said, taking another glass and downing the whole lot in one. I was so thirsty. I know it wasn't advisable to drink champagne to quench my thirst, but it seemed to be the only beverage available.

"Hi, yes, thank you." Another glass of champagne.

I would stop after this one. I just needed a couple of glasses to take the edge off the embarrassment of the ripped dress fiasco; then, I'd rein myself in so I could look as good as possible tomorrow for the grand return of Ted.

As we walked around the gallery, it seemed to us that the pictures nearest to the door were the more 'arty' ones. They looked like someone painted something that exists in the world. Charming portraits and photographs of scenes. Further into the room sat the more modern art – piles of discarded junk with enormous price tags. Perhaps they were clever, but they weren't interesting, challenging or beautiful.

"Oh, thank you, yes, please." Another glass of champagne. I'd stop after this one.

Liz, Veronica and I stuck together as we walked around, trying to look as if we knew what we were talking about, while Janice wandered off deep into the gallery.

Suddenly there was a clinking of a glass, and everyone gathered towards the centre of the room where a small podium had been erected. A man in a black tie stood up to it.

"Ladies and gentlemen, welcome to the Northcote Art Gallery auction. I hope you have received your brochures and have had the chance to look at all the art on sale today. We will be starting with painting one...."

And so began an auction of all the paintings, sketches and weird installations that we had been examining. I know what I'm like, so I stepped right back out of harm's way, away from the crowd, so they couldn't think I was putting my hand up. I wanted to be nowhere near the people who indicated to the auctioneer that they had £40,000 to spend on a collection of twisted-up coat hangers.

I had another glass of champagne.

"Come on," said Veronica. "Let's go for a wander and find Janice."

I could see by the glassy look in Veronica's eyes and the half-smile on her lips that she'd had way too much champagne. It was probably best that we moved away from the auction. We found Janice in the back of the gallery, where the daft modern art display had ended, and a collection of more interesting pictures was on the wall.

"I like this," I observed to Veronica. "Proper art."

There was a picture by Picasso and an odd sketch of a giraffe by Salvador Dali – mad but fun and appealing. There were also line drawings and colourful landscapes – all by artists I'd heard of.

"Are these not part of the main auction?" I asked.

"This is the silent auction," said an elegant lady in black. She was stick-thin. The sort of woman who would never have imagined it was possible not to fit into the biggest dress in Zara.

"Is that different from the auction out there?" I said.

"Yes, that's the public auction. Here you write down your bid, and the person who writes the largest amount wins the lot."

"Oh, that sounds fun," I said. "How much has been bid so far?" I'd seen the extraordinary amounts that had been bid in the public auction; I imagined these drawings would attract millions.

"Nothing yet. They will all be along when the public auction has finished."

Veronica and I looked at the clean sheets beneath the pictures. The minimum you could bid was £5,000.

"That seems cheap," I commented. Some of the pictures around the corner had gone for hundreds of thousands.

"Oh, they won't go for £5k; it's just the minimum you can bid. There would be no point in bidding at that level – the financiers in there will just outbid you later."

The lady with the champagne came back again, so I finished my glass, put it onto her tray and took another one. This was the last one. Definitely the last one. Everyone was looking blurred, and the art was all starting to look like it was coming off the walls.

"You know what we should do," I said to Veronica in a half-whisper. "We should bid, so we can say we bid on Picassos."

"But we can't afford £5,000," said Veronica.

"I know! We won't get them for £5,000, but at least we can tell everyone we bid. We can take a photo of the bid and put it on Facebook. It'll be so funny. Come on, come on."

This was the most fantastic idea ever. We put down our glasses of champagne and signed our names, placing our bets, safe in the knowledge that we would never win these works of art. It was just so funny, and the champagne was so lovely. And Veronica put the picture on Facebook, and everyone was commenting. We laughed a lot. Then we had more champagne; then finally, finally, we decided it was time to go home.

BATTERED AND BRUISED

*O*h, Good God Alive, why do I do this to myself? Why? I clambered out of bed while a dozen men armed with drums and drills danced and fought in my skull. I held onto the sides of my head, worried that it would split in two. All I had to do now was find a clock.

The kitchen. There was a clock in the… Shit, shit, shit, shit, shit. It was 9.15 am—bloody hell. I was supposed to get up at 7 am to be at work by 8 am, but I didn't set my alarm. Of course, I didn't.

I rushed to the bathroom, not letting my hands drop from the sides of my head. On the wall in the hallway, there was a notice board with my LFBTTTCB campaign notes. If you're wondering what that collection of letters stands for, it's: Look Fabulous By The Time Ted Comes Back. Not catchy, but it worked. Except for this morning when it hadn't worked at all. The very day he was coming back I managed to wake up two hours late, feeling like shit.

I couldn't work out what to do. I went to the loo, brushed my teeth and sat down heavily on the edge of the bath. Everything was hurting too much for me to think properly.

On my phone, there were lots of messages. One from Veronica in which she appeared to be singing, or she was being attacked and was shrieking to frighten her attackers. It wasn't clear which.

Then there was the predictable message from work in which my sarcastic and downright miserable boss explained the importance of punctuality and how vital it was to call in and explain if you were going to be off. "I'm trying to run a business, Mary," he said like I didn't know. "Please behave professionally."

Christ. I had to call in straight away. I picked up the phone and dialled the number, hoping that some excuse for why I was late would come to me before he answered.

"I had a dentist's appointment," I said. "Sorry I forgot to tell you."

"You need to have dentist's appointments in your own time," he replied firmly.

"I would have, but this was at the hospital," I replied. I felt very hungover and very sick.

"At hospital? Why, what were you having done?"

And that was where it started... I invented a tale about having a back tooth removed because of an abscess in the side of my cheek, and I heard him go quiet.

"It's very swollen," I said.

"I'm sorry to hear that. It would help if you had told me," he said.

"I'll be in as soon as I can get there."

"Are you sure you're OK to come in today?"

"Yes, I'll be fine. I'm just waiting to get checked over by the nurse, and then I'll be there."

"You're still in hospital?" He sounded worried, and I felt very guilty.

"Yes, but I'm fine, honestly."

"OK, but don't come in unless you're sure."

I had a quick shower and dressed in the lurid green uniform that made me look like Kermit the Frog, then I rushed out of the door, forgetting my hat (yes – we had to wear green and white stripy hats because the uniforms on their own don't make us look stupid enough). I pinned the hat to my hair and piled back out of the door, straight into Dave, the bloody gorgeous guy from the flat downstairs.

"Looking good," he said.

"Yeah, right," I replied, curtseying before dashing off for the bus stop.

"You can come down tonight wearing nothing but that hat if you like."

I didn't stop to reply. Not too long ago, there was a time when I'd have been down there, wearing nothing but the hat, before he could finish his sentence. No longer. I now have a boyfriend (I like saying that).

It was 10 am by the time I got to work, but everyone was too concerned about my awful dental treatment to give me much grief. They'd heard the story of abscesses and hospitals, and, frankly, they were amazed to find me still alive.

"My aunt had that; it was horrific. She was off for two weeks," said Ned, the young gardener who'd joined us a few weeks ago on the apprenticeship programme.

"My aunt's face was swollen and all blue," he added, and I realised that I hadn't faked any swelling or discolouration that would surely accompany major dental surgery.

I should have thought about that…I could have at least held a blood-stained tissue in my mouth or something. As I stood, thinking about how I might sneak out to a joke shop to buy some fake blood, an announcement came over the tannoy telling me to go and see Keith, my boss. Oh no. Now I wished I hadn't lied. I wished I hadn't drunk so much and been such a horrible mess last night.

"Can you tell Keith I'll be there in five minutes," I said to his assistant before I rushed out and went into the Ladies' loos to do a frank appraisal of my appearance. I looked at myself in the mirror: I didn't look wonderful by any stretch of the imagination, but I didn't look like I'd had an operation. I took a wad of hand towels from the dispenser and soaked them in water, wringing them out and then moulding them into the side of my mouth to create a lump. I didn't have any blue eye shadow on me, but I did have blue mascara, so I stroked it against the back of my hand, added a little moisturiser and wiped the resulting blue crème across my cheek to create a bruise-coloured sheen. I dabbed on some pink blusher, and – I swear to you – it looked bloody realistic. The paper in my cheek pushed towards my eye, leaving that half-closed. I looked like I'd undergone some emergency operation on my mouth. It was perfect. I was a genius. I should be working in the makeup department at Casualty.

I left the toilets and headed to Keith's tiny office at the back of the centre, right next to the cafe, which always smelled so good. I ignored the smell of bacon and had a quiet smile as I remembered that I hadn't eaten anything last night and hadn't eaten this morning. Sure, I'd drunk about 40 million calories worth of alcohol, but no food. Result!

"God, Mary, you look bloody awful," said Keith when he saw me standing in his doorway. "Come in and have a sit-down."

I strolled into his small office and sat down on one of the plastic chairs around a small round table. Every time I came into Keith's office, I thought about how poorly decked out it was for the manager of a centre that sold so much lovely furniture. And why didn't he have fresh flowers in here? The gardening section was full of beautiful flowers. This room contained the sort of furniture you'd expect to find in a classroom from the 1950s.

"What the hell have they done to you?" he asked, peering at me through his large glasses.

I couldn't talk terribly well with the paper in my mouth, and I didn't want to attempt to articulate with too much animation in case I dislodged the fake swollen cheek, so I just stood there and nodded at him and spluttered something about a dentist.

"Oh my God, your hand. Why's that so badly bruised?"

I looked down at the back of my hand. It was bright blue – like the sea when you go on holiday to Greece, like the sky on a summer's day.

Not like the colour a hand should be at all.

"Is it bruised from where they put in the needle?" he asked kindly. He looked so concerned that I felt more guilty than ever. I almost wished I'd had a terrible mouth-related incident to justify such attention. I nodded at the needle question, and he shook his head in dismay. "Mary, if you had an anaesthetic this morning, you should take it easier. Why don't you keep an eye on the plants in the greenhouse today and head off early if you need to." I nodded.

I felt like such a fraud. I hated lying. Hated it.

As I walked out of the meeting with Keith, my mobile rang in my pocket. I had no idea what to do. I couldn't answer it with Keith watching because I'd just given an Oscar-winning performance of a woman who couldn't speak. I pulled it out and looked at it. I didn't recognise the number and wasn't altogether sure what to do.

Keith strode out of his office and to my rescue.

"I'll get that for you, shall I?" he said, taking the phone and answering in a brisk voice: "Mary's phone. How can I help you?" The caller spoke, and Keith's eyebrows raised.

"No, Right. Yes. Of course, I'll tell her. Yes. Indeed. I'm sure she'll be delighted. Of course. Yes. Thank you very much for calling."

Then he handed me the phone with a quizzical look on his face. "You've just won a secret auction," he said. "A Dali painting for five grand."

"Ohmmmmghhn," I spat, feeling myself turn red with embarrassment.

"You'd better call them when you're feeling better," he said. "We must be paying you too much.

BANNER WAVING

It was 7 pm, and I was standing at Heathrow Airport waiting for Ted to appear. He was due at any minute. The board said that his flight had landed and that baggage was available to be collected.

"Why's it taking him so long to get his bag?" I spluttered at Veronica. I still had the paper towel in my cheek because I was terrified someone from work would see me without it and realise what a fraud I was.

"They're probably trying to find the luggage carousel; it's always miles away from the plane. It's the worst thing about flying…all the faffing around in airports.

"Yesh," I said, spitting all over her.

Please take that out. No one from work is going to see you here. I thought the plan was for you to look as good as possible for Ted. You look like you've been bare-knuckle fighting or something."

"But what if someone from work comes? I want to keep my job."

"Take it out," she insisted. "No one's going to take your damn job away."

She could be harsh sometimes, could Veronica. Being an ex-model, she openly accepted that there was a catwalk bitch tucked away inside her that emerged on occasion. Luckily, she was bloody lovely the rest of the time.

I dropped the soggy mess of tissue into my hand as surreptitiously as I could and slipped it into my pocket. They didn't have any bins in the airport, so I was stuck with the damn thing.

"Well done," said Veronica, with a smile. "You look a lot better without it."

She had been kind enough to come with me to meet Ted because I can't drive. She stepped into the breach and said she'd take me down to meet him; then, we'd all drive back together. It was very kind of her, especially after the night we'd had. We both stood there in the harsh, deeply unflattering airport lighting, feeling as wrecked as each other.

"Last night was bloody nuts," I said. "Can you believe it? We were only supposed to meet for coffee."

"I know," she said. "I woke up on the sofa with music blaring out. God know what I was doing when I got back."

I shook my head in sympathy. "And that auction. My God. What possessed us to start bidding? And how did I win?"

"I don't know. It seemed like such a fun thing to do at the time. What are you going to do?"

I shrugged. I didn't know. I couldn't think of anything to do other than ignore the calls from the gallery. I could no more afford to spend £5k on a piece of art than I could walk across the Thames. I couldn't afford to buy a newspaper in the morning some days, never mind purchase limited edition glorious sketches from the world's greatest painters.

"We'll worry about that later," I said. "For now, I want to concentrate on Ted's homecoming. Do you think the sign's too much?"

Veronica shook her head at me. I knew she didn't think holding a sign was a good idea. She had already made that very clear. She hinted that it was unsophisticated and that I should be projecting myself as classy and desirable at this stage in the relationship.

The thing is, though, I wanted Ted to know how much I had missed him while he'd been away. If I rushed up to him waving a banner which said 'Welcome home, lovely Ted. I've missed you.' Then he'd know.

"Here he is," Veronica said. She sounded almost as excited as I was. We both looked over at where a line of people were walking out of the terminal. I expected Ted to be looking around and trying to see me, but he walked along sombrely, looking remarkably thoughtful and serious. I'd soon cheer him up.

"Take this," I said to Veronica, throwing my handbag at her and bounding towards Ted, trailing the banner in the air behind me and chanting the letters of his name while dancing along. I felt a thrill of love and desire run through me. How could any woman resist this gorgeous bundle of masculinity? And he was all mine. All mine!

Ted trundled along, looking careworn and tired. Despite being several stone overweight and dressed in an ill-fitting suit, he looked like a superhero to me—my lovely, handsome, perfect Super Ted.

"Give us a 'T', give us an 'e', give us a 'd'," I shouted, shaking my wrists to flutter the banner and smiling like a fool.

As I got close, I saw the look of horror on his face. He glanced to his side at the man standing next to him. A very serious-looking man who I recognised immediately from the briefing notes that Ted had shown me. Oh God, this was the important businessman whom Ted had been to Amsterdam to visit. I stopped in my tracks just in front of them. What the hell should I do now?

In hindsight, I should have said hello and given him a hug, but I knew I was embarrassing Ted; that was the last thing I wanted to do. So, instead of greeting him warmly, I completely ignored him and skipped past him as if I was heading for someone else. I continued to shout random letters as I skipped along until I'd gone around the arrivals hall and was almost back where I started.

Ted and the serious-looking man stood next to Veronica and watched me as I skipped along. There was no good way out of this; I'd just have to skip right up to him.

"Hello," I said nervously. "I was just doing that to help a friend. A bit too complicated to explain. All done now."

I quickly turned to the man with him. "Hello, how nice to meet you."

"Iars, this is Mary, my lovely girlfriend who I've been telling you all about."

"Oh," he said, with alarm ringing through his voice. Clearly, he hadn't been expecting Ted's girlfriend to be a certifiable lunatic. "Very happy to meet. Ted is talking much about you."

"You too," I said as we headed towards Veronica's car. This hadn't been the grand reunion I'd hoped for, but at least Ted had been talking about me while he was away.

"What's the matter with your face?" asked Ted as Iars and I climbed into the back of Veronica's car.

"Yes. Your cheek is blue," said Iars.

"Yes, that's just makeup," I replied. "It's all very complicated. Don't worry."

Iars smiled and nodded, then stared at my face for the entire journey, sometimes leaning in and scrunching his eyes up to get a better look.

He was staying at the Hilton Hotel at Heathrow, so we headed there first with all of us trying to engage him in small talk but struggling to communicate with his broken English.

Veronica's phone rang as we drove along, and I saw the panic register on her face. She was a real stickler for driving sensibly and would never take a call while behind the wheel, so she passed the phone to Ted. "Would you answer that for me? It'll just be Mum – tell her I'll call her later." While my boyfriend took the phone, Veronica turned into the hotel's driveway.

"Right," Ted was saying. "OK…"

Then he turned around and looked at Veronica quizzically. "Some guy says he needs to talk to you about the Picasso print you bought yesterday. He's been trying to reach you all day."

"Oh no," said Veronica, looking at me in the mirror.

"Oh good Lord, no," I replied.

That was ten grand we needed to find between us.

LUNCH PLANS

"Mary, you are bonkers," said Ted when I finished explaining my ridiculous day: the ripped dress, the art exhibition and the silent auction. I told him about the fake operation and the blue makeup. I also tried to explain why I went galloping across the concourse, singing his name without stopping when I saw him.

He pinched my nose affectionately and ruffled my hair. "You're very sweet," he said. Suddenly everything felt OK.

Here are the five reasons I like Ted:

1. He is kind
2. He makes me feel special
3. He doesn't criticise me for doing completely insane things all the time
4. He's fatter than me
5. He has bigger thighs than me.

That last point is important. Indeed, if I were honest with you, I'd say that 'bigger thighs than me' has been the holy grail when looking for a man. I've had boyfriends with legs like sticks, and when I've looked at us lying on the bed, legs entangled, it looks like nothing so much as an elephant mating with a stork. It's not a good look. Not for the stork, not for the elephant, and certainly not for me.

"I've got something to ask you," he says. "What's the LFBTTTCB campaign?"

Oh, dear Lord. I meant to take that note off the wall before he returned. He must have seen it last night. "Just a thing I'm doing for work," I said. He didn't know the lengths I went to in the battle to look as good as possible for him.

"Oh, I see. What are you doing today, then? Buying more art or going to work?"

"Haha. Very funny. Neither. I'm not going to work today, I've got a day off, but I'm definitely not buying any more art."

"Perhaps I should also take the day off today?" he said.

"Ooooo," I replied, looking up at him wide-eyed. "I'd love that, but don't you have to go to work?"

"I was supposed to be going to lunch with Iars and five others from the office, but it's just a social thing. The deal won't be done today."

"That would be wonderful," I squealed.

"One moment," he said, and I heard him coughing and spluttering in the hallway as he explained his sudden onset of flu to his bosses.

"All sorted," he said, coming back to bed and pulling me close to him. "So what are we going to do to kill time today?"

The morning flew past in a whirl of passion, cuddles and chatting. We could happily have stayed in bed all day, but hunger eventually drove us from the sheets, and I headed into the kitchen.

"I don't know what food I've got in the cupboard," I said. "I was trying to diet, so I didn't buy anything."

"We could go out to lunch?" suggested Ted.

"Oh yes, yes, yes." I was thrilled with his idea. I've always loved eating out, but lunch is my favourite. Oh, and breakfast. Breakfasts are great. And brunches. Actually, I think brunches might be my favourite of all. But then dinner is delicious, isn't it, because you can have three courses at dinner, but you can't at breakfast. I wonder why that is.

"Can you ever have three courses for breakfast?" I asked Ted.

"Um…I don't know. Why? Are you hungry? We've kind of missed the breakfast slot."

"I know, but I was just wondering. You can't have three courses in the morning with the whole day ahead of you, but you can have three courses in the evening, just before bed. I might mount a one-woman campaign to have starters and puddings with breakfast."

"That's a good idea," says Ted. "You could run around the airport with a banner."

"I might just do that," I replied, still pondering the nonsense of huge amounts of food before bed versus a simple croissant when you wake up.

"Any thoughts about where you fancy for lunch today?"

"There's this lovely pub where they do enormous jacket potatoes stuffed with cheese and bacon, or why don't we go to that place with the salad bar with all the lovely coleslaws and dressings on it, and those potato wedges they do as well and the delicious steaks."

"I've got a better idea," said Ted. "Why don't we go somewhere different, somewhere we've never been before."

"OK," I said. "That sounds like a good idea, but please, let's not go anywhere near the garden centre. I don't want to bump into anyone when I haven't got my swollen face on."

"We won't go anywhere near Cobham," said Ted. "Why don't we go to Putney, Barnes, or somewhere else? Let's go into London and see whether we can find somewhere wonderful."

"Perfect," I replied.

"We don't have to go quite yet, though, do we?" he said. I could feel his hands moving down my body.

"You are insatiable," I said, but inside I was delighted with this lovely man's attention, passion and adoration.

After 10 minutes of Googling (no – that's not a euphemism - we did the euphemism bit first, then googled), we discovered this gorgeous little place on the river in Fulham that sounded perfect. I printed off the directions, and we went in Ted's car, with me navigating. I was starving. I'd start eating my hand if we didn't get there soon.

"Left here," I shouted, sure that we could miss out on loads of traffic if we went down a side road and cut out the main road.

"Good idea," said Ted, swinging the car left. "Oh look, that's Fulham Football Club."

Ted seemed to be waiting for me to comment. I didn't know what to say. I know absolutely nothing at all about football.

"We were talking about Fulham the other day, weren't we?"

"I don't think so," I replied. "To be honest, I don't think I've ever had a conversation about football with anyone in the world ever."

"Who on earth was I talking to about Fulham Football Club then?" he said. "I can't for the life of me remember. I know someone was talking about the club."

"Can't help you, I'm afraid," I said, continuing to direct him to the pub on the river. I should point out at this stage that I have absolutely no sense of direction, I can't drive, I'm useless with maps, and I've never accurately directed anyone anywhere. This was a triumph of unprecedented proportions. Ted pulled into the car parking space, put on the handbrake and smiled at me.

"We're here," he said. "You did well."

Did well? I was expecting a round of applause.

"That's the first time I've ever directed anyone and got them to the right place," I said. "Surely you have a brass band waiting to burst into a chorus of 'Congratulations'!"

"I might reward you with wine and food if that's OK."

We walked into the pub garden and sat at the table on a wooden deck near the river. It was so beautiful. I do love London. I live on the edge of it. I should come into town more often. We picked up the menus and started perusing them.

"I'm having the steak sandwich," said Ted after mulling over all the offered items. I've no idea why the man looks at the menu. I've only been for a handful of meals with him, but I can safely say that he always has the same thing. He spent half an hour in one bar asking questions about the dishes. "Does the chicken come with pasta? What sort of sauce is this? Would it be possible to have the braised beef with rice instead of potatoes?" Then, after he'd asked a host of questions about all the food available, he had the steak.

"I'm going for the chicken and bacon salad," I said nobly. I wanted the fish and chips as I've never wanted anything before, but I reined myself in. I could easily nick some of Ted's chips.

He headed inside to place our orders while I sat back in my seat and looked out over the river with the sun on my face. This was the most relaxed I'd been for ages. A boat chugged slowly up the river. If only life could always be like this. The gentle sounds of the water and the friendly chatter of people in the garden. It was lovely.

"Hide, hide..."

My silent observations were ruined by shouts from the doorway and the sight of a large man running out of the pub towards me. Ted hurtled through the garden, his face a picture of tortured concentration as he tore out of the pub like Usain Bolt. He plonked the drinks down, threw himself under the table and shouted for me to get under too.

"What on earth is the matter?" I asked.

"I'll tell you in a minute. Just make sure you can't be seen."

"OK," I said, slithering underneath. "Did you order our food?"

"Yes, but then I saw Iars."

"Iars? Shit. What is he doing here?"

"He's with the guys from work, including my boss, who I lied to this morning, pretending I had flu. This is a nightmare," said Ted. "He mustn't see me. Why would they bring him to this place, of all the London pubs?"

"Well, it is very pretty on the river; perhaps they wanted to show him a nice part of London?"

"No, damn!" Ted shook his head as we sat crouched under the table, bent over so we wouldn't bash our heads on the wood above us. "I remember now. He's a Fulham Football Club supporter. He was the one I was talking to about the club. Damn. They must've brought him to see the ground, then taken him to lunch."

"What are we going to do?" I asked. I was full of sympathy for Ted and his plight, and I could see that he needed not to be seen by his work colleagues in the pub, but I was also bloody uncomfortable and starving. If I didn't get my chicken and bacon soon, I might shrivel and die.

"I don't know; let's stay here a bit longer and then work out what to do."

I reached for my glass of wine, scrabbling around on the tabletop to find its stem, before pulling it down to drink while squatting on the wooden decking under the table. It would have been much nicer to sit in the chair with the sun on my face and the view of the river, but one glance at Ted's pained face reminded me not to comment, so I tried to make the best of it and eased myself into a semi-comfortable position.

As we sat, chatting quietly and dearly hoping not to be seen, a gang of people came along thinking the table was empty. They pulled out the chairs and went to sit down. Ted closed his eyes and shook his head. It was all too much for him.

"Um, hello, this is our table," I said, causing a woman clutching a bottle of wine to scream and leap back.

"What are you doing there?" she asked.

I had no idea how to answer her.

"Nothing," I said. "Could you please go to a different table?"

"This is ridiculous," he mouthed at me. "This is the stupidest thing ever to happen to me in my entire life."

I just shrugged. It wasn't the weirdest thing to have happened to me this week, so I wasn't in a position to comment.

"One steak sandwich with fries and one chicken and bacon salad," said the waitress. She could see us under the table but was unsure where we'd want our food to be placed.

"Under here, please," said Ted, as if it was the most natural thing in the world to sit underneath the table in a pub on the river in Fulham.

The waitress bent down and handed us our plates and cutlery. "Shall I put the condiments here?" She pointed to the floor, and we both nodded. "Is there anything else?" she asked.

I could see she was very relieved when we both said no. I was also aware that she would go back inside and tell the other waiters and bar staff that mad people were sitting under the table in the garden.

Meanwhile, Ted and I sat and ate our food like toddlers who'd had tantrums and refused to sit with their parents.

"We'll see the funny side to all this soon," I said to Ted as he tore the steak sandwich apart.

"I'm never, ever, ever pretending to be ill again," he replied. "I'll have to pull out all the stops at the weekend and make this deal happen; then, if they have seen me under the table, they won't care; they'll just focus on the fact that I've made them a fortune."

"At the weekend?" I tried not to sound alarmed. "You have to work at the weekend?"

"Didn't I say?" he replied. "I have to go back to Amsterdam to finalise the deal."

YOUNG MAN, YOUR TESTICLES ARE IN MY FACE

*ater that day, having made a swift exit from the pub without being caught, Ted and I were back at my flat. "Fancy a glass of wine?" he asked. "Or are you still feeling rough from yesterday's champagne overload and today's lunchtimes madness?"

"I'm still feeling rough from yesterday, but I would love a glass of wine," I said as Ted ruffled my hair and walked towards the kitchen. He opened a bottle of wine from the fridge, pouring generous helpings into two large glasses.

"As a special treat, can we sit on chairs tonight and not under the table?" I asked him.

"Too soon," he said, handing me a glass of wine. "Way too soon. I'm still sore from squatting for half an hour. We should have left immediately, but I wanted my steak sandwich."

"Yes, I wanted my salad and half your chips. Anyway - it was more fun the way we did it. Everyone sits on chairs - very passé," I reassured him.

He kissed me on the cheek and looked deep into my eyes. "Have I told you how beautiful you are?"

"And have I told you how handsome you are?" We clinked glasses. I

BERNICE BLOOM

took a large sip, and that was when I had the best idea I'd ever had in my life.

Why didn't I go out to Amsterdam and meet Ted there? I could surprise him by turning up at his hotel. That was a brilliant idea.

As I drank more, I refined the plan in my mind. Perhaps Veronica and I could go over and have a girly night on Friday and Saturday, then I could find Ted and surprise him, and we could all come back together on Sunday. It felt like the best idea anyone had ever had.

"Where are you staying in Amsterdam?" I asked.

"Hotel Sebastian. Why?"

"No reason."

"And what are your plans while you're there?"

"Meetings during the day, dinner in the evening, then drinks in the hotel bar, that sort of thing," he said. "Nothing too wild. Why?"

"No reason."

What could go wrong?

The following day my imaginary toothache had subsided completely, and the non-existent swelling had gone right down. It was nothing short of a miracle. Ted's imaginary flu symptoms had also disappeared, so he was in his office preparing for his weekend trip to see Iars in Amsterdam. Little did he know that I was making similar plans to go to the capital of Holland.

Indeed, my day passed in a whirl of explaining to people that my injured mouth was much better and working out how to get Veronica and me to Amsterdam for the least expense possible.

"By boat?" I texted Veronica.

"Sure," she texted back. "Just as long as it's cheap."

The most economical way to travel was to get an overnight boat on Friday, followed by a train to Amsterdam on Saturday morning. It was so much cheaper than any other possible route. All we had to do was get down to the port on Friday night after work.

"I'll drive," said Veronica, and suddenly the whole thing was taking shape. The trip was cheap because we didn't need accommodation on Friday night since we were on the boat. I just needed to find a cheap hotel room on Saturday night, and we'd be OK. But that was where I was coming unstuck. I kept rushing into the Ladies with my phone to Google hotels in Amsterdam, but they were all so damn expensive.

Then Veronica stepped into the breach once more. "I have a tent," she said.

A tent? Perfect.

I booked us into a campsite, and I felt a thrill of excitement run through me. We were going to bloody Amsterdam.

At 6.10 pm on a busy Friday night, two portly ladies stuffed themselves into a tiny Vauxhall Micra and headed for Harwich. The tent and many bags, sleeping bags, and pillows were safely stowed in the boot. We had the tickets, passports and some hastily changed Euros, and we were off for a fun-filled weekend. We'd checked the luggage about a hundred times…the tent was there, the bags were there, and we had passports and tickets. This was going to be brilliant.

Pink came on to the radio, and Veronica whacked up the volume. We were rock stars, singing along, laughing, cheering and clapping. This was going to be the best weekend of our lives. Guaranteed. And the great thing about it was that Ted had no idea we were coming. He'd have the surprise of his life and be so delighted when he saw me there. It was going to be enormous.

I'd been cautious in the days running up to the trip and had resisted the urge to post anything about our weekend on Facebook in case he saw it. I'm usually the sort of person who charts her entire life through social media. This time I just posted:

"Quiet weekend ahead, looking forward to relaxing and doing nothing."

I got some offensive comments on the post, with friends writing: "Possibly the most boring update ever on Facebook?" and "Could you be any duller, Mary?"

But they didn't know… They had no idea what we would get up to in the land of clogs, bicycles and Edam cheese.

Veronica pulled into the car park, and we clambered out and retrieved all our gear from the boot, checking it again: tent – check, bags – check, sleeping bags – check. We had everything. We could barely carry it all, but we had it.

Having thought I should go for comfort rather than glamour on the boat, I now felt quite ridiculously dressed. We didn't have a cabin, so we were sleeping on reclining seats, and I thought getting to sleep would be much easier if I wore something soft and snugly. My baby pink velour onesie was just the ticket (don't judge me, I know onesies are awful, but it was comfortable, and I wanted to sleep on the boat to look fresh and adorable when we saw Ted). I thought I'd get away with it, but I felt stupid as we walked along, especially since Veronica was much more soberly dressed in white shirts and jeans. Her great poise, elegance and height could all be a bit distressing at the best of times, but more so when I'm head to foot in powder pink. Every time I caught sight of us in the shop windows, I looked as if I was her overgrown toddler. I wished I had worn something less obvious.

Hopefully, my decision to opt for comfort over any semblance of style would yield rewards when it was bedtime, and Veronica struggled to get comfortable in tight jeans while I was sleeping like a baby.

We boarded the boat and easily found a good spot to base ourselves - near the bar, but not so close as to be noisy and crowded out, near the action, but not in the centre.

"This has all come together much more easily than I thought it would," I said to Veronica.

"I know," she said. "Honestly, I thought it would be a miracle if we made it to the boat...let alone with all our luggage and on time!"

"We should celebrate," I declared, and Veronica gave me the thumbs up. "Wine?"

"Yes, please, my lovely," she said. "But let's try not to drink too much."

"Agreed."

We had spoken earlier in the week about how we would try our hardest not to get drunk overnight on the boat. We had a big day ahead in Amsterdam, then a Saturday night with Ted. We didn't want to ruin the whole weekend because we had hangovers.

"Let's have a rule," I suggested. "For every alcoholic drink, we must have a soft one, so we alternate and don't just drink booze all night."

"Good idea," said Veronica. "That's an excellent idea. Yes." So I went up to the bar to buy our wines, knowing that the next round would consist of soft drinks to keep us straight and narrow.

We finished our first glasses, cheered as the boat left, and were on our way to the Hook of Holland. I'd soon be in the same country as Ted. It was all fiercely exciting.

Veronica went up to the bar and came back with our second drink. You'll remember that these were supposed to be non-alcoholic, but I fear that my lovely friend didn't quite understand the plan. She returned with a whole tray of drinks: soft and alcoholic beverages.

"We down the soft drinks as quickly as possible so we can get on to the wine." She plonked the tray onto the table.

"Great," I said, and this was how we proceeded through the evening, with me going to the bar next, buying two large glasses of wine and a small lemonade. We split the lemonade between two glasses, knocked it back, and continued drinking wine. My grand plan to cut the number of alcoholic drinks in half was failing miserably; we were just consuming sugary soft drinks as well. But we were having such a great time that it was difficult to feel too upset about it.

"What will Ted say when he sees us?" asked Veronica. "Will he be shocked?"

"Definitely," I replied. Our appearance would utterly throw Ted. But I knew him well enough to know he'd be pleased. He'd be shocked and speechless but happy.

Veronica and I had relaxed into our new environment and were confident we could sleep in the reclining chairs, especially given how much wine we were drinking. The only thing we weren't so keen on was how young everyone on the boat was. Most of them were in their teens or early 20s, packed around the bar, knocking back shots and chasers and getting hammered far more quickly and noisily than we were.

"I feel like a bloody pensioner," said Veronica, and I knew what she meant. It was a very odd experience. If there's one thing that can be guaranteed in this world, it is that when I'm drinking, I usually drink more than anybody else. Look at the size of me, for goodness' sake. You don't get to my size drinking water and nibbling ice cubes. But her I felt like a complete lightweight. People were walking around clutching large bottles of vodka that they were knocking back neat.

Veronica returned from the bar with our latest trayful and plonked it down.

"This is a party boat," she said.

"What do you mean, a party boat?"

"That's what it is. It's a booze cruise, and most people on it are either celebrating their 18th birthday parties or 21st birthdays. No wonder we feel like two little old ladies."

"What happens on party boats?" I asked, fearing the night of debauchery ahead of us.

"According to the barman, there will be wrestling in jelly and naked bar walking later. The barman asked me whether you plan to enter the wet t-shirt competition later."

"Good God, is he insane?"

"I told him you wouldn't want to, and he looked disappointed."

By 3 am, there was no doubt we were on a party boat.

Veronica and I had tried to be good sports, but we were too old to want to dance the night away or be fondled by amorous teenagers. But I had won a bottle of unbelievably disgusting 'champagne' from having a bloke's testicles dangled into my face.

Before you judge me, I wasn't aware that I had agreed to this or that it would happen. The barman announced something, and everyone started chanting and looking over at us, so I waved. Veronica smiled and waved too. We were being friendly. Next, everyone was slow-clapping, and he shouted, "Will you?" I looked at him hopelessly, and he repeated, "Come on, the lady in pink – say you will."

I said, "OK", fearing that I'd have to dance with an 18-year-old, but instead, there was a loud cheer, and a young man clambered onto the table next to our reclined seats. He pulled down his trousers and straddled me, I had his horrible, wrinkly teenage balls in my face before I could think straight. Then I was stuck. What could I do? Sitting up would have brought me into even closer proximity, so I closed my eyes, ignored them, and waited for him to get off.

When he finally dismounted, I turned to Veronica; her eyes were on stalks.

"What the fuck are you doing?" she asked.

"We must never speak of this again," I said. "Never."

"OK. But…what? Why did you do that? Who are you?"

"I got stuck," I said. "I was embarrassed and confused. I didn't know what to do."

The guy who'd dangled his bits in my face handed me my bottle of 'champagne' and then turned to his friend. "That's the first time I've had my bollocks in a fat girl's face," he said, and they both laughed heartily as they walked back towards the bar.

I rolled over on the seat, curled up and pretended to go to sleep. I was drunk, tired and felt horrible. It was all my fault, so I wasn't looking for any sympathy, but as I closed my eyes against the wild partying on the boat, I thought about how horrible it was to be 'the fat girl' that they were all laughing at, and I started to cry.

I'd been *the fat girl* for years. And I knew why… it was because whenever anything went even remotely wrong, I'd find myself eating vast amounts of food before I realised what was happening.

My mum would say something about my hair looking funny, or someone at work would tell me I hadn't put the plants in the right place, and I'd feel devastated and the need to stuff myself with food until I couldn't feel anything more would completely overwhelm me.

I couldn't cope until I'd forced the feelings down with food.

Sometimes, I thought I must be missing some essential parts of my character makeup. Where was the resilience? Where was the ability to shrug off harsh comments or barbs?

I suspected I knew where that lack of resilience came from…from an incident in a gymnastics club many years ago when I was an innocent little girl.

I wiped my eyes with my hand and tried to fall asleep before Veronica could see I was upset. We'd soon be in Holland. Everything would be OK. I'd lose the weight. I'd lose it, and no one would ever laugh at me for being fat again.

. . .

Morning came with all the subtlety and elegance of a nuclear missile landing on my face. The sun streamed in through the windows, lighting up the interior of the boat, which, frankly, couldn't have looked in a worse state if it had crashed in the night.

If you moved anything, it would be tidier.

Bottles, cans, clothes and bodies were lying across the seats, on the floor and on the bar. Two hardy young men still stood at the bar drinking, while all around them, people had collapsed.

Two cleaners had attempted to enter the fray and were trying to impose a modicum of order over the place, but the bodies lying all over the floor prevented them from doing anything but pick up litter and collect glasses to return to the bar area.

The loudspeaker announced our arrival in Holland as Veronica and I squinted into our compact mirrors and reapplied makeup we had never taken off the night before.

"Well, I've looked better." Veronica licked her finger and wiped it across her eyelid. "This is not a luxurious way to travel."

"No," I agreed quickly. "This booze cruise might be our worst decision ever."

We joined the line of people exiting the boat, all looking as ropey as us. Men were unshaven; women had smeared mascara across their faces, all piggy-eyed and regretting last night's excesses.

"Right," said Veronica, putting the bags down to give her arms a break. "We can do this; all we have to do is get on the train to Amsterdam. That can't be too hard, can it?"

"It can't be," I agreed. "Once we're in Amsterdam, we can set up our tent and relax. The hardest bit's over now."

We walked towards the train station and saw a big sign saying 'trains to Amsterdam'.

"Brilliant," I said. Even we couldn't mess this up. All we had to do was get on the first train that came.

But Veronica had stopped and was looking open-mouthed at her bags.

"What's the matter?"

"It's the tent," she replied. "I've left it on the boat."

"Oh God, no. We need the tent. We can't afford any of those hotels. Run back and get it, and I'll wait here with the bags."

"Don't go anywhere." She turned and legged it back to the boat, weaving through the teenagers disembarking around her.

I had no idea whether they would allow her back on or whether the tent would be there when she got to our seats. It might have been cleared away by the cleaners or nicked by drunk teenagers. I crossed my fingers that she would find it. We were buggered without it.

I heard Veronica running back onto the platform before I saw her. She had the tent in her arms and a look of sheer victory on her face. "Got it," she announced, holding it up like the FA Cup. "Let's go to Amsterdam."

The next train was only 10 minutes away, so we sat on the platform and discussed how much we never wanted to go on a party boat again.

"I've never felt so old and unadventurous before," I said.

"You were quite adventurous." Veronica raised her eyebrows at me.

"We said we would never speak of it," I chided.

"We won't," said Veronica. "Never."

MORE CAKE, PLEASE

Gosh, Amsterdam was beautiful. I wasn't expecting it to be quite so stunning. I'd heard all the stories about the sex museum and prostitutes around every corner and feared I might get drafted into some whorehouse. As it turned out, it was all gorgeous waterside cafes, people cycling around without fearing for their lives, and an air of friendly sophistication. It was a joy. I loved it.

We stood on Magere Brug, otherwise known as the skinny bridge, so highly inappropriate for us two, and we looked out across the water to the little boats sailing along and the cafes on the bank opposite us. I pulled out the guidebook, hoping to learn more about the place.

"Legend has it that the skinny bridge was named after the 'magere zussen' - the skinny sisters. They were very well-off sisters who lived either side of the river and decided to have the wooden bridge built to make it easier to visit one another," I read.

"Maybe we should rename Hampton Court Bridge the Fat Bridge?"

"I think we should."

"Before we do any more sightseeing or learn about any more sisters - skinny or otherwise - I need coffee," said Veronica.

"Me too," I agreed, so we stumbled, with our many bags in hand, over the beautiful bridge and into the nearest cafe.

The weekend had got off to a captivating start, but we were both feeling the effects of last night. I felt like I'd just been through the D-Day landings as we walked along, hunched over and unwashed, desperate for a coffee. Honestly, I'd never felt so rough in my life. Well, not since the last time I felt this rough. Which, now you mention it, was only a few days ago.

"You have got the tent, haven't you?" I said to Veronica for the five hundredth time that day. She was carrying it in front of her, and I was following behind, so I couldn't see it. I was so paranoid after she'd left it on the boat that I felt the need to keep checking.

"Yes," she said, holding it up for me to see. "I won't lose it again. I know we're buggered without it."

We walked into the first cafe we came to. We just needed coffee inside us, and fast. The place we wandered into was shabby-looking, with a slightly wonky canopy over a small courtyard packed with metal chairs. Inside was very dark, with lots of austere-looking art on the wall.

"Two coffees, please," said Veronica in her best Dutch (obviously – no Dutch at all).

"Anything to eat?" said the waiter, his accent beautifully Dutch but his words English.

"Oh yes, please. I'm starving." Veronica looked at me nervously. "I have to eat something."

"Yes, me too," I said nervously.

The subject of eating was always a difficult one for Veronica and me to negotiate. We met at Fat Club, for God's sake. We were only there because we had problems controlling our eating, so it defined our relationship from the start to some extent. It was the ever-present third wheel in our friendship: this knowledge that we could not control ourselves around food.

"What have you got that we could have for breakfast? What's typically Dutch?" I asked. "I mean – what are you famous for here?"

"Maybe this cake?" said the waiter, indicating some fairly unappetising cakes sitting in a cabinet behind him. "We are very famous for this space cake."

"Special cake? Which special cake?"

"This one."

He pointed to the unappetising cakes.

"Is it good?" I asked, unconvinced. If I was going to eat something, I wanted it to be tasty. I hated to waste calories on boring food.

"Very good indeed," he said.

"We will have two and two cappuccinos," I said. I felt so guilty that I couldn't look at Veronica.

"Don't worry," she reassured me. "We'll get back on that diet soon." The waiter came to our table with a tray laden with our goodies.

"Enjoy," he said.

Veronica peeled off a piece of the cake and put it into her mouth.

"Yum, I'm bloody starving," she said.

I took a large sip of coffee and watched Veronica nibble at more of the cake.

"Is it OK?" I asked. She just shrugged, which wasn't the best recommendation in the world. Still, we needed to eat something to soak up all the alcohol still lingering within us. First, though, I needed to go to the loo.

"I'll be back in a second," I said, heading through the side door and out to the bathroom, where I was entertained by a large map of Amsterdam on the door, with the key places to go circled with what looked like bright red lipstick. I looked at them; they were all places we'd considered going. Perhaps we should hire bicycles? Once we'd dropped our stuff off at the campsite, we'd be free to cycle around all day. I rather liked the idea of that. It would be worth checking with Veronica.

But when I walked back into the cafe, Veronica was not in any fit state to discuss the hiring of bicycles. She took one look at me and burst into laughter. "Where the hell have you been?" she yelled out.

"I've just been to the loo," I replied, far more quietly than she. "Why are you shouting?"

"Shouting? Me?" she screamed back at me before laughing so

much she nearly fell off her chair, banging the table with her hand as she creased over. "I've been to the loo?" she said, mockingly "I can't believe you've been to the loooooo."

What the hell was going on?

Veronica turned to the waiter serving the only two other people in the cafe. Thank God it was almost empty. Veronica screamed at the top of her voice: "My friend has been to the loo," before dissolving into peals of laughter again.

I sat down nervously and began to sip my coffee.

"Why are you screaming and shouting?" I asked.

"Why is your head not on properly?" she responded. "Your head is all wonky, and it looks like it will fall off."

Before I could answer, she ran round the table and held my head between her hands. "I'm here just in time; I got here just in time," she said. "Your head nearly fell off. You haven't thanked me for saving it."

She rushed back to her chair and sat back into it, nearly falling off backwards.

I nibbled at the cake and drank my coffee while Veronica examined her thumbs, occasionally laughing about how they weren't hers. She wrote, 'I love you in the air with her finger, and I ate my cake as quickly as possible so we could get out of there and get Veronica into the fresh air.

But no. NO. Veronica was right. It was very funny. My thumbs were on backwards. Wooow…how did that happen?

It was so funny. I roared with laughter as I watched Veronica writing in the sky with someone else's fingers.

"Are your thumbs from a magic bird?" I asked her.

But there was no time to wait for the answer; her head was wobbling… I rushed over. Perhaps if I brushed her hair, her head would stay on her shoulders. I would try. I needed to try. But when I got to her head, the sight of all the hairs coming out of it was the funniest thing I'd ever seen. "Why have you got so much hair?" I said, laughing so much my stomach was hurting as I fell to my knees behind her, clutching a hairbrush. "You've got so much hair it's ridicu-

BERNICE BLOOM

lous. I will count them one by one and see how many there are. I'll start at the top."

I tried to stand up to begin counting, but the floor was moving, and I kept slipping, and Veronica was laughing so much that I couldn't concentrate. Was she laughing because she had so much hair? Probably. The waiter helped me to my feet, taking me to my chair and sitting me down. I looked at him and suddenly realised that he was the guy who played Superman in the film. Wow!

What was he doing here?

"I need your autograph. You are Superman," I said. "How did you get to be Superman? Wow, I can't believe it, you're serving coffee, and you're Superman."

"Just you have a sit-down. I'll bring you some water," he said.

"Go, Superman, fly through the air; get me some water."

At the next table, the man and woman looked over at us like we were insane. They probably recognised the waiter as well.

"She has loads of hair all over her head, and he is Superman!" I screamed across the cafe. They seemed uninterested. They just smiled at me and went back to their drinks. How could people not be interested that Superman was serving coffee?

"There you go, ladies," said the waiter as he brought us large glasses of water. He was definitely Superman. "Next time, maybe just have one hash cake between you?"

How we left the cafe is a mystery to me. I remember crossing the road and thinking it was funny when the little green man appeared and collapsed into a heap. Veronica and I clutched each other in the street – howling, laughing and pointing at the little green man.

Then we seemed to have found a bench and were sitting there, laughing. And we couldn't move from the bench, so we closed our eyes and drifted slowly off to sleep.

We woke a couple of hours later, disorientated and confused.

"What the hell?" I asked. "I mean...what happened then?"

"Hash cake," said Veronica. "It's a cake with cannabis in it. They call it space cake."

"It was the weirdest experience of my life," I said. Not particularly unpleasant, just weird. "And you do have a lot of hairs on your head."

"You are probably right," said Veronica.

It was at that point that we realised we'd lost the tent.

It fell to Veronica to return to the cafe in search of the tent since she was charged with looking after it. She stood up from the bench, stumbled a little, and then weaved across the crowded street and back to the cafe.

I dozed on the bench while she was away, to be woken up by her, grinning from ear to ear. She held the tent in one hand and a white paper bag in the other.

"I couldn't resist it," she said, waving her grocery bag before me. In it, she had two more hash cakes. "Let's have these later after we've set up the tent."

CAMPING CATASTROPHE

We left our bench (with the tent) and wandered off through the streets of Amsterdam in search of our campsite. The more I saw of the city, the more staggeringly beautiful it appeared - a gorgeous maze of cafes, bars and canals. I'd read the literature about how lovely the city was before we went, of course, and I knew that it had more canals than Venice, but what the tourist brochure couldn't explain was just what an incredible impact those canals had on the look and feel of the place. They weaved through the city like living, breathing animals decorated along the route with bridges of all shapes and sizes. We could see the water snaking through as we looked across the city. with gabled houses dotted along the way. I had a sudden desire to come and live in the city. I might never go home. Perhaps Ted and I could move out to Amsterdam?

I pictured myself cycling around all day and losing weight, rowing down the river with Ted in the evening and meeting up with friends for supper in one of the fabulous cafes. There was such a lovely feel to the city, perhaps because it was quite small, so nowhere was too far away, and you kept seeing people you'd just met. It meant that within hours of being there, we felt like we knew people and understood the place.

The best part of it all was the cafe culture. Cafe after cafe next to each other, with people just chilling, reading their books, and minding their own business. In England, people would sit at home, watching daytime TV and feeling lonely. Here, people came out and listened to their music, read books or chatted with passers-by. It all felt so much healthier than how we live in England. Because everyone seemed to be out, there was so much to see, with people cycling past and tourists walking over the bridges, stopping to stare at the beauty of it all.

Our campsite was on the edge of town, a short bus ride from all the city centre attractions and just a couple of miles, by my reckoning, from the hotel where Ted was staying. In other words, it was perfect. It also looked clean and buzzing as many people arrived and set themselves up. We went to the reception area and collected the token, allowing us to proceed.

"Here we go; we could set up here," suggested Veronica, pointing towards a lovely vast space where we could pitch the tent and have plenty of room to sit out on deckchairs, chat and put the world to rights. It was quite near the toilet block where we would want to go and change into our finery later, but not so close that the stench of urine would always greet us.

"Perfect," I said, noticing no children nearby, no groups of rowdy men, and a little pathway to the toilet block and exit. "I think you might have just found the perfect place in the world." We high-fived in our excitement.

I opened my bag, which contained the sleeping bags rolled up tightly and the small pillows we could blow up. No luxuries had been spared. This was going to be magnificent.

"Let's get this tent set up, then we can go off and explore for a bit," said Veronica, pulling poles from the tent bag and the canvas sheet.

I looked at it all and was filled with fear.

I remembered my camping holidays as a child, with my parents on the brink of divorce by the time they got the tent up.

"No, that is not where it goes," my dad would howl.

"If you're so brilliant at this, why don't you do it yourself, and I'll take the children for a walk along the beach," Mum would yell back.

"I'm not saying I'm brilliant," Dad would reply. "It's just that if you hold it there, we won't be able to stretch it over the poles...." And so the arguments would continue for what felt like hours. My parents would battle with the tent and then with one another until, finally, the tent was up.

But that was my parents...and I had confidence in us: Veronica and I were reasonably intelligent women, and the tent was much smaller, so it would be far less hassle. I looked at bits of rope, canvas and loads of poles, and I couldn't for the life of me work out how we would turn this collection into a beautiful tent that would house us overnight.

"Do you want to take the poles and assemble them?" Veronica said.

I couldn't help but think I'd been dealt the short straw. Wasn't it all about the poles? Wasn't I now in charge of the whole tent?

"I'll sort out the pegs and the canvas," she said.

I had no idea what to do. I assumed there would be enough poles to create a base square, and then I would build two arches over the top onto which the canvas would be stretched and pinned down with the pegs. But basic maths indicated there were nowhere near enough poles for this to happen. Perhaps there was just one arch over the top?

I looked at the poles again. I couldn't see how there was even a base square, let alone an arch.

"I don't know how to do this," I said. None of the poles seemed to have bends in them. How would I make them into anything? And there were so few of them. There appeared to be a lot of string. Perhaps the line linked between the poles or something?

I turned to Veronica, who looked as puzzled as I was feeling.

"There don't seem to be enough poles," I told her. "There is a lot of string, does the string link the poles together or something? If so, we will need instructions because I've no idea how to do it."

"I don't know," she said in dismay. "There doesn't seem to be anything like enough canvas. And the tent is blue. I thought it was red before. I don't understand."

We stared at the poles, which would no more make a tent base than I would make a nuclear scientist and the square of canvas that wasn't big enough to make a dress. A young family walked past, nodding, smiling and wishing us a good morning, as people on campsites are prone to do.

They sounded English, so I ran towards them, asking for help.

"I'm sorry to interrupt your walk, but we are completely baffled here. Have you ever seen a tent like this before?" I asked. "If you could point me in the right direction as to how it comes together, I'd be grateful. I can't make any sense out of it."

"Sure," said the man. "I'll take a look."

The woman was a bit pissed off, but we wouldn't keep them long; I just needed a steer as to how this thing came together.

As he looked at our collection of poles and canvas, a loud guffaw from the man indicated that things weren't going to run smoothly from here on in.

"Is there a problem?" I asked.

The man laughed again. "Well, it depends whether you want to camp tonight."

"Yes, this is our tent," I replied.

"You won't be doing any camping in this. This is a kite," he said. "It's quite a nice kite, the kids would love to come over and play with it later if you're taking it out on the beach, but you're not going to make a tent out of it."

"Oh God," said Veronica. "I must have picked up the wrong bag. My mum said it was in the loft, so I went up and got it."

"It did seem quite small." I remembered that I had commented on how compact it was, but Veronica had said it was the latest in modern lightweight camping equipment.

"Do you like flying kites?" she asked.

"No," I replied. "I can't think of anything I'd less like to do right now than fly a kite on the beach."

"Hash cake?" said Veronica, palming off half a cake onto me.

I looked at her and smiled. "Yep, let's eat hash cake," I replied.

And so that's how we ended up in the sex museum.

STATIC TENTS

I have no idea how we got to the Sex Museum. Honestly, I have no recollection of us deciding we wanted to go there. It was never on my bucket list, and, as I discovered, there were only so many times that you could witness sex acts of extraordinary weirdness in the course of a gentle afternoon in Amsterdam before you started to feel a little queasy. Even when we'd had half a hash cake each and found our own feet so funny that we were crying with laughter, it still wasn't that entertaining.

The bizarre views on display in the museum were just obtuse. Perhaps I'm a big prude, but I don't need to see animals of different breeds with one another, and I certainly have no desire to watch humans frolicking with farmyard beasts.

Veronica and I fumbled through the museum's ground floor, then decided the escalator to the upper floors was too much for us. Things were spinning, and I'd taken against the darkness. I needed fresh air, or I was going to be sick, so we staggered back through the art section, the toys section and another section which didn't seem to have any unifying theme (or any redeeming features, to be honest) and left the museum. I'm not saying we didn't enjoy it – it was fun – it was just that once you'd seen one man on all fours, bound and gagged and wearing a fake penis, you'd seen them all. You certainly didn't need to see another 20.

"What now?" asked Veronica.

"We could try and see whether there's a cheap B&B, youth hostel or something?" I said.

She shrugged her shoulders and raised her eyebrows, which indicated that was the last thing she wanted to do with an evening in Amsterdam.

"A bed-and-breakfast sounds better than a bloody youth hostel."

I couldn't disagree. I pulled out my phone and started googling reasonably priced B&Bs in the centre of Amsterdam. The only ones that came anywhere near the descriptor 'reasonable' were buried deep in the heart of the red-light district.

"Can you rent tents?" I asked.

"Oh, that's not a bad idea," said Veronica. "That's an excellent idea. I wonder whether you can?"

Back onto Google we went. It turned out that - yes, generally speaking, you could hire tents, but could you hire one without notice in the middle of Amsterdam? It seemed not. Then, I saw it.

"There's a campsite with fixed tents in it," I said. "That would be good. We wouldn't have to put it up or anything."

"Is it glamping?" asked Veronica.

"I have no idea what that is," I replied.

"It's posh camping…glamorous camping…nice tents with fridges and televisions and heating and stuff."

"Oh. I don't know. It doesn't say. It just says that the campsite we were at earlier has tents there that are permanent, so you don't have to bring one with you."

"So, the choice is – go back to the campsite and set ourselves up there, or ring Ted and explain that we're here and don't have a tent," said Veronica

It was clear that Veronica thought I should ring Ted, but we were here to surprise him. In any case, I couldn't see him while still dressed in a pink onesie I'd been wearing all night.

I was also aware that Ted was working out here. He was signing a huge deal and didn't want big distractions in the shape of Veronica and me.

"This is Ted's big break," I said to Veronica. "You know, he's worked his way up from post boy to become an important salesman in the company, and he takes it all very seriously. When he came back from Amsterdam last time and took a day off to spend with me, he felt so madly guilty about it that he's been working 20-hour days ever since."

"Yeah, but that's because he was almost caught red-handed, and you had to hide under the table."

"Well, yes, this is true."

"SO what's he *actually* doing here?"

A big Dutch company is interested in buying his company's software, and if they do, it'll be a multi-million-pound deal for them. I can't rock up there dressed like a giant pink teddy bear and ruin it for him."

"You look fine," Veronica insisted. "Please call him, or we'll end up sleeping on that bench all night."

"I haven't showered or washed my hair, and have eaten nothing but hash cakes and alcohol since midday yesterday. I don't want to see him like this."

"OK," said Veronica. "So, shall we eat the other hash cake while we think about it?"

"No," I said determinedly. "Let's return to the campsite, get one of their fixed tents, stick our stuff in it, and then eat the hash cake." I was becoming so sensible I was scaring myself.

The day was getting on. It was almost 1 pm, and I wanted to look bloody brilliant by tonight. We needed to get to the campsite and showered and changed, or this weekend would collapse around our ears.

"And we should probably pick up something for lunch," I added.

"Yes," said Veronica. "Let's do that."

We nodded at one another proudly.

"We can be sensible if we try," she said.

"Yes," I agreed.
But then we ate the hash cake.

FINALLY WE GET TO SEE TED

At least we were in the tent when we woke up. Neither of us could remember how we got there. I vaguely remember looking at the map and declaring that we should leave and find the campsite. I remembered Veronica finding this funny, of course, but then Veronica found everything funny by this stage. I couldn't remember how on earth we knew which bus to get when to get off, or anything like that.

I could sort of remember arriving at the campsite. Yes, it was beginning to come back to me…there was confusion at the reception because we couldn't stop laughing enough to tell the man that we had booked a static tent.

"You have a tent," he said, pointing to Veronica's bag.

"It's a kite," we said, roaring with laughter. Really, everything was funny.

Somehow we made him understand that we needed a static tent, and somehow we found the right one and were now in it.

We must have bought food along the way because two paper bags lay next to us. I sat up and pulled one towards me, waking Veronica as the paper rustled.

"I'm so starving I'm going to die," she said.

"Don't die," I replied, handing her a bag.

"Oh wow, thanks, you've been out to get food. You superstar."

"No, we bought it earlier, I think," I said. "It was here when I woke up."

It was worrying that neither of us had any recollection of buying the food, but remembering anything had been a struggle since we went into the cafe that morning.

Inside the bags were sandwiches (carbs, calories) with butter on (fat, calories) and stuffed with ham and cheese (more fat, more calories and some protein); there were crisps and cans of Coke (of the non-diet variety).

Veronica and I froze as if we'd found live snakes in the bags. "Full-fat," I said.

"But we have to eat," she said. "We'll both be ill if we don't."

"OK," I said. "But this has to stay between us. We must never mention this in front of Fat Club people."

"I swear," said Veronica solemnly. "I'll tell people about the hash cakes and the sex museum, but I will never talk about the full-fat Coke."

"Or what happened on the boat," I said.

"I've already forgotten about the bloke on the boat dangling his testicles in your face, so don't worry about that."

"Good," I replied.

The food was delicious. You know how utterly lovely it is to eat when you're starving, and oooo...we were hungry. I loved every last bit of our little picnic.

"I feel so much better now," said Veronica.

"Good, me too. The food's great, isn't it? I mean – it really is great."

Veronica nodded and pushed back her sleeve to look at her watch. "Christ. It's 4 pm," she said. "How did it get to 4 pm?"

"I don't know. We could do with making a plan of some sort."

Veronica pulled out a map of Amsterdam.

"Right, this is where Ted is," I explained, pointing out Hotel Sebastian on the map.

Veronica marked it with a red pen. "Here we are," I said.

She marked our campsite with her red pen.

"I think it will take us about 45 minutes to get to his hotel," I concluded.

"When should we leave?"

"Ted is going out for an early supper with Iars, the guy we met at the airport, and will be back at the hotel by 8.30 pm."

"He gets back at 8.30? Are you sure? That's an early supper," she said.

"Iars is on the red-eye to New York later, so they have to meet early. Why don't we get to his hotel while he's out at his dinner and have a few drinks in the bar, then when he comes back we scream 'surprise', and he'll be so pleased to see us he'll almost wet himself."

"That seems to be a simple, logical, straightforward plan." Veronica's eyes were brimming with trust and respect.

I raised my eyebrow at her.

"No, seriously," she said. "It's the sort of plan that won't go wrong."

And at that moment, something deep within me screamed: 'THE PLAN IS GOING TO GO WRONG!'

My first job was to go to the toilet block to shower and dress. I'd been dying for a shower all day and was starting to feel pretty revolting in my grubby, stained pink onesie, so I was delighted when we made our way there and found the block clean and empty. Hooray! No queuing for the showers. We each went into a cubicle, and I laid out my shower gel, shampoo, conditioner and shaving foam. I retrieved my razor from the bottom of the toiletries bag and put that on the end of the line.

"Is your shower working?" asked Veronica.

"I don't know yet." It had taken me a couple of minutes to lay out my tools. I pressed the red button, and nothing happened. I turned it.

Still nothing. "There's no water coming out," I shouted.

"I know," said Veronica. "I'm just trying another one, but that's not working either."

Bollocks.

I slipped on my pink onesie, gathered my rucksack and other possessions and walked outside to meet Veronica.

"What are we going to do?" I asked.

"Let's go to the reception and tell them," she said.

The reception area was busy with people chatting away in Dutch.

"Excuse me," said Veronica, spelling out her question, using mime and exaggerated language.

"Only seven and nine," said the man.

Veronica and I looked at one another. Neither of us had a clue what this meant. Was he trying to tell us that only showers number seven and nine worked? But there weren't that many showers there.

"Showers," I tried, moving my hand above my head to mimic the falling water.

"Seven and nine, two times," said the man.

Finally, a kindly English-speaking man explained. "The showers are only open between seven and nine in the morning and seven and nine in the evening at this time of year."

"Seven?" Veronica shouted at him as if the shower situation was wholly his fault.

"Yes," he replied. "It says it in all the literature. Most campsites are the same."

"Bugger," said Veronica. "Is there no water at all? I mean, even cold water?"

"No shower," said the man behind the counter, turning to the next person in the queue.

We walked off back to our tent. Back to make a new plan.

We seemed to be going through plans like we were going through hash cakes…at reckless speed.

"OK," said Veronica. "We must be showered and changed before we go out tonight." "Yes," I agreed.

"But there are no showers here."

"Indeed not."

"So I suggest we go to Hotel Sebastian and shower there. What do you think?"

I wasn't convinced it was the greatest plan, but I struggled to think of an alternative. "We'll have to get there early," I said.

BERNICE BLOOM

"Yes, we'll get there for 6 pm; then there'll be no way to bump into Ted because he'll already be out to supper."

"True," I said.

"We'll use the hotel showers (we'd Googled this; there was a spa section in the hotel that we planned to sneak into). We'll get ready, sit in the bar, looking awesome, awaiting Ted's return."

To be honest, we'd had worse plans that day.

At 6 pm, we went to Hotel Sebastian and strode in, trying to look as natural as possible and as if we were guests of the hotel. The only problem was that we were still dressed in yesterday's yucky clothes and carrying backpacks. We didn't blend in with the smart Dutch women who drifted through the reception area.

"There," said Veronica, seeing a sign for the spa.

We walked over to it as nonchalantly as possible, but when Veronica tried the door, it didn't open. She tried again. I tried. Nope. It wasn't opening. Suddenly it dawned on us…you needed your room key to access the spa.

There was no sign of any other showers anywhere.

"OK," said Veronica. "Don't panic. This is going to be OK. Let's sit on this sofa and wait until someone comes to use the spa; when they open the door, we'll pile in."

"A bit like we did with the art gallery?" I suggested.

"A bit like that."

"Because that ended up being so successful," I said.

But there was no alternative. So we sat there.

"I wish we had some hash cake," said Veronica.

"You have a problem," I said. "Forget Fat Club; you must go to Hash Cake Club."

Then, finally, along came an elderly couple. The man flicked his room key against the lock, and the door flew open. Veronica and I flew up; we dashed towards the spa and bundled in behind them, arriving just in time to get in before the door closed. Inside we were greeted by a woman in a white shirt and trousers, ticking off room numbers in the book.

"We're with them," said Veronica, pointing at the elderly couple.

"With whom?" asked the assistant.

We both looked up to point at the couple in front of us. They were disappearing into the changing area as two men walked out.

"Oh hell," Veronica said.

"Oh bloody, bloody hell," I said.

It was Ted and Iars.

This was a hellish situation. I was dressed in a dirty pink onesie, hadn't washed all day, and my hair was all over the place. I'd had a conversation with Ted earlier in which I'd told him I was in Tesco's in Esher. Now, I was, standing before him, about to get thrown out of a spa in Amsterdam.

Veronica and I instinctively stood still...like you're supposed to do if you see a bear in the wild. It was as if we were hoping he wouldn't notice us if we didn't flinch.

Except Ted isn't a bear, and he could clearly see us.

"Mary, what the hell are you doing here?" he asked. "And what on earth are you wearing?"

"Oh God," I said to Veronica as quietly as possible. "I don't know what to say…"

"You need to say something," she whispered. "I'll back you up. Just say anything."

"It was all Veronica's idea," I said. But judging by the alarm on Veronica's face, that wasn't what she expected when she said 'anything'. "Veronica had to come to Amsterdam for work, so I thought I'd come with her. Sorry, to take you by surprise; I was planning to call you later and see whether you wanted to meet for a drink."

I looked at Veronica, appealing with my eyes for the help she'd promised me earlier. She looked like she'd just been punched. "Yes," she said, eventually. "All my fault."

"Oh no, no one's fault at all. It's lovely to see you both. You just took us by surprise, that's all. You should have called earlier. Are you staying in this hotel?"

"No, not quite," I replied. "We had a problem with our accommodation, to be honest. The hotel that Veronica's work booked us into burned down. Completely burned to the ground. Nothing left of it – just ashes."

It was alarming how easily I was able to conjure these lies. I'd always thought myself a terrible liar, but it turned out that they came streaming out of me under pressure. It was a relief in many ways. It meant that if there was ever another world war and the Germans captured me, there was every chance that I'd instinctively lie and not give away the whereabouts of the British army.

"Do you two want to come up and use my room to change?" asked Ted. "I'll go and talk to the receptionist and find out which room Mark was in. He never showed up because his mum was ill, so there's a room we've paid for and aren't using."

"That's brilliant," I said, looking at Veronica, who had happily shaken off the look of utter disconsolation and was now smiling and nodding. "Then come out to dinner with Iars and me. Is that OK, Iars?"

"Of course," he said, smiling warmly at Veronica. Ted walked over to the reception area to sort out the spare room, and I looked at Veronica, blushing to the roots and glowing in the heat of Iars' stare.

There was every chance we wouldn't need that room after all.

What a bloody marvellous ending to a fraught couple of days.

At least I'd learned a few things.

1. Avoid booze cruises. It's better to swim to Amsterdam than get on a booze cruise

2. Don't wear something just for comfort…you might end up stuck in it all weekend

3. If a tent looks too small to be a tent, it probably isn't a tent

4. Look out for the cakes in Amsterdam; they do dreadful things to you.

5. Amsterdam is a beautiful city

"Right, all sorted," said Ted, returning with a key.

"This is for you," he said to Veronica, putting his arm around me. "You, my dear, will be staying in my room."

"Oh good." I let my head rest against his shoulder as we walked along. "I'm very pleased about that."

NO KNICKERS AND A RED FACE

As soon as I got back from Amsterdam I threw the pink onesie away. I'm a woman of great style and sophistication, I shouldn't be wandering the streets dressed like a Care Bear mated with a TellyTubby.

From now on I would ooze glossy glamour. With that thought in mind, I decided to treat myself to a much-needed trip to the beauty salon. I hardly ever go to the beauticians but I always love it when I go. I like every part of it, from the moment I step through the magical doors that tinkle gently as if a wonderful world of fairy magic lies beyond them; to drifting out on a cloud of lavender-scented pillow spray afterwards.

It's one of my favourite things in the whole world. All the gorgeous smells and the wildly over-made-up women in their nurse-like outfits drifting around talking in warm and calming voices; I think it's that combination of a woman who really loves her makeup (I mean really loves makeup – some of them wear so much of the stuff that their foundation enters the room five minutes before the rest of them), and a pseudo-scientific approach to the job, that makes them so appealing.

You know what I mean about the science – those uniforms they wear and all the talk of alpha hydroxides, illuminating particles and oxygen-carrying molecules – I'm convinced every time that my life will be transformed by these women and their alluring potions and endless promises.

"This will make you look 10 years younger," a beautician with a sleepy smile will say. "I will make your pores invisible and your wrinkles vanish…I will make you grow six inches taller and you'll become President of the United States of America."

OK, maybe not the last two, but you know what I mean. Who doesn't want to be in a world in which everyone is telling you they will make you look better? It's like the most perfect world ever.

The science is great, and very compelling – the beautician peers at your skin under a light so bright that it could light up the sky, staring at your skin with an intensity and determination normally reserved for nuclear fusion and brain surgery. It is as if the beauty technician is solving all the problems of the universe: you expect her to make a pronouncement about string theory or black holes, but she doesn't do that, she declares that you need a deluxe, rabbit ear facial or some other such tosh and your skin will be perfect. And you believe her. Well – I do. She could suggest absolutely anything to me at that stage and I'd be fine with it.

"We will spray the essence of sea breeze onto your skin along with crushed crab heads." Fine.

"We'll cover your face in horse manure and dance around you, waving tea towels." Great.

"We'll put salt in your eyes and vinegar in your ears and sing the national anthem." Perfect.

Christ. It's so ridiculous.

And I'm absolutely sure every time that they cover my face in something like mashed-up beetles' legs, sea moss and elephant semen I'll emerge looking like Cameron Diaz. Because that's the thing about going to the beauticians – it's all about hope. Hope of a prettier face, better skin, and a tighter jawline. It's all about the triumph of optimism over common sense.

I always think that this appointment might be the one time that I leave looking really different, really special. Alas, dear readers, I have to report that – to date – no treatment I've had has ever made the blindest bit of difference to the way I look. But I keep going. I keep turning up at the door with the tinkling sounds in the hope that it will work this time.

So, I went to the beauticians for a facial. They showed me through to a small 'consulting' room. I wasn't sure whether I should get undressed and lie down on the bed, or wait for the beautician.

No one told me to get undressed, but clearly, I knew I had to remove my top and I didn't want to look like a complete beauty amateur by waiting to be told everything, but – equally – I didn't want to be presumptuous. On balance I'd rather wait to be told, so I sat down and looked at the rows and rows of lotions, creams and sprays on the side, and enjoyed the strong smell of lavender sitting heavily in the air. The creams and lotions had alluring names – all of them promising to have a transformational effect on the user. Whether you wanted to look younger, tighter, plumper or glossier, you could do so by simply picking up the relevant bottle and smearing the contents on your face.

I reached over and took one of the bottles. It said 'youth serum'. I couldn't resist it. I glanced at the door, then twisted the cap and attempted to put a couple drops of the serum into my hand. But I twisted the cap too much and tonnes of the bloody gloopy stuff came out. The liquid smelled like almonds but had the consistency of semen, which unnerved me a little. I rubbed the semen serum into my face. I'd just covered the right side of my face when the door opened and the beautician walked in. I quickly rubbed my hand against the towel on the bed next to me so she didn't know I'd been pinching her almond semen.

"Hello," she said, extending a very tiny, perfectly manicured hand. I reached out to shake it and watched in dismay at how much bigger my hand was than hers. Mine looked like a man's hand. A fat man's hand. Who on earth wants a fat man's hand? I bet even a fat man doesn't want a fat man's hand.

While we shook hands and exchanged polite greetings, I could feel the right side of my face tingling. It wasn't unpleasant – just a gentle feeling of warmth spreading through it. It felt nice. It felt like the serum was working – yay!

But no. No. I began to panic.

I only had the serum on one side of my face. I became paranoid that one side of my face would look years younger than the other. I pictured half of me looking like Taylor Swift and the other half as Theresa May. Not a good look.

Hopefully, the beautician would cleanse my skin before the transformative effects of the lotion kicked in. The beautician was very exotic. If she were a smell, she'd be cherry blossom and magnolia or lemon grass and pear (see how obsessed I was becoming with the smells? See how this place has got to me?). She sat down and asked me what my concerns were about my skin. Really, I didn't know how much time she'd got, but I did have a lot of concerns. I began to reel them off…the redness around my nose, the puffiness around my eyes, the spots on my chin, the oily patch down the centre of my face. And the open pores. My God! My pores were so open I could store things in them. And wrinkles – don't forget the wrinkles!

"You're being very hard on yourself," she said in a foreign accent so strong that I could barely understand her. She sounded like she was from South Africa. "You have lovely skin and it will look even lovelier after the facial."

There we go…the promises, the hope, the optimism…

She had the most beautiful, caramel-coloured skin and gorgeous shiny black hair. There was more fat in my thumb than she had in her entire body.

"I'm going to go out of the room to let you get yourself sorted. Could you remove your knickers and lie back on the bed? Get yourself comfortable and I'll be back in a tick."

The lady moved to leave the room.

"Sorry, could you repeat that?" I said. She couldn't really want me to remove my knickers, could she?

"Just lie back on the bed," she said in her clipped accent. "Make yourself comfortable, and remember to remove your knickers. I'll be back in just a minute."

I knew I should run after her and ask her why on earth I had to remove my most intimate piece of clothing when I was having a facial. But I didn't, of course. In the same way that I don't scream "It's too bloody hot" if I'm at the hairdresser and they wash my hair in boiling water.

"Is the temperature OK?" the girl will ask, and even though my scalp is melting under her fingers, I'll say "Yes, it's fine," knowing I'll have to go straight to A&E for a scalp transplant afterwards.

So, I took my knickers off and settled down on the bed with a small towel covering my embarrassment.

A few minutes later the lady came back in, smiled at me and took the towel off me.

"Whaaaaa…" she said, staring at me. "Why the hell did you remove your knickers?"

"You told me to," I insisted.

She backed away, towards the door, and looked at me as if I was completely mad.

"I said remove your necklace. Your necklace. Not your knickers."

"Ohhhh…"

I struggled back into my underwear and lay back on the bed. "Sorry," I muttered, as the smell of ylang-ylang and sandalwood filled the room. "I thought you said knickers. I wouldn't have taken them off otherwise. I'm not the sort of person who…"

"Sssshhh… just relax," she said as she massaged some sort of concoction that smelled like the earth into my face. "Relax and think about how beautiful you are going to look."

"OK." I sensed myself drifting away. "OK, I'll relax."

The facial was lovely. I almost fell asleep as she covered my face in a thick, heavy paste and said, to my delight, "I'm going to give you a massage while the face masque is doing its magic. She started to apply oil to her hands, which she then began to massage into my legs and I began to really relax, but then I couldn't help but think about her tiny, delicate hands and how horrible it must be for her to have to massage my enormous, fat thighs. I wondered whether she was repulsed. She was so tiny, so small and delicate, I bet she'd never seen thighs as

BERNICE BLOOM

enormous as mine. As she massaged away, I experienced an overwhelming urge to explain (lie) to her about why I was so fat.

Of course, the reason I was overweight was because I ate too much, but that's not much of a story is it? So I told her all about my baby that had just been born. I told her I'd just had twins.

"How lovely," she said. "I'm so envious. I'd love to have a baby one day. Twins would be amazing. I'd love that more than anything in the world. How long ago did you have them?"

"Yesterday," I replied. (I know, I know, stupid answer, but I was under pressure and not thinking straight…what, with all the lavender, massaging, and everything.)

"YESTERDAY?"

"Yep."

"My God. Really? That's amazing. I'll be gentle with the massage," she said. "You probably shouldn't be here so soon afterwards."

"I'm fine. Honestly," I said, wishing I'd never embarked on this line of chatter. I wanted her to carry on massaging me firmly. I love firm massages.

"Where are the twins now?"

"Sorry?"

"The twins…I wondered where they were."

"My friend has them outside."

"So sweet," said the beautiful therapist and I nodded in agreement in the darkness of the room. My imaginary babies were, indeed, very sweet.

"What are their names?"

"Pardon."

"I just wondered what their names were?" she asked.

Bugger.

"William and Kate," I said, without thinking.

"Oh. Nice. Very patriotic," she replied.

"Yes."

"OK, that's the end of the treatment. Has everything been OK for you?"

"Lovely," I mumbled. My skin was tingling like crazy, my shoulders were relaxed, and I had two amazing imaginary babies named after a future King and Queen of England.

"I'm just going to turn the light up slightly."

She padded gently towards the door. "Don't get up quickly; take it easy, especially since you had your babies yesterday."

"Don't worry too much about the whole baby thing," I said. "It was quite simple, no aggro."

"Holy fuck," she said.

"What's the matter?" I asked as she stared at me, her face in her hands, her eyes wide as saucers.

"It's your face. Something weird has happened to your face – it's absolutely scarlet."

THE TROUBLE WITH TED

It would be a lie to say that my skin looked better after the facial; it would be more accurate to describe me as looking like I'd been peeled and pickled.

The beautician said that the 'blush' (BLUSH? I looked like I'd been boiled!) would go down within a few hours and I should make sure I didn't put any makeup on for 24 hours to get the full benefits of the treatment. So I was heading off to my friend Charlie's house looking like someone had rubbed a cheese grater against my face and then sprinkled vinegar on top. Great! And I'd paid for it. And couldn't put any makeup on it to make it less angry looking. Marvellous.

Charlie's my best and oldest friend. She's known me forever; we did everything together when we were younger. She opened the door and gave me a huge hug, then she released me and glanced at my face before jumping back in horror. Her hands flew to her mouth.

"Good God, you look like wolves have attacked you!" she said.

"No, no, I'm fine."

"Car crash?"

"No, honestly, I'm fine."

"Late-onset meningitis?"

"No, really, I just went for a facial today, and I seem to have reacted to some of the products."

"Yeah, I'll say. Reacted is a bit of an understatement. Why's it so much worse on the right side of your face?"

"No idea."

"OK. And you're sure you don't need a doctor."

"Positive," I said. "The beautician wasn't alarmed, nor should I be."

This was a lie – the beautician was very alarmed; she screamed when she saw the colour I'd gone and called for urgent assistance. The beauty salon owner came running down the corridor as fast as her Chinese silk slippers would allow her and threw cold water on my face. The red didn't fade. It looked worse when wet. The two women looked at one another – entirely out of options. "I think you need to go home and relax and it should fade," said one of them.

"Yes," said the other enthusiastically, as if her colleague had just solved the mysteries of the universe. "Sandra's right; it should fade. Just go and relax."

Despite their apparent conviction that going home (i.e. getting out of their salon before anyone saw me) was the best thing to do, they kept glancing at one another in a way which screamed 'What the fuck do we do now?'

"OK, well I guess the beauticians know what they're talking about," said Charlie. "Come on, come in." She swept her arm into the house for me to follow her inside, still staring at my face in a squinty fashion as if she couldn't quite believe what she was seeing.

"How are you? I mean – besides the raw tomato face thing."

"I'm fine, really. I'm a lot better than I look."

"Christ, yes, I should hope you are. How is Ted?"

I was dreading this question. The truth was that Ted was great. He was kind and decent and honest, and he loved me. But for some reason… I didn't know why…we were drifting apart. I didn't feel as madly in love with him as I used to, and he was starting to annoy me quite a lot.

"Everything OK?" she repeated. "I mean – Ted-wise?"

Charlie had heard everything she needed to know in my silence.

"Everything's not OK, is it?" she said. "Do you want to talk?"

"Everything's sort of fine," I replied. "I mean it's not not fine or anything."

"Sort of fine? Not not fine?"

"Sort of," I repeated.

"Glass of wine?"

"A large one would be great, thanks."

I followed her into the kitchen, jumping as I saw my bright red face in the hall mirror. I looked as if I was in a permanent state of extreme anger.

Charlie handed me a drink, and we clinked glasses affectionately.

"So, things aren't going well with Ted?" she said.

"I don't know, Charlie. I'm not being evasive or anything, I just don't know. It's not that things aren't going well; it's just that I'm not feeling it… Do you know what I mean? I don't know…"

"Have you spoken to Ted about this?" she asked. "Last time we had any sort of conversation about him, you were ludicrously happy and heading off to stalk him in Amsterdam while wearing a pink onesie and clutching a kite. What happened to change your mind?"

"That was ages ago. Things have changed a bit recently. I haven't spoken to him because I don't know what to say. I mean – it's not like I don't love him. And, yes, I know, I was obsessed with him… could think of nothing else. And he has done nothing wrong, and nothing has changed, but I've done this mental thing where I've switched off and gone off him. I don't know…it's nuts. Perhaps I'll get over it."

Ted and I have been inseparable since we met, spending most nights of the week together and all weekends. To be honest, we rarely went out. We seemed to spend all our time inside cuddling up together, watching TV or watching films. If it weren't for Fat Club, we'd have spent most of our time eating takeaways and drinking wine because – let's be honest – that's a bloody marvellous way to pass the time, but we were good, and we cooked instead of getting takeaways. I even persuaded Ted to try salads against his better judgement (believing green food was the devil's stuff). I gave him an apple once, but when he bit into it, he made the most extraordinary face – full of pain and anguish. "There's no chocolate in mine," he said, like a seven-year-old woken up on Christmas morning to no presents.

"It's not supposed to have chocolate in, you buffoon," I said.

"So why do people eat them then?"

We had fun, though – we had BBQs in the summer, sometimes inviting friends, but usually with just the two of us. In fact – yes – it was just the two of us. Now I come to think of it, we only talked of inviting other people over but never actually got around to it, preferring to spend time alone, together. It was lovely – lying in the garden when it was warm or in front of the TV later in the summer when things got colder. To be fair, we spent most of our time lying around. I wonder whether that was why the spark went. It's early November now, and we are still lying around.

When you think about it, I suppose it's not hard to see why things have gone awry with Ted and me. Fundamentally, it's pretty boring to do the same thing every day. The other thing is I realised that I stopped making an effort. In the early days of the relationship, I only had to think he might be coming around, and I'd be thrown into a wild frenzy of cleaning and organising the house, then shaving, moisturising, fake tanning and making myself up. It was exhausting. But fun. And seeing Ted's face when I opened the door made it worthwhile. I guess somewhere along the line, I stopped trying. I stopped dressing up for Ted. After all, what was the point? We were just lying on the sofa. I'd have a quick shower and brush my hair, but I was always in leggings and oversized, baggy t-shirts, not the lovely 50s-style dresses I'd worn all the time when we first met and that Ted had loved so much.

I had to face the truth; as the summer had slipped into autumn, I'd stopped making an effort, and - to be fair - so had Ted. This wasn't a one-way abandonment of the relationship. I think we were equally to blame. Ted would come round and let himself in, and I'd be sitting on the sofa, watching TV or sorting things out in the kitchen. I'd make a cup of tea or (more likely) pour us a glass of wine, and we'd both sit back and relax for the evening, and that was our life. Gosh, when you look at it in black and white like that, it's amazing we lasted so long.

The truth is that Ted and I had drifted into this space of existing together without really living or loving one another. It was a space that was – well – a bit empty.

"It sounds like you need to talk to him," said Charlie. "Tell him you still love him but are concerned…you're not sure things are as good as they were."

"But that'll worry him. You know what he's like…he'll be in a real panic. What would I say? 'You are as lovely as ever, as considerate, kind and loving as you've ever been, but I no longer feel one bit excited when I think of you.'"

"No, maybe don't say that to him…that would be a bit harsh. But tell him that the two of you need to talk."

"Talk? All we do is bloody talk."

Charlie looked at me over the rim of her wine glass. It was quite a stern look that said, 'don't fuck this up; Ted's a good guy.' And she was right. Ted was the all-time, ultimate good guy.

"Perhaps it's a passing thing." As I spoke, I recalled the million butterflies I used to feel every time I saw him. I wished it was still like that. I wished I prayed it was him every time the phone rang, but I didn't. And I didn't know whether that was because we were settling into a relationship in a normal, healthy way or whether this was the end of the infatuation period and the end of Ted and Mary.

How does anyone know?

"I guess it's just become predictable and unexciting," I said. "That's not only his fault…it's my fault as well." As I spoke, my phone vibrated on the table, and I knew straight away that it was Ted.

"You see – this is the problem – there's no mystery or excitement. I always know it's him," I said, turning over the phone to show Charlie what I meant, but instead of Ted's name on the screen, it was Dave's.

More specifically, it said, "Dishy Dave – hottie from downstairs."

"Oh," said Charlie. "The hottie downstairs appears to be calling."

If I hadn't already been the colour of hot chilli, I would have gone red. Why was Dave calling?

"So, are the problems with Ted anything to do with this Downstairs Dave?" asked Charlie.

"No," I said, in all honesty. "Nothing to do with Double D." I hadn't been near the delicious man in the flat below me since I'd started seeing Ted. I hadn't wanted to.

I didn't know why Dave was ringing me, but it had to be something to do with him borrowing something, needing something or wanting me to keep an eye out for the latest glamorous blonde in his life. Sadly, it wouldn't be to fix up an illicit meeting with me.

The times he'd called in the past had been notable for their lack of any actual interest in me.

There was one occasion when he called and said: "Tesco's are bringing my shopping, are you in to collect it?"

The honest answer was: "No, I'm not in." But is that what I said to him?

Of course not. I wanted to be useful. I wanted to be the one to whom he turned when he needed anything. All in the vain hope that he'd realise one day, like the characters in every decent romantic comedy ever made, that the woman of his dreams was right beneath his nose all the time.

So, I said: "Sure, no problem. I'm here. I can help." Even though I wasn't, not by a long way, I was bloody miles away at Mum and Dad's house and had to leave mid-sentence with barely an explanation and break the land speed record to get home in time for the Tesco man.

"I'll call you later to explain," I'd shouted to Dad over my shoulder as I moved at speed through the streets like a woman possessed. I'd flown towards the shared gate that led to mine and Dave's flats just as the Tesco lorry drove off.

"Stop," I screeched, and it came to a halt, reversing back into a parking space and beginning to unload shopping bags. I signed for it all, found Dave's spare key under the dying plants, and let myself into his filthy flat.

I put the shopping away (to be fair – it was mainly beer), then had a massive tidy-up and sat down to wait for Dave's return. In my head, he'd be so delighted that I'd stepped into the breach and not only brought in his shopping and put it away but also tidied everything up that he would instantly fall in love with me and ask me to marry him.

In the end, he didn't get home until 2 am and had a glamorous blonde on his arm. I was six or seven stone heavier than her (I mean that – the woman can't have been more than eight stone, for God's sake).

"What are you doing here?" asked Dave, quite angry, not mentioning the vast amount of tidying up I'd done.

I slinked back to my flat, cried, and ate a load of crisps.

Things like that happened a lot with me and Dave.

In fact, you could say that the only things that ever happened between me and Dave were like that.

So, I didn't take the call on this occasion and switched my phone off.

"Right," I said to Charlie. "Let's talk about you; tell me what you've been up to."

"Well, it's funny you should ask," she said. "Did I tell you about Sam? The guy I met on Tinder."

"No." I poured more wine into my glass and went to put the bottle down when the glass was half-full.

"I strongly think that this is a large glass of wine sort of story," said Charlie, grabbing the bottle off me and tipping so much wine into my glass that it was full to the brim, and I could barely lift it. She filled her own glass.

"Well, he seemed nice...seemed normal," she said. "The picture on the site was good – he seemed to have hair and teeth and no facial tattoos...always a good start."

Charlie told me they'd met at the train station and he had a small bunch of flowers for her.

"A nice touch," we agreed.

They went for a drink first, and he mentioned his wife, who died in a car crash ten years earlier.

"Christ, how awful," I said. "How did she die?"

"She died when a car veered onto the pavement and hit her. She was taking their son to the nursery at the time."

"Bloody hell, mate. That's awful."

"Yep. It's unbelievably awful. I felt so sorry for him. The trouble was, the whole date was all about his tragic story of lost love. He didn't ask me anything about me. He didn't seem interested in who I was or what I wanted; he was just glad to have someone to talk to about his late wife. Does that sound really harsh or selfish? It probably is, isn't it?"

"No, I know what you mean. It's a very sad story, but you still have to find a way to have a relationship. He has to ask something about your life and not use you as free therapy. Tell me what happened afterwards. Did he take you home?"

"We went for dinner, which was nice – just at a pub in Esher. The food was amazing... delicious. Then I invited him back to mine for coffee."

"Ooooo. Now it's starting to sound exciting." I bent over in an ungainly fashion to sip from the top of my wine glass because I couldn't pick the bloody thing up – there was too much wine in it.

"He said he'd love to come in for coffee and would drive me home. I commented that I'd noticed he wasn't drinking anything, and he said, 'I haven't drunk a drop of alcohol since the moment that car hit my wife,' and that was it – he was off again with all the detail...all the bloody, gory detail about her blood-stained sweater and going limp in his arms. It kind of killed the mood, to be honest. I didn't feel very sexy when he was moodily moaning about blood on the street.

"Then, just as I thought things couldn't get any worse, we get into the car, he turns the key, and we head off in slightly the wrong direction. 'I think we're better off turning right here,' I say to him, pointing to the next junction.

"'No, let's go this way,' he insisted. 'I want to show you where the car hit her.'"

"Fuck," I said, downing the rest of my wine in one huge mouthful and struggling to swallow it without choking and spluttering.

"That's what I said. I asked him not to take me to where she bloody died, but he insisted. He drove to the spot and made me get out of the car. He showed me where it happened and recalled the sights, sounds and smells of the moment to make it come alive for me. It was horrid.

Honestly, Mary, hang on to Ted, he's a good guy, and there are lots of nutters out there."

"Yes," I replied, rendered almost speechless by her tale. "Yes, you're probably right."

I got home that evening and forgot that my phone had been off. It's weird when you're used to having it on all the time. So, I switched it on and waited patiently for all the beeps and rings to indicate that Ted had rung about ten times and left eight messages.

Silence.

I checked through the message folder: nothing.

I rang the answer phone: nothing.

Oh.

Ted hadn't phoned.

I wasn't expecting that.

HAS HIS PHONE BROKEN OR SOMETHING?

No call from Ted in the morning. Nothing at all.

I didn't care, to be honest. The relationship was dying, so I guessed it was best that he had lost interest. But I wondered why he'd lost interest. I rechecked the phone—no missed call. Perhaps my phone was broken? I rang myself from my landline and the mobile began singing in front of me. It was working OK. I texted myself. Yep – the text came bouncing through.

Bugger.

Whatever. I didn't care.

Except…I kind of, sort of, did care…just a little bit. This was weird. I did like him, and I wanted him to like me. I didn't want him pulling away…that wasn't in the plan at all.

The good news was that I'd see Ted tonight at Fat Club. The second course was starting and not before time. I needed another injection of Liz's therapy to get me back on course. I'd made loads of great friends on the first course, but we'd lost touch over the summer - it would be nice to catch up with everyone again.

So that evening, when gentle darkness descended on Cobham, I was on the bus heading to the crumbling community centre that passed as the home for Fat Club. I got a little shiver of familiarity as I approached. I remembered walking in on the first day and thinking this wasn't for me, but by the end of the course, I was totally sold on it. Suddenly my mind was flooded with memories of meeting Ted there. He was so loveable, kind and gorgeous. Fat, of course, or why else would he have been there? And not conventionally good-looking at all – kind of half-shy, half wildly over-confident. Sometimes he would smile at me and nudge me quietly when no one was looking, and I'd feel a shiver of excitement run through me. God, it's always so amazing at the beginning of a relationship. Pity so many of them turn to shit after a few months.

As well as seeing Ted at Fat Club, I'd also see the other friends I'd made because they were all coming back for this second course. The first course was about losing weight – this one was about losing more weight. Guess what the next course was called? 'Losing even more weight.' Not sure what would happen after that: 'Losing so much weight it's unbelievable', 'Coping with being too thin'? I don't know. All I did know was that the first course worked like a dream – I felt happier, more confident and – crucially! – thinner after it, so I was going in again.

I walked inside and saw I was the third person to arrive. Liz, the course leader, was in the room, standing at the front in an apple green jumper and a purple skirt, sorting out her notes while Janice chatted with her.

"And then he killed his wife and ran off with the butcher's son!" she was saying. "Can you believe that?"

"Blimey," I said. "You don't half socialise with some colourful characters."

"No, not my social life. This is the plot of the book that Liz told me to read."

"That's a relief." I walked over to Janice and kissed her on the cheek. "I was worried about you for a minute then."

"Hi, Liz, are you OK?" I kissed her on the cheek as well. "What have you got planned for us then? Anything weird or complicated?"

"Nothing weird," said Liz. "We'll just be doing more of what we did on the first course, but probing, trying to find out why people are overeating, why it's become a crutch. We will be leaning on each other for moral support."

"OK – sounds good," I said. "I never thought I'd say this, but I've missed the regular group meetings; it'll be nice to get into them again."

"That's good to hear," said Liz. "Most people come back for the second course after they've been successful on the first one, and they always say it's because they find it such a supportive environment, and they miss it when the first course stops."

"Yep, that's me." I watched Liz as she continued to remove things from her large bag. She pulled out a set of weighing scales.

"What the hell?" I said.

"You're not going to weigh us?" added Janice.

"That's the spirit," said Liz, the sarcasm dripping off every word. "Be enthusiastic and encouraging."

"But – they are weighing scales," I pointed out. "Weighing scales! I'd be less terrified if you pulled out a gun."

"You're not going to weigh us?" said Janice.

"No, of course not."

"Then why would you have weighing scales?"

Honestly, bringing out weighing scales at a Fat Club is like bringing out a bomb or something. I noticed that Janice had physically recoiled from the sight of it.

"Can you put it away," she said. "You're making me feel queasy."

"Don't be silly now, ladies," said Liz, shaking her head, pushing her hand into her bag and pulling out a tape measure.

"Whooooah. And you can put that back from where you got it as well," said Janice.

"I'm not going to use them to measure you if that's what you're worried about."

"That's what I'm very worried about," said Janice. "Why would you have them if you weren't going to use them on us?"

"Yes," I added in a slightly trembling voice, unable to take my eyes off the scales.

"Oh, for goodness' sake." Liz put them back in her bag. "You two are ridiculous. You've both done so well and lost so much weight. Isn't it time to be proud of how much you weigh?"

"Proud?" I said. "I'm six bloody stone over fighting weight; proud is certainly not how I'm feeling."

"You've lost weight, Mary. Please focus on the positives."

"Yes, boss," I said, smiling over at Janice.

It's one thing to discuss our difficulties with food and try to learn to readjust and alter our mindsets, but it's quite another thing to be humiliated publicly. If people knew how much I weighed, they'd be astonished I could walk properly without my legs breaking beneath me.

"Hello lovely," I said as Veronica walked into the room and saw us all staring at Liz as she stuffed the scales and tape measure into her bag.

"Hello, beautiful people," she said, smiling broadly at us. Then she saw the scales. "Woooo…What are they for? I'm not being weighed, not for anyone."

"Not another one," said Liz. "They're not for weighing."

"What on earth are they for then?" asked Veronica, giving me a big hug. "I'll protect you from the scales," she whispered.

Liz continued to put the scales into her bag and remove notes, books, and what looked like a skipping rope.

"I'm not skipping either – you can forget about that. With boobs this size, I'd knock myself out."

"Will you lot stop worrying? Nothing terrible is going to happen. You're not going to have to do anything. These are for my next class – not for you. I was checking that I have everything I need. So you can all relax."

"I can't relax with that skipping rope on the table…it's terrifying. I feel like I'm back in school and not invited to join the skipping games."

"Bloody hell, ladies – you're hard work tonight." Liz put the skipping rope back into the bag with the scales and tape measure. She looked up. "Happy now?"

"Much happier," said Veronica with a smile that lit up her face. She was so beautiful. Today she looked more lovely than ever, with her doll-like features and porcelain skin...kind of like Sophie Dahl used to look before she lost all that weight and let us all down.

"You OK, gorgeous?" she asked.

"I'm fine, thanks."

She sat next to me, so I had Janice on one side and Veronica on the other. For a fleeting moment, I thought I should ask her to move so Ted could sit next to me. But then I remembered that Ted hadn't called or texted or made any effort to get in touch with me for two days. TWO DAYS! He was dead to me. I was glad to be in the middle of a Janice and Veronica sandwich.

"Where's Ted?" asked Veronica, as if she could read my mind.

"He's not here yet." I tried to sound as neutral and unbothered as possible. "I'm sure he'll be here soon."

"Hello," came a voice from the doorway – it was Phil and his wife. They were both elderly and the only people I didn't really get to know on the last course. They sat quietly and didn't chat with us or join in our post-session drinks, and they were quiet during the sessions themselves. All I knew about them was that they were both called Phil: Philippa and Philip, known as the Phils. They said that at their work (because not only did they have the same name, but they also worked in the same place), they were known as the Fat Phils. I felt sorry for her when she said that and told her that she should complain to HR, but she just shrugged and snorted.

I was determined to make friends with them on this course and spend some time getting to know them. It seemed a shame they weren't properly part of the group simply because they arrived as a couple and not on their own like the rest of us. I was determined to pull them into the centre of our little group. I'd be the club's social secretary.

The masculine Phil was resplendent in a large overcoat, and the feminine Phil sported a sturdy-looking winter coat in a kind of boiled wool dyed olive green. Possibly the most unflattering jacket ever made. She wore brown tights and lace-up shoes precisely the same colour so that her legs seamlessly blended into her feet – like she'd got hooves. The shoes were deeply unattractive – the type of orthopaedic shoes that might be given to a child with an unfortunate birth condition that has resulted in one leg growing longer than the other.

Veronica watched as I stood up to walk over to them. She wore a quizzical look on her face. "I'm the social secretary," I whispered to her and Janice.

I reached the Phils, and smiled: "We never really got to know each other on the last course," I said.

"No," said Phil, in a way which made it sound as if that was entirely by design, and he was eager to avoid us getting to know one another on this one.

"I'm Mary," I said, smiling broadly.

"You have lipstick on your teeth, Mary," said Philippa. Could she not just smile and shake my hand, for Christ's sake? I was trying my hardest here.

I rubbed my tongue across my front teeth.

"We should all make more of an effort to get to know each other this time," I said, and Philippa looked quite terrified. "We hardly spoke to one another on the last course…why don't you come out for a drink with us one night?"

"We don't drink," said Phil.

"Well, come and have a Coke or coffee or something?" I tried.

"I don't think so," he said. "Thanks for asking."

I turned round to return to my seat and walked straight into Janice. "I don't want to be social secretary any longer," I told her. "The job's yours."

As I sat down, I was still running my tongue along the front of my teeth to ensure the lipstick had all gone. This was the problem with bright red lipstick – if it got anywhere but your lips, it looked bloody awful…collars, sleeves and especially teeth.

I decided on red lips today to match my red dress. I was wearing it to show Ted what he was missing. He liked me in red. I liked myself in red. So I was slightly confused about why I'd been wearing grey leggings and T-shirts all summer. It was quite a figure-hugging dress for me, and I felt ever so slightly self-conscious, but I knew this was a dress that Ted liked, and even though I didn't care a damn about him and, frankly, didn't care whether he turned up or not that night, I wanted him to be impressed if he did.

Oh, God. He was here.

I subconsciously tidied my hair as I saw him appear through the door. My stomach was in knots…probably because of the food I'd eaten earlier. I'd made a spicy chicken salad. Not the best decision in the world for someone who was rubbish when it came to eating spicy foods. Then I noticed. He was wearing the blue jumper I'd given him. Ahhhh, he looked nice. God, I'd missed him. Why had I decided I didn't like him anymore? I did like him…I really liked him – look at him – he was just lovely.

Ted walked towards me, and I didn't know what to do. We'd been ignoring each other, and I didn't know why. I had butterflies in my stomach, and I felt madly self-conscious. I looked down and started pretending to dig into my bag for something. When I looked up, he had gone over to talk to Liz, kissing her on both cheeks and asking her about the course. Fuck. Why was I behaving like such an idiot?

Ted looked good, I had to admit that. He took the jumper off, and you could see clearly that, in common with most of us, he'd lost a few stones since the first course, which suited him. He had jeans on with the shirt tucked into them, and while no one could accuse him of being too thin, I could remember the days when he would only wear the baggiest of shirts, always hanging outside his jeans. He used to walk around with a look of desperate embarrassment at his own existence. That had turned to mild confidence. He looked like a man who was comfortable in his skin. It was amazing what losing weight could do for a person.

It was great to see everyone back in the room where we'd first met; there was a real familiarity, warmth and happiness in being with these people with whom I'd been through so much.

We'd all lost weight since the last course, but more importantly, we'd all realised why we ate so much. We'd all listened to the lectures and heard each other's stories. We understood that we had convinced ourselves, somewhere deep down, that eating would make us feel better, loved, or so full that we wouldn't worry anymore about the problems that seemed to haunt us like ghosts in the night.

I was trying to smother all the problems I had through my eating. The great irony for me was the discovery that the 'problems' I had were largely related to my self-esteem and that self-esteem hinged on my appearance. So – for heaven's sake – every time I ate to hide my problems, I was making my problems worse because I felt more unattractive to myself as I got bigger, which ate away at my diminishing self-esteem.

Coming onto the first course helped me recognise that and stop it. I did some psychological switch whereby I knew I wasn't eating because I was hungry – I was eating to make myself feel good, and I stopped it. I did other things that made me feel good, like walking and swimming, and the weight started to come off. The more it came off, the happier I felt and the less inclined I was to eat.

I hadn't been perfect, and I had strayed from the straight and narrow at times, which was why I'd been eager for the class to start again, but I'd been pretty good. Sure, I could eat a packet of biscuits in one sitting, and if you saw me wolf down a bag of chips, you'd think that my psychological problems were as bad as ever, but they weren't. I'd eat and eat and eat and then have a moment of clarity when I realised what I was doing, and I'd stop. I'd never had those feelings of clarity before. Honestly, I never stopped until I started crying or feeling sick. Since the first course, I could still eat loads and loads, but then I'd think, 'what the hell are you doing, woman?' and I'd stop. And I didn't do it again the next day and the day after.

THE NEW GIRL AT FAT CLUB

"Just waiting for one more person," said Liz, with a gentle shrug of her shoulders and a warm smile. Liz had been such a support to me since the last course ended: phoning up to keep me on track, and making sure she checked in with me from time to time to ensure I was OK.

"No, we're all here," I said, looking around the room and smiling at everyone except Ted. I still couldn't look at him. He made me feel all nervous and jittery.

Why didn't he call me? He was supposed to like me. People who like you; call you.

He half-smiled at me, then sucked the smile in as I looked away, and I wished immediately that I hadn't looked away. Why the hell did I look away? And why didn't he just come over and say hello, talk to me, or behave as any half-normal human would?

"Ah, but we're not all here," said Liz. "Because we have a newcomer attending the session tonight...."

Everyone in the room looked at Liz. This was the most unwelcome news. We'd become such a tight-knit group, sharing details of our issues with food and stories about failed weight loss and bonding over our shared problems and fears. We trusted each other and felt comfortable with each other. We'd delved deep into our psyches and shared information with the group that was personal, sad and touching. There had been tears, smiles and anguish as we'd talked about the deaths of those close to us and how they sent us spiralling into despair and overeating. I felt I knew more about some of the people in that room and what they'd been through than I knew about members of my own family. How could someone new be joining us?

The door at the back of the hall opened, and in walked a large woman (of course…she'd hardly be here if she was Kylie Minogue size). She was dressed beautifully, in a pair of cut-off jeans and an off-the-shoulder red and white polka dot top. She looked like she ought to be in St Tropez or something with her incredible suntan and lashings of red lipstick. I looked down at my outfit, and suddenly I felt dowdy. Her red was brighter, and her lips were like glistening cherries. I was not the brightest, most eye-catching person in the room anymore, and it disturbed me more than it should.

"I'm Michella," she said with a massive smile stretched across her face.

I hated that she was so pretty, and I hated that she seemed so lovely with it.

"Come and sit here," said Ted with a smile, indicating the seat next to him.

What?

Fuck. No.

She ran her hand through her blonde hair. It was a shade or two lighter than mine, which made me really cross. I wanted to be the brightest blonde in the room. I loved having blonde hair. I'd always loved it.

I remembered being at school, sitting on the benches at the back as a fifth former, slightly elevated from the rest of the children and looking down at the heads in front of me. All the heads were shades of brown. Sure, there was the occasional blonde head, but it was mainly brown. Any blonde head would stand out like ripe corn in a muddy field, and I vowed always to be blonde.

When I first dyed my hair, my mum and dad were cross, but I

loved it... I thought I look like a movie star. I thought I looked like the Barbie I'd played with as a little girl. I thought I looked like a woman should look – bright, pretty and alluring but with an edge of vulnerability. I thought I looked fantastic, and I've been dyeing my hair ever since. In some ways, I was pretty envious of people like Janice, with her mousey hair and the fact that she felt no compunction to hide her natural state. I was all about hiding mine. I didn't want to be natural and 'myself' on the outside. If you are a mouse inside, I think you feel drawn to becoming a peacock on the outside.

"Hello, nice to meet you," she said, having thoroughly ingratiated herself with my boyfriend.

"I'm Mary," I said, ignoring how Ted was smiling at me. I was sure Ted's smile was screaming: "Look, look – a pretty girl. You have been replaced..."

And no – I wasn't being paranoid.

"Have you been on a sunbed?" she asked.

"No," I replied. Most of the redness had gone out of my skin following my disastrous beauty treatment, but clearly not all of it.

"Oh, an allergy of some kind?"

"No."

"A rash?"

"No."

For God's sake, woman. Let it go, will you?

"OK, let's get started," said Liz, rising to her feet and smiling at us. "You'll have noticed that we have a new girl in our midst...."

Yes, we've all noticed, I thought to myself. Nothing was interesting about a new girl turning up; it was a positive distraction. I wanted to get on with the session and not obsess about someone new being here. But – no – of course, they couldn't do that. We all had to get to know this glamorous young creature who'd crawled into our little group. To make it all worse, Michella was invited to go straight to the front of the room and give a small talk to us.

I looked at the way she walked...it was positively sick-making. Silly cow with her wiggly hips and big bottom. No one's impressed love. No one's impressed.

"Hello, my name is Michella," she said, running a hand through her blonde hair and pushing it back over her shoulder. She was very pretty – disturbingly so. I was sure she was exactly Ted's type. Let's be honest; she looked like a prettier, younger version of me. Bitch.

"People call me 'Mich' for short," she said, looking around the room with big blue eyes framed by long eyelashes that I was sure she kept fluttering in the direction of my boyfriend. Did she need to do that?

"OK, where do I start? I'm overweight, as you can see. I look horrible and feel horrible, and I'd go as far as to say I hate myself. I want to do something about it, but for some reason, I can't sort my head out and I sabotage myself whenever I try to lose weight. I thought that by being in a supportive environment like this, I might be able to change the way I am and eventually lose weight. You all seem nice, so that's a good start."

She looked around the room, desperate for encouragement, and I know it was evil of me, but I was silently praying that no one offered her any.

"We're all here for you," said Ted kindly, and I felt like punching him.

"Yes," added Janice. "We look after each other in this group." I feared I might explode with anger. She was such a traitor.

"I know why and when I started putting on weight – it's not a very happy story, but I feel I ought to tell you so you fully understand me and what I've been through."

Oh great. This was obviously going to take bloody hours.

"I had a twin sister called Emily," she said, pausing for a moment before giving a faint laugh to cover up the fact that she was getting emotional. "Phew. I knew it was going to be difficult to tell you about this.

"Anyway, Emily got ill when we were young. She had leukaemia aged 12; I remember it like it was yesterday, like it was this morning, like it was two minutes ago. I remember it all so clearly; it's like she's still here with me now. It's like she'll walk in any moment and hug me, and we'll carry on playing with our dolls, and everything will be OK.

But it won't because the leukaemia took her away from me. We can't talk about boys anymore, moan at each other for stealing each other's clothes or dance to our favourite pop music. We can't do any of it. She died, and I couldn't cope; looking back, I was left alone a lot after her death because my parents were also struggling. They comforted each other, and they cried and screamed together, and then they threw themselves into organising the funeral and setting up a charitable foundation. Me? I just ate."

Michella burst into tears, holding her sides and sobbing with all her heart. I did feel sorry for her – I'm not that insensitive. It must be unbelievably hard to lose a twin. Losing a sister would be awful, but a twin sister…that must be so much worse.

"I'm sorry, I'm really sorry; I thought it was important to talk through this because I think that's why I eat so much – because the pain is killing me, and I still try to bury it under food. Even talking to you today has made me think that now I could do with a big cream cake!"

Everybody laughed, and there were more mutterings of support and people telling her how fearless she was.

Michella then went on to describe the painful death of her sister. The two of them played together until the day before she died. She spoke about how brave her sister was, never complaining, always enthusiastic and talking about the future. "She must have known that she wouldn't be here to enjoy so many of the things we spoke about, but she continued to plan and to talk about it, and we wrote to Top of the Pops and said we wanted to be in the audience, and we wrote to our favourite pop stars and asked them for autographs, and in none of the letters she sent did she mention she was ill. It was like she didn't want it to affect anything. When she died, it felt that everything was pointless. The only thing that made me happy was food. The weight piled on, and I didn't care, I'd get exhausted running for the bus, and it didn't bother me in the least. Now, though, it does. I lost my sister half a lifetime ago, and I need to start living again for her. She's not here to enjoy life, so I need to enjoy it doubly as much… I need to start enjoying life for her as well as for me."

When she finished, there was a massive round of applause and a standing ovation, and she stood in the middle of it all, beaming from ear to ear.

The rest of us went up one by one and gave short talks about what we'd done since the last course. I kept mine brief. I just talked about my weight and my eating. Then Ted went up.

"It's been the best few months ever," he told everyone. "Because I've spent so much of it with Mary."

I looked up, stunned.

"She's changed my life. I'm a better man when I'm with her."

I could feel myself staring vacantly at Ted as he spoke. Everyone was staring at me; this was surreal. Ted came up to me afterwards and wrapped his arms around me.

"I know you've been busy, so we haven't been able to see much of each other, but I adore you, and I miss you," he said.

"I thought you'd gone off me," I replied. "When you didn't text me last night, I thought you didn't want to go out with me."

"I was giving you space," he said. "I thought you wanted some head space. I thought I was doing the right thing."

"Yes," I said. "You were. I'm an idiot."

"Are you coming for a drink?" he said as Liz packed her stuff away and told us she'd see us next week.

"Yes." I smiled up at him. He put his arm around me.

"And are you?" he asked Mich.

"I'd love to," she said cheerily, taking his other arm in a way which REALLY annoyed me.

"Come on, you handsome hunk," she said to Ted, and I could feel my blood pressure rising. Why did she annoy me so much? She was so flirty; it was bloody horrible.

We got to the pub, and she was no better, asking Ted to choose a drink for her and stroking his hair while he did. To his credit, he looked uncomfortable with all the attention, but he didn't push her away. He didn't tell her it was inappropriate.

Eventually, I couldn't do it any longer. "Right, I'm off," I said to a

THE MARY BROWN BOOKS

bewildered-looking Ted, stomping out of the pub without saying goodbye to anyone else. I shuffled out into the cold night air and hid around the corner from Ted, who had followed me. I didn't know why. Even I was confused about the way I was behaving. If I'd gone and spoken to Ted and told him I wanted to go home, he'd have taken me. And that would have been all my problems solved – I'd get him to myself and away from Michella. Bingo! But for some reason, I couldn't bring myself to make life easy. I couldn't bring myself to run into his arms and make everything right. I didn't know why. Something was stopping me.

After a while, Ted went back into the pub, and I stepped out of my hiding place and got on the bus home. All I could think about was eating. It was the ONLY thought in my mind. I got off the bus right by the off-licence, Tesco's and the chip shop – one next to the other: an unholy triumvirate of temptation.

I stood outside the chip shop, looking mournfully through the window and feeling anger and frustration rising inside me. I wanted to go in there and buy about six packets of saveloy and chips with a side portion of curry sauce; then I wanted to buy bread and butter and wine and swig the wine from the bottle without pouring it into a glass.

The thought of it all thrilled me. The more I could eat and drink, the more I would bury all the anger and frustration inside me. I stood in the cold night air for what seemed like hours, just smelling the vinegar. I wasn't hungry, and the smell wasn't making me think 'ooooo...delicious', the smell was making me think 'ooh...here is something that I can use to make myself feel better...here is something that will make the pain go away...not for long, but for a short while, and right now any break from my mad, whirring thoughts will be good.'

"Can I help you, Mary?" asked the lady inside.

Oh, God.

Her knowing my name made me feel like I'd been shot.

How could the lady in the chip shop know my name?

"Everything OK?" she asked.

BERNICE BLOOM

"Yes," I said, retreating from the alluring smells and warmth. "Everything's fine."

And I knew what I had to do. I had to reach out for help. I pulled my phone out of my pocket. There were lots of missed calls from Ted, and I felt a low pain deep inside me when I saw his name on the screen. Tears started pouring from my eyes as I dialled Liz's number. She should have finished her next class by now. Relief flooded through me when she answered on the second ring.

"Are you alright?" she asked.

"No," I said, bursting into tears. "I feel terrible, I'm messing everything up. I'm standing outside the chip shop and dying to go in, I want to eat. I've ruined my relationship with Ted, and I don't know why. Everything in my life feels out of control."

"Well, that's simply not true, is it?" said Liz calmly. "Everything in your life is not out of control because instead of buying chips, you rang me. Instead of falling into food as the answer, you reached out, and I will try and help you. I want you to walk back to your flat, go inside, put the kettle on and wait for me to arrive. We're not going to let you sabotage this lovely relationship you've got, and we're not going to let you sabotage your weight loss campaign – we're going to talk this through and sort it out, OK?"

"Yes," I muttered.

"You're just feeling insecure and unworthy, and you're pushing Ted away because your self-esteem is struggling. I could see it all over you tonight. We can sort this out. Go and put the kettle on: I'm on my way."

"Thank you," I said, all tears and snot. "Thank you so much."

LIZ IS MY HERO

"Right, young lady: first question – did you get chips?"

"No," I said, in all honesty. I did buy two bottles of wine, just in case, but she didn't ask me about wine, so I kept that to myself.

"Well done, lovely," she said, giving me a huge hug. "I'm very proud of you."

"I don't feel very proud of myself." I burst into tears again. "I've been treating Ted appallingly, and I don't know why. What's wrong with me? He's the nicest guy ever. I'm such an idiot; I'm such a loser. Why am I doing this? Look at the state of me. It's not as if men are queuing up to be with me. For God's sake – I'm ridiculous. I don't deserve him."

While I collapsed in floods of tears, Liz stroked my back gently.

"Do you want me to tell you what I think is going on?" she said.

"Yes, please," I spluttered through a veil of tears.

"Right. Well, I think all the answers to every question you have are tucked away in what you've just said."

"Are they?"

"Yes, what drove you to eat a lot in the first place were your emotional issues, am I right?"

"Yes," I said. That was undoubtedly the reason we identified on the first course for my overeating. Though I still hadn't explained which emotional issue.

"Now, we've learned on the course so far that eating to excess is not the answer. Eating gives you a reprieve from your feelings, but it doesn't change them, so there's no point in stuffing yourself full of food to bury feelings – the feelings will still be there, and you'll get fatter and fatter."

"Yes, I know, and I've been good – I had a breakthrough on the course and learned to completely accept that eating doesn't change anything when it comes to feelings and emotions."

"You've been amazing," confirmed Liz. "Now, let's think about those feelings and emotions that are all churned up. They are still there. You are learning to live with them and not to suppress them with food, but they haven't gone anywhere. So, what happens is, from time to time, they get the better of you – they rear up, and they attack you as sudden panic, anger, frustration or plain madness. I'm the same. I can act in the most obscure of ways when my emotions kick-off or someone says something, however innocent and benign it may appear on the outside, but for some reason, it starts something off in me, and I fall into a whirlwind of confusing emotions. Unfortunately, when you feel like that, you often take it out on the person closest to you…as you have…with Ted."

"Yes," I said, feeling calmer all the time at the news that I wasn't bonkers and what I was going through was something that even Liz herself had struggled with.

"It might be worth talking to someone," she said.

"I'm talking to you."

"No, I mean a psychiatrist…someone trained properly to help you."

"Is that expensive?" I asked. It certainly sounded like it would be.

"No, if you go through your GP, you'll get it on the NHS. It would help if you were clear with the GP about how bad you're feeling. Tell him or her everything, and you'll get a referral and should see someone soon," she said. "In the meantime, I want you to follow these instructions if you feel down, concerned or worried."

She placed a list of actions to follow on the corner of my desk. "They will help."

"Thank you," I said to Liz, giving her a big hug as she stood up to leave.

"That's - um - interesting," she said, pointing at the sketch on the wall.

"Er, yes," I said. "A symbol of the more reckless side of my personality."

"Go on…"

"Do you remember that art gallery we gate-crashed when we met up soon after the first Fat Club course finished?"

"Oh no, no. Is that the…"

"Yes, it's the Picasso sketch. I ended up having to buy it. Well, Mum and Dad stepped in to help me out. The auction house threatened to take me to court if I didn't come up with the money."

"Oh, angel," said Liz, enveloping me in a big hug. "Well, it looks good there, anyway."

"So it bloody should. It's worth more than everything else in this flat all put together."

I didn't know whether the process of talking helped me or whether it was laughing with her about the Picasso print, but I felt much better after she left. I could go and get help. Everything would be OK.

I walked to the fridge and poured myself a large glass of wine to celebrate. Everything was going to be OK.

BUGGER, BUGGER, BUGGER

Well, that didn't go brilliantly. It was hard, in many ways, to work out how it could have gone worse. You know that one glass of wine I had after Liz had left? It turned into two. Yes, I know what you're thinking – two glasses is OK – stop worrying.

Mmmm... I wish!

I had two bloody bottles.

Two bottles.

It was now 5 am, and I was wide awake and struggling with the worst hangover in the world. My head was pounding inside my skull, so much that I didn't want to lift it off the pillow because I was worried my brain might burst through and bounce across the room. I knew I had to get some water, or I'd get worse and worse and never get back to sleep again.

OK, here we go... I stepped out of bed and saw my phone on the bedside table.

Oh shit. That was when I remembered.

I texted Ted last night. Shit. Shit, shit, shit. Why did I think it was a good idea to text anyone at 1 am? Why didn't I go to sleep after Liz left? I felt great then – energised and happy. But for some reason, I started drinking, which made the emotions darker, and I drank more to cover them… I did everything that I knew I wasn't supposed to do.

I picked up my phone, and the text was there – sitting on the screen, looking up at me:

"What the fuck am in wine and drinking and that stupid woman Michella fuck her. Am in wine."

Oh, God. Really? I was sure I used to have some self-preservation that kicked in when I was drunk and stopped me from sending texts like that. When I was young, I'd go out to nightclubs and get blind drunk with my friends but still somehow return home in one piece without sending absurd texts to men.

I sat down at my desk and looked forlornly at the computer, open on Ted's Facebook page. Oh, God. I hadn't messaged him through Facebook as well, had I? I clicked onto Facebook Messenger…thankfully I hadn't attempted to contact him. I came back out onto his page. Then I saw it: "Ted is now friends with Michella Bootle." Great! He'd befriended her on Facebook.

And that was it. I was off again…my mind spinning and my stomach churning.

I bet he walked her home after the drink last night, went in for coffee, snuggled up on the sofa, and perhaps even had sex. I bet they did have sex. I bet it was better sex than he'd ever had with me. Then he climbed out of her bed, headed home, and immediately befriended her on Facebook.

I decided that I, too, would befriend Michella on Facebook. You know what they say – keep your friends close and your enemies closer. Michella was about the biggest enemy a woman could ever have. I would keep her close.

I sent her a friend request, which allowed me to add a message, so I tapped out a friendly note: "Hi Mich, it was lovely to meet you last night. I'm sorry I had to rush off, but I felt unwell. I hope you had a good time and look forward to seeing you next week."

Then I stared at the screen like a woman demented. I hit refresh several times. Why wasn't she responding? I decided it must be because she was with Ted. They were in bed together at that very moment. I carried on hitting refresh in a maniacal fashion. Then I saw the piece of paper that Liz left me with last night, and I followed her instructions…

1. Breathe deeply
2. Put two feet firmly on the floor.
3. Clear your mind
4. Think about the earth beneath you and the walls in front of you…ground yourself.
5. Repeat to yourself that this will pass…everything will be OK.

"Everything will be OK," I said. "Everything will be OK," I repeated until my eyes were closing and my bed was calling. I staggered through the apartment and flopped onto my bed, disgusted with Ted and disgusted with Michella, but calmer…much calmer.

By the time I woke up in the morning, there was a message from Michella: "Lovely to be friends on Facebook, Mary. Thanks so much for the invitation. I only stayed for one drink last night; my boyfriend picked me up.

Looking forward to seeing you next week… Ted was telling me how madly in love with you he is. X"

MAKING IT ALRIGHT AGAIN

"I'm sorry."

Little words that should be easy to say but were so hard in practice.

I looked into the mirror and repeated the words: "I'm sorry."

Christ, now all I had to do was say them to Ted. This was going to be much harder than I thought it would.

I picked up my phone and started pacing around the room. "Come on, Mary – you can do this," I said to myself in the manner of a boxer, revving himself up for the fight of his life. "You can do it, girl. You can do it."

Ah, but I couldn't. I put the phone down.

This man meant the world to me; why couldn't I just pick up the phone and talk to him? Why couldn't I stop this madness? I wanted to be with him. But I couldn't phone him – I was too scared. Too scared he might dump me as soon as he heard my voice.

WhatsApp. That was what I'd do – I'd send a message.

I knew that was wimpy, but it was better than doing nothing, and I wanted to get a message through to him sooner rather than later.

"I'm sorry," I typed into the phone and hit send before I could change my mind.

"What are you sorry for?" he replied straight away.

"I'm sorry for everything. I'm sorry I have been so horrible to you; sorry I rushed out last night and sent a horrible text. I'm sorry. Ted – I'm sorry you're not in my arms right now. I'm just sorry."

Tears were in my eyes as I hit the send button.

"Are you at home?" he texted back.

"Yes," I replied.

"I'm on my way if that's OK," he replied.

"Yes, of course it is!" I messaged back, and it felt like the greatest day ever.

I sat back and smiled to myself. Ted was coming over. Then I realised TED WAS COMING OVER. The flat looked a mess.

I threw myself into a tidying and cleaning routine with terrifying and reckless speed, running around with furniture polish and cloth and dragging the vacuum cleaner across the carpets and the wooden floors.

Next, it was time for me to sort myself out. I washed quickly, shaving every part of my body that he was likely to come into contact with and covering myself in the body lotion which I knew he loved. Then I dressed in casual clothes so it didn't look like I'd just charged around and prepared myself for him. I wanted to look simple but beautiful...natural and glamorous all at the same time. I put on lipstick (because I didn't want to look THAT natural) and brushed my hair. The doorbell went, and I looked in the mirror. Not too bad, even if I said so myself.

Ted certainly seemed to think I looked OK. He charged in and grabbed me, sweeping me into his arms, hugging and kissing me, and I burst into tears. It felt like the most beautiful thing ever to happen, better, even, than when we first got together.

"Liz explained how bad you were feeling and that you were confused and guilty. I understand," he said.

"But what about that text I sent?"

"I didn't get a text," he replied.

"Oh, perhaps I didn't actually send it," I said. "Phew – it didn't make any sense anyway, so that's OK."

Ted was looking right into my eyes. "I was going to write 'I love you' in rose petals on the ground outside your door," he said. "I was trying to think of the most romantic thing to do. I didn't know what to do… I'm not very good at this stuff."

"You're amazing at this stuff," I said, kissing his neck.

"Bed," he replied, practically dragging me to the bedroom and tearing at my clothes. His hands shook as he tenderly pulled my bra straps down and cupped my breasts. He was just about to pull my trousers down and begin doing what a man and a woman do when they're on their own and feeling randy when he stopped suddenly.

"I love you," he said. "I really love you."

"I love you too," I replied.

And after that, we fell into a deep silence, punctuated only by gentle moans from me and occasional growls from him. It was all marvellous, dear reader, bloody marvellous.

MEETING THE FAMILY

After our initial bed-centred reunion, I explained everything to Ted, and – to his credit – he didn't judge, criticise, or complain. He listened to what I had to say, nodded and told me he loved me and not to worry.

I told him all about what happened when Liz came around, and he said he was proud of me for reaching out for help, but he wished it had been him that I'd turned to. That was a good point... I didn't know why I hadn't. Perhaps Ted meant too much for me to make myself vulnerable and confess my emotions to him, or maybe it was just that Liz had always told us to call her if we were in distress, so that was the call I made. Either way, Ted and I reached a happy place.

In fact, we reached such a happy place that Ted sat me down to ask me the question. "Mary," he said, holding my hand gently. "I don't know how you feel about this, but my parents would love to meet you..."

"Would they?"

I couldn't work out whether to feel delight or fear.

"Yes, they would love to meet you. I

. . .

WHAT IF THEY HATED ME? They might think I wasn't good enough for their precious son, and the truth was – they'd probably be right.

Ted knocked on the door of their lovely semi-detached in Esher. It was a nice-looking house on a tree-lined street...very suburban but neat and tidy.

Ted let himself in through the front door and wandered into the sitting room, where I met Ted's mum and sister. They jumped up when we walked in and rushed over to embrace Ted and shake my hand. They were both unnervingly slender and well-dressed. His mum had a genuine warmth about her. His sister – not so much – she was a little sour and gave me the feeling, as she slowly looked me up and down, that she didn't like me at all.

"This is Mary," said Ted, and his mum grabbed me in a tight embrace. I was (not for the first time) embarrassed to be so large. The woman could barely get her arms around me. She felt so tiny and delicate. I experienced a longing to be the same way.

His sister smiled a half-smile. "Nice to meet you," she said. "Ted has told us ALL about you, ALL the time. He never stops talking about you, to be honest. It's quite nauseating."

"Oy!" said Ted, smacking his sister.

"You're both so tiny," I said. "I'm very envious of how you keep so thin."

"You need to eat less," said his sister bluntly. "Like Ted – he needs to eat a lot less too."

There was a horrible silence between us that no one knew how to fill.

I needed to keep things light, so I affectionately prodded Ted in the stomach. "Well, we certainly know who eats all the pies in this house, don't we?" I said.

I didn't think the comment per se was particularly offensive...it was designed to lift the mood and add some joviality, but what made the comment offensive and wholly inappropriate was that – exactly as I said it – Ted's dad walked into the room. I say walked; what I mean was waddled. Ted's dad was huge. Massive. He was probably the same size as Ted and me together.

"Someone talking about me?" asked his dad. "Someone saying that I eat all the pies?"

Shit. "No," I said. "Of course not. Definitely not. God, I'm sorry – I was talking about Ted."

"Thanks a lot," said Ted.

"No, I mean – you're a lot bigger than your mum and sister. I was only trying to be nice to your mum and sister. I'm sorry."

Ted's dad shoehorned himself into a large armchair which suddenly looked tiny beneath his massive girth.

His mum removed his shoes and pulled out the bottom part of the chair, forming a footrest. She lifted his legs and put them onto it. Ted's dad stared into space. I decided I didn't like him very much. Not just because I'd inadvertently insulted him, but because he seemed so different from Ted's mum. He seemed distracted and uncommunicative—the opposite of my smiley, happy, chatty Ted.

"I'm sorry if that seemed offensive," I said. "I didn't see you coming; I was talking about…."

"Didn't see him coming," said Sian, Ted's sister. "How could you not see him coming? Look at the size of him."

"Oh God – they all hate me. They all hate me so much," I said to Ted later that night when we were curled up in my bed, recalling the day with wine and slices of melon (I have a theory that fruit cancels out the calories in wine).

"No, they don't – that's how they are. Mum thought you were wonderful, and she's the only one who counts. Dad is just miserable, and my sister is madly jealous of any woman who comes anywhere near me, so you're never going to have a chance with her, but Mum – Mum is special, lovely, kind and wonderful and looks after the family. She's the only one who matters, and she thinks you're great."

"Thank you," I said and felt much better about everything.

SEAT BELT TRAUMAS

"Cheer up, sunshine; it might never happen."

Dave was standing in his garden looking dishevelled, filthy and bloody gorgeous. How is it that some men look better the less care they take of themselves? If Dave lived in a bin for a week, he'd look like a bloody film star. He'd get more manly and desirable as he got stubblier and dirtier. The man reeked of masculinity. It was very distracting.

"It has already happened," I said. "I've booked my first ever driving lesson for this morning, and I'm dreading it." "Why?" asked Dave.

"Because I need to learn to drive."

"No, not – why have you booked a lesson. I meant – why are you dreading it? Learning to drive is a great thing to do."

"Because I'll be rubbish and probably crash the car and kill us all."

"No you won't – driving's easy," said Dave. "Look around at all the idiots who can drive. If they can do it, so can you. I can even drive drunk, so it can't be that difficult." "Ha ha," I replied.

"No, I really can," said Dave. "I did last night. Well, I say I did – I don't remember doing it, but I must have because the car is here." "Really? You really drove home completely drunk?" "Yep." There was a strange pride in his voice.

"You could have killed yourself." I was eager not to encourage or celebrate his reckless behaviour.

"But I didn't," he said proudly. "There's not a scratch on me."

"You could have hurt someone."

"But I didn't. I don't think so anyway. Hard to know for sure, but I don't think so, or the police would have been round."

"It's not funny," I said. "Lots of people are killed by drunk drivers. It's not a laughing matter at all."

"OK, killjoy, calm down. How am I supposed to get home after a few pints if I don't drive?"

"Er – walk? Get a cab? Get a train? Get a bus? Lots of options."

"I was too drunk to walk," said Dave. "Too drunk for all of those things. That's why I drove. Anyway, I'm going to bed. Good luck with your lesson. And remember – if I can do it drunk, it can't be that hard."

"No, indeed," I responded, and Dave went staggering back into his house, weaving across his small patio and stumbling through his front door.

A couple of minutes after Dave's manly frame had disappeared from view, a small yellow car appeared on the horizon, with 'Sunny-side Driving' plastered across the sides and ridiculous primroses on the bonnet and eyelashes on the front lights. No one would be able to miss me in this thing…assuming I could get into it: my arse was bigger than the boot.

"Is it Mary?" asked the driving instructor, waving to me through the open window. He looked like he was going for his first day as a children's tv presenter. He wore a yellow tie to match the car and a V-neck jumper with a yellow jacket over the top. He stepped out of the car looking slightly nervous. I noticed that his trousers were a fraction too tight…like school trousers he'd grown out of, but his mum hadn't replaced.

"Yes, I'm Mary." I lifted myself off the small wall.

Standing up and sitting down are two things I find hardest to do since I have put on weight. I had to use my hands to lever myself off the wall, and as I leaned forward, my protruding stomach got in the way. The other thing I hate is doing my shoelaces. The agony of bending over to do anything, anything at all, when you're heavy cannot be overstated. I feel a wave of nausea and sickness wash through me whenever I bend over as if my stomach is pushing up against all my internal organs and stopping them from working properly. I know I'm making my life sound very dramatic and uncomfortable, and you're probably thinking, 'you're not that fat,' but the little things feel challenging when you're overweight. The things that other people take for granted.

I walked to the car, and the driving instructor shook my hand and told me to get into the passenger seat.

"We'll head out to a disused shopping centre car park and have a chat and get started," he said. "That way there'll be no pressure and no one to see you. OK?"

"OK," I said and felt massively relieved. The guy seemed calm and in control, and I liked the idea of going to learn in an old disused car park rather than on the road. Nothing could go wrong if I was miles from other people and cars. Could it?

I sat down heavily in the seat and the whole car felt like it had dropped beneath me – like a fat kid sitting on the see-saw.

"Seat belt on then," he said.

Ah.

I pulled the seat belt as slowly as possible, hoping it was long enough to go around me, but it jolted to a stop a considerable way short. Damn. I pulled again, ever so slowly, in case it stopped because it got caught up or triggered the stop mechanism, but – no – it had stopped because that was the end. The seat belt didn't get any longer. I was too fat for the seat belt. It was mortifying.

"All done up?" asked the driving instructor, unaware of the crushing few seconds I'd just endured.

"Yes," I replied, tucking the seat belt beside my thigh and pretending it was done up.

"OK, I want you to watch me as I drive, then we'll talk about it when we get to the car park. See how the first thing I do is to put the key into the ignition and turn it." He did this, and the car immediately started beeping like we were out of petrol or something.

"Ah, that beeping is to say that the seat belts aren't done up. Can you check yours is properly clicked in," he said.

Oh hell. This is horrible.

"Yep, all clicked in," I replied. But I could see that this strategy wasn't going to get me very far. He was going to start investigating.

"Are you sure?" he asked.

"Yes, all fine. Just drive."

"I can't drive while the emergency warning light's on. It means one of the seat belts isn't done up properly, which could be extremely dangerous."

Oh for God's sake, man.

"We're not travelling far though, are we? Let's go," I said.

But Mr Health & Safety was out of the car and over to my side of the vehicle to examine the seat belt situation.

"Oh it's not done up at all!" he said. "Look, can you see? It's not plugged in, that's what the problem is." Silly me.

Then he started pulling it and fiddling with the seat belt container, trying to figure out why the seat belt wouldn't go in and end the interminable bleeping still belting away inside the little car.

"It seems shorter this side than the other; I can't get enough of it to come out," he said, baffled. Bless him. Could he not see that I was fucking huge and that it simply wasn't big enough to go around me? We could blame the seat belt all we wanted, but the truth was that I was so large that a conventional seat belt wouldn't go around me. It wasn't the first time this had happened, and I was sure it wouldn't be the last, but it was still mortifying.

I could see my poor, dear driving instructor suddenly working out what had happened. I could see it in his body language as he pulled himself up short, and stood with his hands on his hips, looking down. I also sensed that this was probably the worst thing that had ever happened to him. It was like he felt personally responsible for the seat belt not working, even though it was entirely my fault.

He had no idea what to do. On the one hand, there was his absolute horror of having to tell me that I was too fat for his seat belt; on the other hand, there was his absolute horror of breaking any of the rules of the road – so he didn't want to drive off with me unable to wear a seat belt. If he'd had any more hands, I imagined that on the third one, there would be the issue of him not wanting to lose my business. The invisible third hand won, he got back into his side of the car, and off we went, searching for an empty car park so that the fat girl could drive around without killing anyone.

When we reached the car park, there were children playing football on the far side of it.

"Be careful," the instructor screamed out of the window. "Learner driver here…"

"I'll be fine," I told him, but the instructor didn't look as if he thought it was going to be at all fine. He gripped the sides of the door as he encouraged me to look in my mirror before moving off, and then he told me to keep looking in the mirror. "It's the most important thing," he said, though I didn't think that looking behind me could be that important, could it? I felt I was using the mirror so much that I was looking backwards more than I was looking forwards. And all the while, the beeping noise was driving me nuts as I tried to concentrate on moving in a straight line while looking in the mirror. It seemed unlikely I was going to be a natural at driving.

DODGY DRIVING AND AN ANGRY POLICEMAN

"I could easily teach you to drive," said Dave. "Easily."

I was sitting on the top step with my head in my hands, shaking my head forlornly.

"Don't worry about the driving instructor," he added. "Really, it's easy."

"But everything went wrong, Dave. I mean EVERYTHING. I couldn't get the fucking seat belt on, then my feet wouldn't touch the pedals unless I had the seat all the way forward and then it was so far forward that my stomach was in the way when I tried to reach down to put the key in the ignition. It was all an embarrassing disaster. I'm not cut out for driving. I don't know what I am cut out for, all I know is that it's not driving."

"Yes you are, everyone can drive. You can drive, I can teach you to drive – driving is easy. You know what, mate, I'm not great at much: I can get girls to drop their knickers at my door and I can drive. There's no question that I can teach you to drive, so get in the seat and let's get going."

Dave insisted that I needed to be in the driving seat and that we weren't going to a deserted car park. "We'll just get going, everything will be fine," he insisted. He was an absolute darling to make an effort to teach me, but to be honest, I didn't hold out a great deal of hope. Ignore that, I didn't hold out any hope at all.

The good news was, that Dave had no complicated beeping situation going on and no lights that flashed when I failed to connect the seat belt.

"OK, what do I do first?" I asked.

"We need to get going, sweetheart," he said. "Put the key in the ignition and let's get this baby moving."

His was an altogether less sophisticated approach to the one I'd endured with the driving instructor.

"Turn the key then." I did as I was told and edged the car forward on Dave's command, juddering and faltering as it hopped along like a bunny rabbit.

"OK," said Dave. "So we're moving, but now can we drive it so it's like a car and not a fucking woodland creature."

"OK, how do I do that?"

"Didn't the driving instructor tell you?"

"No, we didn't get that far."

"How far did you get then?" he asked. "I mean – if driving for a bit in a straight line wasn't touched upon, what exactly were you doing?"

"We were doing things like mirror, signal, manoeuvre," I said.

"Oh yes, yes, yes you need to do that. I forgot about all that stuff. Yes, do that as well…before you start driving around."

"OK." I was starting to wonder now whether Dave was absolutely the right person to be teaching me to drive.

Still, we set off, with me trying to remember everything the driving instructor said about mirror, signal, manoeuvre, and how to proceed cautiously. I kept looking in the mirror to make sure cyclists weren't passing and made sure I knew what cars were behind me.

Dave seemed strangely unaware of these simple rules of the road.

One thing I was struggling with was driving a different car from the one the previous day. I didn't know how you were supposed to remember how much force to use in different vehicles. The driving instructor's car was somehow slower, everything took a little longer. It meant that when I turned the wheel in Dave's car with the force I

BERNICE BLOOM

used in the instructor's, the car went up and onto the pavement until I brought it to a juddering halt within inches of a lamppost.

"Well." Dave grabbed the steering wheel and redirected it back onto the road. "That wasn't great. And just as I was starting to think you were getting the hang of it. And slow down, for goodness' sake, why are you going so fast? It's like being in a car with Lewis Hamilton."

"OK, I'll try," I said, once firmly back on solid ground and driving at a sensible speed.

"You're still going too fast; you must slow down," Dave said. "Slow right down… You need to slow down, Mary."

"I am going slowly."

"No, you're not," said Dave. We approached a zebra crossing as someone walked out, so I slammed on the brakes, sending both of us flying forward so we had to put our hands out to stop ourselves careering through the windscreen. I had no seat belt on because I was terrifyingly fat, and Dave had no seat belt on out of some inexplicable sympathy with me (he'd said, "I won't wear one either then." A decision he was coming to bitterly regret).

"What was that for?" said Dave with considerable aggression. "I told you to slow down earlier. You can't just drive full pelt and put your brakes on at the last minute, it's not fair on the drivers behind you and it's not fair to those walking across the zebra crossing. Also, it's not fair to me. I'm a bloody nervous wreck here, doll face. Now slow down."

"OK, OK."

"Go on then, the traffic is waiting behind."

I wasn't very good at starting yet, so I put my foot flat down on the pedal and the car leapt forward.

"Bring the car to the side of the road," Dave said, in measured tones. He sounded quite scared now.

"Sorry?"

"I want you to park the car at the side of the road."

Parking was something we hadn't done yet, so I brought the car to an emergency stop.

"Not in the middle of the road," said Dave, pointing towards the curb while holding his head in the other hand.

"I don't know about bringing the car to the curb," I replied. "If you remember, you're supposed to be teaching me how to do all this stuff."

"OK, turn the steering wheel towards the curb, put your foot down on the accelerator gently, and it will go towards the curb… It's not that hard."

"OK, I'll give it a go."

Anyway, that was how we ended up with the car half on the pavement and half on the road and Dave instructing me to reverse off the pavement back into the road.

"I've never done reversing before," I said. "Where is the reverse button?"

"Oh God," he said as he began to talk me through the process of reversing, telling me to put my foot down on the clutch as he moved the gear stick to reverse. I then put my foot down on the accelerator in a manner that I believed to be gentle but was more aggressive than it should have been. The car flew back. I braked suddenly, and Dave and I went shooting forward. I bashed my head on the steering wheel, which emitted a loud beep.

"Don't beep the horn," he said. "You're bringing enough attention to us as it is."

"I didn't beep the horn," I said. "My head hit the horn when I went flying in my seat."

"OK then, well, you better move us forward a bit, you're sticking out into the road, and the cars can't get past."

I suppose it was inevitable, but the next car was a police car. "For the love of Christ," said Dave, as the panda car pulled alongside me and the officer wound down his window. "Everything OK?" The police officer raised his eyebrows dramatically as he spoke, indicating that, to his mind, things were far from OK.

"I'm sorry, officer, I'm learning to drive," I said. "It's harder than it looks, isn't it?"

"Indeed it is," said the officer. "For starters, you should have L-plates on the car."

"I forgot to put them on," said Dave. "I will put them on next time we come out."

The officer didn't look convinced, but he could see we were in a perilous situation, and he needed to leave us so I could remove the car from its position, sitting diagonally across the road. So he just nodded and said, "Make sure you do."

And at this stage – I promise you – everything was OK. All we had to do was get out of the ridiculous position I'd got us into and continue on our journey. But Dave, being Dave, couldn't let it lie like that...

"Dickhead," he said, thinking the policeman was out of earshot. But the policeman wasn't out of earshot. He reversed the car back alongside my car and looked over at Dave. "Sorry, did you say something?" he asked.

And this was when I made the biggest cock-up ever. I figured it would be good to diffuse the situation with a light-hearted joke—big mistake.

"Honestly, officer, he had three pints at lunchtime – you can't talk to him when he's like this." I looked over at Dave and nudged him playfully.

"She's joking," he said plaintively.

"Of course, I'm joking." I looked back at the policeman who was getting out of his car and coming round to open the door.

"Get out," he instructed, all of the gentleness from his voice.

"OK, officer." I stepped out of the car.

"Why aren't you wearing your seat belt?"

"I was," I lied. "I took it off when you came up alongside us."

"OK, you get out of the car too," he said to Dave. "And blow into this...."

The police officer handed Dave a breathalyser.

"I'm not blowing into that," said Dave. "Not without my lawyer present."

"Dave, just blow into it," I said. Then I turned to the officer: "Really, I was joking, this is getting way out of hand... It was a little joke."

"It wasn't funny. Drink-driving is serious."

"You'll have to take me to the station; I'm not blowing into that bag," said Dave. The policeman was getting very agitated, and everyone was getting angry and cross with one another.

"Mary, can you call my lawyer on this number…"

He handed me a piece of paper with 'I can't blow into that thing, I've been drinking all morning' written on it. What the hell were we supposed to do now?

"I was joking," I said to the officer. "This is going to look ridiculous when it all goes to court, and I say I was making a little joke, and you took it way too seriously. The police have a bad enough reputation for being hard-headed at the best of times. I'm sorry I made a joke…it was in poor taste. I promise I'll never make a joke like that again."

"OK, OK," said the police officer. He turned to Dave: "Make sure you get those L-plates."

"I will," said Dave, and the officer drove off.

"Bloody hell!" I walked towards Dave. "You were drinking this morning?"

"Yes." He wrapped his arms around me as we clung to one another in relief.

"But you can't drink, drive."

"I didn't drink drive. You were driving."

"Oh, bloody hell," I said. "You're such an idiot."

Behind us, there was traffic chaos. Cars were beeping, drivers had got out, and were standing on the road shouting at us to "move the f**king car."

"I better move it." I extracted myself from Dave's arms…he'd been holding on to me longer than I'd expected him to.

We got into the car. I reversed out and nearly hit three people, Dave held his head in his hands, and people all around us shouted angrily.

Later that night, Ted phoned. He'd been due to come round for the evening but said he wasn't feeling well.

"Oh no, sorry about that," I said.

"What did you do today?" he asked.

"Nothing much." I couldn't possibly tell him about the driving lesson. He'd have a fit if he thought I'd done a driving lesson with a drunk bloke.

"See anyone?" he asked.

I decided not to mention Downstairs Dave.

"No," I said. "I just hung around at home and did some chores. How about you?"

"I have to go," he said, disappearing from the line.

Poor thing, he sounded unwell.

HUGGING DAVE

I woke in the morning to a text from Ted.
"Are you awake?" it said.
"Yes," I replied.
A minute later, my phone rang.
"This is awkward," he said. "It's awkward, and it's fucking awful."
"What's happened?"
"I know you and Dave are having an affair," he said. "Don't deny it because I know for sure."

I sat up in bed. "What the hell are you talking about? Of course, I'm not having an affair with him or anyone else – I'm in love with you."
"My sister saw you," he said.
"She didn't."
"She did."
"No, she didn't because I'm not having an affair with him. It must have been someone else. To be honest, Ted, I've seen a lot of women go in and out of his flat – it could be any one of them."

"Don't lie, Mary," he said, and I could hear how deadly serious he was.

"Ted, I promise you, I'm not having an affair with Dave. I don't know how to make it any clearer."

"Then explain this," he said, and my phone bleeped to tell me there was a text. I went into my texts and retrieve one from Ted. It consisted of a picture...of Dave and me with our arms wrapped around each other, caught up in a huge hug. Oh, God. It looked really dodgy.

"Have you got it?" asked Ted.

"Yes."

"You told me you'd spent all your time in the house doing chores, so you're lying to me. I can only assume you lied because you're seeing Dave. Thanks very much."

"No, no, it's not like that," I tried.

"So, you didn't lie to me?"

"Well, yes, I did, but not because I'm having an affair. I lied because Dave gave me a driving lesson, and I discovered afterwards – after the police stopped us, but that's another story – that he'd been drinking all morning. Dave's an idiot, and I shouldn't have got him to teach me to drive, but he offered, and I want to learn."

"Why didn't you ask me?" said Ted. "Why do you always turn to other people for help?"

"Because I don't want to look an idiot in front of you."

"And it doesn't look like much driving's going on in the picture... you've been kissing him."

"No. I hugged him in relief because the police didn't arrest him."

"This is all ridiculous," said Ted. "I'm going now."

"No, don't go," I said. "Ted, I love you. This is all a silly mix-up."

But it was too late. Ted had gone, and I was left holding my phone, on which there was a picture of Dave and me in an embrace. Oh, God.

There was only one woman to call at a time like this.

I dialled Charlie's number. Luckily, she was in and answered straight away.

"Send me the picture," she told me when I'd explained my predicament.

"Mmmm...that's not great," she said. "What are you going to do?"

"I've no idea," I said. "That's why I'm calling you."

"Probably time for an old-fashioned committee meeting, don't you think?"

"Blimey, we haven't done one of those for ages."

We always used to call a committee meeting if one of us was struggling with something (usually involving a man). All the girls would descend on the stricken woman's house and jointly work out the best course of action.

"Your place tonight at 6 pm; I'll let the girls know. See you later." See – I told you Charlie would be the right person to talk to.

There was wine, low-calorie, fat-free nibbles, and fresh flowers filled the room with a soft, rose scent. I was all prepared but feeling dreadful. I didn't want to lose Ted. Charlie nodded her approval as she surveyed the scene and helped herself to a cheese puff.

"Don't worry, angel, we'll sort this out," she said.

"I hope so. I'm such an idiot."

I put some music on and read through the agenda I prepared in advance of this critical tactical and strategic meeting.

It was headed 'operation MATT' (Mary and Ted together), followed by the list of people who'd be there later: me, Charlie, Janice and Veronica from Fat Club, and Sandra, the beautician whose arms I cried in when I bumped into her on the High Street that afternoon. Honestly, I think she was relieved that she hadn't received a legal letter after turning my skin the colour of boiled beetroot. Anything else was a bonus.

1. Convince Ted that Mary still likes him

2. Convince Ted that Mary is trustworthy and that nothing happened with Downstairs Dave

3. Approach Ted's sister?

4. Infiltrate Ted's friend group to convince them that Ted and Mary should be together

5. Get Ted and Mary together whenever possible.

6. Drop lots of hints to Ted about how great the two of them are together

Obviously, in the end, there would be time for Any Other Business, and someone would take notes and ensure that all the things discussed were implemented. There would be follow-up meetings, more strategising, and regular catchups. It wasn't exactly the United Nations, but it wasn't far off.

The girls began to arrive, streaming into my house, taking a glass of wine and chatting amiably while we all collected in the front room. Madonna sang out from the stereo as hands disappeared into bowls of low-fat crisps, and glasses were replenished.

"Right, if everyone could take a seat, we will begin," said Charlie, taking the lead and addressing the assembled guests. "We have a terrible situation on our hands. Our lovely Mary has managed to behave like a giant buffoon, and spend time in the company of Downstairs Dave, hereafter to be referred to as Double D. Their liaison has come to Ted's knowledge. He has told Mary that he is unhappy. A small argument ensued, and now Mary and Ted have split up. Today's meeting aims to work out how to get them back together again."

"What have you done so far?" asked Sandra as she finished her wine and laid her glass on the table.

I reached out to refill her glass. "I haven't done anything," I confessed. "I don't know what to do." "Tell us what happened," she said.

"Well, Dave offered to teach me to drive; I thought it would be an excellent idea because I'd had a terrible driving lesson the day before. Dave said he was a good teacher. It turns out he is a crap teacher and a really crap driver; the whole thing was a disaster. He nearly went into shock when I mounted the curb, and he was rude to a police officer; then, I told the police officer that he was drunk. He refused to blow into the breathalyser because it turned out he was drunk, then we were so relieved when the policeman went away that we hugged. I didn't realise that Ted's sister had seen me and taken a picture which she showed to Ted."

"Oh," said Sandra. "What a pickle. And where were baby Kate and baby William when all this was going on?"

"Oh, don't worry about them. They were fine. With the Nanny," I said. I'd completely forgotten about that ridiculous story I told.

"A man not trusting the mother of his newborn twins. Terrible" continued Sandra.

"Nope, all good. Not to worry. Let's move on." "What twins?" asked Charlie.

"No twins. Just the need to get Ted back on side."

"For what it's worth, I think his sister is a bitch," said Veronica. "I mean – really? That's such a tosser-ish thing to do."

"It is," said Charlie. "His sister knows nothing about what's happening and decides to intervene. She doesn't like Mary."

"But I can't slag off the sister to Ted, the two of them are very close, and he is sure that his sister was acting in his best interests," I explained.

"OK," said Janice. "The first question, then, what have you said to Ted so far?"

"I told him the truth," I replied, smiling inwardly with pride. I'm the sort of person who always manages to make a mountain out of a molehill…the kind of person who opens her mouth and makes everything 50 times worse. But I didn't seem to have done that on this occasion. I'd just told the truth.

"And what did Ted say?"

"He was sceptical. He didn't understand why I'd lied originally about it…which I hadn't…I didn't tell him the whole truth, which, as everyone knows, is different from lying."

"OK, OK," said Charlie. "Enough of what has happened. What are we going to do to put it all right again? Has everyone got an agenda? Let's bring this meeting to order."

There was a shuffling sound as everyone picked up their papers.

"OK, the first item on the agenda – convince Ted that Mary still likes him. How are we going to do that?"

"I'm friends with him on Facebook," said Janice. "I could send him a note on there. I could say that I'm checking he's OK and that I'm sorry that he and Mary have split up because I know how much she loves him."

"Good. Excellent. Anyone else?"

"I'll talk to him at Fat Club," said Veronica. "I'll pull him aside and make sure he knows how much she likes him."

"Good." Charlie struck off item one on her agenda. "Now, what's next?"

"Convince Ted that nothing happened with Downstairs Dave," said Janice. "Well, I can do that when I chat to him on Facebook. We don't want too many people approaching him; he might suspect it's all planned."

"He'll never suspect that we have a bloody working party set up, though, will he? Men would never think of doing something like this," said Sandra with a snort. Oh God, she was very drunk. "You know what we should do – get Downstairs Dave to join us. Maybe he'll be able to give us a man's perspective on the whole thing. Or perhaps he'll offer to talk to Ted."

"No, I don't want him talking to Ted," I said.

"Might not be a bad idea to have a male point of view, though," offered Charlie. "I mean – if we just invite him for a glass of wine and pick his brains for 15 minutes, that would be OK, wouldn't it?"

"I guess so." I wasn't wholly convinced that we needed a male point of view, and I didn't feel great about DD – the cause of all the anguish – being in my flat, but it was decided that he really should contribute to the meeting, so Charlie rushed off to find him, and I pondered the situation.

"What if Ted finds that he was here?" I said. "I mean – this could make everything worse."

"If he finds out that DD is here, just tell him you invited him so you could get a male point of view at the planning evening."

"Yes, but then I'll have to tell him about the planning evening. He'll think I've lost my mind if he knows what's happening tonight."

"Good point," Janice conceded. "He can't know about any of this, or he'll have you carted off to a mental home."

On that note, Downstairs, Dave walked into the room, and there was an audible sigh as all the women swooned in his wake. He did look lovely…really sexy and dishevelled as always. I finished my glass of wine and steadied myself by gripping hold of the mantelpiece as he leaned over and planted a kiss on my cheek. Well, I say 'cheek', but I turned round suddenly, and he caught me on the lips by mistake (yes – mistake!), and there was another audible sigh from the girls in the room as they all contemplated the idea of being kissed by Dave…he really was a spectacularly good-looking man.

"You need to help us," said Charlie, as Dave took handfuls of peanuts and rocketed them into his mouth by slapping his hand against his lips. "We need to get Mary and Ted back together." "The fat guy?" said Dave, looking at me.

"Yes."

"Cool. He seems nice. Why don't you tell him you want to go out with him?"

"Well, we were going out together, then he saw me with you when you gave me a driving lesson, and he thought something was going on with us, so the relationship ended."

"He thought something was going on with us? With you and me? Really? That's so funny."

"Yes, his sister saw us. Do you remember when the policeman left, and we had a hug? She got the wrong idea, told him, and he thinks we're having an affair."

"Just tell him we're not," he said. "Keep saying it…every time you see him. Don't play silly games and get your friends to drop hints – tell him the truth. Be honest and straightforward. You haven't done anything wrong."

We all looked shell-shocked. Dave leaned over and picked up my phone, playing with it as he talked.

"But we've got a complicated plan."

"You don't need a complicated plan – just tell him the truth." Just tell him. Really? It couldn't be that simple.

ROSE PETALS ON THE BREEZE

So...once again, I was sitting at home wondering how to apologise to Ted. It was becoming quite a regular thing in my life. This time I felt like I had to phone him rather than text. Texting after the trouble I'd caused would be wrong, so I picked up my mobile. I'd been thinking about this all night...since the meeting when Dave was adamant that I should talk and not play games.

"Hello," he said, all jolly. "Cheered up now?"

"No," I said miserably. "Why would I have cheered up?" "Have you been outside today?" he asked.

"No, I haven't. Look, Ted. I really love you. I don't want us to split up."

"Where are you?" he asked. "I mean – have you left the house yet?"

"No," I replied. "I'm still in my pyjamas... I can't face work."

"Open the front door."

"Why?"

"Just do it," he said.

I walked up to the door and swung it open, and there, in front of my house, was 'I love you' written out in rose petals., all held down with tiny white stones.

"Oh God," I said. "That's so lovely. Oh, Ted, that must have taken you ages. Why did you do that? I thought you hated me. You thought I was having an affair with Dave."

"I don't hate you. Of course, I don't hate you. I didn't understand what was going on. It's like you push me away, and I think you want space, then as soon as I give it to you, you think I want to leave, and then you're hugging men in the street. I didn't know what was going on.

"Then Dave called me yesterday night. He told me he'd taken my number out of your phone when he was at the meeting. He told me what had happened. He also told me how upset you were and about gathering all your friends together. It turns out he's a pretty decent guy. I'm sorry I didn't believe you. It's just – you know – I was hurt and scared. I don't want to lose you. You don't make it easy, Mary Brown."

"I don't want to lose you." I bent down to gather up some of the rose petals.

"I love you," he said. "I'll always love you."

And every care in the world drifted away on the breeze, followed by dozens of pale pink rose petals.

"Come round," I said.

"I'm on my way," he replied.

THE TRUTH AT LAST

Ted was able to move at a speed which belied his size. It was minutes before he ran up my pathway and swept me into his arms. I was dying to relax and have a gorgeous day with him. But I knew there were things I needed to tell him, things that he needed to know to understand why I behave the way I do.

Ted tried to lead me straight into the bedroom when he walked into the flat. I had to stop him and pull him into the sitting room.

"I want to talk to you," I explained.

"We can talk in the bedroom."

"Not this time."

I sat him down on the sofa and perched next to him…not draped all over him as I usually was, but with my legs tucked up to my chest and my arms wrapped around them—kind of a foetal position, to be honest.

"I want to tell you about what happened to me," I said. "I think it will help, and I want to share it with you."

"OK," he said, reaching over to touch my shoulder in a supportive way. I was immediately thrown back to when I first met Ted at Fat Club, and he reached out to touch me and offer comfort when I was talking about my issues in front of the group. On that occasion, I went bright red. This time I took his hand before he could pull it away and held it tightly.

"I was a gymnast when I was younger, as you know. It's a tough sport at the best of times: it's not like other sports in which you train in the week and play at the weekend. Gymnastics is all about training. You train for months for one competition. There are only one or two big competitions a year, and the Olympics and Commonwealth Games every four years. The rest of the time, you're training... and hoping you don't get injured. Avoiding injury is a crucial part of being good at an Olympic sport. The history of the Games is littered with the broken dreams of gymnasts...stars who got injured at the wrong time and never got to compete. Just think about it - the competitive life of a gymnast is short, and the Games are every four years. It's hard to be at exactly the right age and at the peak of your performance to win that elusive gold medal. Gymnasts who do it more than once are superheroes.

"Anyway, sorry, I'm getting a bit distracted. The issue is that staying injury-free is vital, so we have regular check-ups with the medical staff, and everything is monitored to check that we're in the best shape.

"I went to see the doctor one day when I was around 15, and our regular doc wasn't there. A male doctor was sitting there. I smiled at him, explained that my Achilles heel hurt, and he told me to take off my t-shirt."

"Your t-shirt? To fix your ankle?"

"Oh, he made up some rubbish about needing to check my alignment. That also involved him touching me everywhere...."

I started crying at that point as Ted wrapped his arms around me.

"It was awful and terrifying, and I didn't know what to do. I could have screamed, but it felt like fear had stolen my voice. Anyway, who would have believed a young girl over a middle-aged doctor? So I lay there and let him touch me. Then he undressed, and I panicked. I tried to get away, but he was so much stronger.

"I remember it all so clearly. The gymnasts in the main hall were warming up, and we had this routine we did to the Star Wars music, and I could hear the music playing as he held me down and raped me. And I never told anyone. Not anyone."

"Oh Christ, Mary. We need to go and find this guy. Let me spend half an hour with him."

"No, he died years ago. But what he did is always there. It's there in lots of different ways. Even when I hear that damn music, I feel threatened. It's awful. And I never brought him to justice. I feel so bad about that. He might have gone on to do the same thing to hundreds of gymnasts because I didn't speak out."

"That's not a helpful way to think, angel. You did your best to cope in a tough situation."

"I gave up gymnastics soon afterwards and never kept in contact with any of my old gym friends. Mum and dad never understood why I gave up. No-one did. I coped with it all by eating and not coping, if you know what I mean - just surviving by pushing down the pain and guilt with food and never quite trusting people. And I know I do completely mad things from time to time, and I'm sure it's because part of me doesn't care all that much. You know - why should anyone care about anything when someone in a position of such responsibility can take everything away from you in a moment? You can't trust anyone if you can't trust a doctor."

"I understand. Thank you for telling me all this."

I sit quietly and look out of the sitting room window; a gust of wind lifts the rose petals into the air. I watch them as they drift away into the Autumn skies. The rose petals that Ted put there for me. My lovely Ted. I'm glad I told him. I have a feeling that the future with him is going to be pretty awesome.

"We can go to the bedroom now if you want," I say. "Just to lie down and cuddle and chat."

He looks at me with eyes full of love.

I'm so lucky to have found him, and I know we will have a wonderful time together. Hopefully a beautiful life together.

"Come on, beautiful. Let's go and cuddle," he says.

ADVENTURES OF MARY BROWN

AN OLD SCHOOL FRIEND AND A BIZARRE INVITATION

I should have known that it was the most ridiculous idea in the world. It had 'bonkers' written all over it from the start. Going off on a safari with a woman I didn't know. What was I thinking? It was weapons-grade madness. But somehow, it didn't seem like that at the time. Certainly, I had no idea as I sat there on that chilly September evening that things would get so out of hand.

I had no inkling that I'd be on a continent far away by the end of the month, stuck up a tree in my knickers with a couple of baboons screaming up at me while gun-toting rangers rushed to the scene. Nor did I realise that the video of my embarrassing episode would end up trending on Twitter. But - let's not get ahead of ourselves - we'll get onto all that. First, let me take you right back to the beginning...

It began on a cool autumn evening with a phone call completely out of the blue.

"It's Dawn Walters here," said a voice. "Remember me - we bumped into each other in the garden centre last week. I know you from school."

"Of course," I said. I remembered her very clearly from Rydens High School - this huge, jovial, loud, larger-than-life girl who everyone liked but no one wanted on their netball team.

"How are you?" I asked. I had no idea why she was phoning. She'd been very friendly when we'd bumped into one another in the centre. I work there as a supervisor, and she'd come in looking through the outdoor plants for something to give to her mum on her birthday. I suspected her great friendliness towards me was motivated by her delight at seeing how much weight I'd put on since we last saw one another. I was always so slim and fit at school; she probably assumed I'd gone from a skinny-legged child to an elegant, size eight woman...then we locked eyes over the potted plants 12 years later, and she saw that the girl who once weighed eight stone was now around 14 and a half. She must have been overjoyed. I know I would have been in similar circumstances.

"You've changed," she said, almost delirious with happi- ness. "I mean - you've really changed."

"You're just the same," I retorted. She was about 18 stone at school and was now about 25 stone, so I was being generous.

We exchanged numbers and muttered something about keeping in touch, must go for coffee, lovely to see you, and that was that; I hadn't really expected her to call. To be honest, I'd thrown away the scrap of paper with her number on it. I thought we were being polite when we promised to keep in touch. But Dawn had followed through. Not only that, but she had a peculiar proposition for me.

"Look - this might sound odd, but do you want to come to Sanbona with me? It's a safari in South Africa?" she said.

I sat there in silence, realising I must have misheard her, but not quite sure what she actually said.

"Are you still there, Mary?"

"Yes," I replied. "I didn't quite catch what you said though."

"I know it's mad, but I just wondered whether you fancied a free trip to South Africa...with me...to, you know, see animals and stuff."

"Um. Gosh, yes," I replied, still not sure that I could have heard her correctly. I mean...who would do that? Who would invite someone on holiday when they hardly knew them? "When is the holiday?" I asked. "What will we do? How will we get there? Um - why are you inviting me?"

BERNICE BLOOM

"I get free trips. I told you - I'm a blogger these days. I write a travel blog called 'Fat & Fearless' and I get invited to experience holidays and write about them."

"Yes, I remember," I said. "It all sounds amazing, but why would you want me to come? We don't know each other, except from Mrs Thunder's French class, and that was over a decade ago."

"I get invited to loads of places, and I try to invite different people to come with me every time. I just thought you might fancy it?"

"Yes. That would be amazing. Of course, I fancy it; I'd love to come. If you're sure?" I said.

"I'm positive."

"Great then," I said. "Great. I'll definitely come. Tell me a bit more about it."

"Well, it's a safari so it's full of animals."

"What sort of animals?"

"Hang on, let me just look it up," said Dawn, and I could hear her tapping away on the keys while I waited, wondering what my boyfriend Ted would say when I told him. To be honest, we hadn't been getting on very well recently, so he'd probably welcome the break. We didn't live together but we spent a lot of time at one another's flats. Both of us would benefit from spending time apart rather than continuing to see one another every night when we both knew that things weren't right.

"There are lions, giraffes, cheetahs, oooo, look - elephants," she said.

"Elephants? How cool! Can we ride them?" I asked. I don't know why I said that...I guess I didn't know how to conduct a conversation about elephants.

"No, Mary, we can't ride them. Have you seen me? I'm 25 stones. My car struggles to move with me in it, I wouldn't subject an animal to that sort of brutality."

"Fair point," I said, thinking of the terrible groan that my suspension offered up every time I got into the driver's seat. Dawn was about 10 and a half stone heavier than me, so I imagined her suspension must really have screamed every time she got in. Ten and a half stone!

That was a whole person. Dawn was taller, wider and heavier than me. I felt petite next to her. I'd not felt petite next to anyone for about 15 years. I used to be a bit scared of her when we were at school...forever fearful that she might fall on me and crush me. Now I just thought it was nice that there was someone out there who was bigger than me.

"Look at their website," said Dawn. "The wildlife park is in the Karoo outside Cape Town, it's called Sanbona. That's S-a-n-b-o-n-a Wildlife Reserve. Take a look; it's bloody lovely."

I called up the pages as I chatted to Dawn.

"Bloody hell!" I said. It looked like an incredible place.

"There are lions, cheetahs, hippos and rhinos," it declared, showing them moving across the screen under the warm African sun. Birds swooped through the cloudless skies as panpipes played. If the reality of the place was anything like as captivating as the marketing films on the website, it would be sensational. "We also have leopards, giraffes, zebras and elephants," I read. It looked bloody great.

"This place looks amazing," I said, clicking onto the section called 'our people'.

"Really, Dawn, it's amaz..." I stopped short as a picture flickered across the screen. Not a wonderful animal, but an achingly beautiful man... dressed in khaki and clutching a rifle. It was one of the rangers who'd be looking after us on our trip. He smiled slowly at the camera, a vision of masculine beauty in a branded baseball cap.

"Dawn, get onto the 'our people' section now," I cried, my voice several pitches higher than usual. "I'm not joking. Go on there now. Take a look at the bloody wildlife they've got there. This one's called Pieter. He's based at Gondwana Lodge. Please tell me that's the lodge that we're going to. He's perfect."

"Oh Good God, Alive," said Dawn, reaching the short video on the website. "Oh hell, he's lovely. Wow. You know what, Mary Brown - we are going to have the best week of our lives."

ON THE WAY TO SOUTH AFRICA

*E*xcitement about my impending trip carried me through the next few weeks. I booked the time off work and gleefully told everyone where I was going. Those I get on well with were chuffed to hear of my good luck, and those I don't care much for wrinkled their noses in distaste and pretended that they wouldn't give their right arm to be going on such a trip.

Ted was decidedly unimpressed by it all. Certainly, he didn't seem in the least bit bothered about me going to the other side of the world without him.

"I'm so stressed at work, babe," he'd said. "You know - there's loads going on, and I need to get my head down and really get a handle on it all if I'm going to make salesman of the year again. The financial year ends in a month...I'm up to my neck. You go, have loads of fun, and I'll see you when you're back. OK?"

"Yes," I said, both relieved that he seemed so fine about me going away without him and really unnerved that he seemed so fine about me going away without him. Couldn't he just have pretended to have been bothered? Couldn't he have pulled a pretend sad face and said how much he'd miss me?

Mum was mainly just confused by the whole thing, and I admit

THE MARY BROWN BOOKS

that I completely understood her confusion. I was still none-the-wiser about why Dawn had asked me rather than anyone else in the whole world. Don't get me wrong - it was incredibly lovely to be asked on the trip of a lifetime by a virtual stranger, but it was also really fucking odd.

"Dawn?" queried mum. "I don't think I've met her, have I?"

"I was at school with her. Her mum was a dinner lady, and her dad had an affair with her aunty."

"Oh yes," said mum. It's coming back. Fat Dawn?"

"Yes," I replied, wishing mum hadn't called her that. I suppose it felt fine to call her Fat Dawn when I wasn't fat, but it felt far too close to home to call her that now.

"Blimey. Is she still as fat?" asked mum.

"She is," I confirmed.

"Well, you better make sure you don't ride any elephants then...you'll break them," she said

"I promise we won't ride any elephants," I told her. What was it with our family and riding bloody elephants?

"And behave yourselves – don't go getting drunk and silly like you do every time you go anywhere with that Charlie...I know what you two are like. Every time you two go anywhere, it turns into a scene from The Hangover."

"Indeed," I agreed, and it struck me, not for the first time, that I had no idea what it would be like to go away with Dawn. I knew nothing about her. Would she be any fun? Perhaps she was a lesbian? Oh My God. Had I done the right thing? This could all go so horribly wrong.

"Send me pictures of tigers, won't you," mum said while I was still panicking and running through scenarios in my mind where we were deep in the Karoo and Dawn made a move on me.

"Yes," I promised her. "I'll definitely send pictures of tigers."

"And I'll read the blog every day so I can keep up with what you're doing." I made a mental note to tell Dawn to keep the blog as clean as possible. I'd looked through it several times since she'd asked me to go on safari, and - I must say - it was very good. Quite witty and professional-looking, full of pictures, dry comments and clever observations. She'd obviously done a lot of travelling over the years, so the site was brimming with colourful tales from across the globe. It was also quite filthy. She didn't hold back on the swearing and wasn't averse to telling the world when she fancied someone...and what she might do to them if she got close enough.

Leaving day came around very quickly after the initial shock of the phone call. I'd had the immediate panic about Dawn being a predatory lesbian, then the panic that I had nothing in my wardrobe that was in any way suitable for safari life. The latter of these two issues was easily solved with some light shopping in Marks and Spencer's. Prior to my clothes-buying expedition, I'd read lots about safari life and watched films about colonial Africa. I had even printed off pictures detailing elegant safari wear. I'd bought the items I thought would be most suitable for the trip and packed them all carefully.

Now it was time to go, and I found myself standing by the front door of my flat, mentally running through everything I should be taking with me.

"Passport, ticket, safari clothing, toiletries," I said to myself. Was there anything else? I was paranoid that I'd forget something. I rummaged through my case one last time. Yes - all good. I must stop worrying.

All I needed to do now was to get to the airport, picking up Dawn from her flat in Esher en route. I'd promised to pay for the cab; it seemed like the least I could do when she'd organised a bloody holiday for me. To make the journey as hassle-free as possible, I downloaded the Uber app onto my phone.

We needed the cab for 4pm, so at around 3.45pm I put the destination details into the phone and waited for the car to show up. It told me that Ranjit Singh was nine minutes away in his Vauxhall Corsa. I was wearing my comfortable leisure wear, ideal for long-haul travelling. My outfit was in a muted, fudge colour. I hadn't gone for bright colours, having felt such a fool the last time I went on holiday. I had a very comfortable pink onesie, which I wore when I went to Amsterdam last year, but I spent the whole time feeling like an over-

THE MARY BROWN BOOKS

grown toddler or a Care Bear or something. This time, I wanted to ooze style and sophistication.

I checked in my bag for my passport one last time; then the phone bleeped to tell me that the car was outside, so I dragged my luggage out of the flat, bouncing it down the steps and making such a racket that Dave, my drop-dead gorgeous neighbour, came out of his flat downstairs to investigate.

"Going somewhere?" he asked.

"No Dave, I just like taking all my possessions with me wherever I go."

"Ha, ha," he said, unimpressed by my witty repartee. "Where are you off to?"

"South Africa," I said.

"What are you going there for?" he replied.

"To see herds of elephants!"

"Of course, I've heard of elephants," he replied. "What do you think I am? Some sort of dimwit?"

"No - a herd of elephants - like a flock of seagulls or a litter of puppies."

Honestly, it was like talking to a 90-year-old dementia patient sometimes. I can't believe I used to fancy this guy like mad; now I just feel half sorry for him and half maternal towards him.

"Oh. Herd of elephants! Yes," he said as I bumped my bag to the side of the steps and brought it to rest. Not once did he move to help me; he just seemed to be looking off into the distance. "The babies are lovely."

"Babies?"

"Baby elephants," he said. "Real cute."

"Yes," I agreed.

"Want a hand with that, by the way?" Dave raised his eyebrows and pointed in the direction of my case.

"I'm good, thanks," I said as I looked up and down the street for the Uber driver. I couldn't see a car with just a driver sitting in it anywhere. The only car I could see had loads of blokes in it.

I went back onto the app to check. It seemed like the right car, in terms of its colour, but I couldn't see its registration. It couldn't be right, though; it was full of people.

I stood on the curb as Dave watched me; for some reason, he seemed entranced and amused by the fact that I was going on holiday.

The car was close enough for me to see that it was definitely the right one; same registration number as the little car moving along the map on my phone. Presumably, the men in there were about to get out.

I put my hand out to indicate my presence to the driver, and he waved and pulled over.

"Hi," I said, and the three men in the car said 'hi,' back. None of them moved.

"Are you for me?" I asked. "I'm Mary Brown."

The driver nodded and jumped out of the car to help me put my bag into the boot. "Join the party," he said.

"Right," I replied, cautiously. There were three passengers on board - a large builder called Terry (who, it would turn out, knew everything in the world about sumo wrestling), a window cleaner called Ray who had his bucket and mops with him (his wife left him last week after 40 years of marriage but he never missed one window cleaning job), and a very large painter and decorator in his overalls, called Andy, who didn't talk much but snorted a great deal.

I squeezed into the back next to them. This was odd, but it was my first Uber. Perhaps this was how they worked? Little minibuses.

"We need to pick up my friend Dawn," I said, as the car trundled along, straining beneath the weight of us all. I waved at Dave, who stared back, confusion written all over his face.

"This friend of yours...," said the driver. "She is small, isn't she? There's not a lot of room for anyone else."

I didn't answer. And so, we sat there, me in my smart leisure wear with my handbag and travel documents perched on my lap while Terry demonstrated how he could talk in Japanese.

We were later than planned arriving at Dawn's house, so I phoned from my position cramped in the corner at the back of the car to apologise and say that I was on the way.

"Sure, heading out now," she said.

As long as I live, I will never forget the look on her face when she saw this tiny, overburdened car screech up outside, with me squashed into the back of it next to the large men. The painter climbed out along with the window cleaner, dropping his mops as he went, then the builder from the front, still snorting.

"In you get," I said. I tried not to look at the driver's face. Dawn was dressed in tight green trousers and a t-shirt and looked way fatter than I remembered.

"What the hell?" she said, easing herself into the front seat next to the driver, while the builder climbed into the back. "Why do we have a bunch of construction workers in the back of the cab? We're just a Red Indian short of a Village People tribute band. I can't arrive at the airport like this..."

"Konnichiwa." said Terry in his finest Japanese.

Ray scratched himself; Andy flicked through his phone, looking at pictures of his recently departed wife, sighing occasionally, and the car trundled along through the afternoon traffic, dropping off people along the way en route to Heathrow Airport.

"What was that all about?" asked Dawn as we took our bags from the boot and bid farewell to the driver.

"I don't know," I said. "I've never used Uber before. I wasn't expecting there to be people already in the car."

"Show me what you did," instructed Dawn, taking my phone out of my hand.

I showed her the app and how I'd just pressed the button for an Uber and put in the destination details. It was quite straightforward; even I couldn't have cocked this up.

"That's a bloody Uber pool car. You need to press this button," she said.

"Ohhhh..." I replied. "And what's an Uber pool car?"

"It's like a bloody minibus, for God's sake. Uber pool cars are for people who can't afford Ubers. They are for poor people. Don't ever tell anyone what happened, will you," she said. "I can't have people thinking I travel in uberpool cars with random builders. I won't put it in the blog, and let's not ever speak of it again."

"Sure," I said as Dawn wandered off towards the terminal, leaving me with all the bags. I wondered idly and with a certain degree of concern whether I was about to go on a long-haul flight and the holiday of a lifetime with the world's dullest person.

SCREAMING MONKEYS AND WILD RAINS

In the end, I didn't sit next to Dawn on the flight...would you like to know why? Because Dawn made the most astonishing fuss and got herself upgraded to business. At no stage during the incredible fuss did she suggest that I might be upgraded as well. So, I was stuck in economy, wedged between the window and a man and his wife who could not have looked less happy to be sitting next to me if I'd been carrying a bomb.

I do understand that it's a pain when someone is big and takes up more than their share of the room on a plane but - really - the snide looks and aggressive posturing weren't going to make me thinner, were they? They just made me feel desperately uncomfortable and ruined my whole journey. The rudeness also made me sad so I ate every morsel of food that was given to me to make myself feel better.

As I tucked into some terrible knitted chicken and plastic pasta, I could see the two of them whispering, and I just knew that they were talking about me and what terrible bad luck that they were next to a fatty and how appalling I was eating. Eating! How dare I?

I pulled my book out of my bag and read it aggressively. Can you read aggressively? Well, if you can - that's what I did. Although it wasn't so much reading as staring at the page and letting the words swim in front of my eyes while I tried valiantly to ignore the hostility brewing next to me. They would surely tire of feeling sorry for themselves sometime between now and South Africa hopefully before we left European airspace; then we could all just relax, watch films, eat the terrible food and arrive in Cape Town without me strangling either of them.

I didn't sleep much on the flight because of Mr. and Mrs. Angry next to me, and when we arrived at Cape Town airport, I was exhausted. My tiredness wasn't helped by hearing all about Dawn's magnificent business class experience.

"It was quite wonderful," she said, then began reading out loud what she'd written about it for her blog. The way she wrote about the champagne, the characters, the lovely beds and the nutritious food was really good. The whole thing made me feel jealous because I'd had such a horrible journey, but the writing was really classy. She might be an inconsiderate friend and a self-opinionated oaf at times, but I could see why people wanted to read her blog; she wrote with humour and warmth that was quite compelling. In the piece, she'd written about how she was looking forward to our gentle meander down through the spectacular African countryside to the game reserve. She'd made it sound fantastic, and I was cheered by the prospect of the picturesque journey despite my tiredness.

"Will it be a nice car for the trip to the safari?" I asked, charitably setting her up with the opportunity to tell me how special she was and how companies would always send the best.

"It'll be a lovely limousine," said Dawn. "I'm quite a big deal in the blogging world, so they always send the best."

"Excellent," I said. "This is really exciting, isn't it?"

"It is, actually," she agreed. "I've never been on safari before. I hope I've brought the right clothes with me."

"I watched some films about Africa for inspiration," I said. "Me too," said Dawn. "Out of Africa was beautiful."

"God, yes, amazing," I agreed.

Dawn called the limousine company while we were chatting to ask about the car. There was certainly no sign of a plush limousine or a driver in a peaked cap.

"A what?" Dawn said, turning away from me and pacing around. She wandered off towards the money exchange places and hire car booths, articulating wildly with her hands as she went. I could hear her raised voice but not the words she was saying.

All of a sudden, she spun around and walked towards me, grabbing the handle of her wheelie case and shouting, "Follow me!" I grabbed my bag and ran after her as we waddled across the concourse and onto the street.

"You need to know that this is not the way I normally travel, but there's been a cock up," she said, scanning the road for our transport to the Safari.

"Here it is," she said. "Oh my God, it's worse than I thought..."

Juddering to stop just next to us came an ancient Nissan Micra. It was small and dilapidated looking and covered in dust. The driver looked about 14.

"Oh my goodness, two big ladies for my car," he said in a rather ungentlemanly fashion.

"How far is it to Sanbona," I asked Dawn.

"About three hours," she said. "This is a disaster."

I couldn't be sure the suspension on this damn thing would cope with the combined weight of Dawn and me for three hours.

"A complete disaster," repeated Dawn.

It wasn't a complete disaster, of course. Dawn had a habit of making everything that happened into a drama, but it wasn't the best of times - I'd had absolutely no sleep on the plane because I was cramped in economy next to anti-fattists, and now we'd emerged into the blazing heat to discover a dilapidated old car with no air conditioning was to take us down to Sanbona...which was three hours away. The plastic seats were already hot when we slid onto them. The temperature reading hovered around the 40*C mark. It was going to be the most sticky and unpleasant journey imaginable, and I was going to have to endure it all while sitting next to Dawn. There was no point in being miserable, though - I decided the mood needed lifting a little.

"It's not a complete disaster," I said. "I've got a couple of those little bottles of wine from the plane in my bag. We can stop for refreshments if it all gets too much. Come on we can do this."

I reached into my bag and handed her a warm bottle of Sauvignon Blanc. "Thanks," she said, giving me the first smile I'd seen that day.

"Cheers," I said as we clinked the bottles together. I saw the driver shaking his head at us in the mirror. Had he never seen two enormous women drinking at 6 a.m. before?

The wine soon worked its magic, and we glanced at each other as the car flew over yet another bump on the ancient roads. "This is fucking ridiculous," said Dawn.

"Yep," I said in agreement as we sat there sweating and laughing as the sun beamed down on the little car driving through the Karoo.

The journey that was supposed to take three hours ended up taking closer to five in the dilapidated old excuse for a car.

By the time we arrived at our destination, the two of us looked like we'd been to war. The windows had been wide open because it was so scorching hot, and our sweaty faces had attracted the dust thrown into the air by the travelling car, so we looked as if we were filthy. I glanced over at Dawn; her dark hair was standing up on end, and her eye makeup that she had reapplied so carefully on the plane before disembarking was streaked across her face so she looked like Alice Cooper in one of his more aggressive videos. Sweat patches stood out on her tight-fitting khaki outfit. I hoped I looked better.

"How do I look?" I asked her.

She burst out laughing. "No one has ever looked worse."

The only thing that kept us sane on the journey was the captivating landscape and incredible scenery. It became easy to forget about the heat as we passed through the most glorious countryside... we watched baboons playing in the trees and birds dancing in sunny skies. When we arrived at Sanbona, the tensions of the flight and the heat of the journey melted into calmness and serenity. The beauty of the place was breathtaking.

THE MARY BROWN BOOKS

The driver told us on the journey down that it hadn't rained for weeks, so the animal and plant life were struggling. The difference between rain and no rain in the UK may amount to little more than the difference between taking an umbrella and leaving it behind. Here it was a serious business, a matter of life and death. When there was no rain, the plants died so the herbivores couldn't eat, they grew weak and became easy prey, so the predators thrived. The very balance of nature shifted a little on its axis with a turn in the weather.

As we drove past the guards and into the game reserve, we could see baboons all over the rocks. As we drove past, some of them started screaming.

"Why are they doing that?" asked Dawn.

"They have seen the lions coming; they are warning the other animals," said our driver.

"How clever," I said. "All the animals looking out for one another."

"To a degree," said the driver. "Not always. Now, keep your eyes peeled. If we are really lucky, you will see the lions."

It didn't strike me as all that lucky to see lions, but I knew what he meant...seeing any of the magnificent big creatures that we only ever read about in books would be amazing. To see one on our first day would be great.

Sanbona was set in a beautiful 130,000-acre wildlife reserve at the foot of the Warmwaterberg Mountains in the Karoo region, an area rich with vast plains, rivers, lakes and a huge array of animals.

My heart was pounding a little in my chest at the thought of the days ahead and everything we might see. I looked over at Dawn, and she grabbed my hand and gave it a small squeeze. "I'm so excited," she said.

"Me too. Thank you for inviting me," I said.

"That's okay I couldn't have invited anyone else," she said. I had no idea what that meant, but I was just thrilled to be there and delighted that I was the only person she thought she could invite. It was kind of sweet.

That night, we went to our rooms to unpack. I was relieved that we had separate rooms, but a shared bathroom was linking them, which wasn't such great news. I hoped that she was clean. I could tolerate mess, but not a dirty bathroom.

Dinner was to be in the outdoor restaurant, looking out into the magnificent countryside. We would be met by Henrique, the manager of the reserve, who would run through how things would work. Then we'd know exactly what the plans were for the trip, and hopefully, we'd get to ogle some of the rangers.

We walked down to the reception area to catch up with Henrique - a tall, slim, gangly man who looked like he'd never had a decent meal in his life. The polar opposite, in fact, of Dawn and me. He greeted us warmly and told us about the days ahead. There would be very early starts, so we would see lots of animals. Our ranger would meet us at breakfast at 4 am to tell us about the route we would be taking. I glanced at Dawn. We were both thinking about Pieter...wonderful, fantastic Pieter, who we were about to meet.

"There will be four other people in your group...a newly married couple called David and Alexa and two men, Patrick and Chris."

Dawn looked at me; I looked at Dawn. One handsome ranger and two unaccompanied men. Let the party start.

We sat there, enjoying pre-dinner drinks and looking out into the starry sky. It felt like we were the only people on earth. It was all so beautiful, so serene. Then, we saw flashes of lightning ahead of us, growing brighter and more intense as the evening wore on. By the time we had dinner, the wildest light show played out in the darkness, then thunder's heavy drumbeat joined the cacophony, and the rain came...a little at first, then tumbling down to the delight of everyone.

"It's rain!" screamed the head chef, running outside and praying up to heaven. "Thank God. It's rain."

OUT OF AFRICA

"Dawn, Dawn," I said. Silence. "Dawn?"
Still nothing.
Oh God. This holiday might have been the biggest mistake of my entire life.

"Dawn," I tried again, louder this time. Still nothing.

It turned out Dawn snored. When I say 'snored', I mean she made such a bloody racket that she could have woken the dead. It was a loud honking that left the room reverberating to its tune. I was surprised the whole place didn't wake up. I'd been standing in the bathroom shouting to her, but it was no good, so I walked through to her room and saw her lying sprawled across the bed - a hefty woman in a pair of men's pyjamas, wearing an eye mask that she'd clearly nicked from the plane.

"Dawn?"

It was no good...I couldn't rouse her at all. At least it didn't seem quite as loud now. When I'd been lying in bed, it had been unbearable. I walked back into my room, opened the doors, and strode onto the balcony. Once I opened the patio doors, though, the noise became even louder. Good God, alive - what on earth was going on with that woman...her snoring was so catastrophic that it somehow bounced through the walls and appeared to be coming from the lake outside. What sort of woman made that level of noise? I looked out over the water, shaking my head in disbelief, and that's when I spotted them: hippos...a whole load of them...honking wildly.

Ahhh...it wasn't Dawn at all. I smiled to myself. It might be judicious to keep to myself the fact that I'd confused her with a whole load of honking hippos. I scuttled back to bed, walking passed the gorgeous cream outfit I'd laid out for tomorrow. My size 20, elastic waist trousers in a soft cream colour, a white chiffon blouse, a long white, flowy jacket and a straw bonnet that I had tied a cream ribbon around. Next to them sat my enormous knickers and heavily constructed support bra. I was really excited about striding out in my finery tomorrow. I knew it was a bit over the top, but I was sure the others would be dressed up - it wasn't every day you went on a bloody safari, was it?

Morning arrived with all the subtlety of a nuclear explosion. It turned out that Dawn had the world's loudest and most annoying alarm clock. Really, it was absolutely terrible; it made the honking hippos from last night sound like choirboys. I took my eye shield off, sat up and looked into the darkness.

"We've got to get up," I shouted through to Dawn. "It's 3:45 am."

This was the sort of time I should be coming in from a wild night of dancing and drinking, not getting up. But this was the thing with safaris; it was all about early mornings if you wanted to catch the animals before the day got hot and they disappeared from view - into the undergrowth away from the hot African sun.

There was no sound from Dawn. "Hello, are you awake?" I asked.

As I prepared to get up and go and find her, the bathroom door swung open, and Dawn walked out.

"Oh," I said. "You're up already?" Then, "OH!" When she put on the light, I saw her in all her glory. She was dressed in cream...like Meryl Streep from Out of Africa. Exactly as I'd been planning to dress, she even had cream-crocheted gloves and a ribbon trailing from the hat perched on her newly styled hair.

"What the hell are you wearing?" I asked.

"You can see what I'm wearing," she replied. She was wearing tonnes of makeup as well.

"I can see that you're wearing the same thing that I was going to wear. Exactly the same clothes as I'd planned to."

"Well, not exactly the same," she said, indicating the cream shawl and the fact that she was wearing a long white skirt and not trousers.

"OK, not exactly, but - you know - you've copied my look."

"How can I have copied it if I was dressed first?"

"Oh God, forget it," I said, clambering out of bed and heading for the bathroom. I did my make-up as carefully as possible, determined to look better than her. At least I was thinner, and there weren't too many people I could say that about.

We descended the stairs, and I knew how ridiculous we must look: two heavily overweight ladies with piles of makeup on, draped in ridiculous amounts of cream lace and white cotton. I was cross that we both had the same hat - bonnets bedecked with ribbons. Down below us, the others in our group looked askance. They were in fleeces, woolly hats and jeans.

Everyone was staring at us. I mean everyone...just staring open-mouthed in disbelief at these two heavily overweight women who looked like they'd stepped out of a coffee plantation from the 1920s.

"Hello, ladies," said the hotel manager, breaking the silence. Her name was Carmella...we'd seen her briefly when Henrique had introduced her last night.

"How lovely to meet you properly. You both look - well - amazing. Gosh. I am looking forward to seeing your blog. It's very exciting to have two famous British bloggers with us," she said.

"I'm the blogger; Mary is my friend," said Dawn, territorially. I had no desire to take any damn credit for her blog.

"But didn't we agree that the blog from the safari would be called 'Two Fat Ladies'?" said Carmella.

"Um, yes," said Dawn.

"Two Fat ladies?" I said.

"Yep," said Dawn.

"Really? Is that why you want me to come? Because I'm fat?"

"Well, kind of," she replied. "I needed someone fat to come with me to get the gig. And also, you're fun too. I always liked you at school."

"Bloody hell, Dawn," I said. I don't know why I was offended. It's not like I could insist that I wasn't fat; it just seemed a bit - well - cruel - not to tell me why she'd invited me.

"Do join us for a cup of tea before we head out to meet your ranger," said Carmella, papering over the awkwardness. "Let me introduce you to the group."

There were two couples coming with us on the trip: David and Alexa, who were on their honeymoon and seemed to want to be alone, understandably. Alexa was a very beautiful and very young girl; David was much older...a good 20 years older, to be honest. And he seemed wildly possessive of his young bride. I tried to talk to her twice, and he all but shooed me away from her, wrapping his arms around her and claiming her as his own.

"He's bloody nuts," said Dawn. She was talking to me much more now, presumably spurred into social interaction by her embarrassment at getting caught out with the blog name.

"What possible danger does he think Alexa will come to just by talking to us?"

"God knows!" I replied. "It's not as if she's that interesting in any case. I'm quite happy not to talk to her; I was only being polite."

As well as David and Alexa there were the two men that we'd been told about: Patrick and Chris. They seemed really nice, and I had high hopes of friendships and maybe even something more if they played their cards right.

Chris was an artist of some sort - he said he did modern, progressive art, and his most recent works were shortlisted for the Turner Prize, which even I know is a big deal. He was great fun. Patrick was a food writer who did columns for men's magazines about restaurants and recipes.

Chris was quite gnome-like, with a full beard and sparkly, mischievous eyes, and there was nothing particularly handsome about him; Patrick, on the other hand, was gorgeous...classically beautiful with a square jaw and deep set, dark, brooding eyes.

The thing was, though, even though Patrick was 50 million times more handsome, I found myself much more drawn to Chris - he had such a fabulous personality that he seemed good-looking. Attractive personalities can make people seem so much more beautiful, can't they? In fact, there's nothing more attractive than a lovely personality. Kindness and funny always beat square jaws and muscular torsos. Well, usually. I suppose it depends on how muscular.

Patrick smiled at me and offered an Elvis Presley-type sneer as he shook my hand; Chris wrapped me in a big hug. That was the difference between them.

The other difference was that Chris was wildly politically incorrect and seemed to embarrass Patrick constantly.

"Does anyone want to ask anything before we go out?" Carmella asked.

"Any lesbian animals?" asked Chris, with a glint in his eye.

We watched as Carmella raised her eyebrows and racked her brain trying to remember anything she might have learned about animal lesbianism at ranger school.

"I think it might be time to head out now," she said, her cheeks scorched red and the question lying unanswered in the air.

A FEMALE RANGER

"OK," said Carmella. "Your guide will be here soon, and we'll be going out. I'd just like to tell you a little bit about Sanbona. You'll find this a fascinating holiday...in many ways, all safari holidays are exactly the same in structure: you get up early and go out to spot as many animals as possible before returning to relax awhile. Then we go out to look for more in the late afternoon. After that, you enjoy sundowners and a magnificent sunset before a lavish dinner."

"Ooooo," said the assembled guests.

"But here's the rub," she continued. "The reality is that every safari you go on is completely different. Every time you go out, you see something new and hear something you haven't heard before – honking hippos, roaring lions or singing birds.

"You are moved in a different way with every trip. Safaris are living, breathing holidays that create their own drama as they unfold. They're an unwritten script, an unfinished symphony – a blank page on which your story unfolds daily. Every time you head out you have no idea what awaits you. That's why they're so magical and unique."

The lady had such a lovely, lyrical way of talking; it was a joy to listen to her, and I found myself lost in her words. Even Chris had shut up and stopped with the stupid questions.

"Now, the important job of the day: I need to find out what you want for sundowners. Mary - what do you fancy?"

Damn, why did I have to go first? I find it hard enough to think of what drink I want when I'm standing at the bar and about to drink it. The idea of deciding now what drink I might want at 6 pm tonight was very tough to come to terms with.

"A white wine," I said, and Carmella made a note in a pad adorned with giraffes.

"No, no. I'll have a Bailey's. Do you have Baileys?"

"We do," said Carmella, crossing out wine and turning to the others to take their orders.

"No, I will have wine. Red wine, though. That's what I fancy - a red wine."

"Right," she said, beginning to look as if she was losing patience with me. She crossed out Baileys with real vigour and wrote in my latest fancy.

"OK, next," she said, and I knew that what I really wanted was a gin and tonic. I hovered on the edge of the group until she had done everyone but Dawn then raised my hand like a schoolgirl.

"Sorry, but can I have gin and tonic instead? I promise I won't change my mind again."

"OK," she said, grimacing.

"I'll have a vodka and Red Bull," said Dawn.

"Ooooo..." I said, but Carmella was having none of it. The notebook had been put away, and she was gathering up her things.

"Now then, let's go outside and introduce you to the ranger who'll be looking after you during your stay."

This was the moment that Dawn and I had been looking forward to since first seeing Pieter's heavenly smile on the website. We both adjusted our outfits and straightened our bonnets. I hoped the fact that we looked like extras from a Jane Austen serialisation wasn't going to put him off.

"Do go outside, and we'll get going," she said, ushering us towards the door where an attractive, dark-haired woman was standing.

"This is Cristine; she will be your guide while you are staying with us at Sanbona."

"What?" Dawn and I looked at one another in amazement. A WOMAN. This was not right at all.

"It's lovely to meet you all," said Cristine. "I'll be looking after you during your stay. As long as you do what I say, I will be able to show you all the amazing animals we have here at Sanbona, and I'll be able to protect you and keep you safe. Please remember that this is not a zoo; these animals are wild. It's important to treat them respectfully and follow the basic rules I will outline to you as we go around. The first rule is always to stay on the Land Rover; don't get off for any reason. If you drop something, tell me - don't try to get out to retrieve it. Understood?"

There were muted sounds of agreement from us all, but I was too alarmed to join in.

"Any questions?" she asked, but my only question was WHERE THE HELL IS Pieter?

We left the luxury of the lodge and were immediately confronted by a muddy and filthy-looking vehicle. I realised in that second that I could not have been more inappropriately dressed. The Land Rover seemed terrifyingly open to the elements and rather too exposed, considering I was dressed like a bridesmaid, and we were going off to see animals that could tear us apart with their teeth.

I stood near the side, waiting for them to lower the steps for me to climb in.

"Just hop on board," said Cristine. Everyone clambered onto the vehicle except for Dawn and me. I knew there was no way on earth to get on there.

"Up you get," said Cristine.

"I'm not sure I can," I said.

I gave it a go, grabbing the handrail and trying to lumber myself on, but I just couldn't manage it.

. . .

THE MARY BROWN BOOKS

"Hang on," said Cristine, running around to assist me. She stood behind me and pushed on my bottom, trying to heave me on board. Embarrassingly, it wasn't enough. Dawn joined in, and the two of them pushed with all their might as if trying to load an old sofa into a skip. Finally, I was in - headfirst, and with all my dignity gone, but I was in. Next, it was time to get Dawn on board. Carmella was called, then a guy sweeping the pathways came running, and the chef who'd been dancing in the rain the night before...together they huffed and puffed and loaded Dawn on board.

"OK, lovely, no problem," said Dawn, doing her best to hide the embarrassment we were both suffering. As we were about to set off, Henrique came running along with a step ladder. "Just to make things a bit easier," he said. Cristine stored it in the back, and we were finally ready to hit the road.

"Everyone comfortable?" she asked when she'd returned to her seat.

"Are there lots of rangers?" I asked, completely ignoring her question about our comfort. Of course I wasn't comfortable, I was squeezed into a ropey old four-by-four next to a huge woman with thighs the size of fridges. My elegant bonnet was precariously placed, and my clothes were dishevelled and certainly weren't comfortable. Even the elasticated trousers felt like they were digging into me, which is against all the rules of elasticated clothing; their very existence depends on them being comfortable.

"There are 12 rangers here at Sanbona," she replied.

"All men?" I ventured.

"Yes, I'm the only woman. Though around Africa, there are increasing numbers of female rangers. You'll find that..." "Do you know a ranger called Pieter?" I asked, cutting through her speech about female emancipation.

"Yes, he's the head ranger," said Cristine.

"Will we get to see him?"

"Sure you will," she said. "Is there any particular reason? If there's anything you need or want, you can just ask me. I can help."

"No, that's fine. Just checking then. Um, so, when are we likely to meet Pieter? Do you know?"

"Will we see lots of animals?" asked Alexa.

"It's impossible to know," said Cristine. "The thing with safaris is..."

"Right," I interrupted. "Just so we're clear - is it impossible to know whether we'll see Pieter or not sure whether we'll see animals?"

"Animals!" said Cristine quite sharply. I could tell she was getting fed up with me. To be honest, I think she was fed up with me the minute she saw me. Cristine was thin and wiry and dressed in khaki shorts and a shirt. She was a no-nonsense, outdoorsy sort of woman, and I don't think she'd ever seen anyone as fat as me in her life. Or as oddly dressed. Or as utterly useless at getting into a Land Rover.

"OK," I replied, sitting back in my seat.

"Good try," said Dawn, expressing a sliver of solidarity.

I'd positioned myself so I was near to Chris and Patrick...they were on the seats just in front of us. It meant the lion would get to them first, which was reassuring. It also meant I could talk to him as we bumbled along the bumpy roads. I might have to turn my attention to one of them if Pieter wasn't going to appear. That's when I noticed they were holding hands.

Fuck! Two-thirds of the single men were gay, and the other third hadn't appeared. This wasn't going at all well.

A WHITE LION AND ELEPHANTS GALORE

"Now, the thing with a safari," said Cristine. "Is that you never know what you're going to see or not going to see."

"Too bloody right," I whispered to Dawn. "You head out expecting to see a gorgeous ranger with big thighs and a deep voice and end up with a woman."

"Don't make the mistake of thinking this is like going to the theatre or something," Cristine continued. "The animals don't come out and perform for you. To be honest - we might see nothing at all today."

"We saw nothing yesterday," said Chris. "No bloody animal in sight yesterday." His voice rose theatrically as he spoke, and he stroked his beard like some great Hollywood actor. Kind of how Brian Blessed might look if he lost about ten stone.

"We saw birds, but they don't count, do they?" said Patrick, shaking his head as if the lack of animals was entirely Cristine's fault.

"Well, hopefully, we'll see something today," she replied. I had no idea how she kept her cool. She must have seen all manner of strange people gathering on the back of her Land Rover over the years, but we seemed like a particularly motley crew. I vowed to be as nice to her as possible for our trip.

"So, we'll head off now," she said, pulling away from the safety of the lodge and driving through the huge fences into animal land. "No one must get out of the vehicle under any circumstances. As long as you stay inside, I can protect you. I have a gun here and I've worked here for a long time. I know what to do, but whatever happens, you must not get out of the Land Rover. Do you all understand?"

We nodded mutely.

"What animals are you hoping to see?"

There were mumblings about cheetahs and lions, and Dawn rather alarmingly growled that she'd love to see a kill: "I'd like to see a lion tear down an animal twice its size and drag it off while it's still alive."

"Blimey - I'd just love to see some giraffes and elephants," I said plaintively. I've always thought that giraffes were sublimely elegant creatures - their gentle movements and that elegant long neck...kind of what I'd love to come back as if I had the choice. Elephants are great, too, with their long trunks and comical flappy ears, and baby elephants are adorable.

"OK, I'll do my best," said Cristine.

Within minutes, as if ushered onto the stage by an almighty director, giraffes moved ahead of us, gliding with such gracefulness through the trees that tears sprang into my eyes. They had lovely long necks and tiny heads...the supermodels of the animal world.

Without being able to help it, I squealed a little. This was amazing. I mean AMAZING. If you've never been on a safari - go on one. They are bloody fantastic. I mean fantastic. To be fair, I only came for a free holiday, and to ogle the handsome rangers, I didn't think about how properly captivating it would all be.

Next came the elephants.

"You're good!" I told Cristine as a herd of elephants trooped past us. The two animals I most wanted to see had appeared one after the other.

They lumbered close to the vehicle, and Cristine seemed quite comfortable. I was expecting her to drive away but she didn't move. I was so pleased. I wanted to stay here forever, close to these majestic, beautiful creatures. "No sudden movements and no sudden noises," she dictated. "But, besides that - don't worry - elephants are gentle creatures. They express all sorts of emotions. Elephants cry when other elephants die...you see tears in their eyes when they are sad. They are very lovely. So intelligent, kind, sensitive and emotional, as long as you don't do anything to frighten them, they will be quite comfortable in your company."

It turned out that Cristine was a world expert on elephants (how cool is that? Fancy being a global expert in elephants - that's the coolest thing in the world). She explained that she was studying their behaviour for a master's degree.

"Oh, hang on." With that, she jumped out of the driving seat and excitedly collected their droppings, displaying them for us to see. "Look," she said, as if showing us a diamond ring. "Aren't they lovely?" The droppings carry information about what the elephants have been eating that is useful for her research.

"I'm a very happy girl now," she said, dropping the contents of her gloved hand into a metal dish. "Lovely to have some fresh dung to play with tonight."

We saw so many animals that morning; it's hard to recount them all...a young tawny male lion trying to bring down an eland, failing miserably and having to wander away with his tail between his legs. Then, another lion had been spotted by a fellow ranger, so we were invited to go along and take a look. This was a white lion – a beautiful beast - white of fur and with the pale blue-green eyes of a film star. When we reached him, he was stretched out in the sun, his handsome face framed with a great mane of white fluff, his protruding belly testament to a good feed. A couple of feet away from him, under the trees, out of the sun, lay the remains of a baby giraffe he had killed that morning. "Can we get closer?" said Dawn, practically hanging out of the Land Rover to get a better look. "Can we go down there and take a look?"

"Really?" asked Cristine, losing her relaxed aura for a minute and giving Dawn a confused grin. "You want to go and stand between a male lion and his kill?"

"But he's lying down, he's full up, he's not going to be bothered by me. He'd have come up here and attacked the vehicle if he was.

"It doesn't work like that," said Cristine. "Lions completely ignore safari vehicles. They're just large, unthreatening, moving things that don't look very appetising and smell strange. If you get out you instantly look like a meal – with a head and legs and a tasty aroma of meat."

"OK," said Dawn, suitably chastised. "But if it's a slower animal that we could outrun, can we get out and see them?"

"No," said Cristine. "I want you to remember that for these animals - food runs. If something runs away, they'll assume they can eat it. And don't be fooled into thinking you can outrun anything. It may look big and fat, but even a hippo can run as fast as Usain Bolt and swim faster than Michael Phelps and a rhino can run over 30mph. You wanna take on one of those?? Not on my watch."

"What should we do if we're chased by a hippo then?" asked Dawn.

"Well, hopefully, you won't be, but if you are, I'd suggest climbing a tree."

We all nodded to ourselves, thinking this wise advice and words that we would be heeding should rhinos or hippos get in our paths.

We were only out for a few hours in the morning, and Cristine told us it was one of the best mornings of sightings she'd ever seen. I tried to persuade her that the animals had come to see Dawn and me in our finery...I even doffed my ribbon-bedecked straw hat in her direction, but she wasn't having any of it.

"It's because of the rain last night," she concluded. "It has brought them all out for the first time in ages.

In the late afternoon we went back out and saw rhinos and buffalos aplenty. I learned all about the safari world...how the buffalos die off first if there is a drought because they need so much water.

We saw birds and plants as well. My God, the birds were spectacular - from secretary birds which take off like aeroplanes, with a giant run-up, spreading their wings and swooping into the sky, to the huge fish eagles and the staggeringly pretty smaller birds in jewel-like colours, singing beautifully through the warmth and silence in this lovely part of the world. By the end, I was hopelessly in love with Cristine and wanted to stay here forever, learning from her and mixing with these fabulous animals.

A TERRIFYING SNAKE AND GUN-TOTING RANGERS

It was 6 pm, a very special time of day...sundowner time. This, in case you were unaccustomed to the ways and mores of the Safari set, was shorthand for drinking! It took place when the sun was just going down, so the ranger headed for the most picturesque spot imaginable, and we all consumed the drinks we'd selected that morning. Cristine had chosen the place with the best view of the sunset, and we were all set to enjoy assorted snacks and large drinks in front of the magnificent view.

We pulled up at the breathtakingly pretty spot, and Cristine began unloading the goodies she had packed into her cool bag. There was an alarming moment when it occurred to me that the pots containing crisps and nuts were astonishingly similar in appearance to those she had used earlier to capture elephant dung. I decided to share this with the group. It didn't go down well. We all steered clear of the chocolate peanuts after that.

Cristine handed me a gin and tonic and handed Dawn her vodka and Red Bull. As soon as I saw her drink, I immediately wished I had also ordered one. My gin and tonic seemed far less exciting in both colour and flavour. I grimaced at Cristine like it was her fault, but she seemed oblivious to my facial expressions, so I took a huge gulp and felt the warming drink move down my throat like an anaesthetic and into my stomach, where it warmed me from within.

"Cheers," said Patrick, and we all raised our glasses. I realised that I was the only one to have taken a huge gulp before the 'cheersing' had been done.

"Cheers," I joined in, raising my glass with everyone else. We all sipped our drinks while zebras moved easily across the plane in front of us.

"See how the baby zebras stay close to their mums," said Cristine. "That's so that the mum's stripes camouflage the calf. Look...you can't see the baby next to mum...the stripes blend."

We looked over, and I could see what she meant. Nature was so clever.

"Wouldn't the lion attack the mum anyway?" asked Dawn.

"Could do...but mums are harder to attack than babies, and babies taste better. Younger meat."

"Down in one," said Chris, slightly ruining the rarefied atmosphere. "Come on - 1,2,3 and we all down our drinks."

"Excellent. Is there any other way?" I said, throwing my gin and tonic down my throat and smiling broadly. Chris downed his, too. The others just looked at us while they sipped theirs.

"We're not 14," said Alexa, which felt slightly ironic since she was the only one in the group who looked like she might actually be 14.

"It's a holiday," I said, exasperation dancing through my voice. "Chill out."

The only problem with downing your drink was that it was then all gone. Chris and I looked at one another, as the others continued to sip. Then there was a quite magical moment. A second of pure joy. Cristine unzipped her cool bag and revealed that she had more drinks in there.

"Another G&T?" she asked. "And a red wine for you, Chris?"

Honestly, I could have kissed her. We both nodded vigorously and laughed as we caught each other's eyes. Suddenly, it felt like Chris and I would become best friends after all this.

"Cheers!"

We both downed our drinks again. The others had wandered off to the other side of the small area we'd stopped in. It was a lovely little place...a little grassy area with a couple of trees, three benches facing out towards the most beautiful views and a big, wooden table. Buried deep in the undergrowth in front of the area was an old shack that we could just about make out; it was surrounded by trees and apparently contained an ancient toilet. I decided to hang on until we were back in the room before going to the loo. I didn't fancy wandering down there through the undergrowth.

Though the others wandered around to look at the views from all sides, and compare notes on the incredible day we'd just had, Chris and I stayed close to Cristine and her cool bag. Our devotion to her paid off when she unzipped the bag and took out more drinks. Jesus, how big was that bag? It seemed to have an endless amount of drink in it. I vowed to ask her where she got it and buy myself one.

"I only brought three of everyone's drinks," she said as she pulled out gin and wine. "I didn't think people would want more than that since this is just a quick stop to see the sunset, not a massive piss-up or anything."

Alright, alright, I thought. Cut it with all the judgment. "Perhaps we should drink these more slowly," said Chris.

Cristine looked out at the others, chatting happily in the distance.

"Unless the others don't want theirs, of course," she said. "Then you could have more."

"They definitely won't want theirs," Chris and I said at exactly the same time.

The thing was, I didn't imagine that the others did want their drinks...they were too busy chatting and admiring the views.

"I'll go for a vodka and red bull," I said.

"Yeah, I'll have Patrick's red wine," said Chris, and we downed them both while Cristine looked on, eyebrows raised and hand poised on the cool bag so she could replenish us when necessary, looking increasingly alarmed at the speed of our drinking, despite her professional demeanour.

"What's next?" asked Chris.

"What did the Americans order?" I asked.

I felt quite drunk. It felt lovely, to be honest. That adorable light-headed feeling you get before the real feeling of hopeless drunkenness hits.

"Just these dwarf bottles of vodka and coke," said Cristine, pulling them out of the cool bag,

"Dwarf!" said Chris, convulsing into laughter. "Dwarf. That's so funny."

"Yes, funny word," I said, though I didn't think it was funny at all. Perhaps Chris was way drunker than me?

"No - not the word. It's just the...ah, it's hard to explain." "Try," I said.

"OK, well I need to tell you about our parties."

"Good, then tell me," I said, indicating to Cristine that we'd like the bottles of vodka and coke despite Chris's hysterics.

"Well," he said, smiling to himself. "We really like to party... Or, should I say, I like to party, and Patrick just tolerates it."

"Go on..." I said, taking a big sip of my drink.

"We have these parties, and they're full of great people. You know, writers, artists, musicians... Just brilliant people who are so talented and artistic, and I want to make sure they have the best time possible, so the food I prepare is always magnificent – I will get someone in to make sure the food is restaurant quality, and I serve the best wines and champagne, and then – when everyone is drunk and having a great time and I think things just can't get better... that's when the dwarves come."

"Dwarves? Why?"

"Tons of dwarfs. Dwarves everywhere."

"I'm still really confused; you must tell me what the dwarves are there for."

"So people can snort cocaine off their heads. Why else would they be there?" he said.

I just looked at him, eyebrows raised, mouth open.

"Have you never done that?" he said, genuinely surprised.

"No, of course, I haven't. What's wrong with you?"

BERNICE BLOOM

He laughed like a drain. "Gosh, you are funny. You have to try it. Snorting cocaine off the head of a dwarf is the best fun you can ever have. You are coming to the next party; just don't bring that bloody friend of yours; she is no fun."

"Okay, I will come," I said tentatively.

"Brilliant," he said. "You won't have to bring anything. I will supply the food and the booze. Oh, and the dwarves."

It wasn't long before the effects of the alcohol kicked in, and I found myself staggering, swaying, slurring and unbearably desperate for the loo. I knew that going for a wee here necessitated me striding through the undergrowth toward the small wooden shack. Before, I'd been quite worried about it, but with the false confidence granted by alcohol, it didn't seem to be half the problem.

"I'm going to have to go to the loo," I said to Cristine, shuffling a little as I lost my balance.

"Of course. It's all open - so just go inside but remember to shut the door afterwards so snakes don't go in there.

"Snakes?" I gasped.

"You're on safari," she said. "There are snakes everywhere."

Chris did a sort of little jumpy skip on the spot at the thought of them; it made me like him even more.

"I'm not a fan of snakes," he said. I could see on his face that was a great understatement. He looked bloody terrified. To be honest, who is a fan of snakes? Only spotty teenagers with personality disorders who keep them in their bedrooms and feed them live rats.

"It'll be fine," said Cristine; she looked rather amused by it all.

"Will you come down with me?" I asked her, feeling like a lemon but now worried about what I might find down there.

"Okay," she said, leading the way towards the shack, a gun in her hand.

"What on earth do you need the gun for?" I asked.

"To shoot the snakes," she said.

"You are joking!" I squealed, terror, resonating through my voice.

"Yes, I am, hah!" she said. "I've just got my gun with me because we're not supposed to leave them lying around. I didn't fancy leaving it next to a drunk Chris. I'd come back and find he'd shot himself in the foot or something."

"Yes, very wise," I replied. Cristine was quite funny really, once again I felt quite sorry for her having to deal with drunk English people when I'm sure she'd much rather have been studying elephants and talking to people who understood these things far better than we ever would.

She led the way through the undergrowth, knocking it aside as she went, purposefully striding with all the confidence of a woman who does this every day. I stayed close behind, jumping and screaming as every blade of grass touched me, now paranoid that there were snakes everywhere.

"Here we are then," said Cristine, opening the door to the wooden shack, leaning inside and putting on the antiquated light. It was a very basic, outdoorsy sort of toilet, but it was clean, there was a sink, and there was – crucially – toilet paper. To be honest, it was all you could ever reasonably expect from a toilet in the middle of the wilds of Africa.

I walked inside, dropped my cream trousers and crouched down gently. When anything is old-looking, I'm always extra cautious because I know I'm a huge weight and likely to break things. Breaking the toilet into would be too embarrassing for words, so I hovered slightly above it. That's when I saw it...in the corner of the room – a snake.

It's difficult to describe the huge scream that came from my mouth – driven by some inner terror and fear. I've never made a noise quite like it before. I heard rustling outside as someone came down the hill to my aid. I knew I should pull up my trousers and make myself decent, but I was so paralysed by fear, so utterly terrified, I couldn't move. The wooden door opened, and Chris's face peered through, seeing me sitting there with my lovely, frilly knickers around my ankles.

"I'm terrified," I said to Chris. "It's over there..."

I pointed to the corner of the room where the green snake lay.

BERNICE BLOOM

I kept my voice low, eager not to disturb the vile creature in anyway.

"Oh my fucking God!" screamed Chris at the top of his voice, piling back out through the door and running with all his might. At the top of the hill, Cristine had wandered back to the Land Rover and had started packing away the snacks.

I was alone

The only positive thing in this terrible scenario was that Chris's enormous scream didn't seem to have disturbed the snake in any way, and it sat there, not moving, coiled, poised, and ready to strike if my guard should be let down at any stage.

I knew I had to stand up from this uncompromising position and get myself out of the room, but I was terrified to move.

Slowly, I grabbed my trousers and knickers and tiptoed towards the door. I pulled the big wooden door towards me, and it made a horrible squeaking sound. Oh God, that was bound to alert the creature. I threw myself into the undergrowth, convinced the snake was following me but too scared to look behind. All I could think of was Cristine's advice to climb a tree. There was a big tree with low branches just to my left. I kicked off my trousers that were around my ankles and grabbed at my knickers, half pulling them up. From the corner of my eye, I could see that the party of fellow Safari goers was starting to move down the hill. Chris was in the middle, pointing towards me, presumably telling them the story about the snake in the corner of the toilet.

I launched myself into the arms of the tree, sure that if I was off the ground, my chances of being attacked by the horrible bright green slippery reptile were vastly reduced. I sat on the branch and looked down; Cristine was walking towards me; she would save me. She had a gun, and she was used to this sort of thing. I was bound to be safe.

"Are you okay?" she asked. I'd lost the power of speech, my fear had robbed me of any ability to articulate the sheer terror coursing through my veins.

I reached up to the branch just above, planning to climb onto it but unsure whether it was wise. I was drunk, trouserless and terrified;

was tree climbing the best idea right now? I just felt as if I would be safer the higher I got off the ground.

"Stay there, Mary," said Cristine. "Don't move, okay, I don't want you to fall."

I clung on for dear life as Cristine reached for her radio and called for help, asking for another ranger to come and assist her.

I really wished I hadn't climbed up the tree. Every time I looked down, I felt sick; every time I looked out across the landscape, I became convinced that snakes were coming from everywhere to get me, and down below, I saw the fellow Safari-goers assembling. They shouted words of comfort and told me to hang on, and everything would be okay. Cristine was going to get rid of the snake; she was just waiting for assistance to arrive, and then she'd take care of everything.

"You okay?" she said. "I mean – you're not gonna fall, are you?"

"No," I said, with more surety than I felt. I was half-pissed; there was every chance of me falling from the tree.

Over at the top of the hill, Dawn was waiting; she hadn't come down to join the others and reassure me about my fate. Instead, she was taking videos of me for her blog. It struck me that I would either be eaten alive by snakes or featured on a blog wearing my knickers and with my stomach hanging out. I wasn't entirely sure which the worst of the two options was. Perhaps both would happen! I was fairly confident that even if snakes were eating me, Dawn would keep filming.

UP A TREE, KNICKERS ON SHOW, BROADCASTING TO THE WORLD

I heard the Land Rover bringing my rescuers before I saw it. It arrived at the top of the hill, pulling up by the picnic table where we'd been having such a lovely drink and chat just 15 minutes earlier. I could hear a handbrake being pulled on...then I saw him - like a superhero striding onto a movie set: Pieter. The magnificent, gorgeous, handsome Pieter, powering down the hill to save me. I just wished I looked better. This wasn't in any way how I'd hoped to appear when he first set eyes on me. I'd pictured myself like Meryl Streep, reclining decoratively in a wicker chair, sipping champagne, not half-pissed and clinging onto a tree trunk, terrified out of my mind, with my trousers on the ground in front of me.

"There's a green mamba in the toilets and a lady in the tree," said Cristine, her tone was quite matter-of-fact, as if this sort of thing happened every day. "Could you check on the snake first? I'll stay with tree lady."

Tree lady? Is this what I had been reduced to? Pieter smiled at Cristine and looked up at me.

"You OK up there?" he asked.

"Yes, fine," I lied.

He strode manfully towards the toilets as Dawn appeared under the tree below me, still filming.

"He's hot," she said.

I should have realised that it was the arrival of the handsome ranger that had forced Dawn to come down the hill to join us, and not any concern for my well-being.

"Yep," I replied noncommittally. Pieter certainly was drop-dead gorgeous, but it was strange how much that didn't matter when you were stranded in a tree and just wanted someone kindly and non-judgemental to get you down. I guess I was scared, and when you're scared, you want someone who cares by your side.

I looked to Cristine for help, but she watched Pieter's back as he went on a snake hunt. For the first time that holiday, I wished that Ted were there. Sensible, practical, reliable Ted would know exactly what to do...to be honest; he would probably have climbed up the tree by now and be helping me down, carefully and gently, telling me that none of this was my fault and that any one of us could have found ourselves stuck in a tree without trousers. It was to be understood. My tree climb was a sensible precaution, not the actions of a ridiculous, drunk woman.

"Was this the snake you were worried about?" said Pieter, walking towards the tree, holding the giant, luminous green snake in his hands.

"Oh my God, be careful," I said. "Those things are vicious."

I'd never seen anyone so brave in my life. How did he manage to carry it like that without looking utterly terrified? It was beyond me.

"I think I'll be okay," said Pieter with a slow smile. "This is a hosepipe."

"Oh!" I said. To say that I was embarrassed would be a dramatic understatement; I felt utterly ridiculous, crouching in the tree for no reason.

"Was this why you ran up the tree?"

"Yes," I said. "I thought it was a snake... I just ran away and remembered Cristine's advice that it was best to run up a tree."

"From hippos," said Cristine. "Not snakes."

"Pretty weird place to hide from snakes," said Pieter. "Because - let's be honest, you get loads of snakes in trees, possibly more than you get on land."

"I didn't think," I said, panicking a little. "I was scared."

"Do you want to get down now then?" he said.

"Yes, I want to come down, but I don't know how to," I said.

I was aware that my words were vaguely slurring as I spoke. I wasn't full-on drunk, but things were swaying, and I knew there was no chance of me leaving the tree unaided. Not without landing flat on my face and probably doing myself, and perhaps other people, serious injury.

Pieter was just looking at me. "I still feel very shaky," I said. "I'm scared to come down." "Okay then, I'll have to come up."

Pieter dropped the snake-like hose pipe onto the ground and easily climbed up to me. He reached the branch on which I was perching in about a 10th of the time it had taken me to get there. He crouched next to me. "How are we going to do this, then?" he asked, looking straight into my eyes.

He had these dreamy grey-green eyes that seemed to sparkle like a calm sea on a warm summer's day. He had been clean-shaven in the images on the website, but today, he had a rough-looking beard, which just seemed to add to his beauty. He stroked his chin as he spoke, the glint in his eyes growing as he thought through the options for getting a very large lady out of a tree.

"How about if I climb down to the next branch and help you down to it?" he said.

This didn't seem to be a very sophisticated plan, to be honest. But I knew I just had to do as I was told.

"Okay, I'll try," I said.

"OK, move your right leg down towards this branch."

He was issuing simple, straightforward instructions that should have been easy to follow. Perhaps they would've been easy for someone more agile and less drunk. The trouble was that I couldn't lift my leg as he needed me to because my stomach was in the way. Only people who have been fat understand how debilitating it can be.

Eventually, he realised the strategy was not going to work.

"Cristine, can you call for assistance, please? Tell them to bring the winch."

"Oh my God, what are you going to do?" I said.

"I'm going to get you out of the tree," he said.

And so it was that Mary Brown's mum casually switched on the computer on that cool September morning in her suburban kitchen, hoping to catch a glimpse of her daughter enjoying the holiday of a lifetime.

She was with three of the ladies from bridge club when she opened Dawn's blog to see her only daughter being winched out of a tree with her knickers fully on show, her hair sticking up everywhere, and a team of rangers attempting to move her as if she was a bull elephant that had got stuck in the mud.

"Goodness," said Margaret, Mrs Brown's long-standing bridge partner. "What a time she's having."

MEETING THE CHEETAHS

*E*ventually, they got me down from the tree, but I'd be lying if I said it was a simple procedure. By the time I reached the ground, my fingernails and dignity were completely trashed. I'd screamed the whole time, which was very embarrassing - I just became convinced that I would fall and die. The only good thing to emerge from the horrible tree incident was that Pieter promised me that he would take me to see the cheetah close up the next morning.

"Close up," I said through unattractive sobs.

"Close up," he confirmed. "We'll walk up to them so you can see their beautiful coats. OK?"

"OK," I'd said. I realised he was talking to me as if I were a child, but I didn't mind. I didn't mind anything at the time. I just wanted to be back in the room with my trousers on. That wasn't too much to ask, surely?

Pieter was true to his word, and when we got back to the lodge, he said he'd be back the next morning to pick me up. I went to bed feeling a little bit ashamed of the way the day had progressed and a little chafed on my thighs where I'd been dragged out of the tree, but excited. I'd loved seeing all the animals, and the prospect of walking right up to the cheetah the next morning with Pieter was very appealing. It was also nice that I wouldn't have to get up at bloody 4 a.m. to do it. He assured me that if I let the others go off on their early morning drive, we'd leave later and go straight to where the cheetah always lay.

So, at 8 a.m., I sat in the reception area, waiting for Pieter. Cheetahs were his favourite animal; he knew all about them - I don't think he was an academic like Cristine, he certainly didn't seem like someone who did much studying, but he certainly had lots of experience of working with them; he'd been around them a long time. I had a feeling that this was going to be the most amazing morning ever.

I heard the Land Rover pull up outside, and - just for extra measure - Pieter beeped loudly and shouted my name. I jumped up, grabbed my bag and ran outside. I felt like a girl going on a first date.

"Hello there," he said, waiting in the vehicle for me to climb in, clearly unaware what a problem it was for me to get into the damn thing. We'd resorted to using the step ladder yesterday, which had worked well, but Pieter didn't appear to be aware of my difficulties.

"I may need a hand," I said to Pieter, trying not to look too pathetic. "I'm not great at climbing into these things."

Of course, of course," he said, jumping down and running around to help me. Rather than give me a hand up, he pushed my bottom so that I went into the Land Rover headfirst again. This time, I felt like a nervous foal being pushed onto the back of a horse truck against its wishes. Not the most unladylike or sophisticated move by any definition, but at least I was in.

"If we get going, we'll catch up with the others by the rock on the far side where the cheetah tends to spend her time," said Pieter. The words stung like an arrow to the heart. "What do you mean? Meet up with the others? I didn't realise they were coming."

"Yes, Cristine thought they might all enjoy it, so I said I would take them all. That's not a problem, is it?"

"No, no, not at all," I lied.

It was a rubbish idea in so many ways...firstly because if we were catching up with the group, it meant I could have gone with them in the first place and seen more wild animals. Also, it meant that Dawn would now be able to come and see the cheetah with us, and after the way she'd behaved yesterday... videoing me in my hour of great embarrassment, I didn't want her anywhere near me.

"Good – there they are now," he said, smiling and waving at Cristine. The two of them seemed to get on very well.

I'd had about 10 minutes alone with Pieter, and we hadn't even had the chance to discuss cheetahs. The plan to spend time with him and learn everything I could collapsed beneath me.

Cristine jumped out of her Land Rover and grabbed her gun; the others all climbed out after her, waving to me. "Hey stranger, there you are. I was worried about you when you didn't turn up this morning. Are you OK?" said Chris.

"Hi, yes, I'm fine. Ego a bit bruised, but OK," I said.

"Listen, I wanted to apologise...I came to your room last night, but the lights were off, and I didn't want to wake you up if you'd gone for an early night, but I did want to say sorry."

"What on earth for?" I asked.

"For being useless. For bursting into the loo and embarrassing you, then squealing and running out."

"Honestly, don't worry, I'd have done the same," I said, though I knew I wouldn't have. I knew I'd have tried to help.

I saw Dawn grinning wildly on the Land Rover's far side. She waved over and lifted her video camera to her face. Honestly, I was ready to shove that thing down her throat.

Pieter ran through the way things would work. He would lead the way, and we would all stay behind him and not run or move away from him, whatever happened.

"I cannot protect you if you all run off in different directions," he said. "Just stay behind me, and you will be safe. Understand?"

"Yes," we all chorused; it sounded amazing that he would lead us directly up to the cheetah. I shared my excitement with Dawn. But her face had turned a gentle shade of puce.

"He can't just walk up to a cheetah," she said. "That's insane."

"He knows what he's doing, don't worry," I said.

"Okay, everyone quiet," said Pieter. "Stay behind me in a line;

Cristine will be at the back. We are both armed, and you will be safe. But you must not run off, scream, or make sudden movements... just follow and stay in a line directly behind me. Okay?"

"Can I just confirm? Are we going to walk directly up to the cheetah?" said Dawn. "I don't think that sounds very safe."

"You'll be safe as long as you stay behind me and do as I say," said Pieter, a hint of impatience creeping into his voice. I could understand why - he must have told us a dozen times that we'd be safe if we did as he said.

"Right, off we go then." Pieter walked forward, striding up towards the rock.

It was fascinating to be walking up to a wild animal. I felt completely safe with Pieter leading the way. I stayed behind him, feeling the excitement grow as we walked, all of us in his footsteps as we headed towards the cat lounging in the sunshine, slightly tucked into the shade, by the huge rock.

"Can you see," said Pieter, whispering as loudly as he dared so as not to alert the cat to our presence.

I could see the cheetah clearly, its gorgeous coat shimmering in the morning sun. Wow, it was beautiful...I yearned to go closer still. As if sensing my thoughts, Pieter stepped towards the animal, and we all followed suit. We were all silent; all that could be heard was the gentle sound of twigs snapping beneath our feet. Then, suddenly, there was a cry.

"Oh God, I'm terrified," said Dawn. "It's gonna jump up and eat me; I just know it."

"Shhhhhh," said Pieter. "You have to keep quiet."

As he said this, the cheetah opened its mouth to give a giant yawn, and Dawn lost her mind.

"Aaaahhhh," she screamed, dropping her video camera and rushing back towards the Land Rover, screaming at the top of her voice.

"For God's sake," Pieter said, turning sharply and indicating to Cristine to quieten the hysterical woman at all costs. I picked up her video camera, which was still running, and slung it over my shoulder.

I could see Dawn and Cristine fighting down by the Land Rover as

BERNICE BLOOM

Dawn continued to scream and declare that she knew the cheetah would eat us all.

"Aren't you going to video her?" Pieter said, winking at me. "This is the moment to get your revenge."

"That would be cruel," I said.

"She videoed you when you were stuck in a tree yesterday and plastered it all over her blog," he said. "I was watching it last night - it was a nasty thing to do."

Oh no, Pieter had seen the video. I wondered who else had. I couldn't remember whether I'd given Ted the blog address...I really hoped not. Dawn was still shrieking.

"Go on, video her, you're missing it all," Pieter said.

I lifted the camera up and looked at it for a couple of seconds, and then I turned it off.

"I don't want to behave like that," I said. "What she did to me was humiliating. I'd rather go through life without humiliating anyone."

"You are one hell of a woman, Mary Brown," said Pieter, turning to lead us back down towards the Land Rover. "That was a very kind thing to do."

"Thanks," I said, feeling myself turn red.

"Sorry we couldn't spend much time with the cheetah," he added. "I know you were keen to see it, but it would have become terrified with all that screaming. It wasn't safe to stay."

"I understand," I said. "I just really wanted to know more about them. Is it true that you're an expert? Kind of like a professor of cheetahs."

"Ha," he said. "I guess you could say that. I have lots of videos of the cheetah, right from when she was a cub, and pictures of her when she was pregnant and when she had her cubs. There are tonnes of research notes that the conservationists made and left copies of because they knew how much I loved her. I should bring them round sometime for you to see?"

"Oh Pieter, I'd love that." I gently touched his arm.

"OK, why don't you come to mine tonight, and we'll have a cheetah evening. How does that sound?"

"Oh, thank you," that would be amazing," I said.

"No problem, I'll cook dinner or something."

So, that was a surprise. It turned out that Pieter was a nice guy despite being gorgeous enough to get away with being a shit. Who'd have thought?

A DATE WITH PIETER

The next day was really good fun out on safari, but we didn't see as many animals as the first day, and nothing special was planned, like walking up to the cheetah or tracking the lions. We did see some rock art; it was fascinating to think that people were turning to art so long ago to express themselves. It gave a real insight into their mindsets to see what they drew (men with spears, mainly! I guess they were pretty preoccupied with safety back then), but all I wanted to do was drive around looking for animals. I loved seeing them. I even felt sad on the late afternoon drive that day when Cristine talked about going for sundowners. I'd rather have had more time to look for rhinos or drive around searching for the elusive white lion.

Chris nudged me when I asked whether we could stay in the Land Rover instead of finding a place for drinks. "Don't spoil the fun...it's time for a drink," he chided. I smiled back, but the honest truth was that I'd much preferred to have looked for animals than drink gin and tonic...and that's something I never imagined myself saying.

Pieter was picking me up at 8 pm that evening to take me to his house for our cheetah night, so there wasn't too much time to prepare by the time we got back from animal watching and sundowners.

As soon as I got in, I tore off my clothes and lay back in a large spa bath, bubbles frothing all around me, sending soft scents into the air as I lay back and breathed deeply. It was such a huge bath; it covered me completely, which is a rarity. Most of the time in the bath, I'm reduced to splashing water over me to keep myself covered.

As I relaxed and melted into the soapy suds, my phone rang next to me.

"Hi gorgeous, how are you doing?" It was Ted.

"I'm OK; how are things with you?" I asked.

"OK, but missing you like mad," he replied. "It's lonely here without you. Are you missing me?"

"Of course I am," I replied. "I wish you were here instead of Dawn."

"Oh yes - so tell me - what's she like then? Is she good company?"

"She's OK," I replied. "I mean - she's let me come on a free holiday with her, so I can't complain too much, but she's quite - I don't know - she's not the friendliest person ever. I feel like she's trying to make me look an idiot."

"You mean in the Two Fat Ladies blog?" he asked.

"Yes - exactly. She said we'd always got on at school, and that's why she was inviting me on safari, but it turns out she only wanted me for the size of my arse...and there aren't many people saying that about me."

Ted laughed and told me not to worry.

"The blog's funny," he said. "You up that tree was hysterical."

"Really? Wasn't it mortifying? I haven't been able to bring myself to watch it...I imagined it was awful."

"Don't be silly," said Ted. "You looked scared but were still your usual funny self throughout."

"Thank you," I said, feeling a wave of warmth towards him.

"There's just one problem, and that's what I was phoning about - who's Pieter?"

" He's just one of the rangers here. Nothing special about him."

"He looks very handsome in the video."

"Ha!" I said. "Videos can be very deceptive indeed."

"Oh good," he said. "Because there's a whole montage of pictures on the site and it says you've got a hot date with him tonight."

"Whaaat? No - I haven't. It's not a date. For God's sake, Ted. Of course, it's not a date. He's just going to talk to me about cheetahs."

"How appropriate," said Ted.

"Why's that appropriate? What are you talking about?"

"Cheetahs. Seems appropriate when it feels like you're a cheater."

"No, I'm not. This is insane. Ted, please don't make this into something it isn't. He's going to talk to me about cheetahs - the animals - like lions and leopards. I wanted to go and see the cheetah yesterday, but Dawn got scared and screamed, so Pieter had to take us all away. He said he'd show me his collection of cheetah memorabilia tonight."

"His cheetah memorabilia? Really? He couldn't do better than that?"

"He's a ranger, Ted. He's just trying to ensure I have the best possible experience while I'm here, so we write nice things about him in the blog...that's all."

"OK," said Ted. "It's just hard, you know...reading all this stuff about you and seeing pictures of you having great fun with these gorgeous blokes, and I'm stuck at work."

"I would have stayed behind if you'd asked me to," I said. "You told me to go. You said you were busy at work."

"I know," said Ted. "I know. I wish I hadn't. I thought the break would do us good, but I miss you."

"It's only a couple more days," I responded. "And - you know - when you say 'having a great time with all these gorgeous men' - you're talking about me being stuck in a tree and having to be winched out. It wasn't the best time ever. It really wasn't. Whatever the guys may have looked like - it was bloody humiliating."

"No, I know. I'm sorry. Look, you have a great time, OK?"

"I will," I reassured him. "And I'll see you in a few days."

"Look forward to it, angel," he said.

The call from Ted left me feeling a little shaken as I clambered out of the bath and dried myself on the softest, fluffiest towels known to man. I knew tonight wasn't a date, but it was a shock how concerned

THE MARY BROWN BOOKS

Ted was. It was also a huge shock that he was reading the blog so closely. And why was Dawn writing all sorts of nonsense about me and Pieter? Why the hell would she do that?

I had been quite relaxed with her and uncritical while she'd exposed my imperfections and errors to the world, but this seemed a deliberate attempt to embarrass me and upset Ted.

I could see that a video of a fat woman in her knickers stuck up a tree was funny and would attract viewers and followers, which was her job at the end of the day. I understood that. But putting a piece on there about me going on a date with Pieter...how was that supposed to do anything to drive traffic? She'd just got into the habit of putting everything on there and simply wasn't stopping to think whether what she was doing could be perceived as being just a little cruel.

I sent a text to her. "Dawn, can you not put stuff on the blog about me going on dates with Pieter? It's just a pleasant evening talking about cheetahs, not a date. My boyfriend saw the blog update and isn't very happy."

"Boyfriend?" replied Dawn. "I didn't know you had a boyfriend."

"You never asked," I replied.

"No, I suppose I didn't. I just assumed you didn't. I don't really think about people like us having boyfriends. Well, behave yourself tonight, then."

'People like us?' Thanks. By that, I guess she meant 'fat people'. Charming.

Since the entire contents of the wardrobe I'd brought with me to South Africa comprised cream linen, white cotton and lace, I had no choice but to look like Meryl Streep's younger, fatter, uglier British cousin for my cheetah night, so it was on with the lacy white top, and the long linen skirt. The straw hat was a bit much for evening wear, even I could see that, but I had a big cream jumper with me...kind of like a cricket jumper but without the cricket stripes on it...it would be perfect if the evening got cold. I draped it over my shoulders and pulled the lace top down. I needed the top to fall as low as possible to cover my horrible fat belly, but pulling it down meant that a whole

BERNICE BLOOM

load of cleavage was being shown. Given the choice between stomach and cleavage, I chose the latter.

So, just for the record - my cleavage wasn't showing because I fancied Pieter or anything...my cleavage was showing to ensure my stomach was covered. Hope that's clear.

I wandered down the staircase to the reception area where I'd arranged to meet Pieter. It was a lovely old sweeping staircase that you'd imagine appearing in a Hollywood film. It was beautiful, and I threw my hair back and strode confidently every time I walked down them.

"Oh, thank God," came a voice from down below. "Can someone help me?"

"Hello," I replied, walking towards the door from where the voice appeared to be coming. Cristine stood on the other side of it, looking confused and holding out two sets of car keys.

"Can you drive, Mary?" she asked, looking at me appealingly.

"Sort of," I said. "I mean - I've had lessons, but I never passed my test."

"That's OK. I don't need you to go on a public road just to move this car forward while I move the Land Rovers in to get the oil checked. Pieter has offered to help me by bringing the barrels in."

"Yes," I said. "Which car, though - I can't get into those Land Rovers, let alone drive them."

"This one," said Cristine, indicating a small car I felt much more comfortable trying to drive. It was around 100m away from where it needed to be. I could do that.

"Thank you, you're a star," said Cristine.

The road into the lodge was one way, so it wasn't a tough job; there would be no cars coming towards me and nothing I was likely to hit.

I pushed the seat back far enough to allow myself to get it and turned the key in the ignition. The car moved slowly forwards...excellent. I could remember what to do. This was all going to be fine. I drove forwards, heading towards the building that Cristine had asked me to park next to. But then, as I approached the building, I saw a car coming towards me...it was going the wrong way down the one-way street.

I flashed my lights at it, waiting for the driver to reverse so I could go past, but he flashed his lights back at me.

"Move over," I mouthed at him through the darkness. There was no way I would attempt to reverse back to where I started from, especially since he was in the wrong. I inched forward, but he inched forward, too; I flashed him, and he flashed back.

I had no idea what to do. I sat there for a while, then flashed him again, but the guy just flashed me back. This was ridiculous.

Then, there was a knock on my window, causing me practically to leap out of my seat.

I looked up to see Pieter standing there, confusion on his face. "What on earth are you doing?" he asked.

"I'm trying to work out why that guy won't reverse out of my way," I said. "I have the right of way; it's a one-way street, for God's sake."

"What guy?" asked Pieter, looking genuinely surprised. "You're just sitting here, flashing your lights and beeping at no one."

I looked up to point at the vehicle ahead, and at that point, I realised the car ahead of me was exactly the same as mine...and there was a good reason for this - the car ahead was mine. What I'd been looking at was the reflection of my own vehicle in the mirrored exterior of the building ahead of me.

"It doesn't matter; the car is gone now," I said, moving to drive the car forwards a little way and park it where Cristine had asked me to."

"You were looking at your car in the reflection on the building, weren't you?" said Pieter with a loud guffaw.

"Of course, I wasn't," I said, winding the window up and parking where Cristine had asked me. It was a huge bloody relief that Dawn wasn't there to witness it.

I wandered back into the reception, where Dawn was talking to Pieter. He turned to me as I walked in. "That is the funniest thing I've ever seen," he said, laughing uproariously; you just sitting there, flashing wildly at no one in particular and beeping your horn like a loony. So funny."

"Yeah, hysterical," I said. "Really funny."

I was excited to see where Pieter lived, not just because of a natural interest in anyone who's that good-looking and an eagerness to learn more about him, but also because I was genuinely interested in the lives the rangers led. On the surface, they seemed to have such an attractive way of living - out in the wild all day with amazing animals, carrying a gun around and getting to feel like Crocodile Dundee, but I guessed there was a downside to the job, and it seemed most likely to me that the downside was that they didn't get paid very much and they didn't have great places to live.

"Here we are," said Pieter, as we pulled down a dirt track and came to a standstill outside what looked like an old shack. It was a miserable-looking building - so different from the beauty of the lodge where Dawn and I were staying. The fact that it was pitch black everywhere made it all the more sinister looking, so dark and isolated.

"Come on then." Pieter jumped down from the driving seat and moved towards the door. I scrabbled out, stepped down onto the muddy ground and followed Pieter to his front door. He kicked off his boots and put on the light, sending brightness over the sketchy furniture in a rather dim and dirty-looking room. It was the sort of furniture thrown out by students, the sort of stuff a charity shop in England would refuse to take.

"Have a seat," he said, and I perched on the desperately uncomfortable brown tweed sofa, reluctant to sit back for fear of never getting up again. The springs were gone, and it looked like the seat covers hadn't been washed since the 1960s.

"What do you fancy to eat?" said Pieter, walking into the kitchen.

"I don't mind."

The truth was that I'd already eaten at the lodge, but if he were prepared to cook, I'd happily eat a second dinner so that we could sit romantically across from one another and break bread.

"It's not looking good, to be honest," he said, rummaging around inside a fridge containing little except beer. "I've got nothing in here, food-wise, but a little bit of stale bread and some fruit the farmer gave me last week. It's looking a bit mouldy. I haven't even got any milk. I've got one beer; do you want half?"

"Oh," I said. "OK,"

I just assumed he would have gone shopping in advance of me coming over and have some food prepared.

"I'm not much of a one for sorting out fancy dinners," he said, predicting my thoughts. "I tend just to live one day at a time."

It wasn't so much that he couldn't provide a fancy dinner; what was odd was that he couldn't even provide beans on toast...or beans on their own...or toast...or bread, or anything. The man couldn't even provide me with my own beer bottle.

"Okay, well – should we go out somewhere?" he said.

"Is there a pub or anything like that nearby where we could grab a bite?" I suggested.

"There is a cafe in the village. We could have a beer and a sandwich there," he said.

"Okay, let's do that. Then we can come back here and have a look at the cheetah stuff afterwards."

"Good plan," he said, grabbing the car keys and heading for the front door. I struggled my way out of the huge sofa, my knees buckling as I tried to stand up, and pulled my top down to make sure it was covering my stomach before waddling after him and closing the door behind me. He seemed to leave the door open and not be concerned about who (or what!!) might enter in his absence. I'd have been terrified about what wildlife would call in while I was out.

He hitched me up into the Land Rover, and we drove for about 10 minutes into the local village; then he pulled over outside a small but cosy-looking place. He had called it a cafe, but it was so lively that it was more like a Gastro pub or a small family-run restaurant. I could see through the small windows that there were tablecloths and candles out everywhere, and really pretty flowers in the window boxes outside. My spirits lifted straight away.

"I love it when restaurants have white tablecloths," I said. "And candles. I always look for restaurants with tablecloths and candles."

Pieter looked at me as if I'd gone stark, staring mad. "I'd never noticed that. I've been coming here for 17 years and never noticed they had candles. Women are mad."

"This is perfect," I said, clambering out of the Land Rover again in my effective but undignified way. I'd taken to rolling myself out, clinging onto the doorframe as I did so. Honestly, Land Rovers weren't designed for anyone over about ten stone.

Pieter led the way into the café, and I followed close behind. As soon as he swung the door open, the warmth of the atmosphere inside enveloped us. I heard a band playing cover tunes, and the waitresses smiled and said hello to Pieter, each of them drooling a little as he walked past him. He sat at a table which was clearly his regular, and ordered two beers before I could say that I preferred wine. I looked up, and the waitress had gone. It didn't matter – I'd drink beer and have wine next time.

"They do a great steak sandwich," he said. "It comes with chips.

"Great, that will do for me," I said, although I had imagined something a little more romantic... Perhaps some beautifully cooked seafood and a glass of chilled wine.

Pieter ordered our food, and I leaned forward on my elbows and looked deep into his eyes.

"So, go on then, tell me everything you know about cheetahs."

But before Pieter could answer, we were interrupted by a small commotion as three very large drunk men came bundling over to our table.

"Hello matey, what we got here?" they said to Pieter.

When I looked at them more closely, I realised it was three of the rangers.

"Pieter, my old man, so this is where you are. We been looking for you."

"This is Mary," said Pieter. "Do you know Marco, Liam and Steve?"

"No, I don't. Nice to meet you," I said.

"Five beers," said Marco, waving his hand at the waitress. "Hang on, no - make it 10, no point messing around."

"Oh blimey. I think I'd prefer wine," I said, but my words were lost

THE MARY BROWN BOOKS

in the sound of chatter and cheering as the men downed their beers. This wasn't turning out to be quite the night I was hoping for.

"Come on, Mary, down in one."

I confess that I downed my beer, despite not enjoying it, and knocked the next two back with equal gusto, just to keep up appearances. My food arrived, and it was like a free-for-all, with everyone reaching in and grabbing chips.

All that remained on the plate was a little garnish of lettuce and tomato...I nibbled at the edge of the tomato as the men chatted. They'd moved into talking Afrikaans, which meant I was completely excluded. I don't think Pieter was doing it deliberately...it was just habit - beer and steak and a chat with the boys in their native tongue.

As the men chatted on, I looked around the pretty restaurant which had filled up considerably since we'd first arrived. To the right of us was a young, attractive couple and something about their body language drew me to them. I tuned into their conversation and soon realised they were debating whether or not to have an affair.

'I'm really attracted to you...' said the man.

"I'm attracted to you too," said the woman, more shyly.

It was captivating to listen. The man leaned over and took her hands, and they sat there staring at one another. Another beer arrived on the table in front of me, distracting me momentarily. When I turned back to them a large man had entered the restaurant and was storming towards their table prompting them to jump apart quickly. "Holy fuck," I said out loud. Pieter and his mates stopped their conversation and looked at me for the first time in about 20 minutes.

"What's the matter?" asked Pieter.

"It's about to kick off big time over there," I said. "Just watch."

By the time they all looked it was, indeed, all kicking off, with the husband having grabbed the affair guy round the neck. The woman started screaming for them to stop. Pieter raced over to the fighting men, with his three musketeers in hot pursuit. I loved how much of an action man he was, how confident in his own abilities, and how fearless. It was very alluring.

He arrived and easily separated the warring parties, much to the delight of the manager, who told the duo to leave and sort out their issues elsewhere. By the time Pieter returned to the table, I was shaking a little...whether it was adrenalin, excitement or fear, I didn't know. Pieter wrapped my jacket around me.

"Come on, let's get you back," he said, leading me to the Land Rover and heaving me into it. "You can tell me what all that was about on the drive home."

UP A TREE: AGAIN. THIS TIME WITH ADDED BABOONS

Dawn and I were up early and ready for our penultimate day on safari. There was a sort of sadness as we got ready, knowing that so much of the holiday had already gone.

"I can't believe we fly home tomorrow night," said Dawn.

I couldn't either. I'd got so used to life here. "I hope we see some amazing animals today," I said. "And I'd love to see the elephants close up again."

"And another kill," said Dawn. "I'd like to see a load of lions kill something big right in front of us."

"OK," I said with a fake smile. "Yes, that would be lovely."

I was really into this holiday now. It's odd how the rhythm of a safari starts to come naturally after just a couple of days. I don't feel traumatised by the early mornings like I did when we first arrived. I enjoyed waking up early, knowing that the day ahead was an unwritten page and that we might see things that we never imagined witnessing.

"Oh wow. I've got 600 new followers," said Dawn, lifting her head up from where it had been engrossed in her phone. "I was hoping to get 500 newbies in total, so that's good with a couple of days to go.

Although, when I went to New York and bumped into Tom Cruise, I gained about 10,000 followers as soon as I put the video online."

"I guess me in a tree in my pants isn't quite as exciting as Tom Cruise," I said.

We went to breakfast at 4 am, me sweeping down the stairs, Hollywood style, as I'd taken to doing every time. I found it impossible to descend without pretending to be Marilyn Monroe in Gentlemen Prefer Blondes. I wished I'd brought a long red dress instead of just white and cream; then I could have done the staircase routine justice.

Breakfast was a quiet affair...Alexa and David had left the night before while I was out on my 'date' so there were only the four of us left. I regaled Patrick and Chris with tales of the couple from the restaurant the night before and how manly and confident Pieter had been, then we set out on our morning adventure, heading down by the lake to watch the hippos.

Cristine explained that when the hippos open their jaw right up and look like they are yawning, they are not yawning at all but showing signs of being scared. She said we would be backing away as soon as we saw anything like that. I hoped the hippos would play ball and not do the mouth-opening thing because I wanted to stay and watch them for as long as possible; they were such peculiar-looking creatures.

"It's been lovely driving you lot around," Cristine said suddenly, out of the blue.

"Has it?" I asked, the surprise evident in my voice. I imagined she was fed up with us because we were a bit useless, but she said our enthusiasm was real joy.

"And you are keen to learn; that's been lovely," she said. "You seem genuinely interested in knowing about the animals, not like other people I've had to show around."

"Oh, do tell..." I said, dying to hear stories of really stupid people on Safari.

"Well, there was one time when a couple arrived at the wildlife reserve and the guy told one of the rangers that he wanted to propose to his girlfriend. He asked whether a giraffe could bring the ring to them while he was on one knee. It was baffling to all of us that he thought these wild animals could be made to perform circus tricks."

"Tell us more," I said.

Cristine laughed. "There was a couple from Germany who asked whether the animals got bored, and whether we couldn't bring out a TV for them so they could watch it during the day. They also asked whether the animals had access to a fridge."

We all laughed and smiled at one another, united in the warm glow of hearing that other people were much more stupid than we were.

Back in the lodge, I decided to have a shower before lunch. It was so warm that morning that I felt hot and sticky. Also, the shower in the lodge was the stuff of fantasies, so I tended to go in there quite a lot; all these settings allowed you to have it raining on you, pouring on you, dripping on you or coming down at you with such ferocity that it almost bruised your scalp. I once tried the scalp bruising setting and decided it wasn't for me. The other settings, though, were lovely. Rainwater was the best - a fine spray that tingled as it touched your skin - light, airy, and refreshing. I stepped out and wrapped a towel around my hair and around my body, padding into the bedroom to get dressed. Dawn was out on the balcony trying to look for hippos. She'd become utterly fascinated by them since Cristine told her they could run faster than Usain Bolt.

I slipped into my knickers and left the towel wrapped around me while I applied the lovely scented lotion that had been left in a straw basket in the bedroom. It was gorgeous - it smelled of everything lovely - like clouds and rainbows would smell if you could get close enough to sniff them.

I was aware of quite a commotion on the steps outside the room as I rubbed the lightly scented lotion into my thighs. It sounded as if there were loads of guys all jumping up and down. It was very odd. Then, it all went quiet for a moment.

I popped my head out of the door but couldn't see anything. It was a beautiful sunny day, and a lovely feeling drifted through me when the sun's warm rays touched my skin, still slightly damp from the shower and lotion. I stood there awhile, enjoying the sensations.

BERNICE BLOOM

But as I was enjoying the tingling of sunshine on my skin, I noticed some movement in the bushes just in front of the steps to the apartment. It looked like a couple of people were there.

"Hello," I said. I had the sudden feeling it was Pieter. Perhaps he'd brought the cheetah stuff to show me after last night's disaster. But why was he hiding in the bushes?

"Pieter," I tried. The figures stood still but didn't respond; it was the oddest thing. I walked slowly down the steps. "Pieter?"

I pushed my way into the bushes, and that's when I saw them. It was two bloody baboons standing there. One squealed, and the other just stared. I stood there, rooted to the spot, unsure what to do.

One of the baboons crouched, turning his head slightly to one side and staring intently at me. The other baboon moved around so he was standing to the side of me. I had no idea what would make them go away. Perhaps if I threw something, they would turn to look at it, and it would grant me a few minutes' grace in which I could escape back up the steps to the room. I moved to bend down but was terrified of taking my eyes off them. In any case, there was nothing to throw, nothing big enough to distract them. Then it occurred to me...there was only one thing for it...I removed the towel and hurled it with all my might. The baboons looked round as if flew through the air. I panicked and climbed up into the tree, screaming as loudly as I could as I went. Don't ask me why. Don't ask me why I didn't leg it back to the room. I guess my throwing of the towel was pretty feeble so the baboons weren't distracted for long; I didn't think I'd make it back there in time. So, there I was - once again up a tree to escape from an animal that was perfectly able to get into the tree should it want to.

The baboons were screeching up at me, and I was screaming for help. We were making a tremendous amount of noise; surely, someone had to hear us soon.

In the distance, I saw the sight of khaki green shirts running towards me. Thank God. It was Marco, Liam and Steve, the guys I'd met in the pub with Pieter.

"Here," I shouted, waving hysterically.

The baboons shrieked louder and one, then the other, jumped up into the tree next to me.

By the time the rangers arrived all three of us were in the tree, sitting on the lowest branch, me covering my breasts with my hands, them looking at me quizzically. We'd only been there only a couple of minutes, but they had shuffled over so close that we were all sitting next to one another like we were waiting for a bus or something.

Unbeknownst to me, Dawn, the intrepid blogger, had witnessed the whole episode. She had seen the drama unfold, heard the screams, and had done what a reliable blogger would always do in such circumstances - she'd filmed it all. With scant regard for my feelings and no regard for my privacy, Dawn had shown the world the picture of me half-naked in a tree with two baboons. Then, when gun-toting rangers had arrived, she had filmed that too, finishing her recording with the sight of Mary's larger-than-average bottom descending. She marked it 'Fat Girl stuck in tree: Part Two. This time, with added baboons' and loaded it onto the blog.

A NIGHT WITH PIETER

After everything that had happened during the day, the last thing I wanted to do in the evening was to go out drinking. I felt drained. It had taken four rangers to rescue me, and Dawn had again captured it on video. When I spoke to her about it, she hugged me, said she loved me, and was sorry if I offended. Offended? Try humiliated. The damn thing had been trending on Twitter all afternoon, and she now had 10,000 more followers. I'd matched Tom Cruise...or, more likely, the screaming baboons had matched Tom Cruise. It was all bloody exhausting. I just wanted to curl up on the bed, watch some terrible South African television, and get lots of sleep. Tomorrow was the last day, and we were doing something called 'walk on the wild side' in the morning, where we'd go out on foot to get closer to the animals and see more of the insects and plant life. I knew I'd enjoy it much more if I did it without a hangover.

I slipped on my pyjamas, tied my hair back from my face, and prepared to relax for the evening.

I pulled back the sheets and climbed in. I curled up into a little ball and found myself thinking about Ted. The holiday had taught me many things, and one of them was that Ted was a really good guy, and I should be making more of an effort to make our relationship work.

THE MARY BROWN BOOKS

He was worth sticking with, even when things weren't perfect. He was one of life's good guys.

As I was lying there, lost in my thoughts, I suddenly felt water on my legs. I put my hand down and could feel that my pyjama bottoms were soaked.

Oh my God - I'd wet myself; this was a nightmare.

I leapt out of bed, my pyjama trousers wet through, and went to head for the bathroom, but before I could get there, there was a knock on the door. It must be Dawn; probably come back to check I was OK. We had been leaving the door ajar so that neither of us needed to take out keys with us, but tonight, I'd closed it firmly against the world, fearful of baboons and the looks of pity from everyone who'd seen the video.

But, when I swung the door open, Pieter was standing there, clutching a carrier bag in one hand and two bottles of wine in the other.

"I thought you might be feeling low. I wanted to cheer you up," he said.

I stood before him, my large body encased in unflattering, too-tight pyjamas; having wet myself minutes earlier, my hair was scraped back off my face. It's possible that no one in the world had ever looked worse. I smiled at him.

"I wasn't expecting guests," I said.

"Clearly," he said, smiling back.

Then we both burst out laughing, and I swung open the door.

"Come in," I said.

"Look, I saw what happened today, and the blog and everything, and I wanted to check you were OK. He wandered over and sat on the edge of the bed. The bed in which the sheets were soaking wet from me having peed myself. To say it was mortifying was a gross understatement.

"Why don't we sit on the balcony," I said, opening the French windows and trying to tempt him away from the wet bed.

"Oh no," he said, spotting the damp sheets. "Did it break?" "Did what break?"

"I asked housekeeping to put a heated water bottle in the bed to warm it up for you. Looks like it's leaked everywhere."

"Oh thank God," I said, abandoning all efforts at decorum.

"I thought I'd wet myself."

"You thought what?"

"Really - I thought I'd wet myself. That's why I was trying to get you to come outside...to get you away from the sheets." "You're mad," said Pieter, pulling out a broken hot water bottle from the bed before following me towards the French windows. "I'm happy to sit outside, but won't you get cold out here in just your pyjamas?"

We compromised by bringing the duvets out and wrapping them around us while we sat, drank wine, and dunked crisps into hummus.

"This is great," I told him. "I'm so glad you came over."

"I'm glad too," he said, squeezing my hand, leading me to drop a chunk of pitta bread into the dip.

"You know - if I'd realised that Dawn had been filming everything, I'd have said something to try to stop her," said Pieter. "None of us knew she was doing it. She's very sneaky. I think she's behaved appallingly. I told her just now."

"Did you? I didn't feel like I could make a massive fuss because she's the one who got me this holiday, and it was always stated that the point of the trip was to write the blog."

"Yes, but not like this," said Pieter. "I think she's been incredibly cruel."

"Thanks," I said. It felt good to know that he was on my side.

"Anyway - I told her she owes you big time, and she's promised to look after you in future and not stitch you up."

"Thanks," I said again, giving him a small hug. As Pieter spoke, I could hear my phone ringing in the room...it was coming from somewhere deep in the tangled, wet sheets. I decided to leave it. It was probably Dawn, ringing to apologise after her chat with Pieter.

"More wine," he said.

"Thank you," I replied. "This is so lovely."

Ted pushed his phone into his pocket and sat back in the seat at Johannesburg airport. He'd wanted to let Mary know he was turning up. He didn't want just to appear unannounced at her door. He had phoned ahead to the safari place to tell them he was coming, but he had no idea whether Henrique, the guy he'd spoken to, would let him in when he arrived. He'd tried Mary several times, but she just wasn't answering her phone. He'd have to work it all out when he arrived. He would touch down in Cape Town at midnight, so he should be with her by around 3 a.m. Presumably, she'd be tucked up in bed at that time, and he could burst in and surprise her.

"Tell me some of the silliest things that have happened while you've been working as a ranger," I said, pulling the duvet over my shoulders and looking out into the sky, full of the brightest stars I'd ever seen. The lack of light pollution made them quite dazzling.

"Oh, I've seen everything," said Pieter. "I've had baboons open car doors and get in. Just once, but it was quite a shock for these four women sitting in the back. I had to jump over the seats and clamber into the back to shoo them out. They went pretty quickly, but it was all a bit alarming to start with."

"Did they leave the door open or something?" I asked.

"No, but you used to be able to open the doors from the outside...you can't anymore because of incidents like that."

"What's the worst thing people do?" "I guess it's two things - the first is to ask really stupid questions, the second is to be too brightly coloured and too noisy."

"Oooo...so even though I looked like I'd stepped out of the Victorian era, I was OK with my beige palette of clothing then?"

"You were perfect," he said. "It's the multiple neon colours that tend to cause the problems. And the noise that people make, honestly - when you've been out on a game drive for over two hours, searching an area where there was a recent leopard sighting, everybody is craning their necks, looking in all directions to get a glimpse of the animal, then - suddenly - the bloke in the row behind you bellows "LEOPARD OVER THERE" at the top of his voice. You swivel around, and if you're lucky, you'll glimpse a tail disappearing."

"Oh God, that would be a real pain," I said.

As Pieter picked up the bottle to refill my glass, I noticed that one

BERNICE BLOOM

of his fingers was shorter than the other. It looked as if the end had been cut off.

"What happened to your finger?" I asked.

"Ah," he replied. "That was the time I got too close to a lion. I was trying to pull a thorn out of its foot. I gently held its paw, but he turned and bit the end of my finger off."

"Oh no! That's awful. It must have been bloody agony. And you're miles from a hospital here. Where on earth did they take you? What did they do?"

"Nothing. I decided it would be OK, so for a few days I didn't get any treatment at all…I just hung out here with my finger all wrapped up, then I started to feel faint and shivery, and we thought I'd better seek treatment. By the time I did, the end of my finger was completely hanging off and couldn't be saved."

"Jesus Christ. You were lucky not to lose your whole arm."

"I was lucky not to die, to be honest. The lion would have killed a weaker person on that day." He looked so solemn as he spoke, then he smiled from ear-to-ear. "I'm sorry. That's a load of bollocks," he said. "There was no lion. I got completely hammered in the pub and cut it on a pane of glass."

"You rotter!" I said. "But, for the record, the first story's much better. Stick to that."

I looked at my watch. It was 1 am already. How had it got that late? Dawn must have come in and gone to bed, leaving us out on the balcony chatting away.

"Are you warm enough?" asked Pieter.

"To be honest, I'm starting to feel a bit chilly," I said. "Come on, let's go inside."

I followed Pieter into the room, where it was much warmer. We'd finished one bottle of wine, so Pieter grabbed the other one and the remainder of the food, and we sat on the soft carpet, leaning back against the bed, with our mini picnic laid out in front of us.

"Can a kangaroo jump higher than the Empire State Building?" I asked.

Pieter looked at me expectantly. "I don't know, Mary," he replied.

"Of course," I said. "The Empire State Building can't jump."

"Yep. That's the standard I've come to expect from you, Mary Brown."

"OK - another one. What did the elephant say to the naked man?"

"I don't know, but I dread to think," said Pieter.

"How do you breathe through something so small?"

"Oh dear. These are getting much worse. I'm going to need more wine if we're going to carry on like that. Want a top-up?"

"Yeah," I said enthusiastically, even though I'd already had way more than I was planning to. I'd been determined to go to bed early and sober. Now I was at the stage where I couldn't be bothered to worry about it anymore. I felt invincible, as if I could drink as much as I wanted, and all would be fine.

"Why couldn't the leopard play hide and seek?" I said.

"Go on..."

"Because he was always spotted."

Dawn lay in bed, listening to the chatter from Mary's room. She was glad that Pieter and Mary were getting on so well. She felt bad about always videoing Mary and putting it up on the blog, but that's what she did. That's why she was here. That was her job. If she stopped putting funny videos on the blog, people wouldn't look at it, and the lovely life she'd built for herself through her blogging would be over in a heartbeat. She'd always done this when she'd been on holiday; it was just that she'd never been on holiday with someone quite like Mary before...someone who was forever getting herself into stupid scrapes.

She giggled to herself as she thought of Mary stuck in the tree. And to do it twice! It was the funniest thing. She could see why it had so many hits and bounced around on social media all afternoon.

THE UNEXPECTED ARRIVAL OF TED

"I've really enjoyed being here with you," said Pieter, giving me a friendly squeeze of the shoulder.

"Me too," I said. "You're really good company Pieter."

"Thanks," he replied. "I wish all women thought that...I seem to have absolutely no luck at all with the opposite sex."

"Whaaaaat?" I asked. "I mean - really? I don't believe that for a second."

"It's true," he said. "There's this girl I like, but I just don't think she's interested in me."

"What girl - tell me everything," I said.

"No, I can't."

"Well, if you don't tell me, I can't help you, can I? In any case, I'm going home tomorrow night - it's not as if I can do much damage between now and then."

Pieter raised his eyebrows and looked at me askance. "Not a day has gone by since you've been here when you haven't caused a whole pile of damage, Mary Brown. You're very loveable, but chaos does seem to follow you around the place."

"I can't argue with that," I said, nodding wisely. "But I'm always chaotic and disruptive to myself. I'd never do anything to hurt anyone else. Not ever."

"I know, I know," he said. "I realise that. That's why I came around tonight - when I saw your video online, I knew that you would never have done the same to Dawn. I remember you deliberately didn't video her when she screamed at the cheetah. You're a lovely person."

"Well, if I'm so lovely, you can tell me. Come on, Crocodile Dundee - spill the goss..."

"OK," he said, laughing at me. "I like Cristine, but I don't think she's interested in me."

"Cristine?" I said. "Really?"

"Yes, why do you look so surprised?"

"Because I had no idea."

"Didn't you? But I've been really obvious. Rushing to help her out when she calls - only to find you stuck up a tree, helping her with all the oil barrels last night."

"That's not obvious at all," I cried. "You need to make it much more obvious. I bet she doesn't have a clue."

"Oh God - I hate all this," he said. "I wish I'd never told you now."

"Why do you wish you'd never told me? I can help," I said.

"I want to know whether she likes me," he said. I had to stop myself from explaining to him that every woman in the whole damn world probably fancied him.

"I'll find out," I said. "Leave it with me. I'll be subtle, I promise."

"Thank you, you're wonderful," he said, giving me a huge hug. It was a lovely big, warm embrace, but it was just friendly; there was no sense of romance or sexual interest... Just two people who had spent a lovely night chatting to one another and had become firm friends.

"I think you're pretty wonderful, too," I said, and he pulled me even closer to him.

As we sat in the lovely, warm embrace, bonded by mutual respect and a great friendship, the door suddenly burst open, and Dawn rushed in, her hair standing up on end and a look of utter horror on her face.

"Ted's here," she screamed. "The security guards just phoned through to say he's here. Pieter - you'd better hide, quick."

I looked up as Pieter disengaged from our warm embrace and threw himself under the bed. As he did, there was a loud knock on the door.

"God, he's here already," I said, opening the door cautiously.

"Hello, my beautiful angel," said Ted, wrapping his arms around me. "God, I've missed you. I just couldn't stay away any more... I wanted to see you to check you were okay."

"I'm absolutely fine," I said, my voice loud and high-pitched and shot through with panic.

"What's the matter?" he said. "You sound worried."

"No," I said. "I'm just excited. It's so wonderful to see you."

"I'll leave you to it," said Dawn, backing out of the room, and giving me a look which said 'Pieter's under the bed, your boyfriend has just arrived at the door, I don't know what to do, so I'll just get out of here'.

Ted looked up as Dawn left, closing the door behind her. "I haven't seen you all week, you gorgeous woman. You look amazing..." As he spoke, he lifted my arms and removed my pyjama top, pushing me back towards the bed.

"Why don't we go and get some breakfast or something?" I said.

"Let's have breakfast later," he said.

He took his shirt off and began unzipping his trousers as he pushed me back onto the bed. He began kissing me passionately and urgently. I hadn't been to bed all night, I was half drunk and starting to feel exhausted, and now we were going to make love in a bed on top of Pieter. To say this holiday had descended into farce would be to totally underplay the madness of it all.

"You know I love you, don't you," said Ted. "Now let me put my hand on your little muffin."

He pushed me back onto the bed, and I swear to God I heard a squeal from beneath us. While Ted continued talking about my little muffin – his embarrassing pet name for my most private parts- he kissed me more passionately, removing all our clothes and beginning to breathe heavily and tell me how excited he was. All I could think about was Pieter lying under the bed. Ted pushed himself inside me, and I could feel the bed move and push against the wall. Neither Ted nor I was small; I was well aware that the bed would push down on Pieter as he lay beneath the springs. Ted began moaning and pushing harder and the bed rocked even more. Oh God, this was unbearable. Finally, Ted rose to a climax, grunted, roared, and squealed in delight. There was no way I was going to orgasm with Pieter under the bed, so when Ted touched me, trying to raise me, I held his arm away and held him in a warm embrace. "Just cuddle me," I pleaded.

"Are you sure, is everything okay?" he said.

"Everything is lovely," I said. "I'm so glad you are here, but I'm really hungry, let's go and get some breakfast. They have the best breakfast buffet here – it's brilliant. It's open from 2 a.m. for those on early safaris."

"Okay then," said Ted. He jumped out of bed, dressed, and the two of us left the room and walked down to the buffet bar.

Around 10 minutes later Pieter came wandering through the restaurant and said hello, introducing himself to Ted.

"You must speak nothing of what happened just then," I said threateningly when Ted had set off on a second trip to the buffet.

Pieter smiled broadly at me.

"Okay," he said. "You can rely on me... my little muffin."

HOMEWARD BOUND

Neither of us had slept the night before, but the walking safari was one of the week's highlights, so I didn't want to miss it. Pieter said it was no problem for Ted to come with us, so we headed off on the Land Rover together, with Chris, Patrick and Dawn sitting behind us. I could sense that Dawn wasn't happy about Ted being there. She wasn't happy that I had a boyfriend, I don't suppose. Though I was very glad that she had burst in last night to tell me he was on the way.

We had Cristine and Pieter with us for the walking safari because you're not allowed to wander out of the Land Rover with just one ranger to guide you. I knew that I needed to get Cristine on her own so I could find out how she felt about Pieter. After having sex on top of him this morning, that felt like the least I could do.

"Wow, look, elephants," said Ted. "This is bloody amazing. It's like Jurassic Park."

Ted's enthusiasm for the animals reminded me of my own enthusiasm on the first day. I'd kind of got used to them being around every corner now, but Ted was wide-eyed as he watched them.

"A baby elephant," he squealed. "Look."

"Shall we get out and go closer?" said Pieter.

He looked over at Cristine, who nodded and smiled. I knew instantly that she liked him...it was so obvious. Why hadn't I realised that before? Why couldn't he see that?

We all stepped out of the Land Rover. Ted helped me down so I didn't have to do my bizarre rolling routine, and we walked carefully towards the elephants. Honestly, it was the most amazing experience of my life. Cristine led the way, given she was queen of the elephants, and told Ted all about what emotional creatures they were and how she'd seen them cry and respond with real tenderness to their young.

I held back so I was walking with Pieter.

"Everything OK?" he asked.

"Fine," I said. "I'm sure that Cristine likes you."

"She does? How on earth would you know that?"

"I just do...feminine intuition. I can tell. You have to ask her out."

"No way," said Pieter.

"But - why?" "Because...I don't know, just because..."

"Just say to her 'do you fancy going out for a glass of wine tonight?' Just say it."

"Oh God," said Pieter, looking nervous at the thought of it. It was a very sweet moment; this big, strong man with huge shoulders and massive boots clutching a gun and looking terrifying but as nervous as hell about asking a pretty girl out on a date. I'd seen him charge in to break up a huge fight without a care in the world, but the idea of asking someone out had left him crippled with nerves.

"Maybe later," he said.

We caught up with the others, and Ted entertained Cristine with his terrible jokes.

"There was a Mummy Mole, a Daddy Mole and a Baby Mole. They lived in a hole in the country near a farmhouse. Dad poked his head out of the hole and said, "Mmmm, I smell sausage!" Mum mole poked her head outside the hole and said, "Mmmm, I smell pancakes!" Baby mole tried to stick his head outside but couldn't because of the two bigger moles. Baby mole said, "The only thing I smell is molasses. Get it? Mole arses... see!"

BERNICE BLOOM

"Blimey, that's truly awful," said Pieter. "You and Mary were made for one another - your jokes are appalling."

"Oy," I said, prodding him in the side. "Go and talk to Cristine."

"OK," he said, terror written on his face. "I'll go and talk to her now."

The walk on the wild side was great fun...we saw tortoises, birds, flowers, plants, and elephants. We even found some rhinos that we tracked from a distance.

"We have to come back here," said Ted when we were back in the room and packing for our flight home. "Shall we start a blog or something...one fat couple? It might work."

"Ha!" I said noncommittally. I'd loved the holiday, but I think I might have had enough blogs for now.

Ted and I sat together on the flight home...in economy, of course, while Dawn trundled up to business class with a huge grin on her face. The whole thing had been a giant success for her; some brilliant, compelling videos on the site and loads more people signed up. Presumably, that would mean lots more free trips for her and more income from advertisers. The woman was a pain in the arse, but you had to admire her in many ways.

"All things considered, and bearing in mind that the whole world has seen your bottom, would you ever consider going on holiday with Dawn again?"

"No," I said.

"Even if it was a free trip to somewhere exotic?"

"No," I said with a shrug. "It's quite simple, Ted; I've realised that free trips, luxury, exotic surroundings, and all that are wonderful when you're with someone you love. Not so great when you're with a complete nutcase. Having said that, I met some amazing friends – Pieter was great, wasn't it?"

"Yes, he was," conceded Ted. "He's a nice guy, a bit too good-looking for my tastes, though."

Ted nudged me in an affectionate way as he said this.

"It must've been horrifying to be at home and see all those ridiculous videos appearing on the blog," I said.

"It was insane," said Ted. "I made the mistake of telling my mum and sister all about the blog, so they've been looking at it too. My sister wants to know where you got those lacy knickers from."

"Oh God, this is all getting worse by the minute," I said. "Dawn's nuts"

"Yep, she does seem to be. Do you think you'll stay in touch with her at all?"

"I don't think so, but then I didn't think I would stay in touch after bumping into each other in the garden centre, and we ended up on safari in Africa together, so you never know. I thought I should get her a nice present to thank her. I know she only invited me because I'm fat, but it was a hell of a trip in the end, wasn't it? An amazing experience and such an incredibly beautiful place. I'll just ensure I don't go on holiday with her again."

The air hostess appeared beside Ted and asked us to turn our phones off and put our tray tables up before the flight took off.

I checked my phone one last time. I had a text...from Pieter.

"Hey blondie - just wanted to say thanks for making the past week more memorable than any other week I've ever had. You're a very special lady...don't let anyone ever tell you otherwise. Pieter x PS I'm taking Cristine out for dinner tonight."

Yes. Brilliant.

As I was about to turn the phone off, another text popped across the screen. It was from Dawn.

"I've been invited on a cruise in three weeks' time," it said. "Do you want to come?"

Oooooo...a cruise. I looked over at Ted who was engrossed in his phone. I couldn't, could I? But then again...

"I'd love to," I texted back. "Count me in."

I switched off my phone and put it away.

"Everything OK?" asked Ted. "You look thoughtful." "Everything's fine," I said. "I've got one little thing to tell you, but let's get you a nice large gin and tonic first..."

LETTER FROM THE CAPTAIN

*3*rd Sept 2023
   Dear Ms Brown,

Thank you for arranging to come on the 20-day Mediterranean cruise with Angel Cruises. We look forward to welcoming you on board and hope you enjoy the holiday of a lifetime with us.

The ship will leave Southampton at 5 pm (BST), and boarding will start at 2 pm. All the information about your cruise and the ship is enclosed, along with details about our on-shore excursions and events. If you have any questions, please do not hesitate to contact us.

We look forward to seeing you on 7th October.

Kind regards,

CAPTAIN HOMARUS *& the crew of The Angel of the Seas*

REPLY TO THE CAPTAIN

7th September 2023
   Dear Ms Brown,
Thank you very much for your reply to my letter.

I can confirm that there is an 'eat-as-much-as-you-possibly- can' buffet on board, the bar is open all day and there is a mini bar in every cabin. We will make sure that it is stocked with plenty of gin and snacks, as you request.

We look forward to meeting you.

Kind regards,

CAPTAIN HOMARUS *& **the crew of Angel of the Seas***

THE CAPTAIN RESPONDS

10th September 2023
   Dear Ms Brown,
Thank you very much for your letter.

We will certainly ensure that there's a variety of snacks in the room, not just 'those daft peanuts in a tin'. We also take on board your point about leaving measly chocolate pieces on your pillow. If we wish to leave you chocolates, we will, as you suggest, leave you a whole box next to your bed and not in it.

We look forward to meeting you.

KIND REGARDS,

CAPTAIN HOMARUS & the crew of Angel of the Seas

THE ITINERARY

20-DAY MEDITERRANEAN CRUISE

Departure: **Southampton**
  First stop: **Lisbon**
  Second stop: **Gibraltar**
  Third stop: **Tunisia**
  Fourth stop: **Sardinia**
  Fifth stop: **Malta**
  Sixth stop: **Sicily**
  Seventh stop: **Naples**
  Eighth stop: **La Spezia**
  Ninth stop: **Toulon**
  Tenth stop: **Barcelona**
  Eleventh stop: **Valencia**
  Twelfth stop: **Southampton**

MEETING CAPTAIN HOMARUS

The first thing I did was tell mum: "You won't believe this," I said, breathless with excitement, "I'm going on a cruise."

There was an overly long pause while she put down the steaming iron and worked out how to reply.

"A cruise? What - like a big boat?" she offered.

"Yep," I said. "A very big boat. It's got restaurants, a pub, a tennis court and swimming pools on it."

"OK," she said, looking at the basket full of crumpled clothes, then at me.

"Will you be gone all day?"

"It's a 20-day cruise, mum. I'll be gone for most of the month. Dawn invited me. Remember Dawn? The girl I was at school with who's now a successful blogger."

"Yes - of course I remember Dawn. You went on safari with her and it all went pear-shaped."

"Yep - that's the one."

"You wrote a blog called Two Fat Ladies and ended up stuck up a tree in your knickers."

"Yep - that's the one."

"And my bridge club was round here when I opened the blog up to show them, and they were treated to the unusual sight of your bottom as you clambered out of a tree while half drunk. Marjorie's never forgotten it."

"Yes, yes. No need to go back over all that, mum. Well, Dawn's invited me on a cruise ship now, and there are no trees on cruise ships, nor are there baboons, so I'm confident that there won't be a repeat of the knicker-wearing nonsense. It's going to be free because I'm her guest for the trip, and she'll be blogging about it. Dawn gets to take someone with her every time. I've had letters from the captain confirming it. It's happening. There's a massive 'eat all you can' buffet and everything."

"It's called 'eat all you want', not 'eat all you can' - you make it sound like some sort of competition. And you'll need to watch yourself with those buffets. You don't want to put on any more weight. You'll come back 10 stone if you're not careful."

I didn't want to point out that I was over 14 stone, so to come back 10 stone would be a very marvellous thing indeed, probably involving some sort of gastric bypass surgery along the way.

"Do you want to know what countries I'm going to?"

"Go on then," she said, and I listed the glamorous locations where the luxury cruise ship would stop. I mentioned Sicily and Barcelona, and she ironed dad's pants while I told her about Gibraltar and the tantalising thought of Tunisia and Lisbon.

"Pass me those shirts," she said.

"Mum, are you listening to any of this?"

"Yes, dear. Pass the starch as well."

She seemed more concerned with getting creases out of y-fronts and starching shirts than hearing about the glamour of life on the ocean wave, so I gave up and went to put the kettle on.

Two days later, she called me in a state of near hysteria.

"I'm calling from Walker & Sons - the travel agents on Barnes Road."

"Right," I said. "Everything OK?"

"Yes, I'm here with your Aunty Susan. We've been looking at the brochures for cruises. Goodness me, Mary Brown. They are lovely."

"I know. They are, aren't they?"

I was in Marks and Spencer at the time, looking at bright red, plunging bikinis and trying to summon up the nerve to go and try one on.

"They have theatres and ballrooms and EVERYTHING," mum was saying.

"Yep," I said, holding the tiny bikini up against my large frame and trying to ignore the distasteful glances from the assistants.

"Well, you make sure you have a lovely time, won't you. I've never seen anything like this. A pub on a ship! Is that even legal?"

"I think so" I said, putting the bikini back on the rack and picking up a sober, structured swimming costume that might actually fit me.

"I'll tell you all about it when I return."

"OK, dear," said Mum. "Do be careful though, won't you? You know what you're like. You'll have too many cocktails, trip over your flip-flops and fall overboard or something."

"I promise I won't," I said. "I won't wear flip-flops if there's alcohol around."

"Good girl," said mum. "You have a good time."

"I will," I said, putting down the swimming costume and reaching for an outsized kaftan. "Love you lots, mum."

So, all goodbyes had been said, three weeks had been booked off work, and I'd packed a colossal amount of clothing into a massive suitcase. Ted, my lovely, long-suffering boyfriend, had agreed to take me down to Southampton Docks, so we went bouncing into the car park in his dilapidated old Mini Micra. The car's not really stable enough for two adults, let alone two obese ones. I'd taken to wearing a sports bra and clutching my breasts on long journeys because the damn thing bounced so much.

Ted drove round the car park, directed by a series of men in fluorescent vests until he was shown a parking place facing the harbour. "Look at that!" he gasped, pointing to the ship before us. "Wow it looks impressive."

My goodness, it did. It looked amazing. The sun beat down on the sparkling water, and in the middle of it all was this incredible ship:

Angel of the Seas...my home for the next three weeks. It was massive. MASSIVE. It demanded a full head turn to follow it from end to end. I don't know what I was expecting, but this was awesome.

I could hardly believe what was happening...it was a beautiful, warm, early summer's day, and I was going off on a Mediterranean cruise, and it was all free. Dawn had to be the best friend in the world. I mean - she was nuts and had been slightly uncomfortable company when we were on safari, but - a free cruise! I could put up with a bit of Dawn madness for that.

I clambered out of the car and felt excitement rush through me. This was just thrilling. I started to waddle off towards the ship at full speed until Ted stopped me.

"Haven't you forgotten something?" he said.

"Have I? My passport? Sun cream? Sun dresses?"

"No, a kiss. Where's my kiss goodbye?"

"Oh yes - sorry!" I said, rushing back, throwing myself into his arms, hugging him closely. "I'm going to miss you."

"Yes - I'm sure you will," said Ted sarcastically. "I'm sure you'd much rather be in the pub with me than exploring the delights of Tunisia and Lisbon."

"I'm not sure about that," I said. "But I wish you were coming with me."

"Me too," he said, stroking my hair tenderly. "I don't feel like we've spent any time together recently, what with you off on safari and me working so hard. Promise me we can see each other loads when you get back."

"I promise," I said. "And I'll text you and call you to let you know how it's all going."

"Make sure you do," said Ted. "I want to know everything."

"You will. I love you."

"I love you, too," said Ted, finally letting go of me and wishing me a bon voyage.

Bloody hell...it was all real - I was going on a cruise!

A HANDSOME CAPTAIN AND A MASSIVE BUFFET

*B*y the time I stepped onto the ship, I was already head over heels in love with cruising. It's all incredibly easy. You check in quickly and wander onboard, unencumbered by any of your bags delivered directly to your cabin. Easy. None of the faff that's usually associated with international travel. No angry customs officials or mind-bendingly long queues.

There weren't endless shops at the departure point either, which was a blessing. I can't be trusted around those airport shops. I have more orange lipstick, glittery highlighter and green eyeliner from those things than I could use in a lifetime. The stuff you buy when you're all excited and waiting to go on holiday is the sort of stuff you would never normally go anywhere near. I have makeup that would look perfect were I ever invited to perform in the Mardi Gras or join Abba circa 1978, but it is entirely unsuitable for my life as a checkout girl at a DIY and garden centre in Cobham.

Anyway - all I'm saying is that it was a small mercy that there were no shops to drive me wild, and it was lovely that it was so easy to board.

I stepped onto the ship to the sounds of a string quartet playing soothingly in the background. The captain was there to greet us, a strikingly handsome man with all the suave sophistication you'd expect of a man in his position.

"Good morning, Madam. Welcome to the Angel of the Seas. My name's Will Homarus," he said. "I'm your captain for this cruise."

"Good morning," I said back, curtseying slightly, which was highly embarrassing. Something about the uniform and the majesty of the ship made me behave as if I were meeting royalty.

Will was reassuringly good-looking. Big and manly, kind of swarthy, like he might be Greek or something. He certainly looked like he could save us all if things went pear-shaped.

"The boat's not going to sink is it? "I said because I habitually say ridiculous things to handsome men.

"No, you're quite safe," he said, smiling. I knew instantly that I would have to keep right away from this guy when I'd had a few glasses of wine or I'd be wrapping my legs round his neck and asking him to marry me.

"I'm Claire Oliver," said an attractive woman standing next to him. She was tall and painfully thin. I didn't want to talk to her. I was much happier talking to the Greek God with the hairy chest, but he'd turned away and greeted the next passengers: a rather dour-looking woman in a brown dress and an ancient man in a wheelchair.

"I'm the staff captain," she said. "Kind of like the deputy captain. We'll both be around the ship, so do talk to us if there's anything you need or if there are any problems."

"Yes, I will," I said, trying to catch the captain's eye, but he was crouched down, talking to the guy in the wheelchair, so I gave up and told Claire that 'yes, of course, I'll come and find one of you if I needed anything.'

I was very sure which one of them I'd be going to find, and it wasn't Claire.

A lovely young man called David showed me to my cabin, opening the door and leading me into a gorgeous room with two beds, a bathroom, and a joyous sea view. I rushed to the patio doors and flung them open.

"It's the sea," I said.

"It is," said David. "There's sea all around. Is it OK if I go now?"

"Of course," I said, slightly embarrassed that I sounded as if I didn't I understand how boats worked.

I texted Dawn when he closed the door behind him: "OMG. I've just walked into the cabin...it's bloody lovely...see you soon. M x"

Then I did what every self-respecting woman does in a situation like this: I opened the mini bar, pulled out a Toblerone and a mini bottle of gin and tonic and threw myself onto the bed to work out how the TV operated.

My God, the bed was soft...it was like lying in cotton wool. I snuggled into it and watched the video on the screen about life aboard the ship.

There was a beautician that looked amazing...like a proper New York spa. It even did Botox. I rolled over and peered into the mirror by the bed, holding my eyebrows up to see what I'd look like. Was that better? Or did I just look like a fat Chinese woman? It was hard to tell. Probably best not to take the risk, though. They did manicures and facials as well, which I definitely wanted to try.

Next, they showed the gym and fitness suite and the classes that took place every day. If I went to the gym every morning and did regular beauty treatments, I could go home from this cruise looking amazing, especially if I also had some sun on my skin. That would be great.

Then, the video moved to the buffets available for breakfast and lunch. My God! In an instant I knew that far from returning home having lost a few pounds, there was every chance I would return home 10 stone heavier. The meat. All the Chinese food. Ooooo...I just love Chinese food. And the puddings! Have you seen these buffets? Miles of tables groaning under the weight of all the food. On the video they showed a slim, young lady going to the buffet and helping herself to a light salad and a sliver of smoked salmon.

No woman can do that.

It's impossible to go to an eat-all-you-can buffet and return with a sensible plate of food. Whenever I'm confronted by them, I panic and end up with a plate of roast potatoes, chips, pasta, chicken in black bean sauce, cheese, prawn toast, fried egg and sprouts, or something...food that has no right to be sharing crockery.

The sight of all the food had made me a little peckish, so I finished my drink, slipped my shoes on and wandered out of the cabin. When I got outside, my case was sitting there with a little note on it, wishing me an excellent holiday. This was perfect...so easy and smooth. Three weeks of this and I'd return home totally relaxed and stress-free. Assuming, of course, that the rest of the holiday went as smoothly as this first day had.

I walked up to the buffet and saw Captain Homarus. He was putting a delicate collection of olives, little silver skin onions and some fancy cheese onto his plate. He must have been watching the girl on the video. I smiled at him and started placing items onto my plate in a similar fashion. As soon as he was out of sight, I'd start digging into the lasagne and make a serious dent in the chips.

"Do come and join me," he said, indicating the table by the window in the corner.

"That would be lovely," I said, thinking of the fried chicken and potato wedges I'd have to forsake. "I'll just get a drizzle of olive oil and I'll be right with you."

I walked the length of the buffet, picking at delicacies as I went; a spring roll went into my mouth, then a handful of chips. I grabbed a burger to eat while walking around. I bit into luscious beef while dropping two slivers of sun-dried tomato onto my plate. I don't know who I thought I was kidding. No sane person could believe that I ate in the way my plate indicated. I wouldn't be morbidly obese if my diet consisted of delicately flavoured olives and bits of tomato, would I?

Still, one had to keep up appearances. I took a glug of water to wash down the last of the burger, wiped my face, and headed to the corner table. But when I looked, he wasn't there. There were three people sitting there, chatting away.

Where was he? I have a terrible sense of direction and wandered up and down the buffet that ran the length of the boat. Now I didn't know where to go. Which corner was he in? There were so many nooks and crannies. I walked up and down. I asked the chefs whether they'd seen him, but they shook their heads, I asked a couple of fellow passengers, but - no - no one had seen him. I was completely lost. In the end I had to get them to put a message over the tannoy for him to come and find me. By the time he reached me, I'd been gone for 20 minutes. He'd eaten his cocktail onions and had been sitting there patiently, wondering where on earth I'd got to.

"Sorry," I said, exasperated. "I got lost."

"No problem at all," he said patiently. "Come and join me." He was on the other side of the boat entirely.

I stayed with Handsome Homarus until I'd finished my food, then he excused himself and went back to work. The minute he was out of sight I loaded my plate with every different Chinese food on the buffet, and then I ate the whole plateful quicker than anyone has ever eaten a plateful of food in their life before and practically rolled back to my cabin, feeling like I might explode. I lay on the bed, poured myself another gin and tonic, wished I hadn't eaten so much and downed the drink to make myself feel better. Then I read my messages. There was one from Ted, wishing me bon voyage, and one from Dawn.

"Hi darling," it said. "Can you call me urgently?"

I picked up my phone and glanced at the time. It was 4 pm. We were setting sail soon. Where the hell was she? I dialled her number, and there was a terrible noise when she answered it.

"Dawn, it's me," I said. "Dawn, can you hear me?"

The noise stopped. "Yes, sorry - I was just getting a blow dry. How are you?"

"I'm fine, but shouldn't you be - like - on the ship instead of in the hairdressers?"

"Oh darling, I'm so sorry - that's why I was ringing - I can't make it. Something's come up. Could you write the blog for me?"

"Whaaat?"

"It'll be fine," she said.

"Errr...no it won't, because I'm not a writer. I've never written anything longer than a Christmas card before."

"You can do it," she said. "Just send me text updates with what's going on, and I'll load them onto the blog. No one will be any the wiser."

"OK," I said, struggling to keep the concern out of my voice. "So, I literally just send you texts with what's going on, and that's all I need to do."

"Yep," she said. "Simple eh?"

"Yes, that does sound quite straightforward," I agreed.

"Oh, one other thing," she added. "Don't tell anyone that I'm not there. Just pretend I'm in the cabin if anyone asks. OK?"

"What? I can't spend 20 days telling everyone you're in the cabin."

"Tell them I've just left, or I'm in the hairdressers or having a lie-down, or getting my nails done. Use your imagination. It'll be fine. Have fun. Just don't tell anyone that I'm not on the boat though, please or I won't get any more free trips."

Christ.

MEETING THE GUESTS

As the ship prepared to move out of the harbour, we were all encouraged to go onto the deck for a setting sail party. This event involved glasses of fizz, excitement, singing and flag waving - all of which I approve of entirely, so I was there like a shot. It was also a chance to get to know the other shipmates, so I wandered around, introducing myself and sending texts to Dawn, updating her on what was going on and who I was meeting so she could write about it in the blog.

"Pictures!" she texted back. "Send pictures."

"No one mentioned that," I replied.

"We need pictures, and videos are VITAL. The blog will fall flat, and no one will read it, and neither of us will ever get any free holidays if you don't send me videos."

Great. Now I had to be Steven Spielberg as well as JK Rowling. So much for a free holiday.

I held my phone up and took a video of all the guests singing and waving their flags, and then I moved it around slightly to capture the sight of Captain Homarus bending over to tie up his shoes. I confess I lingered on that shot slightly longer than was necessary but panned back out to take in the whole boat before he saw. "Video attached," I wrote, texting it to Dawn.

"Hot, hot, hot!" she replied.

"Thank you."

"Not you. The dude in the tight, white trousers."

"He's called the captain."

"Wish I was there," she typed.

"Glad you're not. I have him all to myself," I typed back, texting it to her with a still from the video of his manly bottom.

The downside of chatting to people was being forced to explain to them about Dawn: "No, I'm not on my own. I'm with my friend, but she's in the cabin, feeling unwell."

"Oh dear," they all said before asking exactly what was wrong with her.

"Just illness, you know," I replied vaguely, looking at them with great seriousness so they didn't probe further. What I lacked in medical nous, I made up for with steely gazing.

I sent Dawn another video of the ship leaving Southampton harbour and of all the happy cruisers cheering, waving and singing Rule Britannia and Land of Hope and Glory, and then I went back to the cabin to get dressed for the evening.

Cruise ships have very strict sartorial guidelines, as Dawn had been at pains to point out to me. Even on the 'dress down' nights, women tend to wear cocktail dresses. On the black-tie evenings, it's full-on long dresses, sparkly handbags, mink stoles and long gloves. I have all of these things...in case you were wondering. I LOVE getting dressed up. My stoles aren't real mink, and my sparkly shoes and matching handbag don't have a diamond on them, but I look the part all the same.

For that first evening, I went for a long red dress designed for a woman with a far smaller bust than I have. I rammed my assets into it and looked in the mirror. "Oh no," I thought. "All you can see is blonde hair, a red dress and enormous breasts."

Then I stopped for a minute and thought, 'No - that's a good thing.

BERNICE BLOOM

I will be very popular tonight if all you can see is blonde hair, a red dress and enormous breasts.'

The positive thinking (coupled with the gin) gave me a real confidence boost, and I walked down to the gorgeous, art deco-style dining room swaying with delight and swinging my hair back. I stopped for a gin and tonic at the bar first, and then sauntered over to the table at which I'd been told I was dining.

It turned out it was the captain's table which meant I'd be having lunch and dinner with Handsome Captain Homarus. Not a bad start to the holiday.

I glanced at the floor-to-ceiling mirrors by the table. I seemed to have 'dropped' a little in the walk over. I shoved my hand down the front and hitched up my boobs so they sat better in the dress, giving me a more attractive cleavage. I did this just as Claire, the deputy captain, came over to say hello. The wide-eyed look and little gasp she gave made me realise that I'd released a little too much flesh to the world. I looked down. Yep - It looked like two small bald men were trying to peek out of the top of my dress. I smiled at Claire and pushed them down again...kneading them as if I were preparing dough for the oven.

"This is your seat here," she said, politely ignoring the rigorous adjustments I was making and pointing to a chair on the other side of the table from her.

I stood next to my seat as other guests drifted over to join us. There was a couple called Edith and Malcolm who looked like they were in their early 60s. They were the sort of people who were very helpful in life. Do you know the type I mean?

You find them on every committee in every borough in the country...real salt of the earth types. Probably members of the tennis club and the church organising committee - she does the flowers and organises the summer fete, and he plays golf on Fridays. Nice people. Like my Aunty Susan. Nice, but not necessarily the sort of people you'd choose to join for dinner.

Next to me was the man who'd followed me onto the boat earlier -

very, very old and frail and in a wheelchair. He smiled weakly and I bent down to introduce myself. He nodded like he couldn't hear me properly and said his name was Tank. An odd name, but quite nice for a little old man to be called something so powerful and evocative - I liked it.

Next to him sat the dour, plain-looking woman who'd pushed him onto the boat earlier. She had mousy hair which fell limply by her face, large, square glasses and was dressed in what looked like a uniform from the Brownies, or a nurse's outfit from years ago - like the sort of thing they wore on Call the Midwife. Her shoulders were massive - like an American Footballer's. Perhaps it was all that wheelchair pushing that did it?

"I'm Mary," I said, and she nodded without offering her name.

"How long have you known Tank?" I asked her.

"Tank?" she said.

"Yes, your friend," I indicated the man in the wheelchair. "His name's Frank," she said.

"Oh, sorry. I misheard." She looked at me as if I'd confessed to killing babies and chopping up kittens. Meanwhile, Frank smiled and nodded, not looking at me or anyone else. His red-rimmed eyes watered as he looked off into the distance. He was warm and friendly but not quite with it, somehow. Very different from the others at the table, most of whom seemed to have been invited because they were regular cruise-goers and knew the captain. They were raucous and lively and sharing jokes on the other side of the table. This side? Not so much. I looked at Frank while Frank looked down at his shaking hands.

"What made you come on a cruise, then?" I asked.

He smiled at me again, and the lady with the large shoulders and bad dress leaned over and fiddled with what I imagined to be his hearing aid.

"I can hear now," he said with a broad smile. "What were you saying, dear?"

"I just asked why you were on the cruise."

"Oh. You don't want to know," he said. "It's a very long story."

"Of course, I want to know," I said, but he just smiled at me and the lady next to him began feeding him. We fell silent as he chewed his food, and I began to eat mine. To be honest, I didn't much want to know. I was only being polite.

Once Frank had finished eating, the woman wiped his face gently. "Tell her your story, Frank," she said. "Tell her why we're on the cruise."

"I'm here because I'm off to Tunisia say a proper goodbye to two old friends...and then to Sicily to apologise to the family of the love of my life."

"Oh. Why do you have to say goodbye to your friends?" I asked.

"My friends died in the war. I fought beside them when they were gunned down on a rainy night. One guy died where he fell; the other died in a military hospital soon afterwards. I want to go back to where we lost them on that bleak hill on that bleak night and say goodbye properly, forever, before I die."

"Oh my God, that's so moving," I said, feeling tears in the backs of my eyes. "Moving and so sad."

"It was war," he said with a distant smile. "Sad things happened."

"And did you say something about the family of the woman you loved?"

"Yes, I need to make amends. I took her away from them in the dead of night. I need to go back and apologise, and hand them the letters from 70-odd years ago that were never sent. It's the right thing to do...I need to give them the letters."

"Come on, Frank," said the woman in the brown dress. "It's time for you to go to bed now."

"No, not yet," I said, now genuinely intrigued. "Can't he tell me the story first? Tell me about the letters...I don't understand."

"In time, my dear," said Frank with a lovely, big smile. "I'll tell you everything. It's a long cruise. No need to rush things."

"Oh, but - I have no patience at all. Please tell me now."

"He will tell you everything, but not now," said the woman in the horrible dress, pushing the wheelchair away.

"OK," I said reluctantly, turning my attention to the glass of wine in front of me and the captivating smile of Captain H, but I couldn't stop thinking about Frank. What letters? What apology? It was so intriguing. And imagine losing your best friends like that. It was beyond comprehension.

EN ROUTE TO LISBON

Oh God. Oh God. It was so bright. Where was I? What happened? My head felt like it was spontaneously combusting from within. My tongue was so dry it was like I'd spent the previous evening licking the carpets. I couldn't have done that...could I? It wasn't beyond the realm of possibility; I'd had worse nights.

The light in my cabin was on full blast, and the sun was streaming through the window. It was bright enough to perform brain surgery. I crawled across the bed and lashed out at the lamp and the main light switch. I was still too drunk to execute any subtle manoeuvres, but eventually, after much swatting, the lights went out, and I crashed across the bed and went to sleep. When I woke up, it was 10.30 am.

There was just half an hour left before the sumptuous breakfast buffet became the sumptuous lunchtime buffet. I needed to move.

Slowly I stumbled out of bed and dressed myself rather like a toddler, picking the first top I saw in the wardrobe (green) and the nearest trousers (pink) with complete disregard for how they would look together.

I wandered cautiously along the corridor and took the lift up to the main deck. Every step made my head hurt more. I needed coffee...and food, but then I always needed food. I stepped out of the lift and saw a man standing with his back to me but with his reflection clearly visible in the glass in front of him.

Oh, my f-ing God, it was Simon Collins. Simon Collins!

It was like being shot back in time.

I reversed into the lift and pressed the button to the lower floor, pushing it a thousand times, urging the doors to close, but they were too slow - Simon looked up and saw me in the mirror in front of him; his eyes widened, his eyebrows raised, and he spun round just as the door was closing.

"Mary?" he said, with incredulity sweeping through his voice. "Mary? Is that you? Mary Brown. In the pink trousers?"

If I was surprised to see Simon, then he was a million more times surprised to see me...for the simple fact that I'd told him I had six months to live four years ago. I know, it's appalling behaviour but I'm rubbish at finishing relationships and I just came out with it.

I'd told Simon I no longer wanted to see him, adding, "it's not you, it's me." And he'd said, 'No, it's not Mary - that's a stupid thing to say - it's me. It must be me. If there weren't something wrong with me, you'd want to carry on going out with me."

Dear readers, I panicked at this stage and said, 'Yes - it *is* me...I've got leprosy.'

"Leprosy," he'd said, jumping back, his little face awash with concern. "Blimey, that sounds serious."

My lies kicked off more lies, and before I knew where I was, I was explaining that I was going off to Fiji in search of a witch doctor. I know - it was bizarre. I don't know what made me say it. I was in a panic because I hate upsetting people. I suppose I thought I could get away with it because Simon lived in Birmingham, where he was working at the university, so there was no chance of us bumping into one another. He called a few times to check I was OK, but I'd begged him to get on with his own life and leave me to my fate.

Now, here he was, on the bloody ship with me, and there was no way of me escaping.

I stepped out of the lift on the cabin floor, went back to my room

BERNICE BLOOM

and texted Charlie, my lovely friend who'd been in on the whole witch doctor thing (if memory serves me right, she'd jumped around in the background, making 'witch doctor noises' one time when he'd called and I'd pretended to be on a Fijian island).

"You are joking. That is hysterical," she said, rather unsupportively. "God, I wish I was there to see this. His face must have been a picture!"

"Yep. He did look very shocked," I said. "How do I get out of this?"

"Tell him you got better. Insist that the witch doctor performed his magic and the illness disappeared."

"Yeah, I could," I said. "Or I could just avoid him."

"Yeah - well, if you can avoid him - do that, but I don't fancy your chances on a 20-day cruise."

"Yeah," I said. "I'll try to avoid him, and if I can't, I'll go for the witch doctor line."

"Perfect," said Charlie. "What could possibly go wrong?"

I couldn't risk going back up to breakfast, so I had to miss it and wait until lunchtime (exactly 20 minutes, so it didn't involve my internal organs collapsing due to lack of nutrition or anything, but it felt quite a long time for a girl who likes her food), then I went back up on deck when I knew that breakfast was over. I used the lifts on the other side of the ship instead of risking exiting at exactly the point where I'd seen Simon earlier. I don't know why I did that; it wasn't as if Simon would have stood in that position all day, but it seemed safer to avoid going where I knew he'd been. I strode out of the lift and over to the buffet, avoiding looking at everyone in the misguided belief that if I didn't see anyone, no one could see me. It's a tactic used by every toddler who's ever played hide and seek.

Once at the buffet, I started loading chicken wings and nuggets onto my plate, and then noodles and curry sauce followed. I figured I was allowed to go a little bit mad because I hadn't had any breakfast. Also, I'd been drinking the night before, and every right-thinking person knows that a little indulgence is a must the day after massive drinking has happened. It's practically the only way to make yourself feel better again.

I wandered over to sit down when I caught sight of Frank and his nurse (I assumed she was his nurse, based on her dress sense and bossy attitude, but to be honest, she hadn't even given me her name, let alone her occupation).

"Hello, do you mind if I join you?" I said, giving them both a big smile.

"Of course not," said Frank, beaming. His craggy face came alive when he smiled.

"I was just hearing about you," he said.

"Were you?"

"Yes, the captain told me you were performing *YMCA* last night and doing high kicks to *New York, New York*. You were quite the party animal by the sound of it."

"Oh God, no."

"The captain said your Elvis impression was one of the best he'd ever seen."

"Oh, hell. Tell me about your evening, Frank. Let's not dwell on mine anymore."

"Well, it was a bit quieter than yours by the sound of it. No doing the can-can round the boat for me."

"Right, good. Glad to hear it."

"I don't think she wants to be reminded about last night," said the lady in the brown dress. "We all drink too much occasionally; the last thing you need is for someone to remind you of all the details of it the next day."

"Fair enough," said Frank, with a nod of his head. "That's a good point."

I smiled appreciatively at her. "I'm so sorry, I don't even know your name," I said.

"It's Janette," she replied. "You can call me Jan."

"I will. Thanks," I said, then asked: "Are you Frank's nurse?"

"No, I'm not," she said. "Not really. I am a nurse, but I'm here as Frank's friend. He knew my grandfather well, and our families have become best friends."

More and more people were coming along to the buffet, and I was sure I could see Simon in the group. Either that, or I was being paranoid. Too many people were wearing navy blue T-shirts and shorts...it would be very hard to avoid him when I couldn't pick him out of the crowd.

I looked at Frank, who was looking down at a piece of paper in his hands.

"What's that?"

"Irene," he said, lifting up the paper. It was a picture of a beautiful woman with dark eyes and raven hair set in an old-fashioned curl around her shoulders. She had a huge smile like a movie star.

"She was the love of my life," he said.

"Is this the woman you mentioned last night? The one whose family you are going back to find and apologise to?"

"That's right," he said. "You have a good memory."

"You were going to tell me why you have to go back there, do you remember? You said you would tell me the whole story. "

"Of course, I remember. Maybe I should tell you this evening, you must have things you want to do now. "

"No, please tell me now," I said. I had nothing else to do, and the thought of wandering around the boat had lost its appeal since I'd seen bloody Simon Collins. Frank squinted in my direction and began to talk. His voice was very soft; it was hard to hear everything he said. I moved in closer to him.

"I'll have to take you right back to 1942 if I'm going to tell you the story properly," he said.

"Suits me," I said. "You can consider me firmly back in the 1940s."

"Well, I was 19 years old, living in a two up, two down in Portsmouth, when I was called up to go and fight in the war."

"God, how awful. "

"No, not at all – I was thrilled. Especially when I was told I'd be going to North Africa with a group of other new recruits. I'd be joining the Eighth Army in Tunisia. The guys over there were known as the "desert rats". I'd heard about them on the wireless. They seemed incredibly glamorous.

"I'd never been abroad, let alone to a different continent. And my family were so proud that I would fight for the country. No one else in the family had ever been to war. My father was injured, so he missed World War I and always hated himself for it. Until his dying day, he felt less of a man because he couldn't fight.

"None of it was his fault; he'd had had an industrial accident and had lost a foot. He also had limited use of his hand, so he couldn't go to war. But he still felt terrible. I grew up thinking that if you were a proper man, you went to war and fought for your country. That's why it mattered so much to get the call-up.

"I was super excited the day the papers came and determined to make my parents proud. I didn't know, when I kissed them goodbye and headed off to war, that I would never see either of them again."

"Oh no."

Frank took a huge breath. "Yes, they were both killed in the bombings."

"Come on, Frank," said Janette. "Time to go now..."

"Noooo.... Stay and tell me what happened. Please, Frank, carry on. You've hardly started." "Later," he said as Janette started to push him away. "We have plenty of time, Mary Brown. Lots of time for story-telling."

FIRST STOP - LISBON

There was something both frightening and exciting about coming in to dock for the first time. We'd all become so friendly on board that it seemed odd that we would be mingling with other people who weren't part of our on-board community. It was also exciting...we'd been cooped up for a few days - it was time to see the world. A frisson of excitement filtered through the group as we all queued up like children on a school trip at the edge of the boat, looking out into the foreign port.

For me, it was a time of particularly mixed emotions because while it was great fun to be coming into port, I also reasoned that this was a time I was most likely to bump into Simon. That's why I had dressed incognito with a chiffon scarf over my head, entirely covering my hair and large sunglasses.

"You look like that actress...what's her name?" said one of the guys. "You know - the blonde one?"

"Grace Kelly?" I said. That was certainly the look I'd been going for.

"No, no - Rebel Wilson," he said. "You look very like her."

"Thanks," I said. "I was hoping I was channelling Grace Kelly."

"Nope. Rebel Wilson before she lost all that weight. That's who you remind me of.."

As people stood, looking across the sparkling waters into the harbour, there was murmuring and chattering about the day ahead and what joys it might hold. People were making plans for what to do. I had no plans at all. I just wanted to see as much of the city as possible and post some interesting items on the blog so that Dawn would think I was a perfectly acceptable stand-in should she ever find herself unable to make a luxury holiday.

It was odd to be facing the day in a strange city by myself, but I'd read about the extraordinary number of ice cream parlours, so I thought I'd probably be OK. One of the places was called Gelato Therapy, which seemed to be the best kind of therapy you could ever hope for.

We left the ship with strict instructions to be back by 5 pm, having been told colourful stories of people who'd missed the ship in the past and ended up having to take flights to the next port. Their woeful antics seemed so frowned upon that we all swore we wouldn't be one of those people who broke the rules. We were advised to take passports and any essential medications with us, though...just in case.

I left the ship and bid a fond farewell to handsome Captain Homarus, walking into the searing Portuguese sunshine with a huge smile on my face. It was surreal to be abroad when all I'd done was get on in Southampton, eaten a vast amount, drunk gallons and had a nice time, and now - ta-dah! – I was in a foreign place.

I walked off the ship with everyone else, clutching my map of Lisbon, and found my way to the narrow little streets leading up to the main road. It was very pretty: a cascade of houses rose up from the sea towards the castle at the top of the hill. From the beautiful blue waters of the harbour to the white houses with their caramel-coloured roofs all stacked higgledy-piggledy, interspersed with lovely cafes, bars and rooftop restaurants, it was beautiful. Lisbon has the sort of buzz that you always get in cities, but with the added loveliness of being by the sea. How many capital cities are by the sea? Not many, I bet.

BERNICE BLOOM

I walked up to a café sprawled across a rooftop and took a seat, looking down on our ship, sitting there majestically in the harbour. I watched the line of passengers snaking up the side of the hill. The café was so pretty that lots of the cruise passengers decided to come in, and it was starting to feel a little like being back on the boat, I kept thinking that Simon would walk in, so I turned quickly to the leaflet that the events co-ordinator had handed out, showing all the things that were happening in Lisbon, and decided it was time to make a plan. It seemed that the best way to see the place was either in a -Tuk-Tuk or by doing a circle of the city on a tram. I'm self-aware enough to know that if I got onto a Tuk-Tuk, I'd break it, so I decided that the tram was the most sensible option.

I grabbed my bag and headed off for the tram stop. According to the literature, there was one due in around 5 minutes.

Once it appeared, I clambered on board, took a seat by the window, and enjoyed the view as the tram snaked its way through the harbour streets, bouncing around on the rough, uneven roads and squeezing between large trucks that had no place to be out on these tiny, narrow lanes.

The tram turned up a hill dotted with houses in a range of chalky pastel colours.

"Well, this is nice," I said, muttering the words out loud by mistake.

"It nice is yes," said a guy behind me. I swung round and found myself looking straight into deep brown eyes.

"Are you Portuguese?" I asked.

"Yes, I live Lisbon all life."

"All life?" I replied. " Oh, you Lisbon long time live."

I do no know why I thought mimicking his Pidgin English would somehow make me easier to understand, but I did it all the same.

"You are film star, yes?" he said.

I smiled at him warmly. "Thank you. No, I work in a gardening centre in Cobham."

"I have not seen this film," he said. "I will go."

"No, I work in a garden centre in Cobham. That's what I do."

"Yes, I always want to meet film star. I will watch all your film. What your name is?"

Now, come on, you must accept that I tried to correct him. I tried to make him understand that I wasn't an international celebrity. I told him twice that I worked in a garden centre, but he didn't understand me. Hell, I was miles away from home… one would know.

"My name is Rebel Wilson," I said.

"Well, I am Ernesto. It is nice to meet you Rachel."

"No - Rebel. My name is Rebel," I said, and then I went back to looking out at the views, examining a large black and white painting of a woman's face on the side of a building. Suddenly, I felt my new friend by my side.

"I sorry, can I get picture with you, Rebel?"

"Of course," I said, adjusting my head scarf and posing next to him for a selfie.

"I will show you castle?" he said. "We get off here and I show you castle."

"No thank you," I said. "I'm going to stay on the tram." "Yes, I show you castle," he said again. I seemed to have acquired a tour guide, but I wasn't really in the mood for old buildings; I wanted to hit the shops.

"I have to be back on my ship at 5 pm," I told him. "So I have no time to see the castle."

"You have a ship! A film star ship."

"Um, well, not really mine. It's the big ship in the harbour. Lots of people are on it…not just me."

"OK," he replied as the tram stopped at the castle. "I go now." He stood up and began backing away from me, bowing slightly and holding his hands in prayer.

"I've just convinced a Portuguese guy that I'm a famous film star," I texted to Charlie.

"Was he blind?" she texted back. I need new friends.

After a few hours strolling through the streets, buying a new handbag and some candles and trying and failing to fit into a cream linen dress, I walked down the hill back towards the ship, loving the feeling of the sun on my skin as I walked.

The sight of the gorgeous white houses with their caramel-coloured roofs hit me again, and the beautiful blasts of pink flowers all set against the bright blue of the sea. I felt quite excited that I would be seeing Frank again. I hoped he'd been OK on the ship without us all. He'd said he was too exhausted to get off and would stay and make the most of having the whole place to go swimming and relax.

As I walked to the ship, I saw dozens of people lining up waiting by the passenger entrance. Why couldn't they get on, was something wrong?

Then there was a shout.

"There she is!"

I looked up and saw Ernesto, running towards me followed by cheering crowds of people.

"Rebel, Rebel, Rebel," they shouted excitedly. "We love you, Rebel Wilson."

There were cheers and screams and begs for autographs and selfies. I looked up at the ship and saw passengers on board, looking down, wondering what was going on.

I felt my cheeks scorch scarlet as Claire came towards me. "Everything OK, Mary?" she asked.

"This Rebel Wilson - famous American film star," said Ernesto.

I looked from him to Claire and back again, unsure what to say.

"Well, Rebel has to come on board now," said Claire.

"I will go see new film," shouted Ernesto.

"We all go see Garden Centre in Cobham," said another voice.

"Good luck," they cried as I followed the incredulous Claire onto the ship.

"Well that sounds like it was an adventurous day," she said. "I hope you had a lovely time in Lisbon and weren't hassled by all your fans too much."

"A lovely day," I replied.

"I'm glad," she said.

And though every fibre of her being must have been dying to ask what on earth was going on, professionalism won the day, and she wished me a good evening and a pleasant dinner and strode off across the ship, the chants from my new fan club, and cries of 'we love Rebel' still audible as she went.

EN ROUTE TO GIBRALTAR

"Hey Frank, Frank," I said as I saw my nonagenarian friend after dinner that evening. I raced up to him at such speed that Janette looked genuinely frightened. If Frank could have seen further than the end of his nose, I suspect he would have looked frightened too. As it was, he just sat straight-backed, staring into the distance as I ran towards him.

"Hello," I said warmly. "It's me - Mary."

Ah, Mary. I heard all about your intriguing day over dinner. Didn't you convince half of Portugal that you were a famous film star?"

"Yes, something like that," I said.

"I don't think it was Mary's fault," said Janette kindly. "I was speaking to the captain earlier. A load of people just decided that she looked like a film star and began running around after her. Not her fault at all."

"Ahhh. Look, don't tell anyone else, but it was my fault. The truth is that I told a guy on the tram that I was Rebel Wilson. God knows why...I regretted it as soon as I'd said it. I certainly didn't expect them to chase around after me and ask for autographs, but it was all my fault. I feel like such an idiot. I'm always doing things like that, Frank. Always getting myself into a complete state."

I looked over at Frank, and he smiled broadly, his shoulders shaking slightly as he laughed.

"Always a joy to meet someone who doesn't take life too seriously," he said. "Your generation can be so serious about the most trivial of things. I've never understood why. Go tell 'em you're Rebel, whatever her name is, if you want to. Tell them you're the Queen of Sheba if you want. Life's supposed to be full of surprises, Mary Brown. Don't let anyone tell you otherwise."

"Yes," I said with a smile. "And when the psychiatric nurses come to take me away, I shall say that it is all your fault."

"Of course," said Frank. "Just blame me. I'm too old to go to jail."

"Can you carry on the story you were telling me earlier? You know...about you going off to war."

Frank laughed to himself. "Are you sure? You don't want to spend half your time talking to an elderly man."

"I'm fascinated. Please tell me everything. PLEASE."

"OK," said Frank, smiling and shaking his head. "I can't remember where we got to. Did I tell you about Jim and Tom?"

"No. Who were they?"

"OK. Let me take you back to November 1942," he said, his voice soothing and calm. "Close your eyes for a minute and think about it. I was just a teenager, and I'd received my call-up, and within a few days, I was on a military flight to Tunisia. In my newly acquired uniform, I sat there surrounded by complete strangers. I couldn't believe what was happening. Before that, I'd worked on the fish market. I'd never been out of the county."

I adjusted myself in my seat, taking a gulp of gin and tonic and resting my feet on the small, glass coffee table in front of me. I closed my eyes.

"OK, I'm there," I said. "I'm on the plane with you."

"Most of the men on the flight with me were older," he continued. "They had been serving for a couple of years and were being redeployed. I felt like the only one going into combat for the first time. I was so much younger and much more inexperienced than the others. It was like they had known a world that I knew nothing of.

"Then I got chatting to two guys, they were called Tom and Jim. Great guys. Like me, they were off to war for the first time. They were a bit older, but not much. Tom was from Birmingham, and Jim was from Slough. Very funny and entertaining on the journey out there they were. Full of mischief. I guess it was what you'd call gallows humour...all of us trying to cope with what might lie ahead, but it was humour all the same. We quickly became close friends."

Frank stopped to take a sip of his drink, which had been poured into a plastic beaker to make it easier. He lifted the bright blue cup with his shaking hand, and Janette rushed to help.

"We all arrived safely, and I remember walking out into the furnace. I'd never felt heat like it before...this burning, intense heat that seemed to blast itself into us. Then, we were taken for a briefing session before being handed weapons and equipment. I'd had a few basic training sessions in England before leaving, but I didn't know what I was doing. When I look back now...I was just a kid. I knew nothing. Nothing at all.

"I remember one time, after we'd been on the move for a while without seeing anything, we were walking across the sand and saw a plane overhead. Jim thought it was a German bomber, so we all jumped into a ditch nearby. We didn't realise that the ditch was full of stagnant water. Nor did we realise that it was a US plane, so there was no need to have hidden at all. We looked up, and all the other soldiers were standing, looking down at us. They had more experience; they knew a US plane from a German bomber. We stank after that for days and days because it was hard to wash. God, we stank.

"I remember the first people we came across were Arabs sitting on their camels and making their wives walk by their sides. Tom made the Arabs get off and put the women on the camels! He was a big lad, Tom, you wouldn't argue with him.

"The Arabs were nice guys. We got to know them fairly well before we got into serious combat. We learned to respect the local culture. We struck up friendships with the Bedouin. They were the salt of the earth. They were generous and polite to a fault.

"When we were in camp, though, I felt useless. I was good for

THE MARY BROWN BOOKS

carrying and fetching things, but Tom was a carpenter, and Jim was a chef, so they had proper skills. At one point, Tom created this latrine for us that was a work of art. It was 100m from the main tent lines and faced toward the Atlas Mountains. The only trouble was - the loo got used a lot by a lot of blokes and one day, the main supporting beam gave way with a mighty crack, there was a loud howl, and Jenkins rushed out with his trousers round his ankles. The whole thing had broken. We were back to using holes in the ground after that, but it had been nice while it lasted.

"Me, Tom and Jim laughed all the time, and we went everywhere together, like brothers we were. That was before the fighting started. Do you have any relatives who fought in the war, Mary?"

"No," I said. "No, I haven't."

"Good. I'm glad. War is terrifying. Worse than you can possibly imagine. Don't let anyone tell you otherwise. Don't let puffed-up army generals convince you that war is good for anything, don't let politicians who want to make a name for themselves incite conflict. No one who fought on the western front or went through what we went through can look at their medals without weeping. War is messy and solves nothing. Nothing."

There was a pause, and I wasn't quite sure what to say. I desperately wanted him to carry on with his story, but I didn't feel it was appropriate to hurry him when it was so difficult for him to talk about it.

"Lots of the guys perished; one was right next to me when a bomb blew him to pieces in a second. I saw him explode. Can you imagine what that's like? The noise from the shells and bombs was deafening. Most nights were lit up with gunfire. We were dive-bombed and machine-gunned by Stukhas, 13 of our lads killed, ten wounded.

"Jim, Tom and I stayed tight as anything through all this. We'd seen so many people die and been forced to grow up so fast. It helped that we looked out for one another. Then one day we walked to the hills of Tunisia. It was a hellish journey. We joked about there being pretty girls at the top and flagons of ale for everyone.

"Our mission was to capture Longstop Hill. If we succeeded, it

BERNICE BLOOM

would open up the road to Tunis. We trudged up the slopes of the hill in blinding rain. All you could hear was "slop ... slop" as each foot was lifted from the mud. There was so much noise from bullets; it was dark, and the sheeting rain made it impossible to see anything. You'd hear cries as your colleagues were hit. Many of the wounded sank into the mud and died. The rain and wind muffled the cries of the dying. We got to the top, and there was no sign of Jim or Tom. I ran around screaming for them, crying their names, but it was no good.

"Then two lads appeared carrying Jim; he was badly injured. He'd tried to save Tom, but it was no good. Tom had been hit and collapsed into the mud and died. We got Jim to an MDS - a Medical Dressing Station – but it was too late. He clung on for a few hours, then died. He looked me in the eye and said goodbye."

"Oh no," I said. "Oh God - this is awful. You lost two friends on the same night?"

"I did, dear," he said, his voice croaking with pain. "And Jim turned to me as life slipped away from him and said. 'Look after my wife for me, won't you, Frank? Keep an eye on her. Will you? Please say you will.'"

"Of course, I will," I said. "Jim, I promise you." Then his eyes closed, and he died.

"Frank, I can't imagine what it must have been like to lose a friend like that. When I think of my friends and how much they mean to me...it's heart-breaking."

"It was very difficult," he said, staring off into space into an imaginary place that he seemed to escape to so frequently. "I need to go back to see where I lost them...one last time and to say goodbye properly. Janette will be there with me. It'll mean so much to both of us."

"I suppose you want to go because you've heard all the incredible stores over the years," I said to Janette.

"Yes, and because Jim was my grandfather," she said.

"Oh my God! That's so lovely," I said. "How did you two end up meeting?"

"I kept my promise to Jim. I went and ensured his wife was OK, and I got to know his family and helped look after them."

"Oh, how wonderful," I said, settling into my seat and curling my feet beneath me. "Tell me more."

"Frank's tired now," said Janette, protectively.

"I promise I'll tell you more tomorrow," said Frank as Janette stood up and prepared to push him away. "I haven't told you about Irene yet. We'll do that story tomorrow."

"Yes, please," I said, shouting after him. "Please tell me all about it tomorrow."

SECOND STOP - GIBRALTAR

Cruising has messed with my internal clock. I went to bed early last night and was up early this morning - most unlike me. As the sun rose, I was to be found standing on deck in a large sunhat and dark glasses to watch as we travelled down the south coast of Spain towards the Straits of Gibraltar. It was quite chilly that time of the morning and not at all bright, so the sunhat and glasses were entirely unneeded, but I felt they offered me an appropriate disguise should Simon saunter on deck. I was astonished that I hadn't bumped into him but quite sure that a meeting was inevitable, and I had to always be on my guard.

I WAS STANDING NEXT to a guy called Malcolm as the ship sailed along. He'd been on my table on the first night, a wiry man with a warm, friendly face. He had been talking mainly about politics, so I hadn't engaged much with him. I don't know much about politics, only that Winston Churchill was a large man who smoked large cigars, Donald Trump was a giant, orange loon-bucket, and that having a strong view about Margaret Thatcher is compulsory. You must love her and think she was the greatest Prime Minister ever, or you must loathe her so much that you can't bear to hear her name.

"One of Britain's last remaining colonies," said Malcolm as we drifted along. I tried to look interested in his words, but it was hard. "British colonies," he said, shaking his head. I shook mine too because I didn't know what to do.

"How is your friend?" he asked. "Still not well enough to leave the cabin?"

"No, she's going to stay in there for a little bit longer...until she feels stronger."

"Goodness," he said. "How awful for her - missing all of this."

"Yes, absolutely," I said. "I've been telling her all about it." "Very good. Lots of pictures for her to see?"

"Yes, that's right," I said.

"Would you like to join my wife and me today as we look around?"

How do you answer a question like that? I did not want to spend the day with him or his wife – a wide-eyed woman with mad frizzy hair and the look of a woodland animal that had just emerged blinking into the sunlight.

The only thing I'd really learned about the two of them was that they loved talking politics, were frantic about cleanliness, and spent their whole time wiping down surfaces. I just didn't think we'd get on at all.

"I'd love to," I said warmly. "Thank you very much for asking."

Then I stomped back to my cabin to get my things, feeling very cross for not being able to think up a reason on the spot why I couldn't go with them. I ate a packet of crisps and an odd-looking chocolate bar that I thought was a Twix, but when I bit into it, I realised it wasn't (it was runny caramel with bits of nougat and raisins in it, but I ate it anyway). Then I felt doubly annoyed with myself - first for getting pushed into spending the day with the woodland creatures, then for eating all the snacks in the fridge after enjoying a massive buffet breakfast. If I carried on eating like this, the damn ship would sink beneath my weight.

It was quite an easy walk into town from the port, even for a hugely overweight woman in white Capri pants that were at least two sizes too small (I had bought the size 16s convinced, I mean CONVINCED, that I would lose weight and fit into them but here we were a year later and they were no more able to fit me than they were able to fly to the moon).

We walked along, passing a small statue in the middle of a roundabout which gleamed in the morning sunshine as if it were made of fire. It was quite breathtaking.

"Would you mind taking a picture of me?" I asked, reaching out to give my phone to Mary. "It's very straightforward - just an iPhone...you press there."

But Edith looked very embarrassed. "I'm sorry, we don't do that," she said. "Germs."

"Don't do what?"

"Touch other people's phones."

"Right, OK," I said, walking over to the statue and preparing to take a selfie. "I'll do it myself. I'm fine with my germs."

This day was going as well as I thought it would.

"Don't take offence," she said. "Nothing personal."

But it was hard not to take it personally when someone point blank refused to touch something that belonged to you in case you infected them.

Once I'd got my selfie, we walked across the square to Main Street, where there were lots of bars and restaurants.

"Shall we stop for a coffee and work out what to do next?" I said, but I knew what the answer would be.

"A lot of these cafes are quite dirty," said Edith. "And the coffee on the ship is free; let's wait until we get back before we have coffee."

I tried to be understanding, but this was bonkers.

"I might just get one to take away," I said, more to assert myself than because of any overwhelming desire for coffee. It was very much the Malcolm and Edith show, with me just tagging along behind. It was all making me feel very uncomfortable. I would get coffee whether they approved or not.

"Right, where shall we go next?" I said, leaning on the side of the coffee shop and sipping a ridiculously strong, piping hot coffee I didn't want. It was so incredibly hot already. The last thing I needed was coffee with the consistency of gravy. Also, my white trousers were killing me. I'd undone the button to breathe, but they still hurt. Edith wore tennis shorts and a Fred Perry t-shirt with a sun visor. Her legs were the colour of mashed potato; she looked like she'd never been exposed to the sun before, but she looked fresh and comfortable. I found myself wishing I was dressed like her, and I bet no one had ever wished that before.

Edith produced a map and a tourist information leaflet about Gibraltar.

"Right, here we go," she said. "Gibraltar has a population of around 30,000 and is a tiny 2.6 square miles so it's easy to walk around."

I wanted to point out that nowhere was easy to walk around in these trousers, but that seemed churlish. I looked down at the map, at where Edith had her finger pushed into our current location...

"We thought we'd just head up the Rock of Gibraltar, walk around and see the wild monkeys," said Edith. "I've brought some food from the buffet for a picnic lunch. I'm not sure we'll have time to do much else before we're due back on the ship."

I longed to come up with an alternative suggestion, just to be awkward - this is what having too-tight trousers does to a woman. But I couldn't think of a better plan, so I acquiesced.

"Yes," I said, following behind them, feeling like an angry teenager. I wished I hadn't worn the white trousers, wished it wasn't so hot, and wished I hadn't eaten so much at breakfast.

Despite all my reservations, Gibraltar was really good fun in the end. Edith and Malcolm were nice people. Their obsession with cleanliness was bordering on insanity, but I learned to see the funny side and mocked them gently as they wiped everything down and spritzed their hands constantly.

Most importantly, I saw the monkeys - the best bit by far. They were everywhere...everywhere - scampering around the place, not like the big baboons I'd encountered on safari, which had left me terrified and climbing a tree to escape - these were friendly, perky little things.

I loved them. I loved them so much that I didn't want to leave them, so I stayed and had a picnic lunch instead of heading for a restaurant as I'd planned to. While we dined on bread, cheese, crisps and dips, I told them all about Frank.

"What an incredible story. I have to say we've enjoyed spending the day with you," said Edith, as she attempted to pack away the remains of the picnic while I tried to eat it from out of her hands as she did so.

"Thank you for having me," I said, trying to take a handful of crisps from the bowl as she put them into a carrier bag for disposal. "It's been nice to get to know you."

"Right, enough of this, back to the ship," said Malcolm, standing up and offering me his hand. If I took the hand to help me up, I would pull Malcolm down on top of me, so I was forced to pretend I hadn't seen it, then roll onto my side and clamber to my feet.

"Let's go," I said, charging towards our floating hotel.

CAPTURED BY THE GERMANS

"Hello sir, what a pleasure," I said to Frank as I took my seat next to him at dinner that evening. I'd explained to the captain that Dawn had a terrible migraine, so she would stay in the room. He'd offered to send someone in to check on her, but - as usual - I reassured him that she just needed to rest and that she would be much better off if we all left her alone.

"Such a shame that your friend is unwell," said Frank.

"If I tell you a secret, will you promise to carry on with your story over dinner," I whispered.

"Oh, how intriguing," he replied. "Of course."

"Well, Dawn's not actually with me on the ship, but she doesn't want me to tell people that she's not here, so I'm kind of just saying that she's ill all the time. It's bloody nuts."

"Ha, ha," said Frank, with a smile. "Lots of very 'nuts things' seem to happen around you. I like it!"

"All well," said voices behind me. It was Malcolm and Edith. "I hope you don't mind us intruding, but Edith wanted to meet Frank," said Malcolm. "We loved your story about him earlier."

I made the introductions and explained to Frank that I'd been telling them about him.

"Frank's about to carry on with his story, aren't you, Frank?"

"May we stay and listen?" asked Malcolm and Edith in unison, sitting at our table. "Is that OK?"

"Of course," said Frank. "If you want, but I'm sure there must be other things you want to discuss."

"No, no. We want to hear about the war," I said, and then I turned to Malcolm and Edith: "So - just to recap - he lost his two great friends - Tom and Jim - in Tunisia while trying to capture Longstop Hill. Now - what happened next?"

"My, my, you've been listening," said Frank. "That's cheering for an old man to hear."

"Of course, I've been listening," I said. "It's amazing."

"Well, I suppose I'd better carry on then, hadn't I? OK, we managed to capture the hill position, and the British army marched into Tunisia...it was a very special, very important victory, but I was numb. I felt that nothing in my life would ever be the same again, and in many ways, I was right...it wasn't.

"Everything felt flat and colourless after that. Nothing had quite the same meaning for those days, weeks and months after I lost my friends.

"The battalion headed for Sicily after Tunisia, and I went with them, feeling weary and worldlier than I should have been at that tender age. The seventh and eighth Army combined forces and headed through Sicily towards Corleone. Joining two battalions meant we weren't being properly led - officers vied for position, and the whole thing was a bit of a shambles. The lack of proper leadership came to a head one day when we came up to a river, and no one really knew what they were doing. While we were waiting to cross it, some of us were captured by the Germans."

"Oh no," I said. "After you'd been through so much."

"Well, yes, and I just didn't care anymore because I had been through so much. We were rounded up and put into an army vehicle, and all I could do was to hope that my death would not be too painful. Nothing mattered, nothing at all. Then one of the lads nudged me.

THE MARY BROWN BOOKS

"Follow me," he said. He'd seen a gap we could escape through so we all filed out.

"But as we were escaping, the Germans saw us, and it was mayhem - we all ran off in different directions. I ran down an alleyway and straight into a Sicilian man standing by his car at the front of a small, white cottage. I looked at him, desperation sweeping through my eyes, as German voices filled the streets behind us. He hid me behind his small garden wall and stood over me; that man was Antonio Catania - he saved my life.

"The Germans took a cursory look, but when they found no one there, they gave up and left. I told Antonio I would never be able to thank him enough, and then he invited me back to his house.

"Come, have food," he said. "My daughter will tend to your injuries."

"I looked down to see I was bleeding all down my arm. I had no idea what or how I'd done it.

Once we got into his house, he called for his daughter. I stood in the hallway, desperate not to drip blood on the polished wooden floors when I heard footsteps on the stairs. I looked up and saw her...the most beautiful woman I'd ever seen. Irene. She looked like a movie star. Like Sophia Lauren. Have you heard of her?"

"No," I said. The name wasn't even familiar.

"Look her up," said Frank. "A beautiful Italian actress who was the spitting image of my Irene.

"I stopped in my tracks when I saw her and wiped my dirty hand against my trousers before shaking hers. She had these tiny hands, so soft and delicate. "Hello, I'm Irene Cantania," she said in her lovely Italian accent. For the first time since I'd lost Jim and Tom, I actually felt something. Like life wasn't pointless after all. Like there was someone here who moved me, who mattered to me."

"Oh, that's lovely," I said. "Really lovely."

"Beautiful," chorused Malcolm and Edith.

"It was," said Frank. "It was very lovely and very beautiful, but it was also quite complicated because she had a brother - Alberto - who'd fought with the Germans against us Brits, and although Italy had changed sides and were fighting with us against the Germans by the time I got there, it was tough."

"What do you mean - Italy changed sides - is that true, or are you joking?"

"No, that's true. Didn't you know that?"

"Er...no," I said.

"They changed sides just months before I arrived at the house. It was very difficult. Her brother had fought against us and had lost good friends to Allied guns. British soldiers had killed people in Alberto's battalion. How was he supposed to welcome me into his home?

"Hostility and anger were bubbling away, and real resentment towards me from him and his friends. I wouldn't have stayed more than one night because it was awkward, and I knew I shouldn't be there...I should be back with my guys, but I was quite badly injured, so I stayed longer.

"And I wasn't in any rush to leave because I had fallen hopelessly in love with Irene, and I knew that Marco Vellus, a local boy, wanted to marry her. I was determined that before I left, I would make her mine. Marco was a friend of her brother's...the whole family assumed they would get married.

"It was very difficult. But all I cared about was that in the middle of it all was me and Irene - two people who fell for one another despite all the difficulties. We couldn't help ourselves.

"We got on so well. It wasn't like it is now - we didn't jump into bed together or do anything other than sit and chat, but it was enough for me to know that she was the woman I wanted to marry.

"Irene was tending to me daily - my left arm had slivers of shrapnel in it that are still there today, and I had badly cut my face, arm and leg. Her father was as kind as he could be, but he knew my presence was tearing his family apart. He told me that I needed to leave. I nodded, thanked him for everything he had done, shook his hand and told him I would leave that night.

"I left, under the cover of darkness, heading towards Salerno where my battalion was based. I swore to Irene that I would be back soon, and we would marry, and I would give her the life she deserved. She cried when I left and begged me to come back soon.

"When I left that night, I felt like I had something to fight for, something that was worth staying alive for. I headed for Salerno to rejoin my battalion, feeling like a different person from the one who'd left Tunisia weeks earlier. I'd been devastated by the death of my two friends and was feeling helpless and hopeless. Now, I felt desperately sad about losing my friends, but in their name and for Irene, I would fight on. There was so much that I wanted to live for. For the first time in my young life, I was in love."

LIFE IN A POW CAMP

"Can I interrupt," said Captain Homarus, leaning over to check that my glass was full of wine. "You do know you have a fan on the boat, don't you?"

"A fan?" I said, scrunching up my face in disbelief.

"Yes. A guy called Simon," he said you used to go out together and you became very ill and moved away. He hasn't seen you for ten years, and now you're back, looking lovelier than ever."

"Oh God, no. To be honest, I've kind of been trying to avoid him."

"Oh," said the captain, tapping the side of his nose. "I'll tell him I haven't seen you then."

"Thank you," I said. "That's really kind of you. The relationship ended because we weren't suited."

"And because you were seriously ill, according to him."

"Yes, sort of."

"Who's that?" asked Frank.

"Oh, there's this guy on the ship I went out with years and years ago. It's so embarrassing; he's turned up on the ship and keeps trying to talk to me."

Then I whispered: "To be honest, we used to go out together, and I

THE MARY BROWN BOOKS

wanted to get rid of him. I told him I had leprosy; isn't that awful? Now he's wondering how on earth I recovered so well."

Frank roared with laughter while the others looked on, startled by the strange noise he'd just made.

"I'm trying to avoid him, but I'm bound to bump into him at some stage."

Frank smiled at me while I spoke. "I'm sure you'll be able to talk your way out of it," he said.

"I'm not so sure," I said. "But enough about me and my stupid mouth. Tell me about you. What happened next?"

"Well, the story takes a bit of a sad turn," said Frank.

"No," we all chorused. I'd forgotten that Edith and Malcolm were still sitting there. They were leaning in, with their elbows on the table and their faces in their hands, like little children listening to bedtime stories.

"Blimey - really? It gets sadder? This is already the saddest story I've ever heard."

"I never made it back to my battalion," said Frank. "I was captured again before I reached them. If I had got there, I would have seen there was a letter for me saying that both my parents had been killed. Their lives were taken from them in a moment when a bomb dropped on Portsmouth and destroyed our house."

"Oh no, I'm so sorry."

"I wasn't the only one who this happened to...when you go away to war, you assume you're the one in danger, but there was as much danger for those left behind, and many soldiers returned home, thinking the worst of the war was behind them, only to discover that family back home hadn't been as lucky.

"Anyway, as I said, I didn't know about this at the time because before I could make it to Salerno, I was captured again, but this time there was no escape - and I was sent to Poland to a Prisoner of War camp called Stalag 8a."

"Oh no, how awful. Why Poland? Were they on the German side?"

"No, far from it - the Germans had occupied them. The Nazis controlled the country at the time, so took prisoners of war there."

I'd read about POW camps at school. I remembered that they sounded like hell on earth.

"What's got everyone so animated," said Captain Homarus, pulling up a chair next to us.

"Frank is telling us about his time in the war. He was captured by the Germans and sent to a Prisoner of War camp."

"Goodness, Frank. How fascinating. Mind if I listen in?"

"Of course," said Frank, smiling to himself as his entourage grew.

"Conditions were tough; rations were meagre. It was hard work," he said. "Doing heavy labour while you were weak from hunger was very difficult. You see images in every war film of men escaping from prison camps, but the truth is that everyone was much too exhausted to escape, and those who got beyond the wire ran the very real risk of being shot. Escape never felt like an option.

"You're so weakened when you're locked up like that. The Germans didn't heat our cells, and it was freezing. Night times were difficult. You got to the stage where you'd wake up so cold you were glad just to be alive.

"Daytime wasn't much fun either, I have to tell you - surviving on a daily ration of hot water and barley porridge is tough. I was so skinny. There was nothing of me. It was a horrible, dark, difficult time in which I became convinced every day that I would die.

"I stayed in the camp until the war's end when Russians rescued us. It was May 1945. I've had a great fondness for Russians ever since. I was weak, dirty, cold, and hungry; they looked after me. I was taken back to Italy and reunited with my battalion. That's when I was told about the death of my parents."

"Oh, Frank," said Captain Homarus. "Your parents were killed in the war?"

"Yes, they were."

"As soon as I was strong enough, I went to collect Irene - the woman who had kept me sane as I'd been starved, beaten and freezing in the POW camp. I planned to propose to her and take her back to England."

"Ah, good news at last," said Edith. But Frank was looking down at his hands.

"When I got to Sicily, I discovered that she was engaged to Marco," he said.

"Noooooo," we all chorused.

"Blimey, Frank, when are you going to get a break? This is insane," I said. "Please tell me that's a joke.... I can't bear it."

"No, not a joke...far from a joke," he said.

"Frank needs to go to bed now," said Jan. "He needs to get a good night's sleep; tomorrow, he will be going to Tunisia to say goodbye to Tom and my grandpa."

We all looked at one another, bereft that the story had to end at this point.

"Just a little bit more," I tried.

"Not tonight," said Janette, and she stood and began pushing Frank away.

"Good luck tomorrow," I shouted, and I saw him nod as she pushed him away through the dining room and out of view.

DRAMA IN THE THEATRE

I watched Frank and Janette go, Captain Homarus returned to work, and Edith and Malcolm headed to bed. I thought about everything he had said. It was hard to imagine what he had been through... what traumas and difficulties he must have endured. It was kind of weird that someone alive today had been through all that. His experiences felt like they should be trapped in the pages of a history book, not living in the memory of that lovely, softly spoken man.

I left the table and wandered through to the bar area. It was very busy, and getting busier all time, with couples in their finery coming in after dinner, and groups of newly- established friends gathering at tables. I didn't feel like going back to the cabin just yet, so I took a seat on a bar stool.

"Everything OK, Madam," said one of the crew, seeing me sitting alone.

"Yes, I'm fine," I said.

"Can I get you anything? A drink?"

"I'll have a gin and tonic please," I said. I didn't particularly want a drink, but turning one down was beyond me.

The waiter brought me my drink and I suddenly felt quite lonely, and a little lost. I seemed to be the only person sitting on my own. I'm usually good at making friends but it felt like everyone else was in a couple, and quite settled in their own company. It didn't feel like I could go charging up to them, introduce myself and sit down. I sipped my drink and decided to walk around for a bit, then head to bed.

I wandered through the small art shop where people were browsing and commenting on the art and how much they liked it. The only thing that stood out to me was a bronze sculpture of a ballerina. I thought it would look nice in my flat. I turned it over in my hands; it was cool and heavy. The price tag underneath said £3600. Whaaaat? Who would pay that for a sculpture? I wouldn't pay that much for a car.

How did these people have so much money? How did they make it? I walked out of the shop and past the pub, which was playing some sports match that had everyone cheering wildly.

Next to the pub was a small theatre I'd seen earlier in the day. It looked prettier at night, lit up and with people dressed up, sipping champagne in the boxes and settling down to watch a play. I fancied going in, but I didn't want to see some desperately dull play by some worthy, philosophical type – I just wasn't in the mood.

"What's on tonight?" I asked the guy on the door.

"It' a medley of songs and dance routines...just a load of fun," he said.

"Oh, that sounds perfect. Do I need a ticket or anything? Or can I just come in?"

"Just come in...you're more than welcome," he said. "Take a seat anywhere. It starts in five minutes."

I settled into a seat by the gangway and sipped my gin while waiting for the curtain to go up. People continued to come into the theatre, and the gentle murmur of voices soothed me as I sat there in quiet contemplation. I couldn't remember the last time I felt so relaxed.

The lights began to dim, and I looked round to see how full the theatre was....and that's when I saw him. Shit! Striding into the theatre alone, dressed up to the nines in his tuxedo...Simon. Oh my fucking God. It was definitely him... there was no doubt about it. I recognised how he pushed one hand deep into his pocket as he walked. The slightly mechanical movements...like a giant puppet master was controlling him. There was always something so unnatural about him. I dropped my head so he wouldn't see me and sunk down in my seat. There was no way I could leave without him seeing me, but – at the same time – there was every chance of him seeing me if I stayed where I was. I had no idea what to do.

I glanced over to see where he was sitting, and I'm sure he saw me. He did a dramatic double-take just as the lights went down. Christ, what now? There was a door to the right of me that was marked 'authorised personnel only'. Under the cover of darkness, I sneaked out of my seat and peeled the door open, sneaking through it into a corridor full of dancers. There were dancers everywhere dressed up in fabulous sequined leotards and feather headdresses.

"You're not dressed," said a man in a tight blue catsuit.

"What the hell?"

"I know. I'm late," I said, shuffling from foot to foot, afraid to announce that I wasn't in the cast in case he made me go back through the door.

"Damian....one of the larger dancers here needs dressing," said the man, wiggling off towards the stage while two wardrobe assistants grabbed me and began undressing me. There was a great deal of sighing and muttering as they surveyed the racks of clothes for something for me to wear. I tried to insist that I could just sit in the dressing room and didn't have to be dressed up at all, but this clearly wasn't an option.

"With four dancers ill, we need everyone we can find on stage tonight."

"Right, OK," I said, as they wrapped me in blue sequined robes and pinned my hair up, attaching feathers and jewels. It looked quite good by the time they'd finished. So good that I completely forgot that there was no way I could go anywhere near the stage for the simple reasons that (a) I couldn't dance and (b) I didn't know any of the choreography.

"This way," he called.

I could hear that the performance had begun, with loud music hall songs being belted out on the stage, and the sound of footsteps as the dancers tap danced through their routines.

"You're on next," said a behind-the-scenes assistant, leading me through to the edge of the stage. The headdress was so bloody heavy. I had no idea how I was supposed to dance in it.

"Good luck," said the guy, pulling back the curtain a little for me to go on. "When they sing 'arimbo, arimbo' that's when you pull off your top to reveal your tasselled nipples."

"That's when I what?" I said, regarding him with a mixture of alarm and confusion.

"Go!" he said. I strode onto the stage, trying to keep my head upright so the damn headdress wouldn't come tumbling off and trying to do some sort of steps that could be described as being dance-like. The guy in the blue catsuit looked at me like I was insane as I danced around on the spot, clicking my fingers and stamping my feet while all the other dancers moved together in a lovely rhythmical dance that they had clearly been practising for months and which I could in no way hope to pick up.

Then, it happened. "Ariba, Ariba!" came the shout, and four dancers pulled off their tops. I just looked at them... wide-mouthed and disbelieving. I turned out towards the crowd and saw Simon. His eye caught mine, and he stood up.

"Oh my God – Mary Brown – it's you. It's a miracle!" he shouted. "I thought you were dying of leprosy."

"No, I'm better," I shouted back as the headdress slipped over my eyes. "The leprosy has all gone."

GYM BUDDIES

I woke early the next morning and stretched out across the bed. It was so comfortable I didn't want to move. The sun was streaming in through the balcony windows where I'd forgotten to close the curtains again. I looked out across the white pillow towards the ocean, and then I saw it – a bright blue feather lying next to me along with a sprinkling of glitter – and all the horrors of the night before came bounding back to me.

Juan Pedro, the head dancer, had been hysterical afterwards – laughing uproariously when I told him of my conundrum and that I wasn't a dancer at all.

"No! Really? I couldn't tell," he said, mimicking my little solo dance routine and the look of fear on my face when he'd shouted 'Ariba.'

"I particularly liked the stamping," he'd said, and the way your eyes moved upwards towards the headdress all the time because you were sure it would fall off.

"It's hard work," I'd said. "Dancing and holding the weight of that thing on your head...I have a new respect for dancers."

I told him all about Simon and my efforts to avoid him, and he laughed a lot at the fact that, far from managing to avoid Simon and keep the whole thing quiet, I'd been forced to address it in a packed theatre and announce from the stage, while dressed in glitter and feathers, that I used to have leprosy.

"You must see the funny side," he insisted. I wasn't sure I did, but I was confident everyone else would.

Now it was morning, and my head hurt, and it was only 6 a.m. There was no way I would get back to sleep, so I climbed out of bed and decided to go up to the gym and do a workout before breakfast. A 'wake up workout' session occurred at 6.30 a.m. If I did that, I could justify going completely nuts at the buffet later. So, off I went onto the top deck to find the workout class.

I walked into the glass-panelled room to find Juan Pedro sitting there, legs akimbo, stretching out.

"Ah, you're doing this class as well are you?" I asked.

"I'm taking this class, darling," he replied. "I hope you're ready to work hard."

"No, not really," I said. "Especially not after last night's extravagances."

"It'll do you good...it'll help get the booze out of your system. Also, I hear it helps to do lots of exercise if you've suffered from leprosy."

"Stop it," I said, nudging him playfully.

There were six people in the class – three of them were dancers from last night – lithe, slim and gorgeous young men, the other two were called Bob and Doris and looked about 75. I fancied my chances of being more able than the elderly couple but considerably less able than the dancers.

The music struck up – loud drumbeats that rocked through me, making my hangover feel instantly about five times worse.

"OK, and marching on the spot," said Juan Pedro. "Lift your knees as high as possible; come on, I want to see those knees up by your shoulders."

I did my best, though I have to report that my knees were nowhere near my shoulders. Still, I had a light sweat and was quite enjoying it. That's when Juan Pedro put down steps in front of us and said that we'd do a step routine for the second half of the class.

BERNICE BLOOM

He had us stepping on and off the steps at high speed, kicking out and lifting her arms.

"Don't worry if you get lost – just keep going," he said in an encouraging voice, so I gleefully stepped on and off the step, waving my arms, completely out of time with everyone else in the class.

Afterwards, Juan Pedro came up to me and put his arm around me.

"Well done," he said. "You kept going all the way through."

"Thanks," I said. I was proud of myself too. I can't remember the last time I did an exercise class like that and kept going. "I really want to try and lose weight, but it's so hard when you love food."

"Yes, and these ships are a menace with all those buffets," he said. "They're impossible to resist."

He tapped his rock-hard, not-an-ounce-of-fat-stomach as he spoke as if to illustrate how much weight he'd put on.

"There's nothing there," I said, rubbing my own stomach and seeing how it rippled wildly like it was a separate entity entirely. Like a man made of jelly was lying on my tummy.

"You keep up the exercise, and that will go in no time," said Juan Pedro. "You just need to cut back on the food a little, and exercise a bit more – it's not rocket science...none of it is difficult, you just need to make a promise to yourself to take your health seriously from now on."

"I think I will," I said, standing up and wiping the sweat from my brow.

"Good," said Juan Pedro. "Fancy breakfast?"

Going down to breakfast with Juan Pedro was great, and it made me realise how much I don't like being on my own... how much I like to have company. I live on my own, but I'm at work a lot of the time, and when I'm not, I either have Ted round, or I'm at his. Or I'm out with friends. I never spend a lot of time alone.

The only downside to going to breakfast with Juan Pedro was being so restrained. Having had a conversation with him about how I wanted to lose weight, it felt all wrong to pile my plate high with pancakes, syrup and croissants. But – and this is what people don't understand about fat people – I can't not have those things. If I don't

THE MARY BROWN BOOKS

have a pancake and syrup at breakfast, I'll feel awful and deeply deprived all day, and it will play on my mind until I cave in and go to a sweet shop and eat everything they've got.

I walked to the buffet, piling my bowl with melon and pineapple, and then shoved a couple of pancakes into my mouth while still there so Juan Pedro wouldn't be able to see.

I grabbed a pancake, lay it on my hand and dribbled maple syrup into it before rolling it up and pushing it into my mouth. Then I returned to my seat with my little bowl of fresh fruit salad.

"Well done," said Juan Pedro, looking at the food I'd selected. "That's brilliant. It can be so hard to eat sensibly with so many unhealthy options on offer. That's really good."

So, I ate the lousy pieces of pineapple and melon and took his praise on board. "Thank you, Juan Pedro," I said, the taste of delicious pancakes and maple syrup still strong in my mouth. "Thank you."

"Listen, do you fancy spending the day together in Tunisia? Walking around on your own won't be much fun."

"That would be lovely," I said. "If you don't mind..."

"Mind? I'd love that. Any woman who will rock up and join a dance troupe with no dancing experience to escape from a boyfriend whom she told she had leprosy is my kind of woman. Especially if that woman then proceeds to stuff her face with pancakes and pretend only to eat two small slivers of melon for breakfast. Perfect."

DRESSED UP IN TUNISIA

I'd arranged to meet Juan Pedro on deck to head into Tunis together and explore the sights. I didn't know quite what to expect, but he was good fun and - much as I loved Frank's stories of wartime love and loss - it would be good to have a light-hearted day of fun and frolics with a nutter like Juan Pedro.

"Coming then?" he said, appearing beside me in an odd but strangely flattering clothing combo - skin-tight jeans that were ripped both at the knee and alarmingly close to his crotch, along with a shirt with ruffles down the front of it and a very fancy, patterned, shiny blazer. His hair was combed back.

"Glad you made an effort," I said.

"Well, I'm glad one of us did," he retorted, looking me up and down.

"Cheeky hound. It's not easy to be glamorous when you're nearly 15 stone."

Juan Pedro laughed. "You're not 15 stone," he said.

Actually, I am. But I didn't want to push the point, so I took it as a compliment and smiled at him.

"I bet I could get you a fabulous outfit today," he said. "I could make you look gorgeous."

Dear readers, I should have realised this wouldn't end well. You only had to look at Juan and his bright, shiny blazer and skin-tight, ripped jeans to see that his idea of 'glamorous' would be entirely different from mine. I wanted to look like Grace Kelly; he was clearly going to dress me like Danny Le Rue. But all of those thoughts didn't enter my head. All I heard was, 'I can make you look gorgeous' and I thought 'I'd like that,' so off we went, into Tunis, with Juan talking about the lovely, native dress and describing something called a sefsari - a gorgeous huge scarf he wanted to buy for me. He told me about dresses lined with rhinestones. "A gorgeous bodice studded with crystals would be wonderful," he said.

"Bodice? Have you seen the size of my breasts?" I replied. "There aren't enough crystals in the entire world..."

We decided that a stop in a lovely Turkish cafe was called for before we began our shopping expedition, so we wandered into the first one we came to and ordered drinks.

"Not too strong," I said as Juan Pedro raised his eyebrows. "You might be in the wrong place altogether if you want weak coffee, doll," he said. "They take it strong and dark here."

The coffee came as predicted - tiny cups full of wildly strong coffee that was undrinkable.

"Mmmm..." I said. "Mary loves hot tar in the mornings."

There was an added bonus with the coffee when I stirred it because it had this sludge at the bottom - like the stuff you get on the floor of a river bed.

"Fancy another?" said Juan.

I pushed my cup over to him. "Have mine," I said. "I can't do it. The taste of it is making me want to cry."

I looked at the map on my phone as we talked. I'm a terrible map reader, but I hoped to see roughly where the town centre was. As I scanned across it, I saw a sign for Longstop Hill.

"That's where Frank's going," I said, pointing it out. "You know Frank - the old guy on the ship...in the wheelchair...he fought there in the war and two of his friends died. He's going back to say a final goodbye to them."

"Really?" said Juan. "I know all about the battle of Longstop Hill."

"No, you don't." It seemed very unlikely that Juan Pedro would know anything at all about battles fought in the Second World War

"I do," he insisted. "It was a crucial battle. When they took control of the hill, they could go straight into Tunis."

"Yes, that's right. That's what Frank said." I looked at Juan, amazed.

"I took a group of vets out there. They had fought there too and wanted to go back to see it," he explained.

"Gosh, you must tell Frank tonight," I said. "He'd love to hear that."

"Of course," said Juan. "How interesting that he's come back to see it too. It sounds like it was hell up there. The guys I took up had lost friends - they were hit and fell and died in the mud."

"That's what Frank said. That's how he lost one of his friends, the other one died just after they got him to safety."

"Awful," said Juan. "You couldn't imagine any of that if you look at the hill now. It's grassy and pleasant, with goats roaming over it. There is a new road through the Kasserine Pass - the only sign of the war is when it runs past the rusted ruins of tanks. Farmers find shattered helmets in the fields occasionally, but that's it. There's no doubt, though - the landings in North Africa and the Tunisian campaign were vital in the final surrender of the Germans. Frank played an important role in securing our freedom today."

There was a moment of solemnity as we both looked down in quiet contemplation, and then Juan spoke: "So, shall we use that hard-won freedom by going shopping?"

"Yes," I said. "Let's go shop."

We pushed our chairs back from the table, and Juan leaned over to touch my arm. "One condition," he said. "Whatever outfit we buy for you this afternoon, you must wear at the dinner this evening."

"Done," I said, with staggering naivety, and we wandered off, arm in arm, to the shops of downtown Tunisia.

THE FINAL PART OF THE STORY

"No, "he said. "Go back and put the gold chains on."
"But I look ridiculous with this much jewellery. "
"No – you look very glamorous with this much jewellery. "

I walked back into the changing room and looked at myself in the mirror. My arms were full of gold bangles, I had a dress on which was deep pink cotton on the top and had puffy sleeves and a fitted bodice which fell from the waist into a skirt shot through with gold thread. Over my head, I had a pink scarf studded with crystals and gold necklaces were tied around my forehead with these gold discs dangling down. I had similar necklaces around my neck...lots of them. My upper body was so heavy I could barely stand straight.

Juan was unperturbed by the pain I was in. "No pain, no gain," he said. "You have to suffer for your art. It looks really good; I don't see what the problem is. "

I looked back into the mirror. "You don't see what the problem is? I look like a gypsy."

"You don't look like a gypsy; you look like a very glamorous Tunisian woman. Trust me," he said. "When you wear this to dinner tonight, everybody will think it's amazing."

"I'm not wearing this to dinner tonight, absolutely no way," I said.

"That was the deal," said Juan. "You promised me that if I got you into a glamorous outfit, you would wear it for dinner tonight. "

"Yes, but I didn't realise I'd look so bloody ridiculous."

"You don't. You look glamorous and gorgeous, and you're wearing this tonight."

To say that people looked at me with shock in their eyes when I walked into dinner back on the ship that evening would be to understate the impact I had. Elegant women wandered all around in black column dresses, cream sun dresses and stylish party dresses, and in the middle of it all was me - a woman of nearly 15 stone dressed head to foot in pink with huge gold jewellery dripping from everywhere. I had more jewellery on me then everybody else on the ship combined, and there were a lot of women with a lot of jewellery on.

I'd had a gin and tonic in the cabin to take the edge off it, but the edges were still very much there as I walked onto the dining floor and I caught up with Juan who continued to say how great I looked.

In front of us I could see Frank, sitting alone at a table with Janette. I desperately needed to talk to someone non-judgemental, so I headed over there, dragging Juan with me and telling him he needed to meet Frank so they could talk about Longstop Hill.

"Good evening," I said.

Janet jumped when she saw me.

"I thought you were an exotic dancer then," she said. "I thought you were going to give Frank a heart attack."

"No, it's just me. And this is Juan," I said, jangling as I made the introductions. "He dragged me around Turkish boutiques today, telling me he'd make me look me glamorous, but I feel like a complete idiot."

"You don't look like an idiot at all. You look beautiful," said Frank.

"Thank you," I said. The fact that he was almost blind made his compliments less reassuring, but it was kind all the same. "How was Longstop Hill today?"

"Moving," said Frank, nodding his head. "It was very moving. Quite difficult at times, but I'm very glad I did it."

"I found it moving too, and I never fought anyone or anything in my life," said Juan.

"You were there today?" said Frank.

"No, I went a few weeks ago. I took a group of Vets. They said the same. Very difficult but very, very worthwhile."

"Yes, the memories have never faded, so it wasn't like I went there, and the memories suddenly came pouring back, but being there did cut through me a bit, and made me think of all those brave young men who died. That was very difficult."

Janette and I sat and listened awhile while Frank talked through the day. I jingled and jangled every time I nodded my agreement, and Janette looked at me sternly as if my musical accompaniments were somehow lessening the impact of the story.

"Listen, it's incredible to meet you, Frank, but I'm going to have to head off to dance practice. We've got a show later. Will you come?"

"I won't. I'm exhausted after the trip today, but thank you for asking. Good luck!"

"Thank you," said Juan, blowing me a kiss as he walked away.

"He seems like a nice young man. Is he your boyfriend?" asked Frank.

"Er....no, I'm pretty sure he's gay," I replied. "Anyway, he wouldn't be my boyfriend if he was the straightest man in the world. He's made me look a complete fool. I've dressed like a gypsy thanks to him."

Frank just smiled and shook his head. "You look adorable."

"I look like mad gypsy Rose-Lee. People will be asking me to read their fortunes."

"Nonsense," said Frank, with a smile. "You look perfect."

It was a kind remark, but I was well-aware that he was almost blind.

Over dinner that evening, Frank and I resumed our chat, with Frank picking up where he'd left off...arriving in Sicily to discover that Irene was engaged.

"I felt as if my insides had been churned out," he said. "I didn't even try to see Irene; as soon as I heard the news, I turned and walked away."

"No! Why didn't you try and find her and persuade her? She probably got engaged to him because she thought you weren't coming back...you were away so long. How could you just walk away?"

"I didn't want to spoil her happiness; if she chose him, then who was I to ruin it for them? Remember, her father had saved my life, and her family had been incredibly kind to me. I didn't want to make life difficult for them at all. I just turned and walked away."

"And what did you do then? Where did you go?"

"I left and got the boat back to England, but I couldn't stop thinking about her. I got home, and that's when I realised how much she mattered. Nothing was there; my family had been wiped out, and the house was boarded up. I was offered temporary accommodation but decided to travel to Slough to fulfil my friend's dying wish to take care of his wife."

I noticed Janette smiling as Frank spoke about Jim's wife.

"It was lovely to meet her. What a charming lady. Elizabeth was her name. She was standing there with a little three-year-old girl called Linda at her feet."

"Linda was my mum," said Janette. "Dad never found out that mum was pregnant. He never knew he had a daughter."

"Oh no, that's sad," I said.

"It was a difficult time for mum, but Frank really looked after them. He moved them into his mum's old house as soon as that was repaired and took care of them."

"And your grandma helped me too," said Frank. "It was Elizabeth who forced me to go to Sicily and try to win back Irene's heart.

"I got a boat back a week later and talked to Irene. She was astonished to see me. I'd been away so long she assumed I'd been killed. We talked for hours, and I told her I loved her. She said she loved me too, and we decided to run away together. It wasn't a brave thing to do, and it wasn't fair on this family who'd cared so much for me, but we ran away in the night, leaving a note for her parents and one for Marco.

"We settled in England, and she never went back. I know she missed her home and her family. She wrote to her parents and went over to visit them secretly, but never saw her brother ever again because she was worried he would come over to England and find me if he knew where we were.

"I need to go back to the house in Sicily to see who is there and to apologise for everything that happened. Those guys saved my life. They were kind, decent people. I need to see them again, just to say I'm sorry about how I took their daughter away from them. Even if everyone I knew is dead, I want to apologise to anyone there who knew Irene and explain why we ran away; explain to Alberto why she never stayed in touch.

"She wrote letters to Alberto and I thought she was sending them, but after her death, I found them in a vanity case; she'd not sent them because she was worried he'd come and find her."

"Gosh, what does Irene think about you going?" I asked.

"Irene died four months ago. She'd been very ill. She passed away peacefully. I'm hopelessly lost without her. I miss her terribly. I need to do this for her. I do hope we find the cottage. We will, won't we?" he said.

"We will. I promise we will," I said. And suddenly I realised that I would be going with him to Sicily and that I had to help him find Irene's relatives.

JUAN'S COMING TOO

I didn't see Frank much over the next couple of days after hearing the rest of his emotional story on the boat. His journey to Longstop Hill had exhausted him so he stayed on board, mainly in his cabin, being looked after Janette, while the boat stopped first in Sardinia, then in Malta. I explored them both with Juan Pedro. But I couldn't stop thinking about Frank's tale.

"Hey Juan Pedro," I said as we both sat there, sunning ourselves on the deck one day. "You know Frank - the old guy in the wheelchair who went to Longstop Hill?"

"Yeah," he said without moving his tanned face from its position, staring up into the sunshine. "Nice guy. I liked him."

"I'm going with him for the day when we get to Sicily - he's going to try to find the cottage his wife lived in when he first met her. He stole her away from her fiancé just after the war. He wants to go back there and make amends to anyone who's still there. He still feels bad that Irene was forced to abandon her family."

"Blimey doll. I doubt there'd be anyone there now that was alive then."

"Well, Frank's still alive, so there could be."

"True darling," said Juan. "I suppose it's worth him trying."

"Did you hear about the letters he has...letters that Irene wrote to her brother to explain why she'd left and updating him on her life and what was going on? She wrote hundreds and never sent any of them. After she died, he found the letters in her vanity case with a note saying, 'Frank, I'm sorry - I never sent these - I was worried about Marco finding our address and coming to hurt you. I'm sorry.'"

"Good grief, doll," said Juan, turning slightly to face the sun. "We're in the middle of a Sunday afternoon rom-com; you know that, don't you? Hugh Grant is going to show up any moment."

"Haha. Very funny. It does seem like that. I've been writing all about it in the blog I'm doing for Dawn and apparently, it's got quite a big following back home...loads of comments and tonnes of likes."

"My God. They are going to make this into a film. We'll get back to Southampton and a film crew and director will be waiting there. Who's going to play us? I was thinking maybe Johnny Depp for me and Jennifer Lawrence for you. What do you think?"

"Yep, I'll go with that," I said. "It would make a brilliant film - Frank's story is so amazing...I just love him. I think he's one of the kindest, warmest and most friendly people ever. Considering what he's been through, you think he'd be wary and guarded. I mean, he can hardly see, he's got shrapnel inside him still, his wife's just died, and yet he's lovely and friendly. I have to help him find that cottage...I'm so worried about the effect it will have on him if we can't find it."

"We will. I'll come with you," said Juan. "I've been to Sicily a few times before; I might be able to help."

I smiled to myself at the thought of us: me - this extraordinarily overweight woman, Frank, a 96-year-old widower and Juan Pedro, a flamboyant Spanish dancer - all trekking around looking for a house from the 1940s while being watched by a slightly angry-looking nurse in a brown dress.

"Yes, you should come," I said. "I'll talk to Frank - you should definitely come."

OFF TO SICILY

Finally, the day arrived. I stood on deck as the boat docked in Sicily - looking out towards the cluster of houses nestled in the hilltops in front of us. The thought of tracking down Frank's relatives made me tingle with anticipation. It would be so amazing if Marco and Alberto were still alive and Frank could meet them, shake hands and hand over the letters. I knew how much it would mean to him to make amends.

I looked up to see Janette pushing Frank towards me; he was sitting in his wheelchair looking incredibly dapper, dressed in a brown three-piece suit that looked like it came from the 1930s, along with very shiny shoes. In his lap, he carried a hat and a cane. Like the suit, they looked like something out of a 1930s musical. We were just a burst of incidental music away from a chorus of singing in the rain.

"Wow, Frank," I said. "You look amazing."

"Well, I thought I better be prepared for anything. This is how Irene loved me to dress, so I thought it's how I should dress today."

"It's very hot out there, though," I said. "Are you sure you won't be too warm like that?"

"I have tried telling him," said Janette, with her hands on her hips. "But he won't listen."

"I can handle a bit of heat," said Frank with a shake of his head, as if to indicate that his past involved more discomfort than a warm suit on a hot day could ever threaten.

"Howdy!" came a shout from the other side of the deck. I looked up to see Juan Pedro walking towards us, dressed like something out of a gay pride march. He was wearing rainbow-coloured trousers in some sort of shiny material that gleamed as he walked, along with a flowery, Hawaiian-style shirt in orange with red and white blossom on it. On his feet were these odd kind of winkle-pickers in a glittery material. He was carrying a man bag made of lime-green, crocodile material. Now, I love unconventional people, I'm all in favour of people who don't look strictly normal, but I couldn't imagine what Frank would make of him, and I was slightly worried since this was very much Frank's day, a day on which we had to all behave in a way which wouldn't alarm or frighten him.

"Good lord alive," said Janette, seeing Juan Pedro close up.

"Frank, remember Juan Pedro?" I said.

"Very nice to see you again, son," said Frank, reaching out a trembling hand. Juan Pedro shook it and patted Frank on the back.

"Frank, I hope I can help locate your wife's cottage today. If there's anything I can do, or - Janette - if you need any help pushing the wheelchair or anything, you just shout, and I'm here for you. "

"Thank you, that's very kind," said Frank, and I was reminded that Frank couldn't see enough to judge Juan Pedro on his appearance. Just like he couldn't see how fat I was or how dull Janette looked, none of that mattered. He was just judging us on how we behaved and treated him and each other. It gave me a shot of warmth and reminded me that what matters is not how you look, but how you behave, how you treat people, and how kind you are. I felt a tear come into my eye and instinctively hugged Juan Pedro, and Janette. Juan Pedro seemed delighted, Janette seemed alarmed, I was determined by the end of the day she would've softened a little bit and realised that we all just wanted to help.

Janette, being the only sensible person in the party by a considerable margin, was given the job of carrying the maps and all the information that would help us track down where Irene had lived and where we might start to find her family.

"In this part of the world, people tend to live in the same house much more than we would in England," said Frank. "Houses are passed down through generations. It's not uncommon for children to live in the houses their grandparents and even great-grandparents bought."

"Great. Then let's hit the road."

"Absolutely," said Juan Pedro. "Follow me."

So the rather odd party of an enormous fat girl in loose-fitting separates, a man in rainbow-coloured trousers carrying a lime-coloured clutch bag, an elderly man in a wheelchair dressed as if he'd just dropped in from the 1930s, and a rather stout and unsmiling nurse in a starched brown dress, all headed off into Sicily for the day. It was, I admit, hard to see how this was going to work out well.

EVERYTHING'S CHANGED

We walked up to the main square and jumped into a cab. Well, I say 'jumped' - that's a bit of a lie...what with the wheelchair being folded up and Frank being manually lifted in, and me unable to get the seat belt around me, and none of us speaking a word of Italian...it was all rather a palaver if I'm honest, but we struggled on board, and off we set. Janette clutched the modern-day map and handed me the map from the 1940s to look after.

Frank entertained us with his wartime stories.

"We were called the D-Day dodgers, you know," he said.

"The what?"

"Well, D-Day took place while we were in Italy. Lady Astor said that we were in Italy to avoid D-Day. If she'd seen what we'd been through, she would have realised we'd all much have preferred to be at D-Day. We sang a song to take the mickey out of it all; let me see whether I can remember it...it's to the tune of Lili Marlene. Here we go:

'WE LANDED AT SALERNO, *holiday with pay,*
  Jerry got the band out to help us on our way.

We all sang songs, the beer was free.
We danced all the way through Italy.
We were the D-Day Dodgers, the men who dodged D-Day."

WE ALL APPLAUDED HEARTILY.

"Here is the place," said the driver. "Corleone."

Frank looked through the window, and his face fell. We were relying on a 90-odd-year-old man to remember the place from 70 years ago, and he clearly didn't recognise anything at all. The two maps looked vastly different, so it wasn't hard to see why he was confused.

"Come on, let's get out and look around," I said, trying to fake confidence.

I looked over and caught Janette's eye. I knew exactly what she was thinking...we had no way of knowing how we would do this, but on the other hand, we simply had to do it. We couldn't let Frank go back to England without finding the cottage, saying his goodbyes and handing over the letters. He was an old man - he might never get this chance again.

We walked over to a small wall.

"Let me have a look at that," said Janette, and I opened up the map from the 1940s while she unfolded the current map. We laid them both out in front of us, across the wall.

On the 1940s map, there was hardly anything - just a handful of houses and shops. Irene's cottage was circled. The modern-day map featured a new road system, roundabouts, motorways and loads of houses, shops and offices that weren't there before.

"It looks to me," said Janette. "As if the cottage has gone."

"Really?"

"Yes. Look on this map - see that small hill there, well, that must be here on the modern map."

She pointed at the two maps, and I saw what she meant.

"Yes," I said. "Look - there's the church spire. It looks like the cottage was there - I pointed to where it should be...it was now a cafe next to a garage."

"Really?" said Juan. "You reckon it was turned into a cafe?"

While Juan came over to investigate the map, I went to see Frank. He looked exhausted and sad, sitting there, barely able to see, listening to us talking about how the cottage - his only link to his wife's past - had disappeared.

"Come on, let's go and have a cup of tea," I said, seeing his face brighten up. "We'll go to that cafe over there while they are messing around with the maps, and I'll get myself on Google to see what I can find."

"Good plan," said Frank. "I don't know about Google, but tea is an excellent idea."

We sat at a rickety old table, and the others joined us. Juan had pulled out a pen and was jotting down numbers.

"Are you doing your tax return?" I asked.

"Map coordinates," he replied, tapping the side of his head. "Right, OK. Got it."

"Got what?"

"These are the map coordinates of the cottage we're looking for." He pointed to the map from the 1940s with the cottage marked on it. "And this is where the coordinates fall on this map."

We all looked down. Juan was pointing to the cafe.

"The family must have sold the cottage to a developer who built this cafe," said Janette, scratching her head and looking at the map.

Frank looked up and around the cafe as if hoping to see something that would remind him of the past.

I called the waiter over and asked him, in my best Italian, whether this used to be a cottage. It was no good; my broken Italian and his lack of English were getting us nowhere.

"Wait minute," he said, rushing into the back of the cafe and emerging with a very handsome young man.

"How can I help you?" he said in near-perfect English.

Janette clapped her hands together in relief. She repeated our questions, laying the maps out on the table. The guy looked through them and confirmed that this was the spot we were looking for, but it was never a cottage.

"My parents owned this cafe when I was born, so it's been a cafe for a long time," he said. He shouted out in Italian to his mother, who came out and stood next to him, looking at the maps and chatting to him in Italian. Then she called someone's name, and a man came in from the kitchens in a white overall.

"My parents say that they bought this cafe 20 years ago. It was already a cafe when they bought it," said the young man.

"Damn," said Juan Pedro. "No cottage here?"

"No cottage," they confirmed.

"But it does look like the right area, doesn't it?" said Juan. The young man nodded as he studied the two maps.

"Let me try another tack," said Juan, beckoning over the English-speaking man. "Do you have any documentation from when you bought the cafe? I wonder who sold this property to you. Maybe we can track them down?"

"I will take a look," he said.

The man disappeared for so long that we thought he wasn't coming back, but to our delight and surprise, he re-emerged with a piece of paper, the purchase agreement from when they bought the cafe two decades ago.

"My mother keeps everything," he said.

The name of the person they had bought the cafe from was Monsieur Dalmeny.

"I've never heard of him," said Frank. There was an address next to it.

"Do you have a phone number?" I asked. "No phone number here," he said.

"OK, then, we'll go there," I announced, standing up. I was conscious that we didn't have much time if we were going to get back to the ship by 5 pm.

"Your best bet is to head on the main road. Where is your car?"

"We don't have a car. We'll need to get a taxi," I said.

"No problem," said the man. "I will take you there."

"Really? That would be amazing. Thanks so much," I said, and the four of us climbed (Janette), waddled (me), sashayed (Juan Pedro) and were lifted (Frank) into the car, and the man, who we discovered was called Andreas, dropped us at the end of a pathway which led to the house of Monsieur Dalmeny - the man who'd sold them the cafe.

"Thank you so much," I said. "You've been very generous. Can I give you some money?"

"No, not at all," he said. "I'm just helping. Here is my number...please call if I can do anything else."

So, there we were, wandering down a path to knock on some stranger's door and ask them what they remembered about when they sold a cafe.

The house was quite plush, much posher than the other houses in this heavily rundown part of the country. Two goats wandered outside one of the houses, and children's toys were scattered on the lawns, but the bigger, more imposing house had none of the paraphernalia of family life dotted around the place. It gave the feeling of being totally empty.

I knocked. The four of us stood there in silence. I knocked again. Still nothing.

Damn.

It was hard to know what to do next. We were starting to run out of time, but I knew just how much Frank wanted to track down anyone related to the family that he felt he had let down so many years ago.

"I'll put a note through the door and see whether they respond to it. I'll put my phone number on, and they can call me when they return."

"It's 3 p.m.," whispered Juan Pedro. "We're running out of time here."

I knew he was right. We needed to be back in the vicinity of the boat by 5 o'clock in order to make sure we had enough time to sort Frank out and get onto the ship before it left at 6 p.m.

"We're going to have to go soon, aren't we?" I said. Juan Pedro nodded gently.

I turned to Janette: "What do you want to do?" I asked.

She agreed that we should start heading back to the ship and that Frank would have to send the letters once they'd tracked the family down. Janette leaned over to talk to Frank. He wanted to pass the letters on personally and talk to the family himself, but he knew there was no time today to do that.

"Let's go," he said, his voice barely a whisper, and I felt like we'd all really let him down. I just hadn't thought about how difficult it would be, how much everything would have changed, and how hard it would be to find anyone who knew Irene's family, let alone know where they were now.

To add to our woes, it turned out that getting a cab back was easier said than done. I rang the number for the taxi company and was told by a surly Italian that it would be half an hour before they could get one to us.

"Okay," I said. "But we're heading back to the dock to get a ship, so it can't be any longer than that. Will it definitely be here in half an hour?"

"Yes it will be," confirmed the cab lady.

We sat down on the edge of the grass and talked about how we must all work together once we got back to Britain to try and locate this family. I looked at my watch. It had been 40 minutes, and there was no sign of the cab. I rang the company again, and the woman assured me it was 10 minutes away.

"It's 10 to 4," said Juan Pedro.

"I know, but what can I do? Shall I try calling Andreas at the cafe and see whether he can take us back to the harbour?"

"Yes, do that. If we miss this ship, I'll be shot," said Juan. "I'm supposed to be dancing in the razzmatazz ball tonight."

"We won't miss the ship. It will be tight, but we will get there," I said with a ridiculous amount of confidence, considering there was no sign of a taxi anywhere, and I was struggling to get through to Andreas.

An answerphone came on, and I left a message, explaining we were the guys he'd given a lift to earlier, and we were stuck. We waited

THE MARY BROWN BOOKS

another 30 minutes - no cab, no reply from Andreas. It was almost half past four, and the journey would take at least an hour. Unless the cab came within the next 15 minutes, we were in serious danger of not making the boat.

Finally, finally, a cab came around the corner and we clambered on board. I tried to tell the driver how much of a rush we were in, but he didn't seem to understand.

"Don't worry," he kept saying as we drove at unbelievably slow speeds through the narrow roads, coming up against obstacle after obstacle...there was far more traffic than there had been on our way up, which slowed us down considerably; there were animals in the road as they were being taken from one field to another, then, just as we thought we were there, a diversion which cost us 15 minutes.

We arrived near the docks at five to six. While Janette got the wheelchair out of the car and put Frank into it, Juan Pedro and I ran as fast as we could towards the ship, hoping to alert them to our presence and encourage them to wait. But it was no good. When we reached the boat, out of breath and dishevelled, it was 6.15, and our floating hotel was pulling out of the harbour. On the deck, many of the crew and passengers were gathered. Captain Homarus and Claire were there, along with Simon, waving furiously and shouting my name.

"Mary, Mary," he cried. "Get on the boat."

"How in God's name am I supposed to do that?" I said. "Swim out to it?"

I glanced at Juan Pedro. "Shall I?" he said. "Maybe I should swim to it to save my career."

"No, you nutter," I said. "Look how far it is now. Come on - let's go and find Frank and Janette."

So, the two of us walked back towards our 96-year-old friend while a man I once dated for a few weeks screamed at me. "You must get on the boat". "You've only just recovered from the leprosy. Make sure you don't get ill again. Get on the boat."

"Leprosy?" said Janette.

"Long story," I replied.

AWOL FROM THE SHIP

*J*ust to recap...there was an ancient man in an ancient suit, a nurse in a brown dress, a fat lady in sandals that were hurting her feet and a spruced-up Spanish dancer - all standing on the quayside with no provisions and no luggage while the ship they were meant to be on sailed away.

"Well, this is turning into quite an adventure, isn't it?" said Frank with a smile.

There was no doubting that.

"The good news is that we have another day in Sicily to find the Corleone family," I said. "I suppose that counts as good news, doesn't it?"

"Yes," said Janette. "Let's look on the bright side; that's very good news, isn't it, Frank?"

I glanced down at our elderly friend; he looked exhausted.

"Let's find a hotel as near as possible to where we were earlier," said Juan Pedro. "You Google the area, Mary, and see whether you can find a hotel anywhere, and I'll ring some of the guys on the ship and see what's the best thing for us to do now. The ship goes to Naples next. Maybe we should spend the morning tracking Irene's family, then head to Naples and get on the ship when it docks there?"

"Yes, good plan," I said, feeling a little more relaxed now that there was a plan of some kind, even if it was a plan that involved a trek across Italy with a wheelchair-bound nonagenarian.

Juan Pedro picked up his phone to call people on the ship while I found a couple of hotels near the cafe, and left messages on answer phones.

"We are okay," said Juan Pedro with a huge sigh. "They said getting to Naples tomorrow would be quite simple, and we can jump on the ship there. It leaves at 6 pm again, though, so we must be there this time."

"Great," I said, just as my phone rang. "Oh good, this will be the hotel now."

"Hello, Mary speaking."

"Hello," came a rather gruff voice. "Is Dalmeny here. You put note about buying the cafe under my door. You said someone from the cafe have senting you?"

"Oh yes! Thank you so much for calling back. We want to come and talk to you about it."

"Okay, come now," he said. "I am in house."

"Great. We're on our way."

I hung up, explaining to the group what we would do, and calling for a taxi once more. If we could sort this out tonight, it would make getting to Naples tomorrow much easier. Things were starting to look good. This time the taxi came very quickly, and we clambered on board. Once we were in it, my phone rang. It was Andreas from the cafe returning my call.

"Don't worry, everything's fine," I told him. "We don't need a lift anymore, and things look really good. I'll let you know how it all goes."

We reached the house, and I was awash with positive feelings. The goats still grazed outside the neighbouring houses, as Dalmeny stood in the doorway of his superior abode. He was a large, heavily built, bearded man with hands the size of laptop computers and as hairy as a bear's. He invited us in, and I explained what we were trying to do and showed him the map – both the one from 1940 and the current one. He put on his glasses and looked carefully from one map to the next and agreed that it looked as if the cafe was currently where the old cottage used to be.

Great, I thought. He agrees with us, he's going to help us.

"I can't help you," he said.

Brilliant.

"Why not?" asked Juan.

"I know not anything for cafe," he said.

"Is there anyone who might know?" I tried. "We're really keen to get someone to help us. I'm trying to track down the Corleone family – Alberto Corleone?"

"I don't know them. Maybe my mother know. Come back tomorrow," he said.

"What time will she be here?"

"Maybe come back middle of day," he said.

"Okay. We have to be in Naples by 5pm though," I said. "Is there any chance we can come earlier perhaps?"

"No, she not earlier," he said.

"Is there any way we can call your mum?"

"Tomorrow," he said. "My English not good. My wife here tomorrow. Her English good. My mother will know, my wife will help," he said

"OK. And when will your wife be here?" I asked.

"Middle of day with mother."

It seemed fairly conclusive that we couldn't get any more information out of them until midday, so we wended our weary way out of the house, past the goats and onto the main road. Luckily, he was able to point us in the direction of a local bed-and-breakfast. By the time we arrived, Frank was exhausted, so he and Janette went up to their rooms. Juan and I were also exhausted but decided it would be much more sensible to sit up drinking beer all night instead of going to bed. So, we sat outside in the warm evening air, drank beer, ate breadsticks, and tried to make sense of the whole thing.

"We have to find this cottage, Juan," I said. "You saw Frank's face today - he looked destroyed. We have to find it. How has no one heard of this family? I thought it was a tight-knit community?"

"They might have moved out years ago, though. They could have moved 50 years ago for all we know."

"Yes, I guess," I said, looking at Juan. He didn't look quite himself. "Are you worried about what the captain will say when we get back to the boat tomorrow?"

"I will be shot," said Juan dramatically. "You wait and see...they will shoot me like a dog because I missed the ship."

He grimaced as he wiped bread crumbs off his shiny, rainbow-coloured trousers and shook his head with an artistic flourish. "I have to be there tomorrow. I am leading the cha-cha-cha in the evening. Who will do it if I'm not there? I can't see Captain Homarus doing it. Can you?"

"You won't miss the boat tomorrow...everything will be OK."

THE LONG-AWAITED MEETING

The next morning I awoke, bursting with energy, and walked down to breakfast, utterly determined that we would find Irene's relatives if it were the last thing we did. I arrived in the breakfast room first and was instantly dismayed by the food on offer. I'd been so spoilt on the ship with luxurious buffets every day that seeing a plate of pastries and rather mouldy-looking cheese made me feel quite unwell.

Still, I had to keep my strength up, so I managed to force three croissants down me, along with coffee so strong it made me shoot up out of my seat. By the time the others arrived, I had discovered they had pain au chocolat around the other side and was burrowing my way through those.

We headed off at 11.30 a.m. to go back over to the house. I'd called a cab, and we assembled, ready to climb in and begin our day's searching.

"This is it," I said to Frank. "I'm confident we'll find Irene's relatives today."

Despite a long night's sleep, he still looked exhausted. I noticed he hadn't eaten anything at breakfast. I knew we could do with getting him back onto the ship as soon as possible.

We were back at the big house by 11.50 pm and were let into a much noisier home than the one we'd visited the day before. Children played on the lawn outside, and a baby cried upstairs.

"My wife soon back," we were told, and we set ourselves down in the kitchen while our host went to see the baby.

By 12.30 p.m., we were becoming a little worried.

"My wife is come 2 p.m.," he said.

"Oh no," I said, trying not to catch Juan's eyes. I'd promised him we'd be back on the boat by 5 p.m., but that would be impossible the way things were going. In the end, we heard a key in the front door at 2:30 p.m., and a small, slim woman with long, wavy brown hair walked in. She didn't look unlike the picture that Frank had shown us of Irene, and for one almighty moment, I thought that she might be related, and we might sew up this whole mystery once and for all. It turned out that she wasn't in any way related to Irene, and it was pure coincidence that she vaguely looked like her.

"Clutching at straws, darling," was how Juan described it.

She was helpful, though, and had all the paperwork, which showed that she bought the cottage from Alberto.

"Irene's brother," said Janette, breathlessly, leaning down to explain to Frank.

"I remember that he was selling it because his parents had died, and he was living in his wife's parents' old house or something like that," she said.

"Have you got any details about where the man you bought it from was living?" I asked. Holding my breath for the answer.

"Yes – it's here," she said. I'll write it down for you."

In a beautiful italic script, she wrote down an address. It was about half an hour away.

"If we go there, we will miss the flight," I said, and I heard Juan emit a small shriek, like the sort of noise you hear when air is escaping from a tightly pulled balloon. I decided to ignore it and look at Janette.

"Let's stay in Sicily for another night, then go straight to La Spezia tomorrow, missing out Naples completely," I said.

BERNICE BLOOM

"OK," said Janette. "If that's OK with you two?"

"Oh, fine, no problem at all with me," said Juan. "Don't worry about the cha-cha-cha or the ballet spectacular."

I elbowed him in the ribs to silence him.

"Let's book back into the bed and breakfast," said Janette.

"Sure," I responded. "We'll go back there so Frank can have a lie-down, and I'll ring the phone number on the sheet, and we'll head off to see them later this afternoon."

It seemed that finally, finally, we were getting closer to Irene's family.

We said our goodbyes and thanked them very much for their help. When I looked down at Frank, he looked nervous.

"Everything OK?" I asked.

"Everything's fine, dear," he said. "I'll be glad when this is all done, though. It's been a long time since I saw her family. A very long time."

As we headed out into the bright sunshine, I realised what a difficult thing this must be. I'd appreciated how important it was but didn't realise how difficult. Frank was about to confront issues that had lain dormant for decades. I smiled at him and called the number on the sheet, bracing myself for the sound of Alberto's voice...Irene's brother...the man they'd had to flee Italy to avoid.

Rather anti-climatically, it went straight to answerphone. I couldn't leave a message because I had no idea how to begin describing what was happening, and I had no idea whether he spoke any English at all.

"I'll just keep trying," I explained to Frank. "Don't worry - we'll get hold of them and we'll go and see them."

Then I turned to my panicking dancer friend, "Juan - do you want to ring the guys on the boat and explain that we'll be there tomorrow evening instead?"

"Sure," he said with a shrug. "That'll be a nice, easy call to make."

Juan walked off, pouting and sulking, and the rest of us waited for a taxi on the edge of the road. I wish I'd known about all this before I left England. It would have been so much easier to get on the main computer at home and start searching than sitting on roadsides in

Sicily trying to get a signal in the blasting midday sun while waiting for taxis.

It would also, with hindsight, have been much easier to have hired a car.

In the end, it was the next day before I got an answer on the phone. I'd paced around all evening, reassuring Juan that he wouldn't lose his job and reassuring Janette that we would find the relatives and Frank would be able to hand over the letters. I'd been updating the blog with all the ins and outs of our battle to find the cottage, and Dawn - who never issues an iota of praise to anyone, came back to say how much she loved the updates. It was a bright moment in quite a tense few days.

When I finally got an answer on the phone the next morning, I was relieved that it was a young-sounding man who spoke English. I explained, as best I could, who we were and what we wanted, and he replied that he had heard of Irene and he knew the story of her running away with Frank. He said his name was Louis, and he was Alberto's grandson. I smiled from ear to ear. We'd found them.

"I will get my mother," he said.

A lady called Gisella came to the phone and said she was Alberto's daughter.

"Irene was my aunt," she said. "She wrote to us all the time; we heard from her on birthdays and at Christmas, but we never saw her. I never, ever met her. While my grandparents were alive, she visited them but that was it. It would be lovely to meet Frank...she wrote about him so lovingly in her letters."

"One final question," I said. "Is Alberto still alive?"

"Yes," she said. "He is in a nursing home. I will take you to see him."

"Oh, my Goodness," said Frank when I told him. "Oh, my goodness. We've done it. We've found him. I'll get to talk to Alberto after all these years."

Visiting time at the nursing home was in the mornings. I tried explaining that we'd come so far to see him, but it was no good. We would have to stay another night in Sicily, miss out on the Toulon stage of the trip and rejoin the cruise in Barcelona. It was the only way. I looked over at Juan.

"That's the Viennese Waltz gone then," he said. "And someone else will have to judge the grannies' tap dance competition. And I'll need to buy clothes. It's getting ridiculous."

"Yes, we can go shopping this afternoon, buy some new clothes, then go and visit Alberto tomorrow morning before heading for Barcelona. You'll need to let them know on the ship, though."

Juan looked ashen at the thought. "They'll tie me up and beat me til I'm dead," he said. "Or they'll roast me alive and put me on the buffet table."

"No, they won't," I said. "They'll be mildly pissed off, then get over it."

Juan made the call.

"No," he assured them, for the third day in succession. "We will not miss the boat in Barcelona. I promise you." Then he put the phone down and smiled at me. "He said your blog's very good. They are keeping up with our progress through that. I must take a look at it when we get back on board."

"Oh good," I said, remembering that I'd described Juan's clothing in great detail and diarised all his pouting, huffs and stomps off to the corner when he didn't get his own way. To be fair, though, I had also said how kind, warm and generous he was and what a credit to the cruise company. Hopefully, he'd focus on those comments and not dwell on my descriptions of his vile trousers and ridiculous green handbag.

The next morning, we all assembled dressed in 'I am love Sicily' t-shirts for breakfast. There were no clothes shops nearby, so we were forced to buy the only T-shirts the gift shop had. Mine was turquoise, Frank's was white, Janette's was navy, and Juan's was yellow. We looked like Sicily's entry for the Eurovision Song Contest when we walked next to one another.

"It would be bad enough if they said, 'I love Sicily'," said Janette. "But to say 'I am love Sicily' is just ridiculous."

"Oh God," cried Juan. "I hadn't noticed that."

We headed for Frank's daughter and grandchildren's house, and Gisella took us straight to the nursing home. She explained that she and her children had moved into her mum and dad's house with them. "We needed to look after Dad," she explained. "He fell apart a bit when mum died."

"I know that feeling," said Frank, and Janette touched his shoulder gently.

The nursing home was cramped and stuffy, and like every other building housing lots of people, it smelled faintly of cabbage.

"Reminds me of school dinners," said Janette as we walked along the corridor towards Alberto's room.

"I couldn't call him to tell him we were coming because he's not really up to using the phone," said Gisella. "I'll go in first and explain."

"Of course," said Frank. "Don't want to terrify him."

We watched as she knocked gently and then went into his room, talking in Italian. None of us could speak the language, but we heard her say 'Frank' and 'Irene' in the midst of the unfamiliar, foreign words.

"He says to come in," said Gisella.

I glanced at Janette, and she smiled as she pushed the wheelchair through the door. I wasn't sure whether to follow or stay where I was, so I opted for following.

"Shall I come in?" asked Juan.

"Yes," I said. "Let's support Frank."

Inside the room was a desperately thin old man. He was scrawny and pale as he lay back on the sheets.

"You haven't changed a bit," said Frank.

"You neither," said Alberto in a strong Italian accent but very clear English. "Just the same."

Then the two men laughed. Last time they'd seen one another they had been soldiers; strong, young men in their prime.

"I've waited all these years to apologise to you," said Frank. "What I did...it was terrible. Taking your sister away with no explanation."

"It wasn't terrible," said Alberto. "We all understood. You made Irene so happy. How could I be angry?"

"How do you know I made her happy? We all lost contact."

"My mother showed me all the letters that Irene sent. We knew she was well looked after...we knew she was happy with you, so we were happy too."

"Irene wrote to you, too, but never sent the letters. She was so worried that you would come over to England and find us in those early years when we were settling down to our new life together, so she just kept them all. I found them after she died. I'd like you to have them."

Janette opened the bag and handed the piles of letters to Gisella.

"I'll read them to you," Gisella told her father.

"Yes, please," said Alberto, his voice very weak. "How lovely of you to bring them after all these years."

"What happened to Marco?" asked Frank.

"He ran off with another local girl as soon as Irene had gone. He got her pregnant and left the area, leaving her alone to bring up the child. No one heard from Marco again. Irene made the right choice in you, Frank. Marco was no good; I think we all knew that deep down. Thank you for looking after her."

Frank wheeled his chair close to the bed and reached out to take Alberto's hand.

"Thank you," he said. "Thank you for your strength, and thank you for not being bitter. Irene was my life. We were very happy; thank you for understanding."

Alberto smiled and closed his eyes.

"He's tired now," said Gisella. "We should go."

We all left the room except for Frank, who stayed a moment longer before following us.

"Thank you all. Thank you so much," he said, tears streaming down his face. "I wish I'd come here years ago with Irene. I feel like a weight has lifted off me."

FACING SIMON

"We are in Spain. Viva L'Espania," said Juan Pedro, mincing off the plane like he was walking on stage. "Everyone - follow me."

Janette raised her eyebrows and signalled for me to go after him. She would wait until the airline staff brought the wheelchair to them so that Frank could be taken off.

"See you out there," I said.

I caught up with Juan Pedro to see him pouting into the frosted glass windows. "My lips have shrunk," he said.

"No, they haven't," I replied. "Maybe your brain has shrunk, but certainly not your lips."

"Oy!" he said, interlacing his arm through mine like we were two teenagers in an American soap. "I think we should go clothes shopping. Spanish clothes are the best."

"Yeah, no native dress, though. I'm not looking like an idiot again."

"OK, we just go to fashionable modern shops then."

"I'm not going to Zara, though," I said. I knew Zara was Spanish, and I also knew that their clothes were evil. Even their XL was about three sizes too small for me - it was the most depressing shop on earth.

BERNICE BLOOM

"No Zara," he reassured. "We will go to a fabulous designer market. You will love it. It's full of gays."

"Oh great," I said. "I'm glad you think I'd love that. What do you think I am - some sort of fag hag?"

"Why yes - but not any sort of fag hag. You are MY fag hag."

"We need to wait for Frank, though. I don't think he'll want to go clothes shopping in a gay designer market after everything he's been through, but I want to ensure he's OK."

We waited for them to appear. "Frank's exhausted, so we're going to head straight back to the ship," said Janette. "We'll catch up with you two later."

"We won't be long; I'm exhausted, too," I said.

"Whatever you do - don't miss the ship again," said Janette, and they headed off.

"I think Frank might be one of the nicest people I've ever met," I said to Juan, and he smiled in reply. "A very, very cool man," he agreed, then we went shopping.

I followed Juan around like a little puppy, weaving in and out of the racks behind him while he picked out clothes he thought would suit me. "Right - boyfriend jeans - you need these," he said. "We also want some skinny jeans, and I think some cropped white jeans would look good."

He called over the assistant, who he knew by name. The two of them talked together, looking over at me, before the lady returned with armfuls of clothes.

"Right, follow me," said Juan, leading me towards the changing rooms with his clothing haul. "In you go...tell me what you think."

I slipped the boyfriend jeans on first; they were lovely, quite loose-fitting and comfortable, as well as looking good. "You know your stuff, don't you?" I said.

"This is coming as a surprise to you?" he replied sarcastically.

"Try the white jeans on. I know you won't like them because they are tight-fitting, but they are more stylish than those awful ones you had the other day. These ooze style, and you can wear them with either flats or high heels."

THE MARY BROWN BOOKS

With everything I tried on, I emerged from the changing room to comments, prodding and, on a couple of occasions, a round of applause from Juan. We were making quite a commotion in our matching Sicily shirts, but it didn't seem to matter. Juan had this effect on everyone; everywhere he went he was the centre of attention without ever seeming to try.

"Will you try those skinny jeans on with this white shirt?" asked Juan, handing a soft white shirt to me.

I put the white shirt on and tucked it into the jeans, slipping on a pair of high heel boots that Juan had suggested. I looked in the mirror and even though I felt uncomfortable in tight jeans, given the size of my massive bottom, I looked good; much better than I usually do. I walked out of the changing room, spinning around in front of Juan.

"You look very beautiful," said an English voice. I looked up, and right in front of me, staring straight at me, was Simon.

"Hello," I said, flustered. "Let me introduce Juan."

Juan put out his hand and gently shook Simon's.

"I'm going to get jumpers," he said, running off to the other side of the store.

"Sorry we haven't had the chance to talk properly," I said. "I wanted to come and explain...I recovered from the illness. I'm much better now."

"I can see that," said Simon. "I'm so relieved. I always wondered what happened. It's good to see you looking so well."

"Thank you, you too," I said. "We should catch up for a drink later when we're all back on board."

"Sure, I'd like that," he said. "I've been reading your blog. Frank sounds amazing. Will you introduce me to him later?"

"Of course," I said, looking across the rails and seeing Juan ducked down, hiding behind the bikinis.

"Well, see you later then," said Simon, and he wandered off.

"Come back here now," I shouted over to Juan.

"Sorry - but you needed to talk...you can't just ignore him all the time."

"No, I know – well, we've talked now. I told him I recovered from leprosy, and he was very pleased."

"Nutter," said Juan. "Absolute nutter."

By the time we returned to the ship, I had seen nothing of Barcelona bar the biggest indoor market ever - it was astonishing. I had bags full of clothes, plus a pair of earrings that Bet Lynch would have thought too garish and a pair of pink boots that I knew I would never wear, but with Juan there, egging me on, it had seemed such a good idea.

Juan was in his element...trying loads of things on - coming out of the changing rooms, spinning around and pouting like a model. He had about three bags of clothing; all sold to him at bargain prices because of his astonishing ability to haggle.

Much to the captain's delight, we FINALLY boarded the boat, and I headed straight for my cabin - collapsing onto the bed with exhaustion. It had been the most draining experience - physically and emotionally. I could only imagine how Frank must be feeling.

I'd kept the blog up-to-date throughout the trip...I just needed to add a final update to the story then I could have a quick sleep before supper.

I sent several texts to Dawn, showered, and lay back on the bed. I'd taken a few pictures while out and about in Sicily, but fewer than I had on other days because it was such an intensely personal crusade for Frank. I didn't want to be intrusive; Frank didn't deserve that.

I decided to go onto the blog to see how it all looked on there and whether there was any reaction from anyone.

I called up the site and waited for it to load. My God! There were loads of responses. Thousands of people had been following Frank's story. The whole thing was astonishing. Even an MP had commented.

"Our war heroes are very special people indeed. They should be honoured."

There were hundreds of messages underneath the MP's.

"Help them get home!" said one. "Send the army out to help him find the cottage!" said another. "Knight him!"

It had never occurred to me before that the blog might have been a good way of summoning help. When we were wandering helplessly through the Sicilian countryside, it would have been useful to know that thousands of people were following us, willing us on.

I felt too wide awake to sleep, so I decided to get ready for dinner nice and slowly, really taking my time. I slipped on the huge earrings, looked in the mirror, realised I looked completely ridiculous, and took them off again. Then, finally happy that I didn't look insane, I went out to join the others in the bar. I'd been told that we all had to gather for 7 p.m. that evening, and when we met, I would understand why.

I wandered into the bar area, and as I walked in, everyone cheered and clapped. Juan walked in next, and they cheered him as well, and when Frank and Janette came in, there was the loudest cheer I'd ever heard. It was like being at a football stadium or something. People were clapping, banging the tables and cheering like mad.

"Frank, Frank, Frank," they chorused.

Frank and Janette stood in the middle, looking utterly confused.

"What's going on?" Frank asked.

"They are cheering us for our expedition and cheering Frank because he's so incredible," I said.

"How did they know about our expedition? Did you tell them?" asked Janette.

"No, I assumed you had," I said.

"No," said Janette. "It must have been Juan." We both looked at him.

"Not me," he said.

"Ladies and gentlemen, can I have your attention?" said Captain Homarus. "You've all given the most tremendous welcome to Frank, Juan, Janette and Mary, and I'd like to say just a few words. You've managed to miss the ship three times; you've caused mayhem and great worry and panic here..."

Everyone laughed as he spoke.

"But we have been following the blog and are over-whelmed by Frank's story. We've learned all about your incredible war service and how you lost your friends at Longstop Hill; we've heard about your life as a D-Day Dodger and evading capture once, only to be captured again and be forced to spend two years in a horrific Prisoner of War camp. And we've heard about Irene...the amazing woman you loved so much. Irene must have loved you a great deal too, Frank, to have left her family like that. I think we all understand why you wanted to return and find her family, and we're so glad you found them and that all is well. You are an amazing man, and we'd all like to raise our glasses to you."

There were tears in Frank's eyes, and his hand shook as Claire handed him a glass of champagne. He raised the glass slowly and sipped it, putting his hand out to shake Captain Homarus's hand and waving his thanks to the assembled throng.

"Tell me - what is this 'blog'?" he asked.

"Well, Frank, a blog is a story that someone called Dawn has written about you - to tell the world about your incredible life and the incredible journey you have just been on."

"Who is Dawn?" asked Frank.

"I think we all know that Mary is Dawn," said the captain.

"No - Dawn's in the cabin," I started saying.

"No, you're the one who's been writing this wonderful blog, and you're the one who deserves all the praise."

"So, I didn't manage to convince you that Dawn was in the cabin, then?"

"No, of course not. We knew she wasn't on the ship because she never checked in."

"Oh."

"The blog's great. You're talented," said the captain. "Shall I escort you into dinner?"

"Gosh, thank you," I replied.

VALENCIA WITH JUAN

*A*nother day, another amazing city...the last stop on the cruise. It was incredible to think it was all coming to an end. It had been more astonishing than I could ever have imagined.

We pulled into the port of Valencia, and Juan Pedro raised his arms triumphantly. This was his home city, where he had grown up and learned to dance before his burgeoning profession took him to Paris, New York, and the open seas as head dancer on the cruise ship.

He had promised to take me around his city and tell me all about it...unveil all the hidden treasures that normal tourists never saw..., but when I met him on the deck, he seemed unusually pensive and not as exuberant as I was expecting.

"Everything OK?" I asked.

"Well, yes," he said, but it didn't sound as if everything was OK.

"You sure?"

"Everything is fine, but when I come to Valencia, I always think of Javier. He was my one true love. He was a great dancer. We performed together for Ballet Valencia, and I haven't seen him in years. Last time we met, we made out up against the wall outside the men's toilets. It was wonderful."

"Yeah, it doesn't have quite the romance of Frank's story, does it?"

"It was romantic in its own way," he says, with an extravagant toss of his head. "Maybe I will pop into Ballet Valencia, and if he is there, I will say hello; if not, it was not meant to be."

"Sounds like a good plan. What shall we do first?"

"In Valencia? Why – first we eat."

It turned out that Valencia was the perfect place to have a day to wander around. We spent an hour or so exploring the old town before lunch in Casa Montana - one of the oldest restaurants in Valencia. We ate in the busy front bar, lined with wine barrels, and enjoyed big fried anchovies, brown broad beans stewed with chorizo, roasted piquillo peppers stuffed with béchamel and tuna, and jamón ibérico. I wanted fries as well, but Juan said that was tacky. Coming from a man in tight leather trousers that finished halfway up his calf, I wasn't sure whether that was a compliment or an insult.

After lunch, we went to the cathedral, which was just mind-blowing. We saw San Vincente's withered left arm and two Goya paintings, one of which showed a horrifying exorcism and which Juan seemed particularly fond of. He remembered going there as a schoolboy and being mesmerised by it. The guide told us that the windows were made from fine alabaster because Valencia's light is too dazzling for glass. I know this all sounds a bit 'touristy', but I enjoyed every minute.

We went into Ballet Valencia, but there was no sign of Juan's lover – apparently, he had gone on tour with the company to New York.

"I will see him there," said Juan.

"Yes, I've heard the walls next to the men's toilets are nice there," I said.

We then wandered down to the beach for a little siesta - lying on the sand and looking up at the blue skies.

"I don't want to go home," I said.

"Then don't," he replied. "Get a job on a cruise ship and tour the world with me. We'll have the best time ever."

"No - I need to go back. My boyfriend, my mum, my dad, my job..."

"You hate your job," he said.

"Well, that's true, but I have to do it, or I won't be able to afford to eat...and I do like to eat."

"Ha, you're a nutter. Come and live on a cruise ship, and you'll have all the food you could ever want."

As Juan spoke, I heard my phone ring in my bag.

"Hi, Mary speaking," I said.

"Mary, it's Janette here. Are you on the boat anywhere?"

"No, I'm lying on the beach with a ridiculously skinny gay man called Juan. Why? Everything OK?"

"Not really," she said. "Frank's been taken ill."

CONCERNED ABOUT FRANK

*J*uan and I leapt to our feet, grabbed our bags and raced like lunatics through the streets of Valencia, back towards the harbour and onto the ship. The boat was eerily quiet while it was in port. Everyone was making the most of the sunshine and the markets in Valencia. Everyone, that is, except for Frank.

I ran onto the deck and bumped into Claire. "Where is Frank?" I asked.

"Come with me," she said, leading me to the medical rooms.

"Just wait here a minute." She disappeared behind a closed door, and I heard voices, and then Janette came out.

"What is the matter? Is he okay?"

"He is fine; I think he's just exhausted," said Janette. "I was worried about him when I called you because he seemed extraordinarily weak. I sometimes forget how old he is; our trip took it out of him."

"Oh goodness, I feel terrible," I said. "We shouldn't have traipsed around like that; I just wanted him to be able to put his mind at rest and hand over the letters."

"Absolutely," said Janette. "Please don't feel bad; what we did was amazing. I know we've made him a very, very happy man. He's just tired now and needs to rest."

THE MARY BROWN BOOKS

Captain Homarus walked into the room and looked at me quizzically. "Have you come to see a doctor?" he asked.

"No, just checking up on Frank."

"The doctor says he needs to rest; I suggest you give him a few hours and maybe come down later if you want to see him. at that stage, the doctors will know what is going on. "

Janette and I walked out of the small surgery, back to the medical clinic, and out onto the main deck where Juan was waiting for us.

"Why didn't you come in?"

"I hate doctors," he grimaced. "They make me feel ill. Just can't stand them... The smell, the noise, the white coats..."

"There were no white coats, just Captain Homarus, who told us to come back in a couple of hours."

"OK," said Juan. "When you go back, make sure you say hello from me. I promise you - I can't go down there, doctors give me the heebie-jeebies."

"OK, OK," I said. "No need to go down there then."

I turned to Janette: "Do you fancy getting off the boat for a bit?"

I knew that all she'd been doing was looking after Frank; she might fancy an hour in Valencia before going down to see him again.

"I'd love to go out and buy some new clothes. I thought you looked amazing after Juan took you shopping," she said.

"Whaaaat? Really? Are you taking the mickey?"

"No - really - those bright colours and that incredible jewellery. I'd love to dress like that, but I lack confidence."

"Then I shall take you shopping straight away," said Juan. "You see, Mary - this is a woman who knows good taste when she sees it."

"That would be great," said Janette. "I can't leave the ship though...I have to be here in case anything happens to Frank."

"I'll be here," I said suddenly. "I'll stay on board, and if anything happens, I'll phone you straight away."

"Are you sure?" asked Janette.

"Of course, I'm sure," I said. "Perfectly sure...off you go."

Once they had disappeared, I went back to the medical centre and made sure the doctor had my number in case anything happened;

then I strode out onto the deck to sit in the sunshine for a few hours and enjoy a gin and tonic.

HOME SWEET HOME

I popped back down to the medical centre later in the afternoon, but there was no news; Frank was stable and sleeping soundly. He wasn't in any grave danger, but he was weak, and the doctor planned to get him straight to Southampton Hospital when we arrived back.

I went back up to my cabin, texted Janette to update her and did some updates to the blog; then I dressed in a simple black evening dress and went and sat in the bar before dinner, hoping to see Juan and Janette.

Now, when I say 'hoping to see' - it turned out that it was impossible not to see Janette. She walked into the room with all the style and glamour of Elizabeth Taylor in Cleopatra...and almost as much eyeliner.

She'd been transformed. Sure, she was completely over the top because Juan was styling her, but she looked magnificent. I felt dowdy by comparison and vowed to sneak back to the cabin and put more makeup on before dinner.

"You look sensational," I told her, hugging her.

"Thank you," she said, she was beaming. "I love this outfit...I'm chuffed. Isn't Juan amazing?"

"Don't talk about him like that," I said. "He'll get an even bigger head - we need to be bringing him down, not talking him up."

Dinner was called and the three of us sat together, hoping to sit alone and chat about Frank and everything we'd been through, but it was impossible. The entire ship was aware of Frank's illness. Concern and kindness had driven them to join us to enquire about him.

Our dinner was punctuated by the arrival of guests offering to help in any way they could and offering their good wishes.

Arriving back in Southampton was a bitter-sweet moment. I was looking forward to seeing Ted again, and I was looking forward to seeing my friends and telling them all about my adventure, but I would miss these guys. It was strange to think how close we'd all become. I knew we'd be friends forever.

Frank was taken off the ship and put into an ambulance, moaning that he was absolutely fine, and this was just a fuss about nothing, and how he fought in the war and didn't need all this namby-pambying.

"Bye lovely," I said, hugging Janette and giving Juan a huge squeeze. "Let's stay in touch - OK?"

"Definitely," they agreed, and I strode back through the car park to where I could see Ted: lovely, kind Ted, waiting patiently.

"Hello there stranger," I said, giving him a big kiss, and loving the way he lifted me up into the air. "How are you?"

"I'm much happier now you're back," he said. "Come on; let's go home...I want to hear all about it. By the way - do you know that t-shirt makes no grammatical sense at all?"

"Yes, I know," I said. "But I love it – it reminds me of the most amazing time ever. Come on, I'll tell you all about it."

It was three days later when the call came through. I was back at work, stacking bags of compost in the outdoor plant section when my phone rang.

"Frank has died," said Janette, her voice croaky with pain and choking back tears. "He passed away peacefully in his sleep."

It was horrible news, but at least Frank had died knowing that he'd made peace with the world, and now he was reunited with Irene. I hope he died knowing how much he affected my life and how much it meant for me to me to be with him on his Sicilian adventure.

Of course, I went to the funeral and met his friends, who had all heard about our exploits in Sicily. Back at Frank's house, after the funeral, we raised our glasses and toasted the lovely man with a rendition of the song he'd sung to us on that crazy afternoon in Sicily:

"We landed at Salerno, holiday with pay,
Jerry got the band out to help us on our way.
We all sang songs; the beer was free.
We danced all the way through Italy.
We were the D-Day Dodgers, the men who dodged D-Day."

RIP Frank

I WANT TO BE A YOGA LADY

"Oh Charlie, I don't know what to do," I said. "My life's falling apart."

I was standing in my friend's doorway a few weeks after returning from the cruise, clutching a bottle of wine and wearing a look of dismay and disbelief.

"Oh blimey, what's happened?" she asked, ushering me inside. "Nice tan, by the way."

"That's kind of the problem," I attempted to explain.

"What? The tan is the problem? Doesn't look like much of a problem to me. Wine?"

"Yes, please." I followed Charlie through to the kitchen while I explained that I had a lovely tan because of the cruise, and I was missing everyone from the boat, especially Frank.

"Why did he have to die?" I asked plaintively.

"Because he was very old?" said Charlie.

"I know, but he was incredible. The whole cruise was amazing. Everything about it was fab except the fact that I put on so much weight. Those buffets are incredible, you know."

"I've heard about the buffets," said Charlie.

THE MARY BROWN BOOKS

"There's food everywhere on the boat. I put on 10lbs. Ten bloody pounds."

I usually laughed and joked to hide my embarrassment, but I was genuinely concerned about this recent development.

I had been doing so well with my weight loss until the cruise. At the beginning of the year, when I went to Fat Club, I lost a stone and a half. I felt amazing. But then I started to get a bit bored of it all and found I was eating more, which led to me not caring as much, and the weight piled on. Now I was well over the 15-stone mark, and I felt devastated.

Charlie sighed and shook her head. "Well, you'll have to cut back, won't you," she said.

"Cutting back is for someone who's a couple of pounds over fighting weight, not for someone who weighs more than a mini metro," I said.

"You don't weigh more than a car," she replied. "Cars are really heavy."

"I'M really heavy," I responded.

"You need to do some exercise," she said. "Come and join me on my training runs."

"Mate, you're training for a half marathon. I can't walk across the room without panting like a chain-smoking pensioner. Running with you is going to end up with me in an ambulance on the way to a lung transplant."

"You should try one of the classes at my gym, you might like those...there are loads and loads of them," said Charlie.

"Like what?"

"Well – there is Zumba?" she suggested.

"What on earth is that? Zumba sounds like the name of the leader of a Nigerian tribe, not an exercise class."

"It's a dance class. Look..." she reached for her laptop and called up 'Zumba'. Loud music burst out through her computer as energised, young, fit women in various shades of brightly coloured Lycra danced, pranced and jumped around on the screen while a wildly enthusiastic instructor shouted at them. They just kept moving, dancing and spinning, hollering and shrieking. They seemed much slimmer and fitter than I was.

"I would rather sit there with a Stanley knife cutting the fat of my body," I said to Charlie. "Is this an American thing...this Zumba business? I can't imagine anyone with British blood doing it."

"It's great fun, the classes are always packed out," said Charlie. "You should try these things, they might look scary on the screen, but when you're there and the loud music is playing, you'll find you really enjoy it and get fit without realising you're exercising."

"We both know that is a complete lie. Are there any other exercise classes?"

"Yes, there are the traditional classes like aerobics and step."

"No," I said before she had barely finished the sentence. "I tried those when I was 5 stone lighter and hated them. Step is just ridiculous. Thirty fully grown women stepping on and off a bit of plastic that's been put in front of them to trip them up. No thank you. Anything else?"

"Maybe aquarobics will be for you?" said Charlie. "It's a gentler exercise. You don't have any idea how hard you're working at the time because the water supports you, but you definitely feel it the next day. Also, you are in the water, so you won't get injured. It might be a nice introduction to getting back into exercise."

That did, indeed, sound like a rather nice way to lose weight.

"Call it up," I said to Charlie, and she keyed aquarobics into Google and called up a video of a class.

Now, maybe I was overly fussy, but the image that greeted me, of ageing ladies in swim caps waving their arms in the air while a tinny version of Madonna's *Into the Groove* screeched in the background, didn't seem like a wholly worthwhile use of anyone's time.

"Is this a class for old people?" I asked.

"Well, it's a gentle exercise class, as I said, so obviously, it's bound to attract older people, but you get young people doing it too, and it is a tough workout. "

I looked again at the women in their swim hats...wrinkly faces looking out from beneath flowery plastic headgear. I didn't think it was for me.

"Anything else?" I ventured, realising that Charlie was going to get pretty fed up very soon.

"I don't know...there are spin classes, but they are really hard-core, you sit on a bike for an hour cycling furiously, sweat flying everywhere, I don't think you'd like them."

"Nope, that doesn't sound like my sort of thing."

"What do you think is your sort of thing?" Charlie asked.

"Lying on my back and pointing my toes occasionally?" I suggested.

"I know!" shrieked Charlie all of a sudden. "I know what you should do to get yourself back into exercising slowly."

"And this involves lying on your back, pointing your toes occasionally?" I said.

"Pretty much," said Charlie, tapping away into Google.

Onto the screen sprang a lovely image of lots of people lying down while the instructor told them to breathe in deeply and then breathe out again... Breathe in, and breathe out again. I could do that!

"This looks perfect," I said. "What the hell is it?"

"Why," said Charlie with a flourish. "This, my dear friend, is yoga."

On the screen, they continued to lie there while the instructor issued gentle commands about breathing and stretching. All the women looked slim, toned, happy, and deeply relaxed while the lovely instructor talked kindly to them.

"Where do I sign up?" I asked Charlie. "I want to be a yoga lady."

TACKLING THE TREE POSE

*A*t work the next day, I couldn't stop thinking about our conversation. The more I thought about yoga, the more it seemed like it would be the answer to all my woes. One session of lying on the floor in attractive yoga pants and a funky t-shirt would act as a panacea - somehow transforming me...through osmosis or something...into a beautiful, slim and lovely woman who was relaxed, flexible and serene at all times.

The more we'd sat there last night, watching videos while eating crisps and drinking wine, the more converted I'd become to life as a yogi. It seemed like the key to body transformation. A bit of chanting, some toe touching, and a new leotard and I, too, would look like those wondrous women in the videos. I could hardly contain my new-found enthusiasm for the world. The only mystery was why on earth I hadn't done this years ago.

I had memorised some of the poses they'd done in the class on YouTube, and as I watered the geraniums in the garden centre (I work here; I'm not just randomly going around garden centres watering the plants or anything), I tried to think of the poses I'd seen. There was the downward dog which was pretty much the position I ended up in when I tried to pick something up off the floor when I was drunk. It's one thing bending over when you're drunk and slim, quite another thing bending over when you're drunk and 15 stone.

The women in the video had done things like headstands and bridges, which I knew would be entirely beyond me. It would take a crane to get me up there and 20 highly qualified medical professionals to get me safely down afterwards.

Then there were positions that I probably couldn't do at the moment but with a little instruction and some concerted effort, I thought I'd probably be able to do at some stage. One of those was the tree pose. For all you yoga virgins out there, this is when you stand on one leg and put the sole of your other foot on the inside thigh of the leg you are standing on. You start by putting the foot on the inside of your calf, then the knee, then the inner thigh as you progress, then - ta da! - you have your foot flat on the inside of your thigh, right at the top, and you are doing a tree pose.

I looked up...no one was around, so I put down the watering can and decided to give tree pose a go. I balanced on one foot...not all that simple when you're a larger lady, and attempted to place a foot onto my inner calf. Gosh, much harder than it looked.

I moved nearer to the wall so I could reach out and hold on if I felt myself falling. I tried again. I stood up straight and tried to ground myself, then I slowly lifted my right leg, and attempted to put my foot on the inside of my calf. It was hopeless. I felt myself fall as soon as I took one foot off the ground. How could I be so unbalanced?

Right, one more try...I lifted my leg slowly and, trying to ignore the wobbling, put the sole of my shoe onto the inside of my calf. I lasted about a second before I felt myself start to fall. I moved my arms around to try and balance myself. Still, it was no good. I pitched to the side and reached up quickly, intending to lean on the wall, but I was falling faster than I realised, so I made a grab for the nearest thing - a luscious, flower-filled hanging basket that Maureen had spent all morning designing and planting.

I went flying to the ground, one arm windmilling furiously, the other one still clinging to the basket. I hit the ground first and the basket came crashing down on top of me - mud and pansies everywhere and me in the middle, lying on my back.

I wiped the dirt out of my eyes and looked up...there was Keith, my boss, along with Sandra from indoor plants and Jerry from the carpentry section. They were all struggling not to laugh.

"Are you OK?" asked Keith, while the other two bit their lips and choked back their amusement at my plight.

"Yes, I'm fine," I said. "Absolutely fine. I just tripped on some dirt. People need to make sure they clean up after themselves. Someone could really hurt themselves when there's dirt lying around." I wiped the mud off my face and lifted the lovely little flowers off my uniform.

"What were you doing?" asked Jess.

"Just watering the plants," I said.

"We were watching you on the CCTV cameras in our break," said Jerry. "Were you trying to be a flamingo or some- thing? You kept standing on one leg, it was very weird."

"If you must know, I was practising yoga," I said, rolling over and clambering onto my feet. "That move I was doing was called the tree pose."

"Oh," they said, simultaneously. And Keith added: "Well, as long as you're OK. We need to get on, Jerry."

The two of them wandered off, laughing, and leaving me with Jess.

"Do you do much yoga?" she asked.

"I do," I replied. "And I'm going to be doing much more in the future. Though not at work, obviously."

"No, best not destroy any more hanging baskets," said Jess, crouching down to collect the flowers that were strewn all around. "My friend is brilliant at yoga. She's really strong and flexible and says 'Namaste' all the time."

"Yes, like me," I said, nodding as I spoke.

"I think it's amazing that you do yoga. Good for you. Shall I stay and help you clear all this up?" she asked.

"No, it's fine. I can do it. Thanks Jess. And - Namaste."

"Namaste to you too," she replied.

ALL BOOKED UP

Charlie rang at lunchtime. "Slight problem," she said.

"Namaste," I replied.

"What? Anyway, I've been looking at yoga classes at my gym, and you have to do the beginners' course first before you're allowed to go to the normal, timetabled classes."

"Oh, OK, I'll do that then," I replied. "To be honest, a beginners' course wouldn't be a bad idea, I have a feeling it's harder than it looks." I omitted to tell her that my initial experiences with tree pose had left me covered in mud and pansies and the laughingstock of the shop. I still had soil down the front of my uniform, but she didn't need to know about that.

"Yes - I agree. The trouble is - the next course is in January, and it's already fully booked and with a six-person waiting list. The course after that is in April. Shall I book us onto the April one?"

"No," I yelled. "I don't want to wait til then. It's October now. I plan to be eight stone for Christmas. Is there anything else we can do? I want to learn how to do the tree pose."

"The tree pose? Really? OK, well, there are a few options...we could go to a different gym, join up, and see whether we could do a yoga course there, but all the other gyms in the area are expensive."

"Yeah, I'm not all that fond of doing anything really expensive, and you want to stay at Palisades while you're doing your marathon training, don't you?"

"Yes, ideally," replied Charlie. "There is something else we could do though. We could go on a yoga retreat where they teach you all the basics, then when we come back, we could go along to lessons and tell them we've done a beginners' course, so they'd let us straight on. That would be much quicker."

"That sounds good," I said. "Kind of yoga cramming for the weekend."

"Yeah, I think so," said Charlie. "There's a course this weekend at a place called Vishraam House in the New Forest. Two nights stay...beginners' yoga."

"Let's do it," I said boldly. "Come on, let's get onto this course and into Lycra."

"Maybe I should come around to yours tonight and we'll look through it properly, then book it if you think you fancy it. You know - if you think you're up to it."

"Up to it? I think yoga is going to be the making of me," I said. "Just you wait."

Charlie came around at 7 pm that evening, and I had to unravel myself before answering the door. I was trying the tree pose again, but this time I was using a pair of tights to lift my foot into place while leaning against the wall. Even with the help of the prop it was proving quite a task. My hands were sore from pulling on the tights and my foot wouldn't go into place.

"Come in," I said, still with tights in hand.

Charlie gave me a book about yoga. "For you," she said. "Keep it on your bedside table."

She glanced at the underwear in my hand, but I couldn't summon the words to explain, so I sat her down and began finding out about yoga weekends.

"Show me the retreats then," I said, and I thought how grown-up Charlie and I seemed looking at the images of health, fitness and good living on the screen. All the holidays we'd ever been on before had resulted in hospital visits, altercations with the police, and huge amounts of drinking. This time it would be altogether different.

"Here we are," she said. "Look - there are various different types of courses...you can specialise in different yogas...there's Ashtanga - isn't that the one that Madonna does? And I think Hatha yoga is the Megan Markle one. I don't know which one is better? And what's this Bikram Yoga? Hang on, isn't that the one that Pippa Middleton does?"

"I don't know," I said as I looked down the list...there were so many. "Aerial yoga? What the hell is that?" I asked. Charlie shrugged. We didn't really know what we were doing at all.

"Look up aerial yoga, I have to know," I commanded. For some reason, when it came to any sort of research or planning, it was always Charlie sitting in front of the screen, and me barking orders.

"Oh blimey. Very 50 shades of grey," she said, turning the screen round so I could see. There were lots of people hanging from the ceiling by ropes, with little hammocks at the bottom. They were pulling themselves up the ropes and rolling out of the hammocks. It looked fraught with danger. If the thing took my weight in the first place it was sure to be impossible for me to get in and out of it.

"Na," I said, and she nodded in agreement.

"Oh, how about one of these?" she said. She had pulled up a list of general yoga courses where you did all the different yogas on one weekend instead of having to specialise...they came in beginners, intermediate and advanced.

"Here we go," said Charlie. "A basic introduction to all the different types of yoga as well as meditation, mindfulness and clean living."

"Sounds like us," I said. "Oh, but how about this one?"

Below it were the more advanced courses including one called 'guru-led advanced course.'

"Stick it in the basket. I want a guru," I said, clicking on it and adding it into out virtual shopping bag.

"Oy, stop it. I don't think either of us is ready for an advanced course," said Charlie.

"OK - gurus next time," I conceded, and we booked ourselves onto a beginners' course for the weekend by emailing a woman called Venetta.

"I'm quite excited," I said. "It's run by someone whose name sounds a little bit like an ice-cream...that has to be a good thing, surely."

"Definitely," she agreed, with a small squeal. "This could be really good fun. I hope I don't make a fool of myself."

"Oh come now, Charlie," I replied. "We both know which one of us is more likely to make a fool of herself."

THE LAST SUPPER

In the lead-up to the course, I thought it would be wise to try and start living the life that I would be required to live on the retreat. I couldn't go from full-blown Chinese takeaways and large glasses of sauvignon to slices of air-dried mango, chakras and finding my inner goddess. I needed to ease myself into the new lifestyle gently, so I vowed to try and eat as healthily as possible in the few days before we left.

I started making changes on Thursday morning, the day before departure. I had a mug of hot water with a squeeze of lemon in it. It was supposed to curb my appetite and remove the yearning for a fried breakfast and loads of mid-morning biscuits. It tasted so awful that I could barely drink the stuff. I only had a couple of sips and knew that if I were to have any chance of finishing it, I'd have to add sugar, which would completely spoil the whole point of doing it in the first place.

Instead, I sipped green tea and ate slices of apple. Christ, it was dull. I phoned Charlie.

"This is shit, isn't it?" I said, looking at the limp pieces of peeled apple lying pathetically on the plate in front of me.

"Yep," she said. "But just imagine - we'll get used to healthy eating and return completely transformed. Just try to keep going...it'll do you the world of good. I'm about to have some grapefruit."

"Ahhh..." I said. "That's the most evil of all the fruits. To be honest, I don't know how it has the audacity to call itself a fruit. It's awful stuff."

The whole day was ruined by the thought lingering in my head that I wasn't allowed to have anything nice to eat and that I would be hungry all the time. My breaks weren't any fun, and lunchtime was pointless. Chicken salad? I mean - what's the point? Where's the warmth, happiness or joy derived from chewy poached chicken and a collection of garden leaves?

I got home that evening and slumped on the sofa, feeling out of sorts and slightly angry with the world. Ted, my boyfriend, was due to be coming around for the evening because I wouldn't see him for the next few days, but I couldn't face company, I felt all empty inside. I'm not sure whether anyone who doesn't overeat could ever understand this, but I felt horrible without being able to eat food that filled me up and made me feel all warm and lovely inside. All irritable and like there was no point to anything. The whole world felt prickly. I was unbalanced and cross. I told Ted I had a headache and sat on the sofa to spend the evening feeling sorry for myself.

I know this sounds pathetic, but it was so horrible being hungry. I felt so deprived, which led to loneliness and sadness. The lack of food seemed to signal a lack of comfort and warmth. I started to think that my life was not worth living...in my mind I began to question my job, my boyfriend, my friends and my family.

Eating isn't just about putting food inside me, it's about nurturing, warming and comforting myself and stopping myself from feeling sad and lonely. And - I know what you're thinking - I should address the things that were making me feel sad and lonely rather than just eating myself into an emotional slumber, but doing that would take months of self-analysis and confrontation with my darkest fears. Whereas a cheeky chicken and black bean sauce would take half an hour to arrive, and I'd feel great. That's why - at the end of the day - whenever I felt low, I always ate.

And it was very easy for me to justify overeating to myself. When I couldn't think of anything else but being full of lovely, tasty food, I could easily convince myself that eating obscene amounts was actually the best thing I could possibly do.

On that warm evening, I picked up the takeaway leaflet and told myself that this was the last chance I had to eat a big meal, and it would be a good thing if I ate well tonight because it would make me more committed, and give me the strength to throw myself into the weekend ahead.

So, I ordered the food and felt almost drunk and helpless with anticipation while I waited for it to arrive. The ring of the bell sent electric pulses of joy through me, and I practically danced to the door to collect the food. I had chicken and black bean sauce with egg fried rice, and I ate all the free prawn crackers that came with it. I loved eating when there was a lot of food. When I started picking at the food and could see there was absolutely loads more to eat, it gave me a real thrill.

The food was not quite the same without a couple of glasses of wine, of course, so I did that too. I'm like an animal when I eat. It's always better to be alone when I get the real hungers. I poured myself another large glass of wine, feeling drunk on food and alcohol and completely relaxed like I'd just had that drug you have before an anaesthetic...the one that knocks you out a bit and makes you feel drowsy without rendering you completely unconscious.

There were crumbs all over the place, and I'd managed to get dribbles of black bean sauce on my sweatshirt, but that didn't matter; they could be cleaned. All that mattered was that I felt relaxed and happy, and lovely. I just wanted to lay there and bask in the loveliness for a while. I knew I'd feel rotten later...really low, disappointed in myself, and frustrated at my lack of willpower, but I'd deal with those feelings when they arose. For now, it was all about the feelings of light-headedness, satisfaction and warmth. Mmmm...

When I woke the next morning, the memory of what I'd done hit me in an instant. Shit, I'd had a huge takeaway and a bottle of wine the night before. Damn. I'd bought lemons and apples and all sorts of healthy food so that I wouldn't be tempted over to the dark side, then I'd gone and bloody ordered a takeaway.

I'd just have to try and be good this weekend to make up for it. I sat up in bed and saw the yoga book perched on my bedside cabinet, waiting to be read.

I turned to the section by a woman called Rachel Brathen. In it, the woman was describing all sorts of thoroughly awful things that had happened to her when she was younger. She wrote about how she was drinking too much and being sick and how her life was totally out of control...then she found yoga, and everything came together for her. She felt peace at last. A lovely, warm feeling ran through me as I read the words and absorbed her philosophy.

"There is no need to change your habits to make space for a yoga practice," she wrote. "Start practising yoga from where you are today, and let the practice change you. The more often you come to the mat, on your own or in a class, the easier it will be to make healthy decisions throughout the rest of your day. When you're listening more to your body, you'll find that it's not as difficult to eat well. With awareness of your body, you'll find it easier to stay away from sugar or alcohol or whatever it is that you're looking to remove from your diet. Or perhaps you will realise that the foods you're eating are just fine, nothing to obsess over at all! The bottom line is that you will be more conscious about how your body feels and how sensitive it is to what you put in it, maybe that the second helping of food didn't make you feel better after all.

"When we live more in the body and less in the mind, those choices that were so overwhelming before become easier to make. I know that when I really listen to my body, it very rarely wants two huge helpings of food. If I reach for more, it's probably because I'm busy talking and socialising or I'm feeling emotional. If I stay mindful, I'll be able to tell when I'm full. Much of what we eat in a day is simply a result of boredom. I'm not promising you'll stop wanting dessert or wine or all the good things that come with life just because you start practising yoga. You'll simply be more receptive to what your body wants and needs. And this is the very first step to healthy you."

I wished I hadn't eaten all that food last night. I wished I could think of other ways to cope when I was overcome by this emotional hunger that seemed to suck me into it, so that I had no control over myself. Sometimes the feeling was so overpowering that I felt I had no choice but to eat. Perhaps yoga could help me find a balance. Find peace? It was certainly worth a try.

A MUD BATH IN THE CHICKEN COOP

"I can't quite believe we're doing this, can you?" Charlie said, as I slid into the car next to her and made a token effort to put the seat belt on, knowing there was no way on earth it would go around me. I squeezed, pulled, and then dropped it, letting it fall by my side. Luckily, her's wasn't a bleeping seat belt. Those cars that start beeping at you when you can't do the seat belt up are a pain for anyone over about a size 18. The damn car can bleep as much as it wants, and the seat belt won't go around me, however much noise it makes.

"I think this weekend might be good for us," I said. Charlie raised her eyebrows in amazement. "You know, I read the yoga book you gave me, and it all sounded great. This woman was writing about how much it had helped her spiritually, and I thought - this weekend could be life-changing. It could be the time I get myself sorted, get myself together and really clear my life out. You never know.

"Well, let's hope so," said Charlie. "I can't say I'm feeling as positive. I hate being hungry, and I think they only give us tiny portions. I'm worried it's going to be hard to concentrate on the yoga and do well at it when we're hungry all the time."

"Well, yes, I'm not great with hunger either," I said. "I did treat myself to the most enormous takeaway last night."

"Whaaat? I thought we were trying to detox yesterday so we'd be ready for today."

"I know, but I just couldn't. I feel so miserable when I'm hungry."

"You're gonna be great company at a bloody detox yoga weekend then, aren't you?"

We drove along in silence for a while.

"So, how much food do you think we'll get at this place?"

"I don't know, but all the comments on the website say that it was a great place except that they were all starving the whole time."

"Oh God, this is going to be horrible, isn't it? I'm dreading it now. I don't mind eating healthy foods, if we have to, but I don't want to be hungry. Should we get some snacks just in case it gets desperate?"

"We're supposed to be detoxing," said Charlie, admonishingly. "Maybe we should try and do it by eating their food and see how we go?"

"Really?" I replied, looking over at Charlie. "OK, fine. If you think you can survive for three days on half a cashew nut and a teaspoon of peach extract, I'm sure I can, too. "

"Oh, sod it," she said, veering across two lanes of traffic and into the service station. "Let's get some nibbles so we have supplies in our bags in case things get desperate. As you say, we don't have to eat them all, do we?"

"No, it will be useful to have them, just in case we want them."

"Yes."

We decided that I would be in charge of snack purchasing, so Charlie put petrol in while I went inside and filled up with crisps, nuts, rice cakes and a couple of bottles of wine...just in case. It was all very naughty, but if we didn't eat it, we could easily bring it back with us.

I got back to the car with my bag full of goodies. Charlie was in the shop paying for petrol. I plonked the bag in the boot. Then I panicked...what if we weren't supposed to take snacks with us? I had a

BERNICE BLOOM

big suitcase with me with lots of room, so I decanted half of the goodies I could fit into my case. I shut the boot and got into the car.

"Right, where are we going?" Charlie asked as she took her seat beside me.

"I don't know," I said. "You're holding the map."

"I can't drive and look at it; you'll have to read it."

"I'm rubbish at anything map-related," I said. "We'll end up in Norfolk."

"No, we won't, and we'll have the sat nav on; we just need to keep an eye on the map as well because the instructions from the centre say that it is quite hard to find."

"OK," I said.

"Did you not get any snacks in the end?" Charlie asked.

"Yep, just a couple of things. I put the bag in the boot."

"Great. OK, let's go. The location is plugged into the sat nav; you have the map - we're sure to be OK."

I should point out that no one in the history of the world has ever said that my map reading would mean us being ok.

Still, Charlie seemed convinced, and we settled into driving along the pretty country lanes, guided by the satnav. I sat back and relaxed, wallowing in the tranquil sights as we moved further away from home and closer to our weekend rural retreat. The sun's rays reached through the windows as we drove along, caressing my face and arm. It was lovely.

"Right, this is where I could do with your help," said Charlie. I was half asleep, enjoying the gentle motion of the car, when I was brought joltingly back to reality.

"I think there is a left turn coming up...this is the one that their website said wasn't recognised by satnav. It's called Farm Gate Road."

"I'm on it," I said, peering out of the window in search of the road.

"Can you not see it on the map?" said Charlie.

"No, I can't do maps, I don't understand them."

"Oh God," said Charlie. "Well, have a look out of the window and see whether you can see it. I'll drive really slowly.

So, we trundled along the country lanes at a ridiculously slow speed with a very, very fat lady hanging out of the window looking for the road, while clutching a map that would easily have told her where it was.

"Here, look," I said, spotting a small side road that appeared to lead up to a farm. It had a gate about 20 yards along it. "This has to be Old Farm Gate Road. It has all the ingredients."

Charlie slowed and looked at the road, then at the map.

"It does look like it," she conceded. "It leads to an old farm, and it has a gate. What other clues could we ask for? Yay! I think we've found it."

Charlie indicated and pulled into the lane, stopping just before the gate. I clambered out of the car and waddled over to it, unlatching it and holding the gate open, bowing down to Charlie with a flourish as she drove through. I returned to the car, and we drove around the corner. As soon as we drove to the other side of the house, there was a great big flutter as hens and chickens flew up everywhere. Peacocks came striding up to the car, and geese began to make the most horrific crying sound. Charlie jumped on the brake.

"Fuck," we both said as the animals made a colossal noise, screeching and screaming and flapping all around us.

"Reverse...let's get out of here," I said.

Charlie was just sitting there. I couldn't understand it. "Let's go," I said. "This is the wrong place. This is the farmer next door. He's mentioned in the booklet they get all their fresh produce from him."

"I know we're in the wrong place, but I can't start suddenly reversing, or I'll crush half a dozen peacocks."

I looked in the mirror at the birds gathering behind us. Charlie was right...there were birds all around the car now.

"OK, look - don't panic - I'll get out and shoo them out of the way, then you reverse. OK?"

"You're going to shoo them away? What are you, all of a sudden? Some sort of champion ornithologist?"

"I don't know what that is, and I've no idea how I'm going to shoo them away, but I'm willing to try. Are you ready to reverse when I give you the signal?"

"Yes," said Charlie.

"Right, OK."

I clambered out of the car and found myself ankle-deep in mud. It was like thick chocolate sauce. I pulled my foot out and moved slowly to the back of the car, taking off my hoodie and waving it in the air.

"Shoo, shoo, shoo," I cried. "Off you go, birds, off you go. And you, peacock - be away with you. Go, go." I clapped my hands ferociously, and they ran, flew and quacked away.

"OK, go," I shouted to my get-away driver, and Charlie put her foot down hard on the accelerator. The car growled but didn't go anywhere.

"Take the handbrake off," I instructed.

"I haven't got the handbrake on. The car is stuck. I can't move it at all. It must be because of all the mud."

"Oh God."

I could see two figures in the distance, walking through the field towards us. One of the guys was waving a stick in the air. He was clearly ranting at us, presumably telling us to get off his land and to stop petrifying his birds.

"Right, strategic thinking," I said, trying to sound like I had half a clue what I was doing. I should point out at this stage that I don't drive and know nothing about cars. Still, in the absence of anyone else's advice, mine would have to do.

"OK, I'll try pushing the car," I said, wading round to the front. I now had mud all over my pale pink jogging bottoms, and my beautiful new trainers were completely covered. You couldn't see what colour they were (pink, in case you were wondering).

"Are you ready?"

"Yes," said Charlie, pressing her foot down hard on the accelerator. I pushed with all my might, and mud splattered everywhere. I could feel it in my hair and on my face. There were chickens and hens all over the place, all clucking and making the most terrible row.

In the distance, I could hear the farmer shouting. "Get out of there. What do you think you are doing? Get out of my hen coop."

Oh, Christ, the car wasn't going anywhere, and the angry-looking men were getting closer.

"Let's try again," I suggested, with one eye on the fast-approaching men and the other on the peacocks who kept striding confidently behind the car.

"Are you ready?" I asked and primed myself to push with every fibre of my being.

"Go," I said, and Charlie reversed the car. I pressed my whole body against the bonnet and pushed with all my might; the car skidded a little, then flew backwards, and I went with it, landing with a heavy thump. My lovely pink and white yoga kit was now covered in mud. There was mud on my face and my hair, feathers stuck to me, and chickens looked at me distastefully as they clucked and ran around.

"Quickly, get in the car," said Charlie. I clambered to my feet, sliding in the mud as I attempted to run towards the car. I finally made it over to the passenger side and joined her. I was filthy from head to foot; stray feathers had nestled in my mud-coated hair. I could taste mud and see it lying on my eyelashes. I'd never been so filthy in my entire life; I was caked in it.

Charlie reversed out and onto the road. She stopped for a moment so I could shut the gate. The trouble was that the men were getting closer, and their voices were getting louder.

"They'll shut the gate; let's just go," I said, slinking down into the seat. "Go, go, go..."

Charlie raced away from the farm as if we'd just done a bank robbery or a drugs deal.

"I don't know where to go now," she said, but a minute later, there was a very clear road sign on the right.

"Farm Gate," I shouted, and Charlie threw the car across the road and up the narrow lane leading to Vishraam House.

We drove along in silence. It was a long, gravel drive with pretty pink flowers in pots all along it until the driveway opened out and there, in front of us, was a magnificent country house - a lovely white building with turrets and a huge oak door. It was stunning.

"Wow," said Charlie, stopping next to the half a dozen cars parked

BERNICE BLOOM

outside. All the other cars were super expensive looking. Charlie pulled into the space in the middle of them, and we stopped for a moment to admire the views.

On the right of the house, there were horses and cows in the fields. On the left, near where all the cars were parked, there was a meadow full of wildflowers.

"Just look at that," I said, sweeping my mud-drenched arm across to indicate the bucolic scene. There was a gorgeous lake with trees on either side and lovely, colourful plants and shrubs. I once went on holiday to Corsica, and this reminded me of that place - just bliss, utterly idyllic.

"I can't wait to see what the house is like," I said to Charlie.

"I bet it's amazing," she replied. "I'm so excited now. This weekend is going to be brilliant. Just one problem."

"What's that?"

"You. You're covered in mud. Just look at the state you've made of my car. You can't go into her house like that."

"I'll have to," I said. "I can try to wipe some of the mud off on a towel, but what else can I do?"

Charlie was looking down towards the lake. "You're going to have to go in there," she said.

"No way."

"You can go in, quickly wash the mud off, and then dry yourself. You'll be in there for five minutes, and you'll be clean. What other option do you have?"

"But it will be freezing," I said.

"If you're quick, you'll hardly notice it, she said.

"Hardly notice what? The freezing cold?"

"Yes - it's probably lovely and refreshing when you get in there."

"Yeah, sure," I said. "Why don't you come with me if it's so wonderful?"

"Because I'm not filthy," said Charlie. "Just go in there and wash it off. You could've cleaned yourself in the time you've been sitting here talking about it. We've got towels in our bags; just go and do it."

"I don't want to," I said, looking down at the cold-looking water.

398

Yes, it was very pretty and would look lovely in a photograph, but I didn't want to go *into* it.

"Just go," said Charlie. "You have to, or we'll have to sit here all day. You can't go in there like that."

Just as Charlie and I debated how on earth I would get the mud off if I didn't go into the water, the grand oak door in the middle of the house opened, and a petite, dark-haired lady with a broad smile came dancing out.

"Hello, hello, welcome, welcome," she said in what sounded like a faint Italian accent. Then she stopped in her tracks when she saw me. "Oh, my goodness, what happened to you?"

Charlie thought quickly on her feet. "Mary loves mud rambling, so went mud rambling before we came here," she said.

"Oh, how wonderful," said the lady, smiling more broadly. "I do like adventurous women. I've never heard of mud rambling, but you must come on our early morning rambles; you'd love it. We end up at the top of the farmer's fields, scaling the high hills and wading through brooks, clambering over trees and bushes... Just your type of thing, I'd have thought."

"Yes, just my sort of thing," I lied.

"Great, then I will definitely organise a serious ramble for you on Sunday morning. Now - let's get you into the shower."

If I'd had any sense at all, at that point, I would have got out of the car, turned, walked away and kept walking until I got back to London. But I didn't. I agreed that mud rambles were wonderful and smiled at her, completely oblivious to just how insane the weekend ahead was about to become.

THE BIG HOUSE IN THE COUNTRY

"Hello, you're back," said the lady with a big smile and a fancy, foreign-sounding accent. "My name's Venetta. I hope the water was OK."

"It was great, thanks," I replied. "Much better than the lake would have been."

"Yes, it's very cold in there. Lovely and refreshing, but desperately cold. Much nicer to have a warm shower after a mud ramble."

"Yes, I agree completely," I said.

The shower had, indeed, been lovely. It was in an open-air shower block at the back of the house, near the small swimming pool. The showers were proper power showers, and the water had been beautifully warm. Now I was back in the main entrance hall where Charlie had waited for me. I was wet rather than dirty and wrapped in a white dressing gown that only just about went around me. I imagined these gowns were huge on most people - making them feel swaddled, warm and safe. It barely fit me, meaning there was great danger of overexposure. With every step I took, I held the front of the gown together lest it gaped open. I didn't want our friendly host to see any of my unwaxed lady bits. I didn't want to cause alarm in this serene building in this beautiful part of the country.

"Right then...who's who?" she said, pulling out her notes and taking two sheets of paper out.

"I'm Mary; this is Charlie," I replied, putting out my hand to shake hers, but she just bowed, smiling at me and moving her hands into a prayer position.

"There's no need to shake hands," she said. "We tend to greet each other more simply."

"OK, I'll try to remember that," I said.

"You know that shaking hands is about lack of trust, don't you?" she said.

I gave her a confused look and said I didn't really know anything about that. "Yes, the handshake was developed to prove to people that you weren't carrying a weapon. If they took your right hand, that would show them you were unarmed."

"Oh," I said. "I didn't know that."

"Here, we don't need proof that you come in peace; we don't need proof of your character...we trust you and believe that you will do no wrong."

I had a sudden flashback to the peacocks and the hens in the farmyard, flapping their way out of the car's path, the angry farmer charging down the hill, and the way we'd driven off without closing the gate.

"Take a seat," she said, and I looked for a chair. There weren't any that I could see. When I looked back at her, she was sitting on the floor in the lotus position. Good God.

Charlie and I clambered down onto the floor, Charlie executing the manoeuvre with much more dignity than I managed. I sat with my legs out in front of me. There was no point even pretending I could do the limb origami thing.

Next, there was an awkward silence while she breathed deeply and noisily. Charlie and I glanced at one another, not knowing whether to join in, ignore her or fetch her a tissue.

"Let us rise," she said.

Christ, I was exhausted already. I clambered to my feet. On the table in front of her were rice cakes, low-calorie crisps and wine...

not unlike those I'd brought. She indicted them and looked back at me.

"Yum," I said, raising my eyebrows and smiling. "That's cheered me up!"

"Not really 'Yum' though, is it?" said Venetta, dropping her head to one side and looking at me in what you could describe as a maternal fashion or a patronising fashion, depending on your point of view. I decided to go for patronising.

"While you were in the shower, Charlie brought your bags in from the car," she said. "There was a suitcase which Charlie said belonged to you, and Jonty has taken to your room, along with Charlie's holdall, and there was also a carrier bag.

"I'm afraid that I couldn't help but notice that it was full of food and drink. I don't want to be a spoilsport, but you will get the most out of this low-calorie retreat if you eat low calories. If you don't, I'm afraid you won't feel the benefit in your body, mind or spirit. Do you understand?"

I nodded like a naughty schoolgirl.

"I think it would be best if I took this bag. I will give everything back to you when you leave. If you really want them, you will find them in this cupboard. But I urge you to resist taking them. I think it would do you a lot of good if you tried to stick to the programme and just live a much simpler life while you're here. I think you will feel the benefits if you do."

Charlie and I stood there like naughty schoolgirls while she took the bag over to a cupboard and pushed it inside. "I will leave them here. They are yours to take away with you, but I think you will find that you no longer want them by the end of the course. This is the advanced yoga weekend with raw, vegan, no-sugar, and no-salt food. Under the guidance of the Guru Aaraadhy Motee Ladakee, you will find that you can cleanse and clear and direct attention to your inner self so you can focus on yogic practices. I'm afraid that will be much harder to do if you eat crisps and drink wine every night."

"Of course," I said. I looked over at Charlie. There was so much wrong with what Venetta had just said that it was hard to know where to start. She had taken our snacks - that was one bloody awful thing. Thank God I had a few more in my suitcase. The other terrible thing was that we appeared to have been booked onto the advanced course with a guru.

"Peace be with you," she said as we stood open-mouthed. "Now, let me show you around the house - please treat it like your home. I think you will enjoy your couple of days here very much. I know you will enjoy meeting the guru...we call him Guru Motee for short. His full name is very difficult to remember. Here... look at the house..."

The place was amazing, as we knew it would be from our first glance of it from the outside. We walked around behind her, listening to her sing-song voice describe the place, and I'm sure both of us were thinking the same thing - why didn't we tell her that we weren't booked on the advanced course with a guru? We were booked onto the most basic course in the brochure. But we stayed silent and just watched as we were led around. I was embarrassed about turning up covered in mud, and embarrassed about the snacks, I didn't have the strength to admit that, in addition to all that, it now turned out we were on completely the wrong course.

Venetta took us from the wide hallway with its beautifully polished wooden floors and gorgeous antique-style table to the rooms at the back of the house. She told us that she loved antiques and regularly went to London and Europe on antique-finding missions. It showed... the house boasted class and sophistication. Everything looked so expensive. She must have been making a lot of money from her yoga retreats and investing it in the house.

She took us first of all into the conservatory where the mindfulness and meditation classes were to be held. It had a lovely, warm, cosy feeling... soft rugs piled up at the side, comfy armchairs, and piles of mats and blankets in the far corner. Next to the conservatory was what looked much more like an exercise classroom. The wooden floors, the mirrors, the bar. Everything you expect of an exercise room in a gym.

"This is where the yoga takes place," she said. We walked through

BERNICE BLOOM

that to another small room at the back where one-to-one yoga classes took place. The room had mirrors all around.

"Blimey, this is all quite intensive," I said, trying to ignore the sight of myself beaming back at me from all angles in all the mirrors.

"Well, intensity is what you expect at this level, isn't it?" she said. I glanced at Charlie as I felt myself shrink a little.

We walked out of the private tuition room and back through the main yoga room, out into the body of the house, where Venetta showed us the dining room, a small but rather richly appointed place that looked more formal than previously seen.

She opened the door and showed us the outside area where I'd had my shower so that Charlie could see the swimming pool and hot tub area. There were lots of deckchairs to relax on and an outdoor table for when the weather permitted outdoor eating.

"We tend to eat outside in the summer whenever we can," she said. "But if it gets too cold or it rains, we just head for the dining room."

We walked back through the front of her home, and she showed us a sitting room with a library room trailing off it. It was a lovely house. It was a shame we had to do exercise...it would be a great place to come and chill out, read books, laze around, and eat lovely big roast dinners.

"Feel free to use any of the rooms," she said. "I'd like you to treat this place like your home... borrow any of the books you want to read, and let me know if there's anything I can do to help."

"Thank you," I said. I was tempted to say: "You could help by giving me back my snacks," but that felt a little unfair given how friendly and welcoming she was being, and given that - to be fair to her - we were on a detox yoga retreat, and it did explicitly say in the brochure that we were not to bring any food or drink into the house, and to eat only what was provide..

Venetta wandered up the stairs, pointing out all the rooms on the first floor. We were based in the loft on the top floor, there were just two bedrooms up there. Charlie and I were sharing one of them. It was a lovely big room, very plain, with wooden floors and white bed sheets, white chest of drawers and white towels. There was a kind of wet room - a large shower at the side of the room, equipped - of course - with white soap, white shampoo and white conditioner. I don't know what it was with all the white – perhaps it was about being serene, healthy, and pure. It was perfectly nice, though, if a little plain.

"I hope you'll be happy here," she said. "We have a full complement of people for the course today. The others are all based on the second floor; you are the only ones up here, so you should get lots of peace and quiet if you want to meditate or work on your yoga poses."

"Yes, I imagine we'll be doing a lot of that," I said as Venetta backed away to the door, wishing us a peaceful hour.

"Please report for the introductions at 4 pm," she said as she left.

"Of course," I said, bowing stupidly and sitting down on my bed. "I hope you have a peaceful hour, too," I added.

"You're such a dick sometimes," said Charlie, and I nodded. It was hard to disagree with her.

MEETING THE GANG

"Welcome to Vishraam," said Venetta, opening her arms as if to indicate how welcome we all were before wafting them together again, gently caressing the air between them as she did so. Venetta moved her hands into the prayer position and bowed her head. I noticed that the others in the room were doing similarly, so I kicked Charlie in the shin and we both put our hands into the prayer position and dropped our heads in a way that we hadn't done since we were sitting cross-legged in assembly, aged seven.

"As you will all know, as elite practitioners of yoga, 'Vishraam' means 'relaxation' in Hindu. We all hope you will find this weekend to be the most relaxing and energising few days you have ever spent. We are experts at ensuring the environments we create are full of kindness and joy. Please enjoy everything we have to offer. Treat the house as your own and welcome the hunger you feel on our low-calorie vegan diets. Enjoy how your body responds and lift yourself to the challenge of performing yoga here. It is only by overcoming that we reach a higher place."

There were nods and murmurs from around the room, and I realised that Charlie and I were the only people who'd had no idea what the Hindu for 'relaxation' was. I also realised that this was the second time that Venetta had referred to us as 'elite' and 'experts' which seemed both unusual and concerning. The only yoga I'd ever done in my life had left me face first in the pot plants at the garden centre; calling me an 'expert' in yoga would be like calling Kylie Minogue an expert in street fighting. No, simply not true. The opposite of 'expert', in fact.

"We're supposed to be on the bloody beginners' course," whispered Charlie.

"I know," I said to Charlie. "We *are* on the beginners' course. I don't think she realises. She's eaten too many hemp seeds and doesn't know what she's doing."

"I think we're on the wrong course. She couldn't have got it wrong twice. And look at these people - they don't look like beginners to me."

There were eight of us on the course in total. I looked around the room at them...all looking so sincere. It troubled me how thin they all were; if you stuck them all together, they would weigh about as much as I did. Blimey, yoga people are thin. Have you seen them? All wiry and serious looking. The guys on the course looked as fit and lean as athletes, but I couldn't imagine they were much fun at parties. Or anywhere. I don't imagine they could have had a day's fun in their lives. I really hoped they'd prove me wrong.

Venetta invited us to sit around in a circle while we welcomed one another with serenity and kindness. I glanced at Charlie as Venetta said, 'serenity and kindness;' we both tried not to laugh. I didn't think what they were saying was mad or anything. Nothing wrong with serenity, and who on earth could object to a bit of kindness? I suppose I was just a bit embarrassed; I'd never heard anyone talk in such an unselfconscious way before, and I couldn't help but giggle.

I was trying hard to focus because I desperately wanted to change my life and be fitter, stronger and slimmer. I wanted to be like these people, especially the two incredibly beautiful women on the far side of the room who I found myself staring at, but it was difficult to adjust to all the sincerity. The two women must have been around the same age as me (about 30), but in all other ways, they were completely different - beautiful, elegant, relaxed, composed and slim.

"This is our safe circle," said Venetta.

Everyone was sitting with their bony legs crossed in the lotus position. They were all holding their arms out, palms up, with their hands resting gently on their knees. It was hard enough for me to get myself down onto the floor without me attempting to contort my legs into a fiendish tied-up position. We all sat there in silence.

Just when I was starting to think some of the guys in the group had fallen asleep, Venetta started chanting, and the others all joined in - deep sounds resonated through the room...sounds which made no sense. I sort of joined in, but I felt such an idiot chanting and oooing and ahhing. The loudest noise came from a very handsome man with dark hair; my God, he was good-looking, like a young Elvis Presley.

Finally, it all stopped, and Venetta told us to relax. I immediately lay back and got myself as comfortable as possible, but when I looked up, the others had remained in the lotus position and were looking at Venetta, who was looking quizzically at me.

I scrambled to sit up as quickly as my size would allow. "There's no need to sit up," she said warmly. "Just make yourself comfortable while we introduce ourselves."

There were six people in the group in addition to Charlie and me... a mixture of ages and both sexes were there...the one thing which united them, the one thing they had in common was that they were super slim and super fit looking unlike me.

I looked over to smile at the lovely dark-haired man and found myself staring at the two beautiful women on the far side of the room again...really, they were the most elegant-looking people I have ever seen. They sat there, smiling beatifically in their coordinating leisurewear. They looked simple and comfortable, but their clothing probably cost more than the average family car.

A lady who was introduced as Philippa was the slightly more attractive of the two of them. She was dressed in pale grey leggings and a matching jumper. Her clothes looked like they were made of cashmere or some other luxurious fibre. They were complemented by a soft lilac shawl thrown across her shoulders.

Her friend wore lilac leggings and a winter white woollen tunic with a grey shawl over her shoulders. They lounged next to one another with their matching perfect hair and teeth... Philippa's dark hair fell over her shoulders in waves...she reminded me of Meghan Markle: all dazzling smile and perfect figure. Sarah wasn't quite as beautiful as Philippa but still had an air of wealth, good breeding, and the same enviable taste in knitwear. There was something very fascinating about their perfection; it seemed so complete and absolute. You just knew by looking at them that their bras and knickers matched and had been purchased from some fabulous Parisian lingerie designer. There was no way she bought them in Tesco like I did. I could see Philippa's perfect fingernails, painted in a delicate shade of mocha, which matched her toenails.

As I watched her, she lifted her dark hair into a high ponytail and tied it with a lilac band that - obviously - matched her shawl. How do people manage to do that? She looked like she was living in a magazine spread. I longed to look like her.

Sarah stretched her legs out in front of her and folded herself over them, allowing me to see that her manicure and pedicure also matched perfectly... In bright red, which looked beautiful next to the lilac leggings. Her hair was also long, but it didn't seem quite as long as Philippa's, which had cascaded over her shoulders until she tied it up. Sarah's hair was in an immaculate bun that sat high on her head like a prima ballerina.

"I want to be her," I said to Charlie as Meghan Markle introduced herself.

"I've been doing yoga all my life," she said. "It was something my mother introduced to me from an early age because she ran her own yoga studio."

"Of course she did," I mumbled to Charlie. "While we were eating crisps in front of Neighbours, Miss Perfect was meditating in the tree position...life's so unfair."

BERNICE BLOOM

"So unfair," said Charlie. "But don't mention crisps...you're making me hungry. Still can't believe that woman stole our snacks."

We shook our heads in mutual incomprehension at the fate that had befallen our foodstuffs.

"I spend my time helping people wherever I can," said Perfect Philippa. "I also love to go for walks along the beach, and I like to bathe in the ocean when the stars are out. I sit on the rocks reading poetry at night and practice yoga daily."

It turned out that Sarah was equally well-versed in the art of yoga. She had met the gorgeous Philippa at nursery school, and they'd been best friends ever since. They smiled girlishly at one another, and I expected butterflies to emerge from between them and for tiny cartoon deer to dance around them.

"These people are so perfect," I growled at Charlie with undisguised jealousy.

"I reckon one night Sarah will do one downward dog too many, lose her mind and strangle Philippa to death in the middle of the night using just a pair of fashionable cashmere leggings."

"Ha!" I squealed rather too loudly, prompting Venetta to turn and focus on me.

"Yes, you express yourself however you feel you need to," she said. "Yoga can be a moving experience; feel you can let your voice respond to it if needed. That goes for everyone. If you want to chant or express emotion, just do that. Don't hold feelings in. Would you like to chant?"

"Who? Me?" I said.

"Yes, I wondered whether you needed to give voice to your feelings."

"No thanks."

"OK then. Why don't you tell us all your name and a little about yourself?"

"Er...sure...there's not much to say: my name is Mary Brown and I work in a DIY and gardening centre in Cobham in Surrey."

"Try again," said Venetta. "This time don't tell us about your work. Your job is something you do to bring in money so you can live your life...tell us something about that life."

"OK, well I tend to go to pubs and restaurants and watch lots of telly with my boyfriend Ted. My favourite thing is when we go out to one of those 'eat all you can' Chinese buffets and drink loads of wine. I love that."

"OK," said Venetta, with more of a sneer than a smile. "Well, it's lovely to meet you."

The rest of the room had fallen completely silent during my speech. Now they were encouraged by Venetta to speak up, one by one, and explain who they were and what they did with their time. I noticed that all of them were careful not to say where they worked. Then the focus turned back to Venetta, and she looked at us all.

"I know you have come here for various reasons; some of you are thinking of training to be yoga teachers, and others of you want a dedicated weekend of practice. But whatever you are here for, I want you to remember the fundamental principles of yoga and the importance of treating one another well and, most of all, treating yourself well. It's important that we love each other and love ourselves. You're not here to change your body; you are here to make your health better, and that, in turn, will help to change you and make you a happier, more relaxed and able person. I want you to love your body and feel happy and whole. Only when you do that will you truly be at peace and be able to create the body, relationships and life you desire. Namaste."

"Namaste," we all said.

It was time to head back to our rooms for some alone time before a mindfulness course, a short unguided yoga session, and dinner.

Charlie and I sat on our small, firm beds and looked at one another.

"I quite fancy that dark-haired man," I told her.

"Diego?" she said.

"Yes. How did you remember that?"

"I'm good with names. He's good-looking but spent all his time staring at Philippa."

"Are you saying that Perfect Philippa is more attractive than me?" I questioned.

"No, he was probably staring at her out of sympathy."

"Probably," I agreed. "I didn't think there would be men on the course. It feels quite weird in some ways."

"Why?" asked Charlie.

"The idea of them wanting to come here and leap around in yoga gear for the weekend, eating bean shoots and sun-dried tomatoes instead of going to the football with their mates and then getting hammered."

"Yeah, I guess," said Charlie. "I don't know of any men who'd do this. Would Ted ever come to a weekend of yoga?"

"God, no," I said with a chuckle. I couldn't think of anything funnier. "He would hate it. Imagine him going to mindfulness and then 'free expression' yoga."

Charlie laughed. "I can't believe you told her you like getting pissed with your mates and having huge Chinese buffets. She couldn't have looked more shocked if you'd told her you slept in a chocolate fondue."

"What was I supposed to say then? Make it up?"

"Yes - make it up. Say something impressive like that Philippa woman did. She said she liked to bathe in the ocean when the stars were out; you said you liked to shove your face full of Kung Po chicken and beef curry. She wins."

MINDFULNESS

*C*harlie jogged and I waddled back down the stairs to join the group for the mindfulness session. "At least it'll be dinner time soon," she said to me in an attempt to calm me down. I think she could see the fear etched across my face. Watching the videos of yoga from the comfort of Charlie's sofa and practising the odd move in the garden centre had been OK, but now we were here, I was worried about whether I could cope. Everyone else looked so different from me...so bloody fit and healthy. And mindfulness? What was mindfulness? These were things I never came across in my normal day-to-day life.

"Do you think you're allowed wine on the retreat?" she asked. "You know, with dinner."

"You'll have to ask?" I said. "I imagine that the starter will be a plate of raw vegetables and the main course will be salad and new potatoes and pudding will be fruit salad and some light, calorie-low mousse."

"Surely not on the first night?" said Charlie, appalled at the thought. "They'll break us in gently, won't they?"

We wandered into the exercise room to find everyone in there, going into the cupboard to fetch big air-filled balls, mats and blankets.

"This looks alright," I said to Charlie as we wandered in to join them. "We're going to play on space hoppers, then have a little sleep. I might be better at this yoga lark than I thought."

Philippa and Sarah were already sitting on their balls...both pink. All the balls in the cupboard were green, so I could only assume that they had brought their balls with them. They had matching purple mats and light pink and pale purple blankets. I knew they would drive me insane with jealousy by the end of the weekend.

I collected my green ball, a rather tatty black mat and a greyish-looking blanket from the basket by the side and lay my things down to the far right of the room. Charlie positioned herself just behind me, and the two men on the course set themselves up next to me.

I knew that one of the men was called Martin; he was a rather jolly-looking chap with a warm smile and open, welcoming face. He was a bigger build than most of the others there. Not fat by any means, but less skeletal. He looked like he'd eaten sometime in the last 20 years, which the others didn't. He was completely bald and had a sore-looking rash running up the side of his right leg. I decided that he'd lost his hair because of alopecia or something. Whatever it was afflicting him, I hoped it wasn't contagious.

"I'm looking forward to this," he said. "I don't know much about mindfulness, so it'll be good to find out about it. I mean - when I say, 'don't know much' - obviously I know about serenity through Buddhist chanting."

"Yes, obviously...we all know about that," I said.

"But mindfulness is an interesting idea, isn't it?"

"Yes," I said. "I don't know anything about it either."

"Well, don't worry - we'll struggle through together," he said, and I decided right there that I quite liked Martin.

Next to Martin was the very good-looking guy with the Elvis sneer. He said his name was Diego. I smiled at him, but he looked away and seemed uninterested in talking to anyone. He just sat on his yoga ball, eyes closed, humming gently.

THE MARY BROWN BOOKS

"OK, let's get started," said Venetta, entering the room in grey leggings similar to Philippa's and with a shawl not too dissimilar to the one Philippa had been wearing earlier.

"Oh, you've taken your shawl off," she said to Philippa, immediately discarding hers.

Charlie kicked out at my ball to check I'd seen the exchange and nearly kicked me off it.

"She's channelling Perfect Philippa," said Charlie with a small guffaw. "How bloody weird. Who would copy someone else's style?"

I decided not to share with her my thoughts about running out to buy grey leggings like Philippa's as soon as I got home.

"Yeah, weird."

"I'd like you all to sit on your ball and relax," said Venetta. "Mindfulness is about being in the here and now with no judgements or ill feelings; it's about tuning into yourself and just existing. That is a difficult thing to do when we've all got such busy lives and so much going on, so I'm going to show you some tricks to help you do it. These simple things will help you reconnect with yourself and allow you to be present here and now. They will give you a feeling of complete relaxation, and you'll feel incredibly safe and relaxed if you get it right.

"First of all, I would like you to touch the fabric of the trousers or leggings that you're wearing. Does it feel rough or smooth? Warm or cold? Feel down the seam. How does that feel? Now, feel the skin on the back of your hand. How does that feel different? How does the skin on your knuckles feel different to the skin on your hand?"

Venetta went on like this for about 15 minutes, advising us to touch different things and describe them in our heads. It sounds like a ridiculous waste of time, but it seemed to work...I found myself completely relaxing as I focused on the simple things.

"Now, touch your hair. How does that feel? What about your face? OK, now just close your eyes and think about where you are and how relaxed you are. You're safe, warm and surrounded by friends. No harm will come to you. Just relax."

By the end of it, I felt amazing. I don't know how or why it worked, but I felt completely relaxed and happy.

"Doesn't that feel good?" said Venetta, and I nodded furiously. I was slightly light-headed, like when you've had a couple of sips of wine on an empty stomach, and you just start to feel a little bit woozy and floaty...not drunk at all, just warm and lovely.

"Lots of nods, that's great to see," she said. "Remember with mindfulness that we are trying to bring the focus back to the breath...the essence of life. Caring for ourselves and loving ourselves have to start from within. We must pull our attention inside and connect to our breathing. By doing this, we can keep calm, clear our minds, and have a real understanding of ourselves and our body and what we need from yoga to help us develop awareness and affinity. If we are not fully in the present, then we aren't practising yoga, we aren't existing, we have moved too far into our heads, not in our bodies or hearts. Mindfulness can help us escape our minds when they start limiting chattering.

"Another way of incorporating mindfulness into your everyday life is to stop and look at something and describe it in great detail. Look at all the intricate patterns and try to describe colours, fibres and the way the light dances off glass and marble. By doing that, you put yourself into the details of the here and now and stop wandering off into the future or worrying about the past. I think getting into pairs for this one would be useful."

Venetta pointed at me and the very handsome Diego, which was just about the best thing that had happened to me since the idea of this whole yoga lark started. "You two together," she said. I smiled warmly at him, and he just stared back, looking frightened.

"Once you're settled in your pairs, turn to the person next to you and describe the pattern on his or her blanket. Really look at the blanket and describe the colours, the pattern, the texture... Try to lose yourself in it completely."

"Right," I said, turning to the handsome Diego. "Do you want to go first or shall I?"

He lifted a hand and pointed gently at me. He didn't seem to want to talk to me, or anyone else, at all. I wasn't convinced that was going to get him very far in this talking game, but I continued regardless.

"Okay, sure," I said. "I'll go first. Well, your blanket is kind of browns and greys mixed up together there are some black lines in it, and it's sort of rough. Your turn."

I didn't know whether Diego was going to break his silence or whether he'd taken some sort of monastic vow and was determined to remain quiet for the whole weekend.

"Your blanket is slightly rough to the touch, like touching a cow. Not soft like a cat. The colours are muted shades of earth brown, not quite chocolate, smokier than that, and a rather dull army green. It's a slightly faded-looking green, the sort of colour that an army uniform might go if it had been through a hot wash too frequently. The colours play with one another through a criss-cross pattern, and the whole effect is reminiscent of an old lady wrapped up in a blanket, sitting by the fire on a cold November evening."

"Oh," I said, feeling completely outdone in the speaking game by the man who never spoke. "You've done much better than me."

"It's not a competition," he said. "We're all here to learn, grow, and develop...as individuals and as a group. There's no competition."

"Right," I said. "But you'd still have won if it had been a contest."

"No contest, no winners or losers," he said. "Just peace and light."

"Peace and light," I repeated, uncomfortable with the seriousness and sincerity in his voice.

"If everyone would like to stand up, we're now going to do some unguided or free-wheeling yoga just to get you limbered up and in the right frame for tomorrow's activities. If it's OK with you, I was going to do a short film of the session so we can use it to show prospective guests what our opening session is like. If anyone doesn't want to be in the video and they have clicked the tick box on the application form, then obviously will make sure they're not pictured in the video. I looked at Charlie: "Did we click any tick boxes?"

"I don't think so," she replied. "I don't really know. We booked the wrong bloody course...tick boxes were the least of my concern."

It seemed unlikely that they would want me doing yoga in their

BERNICE BLOOM

video to encourage people to come on these yoga weekends, so I decided not to worry about it too much... I was sure that their video would be full of images of perfect Philippa and her sidekick Sarah doing majestic things in expensive knitwear.

"Okay, let's start with some sun salutations, then you can move into your own work," said Venetta. I wasn't entirely sure what 'my own work' would involve since my whole yoga experience to date had been limited to falling into the pot plants after trying to do the tree position at work.

We did the sun salutations, and I was okay, to begin with: we put our arms up in the air and then bent over to touch our toes. Philippa touched her toes; I just about managed my knees. I had very little flexibility and the small problem of a large, protruding stomach to contend with.

From toe touching, we jumped back into a plank position and dropped our stomachs on the floor (to be fair, this was easy for me because my stomach was already almost on the floor), then went up into downward dog (basically, this is shoving your bum into the air with straight legs), then we went into these lunges and back up again. It all seemed much harder than anything we had watched them do on the YouTube videos, but I still didn't think it was beyond me... I thought I could have a fair shot at doing it, but then the crucial moment came.

"Okay, let's speed up to proper time now then," said Venetta, and they all started doing it at such a pace that I was struggling even to get down to touch my toes before they jumped their legs backwards and moved through the routine, I got myself in a complete mess trying to keep up with them, missing half the poses out to reach where they'd got to. At one stage, I seemed to be doing an entirely different routine to everybody else.

"Okay, let's just leave it there for a minute. Carry on doing the sun salutation if you want to, or you can do other yoga poses if you're more comfortable with those."

While the others carried on, Venetta drifted over to me and Charlie.

THE MARY BROWN BOOKS

"Are you both okay?" she said.

"Yes," I replied. "But I'm finding it hard because I've never done yoga before."

"What you mean – never done yoga before?" said Venetta, looking horrified.

"That's what I mean," I said. "I have never done any yoga before. I've booked onto this course to learn, so that I could go to yoga classes at my local sports centre."

"But this is the supreme advanced class; we have Guru coming into lead yoga sessions; this is the very heights of yoga. Only the best yoga people are here," she said.

"I thought yoga wasn't competitive," I replied. And watched as she blinked wildly.

"No, it's not competitive, of course not," she said.

"They will be fine," chipped in Diego from his position in downward dog. His t-shirt had ridden up to display a magnificent six pack and I was momentarily distracted.

"Look, I thought we'd booked the beginners class; we clearly got that wrong," I said. "We won't get in the way; we will just do what we can at the back. Is that okay?"

"Or we could leave," said Charlie. "If you think we should."

"No, let's stay," I insisted.

"No, stay," said Venetta. "But do remember that some of these advanced techniques are going to be very difficult for you."

"Will try our hardest," I said.

I looked around at Charlie to find her gazing at me open mouthed. "That was our route out of here," she said. "You just missed the exit."

"Come on, let's give it a go," I said, pushing myself back into downward dog. "What's the worst that can happen?

RETURN OF THE CHICKENS

"I don't think we should be here," said Charlie, when we returned to our room. "We should have sneaked out when she told us it was an advanced class. I mean - what the hell are we doing on an advanced course? It's insane."

"Yep, it's insane, but we should just try to make the most of it," I said in what I thought was a very grown-up fashion. "Let's go and have dinner. I'm sure we'll both feel better after having a nice meal."

"Yes, OK," said Charlie, giving me the sort of dejected look that one usually associated with a little girl who's been told she has to go and visit her aunt and uncle instead of going to a party. She and I made a very basic effort to get ready. This was a casual retreat, and we'd been told there was no need to get dressed up for dinner, so we were planning just to wear leisure wear and make no more effort than brushing our hair.

It was a relief to get downstairs and discover that the others had done likewise. Well, most of the others. Perfect, Philippa and Sarah looked magnificent, of course, in elegant maxi dresses. Philippa's was in emerald green, and she wore bright red earrings and bright red ballet shoes. Sarah's dress was knee-length and red. It was tight fitting at the top, then kicked out at the waist to form a lovely full skirt. She wore it with - you guessed - emerald green earrings and green ballet flats. They were truly amazing.

Everyone else was very casual. The men seemed to be wearing exactly the same as they had worn at dinner; the women hadn't dressed up much either - like us, they'd just brushed their hair and cleaned up a bit.

"Please, take a seat," said Venetta, indicating the table in the garden. It was a beautiful setting, under trellises with vines growing over them, like at an Italian villa, with the flames from the candles sending light dancing across the glasses on the table. With the pool lying to the side of us and the silence of the evening enveloping us, it was all completely perfect... until the food arrived.

First, it was the starter...a vegetable broth with so few vegetables that tasted like the water you cook vegetables in. It was dreadful. Horrible stuff. Charlie and I were sitting next to two women who we hadn't talked to earlier: Margaret, who said she worked in high finance (she'd obviously forgotten the first rule of yoga club: don't mention your job), and a lady called Julia who was very weak-looking and complained constantly about how ill she felt. She told us about the flu she'd just had, how she had weak lungs and a terrible immune system, and how she'd been in hospital five times so far this year as she was of a very delicate disposition. The two women were polar opposites; while Julia complained of her frailties, Margaret spoke at considerable lengths of her strengths. She had a first from Oxford and then went to Harvard, then she went into the City and has worked there ever since. High finance suited her because of her combative, confident nature.

"What are you doing on a yoga retreat then?" I asked. "Forgive me for saying this, but you don't seem the type to be here. You're kind of an alpha type."

"Absolutely, I'm an alpha type, 100%. But my husband makes me come here every six months because he says they calm me down. I like coming because I lose weight. It's like a cheap spa. Not that I need it to be cheap. I have plenty of money."

BERNICE BLOOM

"Yes, I got that," I said, rather rudely, but she was annoying. So annoying.

More food came, and I rubbed my hands in joy, then stopped rubbing them because the main course was a side plate with salad on it. No protein, no bread, no anything. Sprouting mung beans and bean sprouts with lettuce, cucumber and leaves from the garden. It was dismal.

Desert was no better...three walnuts and a sliver of watermelon. And that was it. My stomach felt like it was eating itself I was so hungry.

Just as we were starting to feel like things were as bad as they could be, Julia shrieked. "Oh my God - birds," she squealed as a dozen or so chickens came clucking into the garden.

Venetta came out and looked at them quizzically. "How did you get out?" she said, then turning to us. "The farmer must have left his gate open. All the chickens have escaped."

Charlie and I dropped our heads and looked down at the ground.

"Shit," I said. "I bet that was us."

"It can't have been. That was hours ago," said Charlie. "Perhaps the chickens have been wandering around for hours?"

Venetta called the farm, and minutes later, the farmer charged into the garden with his hands on his hips. It was the same guy who'd been shouting at us earlier. He locked eyes with me as he surveyed us all, and I looked quickly away. He must have known it was me he'd seen - I was twice the size of everyone else.

We all helped to collect the chickens. "This afternoon, someone drove into the farmyard and disturbed the birds. Does anyone know anything about that?" he asked gruffly. "I haven't been able to calm them down since, and the gate's broken."

I carried on trying to catch chickens and ignored his question. We hadn't broken the gate; all I did was open it.

"If anyone knows anything about a blue car that came into the farmyard, please let me know," he added.

We all nodded and said that we would. Then we helped to take his chickens out to his Land Rover. As we walked back through the car park, I glanced at Charlie's blue car, covered in mud and feathers.

"Thank God, he didn't see it," I said, relieved that we'd parked it in the middle of the cars so it wasn't instantly visible.

"I know," said Charlie. "What a bloody nightmare. We'll have to sneak out and wash the car later just in case. This is all our fault. Bloody feathers everywhere - look at them."

I smiled at Charlie, but she looked too fed up to smile back.

"What's the matter?" I asked.

"I just can't cope with this little food."

"Do not fear, Mary's here," I said. "Come with me."

I led a dispirited Charlie up the stairs and told her to sit on her bed. I lifted my suitcase onto my bed and opened the compartment I hadn't hitherto emptied.

"When I went to the garage, I bought loads of snacks," I confessed. "Some were in the bag that Venetta took, but some are here..."

I tipped out crisps, nuts, rice cakes and wine. I thought Charlie was going to cry with joy. "Oh my God, I love you," she said. "You're mad and everything - really batty at times, but this is amazing. Amazing."

Then she gave me the biggest hug imaginable, and we opened wine and crisps.

LATE NIGHT CAR WASH

The thing I always notice, when I eat next to someone else, is how different their attitude to food is from mine. Charlie was thrilled that I had snacks in my bag because she felt hungry. I was thrilled that I had snacks in my bag because I love food. Charlie ate some crisps and said, 'that's better'. I wasn't like that. Once the food was open in front of me, I became obsessed with it. If the packets were open, I knew that nothing on earth would stop me from eating it all...my lust for food was like a wave crashing onto the shore.

Charlie sat back and poured herself a glass of wine, and I continued to 'pick' at the food as we sat there. Charlie was full; I don't think I know full...it's not a concept I'm familiar with. My 'picking' in these circumstances usually results in me consuming more calories after we've eaten than I do while we're eating. I had five handfuls of crisps to Charlie's two, but that was the very least of my problems around food. Because after we'd eaten our 'little snack' I continued to 'pick' and I finished the crisps, ate another packet, had some more wine, and ate some nuts, all during the 'picking' phase of the meal.

We finished the bottle of wine and were feeling nicely merry. "Shall I open another one?" I said.

Charlie smiled. "Of course, but I think we should go down and wash the car first. What do you think?"

I knew we should. The farmer was bound to come back round before we left this place, and if he saw the way the car looked - covered in dried mud and feathers, he'd know it was us, and probably make us pay for damage or something.

"Yes," I said. "Come on - let's go and do it now, then we can return for more snacks."

It was 11 pm and the house was eerily silent. Charlie and I crept down the stairs without putting the lights on, trying not to let them creak, hoping not to slip. We tiptoed into the kitchen and found two large pans and a roll of kitchen paper. We filled the pans with hot, soapy water and tiptoed towards the front door. I had a kitchen roll stuffed under one arm and a huge, heavy pan in my hands. I desperately tried not to spill any water as we went. We got to the front door, and I put down my pan and pulled the door open, as I did the most astonishing sound peeled through the house.

"Oh Christ, it's the alarm," I said. "Bollocks, how are we going to explain this?"

We stood there, in our pyjamas, carrying huge bowls of soapy water, while a man who I'd seen around the house but who appeared to have no role came running down the stairs, carrying a baseball bat. Behind him was Venetta screeching, "Be careful, be careful." She was dressed in a frilly, flirty little negligée in baby pink that looked as if it belonged in the 1950s.

When the man got level with us, he stopped in his tracks. "Did someone try to break in?" he asked.

"No," said Charlie. "We tried to break out."

"Oh, my goodness, it's you two. What are you doing?" asked Venetta, regarding the bowls of soapy water with confusion.

"Cleaning the car," said Charlie.

"At this hour?" said Venetta. "Can it not wait until tomorrow? Or when you get home?"

"No, it can't," said Charlie, looking at me for support and help.

"I've got OCD," I said. "I can't sleep unless the car is clean. It's just one of those things."

"Oh, I see," said Venetta, though she didn't look as if she had a clue what I was on about. "OK then, well if it will help you sleep, by all means, clean the car, but you'll need better equipment than that. Jonty, can you pull the hose out for them?"

"Really?" he said.

"Yes, it's OCD. We need to be supportive. You do the hose; I'll get car cleaner and brushes."

The man half sneered at me as he went outside, and it struck me that he could do with coming to one of the mindfulness courses. The way he was wielding the baseball bat wasn't very 'Zen' at all.

"Here," said Venetta, handing me car cleaner and brushes. I gave her the pan of soapy water, and Charlie and I walked outside.

"What? What on earth was that?" said Charlie when we were safely out of earshot. "OCD?"

"I was struggling," I said. "I didn't know what else to say. Now, come on, let's find this hose."

All the security lights had come on outside the house like the place was floodlit. I knew those sleeping in rooms at the front of the building must have light pouring through their windows.

"We better do this quickly," I said. "Or we're going to wake everyone up."

We found the hose and sprayed it onto the car, brushing like mad and tipping car cleaner onto the sides and the back, where the mud was worse. We scrubbed for about 20 minutes until the car was sparkling clean, and we were drenched and sweating like mad. "Come on, let's go get some snacks," I said, replacing the hose and leading the way back inside.

We put the pans back, replaced the brushes and tiptoed back up the stairs. Then I took the carrier bag of snacks she'd confiscated.

"Just in case we run out," I said to Charlie. By the time we reached the room, the security lights had gone off, and the house had fallen into complete silence.

HALF A POUND OF CUMBERLAND SAUSAGES

*S*MACK! Morning came like a thunderclap. The sound of the alarm clock burst into the attic room. It was so loud I had to put my hands over my ears to stop my head from exploding. It felt like the whole place was shaking. Lord above, it was horrific. I sat up, switched off the alarm, and looked around me. Crisp packets were strewn across the floor, and two empty wine bottles lay beside the bed. Yep, that was why I felt so damn awful. We'd stayed up til about 3 a.m. drinking wine and laughing about my sudden-onset OCD. The alarm had gone at 5.30 a.m. Our first yoga class of the day was at 6 a.m.

"Up you get, Charlie," I said. "It's time for yoga."

"Good morning, ladies and gentlemen, welcome to Advanced level Ashtanga," said a small, scrawny woman with short, curly blonde hair tied back into a tight ponytail. "My name is Elizabeth Hill."

There were murmurs of appreciation and delight emanating throughout the room. This was obviously a famous yoga teacher brought in to run a session for us. I hoped no one could sense the panic running through me. I glanced at Charlie; she looked as horror-stricken as I felt. At least we'd placed ourselves right at the back of the room.

Then, the madness began, as we started the class with ten sun salutations. On and on we went. I just copied everyone else and tried to keep out of sight. It was all going so fast that I was struggling to keep up.

I saw Venetta had come into the room. She was dressed all in black and wandered around, looking at everyone, clapping randomly and saying, "Very good, very good." Of course, she said nothing to Charlie and me because we weren't very good. I kept catching sight of the two of us in the mirror...there was no disguising it...we were very bad.

Venetta stopped at the side and watched Philippa and Sarah for a while. They looked beautiful of course...Philippa was wearing cream, loose-fitting shorts and a matching cream top. You could see flashes of her blue crop top underneath when she bent over. Her legs were so long and tanned it was impossible not to stare at them. Sarah wore the same but with a bright pink crop top underneath. They both had ponytails. Philippa's was tied with a pink ribbon to match Sarah's crop top, and Sarah's was tied with one in the same blue as Philippa's crop top.

"I think we should match our outfits like that," I whispered to Charlie, who instantly stuck two fingers up at me and nearly fell out of downward dog.

"Now, could we all turn to face the other way?" said Elizabeth, standing next to Charlie and me.

Aahhh...no. I was at the front of the class. I stood facing everyone in my baggy yellow tracksuit trousers and Daffy Duck t-shirt.

"Turn around," mouthed Charlie.

I spun on my heels, and we were told to repeat the sun salutations...with me at the front, and no one to copy. Nightmare. Do you know how hard it is to copy someone in a mirror? I tried to copy the people behind me by watching them in the mirror. It was awful. I was all over the place. In the end, I wasn't even attempting to do sun salutations, I just moved around a bit - stretching up occasionally, touching my toes occasionally and going down into a press-up position every so often.

"And... drop into child's pose," she said, ending my embarrassment.

Venetta had left the room while we were busy downward dogging and touching our toes. I saw her creep back in again. Rather hysterically, she was wearing white shorts and a matching white top. She looked nowhere near as elegant as Philippa and Sarah, but it was clear that she was dressing like them.

I glanced at Charlie. "Did you see that?" I asked.

"Yes," she said. "The woman's bonkers."

"OK, and come out of child's pose. We're going just roll from side to side. This will loosen up the spine and massage the internal organs before we go on."

I felt I would be good at rolling from side to side. I might play my joker on this one, I thought. We began slowly moving from side to side before we rolled. I had Charlie to one side of me and Martin on the other.

"OK, and roll more; go further over," she said.

Martin had rolled himself up the mat a little, so his bottom was in line with my head. He wore rather skimpy running shorts, and I noticed that the scabby rash on his calf went all up the back of his leg. It was most unappealing. Not that I was ideally placed to go around criticising anyone else's appearance, but it wasn't very nice. And why on earth was he wearing such tiny shorts? He looked like he'd come in fancy dress as a footballer from the 1970s.

"And, have a go at rolling," said the instructor. "Just gently, roll from one side, over you go..."

I just lay there. I was enjoying the rest. I didn't plan on rolling anywhere. But as I enjoyed the short rest, Martin decided to begin rolling; he swung over, rolling his body as instructed. As he finished, there was a slapping sound, like someone had slammed half a pound of Cumberland sausages on the ground. I looked over to see that the entire contents of his shorts had escaped through one of the legs. His substantial penis and balls lay on the shiny wooden floor.

"Goodness me," he said, rolling away. "Very sorry about that."

A GURU AND A HEADSTAND

"I feel sick," I told Charlie. "I really didn't need to see the tackle of some old, bald bloke with a serious skin infection."

"So you keep saying," she replied.

"It was disgusting. Really awful."

"Never mind, we've got the guru-led session in five minutes. That should be fun."

"If Martin's still wearing those shorts, I'm not going in," I said.

We were lying on our beds, exhausted. A long walk had followed the morning yoga session (Charlie ran half of it, which annoyed me), and a swimming session, then lunch. We'd eaten our 'summer vegetable bowl', then darted upstairs for proper food (crisps).

"We should head down," said Charlie, getting to her feet and stretching out a little. I grabbed another handful of crisps and followed her down the stairs.

"Ladies and gentlemen, this is a special time on the course... The time when your meditation will be elevated, and your yoga will be given meaning. I would like to welcome the man who has made my yoga journey much more enlightened and joyful. Guru Aaraadhy Motee Ladakee."

We all looked up at the door as it swung open, and a man walked in wearing a long orange robe. Charlie nudged me, and I knew she wanted me to joke about the madness of the whole thing, but I couldn't keep my eyes off him. He was the most magnificent-looking man I had ever seen. I suppose he must have been around 60 and had longish white hair and very tanned skin.

He was the sort of guy you knew must have been devastatingly handsome when he was younger. He had a look about him that was half John the Baptist and half surfer dude. Not a common combination, I admit, but he looked as if he spent his mornings on the beach and in the waves, his bleached, tousled hair and pearly white teeth set against azure blue seas and skies. He looked as if he'd jumped off his surfboard five minutes ago. His eyes were the brightest blue I'd ever seen, set in this very handsome square face with the most amazing gentle smile. I think I fell in love with him straight away. It wasn't a sexual, *come here, I want to shag you*, sort of love, it was more serene than that. There was something quite magnificent about him. I felt wholesome, warm and happy in his presence.

"Christ, look at the state of him," said Charlie.

"He's amazing," I said, still staring at him, transfixed by the vision before me.

"It's a pleasure to be here with you today," he said, bowing and sitting before us. He dropped so elegantly and flawlessly into the Lotus position, just a small glimpse of hairy, tanned ankle as he sat and bowed over. I could only imagine how strong and flexible he was. Gosh, he was amazing.

"Om sahanaa vavatu Sahanau bhunaktu. Saha veeryam karavaa vahai. Tejasvi naa vadhee tamastu maa vidvishaa vahai. Om Shaanti Shaantihi," he chanted.

Everyone joined in. I did, too. I didn't know any words or the sounds they were making, but I chanted anyway.

"Follow me," he said. And he bent right over in the Lotus position, so his hands were stretched right out in front of him.

I tried desperately to copy what he was doing. I was nowhere near as flexible as him, but – my God – I was going to try.

He went through a series of yoga poses stopping every so often and holding them for such an unconscionable amount of time that I didn't have any hope. I decided to make up for what I couldn't do in yoga by the volume of the chats I didn't know the words to. I was aware this was making me look stupid, and I could feel Charlie glaring at the back of my head as I wailed loudly not knowing any of the words.

He kept going for about 40 minutes, moving from position to position. I was exhausted but determined not to stop. In all the other yoga sessions I'd done so far, I had given up when I couldn't do it and taken to doing my own thing. Now I was absolutely determined to try and impress him, so I would make sure I tried my damnedest to keep up and to do it properly.

"Sirsasana," he said, and around me, people started going into headstands. Oh, Christ on a bike. Well, I'd give it a go. I didn't know what I was doing or how this all worked, but I put my head down, kicked my legs up and hoped to God I was doing it properly.

Turns out I wasn't.

I flew over the top and landed on the mat with a huge slapping sound. If Martin's tackle sounded like half a pound of sausages, this sounded like a whole pig had been dropped onto the mat from a great height. I really slammed my back onto the mat. There were gasps all around the room, and Guru looked up.

"Are you okay?" he asked.

"I think so," I said.

I was far from OK. I felt winded, and my back was stinging like crazy.

"Surya Namaskar, everyone," he said. "While I tend to this little injured bird."

I giggled to disguise the pain as he leaned over and rubbed my back. I could hardly breathe; my head was pounding, and I felt about to cry, but I didn't want to show him that. I looked up, like an injured bird might look at him and he continued to rub my back and chant gently.

The strange thing was that I felt the pain subside. I'm not just saying this because he was attractive or anything; I genuinely think he had healing hands. He rubbed down my back and it felt as if the pain lifted into his hands.

"Does that feel better?" he asked

"That feels much better. How did you do that?" I asked.

"I am also a Reiki Master, I can lift the pain from you. Hopefully, that will be much better now."

"Thank you," I said, clambering to my feet. I bowed, said Namaste, and told him I was fine to continue. I wasn't, but I didn't want to look like a total wimp.

Despite the guru's healing hands, it hurt as soon as I moved my back and attempted to join in with sun salutations. I desperately wanted to make it look as if he'd magically made me better, so he'd like me, but - bloody hell - it wasn't better at all. It was stinging. I swallowed down the pain and just carried on doing the yoga. We went from position to position, and it was tortuously hard; sweat poured down my face as I tried to do everything I could.

It was ridiculously difficult, and I definitely should've been on a beginners' course, but the lovely thing was that I did start to recognise some of the names and some of the positions, and I'd worked out which ones I could do and which ones I couldn't. Because Venetta had said right at the beginning, in her introductory talk, that yoga practice was called that because it was always a practice, there were always things to work on, I knew that no one was expecting perfection. I decided at that moment that as soon as I got back home, I would sign up for yoga classes and try to be the best I could then I would come back on one of these retreats, and the group would be amazed at how much I'd improved.

We got to savasana and I collapsed, exhausted. My back was stinging like crazy, I had a terrible headache, and every part of me hurt, so I just lay back and listened to his manly, authoritative but calming voice as he talked about the power of yoga and felt like everything was going to be okay.

The next thing I knew, Charlie was shaking me. "Where am I?" I asked.

"You're in the yoga class. You fell asleep," she said.

"Oh Christ. Where is the Guru?" I asked.

"He's gone, he told me to tell you that you did very well today and if your back isn't better go and see him, and he will treat it some more. "

"My back's not better!" I screamed. "I need more treatment."

"What is it with the Guru?" said Charlie. "He is just an old man with long hair in a ridiculous orange dress."

I tried to sit up but my back hurt so much that I could barely do it. "God that hurts," I said.

"Can you stand up?" asked Charlie, putting a hand out to help me as I scrambled onto all fours and then eased myself onto my feet.

"Yeah I'm up," I said. "But bloody hell that hurt."

"Why the hell did you do a headstand?" said Charlie. "She told us not to do anything we haven't done before. Why didn't you just go onto your knees and watch the others? That's what I did."

"I don't know," I said, dragging my mat across the room to put it away.

"Don't worry about that, I'll do it," she said, taking the mat and putting it onto the pile with the others. No one else was in the room. They had all left.

"I know exactly why you did a headstand," she said, as we left the studio and headed for the room. "You did it to try and impress him, didn't you?"

"Might have," I said, opening the door and feeling pain run all the way through my back. "Did it work? Was he impressed?"

Charlie burst out laughing. "He certainly looked shocked. I don't know about impressed."

"Fuck, it hurts," I said.

"Well, you better go and find the man with the healing hands then hadn't you?" she said, shaking her head. "If you need me, I'll be upstairs drinking the last of the wine."

"Have we got any more damn yoga today?"

"Yes - we've got Bikram before dinner."

"Christ," I said. "Great Saturday night we have before us."

Then I saw Venetta walking down the corridor. "Venetta, where's the guru? I want him to talk to him about something."

"Ahhh....about your OCD?"

"No, the OCD seems better today. I wanted him to do some more reiki on my back," I said.

"I'm sorry, Mary, he's already left to go to a meditation commune for the evening," she said, apologetically. "Would you like me to look at it? Or maybe try an ice bath?"

"It's OK, I'll go for a lie-down, and see him when he gets back."

"OK, see you for Bikram at 6.30 pm," she said. "Do come, even if your back's sore, and just do what you can. Even if you just stretch out, it would be worth coming along."

I would go along, but only because it was another chance to see the guru.

I wandered up to the room to find Charlie lying on the bed, sipping wine out of the bottle. "Not completely getting into the philosophy of this course, are you?" I said, taking the bottle from her and having a huge gulp myself.

"Mmmm," she said. "I kind of am getting into it. I think I like yoga, it's just that it's all too hard. I don't know what they're saying, and I don't know any of the practices. Unlike you, that's made me want to stay out on the fringes a bit."

"Yes," I said. "I'm not really a stay-out on the fringes sort of person."

"Nooo, really? I hadn't noticed," said Charlie. "What with the wild, loud chanting and the mad thumping headstand."

"Yeah, that really hurt. Can you take a look at my back?"

Charlie lifted up my t-shirt and almost squealed. "Bloody hell - it's bright red. It looks really sore," she said. "Wasn't the guru there to help?"

"No, he'd gone into meditation or something. I'll catch him after the next yoga class. I might just have a cool bath or something now, to try and calm it down."

"Good idea," said Charlie. "Shout if you want anything. I have painkillers here if you need them."

BERNICE BLOOM

"I'm OK for now," I said. "I'll shout if it feels worse."

I had the bath and stepped out. It felt much worse, but nothing would stop me from going to the next yoga class to see my lovely Guru man. I dried myself and styled my hair, doing my makeup perfectly. Neither Charlie nor I had worn a scrap of make-up since arriving, but I wanted to look my best for the guru, so I trowelled it on. I didn't care what Charlie said...I knew I looked much better with makeup. On went the foundation and powder, then more foundation and blusher. Fake eyelashes, eyeliner...the works. I looked good, even if I said so myself. I'm just not the sort of person who looks good au naturel, unlike Perfect Philippa.

I walked out into the bedroom and Charlie almost choked on the wine. "Bloody hell, where are you going?" she asked.

"Yoga," I replied. "Coming?"

"Sure," she said, following me out of the door and down the stairs to our next yoga class. "Which class is this one again? Come as a drag queen?"

HOT AND SWEATY

OK, so there were two things immediately wrong with the Bikram yoga situation. The first thing was that the Guru wasn't taking it. So, I was faced with having to do a yoga class with an absolutely agonising back, made-up to perfection, without any guru to show off to. The other disaster was that Bikram was done in a very hot room, unbeknownst to me or Charlie. I mean VERY hot. Basically, a steam room. Christ, honestly, yoga is hard enough without adding in steam, heat or anything else unpleasant. How the hell was I going to cope with this?

We walked into the room that was right at the back of the house, tucked away, and it was like walking into hell. It was astonishingly hot...absolutely boiling. We could hardly see one another through the haze and heat.

"Does it have to be this hot?" I asked Venetta.

"Yes," she said. "Bikram yoga should be done in a room which is 40 °C. You'll love it when we get started. It's great exercise and very good for your skin and your organs. It allows you to really stretch.

"OK," I said warily, taking my place and immediately feeling the sweat pouring off me. It was so warm that it was uncomfortable...like being in a tropical rainforest or something. You know that feeling when you're on holiday somewhere humid, and you're in your air-conditioned room feeling all lovely, then you walk outside, and the heat and humidity hit you like a truck? Bang. Sweat begins to form on your brow, then trickle down your back, and soon you feel soaking without having done anything. It's like the tube train in summer. You get on there and can feel the sweat running down your back, under your clothes, and your hair getting damp, and you know that by the time you get to work, you're going to look like you've been swimming.

The difference between the tube on a hot summer's day or a rainforest is that no one is making you exercise there. Why would anyone do this to themselves?

We bend and stretch into a variety of poses, most of which I am familiar with now. I am a yoga queen, but I can feel my back stinging as the sweat runs down it and collects at the top of my leggings. It feels awful to be honest.

We do lots of sun salutations and I can almost get all the way through one without looking at the instructor for help, which is a good job because I can't really see the instructor, sweat is dripping into my eyes, I wipe it away. I try to do a tree pose but keep falling over. When I land on the mat, there's a splash. We're all sweating so much that it's accumulating in puddles around us. It is - let's be honest - disgusting and unhygienic. There's also a strong smell. This is what it would smell like if you poached humans. Not nice. Even the minty extract in the steam can't disguise it. It's most unpleasant.

Because we're sweating so much, I feel absolutely parched; no matter how much water I drink, I feel myself gagging for more. I'm chugging it down my throat whenever I can but I'm still hellishly thirsty.

"And relax, lie back. Time for savasana."

Savasana is THE best thing in the world. Well, maybe not THE best, certainly not up there with chips and chilli sauce, chicken tikka masala and chicken and black bean sauce, but it's in the top ten, nestling comfortably between chip butties and pizza.

Savasana is basically lying down. It is when you relax and breathe

THE MARY BROWN BOOKS

deeply after yoga to rejuvenate the body, mind and spirit. Basically, whichever way you dramatise it, what you're doing is lying on your back and having a bit of a rest. Perfect.

We were told to rise after around five minutes of relaxation and to take it easy afterwards. Bikram yoga can be very draining...we should be kind to ourselves. Charlie and I walked out of the room, our heads spinning, completely soaked to the skin with sweat. My hair was plastered down against my skull and my clothes were drenched.

We ambled into the long corridor and back to the main house.

At the end of the corridor, I could see someone waiting. As we got closer, I realised it was Guru Motee.

"Hello," I said.

"Oh my goodness, look at you, my dear," he said. "I've come to see you. Venetta said you were looking for me."

"Oh yes," I replied. "I just wanted you to check my back was OK."

"Would you like to clean up first?" he said. "Or maybe you should try and get a good night's rest, then I could treat it tomorrow after the morning walk, if it's still sore?"

"OK," I said. "Yes - good idea. I'm glad you'll be on the walk tomorrow." I smiled at him provocatively from beneath my luscious lashes, which I batted at him for extra effect. I was glad I'd done the full face of makeup now. At least I knew my face looked good, even if the rest of me didn't.

"Bye, bye," I said, as he turned to leave, bowing gracefully.

We walked back up to the room. "I think he likes me," I said.

"Who?" said Charlie.

"The gorgeous Guru. Who else? Did you see the way he looked at me just now?"

"Yep," said Charlie with a smile.

"What's so funny?" I asked.

"You'll see."

Indeed, I did see. As soon as we were back in the room, I looked in the mirror and saw the state of my face. My heavy-duty make-up was all over the place...half my face was black from mascara and eye shadow and the other half a smeary mess of brown foundation and pink lipstick. I stared at the ridiculous sight for a while.

Charlie was sitting on her bed looking into the mirror on her compact. Obviously, since she hadn't worn makeup, she looked fine.

"My skin looks great," she said. "Training in all that heat and steam definitely reduces your pores. I've just splashed some water onto my skin and it's glowing."

I didn't answer Charlie. I just kept staring at myself. I wasn't glowing. I looked like Alice Cooper had been caught in the rain. I looked entirely ridiculous like some sort of hideously nightmarish clown.

Charlie walked over to join me at the mirror.

"What's this?" she said, leaning in to lift something off my cheek. It was a false eyelash. One of the false eyelashes that I had been provocatively fluttering at the guru earlier.

"Look. At. Me," I said, slowly, emphasising each word. "I've been talking to the guru. Looking like this. He must think I'm insane."

"Well you are," said Charlie, rather unsupportively. "Completely insane, if you ask me."

FALLING FOR THE COUNTRYSIDE

There was a loud banging on the door at 5.30 am. "Good morning. Happy Sunday," sang a much-too-enthusiastic and upbeat Venetta.

"Urghhhh," Charlie and I moaned back.

"Downstairs in 10 minutes," she said, and we both heard her skipping off to ruin someone else's day.

"Christ, does she have to be so happy and lively," said Charlie. "I mean - every morning, she's like this. I have no idea where she gets the energy from. It's quite insane. I'm not sure I even fancy this guru-led walk, to be honest."

"Oh my God - it's the guru walk!" I squealed in alarm, leaping out of bed (that's not true - I kind of rolled, and moaned as I straightened out my poor back, but 'leaping' sounds so much better). "I've been looking forward to this."

"Yeah, only because you fancy him..."

"I don't fancy him at all, I just like the idea of getting to know him better. Is that such a problem?" I asked.

"Nope. No problem at all," said Charlie, rolling back under the duvet, trying to squeeze in a few extra minutes of sleep.

It went without saying that I wanted to look amazing on this walk.

It also went without saying that I knew it was impossible for anyone to look amazing while trudging for 10 miles in fields full of cattle. Still, I had to try. My appearance had been so dire when I'd bumped into him yesterday that I simply had to look sensational, eye-catching and wonderful.

I headed for the bathroom and began the beautification process while Charlie moaned at me from her bed.

"Switch the light off, it's too early for light," she said, while I smoothed on foundation and tried to do Kim Kardashian- style contouring and ultra-dynamic eyes. When I had finished, I went to the wardrobe, making a considerable amount of noise as I pulled out my favourite leggings and t- shirt, wincing as the hangers kept slipping off the rail and clattering as they hit the floor. The leggings were black, and the t-shirt was bright pink. I usually wore a black tracksuit top with the outfit, but the last time I did that, my neighbour Dave told me I looked like a massive liquorice allsort so I don't wear the jacket with it anymore. Instead, I tied the black jacket around my waist. I looked in the mirror and smiled. Not bad for a 15-stone woman who only had three hours of sleep...not bad at all.

"Are you ever getting up?" I asked Charlie, who grunted, threw the covers off and walked hunch-back into the bathroom. She emerged minutes later in running shorts and a t-shirt, hair tied back in a pony-tail, no makeup. We looked like we were dressed for completely different events...her to run a marathon, me to audition for the role of head cheerleader.

"Shall we have a bite to eat before we go?" she suggested.

All this early morning exercise before eating anything was hard core. I found exercise difficult enough without trying to do it while starving to death. I opened my suitcase and pulled out fruit, rice cakes, biscuits and diet coke, and we started munching away. Breakfast was after the run, and would no doubt comprise half a prune and a lemon pip in any case. We needed this sustenance.

We walked down the stairs and into the entrance hall, flooded with early morning light despite the unsociable hour.

"Hello, you two, lovely to see you," said Venetta. "I have some good news for you, Mary. I know how much you like mud hiking, so I have arranged for you to go hiking in the fields with the farmers this morning, instead of the guru-led walk."

Christ no. I had to stop lying. Venetta had the impression that I was a mud hiking enthusiast with OCD. I didn't want to do hiking at the best of times, certainly not in mud or when there was a perfect opportunity to spend time with the guru.

"Go on," said Charlie. "You know how much you adore a mud ramble."

"I do," I agreed. "But my back is so sore, I can't possibly go today; I'll just do the walk with the guru if you don't mind."

"Oh, what a shame!" said Venetta. "Let me tell the farmer then. You two head out and catch up with the others. They are waiting by the gate for everyone."

"Thanks for your support," I said to Charlie.

"I couldn't resist. It was all way too funny. You - mud hiking? With the farmer whose chickens we scared! Just brilliant."

When we reached the gate, the group was just leaving. Guru Motee was leading the charge.

"Hi, hello, Guru. Please wait a minute," I shouted, waddling along at top speed, trying to catch the runaway group.

"Hello there. I thought you gone on a mud ramble," he said with a gentle smile.

"No, I decided to come on this instead. I thought it would be nice to spend some time with you," I said, smiling in a lascivious way that made him recoil slightly.

"Ah, well, I'm glad you could join us," he said. "Have you enjoyed the course? Besides managing to hurt your back. How is that by the way?"

"My back is still a bit sore, to be honest," I said. "Completely my fault though... I've never done a headstand before, so it was probably unwise to charge straight up into one."

"What? Never done one before?" he said.

"No. To be honest, I'm completely new to yoga."

"I see; quite a brave thing to do to come on such an advanced course, then?" he said, giving me that lovely big smile again.

"Yes, less bravery and more stupidity I'm afraid," I said. "We managed to book the wrong course. I think it was my fault. When we were booking the course, I jokingly added the advanced course into our basket, and I think we forgot to take it out."

"Well, at least it's been an introduction to yoga, even if you would have chosen a less intensive one."

"Yes, it has, rather. Although everything seems to have gone wrong right from the start," I told him, just to keep the conversation going. I wanted to talk to him for as long as possible.

"Tell me about it..."

"Well..." I began to tell him all about how I had put on so much weight on the cruise, then we managed to get lost and had almost killed half a dozen peacocks, and that's how I got covered in mud and was about to dive into the lake when I was told to take a shower, then when I was taking a shower Venetta spotted all our goodies and hid them..."

When I look at the guru, he's absolutely crying with laughter.

"You are the most adorable, charming woman," he said. "You seem to give yourself such a hard time about your weight, but you're really a lovely person. Be kind to yourself. Relax and learn to go with the flow a bit more. I'm sure that weight will come off when you start to treat yourself much better."

"I don't know about that," I said. "I find it difficult. I love eating so much. I know it's not good for me, and I know I'm overweight, but I love it."

"And now Venetta has taken all your snacks, so you have to eat tiny amounts."

"No, because I had loads more in my suitcase anyway," I said. "And - in any case - we pinched back our bag of goodies."

He was laughing at this stage.

"So, you been cheating and going up to your room and having snacks every evening after the tiny vegan supper?"

"Yes. Is that terrible?"

"No, it's not terrible, Mary. But learning to eat less food, and to focus on eating food that is good for you, and for the environment, is an important part of the course. The reason the food is given to you in small amounts if because is good for you to be deprived, occasionally, of what you think you need."

"I feel bad now," I said.

"No - you mustn't. I'm explaining why you have been given small portions. Don't feel bad; don't ever feel bad. One of the most important things in life is to spread joy and make people happy wherever you go. I know you have bad feelings about yourself with food, and I can feel the waves of negativity around you even as you talk about it; you must try to see your relationship with food more positively.

"You are a funny, self-deprecating, warm and gentle soul. I think you will go far in this life. If you go to a beginners' yoga class and learn basic yoga, you will start to feel better about your whole body, and that will change your eating habits automatically without you having to force the change. Just start very gently. Stop beating yourself up and worrying about how much you weigh and how much you eat. Carry on being your own lovely self, and do a little bit of yoga as well; try to remember some of the mindfulness work, and if you incorporate those into your life, you will find yourself transformed. I promise you. And when we leave, I'll give you my details so if you need to get in touch with me you can, and I'll help you if you need further guidance. How does that sound?"

"It sounds wonderful I said. "Thank you. There is just one more thing I need to mention."

"Oh my goodness, what's that then?" he said.

"Well, you know I said that we went into the farmer's yard and reversed through his chickens and terrified his peacock half to death?"

"This was the occasion on which you landed face first in the mud and told Venetta you liked mud hiking?"

"That's the very time," I said.

"Well, the farmer who chased after us, and who definitely saw me, is just coming to the field over there... Can you see him?"

"Ah yes, I can see him. Why are you worried?"

"Because I think he's looking for me. He half spotted me when his chickens ran in when we were having dinner, but I managed to back away and hide. I'm quite conspicuous, given my size. He will know it was me who was standing there in his chickens, flapping my arms to move them out of the way. And he is coming right towards us."

"So he is," said the guru, calmly.

"Well he might get cross," I said.

"Remember any of the mindfulness techniques? Relax, think about your environment. Lean over and touch that wooden fence there and feel the texture of it; try to relax, and don't worry."

"How the hell is touching the fence going to help me when a mad farmer comes to kill me?" I said.

"He's not going to kill you; just be calm." Strangely, I feel safer and more protected than I ever have in my life before. Just a few words from this man had put me completely at ease.

The farmer caught up with us and glared at me. He clearly knew that I had been scaring his chickens half to death. He looked at the Guru, taking in the long orange robes and beard. "I'm sorry to interrupt you, sir, but I think this lady here was in my chicken coop, and I want to talk to her about the damage she did."

"Not now, not when we are at one with nature."

With that, he walked on, and I walked on behind him. The farmer just stood there and watched us go. I needed an orange robe and a fake beard; they would get me out of all sorts of trouble.

Guru managed to get a bit of speed up, so I couldn't get close enough to talk to him anymore, so I slowed down and ambled along at a more comfortable pace. I felt great for having spoken to him, as though some sort of magic had touched me, some sort of kindness, warmth and strength of purpose that made me feel happier and more confident. When I got back, I would do beginners' yoga, I would try to remember what they said about mindfulness, and I would start to love myself a little bit more, as he had suggested. For now though, I had a half-hour walk up a steep hill to do before I got back to be greeted by half a raisin and a quarter of a peanut or some other such delicacy. Blimey, this was hard-core.

I got about halfway up that hill before the feelings of love and gentleness departed. Everything hurt, the sun was warm, and I felt uncomfortable and horrible. I was getting tense and angry. Not with anything in particular, a couple of minutes early, I'd been feeling happy and full of joy, but this whole bloody exercising thing hurt so much. My back was stinging, and I wanted to be back in the house. Then it happened. I guess I was dragging my feet, and I caught my trainer on a rock; I went flying. I put my hand out to stop myself, but it was no good. I landed in a heap with my ankle all twisted underneath me. I screamed in pain and heard Charlie shout: "My friend's hurt her ankle."

I heard the guru shout: "Don't worry, we'll carry her back to the house. Then he ran back and saw that I had fallen, not Perfect Philippa or Sarah, who probably weighed about eight stone each. He didn't repeat his offer to carry me, but he did help me to my feet, and he and Charlie supported me while I hobbled back in considerable pain.

Once we were there, he sat me on the grass and lit candles all around me, meditating noisily as I winced in pain.

"I think you need to go to the hospital," he said gently.

"Er, yes," said Charlie. "The candles aren't going to make her better, are they?"

I nodded pathetically. "Will you take me?" I asked the guru.

"It might be better if Charlie takes you so I can run the yoga Nidra class after breakfast, but look - take this..."

He handed me a business card. It made me laugh that gurus had business cards, but I guess they had to earn a living like the rest of us. I glanced at it and saw that he lived in Twickenham. Twickenham!! That was so near to me.

"I'll go and get her bags," said Charlie, running into the house while I lay back and smiled up at Guru Motee, luxuriating in all the attention...candles flickered, the guru chanted, and everyone sat around looking at me. I felt as if I were the body at a wake as mourners wandered around me solemnly, and a priest in an orange robe spoke words of comfort.

TAKE ME TO TWICKENHAM

Charlie helped me into the flat, and I hobbled to the sofa, collapsing onto it and resting my foot on a cushion. My phone was bleeping in my bag with messages from friends. I had written about the injury on Facebook in the car on the journey back. I'd even posted a picture of the X-ray department at the hospital. When I say 'written about the injury,' I wrote: "Just injured myself on an advanced yoga course. The guru offered to carry me, and then lit candles around me. Namaste."

It was technically true. I didn't want to say I tripped over my own feet walking up a hill because I collapsed while trying to do a headstand the day before, so I admit I made it look as if I'd hurt myself doing yoga.

Some of the responses were unnecessarily cruel.

"Carry you?" wrote Dave the guy who lives downstairs.

"What's a guru? A forklift truck?"

"Good God woman, what on earth are you doing yoga for?" wrote Dawn

The guys I went to Fat Club with had also left comments on Facebook. They were kind and supportive.

"Well done you for going, but sorry to hear about the injury."

"You poor thing - let me know if you need anything." "Well done for trying yoga!"

What lovely people. I must catch up with the fat course people again soon. I wondered whether they had had as many problems keeping the weight off as I'd had. I know we all lost weight during our weekly meetings, but it was so damn hard to keep the weight off afterwards. Perhaps we should set up another course?

Charlie appeared in the doorway with my bag, coat and the shoe from my injured foot. "There - that's everything from the car. Fancy a drink?" she asked.

"Sure, I'll have peppermint and dandelion tea, please."

"Really? You know the mad cow isn't watching us anymore, don't you? You don't have to drink that horse piss."

"I know that, but I fancy being as healthy as possible now... you know...to develop on everything the guru was saying."

"You're obsessed with that damn guru. And you didn't seem at all interested in being as healthy as possible when we were downing bottles of wine in the room at night," said Charlie.

"Good point, well made," I replied.

"Come on, it's 4 pm, why don't we get the wine out, have a few drinks, then get a takeaway later, or something?"

"Honestly, I don't feel like it, I want to do my life differently from now on. I'm even thinking I might go on one of those courses again, you know, in a few months when I know a bit more about how it all works, when I've practised a bit more and when my ankles better and my back doesn't ache quite as much."

"You're going to book onto another yoga course that the guru is on; that's what you're going to do."

"I just found him very enlightening, that's all," I replied. "The things he said to me on the walk made me feel good. He made me feel like I can live my life differently."

"Well, if you're going to be all boring, I'm going to go home and unpack and sort myself out for work tomorrow."

"OK, I'll call you later," I said.

Charlie gave me a kiss on the cheek and told me to take care and not do too much heavy-duty yoga until my injured ankle was better.

"OK," I said. I had no plans to do any yoga, heavy-duty or otherwise...I just wanted to track down Guru Motee.

I pulled out his business card and the leaflet that had been handed out to us all at the beginning of the course. The leaflet had a small biography of the amazing Guru. He sounded even more incredible when I read it...he'd worshipped in India and all over South Asia, then had been in California for a while, as well as Bermuda, where he'd met Catherine Zeta-Jones and became her spiritual guide.

"Catherine has a home in Bermuda, and Guru would meet and work with her there." The leaflet said. Bloody hell, I loved Catherine Zeta-Jones. I loved her. Guru Motee had to be in my life. Everything was pointing towards it.

The business card said that his studio was in Twickenham, and I knew from what he'd said on our walk that he lived above the yoga studios. I looked up the address, pulled out my laptop and input the details. It was near Twickenham Green; I could picture exactly where it was. Where they played cricket in the summer, near the lovely pub that I'd been to so many times with Ted. Trouble was, how on earth was I going to get there with my ankle bandaged up and aching like crazy?

I picked up the phone and rang Charlie. "Hello matey, it's me," I said. "I'm sorry I was being so dull earlier; I've had a painkiller and feel much better now."

"Glad to hear it," said Charlie. "It's all very worrying when you decline the offer of a glass of wine."

"Haha, I'm not that bad," I said. "Do you fancy catching up later and going for a drink?"

"Sure, yes – shall I come over to you since you cannot move?"

"That would be great," I said. "I thought maybe we could go out to a pub we haven't been to for a while...there's quite a nice one in Twickenham near Twickenham Green."

"Twickenham? That's bloody miles away," said Charlie. "Why don't we just down a couple of bottles of wine at yours instead?"

"Because I want to go to this pub," I said. "Please."

"Oh, go on then. Why don't I come and pick you up at seven?"

"Perfect," I said. I felt bad, of course, using my lovely friend to go and chase a lovely man, but I knew she'd understand. I'd do the same for her without batting an eyelid.

While waiting for Charlie, I did my makeup, dressed, and wrote a letter to Guru Motee. I planned to knock on the door, and if he weren't in, I would push the letter through, saying I was sorry that I didn't get the chance to say goodbye and how much help he had been to me, and I would ask whether it would be possible for me to meet up with him sometime soon.

Charlie arrived at about 10 to 7, telling me she was gagging for a glass. "It's such a pain to go over to Twickenham though," she said. "I can only have one drink when I'm driving. Let's just stay in the pub for a little while, then come back here to yours afterwards and have a proper drink. I can leave my car at yours and walk back."

"Suits me," I said, hobbling out to the car. As we approached Twickenham Green, I urged Charlie to park the car on the side of the road near where my Guru lived. "Just here," I said. "There is no point going any closer; you can never park near the pub."

"But I can see spaces," she said. "And you can't walk. Let me drop you at the pub, then I can come back here and park if there are no spaces."

"No, I absolutely insist. Park here. I'll be fine," I said.

Charlie raised her eyebrows at me and made a funny face before parking the car. I rolled out and waddled, then hobbled to the pavement. We were parked next to number 47, and I knew the Guru lived at number 27.

"See, I'm absolutely fine," I said, hobbling beside her and counting the numbers to get to number 27.

"Oh! Look at this," I said. "I've just realised this is where my guru lives."

"Oh, I see, said Charlie. "Now I get it. That's why you wanted to come to this obscure pub in Twickenham…because you want to bump into the Guru. And - by the way - when did he become 'your' Guru?"

"Shut up. I don't want to bump into him. I don't think he'll be sitting in The Three Kings in his orange robes, will he? I brought a letter with me to push through the door, so let's go and see if he's in, and if he's not, I'll leave this letter there, and we can head to the pub."

"OK then," said Charlie. "But I do get the feeling that this has got disaster written all over it."

We walked up to the door, and I pushed lightly; it opened up to reveal the smell of incense. Someone had been in there recently.

"He must be in," I said in hushed but excited tones.

We were standing in a hallway with a door leading to stairs, presumably up to his apartment, and there was a door to the right of us which led into a beautiful yoga studio. I walked in and marvelled at the beauty of it. It was lovely, with flowers around the edge, motivational posters, and beautiful soft rugs on the side. "Isn't it beautiful? Just the sort of place I'd imagine he would have."

"Yes, it is lovely," said Charlie, looking around. "Very stylish. More Philippa and Sarah's taste than the Guru's, I'd have thought."

"It's amazing," I said.

"Aren't you going to leave your letter then so we can go to the pub?"

But I was too entranced to go rushing off.

"I really like it here. Oooo, look..."

There was another door at the back of the studio. I pushed it open. It led into a smaller but equally lovely, meditation room.

"Don't you think it's got a nice feeling?"

"Yes, it has," said Charlie. "But we shouldn't have walked in here. He'll have a fit if he sees us."

"It's OK," I said. "He's a guru...he doesn't have 'fits'. I'll leave the letter, and let's go to the pub."

I pushed the letter through the door, which led up to stairs and hobbled away. I urged him to contact me in the letter and said I needed his spiritual guidance desperately. I know it said on the leaflet that we weren't to contact the Guru after the weekend, but he'd given me his card along with special permission to contact him, so I was sure it would be OK.

We walked into the pub, and I went up to the bar to order the drinks while Charlie found us somewhere to sit; then, she joined me at the bar to carry them back, with me hobbling behind her.

"I hope he liked my letter," I said.

"I'm sure he will," said Charlie. "I don't see quite what the fascination with him is though; why are you bothering to contact him?"

"I just think he's amazing; he's got this lovely aura of gentleness and calmness," I said.

"Yeah, I guess," said Charlie. "But still – I wouldn't really want to be meeting up with him regularly, would you?"

"God, yes. I think I'm in love with him," I said jokingly, and we both giggled and downed our drinks, but part of me thought that I did have such a big crush on him that it wasn't far off love.

Charlie went up to the bar for our second round, and my phone rang with a number that wasn't familiar.

"Hello, Mary speaking," I said, full of hope.

"Hello there," said a deep, mellifluous voice that I recognised immediately as belonging to the Guru.

"Oh, my goodness, it's so lovely to hear from you. Did you get my letter?" I said.

"Yes, I did. How are you feeling now?"

"Much better, thanks," I said. "Nothing's broken; just a sprain."

"I'm very pleased, Mary. Now, I can't help you with spiritual guidance. I am working with lots of people at the moment. You need someone who can focus and spend more time on you. I suggest you practice yoga and seek fulfilment through that. I can recommend lovely yoga places in the area where you could go to. Would you like me to do that?"

"Are these places where you go?" I asked. "I'd like to do yoga where you are." I was aware that I was sounding slightly stalkerish.

"No, I won't be there, but many very good teachers will be with you on your journey."

"But I wanted to see you again," I said.

"You are very kind," he said. "I hope our paths cross again sometime. I must meditate now. But I wish you joy, love and happiness."

He said 'Namaste' and put the phone down just as Charlie came back with the drinks. I noticed she had changed her mind and had a bottle of wine rather than a glass and soft drink.

"What happened to you driving home?" I said.

"Let's just get an Uber, shall we? I don't start work till 11 tomorrow, so I can get the bus back in the morning to pick up the car."

"Good decision," I said and waited patiently while she opened the bottle and filled the glasses. "Who was that on the phone?" she asked.

"Oh, just mum and dad to check I got home safely from the retreat," I lied.

"Cheers," she said.

We finished the bottle in record speed.

"Shall we get another one?" said Charlie.

I knew it was a bad idea; we already felt half drunk, but I was also at that stage where I was too drunk to think rationally about whether it was a good idea to get another one or not, so I nodded, gave her my card, and told her to put on that. She walked up to the bar, and I saw she was already staggering. Another bottle, and she would be all over the place.

By 9:30 pm, we were on the wrong side of two bottles of wine, and neither of us could speak properly. We sat there laughing, talking nonsense and generally enjoying ourselves.

"I can't feel my hands," I said, as Charlie laughed.

"Me neither," she replied. "Do you think that means that we should head home?"

"I guess," I said, staggering to my feet. We left the pub and walked outside into drizzly weather. It wasn't cold, just rainy and miserable.

"Let's go back and have another look at that yoga place," I said. "We can sit on the lovely soft rugs while we wait for the cab to come."

"We can't," said Charlie.

"Well, you can wait in the rain if you want. I'm going inside." I pushed open the door and walked back into the gorgeous room with the lovely atmosphere. Charlie followed me. We sat on the yoga mats, pulled the rugs over us and promptly fell asleep.

HOME SWEET HOME

I woke first, blinking myself back to consciousness and looking around in confusion, trying to work out where on earth I was. For a moment, I thought I was back at Vishraam; then it came to me... blimey, we'd broken into the guru's yoga studio and fallen asleep.

"How are you feeling?"

I looked up to see the guru - MY GURU - standing there. He was wearing a short, towelling dressing gown. He looked quite delicious. I mean - old - but very attractive.

"Sorry," I said. "We fell asleep."

"Where do you live?" he asked. "Shall I get you home, or would you rather stay here?"

Oh My God. Was he inviting him to spend the night? What should I do? I loved my boyfriend Ted, and he was way older than me. But he was a guru. He was a flipping guru.

"Home would be great. Thank you," said Charlie, sitting up and running her hands through her hair. "And - sorry - we don't normally break into people's homes like this."

"That's OK, Charlie. I'll be right back," he said, smiling at me and leaving the room.

"Did you hear that? He invited me to stay the night," I said to Charlie as soon as he'd left the room. "I think he likes me."

"I'm sure he likes you, Mary, but I think he meant that you can stay here on the mats if you like."

"Nope, that was a come-on," I replied. "I think he...Oh!"

I was stopped mid-sentence by the sight of the guru walking down the stairs, accompanied by Perfect Philippa.

"Oh hello," I said. "What are you doing here?"

"I live here," she said. "We live together. He doesn't drive, so I'll take you back."

"You live together?" I said, but Charlie interrupted. "Thanks so much," she said. "A lift home would be great."

"He's way too old for her; way too old," I said, whispering to Charlie, as we walked to Philippa's car. "What's she thinking?"

"Same thing you were thinking, by the sound of it..."

We got to the car and – of course – it was one of those which bleeps when you don't plug the seatbelt in. She sat there waiting for me to click my seatbelt. "It won't go around me. They never do," I said, feeling my face sting with embarrassment.

"Would you mind trying," she said. "We can't drive to Cobham with this thing bleeping."

I tried and failed.

"I'm sorry," I said as we drove along, the noise getting louder and louder. Eventually, we reached the area in which Charlie and I both live. Philippa dropped me off first.

"Thank you," I said, rolling out and hobbling to the kerb.

"No problem," she said. "Just one thing; please don't turn up at my house again, or phone us or put letters through the door. OK? Guru is very peace-loving, but me? Not so much. Namaste."

"Namaste," I said as I hobbled away, looking back to see Charlie's face, wide-eyed and startled, beaming through the window. Perfect Philippa and the guru. Who'd have thought?

IT WAS 2 a.m. when I got back, and I crashed immediately. I didn't wake up until midday when Ted came bashing on my door to take me to lunch.

"How was it?" he asked after he'd given me a big welcome-home hug. I gave him the potted version, and he shook his head in disbelief.

"Wherever you go, you get in trouble, Mary Brown. Did you enjoy it, though, despite all the minor hiccups? You know - the lack of food, getting your snacks nicked, scaring the chickens, angering the farmer, getting covered in mud, pretending to have OCD, almost breaking your back and ankle, and being on the wrong course. Despite all that - how was it?"

"The mindfulness was really good," I said. "I liked that because I felt relaxed, warm, and happy afterwards. I'll do that again."

"What is it? How do you do it?" he asked.

"It sounds daft, but you just have to connect with yourself in the moment, and you do that by stopping and looking intently at things, like feeling the seat you're sitting on, and trying to describe little details."

"OK," said Ted, looking totally confused by the whole thing.

"What else did you do?"

"Well, this guru came in to do yoga with us, and he was excellent. Turns out he lives in Twickenham."

"Will you meet up with him again?"

"Na, I don't think so," I said. "I might do some beginners' yoga classes because I think it will be good for me, but I'll keep away from gurus for now."

CHRISTMAS WITH MARY BROWN

FOSTERS DIY STORE

13th December: 12 days til Christmas
'Mary Brown, Mary Brown. Please go to the store manager's office. The store manager's office, immediately.'

Oh, bloody hell, this isn't going to be good. I put down the spades I am arranging in height order in the gardening section (I'm just trying to look busy - there's no reason on God's earth why the spades should be assembled in height order). I walk out of the enormous conservatory, pass the rows of plants and trundle into the main store, heading to the manager's office.

I'm wearing my bright green overalls and a red hat and gloves. I don't think anyone has ever looked less attractive (I resemble a large, wobbly poinsettia). It's just so cold over in the gardening section; any thoughts about appearance have been washed away by a wave of desire to stay warm.

I'm working in the gardening section this week because I want to be around all the Christmas trees. I thought it would be all festive and fun. But, tragically, it's not. They haven't got one tree that's nicely decorated. Not one! And there's no music, lights, or any of the lovely Christmassy things you need to make the place look great.

This state of affairs brings me considerable distress because I love

Christmas; I adore it. If I were running this place, all the staff would be dressed like Santa, giving out presents to kids, singing carols and being jolly and friendly. Others I've spoken to disagree. They say that most people want to come into a DIY shop, buy a hammer and go home - not be confronted by a bunch of idiots singing 'We wish you a Merry Christmas' in homemade tinsel hats.

'Oohh, someone's in trouble,' says Neil as I pass the shelving aisle where he appears to be arranging pieces of wood in size order.

He's heard the announcement calling me to the manager's office and assumes I've done something wrong.

'No, Keith wants to talk to me about a pay rise,' I say.

'Yeah, right. Because Keith is *always* doing that.'

I give him a smile and a shrug of my shoulders, but Neil's probably right. I am bound to be in trouble. Why else would I be summoned over the public address system? It'll be because of my joke yesterday: a guy was buying a screwdriver in the hardware section, and I was working on the tills. He came over to pay, and at the same time, as I put the digits into the card machine, his phone rang. It made me laugh because it was as if I'd just dialled him, so I picked up the card reader and pretended it was a phone...holding it to my ear and saying, 'Hello, anyone there.' In my head, it was hysterical, and to the guy's credit, he did laugh weakly at me when I did it.

But the trouble started when I brushed the machine against my ear, and I managed to add extra zeros to the total, so the screwdriver ended up costing £1900. It was quite a fiasco when the guy's bank rejected the payment. Then we realised what I'd done. He wasn't laughing so much then.

I'm pretty sure that'll be what Keith wants to discuss with me - my wholly unprofessional behaviour.

I walk into Keith's office and decide to front up straight away in the hope that this will minimise the anger he feels towards me.

'Sorry about pretending the card machine was a phone,' I say. 'It won't happen again.'

'The card machine? What are you talking about?'

BERNICE BLOOM

Oh good. It's not that. That's a relief. It must be the other thing I did yesterday.

'If it's not the card machine that you want to talk to me about, then I'd like to say I'm sorry about the lipstick kisses,' I say. 'I know that was unprofessional, but the customers didn't object. No one complained. It was a bit of light-hearted fun.'

'What lipstick kisses?' he asks.

Oh no.

'Um. Well, I was working on the paint mixing counter, and when people place an order, we give them a receipt and tell them to come back in an hour to collect the paint.'

'Yes, I know you do, Mary. I implemented that system.'

'Well, I put *'see you in an hour'* and a lipstick kiss - it was just a bit of fun...I thought that's what you wanted to see me about.'

'Er...no,' says Keith, with a bemused look on his red face.'I'm calling you in because I want you to be in charge of Christmas.'

'In charge of Christmas? What do you mean?'

It sounds like the best job in the world, ever.

'You know - make the store look Christmassy, organise some Christmas events. The place is looking a bit unloved. Could you make it look festive?'

'Oh God, yes,' I say, rising to my feet and just about resisting the urge to throw my arms around his thick, florid neck and kiss his bald patch. 'I've never been up for anything more in my entire life.'

'Good,' he says. 'Have a ponder and come back to me with a list of what you think we should be doing. You have a budget of £250.'

'OK,' I say, beaming.

'Oh, and Mary...'

'Yes.'

'Stop doing that lipstick kiss thing.'

'Of course,' I say. 'I won't do it again.'

I walk out of Keith's office and do a little jig. Not a full-on dance or anything - I'm British, after all - just a little shuffle to reflect the happiness inside me. Then I smile. I'm in charge of bloody Christmas.

BATTLE OF THE PARENTS

When I get home from work, the phone rings in my flat. I always answer the landline with extreme caution because it's usually someone trying to sell me something or convince me that I've been in an accident that wasn't my fault. There have been times when the woman on the phone has been so convincing that I have come away believing I was in an accident. Maybe someone knocked into my car, and I wasn't at fault? It could have happened. Then I remember that I can't drive and don't have a car.

'Hello Mary, it's mum.'

Yes - that's the other thing I should have mentioned about the landline: if it's not a salesman, it's mum. Everyone else in the world now rings me on my mobile, but not my mother.

'I'm in charge of Christmas!' I blurt out. There's a moment's silence.

'Very good,' she says before moving on. 'As a special treat, we thought it would be nice to invite Ted to come to us for Christmas. Do you think he'd like to?'

I have to tell you - this is a most unusual development. My Dad is not fond of visitors. So for mum to invite anyone round, knowing what dad's like, is a miracle, and for them to ask a boyfriend of mine...someone they haven't even met yet...well, that's plain madness.

'I think he'd love to,' I say, feeling a shiver of excitement at the thought of waking up on Christmas morning in my flat with Ted and then walking hand-in-hand with him to mum and dad's house.

'Good,' says mum. 'Then I'll ensure we have enough food for all of us. I told your father I was inviting Ted, and he said he was looking forward to meeting him.'

I know this isn't true. Dad hates meeting anyone new.

'Oh, and we're getting a new freezer. Did I tell you?'

Again, this is surprising news. For most people, a new freezer might not be a huge deal, but for mum and dad - it's more significant news than if she told me that dad was getting a sex change. They don't ever buy anything new. They are all about 'make do and mend' - it's like the Blitz is going on, and they feel duty-bound not to use up the country's precious, dwindling resources.

'We've talked about it for a few years and decided to get one before Christmas. Will you help me choose one?'

'Of course, I will,' I say.

'Very good. Talk to you soon.'

Whenever I speak to mum on the phone, I'm astonished by how clipped her tones are and how formal and professional she sounds; it's as if she's talking on the telephone for the first time. As if phones have just been invented, and she's not at all sure whether they're a good idea. She's not at all like that in real life. Still - nice of her to invite Ted to Christmas. I'm chuffed about that.

LATER THAT EVENING, I arrive at Ted's flat, eager to give him the double helping of good news that I have been put in charge of Christmas and that he has been invited to spend Christmas Day with my parents and me. I'm not sure how he'll react to the latter of these two pieces of information because he's never met my parents. But now that Ted and I have been going out together for six months, it's time he met them, and Christmas will be the perfect opportunity.

He opens the door beaming with delight. It's like he knows my good news.

'You look happy,' I say.

'I'm delighted, young lady,' he says, pulling me into his arms. 'Come in, and I'll tell you all about it.'

Ted closes the door behind me, and I start walking up the narrow staircase to his flat. I hate walking ahead of Ted. I'm always worried that he's looking at my colossal bottom and wondering whether he'd be better off with someone who wasn't the size of a large freight ship. I worry that he'll go off me or something. Not that he's thin. We met at Fat Club and are both...how do I phrase this elegantly?...we're both considerably larger than Kate Moss. We've lost some weight and are on mad diets most of the time, but we still both weigh twice what an average person does.

We get to the top (only about ten steps), and I'm breathing heavily...I need to start exercising as well as dieting.

'I'm in charge of Christmas!' I blurt out.

'OK, you'll never guess where we've been invited,' he says.

Why is no one reacting in how I expect them to act to the news that I am IN CHARGE OF CHRISTMAS? Surely that statement deserves some recognition, but first, mum completely ignored me, and now Ted has completely ignored me.

'I'm in charge of Christmas,' I repeat.

'I know. You said. Well done, you. Now - you have to guess where we've been invited to go.'

No one is anywhere near as excited by my news as I am.

'Buckingham Palace?' I venture.

'Better.'

'Better than Buckingham Palace? Um...The White House? Is that better? I don't know. Tell me.'

'OK. Wait for this...my mum and dad have invited us to have Christmas lunch with them. I can't believe it. It's so exciting. My sister's away for Christmas, and they thought we might like to join them instead. Please, please, please say 'yes'.'

'Um... yes,' I say before I can stop myself and explain that I have already committed to lunch with my parents after they made an extraordinary invitation. But I don't want to let Ted down; he looks so excited. And it is wonderful that his parents have invited me to join them for Christmas. I'm flattered. Perhaps I can pull out later...urge him to change his mind and come with me to my parents instead.

'Brilliant,' he says, gathering me up and kissing me all over my face. 'You've made me the happiest man alive. Now I can't wait for Christmas day. It's going to be the best.'

Shit.

We retire to bed with glasses of wine. Ted is beaming with happiness that we will be spending Christmas at his mum's; I am smiling and trying to look like it's a great idea.

'What did you say earlier?' he asks. 'Something about you wanting to take charge of Christmas.'

'No, I've taken charge of Christmas. I am now in charge. It's official.'

'I think you'll find Father Christmas already has that job sewn up, sweetheart. What are you talking about?'

'I'm talking about work...Keith called me into his office today and told me he wants me to be in charge of Christmas.'

'Wow, that's brilliant,' says Ted.

Finally, someone recognises what a big deal this is.

'You'll be perfect.'

'Yes - I know. I'm beyond excited about it,' I say. 'I have many plans to decorate the store and offer a Christmas tree decorating service and lollipops for children. I have to pitch all my ideas to Ted in the morning.'

'Well done you,' says Ted, kissing me lightly on the cheek before rolling over and going to sleep. I drift off, too, thinking of how to make Fosters DIY Emporium the best Christmas experience ever.

We need a nativity scene...a brilliant one. We should have real donkeys. Where can you get real donkeys? And we need a baby Jesus. Can you hire them? I need to check that. We need a giant Christmas tree with beautiful lights, presents underneath it, and a star on top, and we need lots of Father Christmases and carols playing and sweets for children and the smell of mulled wine and mince pies, and maybe Christmas cards for every customer.

And why don't we have a magical Post Box where people can post their Christmas wishes? Then someone could answer all the letters. I'll make this the best Christmas ever for everyone who comes into the store.

BEING MARY CHRISTMAS

1 4th December
At 9 am the following morning, I am standing in front of Keith with my list of ideas typed out neatly on a sheet of A4.

'I thought we could have a Christmas postbox of wishes and dreams, a nativity scene, lots of decorations and lots of fun,' I say as he scans the list, nodding to himself. What he's worried about, of course, is the cost. He reminds me that he told me to keep to a £250 budget.

'Yeah, the budget is a bit tight, but I thought we could get the local paper to come down,' I say. 'Editors like Christmas pictures in the paper, so if we had an amazing nativity scene, they might photograph it, then we'd be in the papers, and we'd attract more customers. Then your boss would be thrilled.'

You see: I may look stupid in my large green overall and with Christmas decorations hanging from my ears (are they too much?), but I'm not. I know that the prospect of free publicity will be enough to compel him to spend a fortune.

'Indeed,' says Keith, with a sharp rise of his eyebrows. 'Excellent thinking. And then, we can offset the costs against the PR budget. Perfect. Get to it, Mary. Christmas is in six days, so we need to get cracking.'

Tomorrow is the day when celebrations officially start at the centre, so use today to get everything set up.

'Great,' I say, adjusting the tinsel in my hair. 'The only thing is - I'm supposed to be working on the till in the bathroom section this afternoon. It will take a while to do all this. Could someone else cover, so I can sit down and sort this out?'

'Yes, of course,' says Keith, hitting the microphone and buzzer on his desk. 'Could the supervisor in the bathrooms section please come to the manager's office immediately? Thank you,' he says.

'Mary, go and work on the desk next to Sharon. Let's try and get this place Christmas-ed up to the hilt by the end of the day, and I want photographers and BBC news film crews here tomorrow.'

'Right,' I say. Keith seems to have escalated the publicity potential in his mind. The 10 O'clock news has replaced my suggestion of a local newspaper. How do you convince a TV crew to come to a DIY store?

I'd have thought they would have better things to do.

Presumably, they wouldn't come unless a child was kidnapped or something.

Maybe I should kidnap a... But, no, I can't do that.

I sit next to perfect Sharon in her elegant cream suit (not for her the daily humiliation of a green overall), and I start scribbling.

The first thing I have to do is create a very realistic nativity scene. I'll need a baby, a Mary and Jesus, wise men, shepherds and some animals. That can't be too hard to assemble, can it? The average junior school production manages to acquire all of those, so it can't be beyond me.

'It's nice to have a girl working alongside me,' says Sharon, smiling at me warmly.

'Yes,' I say, but I don't want to engage in chit-chat; I want to organise a wonderful Christmas. So I lean over my notebook and scribble away.

Sharon watches me.

'Mary, you might be able to help me with this,' she says. 'Something's been troubling me.'

'Has it?'

'Yes, I saw on the telly last night that they said one in three men lives at home now.'

'OK,' I say. 'That doesn't surprise me. It's a sign of the times...credit crunch and all that. People are finding it difficult to buy their own homes.'

'No, but it's ridiculous...everyone lives at home.'

'Yes, but they mean that one in three men lives in the family home rather than buying their own home.'

'But it's still a home.'

'Yes, but they mean they don't have their own homes.'

'But they do have homes.'

Oh goodness.

'You're right,' I say, eager to return to my Christmas planning. 'How silly of them.'

'Isn't she adorable?' says Keith, standing over Sharon as we chat. 'Mary, I'm fortunate to have someone as smart and lovely as my PA.'

'You are,' I say, looking up at him as he grins down at her, and she turns scarlet in response. Keith does have more than a touch of the David Brents. Everything he does is ever-so-slightly cringey.

'Come on, Sharon, let me take you to lunch as a Christmas treat. Then, Mary, maybe you could cover the office while we're out?'

'Sure,' I reply, as Sharon pulls her brush from her handbag and starts sprucing herself up for lunch with the boss. It's striking the difference it makes to your life if you're pretty, delicate and alluring like Sharon. I see the guys rushing to open doors for her and help her if she has anything heavy to carry. Me? Nope - I'm left to struggle with my arms full - bashing doors open with my enormous arse while men stand by, ogling at women like Sharon.

'See you later,' she squeaks, wiggling her way out of the office and leaving me to my planning.

Their lunch seems like a triumph because they don't reappear that afternoon. So I sit there, lost in my own world, plotting and planning until around 7 pm when I pack up everything and head home.

On the way home that evening, I jump off the bus at a toy store to collect everything I need for my nativity scene, along with decorations for the garden centre. They come to £275. I've smashed through the budget after a little shopping trip. Still, it had to be done. Keith says that Christmas officially starts tomorrow, so I must be prepared. When I get home, I line up all the animals in the hallway and look at them like a proud mother—what a splendid selection. I'm thrilled that I've got this job…bloody thrilled.

TEN DAY COUNT-DOWN BEGINS

1 5th December

The following day, I'm awake at the crack of dawn. 'It's Christmaaaaaaas....' I yell into Ted's ear in the manner of Nodder Holder. He jumps as he wakes up and throws his big hands against his ears, muttering obscenities at me. Then he pulls the duvet over his head and turns away. So my words of seasonal joy haven't had quite the effect on my beloved that I hoped they might.

Most people would take this as a sign that their partner doesn't want to be disturbed and walk away. Not me. I'm not perturbed. Nothing can dampen the Christmas spirit soaring through my veins. So I sit up and start singing *Twelve Days of Christmas.*

'On what planet is it Christmas today?' Ted shouts over the sound of my awful singing. 'It's 15th December. That's not Christmas Day anywhere.'

'No, not Christmas Day,' I say. 'It's Christmas time. Today the countdown to Christmas starts at work. And you remember who's in charge of it all, don't you?'

There's a long sigh and a grumpy noise from the lump under the duvet.

'Meeeeeeee,' I remind him.

Ted sits up and rubs his eyes.

'I can build my lovely nativity scene today and put up the magic *Post Box of Wishes and Dreams*. Also, we'll start giving sweets to all the children who come to the store, which will be lovely.'

'Yeah, I'd be a bit cautious about handing sweets to children. That can end badly.'

'Nonsense,' I tell him as I get changed for work. This morning I don't have to clamber into the terrible green uniform that makes me look like a cross between Kermit and Shrek. No, I'm not working on the tills for the next 12 days, so I put on my red Christmas jumper with big holly leaves on the front. The great joy of this jumper is that, in addition to the fact that it has big holly leaves on the front, it also has Christmas baubles all over the back, and when you press each of the baubles, it plays a different festive tune.

Of course, Ted looks at me like I'm nuts and comments that I constantly moan about having to wear the horrible green uniform to work. He says I complain about not being able to wear nice clothes, then as soon as I get the opportunity to wear my own stuff, I opt for a ridiculous Christmas jumper.

'But this is nice,' I say. 'I like it. It's fun, musical and charming. Now, I need to go. Don't delay me any longer.'

'Don't delay you? I was fast asleep. You woke me up.'

'Oh yes - sorry about that. Right, I'm going. See you later.'

I go to the kitchen and collect a large bin bag to transport all the stuffed animals waiting patiently by the front door.'

Ted follows me, rubbing his eyes like a giant toddler.

'Are these the animals for the nativity scene?' he says, as he watches me laying them carefully into a bin bag.

'Yes.'

'But they're ridiculous.'

'What's wrong with them? They'll make the nativity scene look wonderful.'

'An elephant, a camel and a horse? In the name of all that is holy, where do they fit in? There wasn't an elephant in the stable.'

'That's how the three wise men got to Bethlehem.'

'Yeah, on an elephant? Sure.'

'It's true. One was on an elephant, one on a camel, and the other on a horse. I know I'm right because I phoned the vicar from the toy shop last night to be sure.'

'Was the vicar sober?'

I stand there, looking down at the bin bag, not keen to discuss this anymore because I want to be excited about it and have a lovely time.

'Why are you in a sulk?' asks Ted.

'I'm not in a sulk, I just know how the three wise men got to Bethlehem, and you don't, so keep your nose out of my elephant-related business.'

'OK,' he says, unsure whether I'm serious or joking.

I run out to the bus with my bag of animals and catch it in the nick of time. I sit down but soon realise I have to perch on the edge because every time I move back, my jumper touches the seat and bursts into song. I didn't realise it was quite so sensitive. One little knock and my jumper starts serenading me. I see people looking at their phones, wondering whether an incoming text is causing the sudden musical outburst.

I'm about halfway through the journey when I burst into song without touching my jumper. It takes me a few minutes to realise that it's my phone, with a text from Ted.

'Can you get me some deodorant if you pass a shop? I'm stuck in the office all day, and I'm starting to smell like a horse, a camel and an elephant! Xxx'

Given the unhelpful jibe about my nativity animals, he doesn't deserve any, but since I get off the bus next to Boots, I'll get some for him.

It's one of those tiny branches of Boots that sells nothing but the absolute essentials. I walk in and head to where the deodorants are kept, but there only appear to be women's deodorants. Do you think it matters? I mean - what difference can it make? It must be all the same inside, just with different patterns.

But I know Ted won't be happy if I come back with a pink, floral deodorant bottle, so I ask the somewhat official-looking woman behind the counter, wearing a white uniform, whether she has any men's deodorant.

'The ball kind?' she says.

Ball kind?

'No,' I screech. 'My boyfriend wants it for his underarms, thank you very much.'

Good grief. I didn't even realise you could buy deodorant for your testicles.

When I arrive at Fosters Gardening and DIY centre, I'm still concerned that there are men all over the country rolling deodorant all over their manly bits. But I try to push the unfortunate image out of my mind as I head straight to Keith's office and over to my little desk in the corner, now the centre of all Christmas-related affairs.

It gives me such a sense of importance to have my own desk. I've been working at the centre since I left school. I'm usually out in the store, avoiding customers and their questions and wasting time by moving plants about unnecessarily. But now I have a mission... I'm in charge of something. Christmas is all mine, and I have a desk of my own on which to plan it.

I made a good start yesterday, but I want to discuss things with Keith before proceeding much more. I find him sitting in the cafeteria with horror and sadness etched on his face. He's staring out into the middle distance, contemplative...as if trying to make sense of some terrible event that has befallen him.

'Lord above,' he says when he sees me. 'I drank so much yesterday that I almost killed myself.'

'Oh dear, well, I'm glad you didn't...you know...kill yourself,' I say. 'Have you got five minutes so I can run through some thoughts?'

He looks like he might burst into tears at any moment and slips on his sunglasses.

'Go ahead.'

'I had a good think yesterday while you were out and about, and I made a few calls. This is what we need: first of all - an enormous nativity scene, and I've bought lots of animals with which to fill it. Then we need to decorate eight Christmas trees, have a spectacular light display, and a *Christmas Post Box of Wishes and Dreams* in red and white for people to post their Christmas wishes.

'What I thought we could do is - I could read the letters and answer them from Santa's elf. We know it'll be mainly adults putting notes in there because we don't get that many children in the store. All the same, I think it will be good fun.'

'Sure, whatever,' says Keith. He looks worse now than when I first walked in.

'Is it OK to use Ray and Joe to help me?'

'Why would you do that?'

'I need some help, and in the message you left me last night, you said that they would do the heavy lifting for me.'

'Did I send you a message?'

'You sent lots, but I couldn't establish what you were trying to say in some of them. Shall I show you?'

'No, no. That's fine. Whatever you want. Just go and get on with it.'

'Great,' I say, walking away. I think Keith would have agreed to anything to get rid of me. A perfect scenario. So why the hell didn't I ask for a pay rise?

CHRISTMAS WORLD

I grab a coffee and head out to find Ray and Joe. They are surprised that they are seconded to help me set up Christmas, having not been told anything about the plans by our hung-over boss. But they are pleased to be dragged away from loading fertiliser bags onto the cart at the back of the garden centre.

'First, let's get this nativity scene up and running,' I say, handing each of them a box containing all manner of nativity features, the bag of animals I brought from home, a giant star and some hay.

'I'm afraid we will have to make a new stable. I tried to save the one from last year, but someone had put spider plants on top of it, and it was all dented and horrible, with worms crawling through it. It would have been very disrespectful to expect Mary and Joseph to live in a shabby old stable like that.'

Ray and Joe nod in agreement as I present them with an enormous furniture packing box that I found in the garden furniture department. It is big enough for me to get inside (I know that because I did just that), and I suggest that the guys paint it and move it to my specially chosen location, marked with an 'x' on a map, then fill it with nativity items.

'This area will be henceforth called 'Christmas World',' I say grandly.

'It will contain Santa's grotto and the nativity scene, with Mary and Joseph in the middle, flanked by the three wise men.'

We decide that Ray will work on sorting out the nativity scene while Joe works with me on decorating the trees. I picked up everything I needed for the trees last night and plan to decorate them with my usual verve and individuality by hanging pictures of Rick Astley stuck onto cardboard bells all over one of them.

Rick lives locally, you see, and he has promised to pop in and do a live song for us this Christmas, so it seems appropriate to have one tree decked out with his face. The other trees are slightly soberer, well – I say that, but one has pink elephants hanging from every branch, and the other has a mixture of brightly coloured ornaments. I designed that to be a treat for everyone - a streak of wonder, colour and life.

Lots of the staff gather around as we assemble all the elements of the Christmas scene. As it comes together, it immediately lifts the look of the store (and - to be fair - it's quite a task to lift the appearance of a shop that sells lots of spades and copper piping).

The Christmas World area is now a riot of vibrant hues, sounds and joy. I commandeer a considerable number of lights and the centre's hi-fi system, and we finish this first stage off by playing Christmas music as we string the lights above the whole area, like a sparkly net overhead. The lights move from tree to tree and from the edge of the portacabin to Santa's grotto. You can see the section for miles off. You can probably see it from Mars.

The only thing left to go up is the *Christmas Post Box of Wishes and Dreams*, which I am lovingly creating from numerous cereal boxes and an old Santa Claus outfit made from horrible scratchy nylon. The result divides opinion. In my view, it's pretty spectacular. In everyone else's view, it's ridiculous.

I put a laminated note in front of the post-box saying:

'Ho, ho, ho. I am the Christmas Post Box of Wishes and Dreams. Post

your letters here with all your Christmas wishes, and I will see whether we can make them come true... from Santa's Elf.

'Well, well, well,' says Keith, walking up behind me. 'This looks great.'
'Welcome to Christmas World,' I say. 'Isn't it fabulous?'
'Outstanding, Mary Brown. OOOOh, but I wouldn't put that note on the post box. You'll get all sorts of odd requests.'
'I'm sure I won't,' I say confidently.
'You don't know what guys are like,' he replies as if he were some worldly lothario instead of the inefficient manager of a struggling DIY centre on the outskirts of Cobham.
'You'll be inundated with obscene requests and offensive suggestions,' he adds. 'And that'll be from me. Ha ha. I am only joking. You know I'm joking. Mary. You know I'm joking?'
'Yes, Keith. I know you're joking.'
'Seriously though, I think it's a big mistake to call it a *Christmas Post Box of Wishes and Dreams* – call it a *Christmas Post Box*. You're not going be making anyone's wishes and dreams come true. You are giving them false promises...false hope.'
I try to argue that I am doing no such thing, but Keith's not interested...his attention has wandered, and he's noticed the lattice of lights sparkling above us.
'It's very bright. Very eye-catching. That is a lot of lights.'
'Yes.'
'It lights up the whole nativity scene. Hang on. Why's there an elephant there?'
'That's how one of the three wise men got to Bethlehem.'
'On an elephant? Please do me a favour, Mary. They were on camels; everyone knows that.'
There are sniggers from Ray and Joe.
'One of them came on an elephant. I checked with a vicar.'
My patience is already wearing thin with all the elephant-defending, and I fear this is only the beginning.
'OK. Well, it looks odd. Mary - I've got some of the staff together

for a meeting at 4.30 pm. Can you come and give them a quick overview of plans for Christmas and what to expect?'

'Sure,' I say. I don't know what sort of plans Keith thinks I've got. I had a budget of £250, and I've spent about £400 if you include all the pink elephants and pictures of Rick Astley.'

Still, at 4.30 pm, I head to the meeting and walk to the front of the room, preparing to tell all my colleagues about the extraordinary Christmas events we have planned.

'Hello, everyone. As you know, my name is Mary Brown, and I'm in charge of Christmas,' I say proudly. 'I want to run through some of the exciting things we've planned for this year and answer any questions you might have. Also, if you have any questions relating to Christmas or Christmas products, I'll be around to answer all your queries. So, let's get started....'

I run through all the glorious decorations that are now adorning the walls, trees and plants, turning the DIY store into a spectacle of Christmas joy. There's not much reaction, to be honest. I hoped it would be a bit like one of those Trump rallies where cheers and whoops of delight meet everything you say and waving of arms and chanting accompanies every comment, but it doesn't happen like that.

Everyone sits there, mostly looking down, appearing to pay very little attention to what I'm saying. Meanwhile, I bounce around in front of them, full of the joys of the season, squeezing the back of my jumper occasionally to inject some Christmas music and spirit into the occasion and trying to make just one of them smile.

'OK, I'm glad that's all been received so well,' I say. 'Now I want to tell you about an exciting new development this year.

'We will have a *Christmas Post Box of Wishes and Dreams* so that people can put their Christmas wishes into it, and Santa's elf will reply to them all.'

I look around the audience. Tony-the-Tap from bathroom supplies is playing with his phone, and Gavin from outdoor furniture is scratching his ears. I think that might be because he's got nits, though. Gavin's always sporting some horrible health condition, and we mostly keep away from him in case we catch it. Then I see his hand go up.

'Yes, Gavin?'

'How have you got an elf to answer the questions?'

'No, Gavin, it's not a real elf. That was just a joke.'

'Oh, so why are people going to post their Christmas wishes in the box?'

'It's just a bit of Christmas fun. I'll be replying to them.'

'Will you be dressed as an elf?'

'Probably not. It doesn't make any difference. It's just a bit of fun.'

Tony's hand goes up then.

'Do you have to have a stamp on the letter you put in the letterbox?'

'No, Tony. It's not a real letterbox.'

'What will you do if people put stamps on the letters?'

'I haven't thought about that. Perhaps I will take the stamps off the envelopes and give them to charity.'

'What charity?'

'Honestly, I haven't thought about that. I'll ask Keith what he thinks.'

'Do you think that the Mary and Joseph story is true?' asks Martina, the lady who works in the staff canteen.

'I don't know,' I say. 'I'm not a history expert, and I don't have any religious studies background; they've just put me in charge of making the place look Christmassy. I've got some flashing Father Christmas hats here for everyone to wear. I'd be grateful if you could all start wearing them, so we look as festive as possible.'

Another hand goes up. It's Tony-the-Tap again. 'What's with all the elephants in the manger?"

Keith interrupts and says that, unfortunately, we will leave it there, and he hopes everyone enjoys getting into the spirit of Christmas.

CAR SURFING

'I need a drink,' I say to Belinda as I slump into an armchair in the coffee room.

'There were some full-on, daft questions being asked there,' she says sympathetically. 'Is it always like this?'

Belinda is new. She's the only woman working in the store around my age; everyone else is much older. I don't think she can believe how slow and behind the times some of them are.

'It's always like this,' I say.

She smiles.

'I think you're amazing. You're a sales assistant like me, but you have taken on all the responsibility for Christmas. I would never be able to stand up and talk in front of everyone like that.'

'Thank you.'

'You should be in charge of this place. You seem so much brighter and more intelligent than everyone else.'

'Gosh, that would be nice. Especially the pay rise,' I say.

'Yeah.' She's playing with the rim of her plastic cup as she sits there in silence. It feels like she wants to ask me something, so I sit there in silence, sipping my coffee.

'Can I ask you a question?' she says eventually. But then Tony-the-

Tap walks in, and she looks up, all alarmed. She pulls her chair closer to mine.

'It's quite personal. Can I talk to you away from work? I don't know whether you fancy going for a drink tonight. I'm having a bit of an issue, and I could do with talking it through. A guy is coming on to me, and I'm finding it awkward.'

'Sure,' I say. 'Who is it?'

She glances up at Tony.

'Do you mind if we talk about it later?' she mouths.

'No problem.'

There's a moment's silence.

'Could you give me a clue?'

'No,' says Belinda. 'Let's talk about it tonight. I don't want anyone to overhear. I've got my car; I could drive us.'

'That would be great,' I say. Clearly, I will have to wait until tonight to hear who has been misbehaving. 'Shall I meet you in the car park at 6? My car's a blue Golf.'

'See you then,' I say.

The rest of the day flies past. The staff don't seem to be wildly engaged with my Christmas festivities; some walk around without their flashing Father Christmas hats. To make it worse, they run away whenever they see me approaching, clutching the hats they should be wearing.

Happily, the customers seem to like what they see. First, they come wheeling through the store, then they stop and stare at the festive scene, smiling up at the lights twinkling above them.

People laugh at the Christmas trees and take pictures of my Rick Astley baubles. Then they hover by the nativity scene, humming to the music. There's a genuine feeling of goodwill and delight at the spiderweb of flashing, sparkling lights strung across the top of the nativity section.

By 6 pm, I'm feeling much better about everything. The team meeting put a dampener on things, and the attitude of the staff made me cross but seeing the customers enjoying it has lifted my spirits. I've not seen anyone post a letter in my fabulous postbox yet, but hopefully, by the time I come in tomorrow morning, there'll be a little bundle of them waiting for me.

Now I'm off to meet Belinda for a proper girly natter and also – obviously – to find out which one of our employees has wandering hands.

I've thought about the options since she first mentioned what happened to her. There's Keith - he can be a bit slimy, but I don't think he's the handsy type. The guys in the warehouse are very loud and boisterous when they're all together, but they're pack animals; I can't imagine them causing any trouble when they're on their own without backup.

I walk out to the car park and see Belinda's car straight away...it's all shiny and new-looking, she must have bought it quite recently, or she keeps it looking nice. Funny - she doesn't strike me as the sort of woman who would spend a lot of time looking after her car. She doesn't seem like the sort of woman who spends a lot of time looking after anything. I mean, she's nice but sort of scruffy and poorly put together. I don't mean that as an insult at all; it's just that she's always messy.

As I walk over to her car, I see her coming out of the centre towards us, so I drape myself across the bonnet to await her arrival. I assume an amusing supermodel pose, lying perfectly still, with the poutiest of lips. I lay there for quite a while, thinking that Belinda should be here by now. Perhaps she forgot something and had to rush back inside for it? But, when I look up, she's nowhere to be seen. I'll stay a bit longer but turn onto my other side because this is starting to get uncomfortable. I roll over, feeling the suspension groan beneath me. And then I see it.

Bloody hell.

Sitting in the front of the car, staring at me with a look of wide-eyed confusion, are an elderly man and woman. They look both astonished and terrified. I smile at them to placate them, but judging by how the man flinches and moves back in his seat, he's not remotely reassured.

I scramble off the bonnet, regretting how it dips down as I move across it, and I hope I haven't wrecked their suspension with my antics. Then I wave and run off. I don't know what else to do. I've no idea how to explain to them why I lay across the front of their car for 10 minutes, licking my lips and pouting.

I hear a toot and turn around to see Belinda waving at me while sitting in the driving seat of a scruffy old car. Much more like the sort of vehicle I was expecting her to drive. The thing is practically falling apart. I jump into the passenger seat and instruct her to go.

'Who were they?' she asks, indicating the people sitting in the car on which she saw me lying. It's a fair enough question, but I don't have a sensible answer for her.

'Just old friends,' I say. 'Quick, let's go.'

'I swear they were the guys who bought all that expensive garden furniture today. Your friends have good taste.'

'Yes,' I say noncommittally.

'They're coming to collect it on Saturday before they move into their new house.'

'Good for them,' I reply. 'Now then - let's get going. Shall we try The King's Arms?'

'Sure,' she says, crunching the gears as she moves off and heads towards the pub. Once we arrive in the car park, she parks her car very badly, taking up two spots by parking on the dividing line between the Then she blocks another two by sticking her bumper out so far that she's effectively prevented anyone from getting into the spaces behind her. Four parking spots for a tiny car? That must be some record. I feel strangely proud of the woman.

We walk into the pub, order wine, and sit in a corner booth. We clink our glasses together.

'To Christmas,' says Belinda.

'Christmas.'

'I hope you didn't mind me asking you to come out tonight. I know you must be busy with all your amazing, valuable work,' says Belinda. She talks about me as if I'm running the Red Cross.

'Don't be silly,' I say.

How much work does she think it entails to string up some lights and make a post-box out of cereal packaging?

'It's just so hard to know whom you can talk to. You always seem so professional and on top of things that I thought you might be able to help.'

This is not a common description of me, so I pause for a while to cherish the flattering words.

'I'm delighted to help,' I tell Belinda. 'Honestly, anything you tell me will be in confidence, and if there's anything I can do to assist or make life better at work, you only have to say.'

'No, this isn't at work,' says Belinda, and I regret that I feel a pang of disappointment.

'It's embarrassing, but it's my mum's boyfriend. He keeps telling me how much he fancies me, and I'm unsure what to do about it.'

'Oh no, that's awful. I'm so sorry,' I say. 'That's a tough situation. I'm sorry, but I thought you meant one of the guys at work had been coming on to you, and I was going to suggest all sorts of things, but it's a bit harder if it's in your home.'

'Yeah, it's tough.'

'Weird but harmless,' I say. 'Tell me a bit about this awful boyfriend, and I'll see whether I can help. Has she been seeing him for long?'

'Just a couple of months, and I don't like him. And he's now become a bit, you know, affectionate. Is that the right word? He strokes my hair when he walks past me, telling me how lovely I look.

'Mum smiles when he does it, she thinks it's great that we're all getting on. But we're not all getting on well at all. I'm certainly not getting on well with him. I'm sick to the back teeth of being touched by him.

'Then he got drunk last night and told me he fancied me. I didn't know what to say.'

'Tell him to piss off, and you tell your mum straightaway. Honestly, you don't have to put up with all this. Don't let someone in your home make you feel scared and uncomfortable.'

'But I don't want to upset mum.'

'I promise you; your mum will want to know. And she needs to know what sort of scumbag she's going out with, doesn't she? For her good as well as yours. If you don't tell her, you're not protecting her. On the contrary, you're leaving her vulnerable to more bad treatment from him and making your own life very difficult.'

'Yeah, I guess,' says Belinda. 'I thought that maybe I should move out or something like that. Just get away from the situation.'

'No, you've done nothing wrong. You need to tell your mum.'

'Yes, I'll tell her. I promise I'll talk to her. Thank you. I feel so much better now.'

'And, if things get terrible, call me any time. You can come and stay with me if you need to. I mean that.'

'Oh my God, Mary. Thank you so much; you are so kind. I didn't want to move out and get a place of my own: I get so lonely.'

'No, you don't have to live on your own. But - equally - you shouldn't be drummed out of your own home by this scum bag; tell your mum, and I'm sure everything will be OK. If it's not, you know where I am.'

'Thanks, Mary. Do you live by yourself? I did it once and hated it.'

'I have my place on my own, but my boyfriend Ted is always around, so I never get lonely.

'I'd love to have a boyfriend,' she says. 'It must be amazing to have someone there who loves you, no matter what. And you can tell them anything. And everything's lovely. You have this gorgeous perfect man at home, waiting for you.'

I get the sentiments of what she's saying. But when I think of Ted scratching his balls and picking his nose, the words 'perfect man' don't spring quickly to mind.

'How did you meet Ted? I don't know how to meet anyone. I've never really had a boyfriend.'

'I met Ted at a club I went to.' I don't want to tell her we met at Fat Club, so I tail off before explaining what sort of club and offer her advice instead.

'I think your best bet is to get out as much as possible. You will never meet someone in your house, so you need to join clubs, even go to the gym if you can bear it. I know it's one of the most dreadful places on earth, but it is full of men. Or even go to a cafe, sit, drink a coffee, and look around. You know you can go to many places where you might meet someone. And have you tried internet dating?'

'No, I could never do that.' says Belinda. 'Honestly, I'd hate it.'

'I understand. And, to be honest, I'd focus on sorting out the situation with your mum's boyfriend first. That's the priority. Then I'll help you find a boyfriend if you'd like.'

'Oh, that would be great.'

'OK, promise me you'll go home and talk to your mum.'

'I will,' she assures me. 'Mum and her boyfriend are away this week. They are back on Sunday, and I'll talk to her then.'

'And you'll tell her how upset this is all making you?'

'I will,' she promises, and we clink our glasses together again.

THE POSTBOX OF WISHES & DREAMS

1
6th December

My first task on this lovely, though chilly, morning is to head out to the grotto and switch on the sparkly lights and Christmas music. My original plan was to play carols, but, I'll be honest with you, I don't take much to carols. The thought of listening to 'Away in a Manger' through the second-rate music system all day filled me with horror. So, instead, I decide to play a mixture of Christmas favourites. I don't know what it says about my sophistication and religiosity, but as 'Last Christmas' bursts into life, I'm prepared to admit that I prefer Wham to choir boys.

Next, I turn my attention to the *Christmas Post Box of Wishes and Dreams*, sitting proudly before me. I open the little door I fashioned on the front of it and stick my hand inside.

Oh my God.

There are letters in there. I feel a thrill rush up through my body. I *hoped* there would be letters, but there *are* letters. I count them. There are 12 in total. Oh my God. I pull them out, tie the whole thing back down again, and disappear into the office to read them. I'm pretty good at giving advice and offering kind words; I hope I can help with these.

I sit down at my desk and open the first one.

I swear to God - some people are rude. I'm unsure whether I should tell you what they wrote, but many of the suggestions would not be anatomically possible. And the suggestions about the reindeer's antlers? Who thinks like that?

I put the rude letters to one side and discover, to my great disappointment, that there are only three left that aren't obscene.

The first of these says: 'I wish the store were cheaper.' The second says: 'I wish someone in this place knew the difference between a flat top grind saw and a triple chip grinder.'

I can't do anything about the prices in the store, but I plan to send a formal letter back to the writer of the second letter, explaining that there are lots of people here who can help with particular tools, and giving him the name of a member of staff who he can contact.

I expected to be busy all morning, writing letters and trying to find the answers to problems. I feel a wave of disappointment that I won't be able to help people in the way I thought I would. I've only got one more letter to read. So I put it to one side. I'll save that for later.

'You look miles away,' says Keith, coming into the office to see me. 'What on earth are you thinking about?'

'Rude men, chip grinders and flat-top saws.' I say.

'Not more mad things to go in the manger with the elephants, I hope.'

'No, and elephants have a legitimate place in the manger.'

I'm going to open the final letter. I can't wait any more. The letter sits in a pale blue envelope with neat, slanted and elegant handwriting...as if written by a quill-wielding, sophisticated gentleman from the early 1900s.

The letter inside isn't on matching pale blue paper, which is disappointing, but on plain white A4 paper instead.

Daniel.Johnson@gmail.com
Dear Father Christmas,
I wish I had a girlfriend for Christmas. I feel so lonely sometimes. Can

you help arrange a date for me? I am free on 20th December if that would be possible.

Kind regards,
Daniel

I TURN OVER THE PAGE, but there's nothing written on the back. No address, no phone number. I push it back into the envelope. Gosh. It's a sweet little note, and I feel a rush of desire to help, but I'm unsure how to do that. I suppose I could put a note in the centre asking all single women to nominate themselves for a date. Perhaps I could run a competition...

Win a date with Mr Lonely from Surrey?

Na. There's no way Keith would let me do that. Not in a million years.

I pull the letter out of the envelope again and look at the writing. I have such a lovely feeling about this guy despite having no idea how old he is. He could be in his 50s or 60s, but I see him being a couple of years older than me, romantic beyond his years, courteous and kind. As I ponder the situation, Bev from crucial cutting and electricals walks past and pulls a face at me through the window. I make an equally silly face back.

Then Belinda walks along and pulls a daft face at me. I pull another silly face back. We always do this. Instead of greeting one another like adults, we've all taken to gurning at each other. It's most peculiar.

Hang on.

Belinda is keen to meet someone.

Daniel and Belinda.

That would be perfect.

'Belinda,' I say, rushing out of the office, clutching the letter in my hand. 'Stop for a minute,' I shout. 'I have something to ask you.'

I catch up with Belinda, who has caught up with Bev, and they both stop and turn round as I charge towards them with all the grace of a stampeding rhinoceros.

BERNICE BLOOM

'Look,' I say, brandishing the letter at Belinda. 'Read this letter.'

Belinda reads it and looks up at me. 'Wow. He sounds nice. But what does he look like?' she asks.

'Well, that's the problem. I've no idea.'

'Is he my age?'

'I don't know that either. It's just come...it was put in the *Christmas Post Box of Wishes and Dreams*. Do you want me to investigate further?'

'Does he live nearby?'

'I guess so,' I say. 'He must live fairly near, or he wouldn't come to this centre. And look how neat it all is. He must have seen the post box going up yesterday, gone home to write a letter, and then returned to post it. So I imagine he lives near. If I can find out, would you like to go on a date with him?'

'Er...yes,' she says. 'I mean - yeah, why not. Just make sure he's not, like, 60 or something.'

'Yes, of course,' I say. 'So - you're sure? I can go ahead and plan it.'

'Yeah - what the hell. It's Christmas, and I've had a shit year. So go for it, girl, and let me know where we're going.'

'Great. I'll contact him now.'

'Just make sure he's not too old,' shouts Belinda as I walk away. 'I don't want to date my Grandfather.'

'I will. Are you free on Saturday?'

'I am at lunchtime,' she says.

'OK, I'll try and arrange something for Saturday lunchtime.'

Dear Daniel,

Thank you so much for your letter in the Christmas Wishes Post-box. I'm sorry to hear that you feel lonely. We'd love to set up a lunch date for you, with a lovely girl, here in the DIY centre on Saturday 20th at 1 pm. Do you have a picture that you could send us? Also, I hope you don't mind me asking this, but are you under 40?

Thanks very much, Mary 'Christmas' Brown.

It's just minutes before a reply is forthcoming.

'Thank you. Yes, I'm under 40, and I would love to go on a date.'

No photo, but as long as he's under 40, that'll be fine. Belinda's lovely, but she's not going to win Miss World anytime soon. I know that sounds cruel, but all I'm saying is that looks aren't everything, and if he's in the right ballpark, age-wise, I think we should give it a go.

I email Belinda confirming that the date is on Saturday, and I send a quick email to Keith to tell him about it. He sends a reply to say that he's at lunch, but it sounds interesting. Are there any PR opportunities through it?

'Of course,' I reply.

THE HOT DATE

By the time Keith returns from lunch, I've created a multi-dimensional PR campaign that would rival that of any political strategist. It may not look like an era-defining document... I've just put bits of A4 paper and Post-It notes together. But don't let the unsophisticated look of the thing detract from its power. This pile of papers is designed to impress.

'What the hell's that?' asks Keith, peering at my life's work as if it's something I've picked out of the bin.

'It's a PR campaign to tell the world about the great Christmas stuff we've got here at the store.'

'What great Christmas stuff? You've put up some lights, Mary, and they look great, but it's not exactly Lapland. I don't think the press will be interested.'

'I've done more than just lights. There are loads of things going on.' I feel wounded. Has he not been out there? 'There's the letterbox to send wishes to Santa's elves, who will answer all of them - except the rude ones. And there's the grotto and all the trees with wonderful decorations. And there's the nativity scene.'

'A nativity scene with a bloody elephant in the middle of it.'

He throws his hat and scarf onto the hat stand, and they miss the pegs, slide down the coats and land on the floor. He shakes his head as if it's the fault of the hat and scarf and stomps over to pick them up.

'I'm not criticising anything, Mary. I gave you a small budget, and you've done a sterling job, but I don't think it's a story that the global media will be interested in.'

'Yes, but the date will be.'

'What date?'

'Did you not see the email I sent you?'

'Yes, but I've forgotten now. I've been out with my wife trying to pick carpets, and I don't care what carpets we have. And now I've wasted my lunch break comparing duck egg blue Axminister carpets with seafoam-coloured Wiltons, and I'm fed up.'

I pause for a moment while Sharon brings him his coffee which she puts on the edge of his desk. Keith then swings his legs up, and I swear to God, I think he's going to kick the scalding coffee all over her. We both gasp.

'I know what I am doing,' he says. 'My feet weren't anywhere near the coffee cup. Now, tell me about this date. What's that about?'

'OK,' I say. 'Well, a lonely man put a note into the *Christmas Post Box of Wishes and Dreams* to say that he'd love to meet someone this Christmas. It was a sweet note in which he said he gets lonely sometimes, so I thought it would be a great idea if we fixed him up with someone.'

'And who, pray, are we planning to fix him up with?'

'A member of staff who is single and keen to meet someone. She's lovely, and she's lonely too. So I was going to organise a date to fix them up. A date here in the centre, in the grotto. A Christmas love story. On Saturday…this Saturday, the 20th.'

'Oh. That sound doesn't sound like a bad idea, Mary. Who's the female on the staff?'

'It's Belinda.'

'Oh.'

There's a short silence while I wait for him to say more than 'Oh,' but he doesn't, so I carry on.

'I think it could be a lovely story. It will bring attention to the Post

Box of Christmas Wishes and Dreams and all we're doing at the centre to make Christmas as special as possible for the community.'

'Yes, that's wonderful. I love it. I'm just wondering about Belinda as the date. Do we not have anyone a bit - you know - more attractive? A bit thinner?'

'Belinda's lovely,' I say.

'Yes, I've no doubt. I'm just thinking about the photographs and the centre's reputation.'

'What?'

'Oh, it doesn't matter. I think that if possible, we should get someone pretty. Someone photogenic. How about Selina? She's a lovely attractive girl.'

'Yes, she's also engaged. Belinda is perfect.'

I can see Keith is still thinking, casting his mind through all the more attractive women on the staff.

'I'll get on with setting it up then. I thought we'd do it here in the centre. We can decorate the pagoda with the flowers from the cut stems department and bring out the lovely gardening furniture and make it gorgeous, and a big advert for everything we sell in the store.'

'Oh, that does sound like a good idea. Very well - you plan it all and keep me briefed. Is Mandy single? She's a nice-looking girl.'

'I don't know, but Belinda is keen to go on this date.'

'Very good,' says Keith, picking up his phone. 'Make sure we look good. And stop calling it the *Christmas Post Box of Wishes and Dreams*. It's just a Christmas Post Box.'

'We'll look good. Don't you worry,' I say to Keith, rushing off before he can change his mind.

I need to get cracking and organise this quickly because I'm due to finish work at 3 pm after coming in at 7 am this morning. Mum's coming in after work to take me Christmas shopping which I'm looking forward to, but it means I have to leave on time, no staying late to get things done.

I open a new word document on my computer... OK, so - what are the issues?

I know that Keith will baulk at us spending too much money on this date, so we'll have to get an excellent takeaway or something for them to eat. There's a lovely Lebanese restaurant in Hampton Court; I'll email them now. Perhaps they will give us a discount if I tell them about the publicity.

The decor should be easy enough to do since we're in a store full of lovely gardening furniture and flowers. I wonder whether we could get a snow machine? We could have people dressed as angels and snowflakes so the whole thing is white, sparkling, and beautiful. I jot all this down. Next, I send out press releases, inviting local journalists to meet the lucky shopper who is invited on a magical Christmas date.

It's going to be perfect.

GINGER WINE & GOSSIP

I see mum wandering through the garden centre at around 2.30 pm; she's dressed nicely but clutching a carrier bag. What is it with mums and carrier bags? I've lost count of the number of handbags I've given her as presents over the years, but she still brings a carrier bag because she wants to keep the handbags for best.

'This bag's just fine,' she says, indicating the aged Sainsbury's carrier bag she has wrapped around her wrist.'

'I want you to have nice things and use them,' I tell her. 'There's no point having them if you don't use them.'

'OK, I promise I will,' she says.

'Now come and see the decorations.' I hug her and lead her in the direction of the nativity scene.

I'm happy to say that she's impressed with what she sees. 'You have done very well there, dear. The way you have done those lights is wonderful. And the trees with all those amazing decorations! You do have a magical way with colour.'

This is another thing about mums. They can be desperately nice about you even when you've created what is a complete eyesore to all other people.

'Thanks very much,' I say. 'What do you think of the nativity scene? Don't you love how the children sit around looking at it?'

'Yes, yes,' says mum. Then she goes quiet.

'What's the matter? Didn't you think it was great?'

'You know that I think everything you do is great,'

'But...'

'Oh Mary, you know I don't like to criticise, but I was surprised to see an elephant there. I've never read a bible story about an elephant in the manger.'

'Not you as well.'

'What do you mean?'

'Everybody is telling me that there was no elephant there. But you look back at the Bible. The three wise men arrived on an elephant, a camel and a horse. That's how they got there.'

'Well, in every Christmas card I've seen and every nativity I've watched, the wise men come on camels. It's that part of the world. The part of the world with camels.'

'Yes, but one of them comes on an elephant. You flick through your bible when you get home and check.'

'I will,' she says.

We leave the centre and catch the bus to Richmond, where we wander through the shops, picking up bits and pieces for presents. I find a giant chocolate 'T' covered in marzipan, with nuts sprinkled on the top, to put into Ted's stocking. Then I pick a second one up because I know there is no way on God's good earth that I will make it to Christmas without nibbling on it.

'You should get one for dad,' I say. 'He loves marzipan, doesn't he? He always picks it off the top of the Christmas cake, which annoys everyone.'

'Oh Mary, that's an excellent idea. You're right. He does adore marzipan.'

She picks up the T.

'But dad's name doesn't begin with T? Why would you pick up a T?'

'I don't know. Why did you pick up the letter T?'

'Because Ted's name begins with T.'

'Oh yes, I see what you mean.'

I pick up some lovely earrings for the girls, in Zara, and some other bits and pieces, like a hot water bottle in the shape of a zebra and a pair of gloves that squeal when you clap your hands. Honestly, it must be fabulous being one of my friends at Christmas. Who wouldn't want to wake up to a pair of gloves squealing under the tree?

'Come on. Let's go and have a drink. It is nearly Christmas, after all.'

'Sure,' I say, because - who'd say no to a cheeky afternoon drink? But it's most unusual for mum to suggest alcohol, let alone before 6 pm.

We wander into a bar packed with Christmas revellers, many sporting their finest Christmas jumpers. In the corner, a group of people sits down to a proper Christmas meal. At a guess, I'd say it was a work party, and the people there seem to be at various levels of drunkenness. There is a relationship between how drunk they appear and how much fun they are having. The sober-looking guys glance at their watches and wonder when they can get back to the office and away from all the forced jollity while their more inebriated work-mates throw tinsel at one another and smile an awful lot.

'What do you fancy drinking?' I ask mum.

'Whatever you're having, love,' she says.

'No. You choose what you want. Don't just have what I'm having.'

'I don't know. Your father gets me a glass of wine, but I'm not that keen on wine, to be honest.'

'What do you like?'

'I like ginger wine, but it makes my cheeks bright red...ginger always does that to me. I enjoy it, though.'

'Sit down, and I'll get you a ginger wine.'

The barman pours the glass of Stones ginger wine, and it's such a tiny amount that I tell him to make it a double and decide to have one myself.

Mum has sat herself down on a long table next to a rather drunk-looking man with three pints in front of him. I must be honest - it's the last place I would have sat. I'd rather be next to the festive-jumper-clad work group or the old guys sitting at the bar with no tinsel or decoration. But a man sitting on his own at lunchtime with three pints in front of him? He's going to start talking to us, isn't he?

I sit next to mum and put her glass in front of her, moving my eyes towards the old guy in the coat as if to say to her: 'why are you sitting next to him?'

'I thought he might be lonely,' she mouths back at me. Bless her. We can't even come for a Christmas drink without her trying to help someone out.

I smile over at the man.

'You're wondering why I have three pints in front of me, aren't you?'

'I thought you were probably just thirsty,' says mum, taking a large gulp of her ginger wine. Her cheeks turn bright pink straight away. It's amusing to watch.

The man, meanwhile, takes a sip of one pint, then the other pint, then the third pint. 'I bet you are wondering why I'm drinking them like this, aren't you?'

'Not at all,' I reply.

But he's not put off.

'I have three brothers: one lives in Australia, one in China, and one in the States. We can't be together this Christmas, and it's the first Christmas since our parents died,' he says.

'I'm sorry to hear that.' I take a large gulp of ginger wine and feel my cheeks flush.

'Oooo - it's happened to you too,' says mum, with a giggle. 'Your cheeks have gone pink.'

I touch my cheeks lightly as our new friend continues with his story.

'We made a vow to each other that at Christmas, all four of us would go to bars in our respective countries and drink together. So, my brothers have four Guinness Stouts too, and we're drinking together - all four brothers.'

'I can't help but notice that you only have three pints in front of you, but you said there were four of you.'

'Yes, but I'm not having one...I've given up drinking,' he says.

There's a short pause before he collapses with laughter, banging his hands on the table and creasing over with joy.

The guys at the bar laugh too. 'You've given up drinking, so you only have three pints. It works every time,' they howl.

'Come on, drink up,' I say to mum. 'We're getting out of here.'

The man continues to laugh to himself, raising a glass as we leave the pub.

'Do you think that man has sat in the pub all day, with three pints in front of him, ready to crack that joke?'

I say to mum. 'Because if he has, he's having a dull Christmas.'

'You know, I think he probably has, the daft fool.'

We leave the pub, and mum looks down the busy street. 'I'm going to head back. I've left your father on his own for too long. You know what he's like if I leave him. He'll start putting on old John Wayne films. He needs me there to keep him in order.'

'No, don't go home yet, come with me. Dad will be OK. If the worse thing he's going to do is watch old cowboy films, I'm sure he'll be fine for another couple of hours.'

'I suppose so,' says mum. 'What shall we do then? Look for another pub?'

'Have you got a problem or something? Shall I find you an AA meeting?'

'No, but that ginger wine was nice, wasn't it? I must remember to get us a bottle for Christmas.'

'Good thinking,' I say. 'It does give us both very pink cheeks, though. If we drink too much more, we'll look like beetroots.'

'Look, there's a bench here; let's sit down while we work out what to do.'

I forget that mum's getting older. It wouldn't have occurred to me to sit down, but I guess you get tired when you're over 60. I can't stand the thought of mum and dad getting old.

I take them for granted, but they're my biggest supporters and fiercest allies. They mean the world to me.

I sit on the bench next to mum and smile at her. 'Shall we find somewhere a bit nicer than a pub? How about we find somewhere where we can get afternoon tea and ginger wine?'

'Oh, that would be lovely, dear. But where?'

'I guess one of the hotels will make afternoon tea. Let me check.'

I google the hotels in Richmond and discover that the Hill Crest hotel, about five minutes from where we're sitting, makes lovely cream teas. They look delicious in the photographs. If we add a couple of glasses of ginger wine, we'll have the perfect spread.

'I've found somewhere,' I say to mum. 'There are gorgeous cream cakes at this place.'

We walk up the hill to the hotel, but it turns out it's quite a steep hill and quite a long way. Google lied to me. It's not a quick 10-minute walk but an urban route march. I try not to look like I'm struggling as I power along, carrying all the bags because I am worried about mum being old and not wanting her to be in pain or anything.

Finally, the beautiful old hotel hoves into view.

'Oh, this is lovely,' says mum. 'Worth the 40-mile hike up the hill.'

'Yes, it was a bit of a journey. But you're right…this looks amazing.'

'We'd like cream tea for two,' I say to the smartly-dressed waiter'.

'And we'd like two glasses of ginger wine as well,' mum says.

'Of course, ladies. Follow me.'

He leads us into a beautiful room with breathtakingly high ceilings and enormous chandeliers that twinkle above us in the fading light.

Cream fur blankets are thrown across the back of the seats, giving the whole place an air of comfort and homeliness, despite its extravagance. Next to our table is a beautiful Christmas tree with just a few white lights twinkling at us.

'Their Christmas trees are nothing on yours, love,' says mum, loyally.

'They haven't even got 100 Rick Astley faces on the trees. Rubbish!' I say.

'Good afternoon, ladies,' says a smartly-dressed waiter. 'I understand you would like the afternoon cream tea?' he says.

'Oh, yes, please,' says mum.

'And some ginger wine?'

'We definitely want ginger wine,' says mum, even more effusively.

'Of course. I'll be back very soon with your wine. In the meantime, perhaps you'd like to look through the various tea options.'

He presents us with a menu each, offering a variety of styles of cream tea. They all look lovely.

'I bet this will be lovely,' I say.

'I bet it will,' says mum. 'I love you very much, Mary. And I'm so proud of you. Christmas will be such fun this year with you and Ted joining us. Just thinking about it makes me so happy.'

'I love you too, mum. And you're right…Christmas is going to be lovely.'

Shit.

A KID CALLED OLIVER

1 7th December

By the time Keith makes it into the office the following day, I'm an utter wreck. I'm lying across my desk sobbing uncontrollably. I can't stop.

'Good lord, woman, what on earth is wrong with you?' he says, displaying all the sensitivity and kindness I've come to expect from him.

He's not a man to deal gently with emotional outbursts. To him, every sign of feelings is a weakness that needs to be stamped out.

'It's one of the letters,' I say to him, gasping between sobs and trying to get the words out. 'A young boy. He's only five, and his dad has written to the *Christmas Postbox of Wishes and Dreams,* saying how much he wants to go to Lapland. He was born with one leg and has this horrible illness that will probably end up killing him in the next few years, and there is a photo, and he's gorgeous. Look at him. He's been through so much and has had so many awful operations. We have to send him to Lapland. Look, Keith. Look at him...'

I thrust the picture of the beautiful blonde kid in front of Keith. The child has wide blue eyes and a soft, gentle smile.

Keith looks at the picture and grudgingly admits it's all rather sad before saying: 'That's life, girl. I'm afraid there's a lot of shit around.'

'I know, I realise that. But we have the opportunity to help one child and make life just a little bit less shit for him and his family. Can the company pay for him to go? It would be such an amazing PR opportunity.'

'Yeah right, it's been so tight this year they won't pay for anything, let alone thousands of pounds to send a kid to Lapland. Do you know how much of a struggle I had to get the bathroom section painted? I had to fill in 45 forms for that.'

'Can we try? Please let me contact them and explain how wonderful this would be for us.'

'Send me an email with the details and all the likely costings, and I'll forward it to head office. But don't get too hopeful; the chances of them being willing to foot the bill are about as likely as the chances that one of the three wise men came to Bethlehem on the back of a bloody elephant.'

'Well then, there's every chance they'll say yes because there is no doubt in my mind that one of the three wise men did come to Bethlehem on an elephant.'

I switch on my computer to find out how much the trip will cost.

Ideally, we'd go on the 22nd of December, five days from now, and come back on the 24th of December.

I look down through the figures.

Blimey.

I wasn't expecting it to be cheap at this time of year, but I'm shocked by the cost. I go back into the search engine and suggest going on the 23rd, staying one night and coming back on the 24th. It's marginally cheaper, of course, but still recklessly expensive. The best part of £5k. Shit. Keith is never going to go for this.

Still, I need to try. So I put an email together with all the figures and a summary of why this would be such a lovely thing to do. I include details on how much promotion the shop would get.

Dear Keith,

As you are aware, we had a charming letter appearing in the Christmas Post Box of Wishes and Dreams this morning from the father of a young boy called Oliver, who was born with a degenerative disease and only one leg.

He is a happy, friendly boy who loves Christmas, and the father's wish is for them to be able to take little Oliver to Lapland.

I wondered whether the company would be willing to fund the trip. It would attract lots of positive publicity for us, and show how kind and loving we are as a company.

I have to confess that the trip would not be cheap. I've looked at the most cost-effective way of doing it, and it would still cost around £5000 to get their family of three to Lapland for a couple of days. I appreciate how expensive this is and how tight things are across the entire retail industry. Still, I think we would be more than compensated for by the incredible goodwill generated in the local community and the extraordinary publicity our kindness would bring.

If you need any more information, please do contact me.

To repeat, even though it is an expensive trip, I believe that we would have lots of marketing and PR opportunities as a result, and it would work out to be worth doing.

Kind regards,
Mary 'Christmas' Brown

I email it over to Keith, along with a picture of the child, and then I sit back with my fingers crossed, hoping that this trip can go ahead with every fibre of my being.

It doesn't take long before Keith replies.

Mary, that's just not going to happen. Is there no cheaper trip? Can we not send them to a Christmassy hotel down the road or something? Or send them one of the hampers from the seasonal goods section? If it's more than a few hundred quid, I'm not even emailing Head Office. Keith

PS Don't call it the Christmas Post Box of Wishes and Dreams.

I reply in an email, even though he's sitting a few metres from me.

But Keith, it's Lapland; it's bound to be expensive. My point is that it would be worth it. Pleeeeeease try. Please!

Keith leaves the office without acknowledging my reply to him. I see him stroll through the centre, pass my nativity scene where there's an elephant that absolutely SHOULD be in there, and off to hardware, presumably to have a sneaky fag by the exit next to the nails. He thinks we don't know, but the horrible mixture of stale smoke and mints when he returns gives away the fact that he has been smoking and that he's trying to hide it.

'There aren't huge crowds here,' he says on his return. 'Don't these people know it's almost Christmas? Mary, think of ways we can pull people in.'

'If we sent the little boy to Lapland, we'd get great publicity, and people would hear about the good work we do, and they'd come here for sure.'

'OK, Mary. Let me rephrase that...how do we get lots of good publicity without spending five grand that the company doesn't have?'

'We've got the MCD on Saturday - there's interest in that. Two local papers, Surrey Life magazine and Women Online. They're coming. I'm sure it will show us in a great light and part of helping the community and draw people in.'

'What on earth is MCD? I thought you were running everything past me.'

'The Magical Christmas Date on Saturday. I did run it past you.'

'Oh, that. Yes, of course, you did. Well, that's good. I look forward to that. When is it again?'

'On Saturday. I'll send another press release out in the morning and see whether I can get any more interest.'

'Good, good. Well, I'll leave you to it then. And I will send off that letter you wrote to headquarters. Just in case someone there is feeling very generous, full of the Christmas spirit, drunk, or something. Just don't hold out any hope of it getting anywhere.'

'I'll call Oliver's dad back and tell him we're seeing what we can do,' I say.

'No, Mary. Don't do that, for God's sake. Just leave it until head office comes back. Don't make any promises to him.'

'Sure,' I say, but I feel sad about everything. That little boy's picture keeps haunting me...imagine being born with one leg? I need to get out of the office before I burst into tears, so I leave my desk, head past the nativity scene, and to the bench on the far side of the centre, where I often slip off to while away the hours.

Today I can't stop thinking about Oliver.

I pull the letter out of my pocket and read it once more. The words make me want to cry all over again. Before I can think straight, I have rung the number on the letter. I want to tell the father I have the letter and reassure him that I'll do all I can. I want to tell him that it's difficult, and I'm not promising anything, but I'll do everything possible.

'Is that Oliver's father?' I say to the softly-spoken man who answers the phone.

He mumbles that it is and requests that I tell him who I am.

I go through a lengthy explanation of how I'm in charge of Christmas. I hear him sigh.

'No, I'm not pretending to be in charge of Christmas around the world. I'm not claiming to be Father Christmas or anything. I'm not a nutter. I promise. I just received your letter about Oliver. I'm from Foster's Gardening & DIY centre.'

'Oh, I see. Oh yes. Right,' says Oliver's dad, sounding mightily relieved. 'I thought you were one of those people pretending to be a charity campaigner but just trying to get money out of me.'

'Gosh, no, no. Not at all.'

'You've caught me at a bit of a bad time. I'm in a hospital in Scotland with Ollie.'

'Oh, sorry,' I say.

'Yes, things haven't been great recently. It's three years since my wife died - Ollie's mum - and Ollie's not well at all.'

Oh, My God. His wife died.

'I just wanted to say that we will arrange a trip to Lapland for you and your son to go on. It would be our pleasure. I can email you later with all the details.'

'You're joking?'

'No, I'm being serious.'

'Oh, that's wonderful. Thank you so much. That will make Ollie's day. He'll be so pleased. Thank you from the bottom of both of our hearts. My name's Brian, by the way.'

'It's lovely to 'meet you', Brian. I hope that news cheers Ollie up.'

'Oliver will be delighted. I didn't know whether a store would have the budget for a trip like this.'

'Of course, the management at Foster's are very keen on helping people.'

'Well, thanks again. I can't tell you how much this means.'

'You're very welcome,' I say before ending the call and staring into the middle distance. What have I done? I mean - what in God's name have I done?

There's only one person to talk to when I've done something utterly insane…Juan. He's a nutcase who is always doing mad things himself, so he'll know exactly what to do. I met Juan on a cruise and we struck up a glorious friendship. He's planning to come over and visit just before Christmas; then, he's going to come and live with me for a while later in the year. I can't wait. I call his number, and he answers straight away.

'Ciao Bella.'

'Oh God, Juan. I've just done something completely insane. I promised a guy that he and his one-legged son could have a free trip to Lapland.'

A TREE FOR MR BECKHAM

I hear Juan giggle at the end of the line.

'No, this is not funny. It's not the opening line of a joke. This is weapons-grade stupid. I have behaved in a way that is properly God Damned ridiculous.'

'I have no idea what you're talking about. Explain.'

I hear the clink of glass.

'Are you drinking already?'

'Yes, just a little one, my lovely friend. Tell me what's going on.'

I regal Juan with the story of the *Christmas Post Box of Wishes and Dreams* and my call to the little boy's dad.

'What's wrong with that?' says Juan. 'It sounds like you've behaved perfectly properly.'

'No, Juan. I accidentally promised him a free trip to Lapland, but there is no free trip to Lapland. I made it up. Now I need to provide a free trip.'

I hear spluttering and a small cry of anguish down the phone. 'You made me choke,' says Juan. 'So there's no trip to Lapland?'

'Nope.'

'Well, that's the craziest thing ever. Why would you do that? What

BERNICE BLOOM

are you going to do? He has a disabled son...you can't let him down. You have to provide a trip to Lapland.'

'I know I do. That's what I said. But how? I thought you might have some bright ideas.'

'Fundraise in the garden centre?'

'Keith will never let me. Unless I tell him what I've done, then he'll sack me.'

'Oh, angel, I wish I was there to give you a big hug. We'll make a plan when I come on my pre-Christmas visit.'

'It'll be too late by then,' I say. 'I need a plan now.'

'OK, well - you could write to local companies asking them to donate, write to any rich individuals locally, go door-to-door collecting money. I don't know.'

'Yes. Yes. I'll have to try things like that. Oh, you've cheered me up. I feel better now...I will write to all the big companies in town, work out where the richest people live and put notes through their doors. Thank you.'

'Pleasure, my love.'

I walk over to Santa's grotto and settle myself into the big throne-like chair in the centre of it. It's cosy here. I'll have a little break; then I'll sort out getting the funding I need to send a sickly child to Lapland. So I start to relax, almost falling asleep in the comfort of the place, as the sound of Chris Rea singing Driving Home For Christmas drifts through from the cranky little loudspeaker in the corner.

'ERR... EXCUSE ME.'

I look up to see a man looking over me as I doze.

'Are you the manager?'

'Well, I'm the manager of Christmas.'

'Great. I want to buy a Christmas tree and arrange for it to be delivered.'

'Any of the guys in the gardening section can do that for you,' I say, struggling to sit up straight. 'Would you like me to take you there?'

'No, it's a bit more complicated than that. Do you mind if we talk confidentially?'

'Of course not,' I say. 'How can I help you?'

'The Christmas tree is to be delivered to someone famous,' he says.

I try to stay professional, but I feel my eyebrows raise and my mouth open involuntarily. I wonder who he's talking about.

'OK,' I say. 'We service lots of famous people here (we don't, no one famous has ever set foot in this place), so that won't be a problem. Who is the Christmas tree for?'

'It's for David and Victoria Beckham,' says the man. 'So this would need to be handled with the utmost discretion.'

Victoria Beckham. Victoria bloody Beckham.

'Discretion is our middle name here at Foster's,' I say. 'You can rest assured that we will deliver the best Christmas tree to the Beckhams and do so with every courtesy known to man.'

'Good. OK. The next question is - what's the biggest tree you can get for me?'

'Have you seen the trees we've got outside?' I say. They all seem pretty bloody big to me.

'Those out there? No, no. They are nowhere near big enough. Can you show me some that are bigger?'

'Sure, follow me,' I say, easing myself out of Santa's seat and marching through the centre to the office. Sharon is sitting there, looking utterly adorable in baby blue. She giggles as we walk in. Happily, there's no sign of Keith.

'I have a pile of booklets here,' I tell the man (I'm now wishing I'd asked him his name).

I pull out a pamphlet from *'The Christmas Tree Company.'*

'Here are some massive trees.' There's a picture of one that's so massive it looks like it belongs in a pine forest.

'That's the sort of thing,' he says.

'That is massive,' I say. 'Are you sure the Beckhams want it to be that big?'

'Yes – absolutely sure,' says the man. 'They are having a huge Christmas party at their mansion, and they need the entrance hall to look like the open sequence of every Hollywood Christmas movie you've ever seen.

'So if you can produce Frank Sinatra and have him coming down the stairs while crooning, that would be ideal.'

He laughs at his joke, but I have no idea who Frank Sinatra is, so I smile along with him.

Then I see the price of the tree. It's extortionate. 'I'm afraid that one costs £350,' I say, closing the pages.

'Very reasonable. I'll pay now,' he replies. 'It needs to be delivered tomorrow.'

'I think delivery might be an extra charge. Can I call you when my assistant returns, and I'll confirm all the details and take the payment over the phone?'

I want to run it all past Keith before going further here. I don't even know how we'd get hold of one of these enormous trees, and I've no idea how we'd deliver it.

'Okay,' says the man, standing up. 'Let's do that, but call as soon as you know. I want to get this sorted today.'

'Let me take your name, number, and the tree you want.'

'Sure, my name's Mark Hutton,' he says and starts to give me his number as Keith comes thundering into the room on the wrong side of about four pints.

'Ah, is this your assistant?' asks Mark.

'Yes,' I say as Keith looks at me quizzically.

'Oh, I'm your assistant now, am I?'

'Yes, you are. Now, Keith - this is Mark Hutton. He is here to buy a huge Christmas tree for Victoria and David Beckham.'

'Oh my!' says Sharon, holding her face in her hands. 'David Beckham. Oh my...'

I ignore Sharon's breathless interjection and continue. 'Mr Hutton wants to order it and get it delivered tomorrow. He wants one of these huge ones.' I indicate the tree that he has chosen in the brochure.

Keith knows an exciting opportunity when he sees one, so he stops worrying that I described him as my assistant, and he gets on with

THE MARY BROWN BOOKS

writing down the code for the tree that Mark has chosen. Within minutes Beckham's assistant is placing the order.

'The delivery charge will be an additional £10,' he says.

'Sure,' says Mark. 'That's fine - money isn't an issue. I need to get everything organised.' He looks down at the bunch of leaflets. 'Do they have tree dressers in there?' he asks.

Tree dressers? Really? Do such people exist?

'What would be great would be if you could bring the tree and dress it at the house. Do you have someone who dresses trees?'

'I could do that,' I say. 'I'm in charge of Christmas.'

Silence descends on the room. It's almost as if everyone present thinks that this is a disastrous idea. Almost as if they are all thinking… she put pictures of Rick Astley all over the tree in the centre and an elephant in the manger; please don't send her to decorate the Beckhams' tree.

But Mark looks interested.

'There would be a tight brief, and Victoria has exacting tastes. Her Christmas party attracts the world's most important and glamorous people.'

'Absolutely. No problem at all. 'Tasteful' is my middle name,' I respond, subconsciously touching the giant earrings and metres of tinsel strewn through my hair.

'OK, then we have a deal,' says Mark, offering his hand. I shake it firmly and look at Keith, who looks terrified.

'I'll just put your bill together,' says Keith, scratching his head and flicking through the brochures in front of him in a manner which suggests that he has no idea what to charge the Beckhams for the tree decorating service I've just offered. Once Mark has left, we all sit back and ponder what just happened.

'How much did you charge him for me?' I ask.

'£200,' he says. 'So I hope you're good at this sort of thing.'

'I've no idea: I've never done anything like this in my life before. I did the ones here in Christmas Land but never before that. Mum and dad would never let me near the tree at home in case I ruined it.'

DAY WITH THE BECKHAMS

'You can't do that,' says Ted, rather unsupportively.

'Yes, I can. How hard can it be? I mean - really? How hard?'

'Bloody hard,' insists Ted. 'People do proper university degrees in things like this.'

'What? In dressing a Christmas tree? What are you talking about?'

'OK, maybe not dressing a tree, but - you know - home decor and making the place look good. Isn't it normally those interior designers who do up trees and stuff, do party decorations, and make everything look good?'

'I don't know,' I say. 'All I know is that I've had the brief from the party planning company, and I've been googling 'how to decorate a tree,' and I can't see that I'll have any problem at all, so please be more supportive.'

'Sure,' he says, and we raise our glasses to the task ahead of me. I'm full of optimism and excitement; he's full of dubiousness and concern.

'In all honesty, Ted, I'm much more worried about getting this little kid to Lapland than I am about going to the Beckhams. It's upsetting me that he's having such a difficult time. I think I will pay for the trip myself out of my savings account.'

Ted smiles at me. 'You are such an incredible, kind and sweet person. I don't think you know how much I love you, but you can't pay yourself. You can't, Mary. It wouldn't be right.'

'I don't know,' I say. 'I think it might be the simplest way to get him there.'

'We'll talk about it tomorrow night,' says Ted. 'Try not to worry about it while you're doing your decorating.'

18TH DECEMBER

I rise at 7 am the following day. There's so much going on; I need to get on top. I email Belinda confirming that the hot date is on, and I send a note to Keith with a draft press release to go out to more local newspapers and magazines today. I'll send the press release when I return from the Beckhams' house tonight. I slip the letter from Oliver's dad into my bag with my savings account details. I will pay for the trip to Lapland and give the little boy the trip of his life. After we've done Beckham's tree, I'll go to the bank and sort the whole thing out.

RAY AND JOE have been tasked with accompanying me to the Beckhams, and they arrive outside my flat at 8 am to pick me up. I'm dressed and ready to go when Ray beeps the horn outside. I washed and ironed my uniform last night. I'm wearing it with just a simple white shirt underneath, and I have done my make-up in a discreet, elegant way. No tinsel, no stupid earrings, no madness at all. I'm all over this. No one needs to worry. Mary's got it under control.

'We need to go to a shop to buy the stuff to go on the tree first,' I say, directing Ray towards a boutique Christmas shop in Wimbledon, where we have identified very posh decorations that will be perfect for the Beckhams' tree. I'm aware that I will have to reign myself in here because my inclination is towards the flamboyant and fabulous, and I suspect that Posh and her friends are all about white and cream and all that understated bollocks. In fact, I know they are because of the very detailed brief I received late last night.

BERNICE BLOOM

'Here it is,' I say as we arrive outside the shop. Ray and Joe make it clear that they are staying in the van and want nothing to do with the choosing part of the operation.

'I'm just the driver,' says Ray.

'I've just come to do the heavy lifting,' says Joe.

'OK, I'll go and have a look.' I jump down from the van's seat and waddle to the front door. You have to ring a bell to gain entry. How poncey is that? They are selling decorations, for God's sake.

I survey the beautiful interior of the shop - it looks like a jewellery shop, with the baubles laid out like they are precious jewels. Nothing in the shop has prices on it. I've been told not to worry about the cost, and to pick the best, most classy decorations, and I have Keith's work Amex card in my bag. I start to look through them...they are all lovely, some of the baubles are made from shells and are incredibly delicate (I swerve those - I'm the clumsiest person alive, I'll break them if I so much as breathe on them), others have some sort of expensive sheen. They all look nice, but none of them looks brilliant. Do you know what I mean? None of them stands out or will send the guests home from the Beckham's house full of envy. They aren't right. They are expensive and elegant, but they aren't Christmassy. They are not suitable for a festive party.

'I need to think about this,' I say to the lady in the shop, leaving and walking back to the van to talk to the guys. They see me coming, and Ray winds down the window.

'Everything OK?'

'Yes,' I say, 'But the decorations are plain. I don't think they're quite what I want.'

'It's not about you, doll face; it's about the Beckhams. They like all that sort of shit.'

'I know. But I want to do something extraordinary for them. Can you come in and help me?'

Ray has lit a cigarette and has no desire to leave the warmth and familiarity of his van. Joe is on his phone.

'Mate, I know nothing about bloody decorations,' says Ray. 'I can't tell the difference between the posh ones and those tacky ones there...' he points towards the cheap pound shop next to us, and I follow his finger. That's when I see them...the absolute best Christmas decorations - bright pink with cat's faces and whiskers on them.

'OH MY GOD. I love them,' I squeal. 'They are perfect!'

'What? Perfect for the Beckhams? Are you sure?'

'I've never been more sure of anything in my life,' I say, running towards the shop as if drawn by a giant magnet.

It's so much better in this shop. Way less poncey than the other place, and the decorations are so much nicer.

I buy 30 of the pink baubles with cat faces on, and some which are shaped like pigs. Pigs flying through the Christmas tree with little curly tails that move...who doesn't want to see that on a Christmas morning? I buy tonnes of tinsel because they have it in pink, and I know that posh is all about coordination. I've seen her in Heat magazine - everything she wears matches everything else. I have bags and bags of goodies at the end. Bags bursting with pinkness. This is going to be amazing.

Then, I have a sudden thought...why don't I get some of these for the shop as well? I pile even more into my baskets and stagger towards the cashier.

'Look at this little lot,' I say to Ray when I return to the van. He jumps out of his seat and looks stunned as he puts the dozen or so carrier bags into the back of the van.

'Bloody brilliant, eh?' I say, but he sort of half-smiles and asks me whether I'm sure that pink Christmas baubles with cat faces and pig-shaped decorations are what's required.

Er...yes. They're perfect.

We drive along in companionable silence, into the countryside and toward the Beckham's lovely country house. I can see the black wrought iron canopy leading to the front door in the distance. It looks so familiar. I feel like I've been here before, but all the research I did (mad googling last night) has made the place look so familiar. I know that beneath that canopy lies a cream and black tiled path. I can't wait to see it all.

BERNICE BLOOM

But when we pull up at the gates and ring the intercom, there are problems.

'You can't come in,' says a haughty voice. 'We are having difficulties.'

'Oh,' says Ray. 'We've come to deliver and decorate the Christmas tree. What would you like me to do with it?'

There's murmuring in the background and raised voices, then eventually, the gates open, and we pass through them and head up the driveway towards the house. I'm so excited. I can't wait until she sees the tree when it's all decked out. She will love it, and the two of us will instantly become best friends and probably go on holiday every year with Ted and David.

Fantasies about David and I frolicking on a sun-drenched beach are bouncing through my mind as we pull up in front of the palatial abode, and I shuffle towards the door, preparing to wrap Victoria in a warm embrace. But there's no Posh Spice to greet me, just a large, Polish-sounding lady. She apologises profusely for not letting us in at the gate earlier.

'There is misunderstanding. Problems are here. Harper is bad girl today. Mr and Mrs Beckham are not happy. They are very upset.'

'Oh, I see,' I say. 'Sorry to hear that. Are we OK to come in now?'

'Yes, must come through,' she says, ushering us both into a hallway that is every bit as spectacular as I hoped. It has a wide staircase in the centre, featuring a large window on the landing halfway up, giving a fantastic view of their magnificent garden.

From a distant room, I can hear the sounds of a young girl screaming and stamping her feet in a tantrum.

'You can go in there,' says the Polish lady, pointing to a side room. Ray, Joe and I wander in sheepishly and are introduced to three party planners - all painfully thin, dressed in identical black outfits, and looking very sombre. It becomes clear that they are fed up because they want to be the ones dressing the tree. My arrival has come as something of a shock to them. They think that, because they are responsible for all the other aspects of the party, they should be responsible for dressing the tree, so everything is coordinated.

What is also clear is that I have been billed as the ultimate Christmas expert and the woman who will make the tree look amazing.

'I hear you've done this a million times before.' says the tallest of the women. She has sleek brown hair in a razor-sharp bob and the shiniest, most pointy boots I've ever seen.

'Your boots are lovely,' I say, quite mesmerised by them.

'Thank you,' she replies, and I seem to have escaped without having to answer her question.

'Do you think you should tell them that you've never done anything like this before,' whispers Ray. 'I mean - look around you - everything is white and cream. There's no pink anywhere.'

'Just relax,' I say. 'Don't worry about a thing.'

While Ray, Joe, and three gardeners go outside to bring in the tree, the party planners help me to bring in the bags of decorations. We put them all down in the hallway, and I begin to unload the bags.

'Holy fucking Christ, are you joking?' says the older woman in the group. I think she's probably in charge. She is the prettiest, with lovely auburn tumbling curls and a perfect creamy complexion.

'How do you mean?'

'I mean...flying pigs? Flying pigs? Do you know who's coming tonight? Everyone from Elton John to the Home Secretary will be here.'

'Yay! Elton's going to love the pigs. And the cats. Look at these,' I say, pulling out the cat baubles while waving them around and meowing. 'Great, aren't they?'

There's silence from the three women, all of whom are staring at me as if I've grown an extra head.

'This is unimaginably horrific,' said razor-sharp bob woman.

'No, it's not. They're lovely. Look,' I said, wiggling the pigs in the air and making 'oink oink' sounds. 'It's going to be lovely. I promise you.'

'We're going to find Victoria,' says the third woman. She's very tall and skinny with quite a harsh angular face. Her legs are so incredibly thin they look like they might snap.

Once the women have gone, we get the tree into place. I decide there's no point waiting for them to return. I might as well get on with the decorations, so I climb onto a step ladder and begin making it look fantastic...and - my God - it does. It looks brilliant by the time I've finished. It screams 'Christmas'. I have lined all the little pigs up so they are chasing each other around the tree. They all have lovely prominent snouts. Honestly, it's the best tree ever.

In the background, I can hear the party planner women coming back. Posh is with them. She's much prettier than she looks on television. She has a natural softness about her and these enormous eyes. I decide I want her to be my best friend.

'Oh my God, Oh my God,' she says, her hands flying to her mouth as she looks at the tree.

See, I knew she'd love it.

I wonder whether she's spotted the giant pig on the top. (I forgot to get a star...I can't think of everything).

Then she starts shouting.

'This is the worst day of my life,' she says. 'It's all I need with Harper playing up all morning. Nothing will stop her from crying. This is the worst Christmas ever. Can you all get out of my house.'

'Me?' I say, looking at her with disbelief. 'You want me to go?'

'Yes,' says Victoria. 'Just go before I call security.' The sound of Harper's wails fills the room. She sounds distressed.

'Oh God, this is unbearable,' says Posh. 'I just can't stand this anymore - a screaming child and a ridiculous, cheap, nasty Christmas tree.'

The three party-planning women glare at me as she speaks.

'But it's lovely,' I try. 'It's different and fun and....'

As I speak, Harper stomps in, tears streaming down her face and anger and frustration written into every pore. Then she looks up, sees the tree, and is mesmerised.

'Ooooooo,' she coos. 'It's so lovely. Is it for me?'

She has finally stopped crying. She wipes away the last of the tears as she stares up at the tree, delight replacing the sadness on her face.

Then she smiles the most enormous smile. 'It's the best thing I've ever seen in my life. Thank you, mummy.'

Harper throws herself into her mother's arms, takes Posh by the hand and leads her to scrutinise the tree. 'See the piggies,' she squeals.

Posh turns round and smiles at me. 'Thank you,' she mouths, as the party planners almost faint from the shock. 'You're a star. This is amazing.'

I'm sure you'll agree that it is a clear victory for the fat girl and her gaudy candyfloss pink decorations against the very skinny ladies in black.

FLOWERS & FAME

My unexpected triumph earns me hugs from Harper and a warm handshake from Victoria, who apologises for her earlier sharp words, and tells me that the peace I have brought to her house is very precious to her.

'I am a peace giver,' I say, because I'm enjoying all this love, and I don't want it to end.

I shake hands with everyone, even the horrible party planners, and am preparing to leave their lovely house when I hear a familiar voice behind me. I turn round to see David Beckham standing there. 'Cup of tea?' he offers.

Good God, he's handsome. He's not just good-looking, with nice hair, nice clothes and a sound body. He's properly gorgeous. His face is captivating, with those high cheekbones set in a well-defined jaw and perfect skin. His teeth are all shiny, and his eyes are all sparkly.

'Tea?' he asks again, and I realise I've just been staring at him.

'Oh, yes. Tea. Lovely. Please and thank you,' I say, stupidy.

David turns to look at Ray and Joe. 'Would you like one?' he asks, but my two assistants have lost the power of speech in front of the famous footballer, and they stand there, staring ahead like they are on some psychotic drugs.

'No?' says David. 'OK, well, we'll be through here, in the kitchen, if you change your mind.'

I follow David into the kitchen as Harper takes my hand. It's the most wonderful feeling in the world as she skips and smiles and continues to tell me how wonderful the tree is.

'Do you have children?' asks David.

'No, not yet. I'd love to one day,' I say. 'I love kids.' And then, for some reason, I think of Oliver, the little boy with one leg, and I wonder how he got on in the hospital and whether he's OK.

'Are you OK?' asks David, but I can't answer him because I'm choking back tears.

'Hey, you look upset. What's happened?'

At that point, dear readers, I regret to say that I burst into tears.

'Oh no, have I put my foot in it?' he asks.

'No, not at all; I'm sorry,' I say, and I tell him the whole sad tale.

He listens quietly as I talk, and I tell him I've decided to pay for the trip myself.

'Don't do anything for the next hour,' he says. 'Let me make a couple of calls, and I'll come back to you.'

'Really?'

'Yes, I'll try and help you.'

Before we leave, I get pictures of David, Harper and me in front of the tree and various shots of the different decorations. I know I'll need photos for when I put together the press releases this afternoon.

Then I collect Ray and Joe, still motionless and staring vacantly at David, and I lead them to the van.

Before we head off, I have to do a quick interview with a local news reporter at the end of the road leading to the Beckham's house. He's keen to talk to anyone leaving the house, to ask whether they know any details about the party. I tell him that I don't know anything about the party, but I know all about the tree…

'Come on, let's go back to Fosters,' I say, as Ray starts up the engine and we hit the road. We're about five minutes into the journey when one of the guys from work rings him.

'Oh, it was brilliant,' I hear him saying, 'I was chatting away to

David; we got on really well. Poor Mary was a bit overawed, but I was totally cool. I think David and I will stay in touch for a very long time.'

'Really?' I say. 'Am I going to have to listen to you telling everyone how you and David got on like a house on fire?'

But before he can answer my phone rings.

'Mary, it's David,' says a familiar voice. 'I just wanted to tell you that I've sorted out that trip for you...for the little boy without a leg. A man called Michael Foley will call you this afternoon.'

'What?'

'You told me about the little boy who wanted to go to Lapland? Well, my manager has contacted a company that will give you a free trip - for the kid, his parents, you, and a guest for a few days before Christmas. And I'll come to the airport to meet him when you return. But don't tell him that bit, then it'll be a nice surprise for him.'

'Oh God, I love you,' I shout. 'You have no idea what this means. If you ever leave Victoria, please, will you marry me?'

'Well, um, I. I'm not planning to leave Victoria.'

'I know, but it was worth a shot.'

'So, you'll tell the little boy's mum and dad?'

'Yes, I will,' I reply. He doesn't have a mum, but I'll tell the dad. 'Thank you so much. Honestly, this is just wonderful. I think I'm going to cry.'

'Just a couple of conditions,' says David. 'If Harper wants her own Christmas party in a few days, will you come back and do her tree for her?'

'Of Course,' I say. 'Yes, 100%.'

'The other thing is - could you hold off telling anyone except the boy's dad for now? I don't want any press - everyone will think I'm helping to get press attention which I'm not. If you could tell work and anyone else who needs to know after I call you in a few days when it's all set up.'

'No problem, David,' I say. 'Discretion is my middle name....'

I smile to myself. I'll go back to the office now and sort everything out - the date on Saturday, a press release about today, and the fantastic Lapland trip beginning next week. Bloody hell, Christmas is starting to come together.

THE GLORIOUS RETURN TO THE GARDEN CENTRE

By 4 pm, the story of my great success at the Beckhams' house this morning is spreading through the store like a bushfire. There have been mixed reactions to the news that the Beckhams loved my interior designing skills. Actually, that's not true - scrub that - the reactions have all been the same; everyone is GOB-SMACKED. They can't believe that I could have made such a success of it.

'I'm pleased for you but AMAZED,' says Sharon, while Ray and Bob regale everyone with the details.

'The look on the stylists' face was a picture,' they say. 'They were all there, dressed head-to-toe in some fancy designer gear, and up rocks Mary in her bloody green overalls, which make her look like Kermit, the frog, and she's twice the size of all of them put together.'

'Alright, alright,' I say. 'No need to get personal.'

'Sorry, love, but it was very, very funny.'

I can see that some of the women in the group are wild with jealousy, that I managed to pull it off. I got myself inside the Beckham's house and decorated a Christmas tree in a manner that delighted them. I know that half the people here today were hoping I'd mess up...I am determined to rub my victory in as much as I can.

'Call me Kelly Hoppen!' I keep saying. 'I'm the queen of interior design.'

We've all gathered in the giant gardening conservatory in front of the company Christmas trees that I have just done out in the style of Posh's tree.

We'll trade off the link to the Beckhams to sell as many of these trees as possible. There is a whole row of them, all with the little pigs chasing each other across them and lovely pink cat faces looking out. They are heavily adorned with tons of tinsel that I have just thrown onto them, as I did with Victoria Beckham's, to create an artistic and spontaneous look. In short, my trees look unique.

Next to them is the Rick Astley tree. The whole scene is quite a feast for the eyes.

Sharon isn't convinced. 'What was it about the tree that the Beckhams loved so much,' she asks. 'I mean - I'm not being funny, but you wouldn't imagine Victoria thinking that it was very sophisticated.'

'She did,' I reply quickly. 'She thought the tree was stylish and elegant and leant a certain stylish flavour to the house.' I'm lying, of course. I'm not going to mention to anyone that I only got away with it because of the intervention of a small child.

Sharon nods disbelievingly and continues staring at my mad, pink trees.

The whole shop looks stunning today. Now there are loads of decorated trees and the nativity scene, which looks great with its elephant, camel and donkey. It's a shame that the stuffed donkey is twice the size of Joseph and looms over everyone slightly threateningly. He's also wobbly on his legs, so I've had to lean him up against the manger, which does nothing to diminish his intimidating presence in the scene.

Away from the nativity, there's a beautiful area for Father Christmas to sit and meet children - it's full of fake snow and sleighs and has Christmas music playing and the occasional jingle-jangle of sleigh bells. There are also elves and a couple of fairies (I liked them - I know they're not in the original tale, but they look cute).

Then there's the pile of presents for Santa to hand to children and the sweets and cards I've bought. It all looks great.

'Blimey, how much did this lot cost?' asks Keith. 'Did you get it all for under £250?'

'Yes, of course,' I say (no, I didn't – it was nearer £500).

'Well done,' he says. 'Well done, indeed. This is all fabulous.'

'Thank you,' I say. 'Now I should finish some work and check the Postbox of Wishes & Dreams. Hopefully, there will be lots of lovely letters in there.'

'Yeah, once again, Mary. Let's not call it that. It's just a Christmas Post Box, and you can tackle it in a couple of days. For now, relax. Don't try to do too many things at once. You're a superstar, Mary Brown; we need to look after you.'

'But I'm off tomorrow. If I don't look at them now, it'll be two days before I get to them.'

'That's fine,' says Keith. 'Enjoy your day off tomorrow and then answer the ridiculous requests from customers when you're back. I think this Beckham thing is far bigger than that damn post box you're so obsessed with.'

As we are talking, Mandy from accounts walks across the gardening section towards me, holding the most beautiful bunch of pink flowers I've ever seen in my life. It's an enormous bouquet. She hands it to me, and I lean over and kiss Keith on the cheek to thank him for them.

'What the hell are you doing, woman?' he says.

'I'm thanking you for these flowers,' I say, opening the envelope tucked into them.

'I didn't get you those. Why on earth would I buy you flowers?'

'Because I went to the Beckhams this morning and did their tree and because I made the shop look amazing,' I say, then I read out what's written on the card:

'Thank you so much for making our Christmas tree look wonderful. You are a superstar; much love, Victoria and David Beckham x.'

'Yay! Have you seen this?' I say to Keith, showing him the card.

THE MARY BROWN BOOKS

'Bloody hell!' he says, genuinely impressed with what he's seeing. 'I don't believe you've just had flowers from David Beckham.'

'David Beckham? Really? Has David Beckham sent you flowers?' a young mother comes up to me, having overheard Keith's words. She's at the nativity scene with her son and declares herself a massive fan of the former footballer. 'Can I see the card?'

'Yes, of course,' I reply proudly, showing the greeting buried in the floral arrangement and watching her swoon before me.

Quite a crowd has gathered around me as people regard my flowers admiringly.

'Why has he sent flowers?' asks one man, smartly dressed and a little out of place among the pink trees, tinsel and toddlers.

'I went over and decorated his Christmas tree, just like that one,' I say, pointing towards the large tree in front of us. 'That's a replica of the Beckhams' Christmas tree.'

A lady pulls her phone out and takes pictures of the tree. Others soon join her, all flashing away and capturing the image of my pink, glittery tree in their phones.

'Would you stand next to it,' asks one lady, and then it feels like dozens of people are taking pictures.

You can hear the hum of general chatter in the store, punctuated with 'David Beckham...Victoria Beckham...pink tree...' as they share the information and post their news on Twitter and Facebook.

'Are you available to come and decorate my tree?' asks one lady.

'Oh yes!' says another.

Then there are lots of questions about where I got the decorations from and whether they will be on sale in the store, and I'm filled with a warm glow and a rush of excitement at the thought that flying pigs in Christmas trees are going to be ALL the rage in this affluent part of Surrey this festive period.

'We need to capitalise on this,' says Keith. 'I'm going to get onto the warehouse and order loads of decorations like these, and we'll sell them in the store. I'll make a sign: *'You too could have a Christmas tree like David Beckham.'* You're a bloody genius, Mary. You are.'

BERNICE BLOOM

'That's a great idea,' I say. 'We could sell loads and get some of the money I spent on this place.'

'It was only £250, don't worry about it,' says Keith.

'Have you got a minute?' someone says to me. I turn around to see a small woman dressed entirely in brown.

'Of course. How can I help?'

'I'm from the Cobham Advertiser, I'm here shopping, but I couldn't help overhearing what you said. Is there any chance I could interview you?'

'Yes,' I say. 'Of course.'

There's another woman behind her; she's just arrived and is on her phone but signalling that she needs to talk to me.

'Hi, I work for Vogue magazine. I saw the trees on Twitter. We want to do a shoot here. Would that be possible? We'd bring models and put them around the Beckham Tree for a feature online.'

'Hi, sorry - but I was here first. The interview will only take about 10 or 15 minutes, then we can get the story online in the next couple of hours, and it will be in the paper at the end of the week,' she says. 'The Cobham Advertiser, your local paper. Good for sales.'

'Sure. Fine,' I say.

'And do you mind if I get my photographer to come?'

'No problem,' I say. I look around and see Keith standing there with his thumb up.

'So, that's OK?' says the woman from Vogue.

'Yes,' I say.

'Well done, sweetheart,' says Keith. 'You go off and do the interview, and we'll talk later. Remember the party tonight - it's going to be rocking.'

'Sure,' I say. Works' Christmas party...rocking...Great!

I do the interviews, then sneak back to the office, away from the commotion in the gardening section. And there I sit, quietly smiling to myself. I'm going to be able to send Oliver to Lapland. That matters to me more than anything.

THE OFFICE CHRISTMAS PARTY

'Why are they holding the party in such an odd place,' says Ted. We have to drive over this complicated road system to get to the work Christmas party.

The junction in Hounslow reminds me of when you go over the Severn Bridge to get into Wales. Do you know the one I mean? Is there more fun in the world than when you go over that? Suddenly there are no lanes, and it's a mad free-for-all to get into a lane. I love it. Ted and I went away for the weekend to Cardiff and went over that bridge, and we were both screaming as he drove flat out on the road with no lane markings at all, fighting against all the other traffic to get to the front of the lanes when they arrived.

'Can we go back and do it again?' he asked. 'It's like Thorpe Park.'

And this bloody road system in London is just as bad...it's like wacky races, with cars shooting around us from every direction.

'Left,' I say. I'm in charge of map reading, but I can't make head nor tail of the map or the roads. It's not an ideal situation.

We finally find the place - a big hotel called 'The Fallgate'. Ted pulls over, and I jump out. He's not coming with me tonight because it's a 'no partners' party. They do this so that we are forced to mingle and can't just sit there all evening, chatting to the person we came with. It just means being stuck in a corner talking to Jed from the lighting department about bulbs and lampshades.

'I wish you were coming,' I say to Ted as he kisses me goodbye.

'You'll have more fun without me,' he replies. 'Anyway - I've got the football to watch. Call me later, OK?'

'OK,' I say as I watch him drive off, waving through the open window as he goes. I do love that man, you know. He drives me nuts sometimes, but he means everything.

I pull out my phone and text Ray and Joe to see if he's here...I don't fancy walking into the room alone and having to frantically scan faces, looking for someone I know. There are about 20 missed calls and a whole stack of messages on my phone. Christ. Every journalist in London is keen to talk to me about my experience at the Beckhams. The Cobham Advertiser interview must have gone online...now everyone knows about my Christmas tree experiences. It's like I'm famous or something. I'm unsure what to do, so I tuck my phone back into my bag and decide to sort it out tomorrow. Right now, I need a large drink and a handful of salted, savoury snacks.

In the main foyer of the hotel, there's a sign:

'The Felgate is pleased to welcome all the staff of Fosters DIY stores in the north Surrey area. We hope you have a lovely evening and a very Happy Christmas.'

Excellent, That's nice, except that the sign doesn't say where we have to go. It's nice to get a cheery festive greeting, but some directions would also be excellent.

I wander through the reception area, looking for clues. There's no reply from the guys, and I have forgotten to bring my invitation with me, telling me which room to go to, so I stroll through the marble reception area, hoping to bump into someone I know. Just in front of me is a group of three people - all fat, middle-aged, and shuffling through towards the Queen Anne Room.

Perfect. They look exactly like employees from Fosters, and - yes - Queen Anne room rings a bell. I follow them and help myself to a glass of wine from the guy at the door. The wine is lovely...really expensive-tasting stuff. I sip at it while I wander around looking for my work colleagues, but there are so many people here it's tough to find them. A guy walks past with a tray of lovely wine, so I take another one, putting my empty glass on his tray. I'm so impressed that they have done this party properly, with a beautiful, big elegant room featuring a giant Christmas tree, but I'm disappointed that I haven't been asked to dress it. Great to have proper, good-quality wine and not the usual cheap rubbish that gets served. I might have another one. Still no sign of anyone I know, though.

'Very posh, isn't it?' I say to the couple next to me. 'And everyone looks very swanky out of their green overalls, don't they?'

They look at me the same way that one might look at an axe murderer running down the street, clutching a sharpened blade.

Then, they back off and turn to talk to someone else.

'Right - ladies and gentlemen,' says a toastmaster, resplendent in a uniform of red waistcoat and black frock coat, banging a hammer down to get everyone's attention. 'Welcome to the Christmas dinner and drinks for Parker & Parker Legal services. Please move down through the reception room into the main dining hall, where dinner will be served.'

Shit. I'm in the wrong bloody party.

'Please go through,' says the toastmaster, signalling towards the dining area. I have to admit I'm tempted to stay at this party. They don't look like they're short of a bob or two. I bet the food will be lovely - much nicer than the naff bits of pastry that will no doubt be served at our shin-dig.

'I just need to pop out to make a call,' I say, moving towards the front doors of the room.

'Of course,' says the toastmaster, opening the door and allowing me to go through. As I leave, I help myself to another glass of wine from a tray on the side. Once I'm outside, I check my phone.

'It's the Queen Mary room,' says the text from Ray. Bollocks. Queen Mary, not Queen Anne.

I get to the right place, and it's much more like I imagined it would be; plain and tired-looking with a simple pay bar in the corner...no elaborate decorations, no toastmaster and no delicious free wine.

'Here's to Parker & Parker,' I say, raising my glass and promising myself that if I ever need any legal work, they will be the firm I turn to before any other.

'OK, ladies and gentlemen,' says Keith, taking the microphone and looking for all the world like a low-rent comedian on a cruise ship. 'Let's get this party starteeeed.'

There are a few feeble claps from those who have bothered to gather before him. The rest of us mill around, waiting for what will be an overlong and under-prepared speech.

'Hey, gather round,' he shouts over to us. 'We're really partying over here.'

'There you are, hero of the hour,' says Keith, throwing a cursory Christmas decoration at me for no good reason.

I'm standing next to Ray and Belinda. 'We'd better go over there and pretend to like the boss,' says Ray. 'He's standing there on his own.'

Keith's eyes light up when he sees us coming towards him. He's a nice guy. He's been an excellent boss to me over the years I've been at the company. He's just a bit...I don't know - a bit naff, I suppose. Gosh, that sounds harsh, but do you know what I mean?

'We're going to do a fun quiz,' he announces.

Those of us gathered before him do nothing to disguise our distaste. Fun and quiz are not words that have any right to snuggle up to one another in the same sentence.

Keith divides us into four teams of five people and invites us to get a chair each and assemble in our newly-formed groups to begin the fun. Since trying to organise 20 people when most of them are drunk is a little like trying to herd cats, this process takes about 20 minutes, and by the time we're all finally sitting down and ready to start, I, for one, am losing the will to live. Keith looks more exasperated than any man has ever looked before.

'Finally,' he says. 'Right - now for the quiz...can you nominate a person in each group to write down the answers.'

Again, given the level of alcohol consumption, this takes way, way longer than it has any right to.

'Come on,' says Keith. 'It's like trying to get toddlers to organise themselves.'

It strikes me that this is a pretty good analogy. Drunk people are very much like toddlers...staggering into things, unable to make it to the toilet on time, and babbling nonsensically.

Finally, we are in our groups, and Keith can start his God-forsaken, entirely unwelcome quiz. I'm with Belinda, Ray, Joe and Sandra from catering.

'OK,' he says. 'In the store, we asked questions of lots of people, and I have the answers here. You have to guess what they said. The person who gets the closest wins the prize. Does that make sense?'

'Yes,' we all chorus, hoping there aren't too many of them.

'OK, ready for the first question?'

'Yes,' we all say again, with slightly less enthusiasm. I wish he'd get on with the damn thing.

'OK. What is the worst way to start your day?' he asks. 'Would the appointed spokesperson in each team please raise their hand when they are ready?'

I throw my arm into the air before consulting with the team—Sandra voices her anger.

'Well, do you have an answer?' I ask her, and she mutters that she doesn't, so I turn back towards Keith, waving my arm impatiently.

'OK, Mary's hand was up first. What do you think the answer is?'

'Is the answer: the worst way to start your day is to wake up on the floor and discover that your Siamese twin is missing...the one with the vital internal organs. Is that the answer?'

'No, Mary. No,' says Keith, looking distressed.

'OK - in a prison cell.'

Everyone looks open-mouthed. Well, what did they expect? This is supposed to be the worst way to start your day. It's got to be something terrible.

'Dead,' I say. 'Is that the answer? The worse way you can wake up is dead.'

'No.'

It turns out the correct answer is 'having overslept' - for God's sake. That's not the worst way to start your day...I can think of loads of worst ways.

'Mary, you have a peculiar imagination,' says Simon from customer services. 'Remind me never to be alone with you on a dark night.'

'Next question,' says Keith. 'Let's see if someone other than Mary can answer. Mary - please make your answers less...what's the word I'm looking for?...troubling.'

'OK,' I mutter, but I'm not put off; I'm in my stride now and determined that we should win this game.

'And let the others on your team contribute,' he adds. 'It's a team quiz.'

'Yes,' I say, but I'm thinking ',, *fuck that...I've got a load of dimwits on my team.*'

We play for the next hour. HOUR! At a bloody Christmas party. I contemplate leaving and returning to that lovely lawyers' party on several occasions. That was so much more classy, and no one was asking stupid questions and judging you on your answers.

'OK, this one is the decider,' says Keith, now clearly losing patience with us and confidence in his own game. 'The question is - what was the name of my childhood friend?'

Marty from the kitchen department throws his hand into the air immediately. Marty is an odd-looking creature. He's extremely thin (almost skeletal). He looks like a box of KFC after you've eaten all the chicken and thrown the bones back in. He's also a terrible chain smoker in an old-school way, with roll-ups and yellow fingers to prove it.

'Was your friend called Mike?' he asks.

'No,' says Keith.

'Barry?'

'No'

'Peter?'

'No, look, Marty - you can't just keep shouting out names; you have to confer with your team and come up with an answer. 'Anyone else?'

'I know,' I say. 'Did you not have any friends? Maybe you just had an old cereal box onto which you painted a face and called it Brian the box, which became your best friend?'

Keith looks at me like I'm the most ridiculous person on earth.

'Let's end the quiz there. Everyone has won,' he says. 'Collect your free drink from the bar whenever you're ready.'

There's a free bar running between 9 and 10 pm, so this is not quite the generous gift that it might appear, but I don't want to bring this up with Keith. I've upset him somehow...he's staring at me like I'm some lunatic. Does he need to be reminded that I'm nearly famous?

Behind me, Father Christmas is saying his 'ho, ho, hos' and swigging from a beer bottle.

'Alright?' asks Neil from kitchen appliances.

'I'm fine,' I say. 'I'm just admiring Father Christmas. He's a bloody handsome fellow.'

'I'm going to make a bet with you, Mary bloody Brown. Yes - we're going to have a bloody bet, you and me...a bloody bet.'

'OK,' I say, ordering myself a bottle of wine (the free bar's only there for an hour, I need to fill my boots while I can). 'Go on then, let's have a bet.'

A DAY OFF

Thank Christ, I haven't got to go to work today...I took the day off to do my Christmas shopping, which was the best decision in the world: I don't think I've ever felt so bad.

I stretch out in bed and feel immediately constrained by something. I can't fathom what it is, but it's bloody annoying. I look over to see that I'm fully dressed, and my sleeve is caught on the bedstead. Strangely, I appear to be dressed as Father Christmas. Ow - and my leg hurts. Whichever way you look at it, this is not good. Questions which immediately spring to mind are: where are my real clothes? What did Father Christmas go home wearing, since I appear to have his outfit? At what stage did Father Christmas and I swap clothes, and did I do this publicly? And why does my leg hurt so much? I think Sharon from catering might be the person to ask.

I pick up the phone gingerly and dial her number. She answers straight away with a girlish chuckle.

'Mary Brown. What are you like?' she says.

'I don't know,' I want to reply. 'What am I like? Tell me.'

'So you got home safely then?' she asks, laughing again, clearly at some memory of me that she is not choosing to share.

'Home safely,' I say. 'All dressed as Father Christmas….'

'Ha,' she laughs, giving nothing away.

'I was surprised to wake up in a Santa costume,' I say, hopeful that she'll explain my outfit to me.

'Well, you took the bet,' she says.

'Yes, indeed.'

What bet? What's she talking about? I don't think Sharon hangs around too many people who get hideously drunk, or she'd know with absolute certainty that she needs to spell these things out, or I won't know what is going on.

'Well, I'd better go,' she says. 'It's crazy, crazy here today. Thanks to you, the store is packed. People are queuing to get into the car park. Father Christmas is booked up until 9 pm on Christmas Eve. It's mad. Keith says people are driving hundreds of miles to see the Beckham Tree and to buy the decorations, and there are loads and loads of journalists wanting to talk to you. They are all coming in tomorrow. I hope that's OK?'

'Of course,' I say.

'Bye,' she says, and she disappears off the line, leaving me none the wiser about the bloody outfit I'm wearing and some bet I had.

I text Neil. 'Did I make some sort of bet last night?' I ask him. A couple of minutes later, the phone rings and all I can hear is Neil guffawing and chortling. So, that'll be a 'yes' then.

'Just stop laughing and tell me what I did,' I say.

'Do you not remember?'

'Not a thing,' I say.

'You had a bet with Dom and Pete from the warehouse that you could get yourself onto *This Morning*, the TV show. The bet was that you have to wear that Father Christmas costume until you've been on there.'

'Been on there?'

'Yeah - you either have to be mentioned by them, be on the phone to them...on air, or go on to the show, but since you have to wear the Father Christmas costume all the time, you might not want to do that.'

Oh, for God's sake.

'That's a ridiculous bet. There's no way I can do that. So why did I bet with them?'

'Because you were drunk?'

'Well, yes, that's hard to deny. How long have I got in which to get myself onto *This Morning*?' I ask.

'As long as you like,' says Neil. 'But you must wear the Father Christmas costume until you've been on there, so I wouldn't leave it too long.'

Oh FFS.

Now, if I were a sensible, rational grown-up, I'd take the Father Christmas outfit off at this stage, fold it up, put it to one side, and dismiss the whole thing as a drunken prank at a Christmas party, but I'm not like that. I've got this maverick streak in me, and once I say I'm going to do something, I make sure I damn well do it. Or, certainly, I'll give it a try. This one might be beyond even me, though. Get onto This Morning? With lovely Holly and Phil? Bloody hell.

I make myself a cup of tea and take a banana (I curse my bloody diet on days like this...no one wants to be eating fruit when they're hung over, bacon was invented for the very purpose of comforting drinkers the morning after).

I sit down, peel the banana and switch the television to ITV. As I do, my phone bleeps with a message. I take a look:

'Thank you for your order from Top Shop. Your parcel will be dispatched from our depot today.'

What order?

I go through my emails and find one entitled 'order confirmation'. Scrub that - I see three entitled 'order confirmation' - one from Topshop for three dresses (all size 10, I would be a size 20 in Top Shop clothes if they did clothes in my size), one from River Island for a pair of shoes size 8 (I'm size 5) and one for underwear from Agent Provocateur that would shame a pole dancer. Nipple less? Really? Where the hell was my mind last night? Can it be true that I sat down at my computer at midnight, dressed as Father Christmas, drunk out of my mind, and ordered 'peep panties' and 'nippleless bras'? Yes, it is.

I'm never drinking again. Never. Not ever.

There are also loads of emails from journalists wanting to interview me. I'll have to get back to them all later. My life's just a little bit out of control at the moment.

On *This Morning*, Phil and Holly are looking very serious. With her perfect hair and lovely face, the beautiful Holly makes puppy eyes into the camera lens. 'If you have been affected by drugs, call in now and talk to our experts.'

OK. This has to be my moment. I've never seen drugs, heard anything about drugs, and I don't know anyone who's on drugs, but still - I pick up my landline and dial the number. I have to get myself mentioned on *This Morning*.

'*This Morning*, Annabel speaking.'

'Hi, I was just ringing about the drugs,' I say.

'Of course; how can I help you?'

'I'm addicted to drugs,' I say, biting into my banana. 'I'd like to talk to Holly and Phil about it...on air.'

'Certainly. Can you tell me a little about your problems...'

'I've always had them,' I begin. 'Since I was a child.'

'A child? So, how old were you when you first started taking drugs?'

I can sense that the child angle is good, and she's interested in me because I took drugs when I was young.

'I first took drugs when I was four,' I say, thinking that will pique her interest.

'When you were four? Really? Gosh, that's young.'

Yep - interest is officially piqued.

'How were you introduced to them? I mean - where does a four-year-old come across drugs?'

'Mum,' I say, and there's a short silence.

'That must have been tough,' she says. 'Your mum was an addict?'

'She was,' I say. 'She made me take them.'

'OK, look, we'll put you on air in three minutes. Is that OK?'

'Yes,' I say, grabbing my mobile to text the guys at work. They won't bloody believe this.

'I'm on This Morning in three minutes!!' I text.

BERNICE BLOOM

'So, welcome, Mary. Can you hear me? Also, Mary - can I ask you to turn your mobile phone off - we're getting some feedback from it.'

Lovely Holly is talking to me! It's so exciting. 'Of course, just doing that now,' I reply, switching my mobile off, but already I can see Neil's reply is a whole load of smiley faces, and the message 'am watching it now.'

'Would you tell us briefly what happened to you? Is it true that your mother forced you to take drugs, Mary?'

'Yes, it is,' I say. 'When I was four years old, she started feeding me drugs, and I became hooked on them.'

'That's terrible. Dr Mike joins us in the studio. Is there anything you'd like to ask him?'

The truth is that there's nothing I want to ask anyone, and I don't want to take up too much of their time in case someone is waiting with real issues to discuss. All I want to do is make sure everyone at work knows I'm on the show.

'I just want to say how difficult it is,' I say. 'And I want to urge mothers everywhere never to give drugs to their children because it ruins lives. My name's Mary Brown, and my life has been ruined by them.'

'Indeed,' says Holly, turning to the doctor in the studio to talk about my entirely fabricated life story. 'How hard for Mary. Is that something that anyone can ever come to terms with?'

The doctor explains that I need counselling and drug therapy, and I'm urged to stay on the line so they can talk to me afterwards to offer me the help I need.

'Thanks, I'm OK,' I tell the producer, and I put the phone down, stand up and remove the blasted Father Christmas costume.

'Victory!' I say, laughing to myself. 'A lovely little victory.'

CHRISTMAS SHOPPING

1 9th December

I'm not overwhelmingly proud of myself as I grab my handbag, put on some lipstick and push the front door open. Phoning a national television station and pretending to be on drugs isn't an ideal way to start the day.

Dishy Dave, who lives just below me, leaves his flat as I step out.

'Ah, glad to see you're up and about,' he says. 'I didn't think you'd be leaving your bed today.'

'Why wouldn't I be up and about?' I reply. 'I have Christmas shopping to do.'

'Well, I thought you wouldn't be up today because of the state you were in last night. Don't you remember falling and me helping you up? I'm surprised you don't have a bruise on your leg. You took a nasty fall.'

'Oh,' I reply, pleased to know where the painful bruise came from but a bit embarrassed that Dave saw me.

'You were all dressed up,' he continues.

'Yes, that's right - Christmas party. Now I better get on my way. I've got Christmas shopping to do.'

'You said last night that you planned to do all your shopping on Amazon.'

Christ - for how long did I talk to him?

'I changed my mind,' I say bluntly, offering a cheery wave as I step out onto the pavement. He is right, though; I had planned to do all my shopping online, and my drunk self was quite sure about that, but I'm fed up with ordering things and having to send them back because they're not quite right.

I'm also really fed up with all these advertising emails... I bought mum a book about woodland birds and got an email saying, 'if you liked the book about woodland birds, perhaps you'd like these....' There followed a whole selection of things like tea cosies, screwdriver kits, and children's Postman Pat dressing-up outfits. On what planet does buying a book about birds for your mum mean that you are secretly longing for a Postman Pat costume?

So, today, despite my raging hangover, I will be buying my Christmas presents the old-fashioned way.

The first shop I come across on the High Street is Argos. In common with everyone else in the world, I wonder why the shop is still going or how it ever started in the first place. Still, I go in there and wander around, thinking how utterly bizarre it is. I flick through the catalogue, and a painting set catches my eye. My mum has always wanted to learn to paint...this would be perfect... There is a mini easel, paints and pads, brushes, and all the other paraphernalia of introductory-level painting. It really would be ideal. My dad always rings me before Christmas to ask what he should get mum, this year I told him to book her a painting course, so when I arrive with this on Christmas morning, it will complete the package. She'll be delighted, and dad and I will look like superheroes.

So I write the item number onto the pad, with the tiny little pen, and take the piece of paper to the desk. This is where shopping in Argos becomes a bit like battleships, trying to work out what's on the other side of the wall.

It turns out that they do have the painting set. Bull's-eye! So I pay my money and wait in line under a blue light on the far side of the room, looking up at the screen like I'm waiting for train details to emerge on the phalanx of screens at Waterloo station.

The art set arrives, and I head off feeling very proud of myself that mum's present has been bought. I think how happy she'll be when I give it to her on Christmas Day. But as soon as I start thinking about Christmas, I start thinking that I still haven't talked to Ted properly about what we're going to do. I need to chat with him about the fact that I have accepted two lunch invitations and we must go to both, but the time never seems right.

I wander into Marks and Spencer on the way through the centre to see whether there's anything in there that would be nice for dad this Christmas.

A lady walks up to the shop assistant in front of me.

'May I try on that dress in the window, please?' she asks.

'Certainly not, madam,' I find myself saying. 'You have to use the fitting room like everyone else.'

OK, so it was funnier in my head than when I said it out loud, but - it's Christmas - time for having fun and not taking everything too seriously.

The woman scowls at me as if I've just trodden on her cat or kicked her baby while I offer a reluctant smile and shuffle away.

So, on to the big question - what the hell should I get dad for Christmas? I mean - what does anyone get their father for Christmas? It's the stupidest present in the world to buy. He won't be impressed if I get socks, ties, or cufflinks. But what else do I get?

I pull my phone out of my bag to ring Charlie and see whether she has any thoughts. It's switched off, which strikes me as odd. I'm the sort of person who has my phone on all day and all night. I'd have to go for counselling if I ever lost it. I never switch it off. NEVER. It's so odd that it's not on.

Then I remember that lovely Holly told me to switch it off while we were filing The Morning. I switch it back on and phone Charlie.

'Hiya gorgeous,' I say.

'At last,' she replies. 'Why haven't you returned any of my messages?'

BERNICE BLOOM

'Sorry - my phone was off in my bag; I didn't see that I had any. What's so urgent?'

'What's so urgent? Fuck me, Mary - you were on national television this morning telling the world that your mum pushed drugs on you. Your mum is frantic and is ringing me to find out what the hell is going on. What were you thinking?'

'Oh, that!' I say. 'Don't worry about that - it was just a bet I had with one of the guys in the office. Nothing to worry about.'

'Yes - lots to worry about, Mary. You're mum's going loopy. You have to ring her. Call her now, then ring me straight back.'

'OK,' I say. I didn't think anyone would twig that it was me on the television this morning...perhaps I should have given a false name, but Mary Brown is such a common name; there didn't seem to be any point.

I dial mum's number and prepare myself to get screamed at. But it's a relatively quiet, subdued mum who answers the phone.

'Why did you say those things?' she asks pitifully. 'I don't understand.'

I explain about the bet and me being an idiot and not thinking it through.

'I'm so sorry, mum,' I say when I realise how upset she's been. And because she's my mum, and because mums are amazing, she tells me not to worry and to enjoy my shopping trip.

'Don't waste all your money on your father and me - we don't need anything,' she says.

You get lucky in life, or you get unlucky in life. When it came to mums - I've been the most fortunate person in the world.

PREPARING FOR CHRISTMAS

20th December

'I still can't believe you did that,' says mum, sitting in her little car with her seat so far forward that her nose is practically touching the windscreen. She wipes a small hole in the condensation that she squints through, like a nocturnal animal peering out into the light for the first time.

'Did what?'

'Oh Mary, you know what I'm talking about - when you rang the tv company a couple of days ago and told them I fed you drugs. I think there's something wrong with you sometimes; I do.'

'I'm sorry,' I say for the thousandth time. 'I bet with a guy from work that I couldn't get on the show. I shouldn't have done it; you're quite right. I'm sorry, mum.'

'And what's all the stuff I'm reading about you decorating David Beckham's tree?'

'Yes, it was something I did for work,' I say. 'They bought a tree from us in the garden centre, and I went and decorated it for them.'

'Well, everyone's ringing me about it. It's been in the papers and everything.'

It certainly has. I've done dozens of interviews, and the 'Beckham

Tree' continues to be Surrey's major tourism attraction, with people coming from far and wide to see it in the gardening centre.

We're quite a ridiculous sight this morning - me and mum - driving to the dump in her little car with the old freezer sticking out the boot (tied on with ropes though God knows whether they'll hold).

'I don't know the way,' declares mum. She has no sat nav, map or even the address of the dump with her. She's so bloody disorganised, but I can't complain because in that, and so many other ways...she's exactly like me. We spent yesterday evening at IKEA - bloody hell, that was a performance and a half. Mum wanted a new freezer and had decided she wanted a massive one - the size of a bloody bungalow. She was dead set on a chest freezer, but I managed to talk her out of that; I've seen many horror films in which the body ends up in the freezer and gets eaten by the dinner guests. I wanted no part in encouraging cannibalism. But she did insist on one bigger than most restaurants have. There are only two of them. How much frozen food can one couple eat?

Mum didn't want to pay to have the old one taken away...that's why we're trundling through the backstreets of Cobham with our treacherously large load, hunting for the tip. We've asked three people so far and now appear to be heading in the right direction. Finally, on the side of the road, there's a sign.

'Here, mum,' I say, confident that she won't have noticed it. 'In this entrance on the right.'

Mum swings her car down the small side road, recklessly ignoring all the oncoming traffic as she goes. As we disappear from view, there are beeped horns and shouts, and mum seems oblivious to all of them.

We pull up on the left-hand side in front of a barrier manned by four guys (no wonder the economy is in a mess - why does it need four guys to press a button and raise a barrier).

'What are you dumping?' asks one of them, like it wasn't entirely plain from the freezer sticking out of the back of the car.

'A freezer,' I say.

The man looks down at his clipboard and back up at me.

'And you are hoping to dispose of it?'

'Yes.' What else would I be doing? No - it's full of ice cream. I brought it down here to offer you all a nice tasty snack.

'You know you have to phone us in advance if you're bringing white goods, don't you?' he says.

'Who do I have to phone?' I ask.

'Environmental health department,' he says. 'They are the council's rules, not mine. I don't make the rules; I do as I'm told.'

'Do you have the number?' I ask. There's no way we're taking this freezer back to mum and dad's house. We're leaving it here whether they want it or not. The guy hands me a number, and I tap it into my mobile phone. 'And what's your name?' I ask him.

'I'm Malcolm,' he says. 'Head of refuse.'

As I wait for someone to answer my call, the phone in the hut starts ringing.

'Excuse me,' says Malcolm. 'I better just go and get that.'

He runs into the shed while I wait for the council to answer my call. Eventually, it connects.

'Hello, refuse tip, Malcolm speaking. Can I help you?' he says.

'I want to drop my freezer off at the tip,' I say incredulously. What the hell sort of game is he playing here?

'Sure, where are you?' he asks. 'You can bring it down, but there's a backlog of people waiting. Someone's already here with their freezer.'

'That's me!' I say. 'I'm sitting in the car with my freezer. You told me to call you.'

'Great, then you can come through,' he says, walking back out again and pressing a button to lift the barrier. 'Have a nice day.'

It's late in the evening, and I'm looking in the mirror, holding back my hair to expose my cheekbones and lifting my eyebrows to make my eyes look bigger. God, I wish I weren't so fat. But, you know, the thing with putting on weight is that it affects everything...not just your body. When you think about an overweight person, you think about the size of their arse, how their stomach sticks out and that they have big thighs...that's all true, but it's also the face. When someone puts on weight, it's as if someone has covered their face in uncooked dough...the features become less distinct, and the jawline less clean. There's not a pretty little face with features but a large and rather indistinctive mask. However different you look at fighting weight, once you put on the pounds, you all start to look the same. You look less like 'you' and more like every other fat person who's ever existed. At least, that's what happened to me.

I found that it wasn't just that I got bigger, but my face became a fat person's face. My clothing became that of a fat person - the voluminous dresses and elasticated waists, the retreat into kaftans, always covering the arms, never wearing anything that defines your waist. I'm just a homogenous fat person. I look like every other fat person. All thin people don't look alike, but I fear that all fat people do. No one wants to be like that.

The sound of my phone ringing in my bag distracts me from further contemplation on the state of my face. I answer it and hear the voice of one of my very best friends.

'Hello, it's David. David Beckham.'

'Holy mother of God.'

'No, not the holy mother of God,' he says. 'Though I'm flattered that you've confused us.' I can hear the laugh in the back of his voice. 'I'm calling because it's Harper's Christmas party tomorrow, and we wondered whether you were free to come and decorate the tree for her. She loved it so much when you did it for our party.'

'Of course,' I say.

'It's late notice because the party is at 3 pm tomorrow, so we'll need you here by 10 am if possible.'

'Sure, perfect. Of course. I'll be there,' I say.

'Oh great,' he says. 'Victoria thought you'd be busy with all your other clients at this time of year, being a professional tree dresser, but if you can fit us in, that would be awesome. I can also bring you up to date with all the details for the trip to Lapland.'

'Lovely. I'll see you then,' I say.

I look over at the beautiful Christmas trees; some are decorated like the one I created for Dave and Vicks, and the others have their

Rick Astley bells hanging on them. I think that - yes - one can imagine how he might have confused me with a professional decorator.

David and I say our goodbyes, and I let out a significant squeal before I run as fast as my chunky legs will carry me past the nativity scene and towards Keith's office. Mike from bathrooms sees me fly past him at lightning speed and shouts: 'Oy Mary. All the kids are asking why there's an elephant in the manger.'

And you know, his question doesn't even bother me.

'That's what one of the three wise men travelled on,' I pant back as I tear through the centre like the love child of Usain Bolt and Mo Farrah.

'The three wise men did not travel on elephants - that's complete fantasy,' says Tony the Taps.

'Fantasy? Perhaps it's elephantasy,' I shout back, laughing very loudly at my joke. Indeed, so preoccupied am I with my joke that I go tearing straight into Keith, who is emerging from his office with a clipboard and two pot plants. The clipboard drops to the ground, the greenery goes one way, and Keith goes the other.

'What is the name of the lord is all the rush for?' he asks, as I apologise and help him to his feet, patting him down to get rid of the dirt until he rudely pushes my hand away.

'Why were you rushing?'

'Because David Beckham just called. He wants me to come back over and decorate a Christmas tree again. This time it's for Harper's party.'

'Holy cow,' says Keith. 'My office. Now.'

Later that evening, Ted and I are sitting on the sofa. He's watching Curb Your Enthusiasm and laughing a lot. The other thing he's doing a lot is telling me that I am exactly like Larry David. 'Honestly, Mary - look at the chaos he causes. He's like your twin brother. I mean, you're much more friendly than he is....'

'And prettier.'

'Yes, much prettier, but you create the same level of madness and chaos.'

'You mean that in a good way, right? This guy has his own tv show, so he can't be a complete clown. Perhaps I should have my own tv show?'

'Yeah, because that would work out incredibly well. Just a brief five-minute appearance on *This Morning*, and you managed to bring your entire family into disrepute.'

'Yeah, not my best moment.'

'Are you looking forward to going to the Beckhams tomorrow? Maybe keep it quiet this time, so we don't have the entire world's media camped on our doorstep.'

'Yes, I'm not telling anyone. I'm just going to set about the job with dignity and decorum.'

'You don't seem as excited about the whole thing this time. Last time you were practically swinging off the lampshades.'

'Yeah, well, David and I are friends now. Tomorrow will be a case of two mates getting together. No drama. No excitement.'

BECKHAM-BOUND

18TH DECEMBER

I wake up at 5 am, and the realisation hits me like a steam train. I feel overcome with a desire to wake Ted up and tell him. 'I'm going to the Beckhams today; I screech at high volume. You know David, the guy with the tattoos, plays football, is married to a Spice Girl and is the embodiment of manly beauty? Well - that's where I'm going. Today. Right now.'

'I thought this was just a couple of mates meeting up together…no drama.'

'It's David Bloody Beckham,' I say. 'Why are you not excited about this?'

I leap out of bed like a salmon jumping the falls and hurl myself into the shower where I carefully remove every body hair. I emerge as smooth as a dolphin and slather myself in scented body lotion before I clamber into my uniform. If things get friendly with David, he'll be delighted by my soft, perfumed skin.

I do my hair and make-up, thinking about the task ahead. I feel more excited than nervous because I know what to expect. Also, the tree is for Harper's party; I think I know what she likes. I know what sort of 'look' she'll be expecting. I think I've got the measure of her.

It would help if all the arty-farty interior designers weren't there. They were a painful, sharp-edged, jealous bunch who contributed nothing to my tree artistry.

My driver for the day is big Derek. He is working with the centre on a three-week contract to help shift Christmas trees around. Sales have increased so much since the Beckham story broke that they have had to hire extra workers.

To say that Derek is excited about meeting David Beckham would be to understate his feelings. I jump into the cab next to him, and he looks at me in amazement.

'Please tell me the truth, the absolute truth. Are we going to David Beckham's house today? Tell me, really... Or is this just a wind-up. Tell me if it's a wind-up before I get any more excited.'

'No, it's not a wind-up,' I tell him. 'This is all perfectly above board.'

'I'm his biggest fan,' says Derek in a slightly scary voice.

'David himself might not be there,' I say, eager to dampen the excitement so the poor guy doesn't wet himself.

'But we'll be in his house? Where he lives? I mean... That's amazing.'

'Yes, we will be in his house, and I think Victoria will be there to meet us, and Harper – her daughter – should be there, but I'm not sure about David.'

'Do you think they'd mind if I did videos in the house?'

'Yes, they would mind. You can't do anything like that, Derek. You must bring the tree and all my stuff in and help me when I ask you to. You can't be taking pictures, stealing David Beckham's pyjamas or sniffing his sheets.'

'Okay then,' he says, pulling the van over to the side of the road.

'Why have you stopped?'

'I better take it off Twitter.'

'Take what off Twitter?'

'I put a post up saying that I would be putting up videos giving people guided tours of David Beckham's house. So I'll take him down if you don't think I can do that.'

'Shit, yes – take it down. Why would you think you could do guided tours around Beckham's house?'

'For a laugh,' he says, as he fiddles with his phone, hopefully removing the various posts he's put up. We seem to be sitting there a pretty long time.

'Have you not done it yet?'

'There are about 50 posts on Twitter, Facebook and Instagram,' he says. 'I'm just making sure that I remove them all.'

'Oh dear God, Derek, why would you think that was appropriate?'

While playing on his phone, he shrugs, eventually declaring that all the posts are removed.

'Okay, keep going straight down this road. At the roundabout, turn left, and there is a string of shops along there that sell fabulous Christmas decorations. So that's where I'm going.'

'Is that where David Beckham lives?'

'No, Derek, David Beckham doesn't live at the back of a Christmas decoration shop on a shabby old street in south London. We'll get to Beckham's house; we need to go and buy the decorations I need first.'

We arrive at the shop, and I clamber out of the van and towards the door of the beautiful shop with its pick-a-mix of decorations. For the cheap and cheerful ones, you can get three for £1, but because this is the Beckhams' house, we're going for broke and spending a whole pound on each glossy little decoration.

This is for Harper's party, so it needs to reflect what she loves in life, and I've been through her Instagram account and found that animals and bracelets feature more than anything else. That might sound like an odd combination, and I don't expect it fully encompasses all her likes and dislikes in the world, but it's what she seems to show most of on Instagram. Of course, there are also loads of pictures of her with her dad, hugging and being carried by him, and generally being a real daddy's girl, so I bear that in mind as I scan the aisles.

I go first of all to the bright pink cats with hellishly long whiskers like false eyelashes. Could anything be better? I throw ten into the baskets before spotting teddy bears to hang in the tree. They're a mixture of brown and black ones. Black doesn't seem very Christmassy, so 12 brown bears tumble one by one into the basket to nestle down next to the girlish cats. Of course, I'll pick up tinsel in a mixture of pink, lilac and white. I'm a bit torn on the white; I think pink and lilac are great, but I throw some white because it looks like snow, and I might create a snow scene for the bears to play in. Then I see some beautiful bracelets in an array of colours. The lovely thing about them is that you hang them in the tree, and then friends can come and help themselves to a bracelet that they can wear to go home. I want some of these. They've got 40 in the shop, so I throw all of them into my basket before reaching for candy canes and some sizeable Father Christmases that you hang on the tree and squeeze to hear them say 'Ho Ho Ho.'

Honestly, I'm having an absolute field day. There are huge pink teddy bears in the far corner of the shop. They are huge, but I take one to sit on top of the tree like the star of Bethlehem. Then realise that that might be too unreligious, so I take a star and figure that if the bear is holding the star and then wedged onto the top of the tree with a branch up his bottom, that will look altogether more religious.

I think I've got enough, but I'm never one to under-do things; I'd rather take too much than get there and wish I'd bought more, so I grab handfuls of singing sheep, dancing cows that jiggle and shake when you make a noise and these crabs that crawl around sideways underneath the tree going round and round with flashy lights. I've never seen anything so ridiculous, so I buy 10 of those. Armed with two carrier bags full of £200 worth of tat, I retreat to the van and tell Derek we are ready to go. He's been sitting in the van's cab while I've been choosing ornaments and has taken the opportunity to spruce himself up a bit. He stinks of something musky and old-fashioned, and his hair has been gelled back David Beckham style. It's a style that looks perfectly lovely on the former England footballer, but on big Derek, who is pushing 60, it looks less alluring.

We drive through the countryside to the Beckhams' beautiful country retreat, then through the gates and up to the house. Derek is hyperventilating. It's not ideal.

We're greeted at the door by a collection of staff who lead us through and show us where the tree should go. Derek brings it in, and I start work.

'Can you pass me the lights I brought from work? The ones called 'pulsating disco stars,' I say.

Derek rummages through the box and hands them to me. I explain how I want them to run through the tree, one on every branch.

'I brought five boxes with us, so there should be plenty,' I add.

Derek gets his ladder from the van and begins doing as I've asked. It's quite a big job, and I feel much happier now that he's fully occupied, whistling as he carefully attaches the lights I've asked him to. Everything should be OK if he's within sight and working hard. Can you imagine if he'd gone round the house, videoing the place? We'd have been bloody arrested.

I finish all the decorating in around two hours which surprises everyone. How long were they expecting it to take? Perhaps it would have looked more impressive if I'd worked slowly and made a meal out of it. Finally, I ask whether Harper is available to come and look at the tree so I can talk her through it and make sure she's happy. The assistants look at me as if I've just asked to meet the queen, but they shuffle off and emerge 20 minutes later to say Harper will be down shortly. Only a few minutes later, I see Harper, accompanied by David.

There's an embarrassing gasp from Derek, like a teenage girl at a *Take That* concert.

'Stay calm,' I mutter as he reaches for the wall to steady himself.

I step forward and say hello to David and Harper, and I tell her all about the tree...I explain that the flashing loops are bangles she could take off and keep. I show her the mad creatures running around underneath the tree and the lights woven through it.

'It's brilliant,' she says to David. 'I can't wait for my friends to see it.'

'That's great,' says the blessed David. 'You're very good at this, aren't you?'

'I try,' I say modestly.

Then I introduce him to Derek. What a mistake. I think the guy will keel over and die when David puts his hand out. Instead, Derek stares at it. Then he leans forward and holds David's hand, rather than shake it until the lovely Mr Beckham has to use his other hand to move Derek's hand away.

'I've got this envelope for you,' he says. 'It's got all the information about the trip in it. Of course, you'll also get a call from the organisers, but so you know…everything is there.'

'Thanks, David,' I say, giving him a huge hug. 'This is amazing.'

When I pull back, Derek is there, waiting.

'Hug for Derek?' he says, putting out his arms.

'You know what, I have to go now,' says David. 'You look after yourself, mate.'

THE RETURN OF JUAN

1 9TH DECEMBER

It's 6 am on a cold morning, and I am at Heathrow Airport to collect Juan. My gorgeous little friend from the cruise ship. I'm so excited to see him.

Charlie is outside waiting in the car while I scan the arrivals concourse, looking for him. As usual, I don't need to look too closely amongst all the grey suits and blue coats for Juan as he strides into view in a gorgeous bright pink silky-looking jacket and zebra print trousers. Juan struts when he walks, treating every piece of pavement like a catwalk. He is such a magnificent creature. I wish I had an ounce of his style and confidence.

'I'm here!' I shout, prompting him to swing around and give me the biggest smile as he runs towards me and hugs me tightly. He doesn't do that thing that they do in the movies, where he picks me up into the air and spins me around. He tried that once when we were aboard the cruise liner and almost broke his back, so we stick to hugging these days.

'You look gorgeous, darling,' I say, stroking the silky jacket.

'It was an early Christmas present from my sister, isn't it fabulous?'

he says. 'She said she might come over and visit me when I come to stay later in the year. Would that be okay?'

'Oh my God, of course. It would be lovely to meet her.'

This isn't entirely true. It wouldn't be lovely to meet her because I've seen photographs of her and she's gorgeous. I could do without her swishy dark ponytail and long, tanned limbs striding around my flat first thing in the morning.

We get out of the car when we reach mine, and Charlie zooms off straight away like she's just done some drug deal. 'I've got a meeting first thing, sorry - I have to fly,' she says before Lewis Hamiltoning it down the road.

Juan and I head inside, I put my bag on the sofa and go into the kitchen to make coffee. All the while, my phone is beeping and vibrating non-stop. I know what it is; it is all the tweets and Facebook messages after yesterday's Beckham tree thing. We put together a press release yesterday afternoon and attached the picture that I took, and it was on most of the newspaper websites last night.

'Why is your phone ringing so much?' asks Juan. 'Do you want me to answer it?'

'No, don't worry. It's just because I went to decorate David Beckham's Christmas tree and all the papers ran stories about it this morning.'

'David Beckham? What? Did you decorate David Beckham's tree? Oh my God. Oh my God. Is he gorgeous? Is he bloody gorgeous?'

'Yes, yes and yes. And you haven't heard the best bit - I was going to tell you later, but I can't wait any longer.'

'What?'

'He's sorted out the trip to Lapland. He's found someone to sponsor it so that Oliver and his dad can go.'

'No way. We must go somewhere expensive for breakfast to celebrate,' says Juan. 'That's amazing.'

'I can't do breakfast. I'm working this morning, but why don't you come to the store at 3 pm when I finish, and we can go out then, have a few drinks, and catch up properly.'

'OK,' he says, 'But I want all the details then, every one of them...'

'You will have them, my love, I promise you.'

It's 7.30 before I get to work, despite my official start time being 7 am today. Keith always works nine till six, so he doesn't know when I get to the office. So I go in, switch on my computer, and check the newspapers online to see what they've said about the Christmas tree.

Wow. The photo is everywhere. Every site I can think of is running the picture of beautiful David with his cute grin, standing next to my tree. The only horror is how big I look. I know I should be glad of all I've achieved and revel in the moment of glory, but I am twice as wide as David Beckham. And he's a big bloke. I'm also half his height. I wish I hadn't stood next to him for the photo.

I've got to lose weight. Somehow. I know this is the wrong time of year for worrying about that, but as I look at myself in the picture, I feel a tear creep into the back of my eye. The only thing that distracts me and stops me from staring at the hideous sight of myself is a loud banging on the office window.

I look up to see around a dozen people staring into the office. They cheer when I look up. 'It's Mary Christmas,' shouts one, which makes me laugh.

'How was David Beckham?' shouts another.

'Wonderful,' I say.

Blimey, it's only 8 am, the doors have only just opened, and a fan club has formed. I look back at the pictures and think - yeah, I need to lose weight, and - yeah - I do look big in those, but for heaven's sake, I'm getting some things right. So I wave at them, eliciting another big cheer and a spontaneous round of applause.

I thank them and turn back to my computer but can sense that they are all still out there, so I head into the staff cafeteria to study the coverage on my phone, unwatched by customers. As I walk in, there's a ripple of applause, and the catering staff present me with a free caramel latte and a chocolate doughnut.

Christ. Now I'm going to be three times the size of David Beckham.

I click onto Twitter to find it aglow with discussion about my tree.

Of course, there are a few unkind comments and references to my weight.

I'm surprised there were any candy canes left says Gal3345 from Leeds.

Wow! Have you seen the size of the woman who decorated it? says Peter from Barnsley.

Good grief, she's never turned down a pudding, has she? says Mandy from Bath.

It's hard to read things like that about yourself. I don't know how famous people cope with the constant bickering and nastiness about their appearance. They must have developed very thick skins to cope. Even women who are, by all objective judgement, exquisite and slim are derided and mocked relentlessly. Social media is a cruel place. I close my phone and sit back. Sod them all; I will enjoy my latte and think about the good I'm done since I took charge of Christmas.

First, there has been lots of positive PR for the store, which is excellent. Admittedly I flew beneath the standard I'd expect from Mary Christmas when I honed up a popular tv show and told them I'd had drugs forced on me by my mother. But, happily, no one seems to have linked the woman in charge of Christmas and the hung-over lunatic calling tv stations.

Then there's the *Christmas Post-box of Wishes and Dreams*, through which I've reached out to the local community. Keith may have mocked the idea that global media would cover us, but even he must agree that there has been good coverage of everything we've done, and we still have the date to come here in the store tomorrow. I send Belinda a quick text to make sure she's remembered.

I've been sitting in the cafeteria for around 20 minutes when Keith bursts in and shouts, 'You Beauuuuty!' like he's cheering a goal scorer at a football match. 'The place is packed. It's bloody packed. What are you doing hiding away in here?'

'People were looking at me through the window; I was getting fed up,' I say.

'We'll close the blinds. Anything you want, ask - you're a superstar, Mary Brown. A bloody superstar.'

'I have more good news. David Beckham helped find someone to sponsor Oliver's trip to Lapland.'

'The kid with one leg?'

'Yes. I'm going too. I hope that's OK. Just for a couple of days to make sure it all goes smoothly.'

'Of course, that's OK. Of course. Anything. Anything at all. Can I get you anything?'

'It would be great if someone could go out and empty the Post Box of Wishes & Dreams for me. Unfortunately, I can't go outside, or I'll get mobbed.'

'Of course, of course,' he says, running straight outside to do my bidding. I love how he didn't even react to my description of it as the *Post Box of Wishes & Dreams*.

Keith rushes in with the notes he's found. First, there are a few notes requesting different tin sizes in the paint and suggesting that we do wider planks of wood, then there are ones from kind people wishing us all a Merry Christmas, wishing for world peace, and generally saying nice things about the world. Finally, at the bottom, there is a letter clearly written by a child.

Dear Christmas Elf,
For Christmas, I would like One. Sticks
Two. More sticks
Three. Even more sticks.
PS I really like sticks
From,
Jamie Mason, aged five.

I'm overcome with joy that there is a task here that I could fulfil. It would be no effort for me to go along tonight with piles of sticks for this young kid. And I know exactly the man to come and do it with me.

'You want me to what?' says Juan. 'I thought we would have a few beers and talk about David Beckham.'

'Yes, we will go to the pub, have a few beers and a bite to eat, then around 6 o'clock we will go to the house and leave loads of sticks outside with a note saying they're from the gardening centre for Jamie and we hope the whole family has a very lovely Christmas. Don't you think that will be a nice thing to do? Go and get him loads of sticks?'

'Go on then, I'm in,' says Juan wearily. 'Shall I come to the garden centre at 3 o'clock?'

'I'll see you then,' I say as I put the phone down and scan through the messages left on my phone.

There's a note from the Lebanese takeaway confirming lunch delivery for the grand date at the weekend, then about 20 requests for newspaper interviews from all over the world. Then there is one from Michael Foley, David Beckham's assistant. He tells me the trip has been organised, and we will leave on the 22nd and return on the 24th. 'See your emails,' he writes. 'All the details and tickets are in there.'

Oh brilliant! I forget about the interview requests from papers in China, Outer Mongolia and Luxemburg and rush to my emails. There it all is. All details of the cab will pick us up and take us to the airport, the hotel details and photos of Santa galore. There's a separate email for me to forward to Oliver's dad, Brian, so I do that, and go back to the email for me: there are pictures of reindeer on snowy plains, huskies, gorgeous food and pretty people in bobble hats. I need a bobble hat. Where can I get a bobble hat?

THE ARRIVAL OF JUAN

1 9TH DECEMBER

Juan and I cling onto one another as we stagger towards the small cottage, nestling in a quiet cul de sac off Cobham High Street. Oh, dear. I can't walk straight, and everything's just a little blurry. We drank way more than we'd meant in the pub, I'll be honest with you. We were only going for a couple, but there was such a lot of catching up to do, and then we were celebrating the whole Beckham thing and the trip to Lapland, so a couple of drinks turned into five or six and by the end of it all, well - not to put too fine a point on it - I feel very drunk.

We should have just staggered home to sleep it all off, but instead, we've found our way to this pretty cottage where the boy who wants sticks lives.

The two of us now stand in front of the beautifully decorated house, with the lovely giant wreath on the door and sparkly lights around the window frames. You can see the orange glow behind the heavy curtains, indicating that the lights are on inside. They're in. Now we need to provide them with sticks.

I notice that Juan is swaying a little. Or perhaps I'm swaying: it's hard to know. There is certainly a lot of swaying going on.

'OK, come on then,' I say to Juan. I can hear myself slur, and I notice how glassy his eyes look...you know, that look people have when they've drunk too much? Well, he has it—big time.

'Sshhhh...' he says, waving his finger in front of his face. 'We have to be quiet now.'

'Yes,' I whisper so quietly that he can barely hear me. 'Now we know where the house is, let's go into the park over there and collect the sticks, which we can leave on the doorstep. Yeah?'

Juan nods. I'm not sure he knows what I'm saying. He staggers along behind me as we try to walk towards the park. 'Have you got the letter with you for the little boy?'

'Of course,' I say, pulling the letter out of my pocket.

Dear Jamie,
Here are some sticks from Foster's gardening centre. I hope
you enjoy playing with them.
I know you love sticks, so hopefully, these will be a Christmas
treat. I hope you and your family have a lovely time over Christmas. Lots
of love.
From,
Mary Brown and everyone working at Foster's DIY & gardening centre.

We start gathering as many sticks as we can carry, bundling them into black bags and tipping them onto the doorstep.

I'll be honest, it looks like we've just tipped out a whole heap of rubbish on their doorstep, but once they read the letter and remember the note that their son wrote, they'll be pleased that we took the time to do this.

I smile at Juan. What five-year-old wouldn't be delighted to come out of his house and see all this?' I say. 'I think we've made a kid very happy.'

'And you could make a 35-year-old very happy if you would accompany him back to Cobham High Street for another cheeky pint before we head home.

'Good thinking,' I say, as I see the curtain move slightly in the house as if someone is aware of our presence. 'Let's get out of here.'

THE MARY BROWN BOOKS

The two of us power-walk (power stagger might be more accurate) away from the house, breaking into a mild jog as we hear a sound behind us. Then we go racing down the little country lane, which leads back to the centre of Cobham, laughing all the way. Finally, we emerge onto the High Street and give each other a high five before pausing to catch our breath.

'That was a cool thing to do.'

'It was. That kid will not believe it when his mum and dad show him all the sticks.'

'I know. It would be great to be there to see the boy's face when he realises the sticks are all for him.'

'You know you are covered in leaves and bits of broken branches, don't you? All over your jumper. Look at you...you're filthy.' As Juan says this, he looks down and sees that his jumper is covered in bits.

'Oh Christ, I look like a vagrant,' he says, frantically brushing himself down before picking off the remaining debris bits and starting to help me.

'How have you got so much more than me on you?' he asks.

'There's a bigger expanse of jumper to attract leaves,' I reply, as he plucks bits off me like a cat grooming its kittens.

'Done,' he says, rubbing his hands together to remove the last vestiges of the rubble from his fingers.

'Come on then,' I say. 'It'll be last orders soon.' We start to move towards the pub door when a police car comes zooming towards us at top speed with its lights going, and its nee-naw, nee-naw, nee-naw blaring out.

'Someone's in trouble,' I say to Juan as it screeches to a stop next to us. 'Those boys don't look like they're messing around.'

We stand and watch for a minute as an officer jumps out of the car and runs towards us. I step aside to let them enter the pub, but the officer stops in front of me.

'Don't go in there,' he says.

'I'm not. I was opening it for you.'

'Come over to the police car,' says the officer. Juan lingers by the pub door. 'You too, sir.'

Another officer steps out of the car as we approach it, and the two of them stand in front of us., looking at us as if we're hardened criminals.

'We've had reports of two individuals hanging around in front of a house in Rose Avenue before dumping a load of gardening rubbish. The people described to us look very much like you.'

'Yes, it was us,' I say. 'Not loitering or anything. We weren't causing any trouble. We just dropped off a load of sticks.'

'You dumped a load of branches and mud on the doorstep.'

'Yes. Not mud - not really - we were mainly trying to put sticks there.'

'You dumped your gardening waste on their doorstep instead of taking it to a dump or disposing of it properly. That's fly-tipping. You also frightened the lady of the house by loitering outside in what she describes as 'a loud, drunken manner.'

'No, we didn't. No, you've got it all wrong,' I try. 'That's not what happened at all.'

'So, you didn't dump leaves, sticks and branches outside Mandarin Cottage on Rose Avenue around 20 minutes ago? Because I have descriptions here which match you...a fat, unkempt woman with messy hair and an effeminate-looking man who was jigging around constantly like he needed the toilet. Would you say that was an accurate description?'

'It's a bit harsh,' I said. 'My hair's OK, isn't it?'

'Did you or didn't you dump rubbish outside their house?' 'Yes, we did, but as a gift.'

'A gift.'

'They were sticks for Jamie, the little boy who lives there. Jamie wrote to me and asked whether he could have loads of sticks for Christmas, so we put them there as a present. We left a note with them.'

As I mention the note, it occurs to me that I don't recall leaving the note. I push my hand into my pockets and feel it in there; I pull it out and open it.

'Didn't you leave it with the sticks?' says Juan. It's the first time he's spoken since the police arrived. 'And - by the way - I wasn't jigging around like I needed the loo. I was just cold, that's all.'

I look up at the officer and show him my note. He begins reading it while I delve into my handbag and pull out the letter the kid sent us in the *Christmas Post Box of Wishes and Dreams*. I hand that over as well.

'The family didn't know why you'd dumped a load of sticks outside the property,' he says. 'It was a foolish thing to do even with the note. Could you not have spoken to the lady first?'

'Sorry,' I say, looking down at the floor as he speaks.

'Come with us,' he says. 'We'll go back to the cottage, and you can explain.'

Juan and I enter the police car, glancing at one another nervously.

'Will we have to put all those bloody sticks back?' Juan whispers. I shrug. I didn't know, but it seems likely.

We pull up outside the house, and the officer knocks on the cottage door - a miserable woman with short, badly dyed hair answers.

'That's them,' she shouts, pointing aggressively in my direction. 'They're the ones...'

The police officer steps forward and explains the misunderstanding. I stand there fiddling with my hair. Why did she describe it as messy? I don't have messy hair. Her hair is horrible. How dare she.

The lady looks at the letters. A little boy is sitting on the sofa.

'Jamie, come here and see what these people have brought for you,' she says, bending over to gather a handful of the sticks.' Jamie takes one look and lets out an almighty shriek: 'Sticks!' He gathers them into his arms, smiles at Juan and me and settles down to arrange them in what seems like size order.

'I'm sorry that we panicked,' says the lady. 'But I saw you were hanging around outside, and when I came out and saw all the mess, I was shocked. A police car was driving down the road, so I flagged the officers down.'

'It's OK; we were just trying to be Christmassy,' I say. 'I'm in charge of Christmas at the store. I decorated David Beckham's tree yesterday.'

Oh, God. The lady looks from me to the officers while her husband, sitting quietly on their brown sofa for the duration of the chat, coughs gently to himself as if passing a warning to her that if I think I decorated David Beckham's tree, I am clearly nuts.

'Why don't you stay for a drink,' says the woman.

'Sure,' I say. 'That's nice of you.'

'I was talking to the officers, actually, but you're welcome to stay too.'

Her husband coughs again to warn her about the dangers of allowing two raving nutters into the house. But the lady is not perturbed. Instead, she leaves the room to get us drinks, and her husband flicks on the television so he doesn't have to converse with us. Then she returns with a tray full of glasses. 'It's a little drop of brandy,' she says, handing out the drinks.

'Good heavens!' shouts her husband, forcing his poor wife to jump.

'What's the matter? It's only the cheap brandy, not the expensive stuff.'

'No, I mean - look - on the television.'

We all look past Julie and her tray of drinks to the television behind her, where I stand outside the Beckhams' house in all my festive glory. He turns the volume up, and they listen as I speak about how I decorated the Beckhams' Christmas tree.

They all look at me, awe-struck.

'I told you before that I decorated his tree. I went twice. That was filmed the first time.'

'What's her house like?' asks the lady while Jamie hugs his sticks, and her husband stares open-mouthed at the screen.

'Nice,' I say. 'A nice house.'

THE BLIND DATE GOES WRONG

CHAPTER 21 20TH DECEMBER

I look out the window to see a perfect winter's morning: crisp & fresh: the ideal day to meet the man of your dreams.

'Surprise, surprise,' I sing out in the semi-darkness as Ted stirs beside me.

'I'm Cilla Black,' I add, in case he didn't get the Cilla reference from the song.

'Good for you', he says, moving as if he's going to roll over and go back to sleep, but then he sits up and stares at me through sleepy eyes. His face is stubbly, his hair is all standing on end, and he scratches his chest hair like a baboon.

'Why are you, Cilla? Are you about to do something ridiculous, like take to the stage at the Royal Variety Performance, or develop a Liverpudlian accent?'

'No. I'm organising the blind date today... Like Cilla Black did. Do you remember her program 'Blind Date'?'

'Oh, I'd forgotten all about that. You've worked so much this week, do you have to work Saturday as well? Can they not just get on with the date without you? Do you have to be there?'

'I always have to be there when Christmas calls,' I say, standing on the bed as if preparing to give a Martin Luther King-type speech. 'Christmas doesn't confine itself to the days in the week; Christmas is everywhere. Christmas is all of us. When I am wanted for Christmas-related activities, I must go. And now I must leave...'

'Good God,' says Ted, pulling the duvet over his head and snuggling back down into it while I dance into the bathroom to prepare myself for the exciting day ahead.

Sitting on the bus to work, I think through everything I need to get done before this wonderful Christmas date. I've asked the guys from the warehouse to move the pagoda into the main area by the Christmas nativity scene and to have the beautiful Christmas trees, now decked out in the same decorations as the Beckham tree, lined up to create an alleyway of Christmas trees leading up to their lunch table. On the other side is the lovely Rick Astley team. I make a mental note to contact Astley's people and see whether he'll come and perform for us.

Then Mandy will run natural and artificial flowers through the pagoda. In the middle of it, all will be a table and chairs beautifully laid out with linen, crockery, and cutlery that we sell in the store. Keith is apprehensive about us damaging the things we use, but I've tried to tell him that this is a valuable PR opportunity. I can't lay the table with crockery from Marks and Spencer, can I?

There should be a lot of press interest; a lot of newspapers have been ringing the store to check the timings today. It's an excellent Christmassy story and a bit of fun. It's hard to see what could go wrong. If Belinda isn't interested in Daniel, or if Daniel isn't interested in Belinda, then they don't contact one another again, and they have had a free meal. Everyone's a winner.

By 12.30 pm, everything is ready in advance of our 1 pm sit down. I never expected it to look quite so fantastic. Ted and Juan have even come down to support me, and I've managed to persuade Juan to act as a waiter.

At five to one a rather handsome man approaches me. He must be in his late 30s and has a lovely rugged look, giving him a film star quality.

THE MARY BROWN BOOKS

'Can I talk to someone about this date today?' he says, and I feel as if all my wishes have come true. He's bloody lovely. I smile at Belinda and see her go a deep shade of tomato.

This man is seriously yummy. She must be delighted.

'Of course,' I say to the man and hear Belinda giggling in the background. The familiar sound of Juan's voice saying, 'I would,' makes me smile. It's all going to be OK. The thing I was most worried about was what Daniel would be like. Now here he is. Ah. All panic over.

'Can you tell me what this date is about?' he asks. 'I've received information to be here at one o'clock. But I'm a little bit baffled. I'll be honest.'

'Please don't worry about a thing, Daniel,' I say as I guide him to the table and chairs laid out beautifully. 'You will have the most wonderful date with a beautiful woman. I signal for Belinda to come over, and she sashays across.

'Let me introduce you to your date for today. This is Belinda.' I stand back and open my arms to introduce the couple.'

'There's been some terrible mistake.' he says. 'I'm not Daniel. I'm Tom. The date isn't for me. The person who put the note into the box was my son.'

With that, a young boy walks out looking a bit shell-shocked, to be honest. 'How do you mean your son put the note in the box? I sent emails confirming everything and checking it was all OK,'

'Yes, and you sent them to him, but he's seven, so he doesn't know what a date is. He's seen it mentioned on some tv programme. I didn't know anything about it until this morning. He asked me to take him to the centre for his date with a lady.'

This is a bloody disaster. I look at Belinda, smiling to herself as she waits to join her man at the table. Except her 'man' isn't a man, he's a young boy.'

'But I asked his age,' I say.

'No, you didn't. He showed me all the emails this morning. You double-checked that he wasn't over 40, and he confirmed that he wasn't.'

Shit.

575

Daniel walks over and stands next to Belinda, who looks hellishly confused by the sudden arrival of a young boy. Meanwhile, the photographers start to take pictures.

'Are you single?' I ask Daniel's father.

'No, I am not; I'm married.'

'Are you happily married, though?' I try.

'Yes, thank you.'

'You wouldn't fancy a date with a lovely lady?'

'No, I most definitely wouldn't.'

Damn. OK. I need to act.

'Daniel, would you like a free Christmas tree? One just like David Beckham's?' I say to the boy. Daniel nods, so I move him away from the date area, signalling for his father to follow us. I lead them over to where the Christmas trees are sold and tell the guys there to give him any tree he wants. Then I shake hands with his father and apologise for the confusion.

Belinda is now looking very worried. Oh, God. The poor woman's got enough on her hands with her mum's dodgy boyfriend fancying her. The last thing she needs is to be romantically linked with a seven-year-old and then have it blasted all over the press.

'Are you OK?' asks Ted. 'You look worried.'

'Oh my God, you have to help me. I'm going to ask a massive favour.'

'Sure, go ahead,' he says. 'Ask me anything.'

'Will you please pretend you're the one who's on the date with Belinda and have lunch for the photographers?'

'What?'

'Pretend to be her date. Unfortunately, the real date turned out to be a seven-year-old, and I don't know what to do.'

'A seven-year-old?' says Belinda, joining the conversation.

'I'm sorry,' I say. 'I promise to make it up to you.'

'Come on,' says Ted, grabbing a rose from the pagoda, presenting it to her and walking her towards the table and chairs. 'Let's have a nice lunch, and we can both go and beat up Mary afterwards.'

'Sorry for all the confusion, ladies and gentlemen,' I announce as the two of them take their seats. 'I'd like to introduce you to Ted and Belinda, who are on the Christmas blind date today. They're available for any interviews or questions; then I think we should leave them alone to enjoy their date.'

There are a few questions that Ted battles through before the couple are allowed to sit and enjoy their food, a rather lovely spread from the local restaurant.

Once they are seated, and Juan is serving them, I back away from the scene, drop my head into my hands and wonder how I have managed to get this so bloody wrong. I should have rung the guy and checked him out properly, but all the distractions of Beckham and Lapland...I didn't do the work on this that I should have and I'm cross with myself. So now I'm forced to sit here hoping no one notices that my boyfriend is on a date with Belinda. When I think things can't get any worse, there's a tap on my shoulder.

'Excuse me, do I know you?' asks a familiar-looking man.

'I'm not sure. I work in the centre here. Perhaps you have seen me walking around?'

It's bound to be a David Beckham fan wanting to hear more about his idol, but I can't face any of that right now.

'No, I know where I saw you. You're the lady who walked up to our car last week and lay across the bonnet just as I was trying to leave the centre.'

'What?' says Keith. I hadn't realised he was standing right next to me.

'Oh, right. Yes. Ah, I'm glad you brought that up because that was a complete misunderstanding. I got you mixed up with someone else. Can you believe it? Many apologies.'

'It was strange. You just lay there pouting at me,' said the man, warming to his theme. 'I couldn't work out what was going on. But, really - it was the strangest situation, wasn't it, Emma?'

The woman with him nods. 'We thought you were dead at one point because you didn't move. Our son, Jacob, was terrified.'

'Yes, well - that's terrible. So sorry. Have you got everything you want in the centre today? Can anyone help you with anything?'

'No, we're fine,' says the man, and Keith looks at me quizzically while the two of them walk off.

'I hope you know what you're doing,' he says.

'Yes, of course, I do. The date is going well.'

'You think so? That's your boyfriend up there having lunch with her. I don't know what is happening.'

REMOTE-CONTROLS, CUKOO CLOCKS AND MADNESS

21st December

'Where are you going now? I thought we might have a lie-in this morning before getting ourselves all packed for our trip to Lapland tomorrow,' says Ted.

'I won't be long. I'm just heading into the office to empty the *Post Box of*

Wishes and Dreams to see whether there's anything that needs actioning because I won't be able to do anything for the next few days while we're away, and then by the time we get back from our lovely trip, it will be Christmas Eve. So if there's something in there that needs dealing with, I should go and deal with it now.'

'OK,' says Ted. 'But everything you seem to 'deal with' from that bloody post box brings trouble. So be careful, OK? Don't get yourself arrested or beaten up trying to look after people, and particularly don't drag me into any more of your plans.'

'OK, I promise,' I say.

'And don't be long.'

'I'll be as quick as I can. I think Juan will come with me and help me move some things around because Keith wants the Christmas trees to have a more prominent position in the shop for these final days before Christmas.'

'Juan can't move Christmas trees around; he can barely lift a bunch of flowers. So if there's heavy lifting to be done, I'd better come.'

Ted throws the duvet off and scratches his balls. He's a joy in the morning he is.

'There are guys in the shop who can move them. Honestly, there's no need to come unless you want to.'

I jump in the shower, get myself dressed in casual clothes and wander into the sitting room to see whether Juan is up yet.

He's sitting there on the sofa, painting his toenails a rather horrible shade of green...not a lovely emerald or soft turquoise, but a colour that makes him look like he's got gangrene.

'Why?' I say.

'I thought it would work well and look great with khaki trousers, but now I'm unsure.'

'No. Not great timing either - we're about to leave.'

Juan insists that it's OK: he'll wear flip-flops. It's freezing, but he doesn't seem put off by the idea of getting frostbite. And, anyway, don't toes that get frostbite to become gangrenous? He's short-circuited the whole thing by painting them the colour of gangrene in the first place.

'There's no point painting my nails if no one can see them, is there?' he says as he grabs flip-flops, shades and his man bag and sashays towards the door as if he's going to the beach.

We jump onto the bus and head for work. I'm pretty nervous about going in today after yesterday's fiasco, but I'm reasonably sure that Keith won't be there. By the time he sits me down and talks to me about it, I'll have been to Lapland and got the best PR possible for the gardening centre, so he'll have nothing but praise.

As we walk past Big Terry, who's moving the Christmas trees away from where they were placed yesterday, flanking the romantic meal, to a prominent position in the centre, I'm excited about everything again. This place does look great.

There's a big sign saying:

Want your tree designed like Beckham's? Take a look at this and talk to the staff about how you can copy it at home.

The date may have been far from perfect yesterday, but we just about got away with it, and I'm sure the photos will look good and highlight the merchandise for sale in the store, and I did manage to decorate Beckham's tree, so it hasn't all been bad. And - of course - I'm taking the lovely Oliver to Lapland tomorrow. So it's been a Christmas to remember.

'Juan - do you mind just going over to the post box and taking out the letters in it,' I say, as I help put the decorations back onto the trees, they've moved them around so clumsily that half the Rick Astleys have tumbled off.

'If there are too many letters to carry, there's a carrier bag in my handbag.'

Juan goes to the post box while I reassemble the decorations.

'One bag enough?' I ask him as he returns.

'Err...yes,' he says. 'There's only one letter in there.'

'What? I thought there would be loads yesterday after the date. I expected it to be full to bursting.'

'Yeah, perhaps it will be next week?' he suggests.

'Next week is too late. The Post Box comes down on Christmas Eve.'

Juan hands me the solitary letter from a lady called Agnes, who is writing to the good people of Foster's garden centre to thank them for making it so Christmassy and lovely every year. She says it's a real treat for her to see how full of Christmas spirit the shop is. 'It's been the best place to go at Christmas,' she writes.

Ah, that's lovely. I feel genuinely pleased that we can bring such joy and happiness into the lives of our customers. I think it's an important thing to do. She says she has a present that she would like to give to the person responsible for making the store look so special. And she urges whoever it is to come to the house that evening to receive it.

'Oh God, I'm not going to any more customers' houses,' says Juan.

'Not on your life. Not after stick-gate. That was terrible. Let's keep right away from the customers' homes.'

'I don't know. I think it might be nice to pop round.'

'Have you forgotten that last time we did that, we ended up in the back of a police car? Just write a kind letter to them thanking them, but tell them we don't accept presents at Christmas.'

'You speak for yourself,' I tell Juan. 'I'm all about receiving presents at Christmas. So let's meet the customer, be nice to her, and graciously accept the present. After all, it's what she wants to do.'

'I guess,' says Juan. 'But you got to be a bit careful about these people. There are some right nutters out there. And I bet among the nuttiest are the people who contact the staff of the local gardening centre and invite them around for a 'present'.

'She lives about five minutes from my flat. Why don't we pop around there later? I'll feel better if we respond to as many letter writers as possible.'

'OK, it's your shout. But I'm not coming.'

'What do you mean you're not coming? You're my little partner in crime.'

'Yeah, exactly. That's why I'm not coming. See if Ted wants to go.'

'Oh yeah, Ted's going to want to come and knock on some woman's door.'

'He won't want to, and neither do I.'

At 7 pm that evening, Juan and I head towards the house belonging to the lady who put the letter into the post-box. He didn't take much convincing, as I knew he wouldn't. I think he secretly likes all the adventures I take him on.

He makes me lead the way, so I stride to the front door and knock gently. It says in the letter that her name is Agnes, but she likes to be called Mrs A.B. Walters. I hate to call people Mr or Mrs; it reminds me too much of school. But I don't want to upset her, so when she opens the door, I am reduced to calling her, Mrs Walters. I explain to her that I am in charge of Christmas at the gardening centre and I just wanted to thank her very much for her note, and how kind I thought it was of her to take the trouble to write in.

THE MARY BROWN BOOKS

'Oh, do come in. I've got some cookies here. Have some cookies.'

'They could be poisoned. This house is weird,' says Juan, who is hiding behind me the whole time. From over my shoulder, I see him scanning the place like he's my security detail or something. We're invited to sit down and told to eat some cookies. Not offered them, but told to eat them. I nibble nervously on the edge of one while Juan's action-man eyes scan the place.

The thing is, the cookies are delicious. They are lovely. Any latent fears about my safety are swept away by the sweet taste of delicious, crumbly biscuit.

'This is for you,' says Mrs Walters, smiling in quite an odd way. She must be around 60, but she could be much younger. It's hard to tell. She's wearing an old-fashioned apron, and her house looks like it's from the 1960s, mainly brown and with very retro furniture. Quite awful.

I sit there, wondering what is 'for me' because she hasn't handed me anything. Then she rushes out of the front room and into the kitchen, where I hear rustling paper.

Juan and I stare at the big old television while we wait. I notice there are cuckoo clocks everywhere. I mean *everywhere*. How bizarre is that? It's quarter to six, and I know we have to get out of the place before 6 pm because it'll be mayhem when they all start bursting out of their little wooden houses and cuckooing.

Mrs W is suddenly back in the room. She moves like a wild animal sneaking up on its prey, and she hands me a parcel wrapped so badly that it looks as if a pet terrier did it. I take it and smile.

'Thanks very much,' I say.

I am about to open it as her husband walks in through the door.

'Oh my my, we have visitors. Who do we have here then?' he asks. 'We weren't expecting visitors. You've given them my favourite biscuits as well.'

'My name is Mary, I work for Foster's gardening centre, and your wife sent a kind letter thanking us for how we decorated the garden centre at Christmas. I just came to wish her a Merry Christmas.'

I look at Mrs Walters; she's gone scarlet and is mouthing something to me behind her husband's back. When he goes into the porch to hang up his raincoat, she darts over to me and tells me to hide the present. 'Hide the present quickly. HIDE IT,' she shrieks. 'Don't let him see it.'

I push the present into my handbag. Juan glares at me as if to say - *we all knew this would happen. I told you, they're mad.*

When her husband comes back into the room, he looks at us as if he's surprised we're still there.

'Well, we must be off,' I say. 'Merry Christmas to you both.'

'Merry Christmas,' says Mrs M. 'From Malcolm and me.'

We walk outside, and she closes the door behind us.

'That was odd. Seriously, there is something wrong there. I don't know what, but something was weird. Do you think she's mental or something?'

'I don't know,' I say. 'She told us to come round, but her husband didn't want us there.'

'Perhaps it was a cry for help?' suggests Juan. 'Look at what the present is.'

I pull the bundle of scrunched-up paper out of my handbag and take the wrapping paper off. Inside is some sort of remote control.

'What on earth is that for?'

'I don't know. It doesn't look new. It looks like any normal household remote control,' says Juan, as he leans over and presses a few buttons to see what happens. As he presses, there's a loud shout from Malcolm on the sofa in the sitting room.

'Stop it,' he says.

I press another button, and he shouts again.

'It's a remote control to work, Malcolm,' says Juan. Through the window, we see Mrs Walters come in from the kitchen.

'Why does this TV keep going on and off?' he says.

'Oh fuck. It's their tv remote control,' says Juan, rather too loudly. Mr Walters looks through the window and spots us both standing there just as I press the button again, and the TV volume raises until it's bellowing out.

'Turn it down,' says Juan, but I can't remember which button I pressed, and we're in semi-darkness, so I can't see anything.

Malcolm comes out of his house and stands there with his arms folded. 'What on earth are you doing?' he shouts over the sound of people bellowing on his television. 'Why are you standing there with our remote control, pressing all the different channels and moving the volume up and down?'

'I don't know,' I say because I can see his wife in the background, and she shakes her head viciously, indicating that she doesn't want us to talk to him.

'Is this your idea of fun?' he barks at Juan. 'You: the man with the flip flops and the green toes. Why are your toes green?'

'Oh, I painted them.'

'Did you steal our remote control so you could ruin my evening's television watching?'

'No,' says Juan, giving me a look of pure helplessness.

'Well, what are you doing with it then?'

Agatha is apoplectic now, jumping around behind him, begging us not to reveal that she gave it to us as a Christmas present.

'I don't know what's going on here. I have a good mind to call the police,' he says.

'Oh no. Not the police. Not again,' says Juan, which does nothing to make us look like the innocent party.

'I'm sorry. There's been a misunderstanding. Here's your remote control. I'm very sorry,' I say, handing it over.

He's about to bark something back at us when the neighbour pops her head out of her door and shouts to Malcolm to please turn the television down.

'I'm sorry, Emma,' he says. 'These two nutters from the garden centre stole our remote control.'

The lady comes out of her house and walks over to us. Bugger. I recognise her.

'I know you,' she says. 'You work at the gardening centre, and you threw yourself across my husband's car when we were driving away, and you lay there for about 10 minutes, refusing to move.'

'Right, I'm ringing the police,' says Malcolm, but his voice is drowned out by an almighty clatter as all of the cuckoo clocks burst into life and deliver their sounds. The noise is deafening, with the tv blaring out and cuckoo clocks singing.

'Time to go,' I say to Juan, and the two of us run like the wind.

MARTII THE VIKING & A QUESTION FROM TED

Once we are back at my flat, we race into the sitting room and try to explain everything to Ted.

'And there were cookies, and the house was odd, then she gave us their remote control, and the volume was too loud, and the cuckoo clocks went off, and the neighbour turned out to be this woman whose car I had laid on, so we ran, we ran like the wind, but no police were called this time.'

'I don't understand any of that, Mary, but I'm happy the police weren't called. Now, shouldn't you go and pack for our trip to Lapland tomorrow? And have you filled in all those forms they sent you, the ones asking for shoe sizes and things?'

'Oh yes,' I say as I fill them in. I'd completely forgotten all about them.

It takes me about 10 minutes to pack and about two hours to find my passport; then I fall into bed. Being in charge of Christmas has been quite hard. It's a lot of responsibility, you know. I don't know how Father Christmas copes. No wonder he drinks so much.

22ND DECEMBER

'Do you ever think to yourself, *how on earth did I get here?*' asks Ted as the taxi driver pulls up outside Gatwick airport.

'No, never. I think it's perfectly natural to be on a trip to Lapland with a one-legged boy to meet Father Christmas, all organised by David Beckham.'

Ted laughs and takes the bags out of the boot. 'I don't know how you manage it, Mary Brown, but I'm happy you do.'

So, we're off. Brian and Oliver are travelling separately because they're flying from Scotland, where Oliver has been having treatment, and we'll meet up with them tomorrow morning. For now, it's just Ted and me - off to a winter wonderland of pink skies, reindeer sledges, frosty fir trees, steaming hot chocolate and twinkling lights. And snow. Snow everywhere. I've been looking at Lapland videos online; it's a snow-filled fantasy. We are staying in the capital - Rovaniemi - which is perched on the edge of the Arctic Circle. Most importantly, it's the official home of Father Christmas.

I plan to take loads of photographs and send postcards to everyone I know.

When we arrive in Lapland, it's freezing cold. I realise that shouldn't come as a surprise to me: of course, it's freezing. But I'm talking about a whole new level of cold here. So cold that I'm wondering just how much wear I'm going to get out of the strappy sandals that I insisted on bringing, even though Ted said there was no point in bringing them because I wouldn't get any wear out of them. Damn it. I hate it when he's right.

I wrap my scarf around my neck, push my hands deep into my pockets and look around me. I can't see a great deal… it's dark and bitterly cold, even though it's only 3 pm. I was hoping to take in all the wondrous sights while driving along to Santa Claus Holiday Village, but despite peering out of the window like a small child, I can't see anything.

'You are here,' says the taxi driver. 'In the home of Father Christmas.'

'Thank you,' we both say as we clamber out of the warm car and move to collect our luggage from the boot.

'We will take care of that,' says a sizeable blonde man with a huge beard. He looks like a Viking. He's beautiful. He's an enormous, handsome Viking. Happy Days!

I see Ted standing up extra tall and puffing out his chest.

'I could look like that if I dyed my hair,' he says.

'Of course, you could, dear.' I don't add that he'd also need to grow a few inches and spend the rest of his life in the gym.

Viking man tells us that his name is Martii. 'You have come on the shortest day of the year, which makes it a special day,' he says. 'But also, quite a cold and dark day. We have ski suits here for you to wear, to keep you warm.' A lady steps forward with ski suits. She must be about 20, tall, blonde and fabulous.

'That's more like it,' says Ted.

'Maybe come in here to change?' she says, leading us into the hotel reception and a room just off the main lobby. I try on the ski suit hoping to God that it fits. I find it so embarrassing when things don't fit me. I filled in that form last night and said we both needed extra large sizes. Happily, the Laplandish extra-large is big, so for the first time in my life, I'm able to put on clothes which say they are extra-large and turn out to be extra-large. If anything, mine are a bit too big. And you won't find me saying that very often.

We walk back into the lobby, and Viking Man dazzles us with loads of interesting facts about the area, telling us that the line of the Arctic Circle runs right through the middle of the village. 'You can see it marked with a row of lanterns and blue lights,' he says in that lyrical, sing-song accent that makes me want to smile.

'Now I will take you on a reindeer sleigh ride so you can see some of it for yourselves.'

'Oh great,' I say, smiling warmly at Viking man. 'That would be lovely, thank you.'

'My very greatest pleasure.'

'I bet he takes steroids.' says Ted.

I jump onto Martii's sleigh (not a euphemism, sadly), and he takes us along the Forest Path, through fir trees piled up with snow as Ted and I snuggle up between blankets and reindeer hides. It's a wonderful, magical trip, and I want it to go on and on. We don't see anyone else in the snow as we skate along so gracefully that I feel like the sleigh might lift into the air and glide through the late afternoon sky. Some of the journey takes us through extensive forests of imposing trees; some skeletal, boughs hung with snow, others - fir trees, I think - dressed for the cold, displaying their pine needles like a peacock exposing its feathers.

Martii tells us to come back later that evening because water droplets will have crystallised on the branches creating magical Arctic art. He tells us that the ice looks like 'ladies' fingers.'

'You must see the sparkling icicles,' he says, making it all sound so poetic.

'And here is house,' says Martii, pointing to a small cottage which looks like something out of a fairy tale. There's an elaborate wreath on the door, and you can see the lights from the Christmas tree sparkling and welcoming through the windows.

'All your luggage is inside,' says Martii.

'Wow, thank you so much.'

Martii helps me off the sleigh and puts his hand out to help Ted.

'I'm OK, mate. Don't need any help, thanks,' says my boyfriend defensively.

'Tonight, you may come to see the northern lights with me after Lappish food is delivered to your door. OK?'

'Oh yes, I'd love that,' I say while Ted shrugs and says he's heard the northern lights aren't that special.

'Will you behave, Ted?' I say as we walk down the little path to our home for the next few days. 'Just because you don't like Viking man, doesn't mean you can spoil the whole trip.'

'Sorry, but he's a bit much. Chucking compliments around and driving a bloody reindeer sleigh.'

'You might need to get into the spirit of the thing a bit more,' I say. 'If you think he's too much, I don't know what you're going to make of grown men and women dressed as elves and Santa Claus tomorrow.'

'As long as they're not all 8' tall and with muscles bursting out of their shirts, I'll be OK. Let's go and unpack.'

We've put away all our clothes and adjusted to our tiny home when there's a gentle knock at the door, and an old man with a long white beard hands us a box of food.

'We have put extra pancake,' says the man. 'Any more food needed, call reception, and I'll be back.'

'Thank you very much. That's very kind,' says Ted.

Inside the box, there's a delicious soup with fresh salmon, a kind of pancake to go with the soup and some cookies with hot tea for dessert. We've just finished when there's another knock at the door.

'Blimey, we don't get this many visitors at home,' says Ted, trundling off to answer it.

It's Viking Man. He has arrived to take us to see the northern lights.

'We will go now to try to see the lights. I can make no guarantees about this, though,' Martii insists. 'It is a clear night, but you never know whether you will see them. We will go, but I cannot promise.'

'We understand,' I say, while Ted shrugs. He seems to go quiet and sulky whenever Martii is around.

'The Northern Lights are also known as Aurora Borealis,' Viking man continues, and they are pretty spectacularly beautiful. Very much like your girlfriend.'

I giggle like a schoolgirl at this. A handsome Viking who tells you you're spectacularly beautiful. What more could a girl want?

Ted drops his head into his hands.

It takes a while before we see anything. I mean, it feels like we drive, walk and wait for ages but then a faint grey-green stripe becomes visible in the sky.

'Watch it, watch it,' says Martii.

The stripe soon becomes a vivid shot of green; then, in no time, the sky looks like it's on fire, lit by green-purple flames. Green clouds of light begin to dance above us and smudge outwards, so they're all around us. I don't think I've ever seen anything quite so beautiful. It's entrancing; it makes you feel like you're being drawn into this magic artwork in the sky.

I stare up at it, mesmerised.

'Are you happy?' asks Ted, as we stand, wrapped around each other, watching the magnificent lights swirl around us.

'So happy. I'm the luckiest girl alive,' I say.

'No, I'm the lucky one,' says Ted. 'Look, there's something I want to ask you.'

'Sure.' I'm talking to Ted, but my eyes are fixed on the skies above us. When I eventually glance in his direction, he looks very serious.

'What is it? Is everything OK?'

'Mary - everything's perfect. I love you.'

'Oh, Ted. I love you too.'

'I'd like us to take things to the next step.'

'How do you mean?'

'I think we should move in together.'

'Really? Oh my God, I'd love that.'

'If we both get rid of our flats, we can buy a place that's our own.'

'Oh wow. Wow. Ted, I'd love that so much.'

'So would I,' he says. 'I can't think of anything better, to be honest. I want to be with you forever and ever.'

'Oh, me too, Ted. Me too.'

So here I am: standing in the snow with the northern lights dancing in the skies above me, as a large Viking claps and cheers at the news. I've thought a lot about Ted and I moving in together, but I never envisaged it being like this.

'Shall I take you back now,' says Martii. 'You have celebrating to do. Maybe you like to celebrate in bed?'

'Yes, it's getting late,' I say, ignoring his bed comment. The sky's colours fade away, but it's been incredible. The whole thing was surreal, as if great artists were floating through the sky, throwing paints around and drawing magnificent streaks of colour above us.

'This has been great,' I say to Martii. 'Thank you so much.'

'No problem. I enjoy showing you the lights. Now, I will enjoy seeing you in the morning. So enjoy your rumpy-pumpy celebrations.'

Oh, good God. These guys don't mince their words. Do they?

FATHER CHRISTMAS TIME

23rd December

'I'm so excited to meet Oliver,' I say to Ted when we wake up, all snuggled up in our cosy bed.

'It's a shame he's only coming for two days, though,' says Ted. 'I'd have thought they would have come early yesterday morning.'

'He's not well. His dad said that two days was the most he wanted to take him away for.'

'Yeah, I guess he can't be too far from his doctors. It must be tough. I do feel for him.'

'I know I can't imagine how it must feel. Can you picture having this lovely little boy who means the world to you but is in so much pain, and you can't do anything to help him.'

'I'm sure he looks after him well.'

'Yes, I'm sure he does, and I know Brian is at the hospital all the time with him and struggles to hold down his job because he needs to spend so much like with Oliver, but you can't take the pain away from him. That must be heartbreaking.'

'Where's Oliver's mum?'

'She died,' I say, trying not to cry, so Brian is dealing with this awful situation all alone. No mum to help share the worries and the joys. And how will he ever meet a partner if he can't leave Oliver alone? It must be so hard.'

'Come on now, Mary. Don't cry. We'll ensure he has the best time possible while he's here. Now, shall we get up?'

I nod because I'm scared to speak in case I start crying. Finally, Ted gets out of bed and shuffles off to the shower.

'We're meeting Oliver and Brian at 10 am at the main hotel so that they can get their ski suits.'

'So, how do we get there?' he shouts from the shower.

'I think Viking man is coming to pick us up and take us over there.'

'Oh, joy,' says Ted. 'Bloody wonderful…' Then his voice is drowned out by the water cascading down in the shower room.

By 9.30, Ted and I are showered, dressed in our padded ski suits, bobble hats and gloves at the ready, waiting by our cottage door. But it's not Viking man who turns up to take us out for the day; it's an older man. He looks like a Viking, too, to be honest, but nowhere near as big, hunky and handsome as yesterday's Nordic delight.

'I bet Martii didn't want to come,' says Ted. 'Now he knows we're going to move in together, and he's got no chance with you.'

'Oh, Ted. Honestly, you are so ridiculous. As if a man like that wants anything to do with me anyway.'

'He said you were spectacularly beautiful. And he's right. Then he said we were going to have rumpy-pumpy. He was right about that, too. But he shouldn't have said it.'

'He was being friendly. It's his job to make us feel good.'

'Well, he didn't make me feel very good when flirting with you.'

'Honestly, Ted, you are crackers sometimes.'

We head off to the hotel, and as soon as we arrive and I step off the snowmobile, I see Oliver. He looks just like his photo: incredibly pretty, with big blue eyes and this lovely pale blonde hair sticking out from beneath his furry hat.

'Hello, I'm Mary,' I say, stomping over to him in my big ski boots and waving like a lunatic. 'It's so lovely to meet you.'

His dad, Brian, has a captivating smile, like his son. He is hand-

THE MARY BROWN BOOKS

some in a scruffy way - unshaven and tired-looking with his hair all over the place. But I guess he's got his work cut out with this little one, so, understandably, he's not groomed to within an inch of his life.

I give Oliver a big hug. And then wonder whether I should have done that. Is he unstable? Is he unsteady on his feet? He doesn't seem to be. He smiles and looks at me like he's not quite sure who I am. Brian shakes my hand and tells me he cannot begin to thank me enough for organising everything.

'Really, it's no problem,' I tell him.

'We saw lovely dogs, didn't we, dad?' says Oliver.

'We did, son,' replies Brian.

'We went on a husky ride when we arrived yesterday evening. It was all a bit terrifying. But good fun.'

'Oh my god, that sounds amazing. I'm so glad you got to do that. We had a reindeer ride, which was lovely, but probably not quite as adrenaline-surging as the Husky ride.'

'We went faster than the wind,' says Oliver, swinging his arms from side to side to show me the speed at which they travelled. And you know who we're going to meet now, don't you?'

'Well, I've heard a rumour, but I'm not sure whether it's true,' I say

'We're seeing Father Christmas,' whispers Oliver conspiratorially. 'In his Grotto, which is where he lives. Are you coming as well?'

'I am coming, and I'm looking forward to it. I hope you've been good, so you get lots of presents.'

'I'm always good,' says Oliver. 'The only time I'm not good is when I'm bad.'

We all laugh at this. Oliver is a lovely kid. I'm so glad I could do this for him. He seems to be having the time of his life.

We climb onto the snowmobile that is taking us over to Santa's Grotto, and I sit next to Oliver while Ted and Brian take the seats behind us. Oliver is charming company. He even tells me about his leg and how he only has one and has to wear a 'falsie'.

'I'll show you later if you like, but I can't show you now because it's in my ski suit tucked into my boot, and I can't get to it.'

'That's okay. I think you should keep your ski suit tucked in to keep you nice and warm.'

'You've got to keep nice and warm when it's snowing and cold like this, haven't you?'

'Oh, you have,' I confirm. 'I nearly forgot to bring my hat. My head would have been icy, wouldn't it?'

Oliver laughs and tells me he would have lent me his hat if I'd forgotten mine. I give him a warm hug before we fall into a relatively peaceful, comfortable silence, looking out at the colossal fir trees painted thickly with snow. Before long, we start to see the signs telling us we're approaching Santa's grotto. I hear Ted and Brian chatting companionably behind us as we zoom along. Lovely Ted is asking him how he copes and how difficult it must be to do this alone.

I hear Brian telling him that it's hard but worth it. He says he'd love to meet someone and have a relationship, but he doesn't see how it would be possible.

'I'd have to meet an exceptional woman who would be kind and thoughtful enough to give me the space to spend time with Oliver when I need to. I don't think it will happen while Ollie is so young.'

I hear the words without thinking, but then a thought bursts into my mind.

And you know what that thought is: Belinda. How great would that be?

Belinda is kind and thoughtful and would be perfect for Brian.

Quite how I'm going to bring this subject up with him, and ask him whether I can make an introduction, is something I can't quite get my head around at the moment, but bring it up I must because this, Ladies and Gentlemen, might be the kindest thing I could do for this man and his lovely son.

We arrive at Santa's grotto and are greeted by elves who put down the toys they are making in the toy factory and wave at us like long-lost friends before they rush to help us off the sleigh.

If they're surprised to discover only one child on the sleigh carrying four people, they manage to hide it and treat us all to a charming welcome. The scene is beautiful as we watch dancers,

THE MARY BROWN BOOKS

singers, and elves frolicking in the snow. This is a wonderful place for children, but it feels odd for Ted and me to go in and meet Santa.

'I think I might be too big to sit on Santa's lap,' I say.

'And I'm too big,' says Ted.

'I'm not too big,' says Oliver quickly.

'No, you're the perfect size. Why don't we let you go in to see him, and we'll wait outside and see you afterwards.'

'OK,' says Oliver. 'I will show you all of my toys when I come out.'

'Yes, please. I'm looking forward to seeing them,' I say.

Once the two of them have trundled off, Ted turns to me: 'Fancy some of that gluhwein over there?'

There's a stall on the far side, dishing out a rather pungent-smelling hot alcoholic drink. It feels like the best thing we could do for ourselves at 11 am, so we stroll over, sit on the bench and sip away. It's idyllic, snuggled up to Ted, being warmed by love and alcohol. We only have a couple each, but I soon feel quite drunk; in that hazy, nothing matters; life is wonderful sort of way.

'I sometimes forget how lucky I am, but right now, at this moment, I'm aware of how great my life is,' I tell Ted. He looks a little shocked at my serious tone, so I suggest he gets us some more gluhwein.

Three glasses are too much. I feel very wobbly. I know I'm smiling like an idiot and wobbling my head around because I always do that when I'm drunk, and I can see Ted smiling at me in his lovely, indulgent way.

It feels like we've only been there a short while when I hear a shout in the distance.

'Look, look...'

We both spin around.

'Look at these! I've got presents,' squeals Oliver. He is hugging the biggest teddy bear I've ever seen. His father carries a separate box with a train set in it - something that Oliver has always wanted.

'I'm so excited,' says Oliver. 'I can't wait to show my friends.'

'We're going down to the children's party now. Do you want to come?' asks Brian.

'Yeahhh…party!' I shout, staggering to my feet, but Ted guides me back into a seating position.

'I think we'll give the party a miss and go and get something to eat,' says Ted.

'I don't blame you,' says Brian, being led away by Oliver. 'Hopefully we'll see you later.'

DAVID BECKHAM & RICK ASTLEY

24th December

The following day, I have a terrible hangover.

'Why do I feel as if my life is coming to an end?' I ask Ted.

'I have no idea,' he responds. 'I don't suppose it would be the three glasses of gluhwein followed by wine followed by more gluhwein late last night.'

'Really?'

'Yep. You were a disgrace.'

'I'm so sorry we didn't have dinner with Brian and Oliver last night. Did we let them know that we wouldn't be joining them?'

''You mean you're sorry that you didn't have dinner with them? I went.'

'You what?'

'I met them for dinner, and very nice it was.'

'Where was I?'

'Crashed out, face down on the duvet, dribbling.'

'Nice. Well, as long as I wasn't embarrassing or anything.'

. . .

BERNICE BLOOM

WE FLY BACK to the UK later that afternoon. Oliver clutches his bear, and I clutch onto Ted. As long as I manage not to be sick on the flight, everything will be OK. When we land, I have one last surprise for Oliver: David Beckham will be at the airport to meet him. We've already established that he's a big David Beckham fan, so I'm hoping he'll be thrilled by the surprise.

Ted takes Oliver for a walk at the airport while I sit quietly with Brian. I'm unsure how to address this, but I'm determined to see whether he'd be responsive to a romantic introduction. 'Look', I say eventually. 'I'm sorry this is a bit embarrassing, but I've got this lovely friend who's single and dying to meet someone. Do you mind if I give her your number? You know, put the two of you in touch?'

'Gosh. Really? I'm not sure anyone would want to take on someone like me.'

'I think Belinda would love to take on someone like you. You're kind, fun and an incredible dad.'

'That's very kind of you,' he says. 'Tell me a bit about her.'

I put her name into Google to call up her picture on the company website. 'I can show you what she looks like,' I say, waiting for a picture to download. But the image is not of her at work, but of her on the fake date that went wrong.

'Oh, is that her? What does that say? *A magnificent date for two locals.* But isn't that Ted?'

'Yes, it's a rather long story. I won't bore you with the details, but - yes - that's her having lunch with my boyfriend.'

Brian looks unsure.

'Why would she be on a romantic date with Ted?'

'Don't worry about that - all a big misunderstanding. Just focus on the lady sitting there. Belinda is a sweet, lovely person. I think you'd like her a lot.'

'Okay. I'll give it a go,' says Brian, handing me my phone back. 'But please make sure that she's aware of my family situation. I'm not the easiest person to date.'

'Brilliant,' I say as we board the plane and prepare to head home for Christmas. 'I'll fix something up once we're back.'

I sit next to Ted on the flight home, and we spend much time discussing what sort of home we want.

'I want somewhere cottagey,' I say. 'You know - the whole roaring fire, little garden, pretty cottage thing. Let's look at some more houses when we get back. We could even go out and go round seeing what's on the market.

'Not tonight,' says Ted as the pilot announces that we're coming into land. 'I want you to do me a favour...don't make any plans for tonight. We've had a madly busy week, and we're visiting family tomorrow. It's Christmas Eve, and I'd like the two of us to be home together for once. Alone. OK?'

'Of course,' I say. 'That would be lovely.'

We arrive at Gatwick airport, and the four of us are taken aside and told there is someone to meet us. 'He's someone who really wants to meet Oliver,' says the airport official.

Oliver looks intrigued and Brian looks a little concerned; then, out walks David Beckham, causing Oliver to squeal like a puppy. Next, Ted squeals, and then Brian. I say, 'Hi David, how lovely to see you again', and - I swear to God - I feel like the coolest person ever to walk the earth.

David chats to Oliver and gives him piles of presents, including signed football shirts and tracksuits and some amazing computer games. I stand on the edge of it all, watching with pride and staring at David's bottom in what could be described as an inappropriate fashion.

As Oliver and David talk, my phone rings. I answer the call and hear Keith's dulcet tones on the other end. I assume he's calling to find out how the trip went, but he sounds like he's in a disco.

'Where on earth are you?' I say.

'I'm at work. Rick Astley's just turned up, and he's entertaining the crowds.'

'What?'

'Yes - he saw the Rick Astley decorations on the Christmas trees when the blind date feature was in the paper, and he came down to meet you. Hurry back.'

I look over at Ted, sitting there on his own, patiently waiting for me.

'Actually, I won't be back at the centre tonight. I'm going to head home now, but have a lovely Christmas, and please thank Rick for me, and get lots of pictures of him in front of the Rick Astley decorated tree, OK?'

'Are you serious?' says Keith. 'This is Rick Astley. He's about to sing *'Never Gonna Give You Up'*.'

'It sounds great, Keith. Have a lovely evening. I'll see you next year.'

I smile at Ted. 'Let's go,' I say. 'We've got a whole, wonderful future to plan.'

HOME SWEET HOME

❦

I'm going to be completely honest with you; the minute I put down the phone, I feel a wave of disappointment. I really like Rick Astley, and - obviously - *Never Gonna Give You Up* is my favourite Rick Astley song because it's the only one I know. Perhaps we should head down there and watch him perform after all.

'Ted, if you want to go to the centre to watch Rick Astley, just say, OK. I've told Keith that we won't be there, but I don't mind going if you really want to.'

'Nope. I've no interest in going anywhere near your work today,' says Ted. 'I'm excited about spending the evening with you and waking up tomorrow morning and going to mum and dad's.'

Yeah. Christ. This is where it gets complicated because – as you know – I still haven't told him that we are committed to spending Christmas with both sets of parents. I genuinely believe he should tell his mum that we can no longer go there; I can't possibly tell mine after the disaster of me announcing on This Morning that my mum was a drug pusher. She really will take it personally if I now announce that I'm not coming for Christmas or that Ted can't make Christmas.

The only alternative I can think of is to go to both sets of parents and have lunch with them all. Ted won't be all that delighted; I know

BERNICE BLOOM

he'd like to go to his parent's house properly. But I can't think how else we can handle this without offending.

Later that night, I'm at home with Ted, curled up on the sofa, having wrapped all the presents and feeling wonderful. Ted's watching the news while I laze rather sleepily, sipping my wine.

'You know what I think,' he says. 'I think I wouldn't have a square if I were a dictator.'

'What? A square?'

'Yes - like Red Square and Tiananmen Square...all the problems, uprisings and murders...they always happen in squares. You shouldn't have one. There you go - that's my tip for dictators.'

'Very good,' I say, drifting off to sleep. 'If I become a dictator, I'll bear that in mind. Oh - and - by the way - I've cocked up.'

'In what way?' asks Ted innocently.

'I have promised my mum that we will go for Christmas lunch with her tomorrow.'

'Whaaaat? Are you serious?' he asks. 'You've told your mum we'll be there when you know that I've told my mum that we'll be at hers.'

'Yep.'

'That's a disaster. I can't cancel, mum. She's been shopping and has bought everything already, and she did ask first.'

'Well, no, technically, I don't think she did. Mine did...and I said 'yes,' but when I arrived at yours, you were so excited about going to your mum's that I couldn't face telling you.'

'What are we going to do?' he says. 'I don't want us to spend Christmas apart. And I thought your dad didn't like meeting new people.'

'He doesn't, and he hates having anyone in the house. All he wants to do is watch programmes about Margaret Thatcher. Amazingly, he's said you can come over. I can't cancel. But - I have a plan.'

'Go on.'

'Well,' I say. 'My mum's lunch is at 1 pm, and yours is at 4 pm.'

'Two lunches?'

'Unless you can think of a better plan.'

'Is there ever a better plan than two lunches?'

CHRISTMAS MORNING

25th December

I wake up most mornings and think, 'when can I eat?' I open my eyes and scan the room, and perhaps kiss Ted good morning, but all I can think about is when I'm going to get something to eat. When will I taste hot buttered toast with lashings of peanut butter on top? Thick bread, thick butter, thick peanut butter...big bite. God, I can feel myself salivating at the thought of it.

Food is my overriding concern all the time. If I feel happy, I want to celebrate with food; if I feel sad, I want to fall into food and fill myself with it until I can't feel the pain anymore. The thing I want to do more than anything, all the time, is eat. On 364 days of the year, I am trying to moderate myself and control myself around food. I wake up every day determined to pace myself and not eat all the day's calories before 8 am. I try to leave meals as late as possible, so I don't have time to overeat.

But Christmas Day is the one day of the year when I don't have to do any of that because the day is free of the usual food timing restraints. You can eat what you like when you want - it's the law. No one can tell you off for having three sherbet dib-dabs and five jelly babies or having a bowl of custard before breakfast. It's all allowed.

No one will tell you that you are going to spoil your lunch. Nutty food combinations in unspeakable quantities are positively encouraged; you can delight in it... If you say, 'I'll have a plain boiled egg,' people will laugh, 'no, you won't - you'll have Baileys flavoured popcorn, and pop tarts dipped in marmite - it's Christmas. What's wrong with you?'

In some ways, you'd think this would be a living nightmare for someone like me with a food addiction, but it's not. It's really not. Once all the rules disappear, and I cannot beat myself up for breaking them, I feel much happier and more comfortable with myself. If I have honey ice cream and chips for breakfast, that's fine. On any other day, if I had honey ice cream and chips I would hate myself for it, and feel weighed down with guilt and disgust with myself, and it is those feelings of disgust that will push me headlong into food and cause me problems for days after my one bit of naughty behaviour occurred. It's the disgust that does for me; that's what causes me problems.

But not at Christmas. Oh no. It's 7.30 am on Christmas morning and I've eaten an entire box of After Eights. I mean - how rebellious is that? It's not even after eight in the morning, let alone after eight in the evening, and all that is left of the previously full box are scattered wrappers and the pungent aroma of fresh mint. I wander into the kitchen and see the bottle of ginger wine on the side. 'Oooo...' I think, but - no - even I have some standards. Gurgling ginger wine at the crack of dawn is the route to insanity.

'What are you doing up and wandering around instead of being tucked up in bed next to me?' says Ted, walking into my tiny kitchen behind me and wrapping his hands around my waist.

'Mmmm...you smell nice,' he says. 'What is that? Have you just cleaned your teeth?

'It's After Eights,' I reply proudly. See - no shame, no embarrassment, no disgust, no lying to hide my ridiculous eating habits - I tell Ted quietly and confidently and he doesn't bat an eyelid. 'Excellent start to the day,' he says. 'That ginger wine looks nice.'

'I thought that, but that's a bad idea. We'll be fast asleep by 10 am if we get started on that, and we've got two lunches to go to today.'

'OK, well, why don't I just give you this instead,' he says, handing me an envelope. 'It's a book token...I didn't know what else to get you.'

I try to hide the feeling of disappointment welling up inside me. A book token?

'How nice,' I say, gingerly opening the envelope. I don't want any bloody books. I wonder whether I can swap it for cash. Is that ungrateful?

I pull out the paper inside, but it doesn't say anything about books. It's a ticket to Greece for the holiday of a lifetime. I look at Ted open-mouthed...a holiday? Not books?

'Of course, it's not books,' he says. 'I thought it would be nice if we went away on holiday.'

'Oh my God, oh my God, oh my God. Best. Present. Ever,' I squeal. 'This is just amazing.'

I feel bad now that I only got him a jumper and some boxer shorts.

11.30 AM:

Santa hat? Check.

A massive pile of presents? Check.

A bottle of really strange, green alcohol that I won in a tombola and think mum might like? Check

'Come on then, let's go,' I say to Ted, knowing that by now, mum will be peering out of the window, desperate for us to arrive.

'Coming,' says Ted, walking through the flat with a small bundle of presents.

'What are they for?'

'Well - I might have an extra one or two for you, and I've got presents for your mum and dad - nothing much, just little thank-you gifts for inviting me to join them for lunch.'

Bugger.

I have no extra presents for Ted, and it never even occurred to me to bring gifts for his parents. I'm bloody useless! And I'm Mary Christmas...I'm supposed to be in charge of Christmas.

'Hang on. Hang on,' I say.

I have presents under the bed. I've just remembered.

'Be back in a sec,' I say to Ted, tearing past him and reaching under the mattress, past the dozens of shoes that I never wear because they are too tight or too high (but they look lovely, so I'm not throwing them away).

There!

Nestling between some candyfloss pink wedges and a pair of way-too-small gold sparkly trainers that no one over four should wear, are three little presents. I can't even remember what's in them...they've been here since last Christmas. It's probably chocolates or a book or some other generic present. Enough to make it look like I've made an effort without looking like I've gone over the top. I pull them out, drop them into a carrier bag and rush out to join Ted.

'Let's go!' I say.

We squeeze into Ted's car and head off. Neither of us can get the seat belts around us, but we do our customary thing of trying to do it, then shrugging at one another in despair. I'm looking forward to the day I can get it around me; it will feel like a tremendous achievement.

Ted heads off with us both sitting there, wilfully breaking the law as we ease through Cobham streets, heading for mum's house in Esher. Ted's quiet on the journey; I can tell he's feeling nervous. He hasn't met my mum and dad before, and I imagine that meeting them for the first time on Christmas Day must make it feel all the more daunting.

'Just here on the left,' I say as Ted swings the car into a small space. I look up and can see the curtains flicker a little. I knew it.

Mum's been looking out of the window all morning, waiting for us to arrive. I dread telling her that we have to leave at 3.30 pm (we're going to Ted's mum's for Christmas lunch at 4 pm, but I'm not telling my mum that, so please don't mention it).

'I bet they won't like me,' says Ted sulkily. 'They'll probably think you can do much better than me...and they'd be right. You're so lovely; you could have anyone.'

'Stop it, Ted. That's not true; I couldn't have anyone else. I'm desperate. That's why I'm with you.'

'Oh great, thanks very much.'

'I'm joking, Ted. For goodness sake. You know I'm joking; I love you; I think the world of you.'

Ted hugs me. 'Sorry for being sensitive, but it matters to me that I make a good impression on your mum and dad.'

'I know. And I love you even more for that,' I say. 'Don't expect too much communication from my dad. He's a bit of a nightmare.'

'Mine too,' says Ted. 'Mine too.'

Mum answers the door and throws her arms around me, hugging me closely. 'Happy Christmas, darling girl,' she says, grinning from ear to ear. 'A very merry Christmas.'

'This is Ted,' I say, indicating him, standing nervously by my side, clutching the mountain of presents.

'Hello, lovely to meet you,' says mum. 'Please come in.'

Ted follows me into our hallway, where the smells of Christmas lunch hang alluringly in the air.

'Smells delicious,' he says, and mum smiles warmly. 'Thank you.'

It's not all quite so cordial when we meet my dad. He looks Ted up and down and says: 'Blimey, Mary. You managed to find a bloke who's fatter than you.'

'Indeed,' says Ted, apparently unfazed by dad's rudeness. 'Nice to meet you, sir.'

He then turns to my mum and asks: 'Is there anything I can do to help?'

'Honestly, no - it's fine. Everything is under control,' says mum.

'I'm quite handy with a carving knife,' he says. 'So - please say if I can do anything.'

'Of course,' says mum demurely. 'Thank you, Ted.'

And I swear, in that minute, I fall more hopelessly in love with Ted than I've ever fallen in love with anyone before. I think mum does, too. She kind of swoons and has to hold on to steady herself. Well, it's either a swoon, or she's been at the wine already; hard to tell for sure.

'Ted, please, take a seat,' she says, indicating the furniture in front of us. Dad is in his favourite armchair, scowling at us; there is the small two-seater sofa and the other armchair - old and rundown but madly comfy. Ted wisely chooses the armchair. He sits down heavily and smiles at my mum.

'A little Christmas drink?'

'Please,' he says.

'Ooooo...look what I've got,' I interject, handing her the bottle of bright green liquid that I'd brought with me.

'Great,' she says, unconvinced by the lurid colour of the drink. But mum's unfailingly polite and wouldn't want to dismiss the gift, so minutes later, she reappears with several glasses of the stuff to hand out. Oh dear, this wasn't the plan. The last thing I wanted was to drink it; I hoped to get rid of it here so mum would have it sitting in her kitchen rather than mine.

'Well,' says mum, blinking furiously after taking a swig. 'Is this what the young people are drinking these days?'

'I thought it might be nice to try something new,' I say, taking a swig and stepping backwards in alarm. It sure has a hell of a bite; I feel like a tiger has gnawed my throat.

'I'll get a bit more, shall I?' says mum, and I know, in that very moment, that we are all going to get hammered. The chances of Christmas lunch arriving at anything close to the suggested time or in anything like an edible state are becoming increasingly remote.

But it's Christmas, so we don't worry about those things. Mum comes back into the room, and we get stuck in.

'I'd love some more, please,' I say. Meanwhile, Ted has yet to take a gulp. Everyone is looking at him as he lifts his glass to his mouth and pours some of the acidic solution down his throat.

'No,' he squeals, choking and lifting his legs in some involuntary action to the impact of the liquid. Unfortunately, though, mums old armchair isn't used to quick, unpredictable, violent movements from 25 stone men, and his legs go up just as the backseat goes down behind him. Suddenly he's upside down in a broken armchair, trapped and struggling to get back onto his feet.

'Oh my goodness,' says mum as she and I rush over to try and help him up. Ted looks mortified as he struggles to get his (massive) arse out of the chair and get himself upright. The more effort Mum and I make to assist him, the worse we seem to be making it, so much so that we are forced to admit defeat and step back and watch him struggle and squirm as he scrambles to his feet.

'Well, that didn't go well,' he says, finally. He's got sticky green liquid all down his shirt, and the remains of mum's favourite armchair lie on the floor. 'This isn't the impact I hoped to have,' he adds. 'I'm very sorry.'

But mum and I are too busy laughing to hear his apologies. The impact of the strong alcohol, combined with seeing Ted jammed upside down with legs and arms in the air, has left us crying with joy. 'I don't think I've ever seen anything so funny in my life,' I say.

Mum tries to speak, but laughter gags her, and she splutters and smiles, and when she realises she can't talk at all for laughing, she leaves the room and runs into the kitchen to get more of the terrible drink I bought.

'This is going so terribly badly,' mutters Ted. Dad is sitting there watching the scene unfold, mum's laughter can be heard from the kitchen, and I'm rather uselessly dabbing at Ted's once-white shirt with a tissue I've found on the side.

'I'm very sorry,' says Ted to dad. 'I'm such a bloody clumsy fool.'

Ted looks heartbroken. It's clear he hoped to make a good impression on my parents, and he feels he's completely blown it. 'I'm sure you're probably thinking ', who is this big, fat, useless fool'...I'm not usually so unbelievably careless,' Ted is saying.

Perhaps it's Ted's contrition that gets to my dad, maybe it's the taste of the indescribably bad alcohol, or perhaps it's just the festive spirit, but he does what he's never done before - he smiles, then he laughs, then he says to Ted. 'Well, son, you've certainly broken the ice.'

It's bizarre and unpredictable, but the broken armchair situation has lifted this family Christmas, with mum and dad smiling and laughing while Ted apologises profusely for the mess of an armchair by his side.

Next, it's time to give Christmas presents, and we have this bizarre tradition in our house where my mum gives my dad the same Christmas card every year, and he doesn't remember from year to year. It's always been a joke between mum and me. Dad looks at it, smiles, thanks her for it and puts it on the mantelpiece, oblivious to the fact that he's been given the same card for the past 30 years.

Mum hands the card over to dad and winks at me. Dad opens it (mum invests in a new envelope every year, but that's it). He surveys the dog, reads the message and puts it on the mantelpiece.

'Ted,' he says. 'You see that card?'

'Yes,' says my boyfriend.

'Well, that dog is about 30 years old but hasn't aged a day.'

'How do you mean?' asks Ted. I haven't told him about mum's dog card tradition.

'My wife has given me the same bloody card every year since we married, and she doesn't think I've noticed.'

'Ohhhh,' mum and I both cry. How the hell has he noticed something like that?

'God, dad. We rely on you to be unobservant at all times. It's heartbreaking that you've started noticing things.'

'I notice lots of things,' says dad. 'I've noticed the bloody card coming every year, but I'm too polite to comment. But now you've brought Ted along, and he's started smashing up the furniture; I guess it might be time to speak up.'

'Well, I'm very disappointed,' I say.

'Me too,' says mum. 'I'm going to have to go out and buy a new bloody card now.'

Mum refills our glasses, and we all comment that the sickly sweet, green liquid is rather palatable after a couple of glasses.

'The more you drink, the better it gets,' says mum with a little 'hick'.

'So, tell me about Mary when she was younger,' says Ted.

Mum, Ted and I are sitting in a row on the small sofa without any other seating. The whole thing creaked when we all sat down on it, and I'm hoping it doesn't break. That would be too mortifying for words. The truth is that the sofa is built for two small people - not two enormous ones and one average-sized person.

'Well, there was this one time when Mary went abroad. We don't go in much for abroad in this house, so it was quite an occasion,' says mum, and I know straight away what bloody story she's going to tell...it's her favourite one.

'Mary was going to fly with 'assisted travel' which means someone would look after her on the flight. Now, the way they do this is to clip a tag on the child's coat and give you a code, and you can go online and track your child's journey...see where they are at any time. It's a good system.'

'Yes, that sounds like a perfect system,' agrees Ted.

'But, do you know what our Mary did?'

'No,' says Ted, looking over at me.

'As a joke, she took the clip off her blouse and clipped it onto someone else's bag. That meant that when I went to the site to check where she was, it brought up a map of the world, and I could see her plane taking off, veering the wrong way, and then flying off to Spain. I was beside myself! I had to ring up the company, screaming and saying my little girl was on the wrong flight. It wasn't perfect. Awful.'

'You little horror,' says Ted, shaking his head at me. 'How could you do that to your poor mum? Perhaps I can make it up to you with these presents.'

Ted pulls out gifts for mum and dad. He hands over the one for mum first, and she can't hide her delight.

'How amazing. Thank you so much,' she says, turning a deep shade of pink. She tears off the wrapping to reveal a lovely silk scarf. It's very beautiful, with peacock blue and navy swirls through it.

Mum is thrilled. 'Thanks so much,' she says, wrapping it around her neck. 'That's very kind of you.'

Next, he hands a package to dad. I'm astonished at his bravery. I struggle to work out what to buy, dad. I've no idea how Ted has managed to think of something.

Dad tears off the paper to reveal a book about Margaret Thatcher...he almost drops it in surprise.

'This is great, thanks, Ted,' he says. 'She'd a fascinating woman. I will enjoy reading this. Thanks, son.'

'Lunch is ready,' says mum, as Ted and I snuggle up a little closer on the sofa. 'All come to the table.'

We all sit down and survey the mammoth amount of food before us. Mum has no idea this is the first of our Christmas lunches, so she's pulled out all the stops.

'What will your parents be doing for Christmas lunch?' she asks as if she's reading my mind.

'They'll just have lunch together,' says Ted. 'Just mum and dad.'

'Were they sad that you wouldn't be with them this year?'

'Yes, a little, but they are glad I'm spending Christmas with Mary.'

'How nice,' says mum. 'Turkey?'

We are going to have to leave straight after the Queen's speech to get to Ted's on time, but as the time rolls around and we're all seated on the tiny sofa waiting for it to start, I have a sudden emotional pang, I don't want to leave mum and dad's house. I don't want to go galloping across to Ted's mum and dad's house when Ted's dad can be so funny with me while mine is behaving with such extraordinary friendliness. It feels so cosy sitting next to one another. The absence of an armchair is working out just fine, though it does look like we're waiting for a bus or something. I wish Ted's parents could come instead of us going there, but I know his mum's been cooking dinner all morning. We must make an effort.

The queen's face looms on the screen, and we all lean forward.

'Do you remember when you thought Prince Philip had a huge bottom,' says my dad, laughing away to himself.

'What's this?' asks Ted.

'Mary heard them say 'three cheers for Prince Philip' and thought they said, 'three chairs for Prince Philip'. She thought he must have a massive bottom.'

Thanks, Dad.

CHRISTMAS AT TED'S

I walk into Ted's front room and see that they have had a change around in the furniture. They have a new TV, and - Christ alive - it might be the most giant TV I've ever seen. Most of the living room is plasma.

On the one hand, I feel like congratulating them on having enough money to buy such an enormous television; on the other hand, I'm tempted to criticise them for not having enough money to buy a house big enough to go around it...

We exchange hugs and warm greetings of the season, and I sit on the sofa.

'Here are some nibbles; you must be starving with us having lunch so late,' says Ted's mum, handing me a plate with mini sausage rolls, mini chicken satays and other delights. 'And take this too,' she adds, passing me an enormous mixing bowl full of crisps.

'Yum,' I say. 'Yes – starving.'

Ted looks at me like I've gone insane, but I'm not sure what else to do. I don't want to tell her we've already had one Christmas lunch. I'm sure she'd be offended.

'Shall we play a game before we eat,' says Ted's mum, full of enthusiasm. Ted and I think this is an excellent idea because we've drunk

BERNICE BLOOM

about four pints of green alcohol, but Ted's dad is less convinced. He grunts.

'It'll be fun,' she insists.

'No, it won't,' he says.

I glance at Ted, and he raises his eyebrows. Ted's dad makes my parents look positively friendly. I feel sorry for Ted's mum; she's trying so hard. Ted's dad sits there and doesn't engage us. It's all down to her to make the day work.

'I'm not playing any bloody games. Let's eat.'

'Sure,' Ted's mum says, leaving the room and rushing into the kitchen. My God, I feel sorry for her. I run after her and offer to help.

'No dear, honestly, you go back in there and have a good time....' But she looks sad and broken down by the pressure of dealing with Ted's dad.

I go back into the sitting room, where Ted and his father are in uncomfortable silence.

'I have some presents for you,' I say, digging into my bag and pulling out the wrapped Christmas presents I had retrieved from under the bed earlier.

'Here you go,' I say, handing a gift to Ted's father.

Ted's mum has come into the room behind me, so I turn and hand her a carefully wrapped package as well.

'Thank you, dear,' she says, turning to her husband: 'Isn't that kind of Mary?'

'But what is it?' says Ted's dad. He opens his package to find a pretend aeroplane inside it. It's brightly painted and made of plastic. He throws it across the room, and we watch as it glides, dips, and flies.

'That's a lovely present,' says Ted's mum, though I detect the confusion in her voice.

I feel myself go scarlet. Why the hell have I got kids' presents under my bed? I don't know any kids... Oh! I remember now; the presents were from when I played Father Christmas at a friend's party last year. They were the gifts I was giving out in the grotto, and there were too many of them, so I brought a few home. There is no chance on earth that the present that Ted's mum is about to open will be any more appropriate for her than the aeroplane was for Ted's dad.

'Goodness, that's nice. It might be a bit small, though,' she says, having opened the package to reveal a cowboy outfit.

Ted is just staring at me. 'Do you want to talk us through this?' he says as his mum makes a valiant attempt to wear a cowboy hat and pin the sheriff's badge onto her dress.

'I'm so sorry,' I say. 'I saw Ted had gifts for my mum and dad, and I wanted to bring something for you. I knew there were presents under my bed, so I went to get them. I've just remembered that they were presents for children. I'm such an idiot. I thought they were boxes of chocolates. I'm sorry.'

'No, not at all,' says Ted's mum. 'You know what they say; it's the thought that counts.'

'Don't worry,' says Ted, hugging me. 'Mum's going to look cracking in her new outfit.'

Ted's dad is just sitting in an almighty, slovenly heap. I'm starting to miss the relative warmth and happiness of my house.

'You know what we should do after lunch,' I say. 'We should invite my parents to join us...then we could play games and have a lovely time.'

'Oh dear, that would be marvellous,' says Ted's mum, positively beaming with excitement.

'Let me go and call them,' I say.

'Are you sure?' asks Ted. 'I mean - will they want to come?'

'I'll find out,' I say, and I head out of the room to make the silliest call ever. I have to confess to mum and dad that we are at Ted's for our second Christmas lunch of the day, and I have to ask them to come over in an hour and join us, but they mustn't mention the first lunch.

'Please, mum,' I say. 'I know it's a lot to ask, but it would make Christmas wonderful. I promise I'll explain all afterwards. Is that OK?'

'Of course, it is, dear,' says mum. 'I'll tell your dad.'

She takes the address and says they will be here in an hour.

I walk into the kitchen where Ted's mum is shaking a pan laden with roast potatoes. 'They are coming,' I tell her, and the look on her face says everything...she's delighted not to have to spend the day coping with her husband's miserable attitude and to have lots of other people to entertain.

'Let me tell everyone.'

She runs into the front room and announces that my parents are coming over.

'Oh great,' says Ted's dad, unenthusiastically.

'Oh,' says Ted. 'I see. Mary, can I have a word?'

Ted and I disappear into the back room, and I tell Ted how sad his mum looked and how much I'd like to cheer her up.

'If my parents come, we can play games, and it'll be noisy and fun and Christmassy. Your mum will love it.'

'You are lovely,' says Ted, hugging me. 'But won't they tell Mum that we were there earlier?'

'Mum's promised not to say anything,' I explain. 'Let's just make Christmas come alive for your mum.'

'Thank you,' says Ted. 'Now, can I ask you something?'

'Yes,' I say.

'Will you move in with me? Can we live together...you know - sometime soon? I mean - not immediately - but...in the future?'

'Oh my God, Ted, I'd love to. I'd love to.'

'That's sorted then,' he says. 'You and me - setting up home together. Happy Christmas, Mary Brown.'

'Happy Christmas, darling Ted,' I say.

Best. Christmas. Ever.

WANT TO KNOW WHAT HAPPENS NEXT?

OF COURSE, you do!

MARY BROWN IS LEAVING TOWN is available on Amazon NOW:

UK: My Book
US: My Book

OR – see the next Box Set, which carries on from where this one left off – with three fab books to entertain and delight you.

THE SECOND BOX-SET:
UK: My Book
US: My Book

The second box set opens with 'Mary Brown is leaving Town.' DETAILS BELOW…

* *"It was hysterical, some bits made me laugh out loud, and other parts made me blush with recognition."*
* *"This is definitely one of my favourite of Mary's adventures so far! I feel like they're just getting better and better! Can't wait for the next one!!"*

Mary Brown heads to Portugal for a weight loss camp and discovers it's nothing like she expected.

"I THOUGHT it would be Slimming World in the sunshine, but this is bloody torture," she says, after boxing, running, sand training (sand training? what fresh hell is sand training?), more running, more star jumps and eating nothing but carrots.

. . .

MARY WANTS to hide from the instructors and cheat the system. The trouble is, her mum is with her and won't leave her alone for a second... Then there's the angry instructor with a deep, dark secret about why he left the army. The mysterious woman sneaks into their pool and does synchronised swimming every night. Who the hell is she? Why's she in their pool?

MARY TAKES snacks in with her. Will they prevent her from losing any weight at all? And what about Yvonne - the slim, attractive lady who sneaks off every night after dinner? Where's she going? And what unearthly difficulties will Mary get herself into when she decides to follow her to find out...

While Mary's away on her retreat, she and Ted are forced to rethink their relationship. Ted doesn't have the time to see Mary because he's always working, and Mary is getting very fed up with the situation. Reluctantly, our lovely couple decide to separate, leaving Mary alone.

She decides to try online dating sites.

Aided and abetted by her friends, including Juan Pedro – the flamboyant Spaniard she met when he was a dancer in sparkly trousers on a cruise ship- and her best friend Charlie, Mary heads out on NINE DATES IN NINE DAYS.

She meets an interesting collection of men, including those she nicknames: Usain Bolt, Harry the Hoarder, and Dead-Wife-Darren.

Then just when she thinks things can't get any worse, Juan organises a huge, entirely inadvisable party at the end.

It's internet dating like you've never known it before...

'SO INCREDIBLY FUNNY. **Read this book before you go on any internet dates.**'

'I loved it. If you join an online dating site and go on dates, then make sure the guy doesn't have a big bag with him or a young kid. This really made me laugh.'

'I just loved it.'

'A wonderful book.'

'It was hysterical, some bits made me laugh out loud, and other parts made me blush with recognition.'

'This is definitely one of my favourite of Mary's adventures so far! I feel like they're just getting better and better! Can't wait for the next one!!'

THE ORDER OF THE MARY BROWN BOOKS & ALL THE LINKS

(Ebook readers can click 'My Book' for more details):

1. WHAT'S UP, MARY BROWN?: My Book
2. THE ADVENTURES OF MARY BROWN: My Book
3. CHRISTMAS WITH MARY BROWN: My Book
4. MARY BROWN IS LEAVING TOWN: My Book
5. MARY BROWN IN LOCKDOWN: My Book
6. MYSTERIOUS INVITATION: My Book
7. A FRIEND IN NEED: My Book
8. DOG DAYS FOR MARY BROWN: My Book
9. DON'T MENTION THE HEN WEEKEND: My Book
10. THE ST LUCIA MYSTERY (out 2024): My Book

Or, see them all together here:

UK
https://www.amazon.co.uk/Bernice-Bloom/e/B01MPZ5SBA?ref=sr_ntt_srch_lnk_1&qid=1666995551&sr=8-1

US
https://www.amazon.com/Bernice-Bloom/e/B01MPZ5SBA?ref=sr_ntt_srch_lnk_1&qid=1666995644&sr=1-1

Printed in Great Britain
by Amazon